*A lifetime seemed to pass between them
in that first moment of their meeting.
Their eyes met and locked across the room.*

Her damp shift clung, outlining every rounded curve
of her slender body. Her long, blond hair lay tousled
about her as though a lover had caressed it, wrapping
his strong hands amidst the cascading mass.

Hunter wanted her, and his heart quickened at the
thought.

Mary stared at the stranger who had awakened her,
her earlier panic giving way to a sickening dread that
crept upon her like an icy death as she recognized the
MacBeth plaid he wore. She was alone—trapped—
with one of *them!* If he knew—dear God! He must not
find out! She lowered her violet eyes quickly. He
would know! The moment he saw their color he would
know. The crofters did not call them ''Carmichael
eyes'' for naught. This man of the clan she had feared
every day of her life would rape her. Kidnap her. Slay
her. She studied him from under half-closed lids. God's
wounds! What should she do?

Novels by Rebecca Brandewyne

*No Gentle Love*
*Forever My Love*

Published by
WARNER BOOKS

# Forever my Love

# Rebecca Brandewyne

**WARNER BOOKS**

A Warner Communications Company

For two brothers:

Thomas,
who made it all possible,

and

Daniel,
who showed me the way.

# The Players

## THE CLAN CARMICHAEL

Lord Magnus, Earl of Bailekair
Lady Margaret, Countess of
   Bailekair

Their children:

   Lord Ian
   Sir Andrew
   Sir Harold  (the twins)
   Sir Gordon
   Sir Charlie
   Lady Mary

Mistress Joanna, a relative
Lord Hugh, heir to Dùndereen
Squire Edward, half brother to
   Lord Hugh

## THE CLAN MURRAY

Lady Alinor, wife to Sir Charlie

## THE CLAN MacDONALD

Lord David, Earl of Wynd
   Cheathaich

## THE CLAN MacBETH

Lord Angus, Earl of Glenkirk
Lady Sophia, Countess of
   Glenkirk

Their children:

   Lord Stephen
   Sir Blair
   Lady Euphemia (Effie)
   Sir Francis

Lord Duncan, Baron Torra nam
   Sian
Sir Ranald, a relative
Lady Laureen, wife to Sir Ranald

Their son:

   Sir Hunter

Sir Cadman, foster brother to
   Sir Hunter
Lady Grace, half sister to
   Sir Cadman
Grizel, a nanny
Old Bethia, a villager
Mistress Sybil, a servant
Mistress Winifred, a servant

## AT HOLYROOD PALACE

King James IV of Scotland
Lord Patrick Hepburn, Earl of Bothwell
Lady Jane Gordon

## IN HUNGARY

Ashiyah, Queen of the gypsies

# Contents

The Isles
Of
Orkney

Torra nam Sian

Wick

North
Sea

The Minch

Rath na Mara

Abergorra

Feoghail

Moray
Firth

Glochiomond

HIGHLANDS

Inverness

R. Spey

Moy Heath

Glenkirk

Loch
Ness

Dùndereen

R. Don

Aberdeen

The
Islands
Of
Hebrides

The Kirk

Ballekair

Mheadoin

R. Dee

Leabaidh a' Nathair

Dumbarton

Wynd Cheathaich

R. Tay

Dundee

Oir Uisge

Glasgow

Perth

SCOTLAND

Eadar Da Voe

Firth
Of
Forth

Kirkaldy

R. Forth

Stirling

R. Clyde

Leith

Edinburgh

Dunbar

LOWLANDS

R. Tweed

Berwick

Dumbritan
Firth

Càrnwick

R. Teviot

![Castle] Castle

● Town

![Church] Church

R. Nith

BORDER
LANDS

ENGLAND

# Forever My Love

'Cross rainswept moors,
One Highland morn,
Two bold MacBeths did ride.
There far away,
On coal black steed,
A maiden gold they spied.
One claimed her for his own,
They say,
But she couldna be his bride,
And so began the legend,
Which sweet song
Has never died.

Haunting Mary,
Weep thy sad lament
For those who loved and lost,
And those who sought
To keep ye free,
Wie dear their lives the cost,
Who lie beneath
The foggy dew
In graves so cold and mossed.

Dark Hugh, and Hunter,
Thy enemy,
And Edward, fair and pale—
For ye they offered
Everything,
And some were bound to fail.
Listen whilst I
Sing to thee
A mournful Highland tale.

One of passion's woes
And wildest hearts,
Which beat wie lonely pain,
Of two whose love
Still echoes clear.
Forever its refrain
Will haunt the purple
Scotland moors,
Where legends yet remain.

# BOOK ONE

*A Maiden Gold*

# One

If one stands on the edge of the cliff overlooking the clear blue waters of Loch Ness, one can see three castles in the distance. Three castles standing like sentinels against the grey of the morning sky, towers shrouded by the Highland mist that never quite seems to fade, as though some strange and mythical magic would disappear from Scotland herself without the shelter of the lingering haze. Three castles, fates forever intertwined, like the fragments of a puzzle, the passages of a maze.

To the east lies Bailekair, grandest of them all. Its massive stone walls rise in the shade of the purple mountain whose darkness, even in the golden sun, seems to foreshadow the doom that waits for Bailekair. Farther on, in the hollow of the sweeping hillside, bides Dùndereen, the smallest of the three, the most deceptively serene: for one day, inside its high battlements, blood will stain the cold rock floor of the long hall within its keep, never to be washed clean as long as the castle stands. To the west Glenkirk, with its tall, graceful spires, springs up from the craggy chasm for which it was named, as dark and mysterious as its old servant Grizel, who once laid her curse upon them all.

If one turns from the edge of the cliff toward the south, one can see the blackened ruins of the village of Mheadhoin and perhaps the very place whence she delivered her chilling prophecy. The words were wrenched from her grieving, tormented heart in avenging wrath; for bonnie Anne MacBeth of Glenkirk, the young lassie Grizel had reared from childhood, had been taken captive by James Carmichael of Bailekair and his brother, Robert of Dùndereen.

The two men held the girl for ransom; but, deciding against paying, Kevin MacBeth undertook to regain his only daughter in a long and fierce siege. At its end Bailekair, where she was kept prisoner, still stood strong, its walls unravaged: and the dead of the MacBeths lay futilely upon the ground among the crude battering rams and broken shields the few survivors of the battle left behind them in despair.

Anne was never seen again, but as the traveling bards, the wandering minstrels, and the Royal troubadours of Scotland are many, so are the tales surrounding her disappearance. Some sing the version that James slew Anne with his mighty claymore and delivered her body up to the beaten MacBeths with a mocking note pinned to her breast. Some claim Anne flung herself from the high walls of Bailekair, as penance for her kinsmen's terrible suffering, after she'd helplessly watched the siege. Still others swear she vanished from the ramparts only to appear moments later astride a huge white stallion riding out through the iron portcullis and the solid wooden doors of the castle to fade into the Highland mist forever.

To this very day in the small taverns of the neighboring villages the crofters whisper that Anne's ghost haunts the sandy shores of Loch Ness and weeps mournfully in the night, forever torn between the massive walls of Bailekair and the graceful spires of Glenkirk. If pressed and in their cups, the serfs will even relate the legend of Grizel's revenge upon the three castles and the story of the bitter feud between the Carmichaels and MacBeths that has continued these many years past.

Aye, Mheadhoin was the place where the old woman cursed them. *Village of death*, 'twas called even then, for 'twas naught save a scattering of old, abandoned huts and shops, long since decayed and fallen to ruin. Years before Grizel sought it out, the Black Plague had come upon the town, leaving nothing but rows of crosses in the graveyard near the kirk and, here and there in the cobblestone streets, the bleached bones of those who had been the last to die. No one ever went there anymore, for fear the disease still lingered.

But Mheadhoin served Grizel's purpose well, for it lay between the three castles, overlooking the still waters of the loch that would carry the sound of her haunting prophecy to the towers of the keeps.

Tiny, wizened, all sharp angles of jutting, pointed bones, she trudged her way slowly up the hillside to the village. Her wrinkled cheeks were sunken in her face, for she had no teeth, and her chin protruded from her jaws in the manner of a small spike; a mole from which several coarse hairs grew sat upon this last like a beetle upon some crumb. Her jet black eyes sparkled maliciously in the light of the torch she carried. Her upper lip was scarcely visible, but the lower one hung out over her chin slightly, a stain of tobacco or tea at its center; a bit of spittle drooled from one corner as the crone panted raspingly for breath. Gnarled blue veins showed plainly in her aged hands as she reached out to lay the torch to the town.

The rotten thatched roofs of the forgotten buildings caught fire quickly, and soon Mheadhoin was ablaze with the flames. When Grizel heard the shouts begin from the castles and saw the figures scurrying rapidly upon the ramparts of the fortresses, she made her way to the cliff at the edge of the village. There she flung her arms wide, palms outstretched toward the night sky, her eerie form silhouetted against the licking orange and yellow of the burning town. Her great cloak flapping wildly about her in the high wind, she stood like an angry, evil raven beating its wings against its prey. Her voice rose to a shrill piercing across the waters of the loch, and the shadowed figures upon the ramparts of the castles froze in terror as they listened.

"Hear me, thou marauders of Bailekair, thou scavengers of

Dùndereen, thou cowards of Glenkirk, for I, Grizel, in painful lament for the bairn thy foul deed has wrested from my breast, do lay my curse upon ye!

"The spawn of the devil will walk amongst ye, accursed amongst thy people for another's sin, the same of which will be his own in the end. Aye, accursed," Grizel croaked slyly. "Look to his eyes, and ye will know the truth of which I speak. What he takes will be gi'en him and will be holy, just as what once was, was holy also. What he steals he will ne'er relinquish, for what he holds he will keep unto death; and all that he gains will be his from the beginning.

"Beware, thou castles three. Thy sorrows will be many for the sadness ye hae wrought, spire for spire, kirk for kirk. As 'twas in the beginning, so will it be again. Woe unto him who doesna listen! Thy enemies will falter by sickness and the sword; and as they die, so will ye die also. As they are betrayed, so will ye be betrayed. As their tears flow like rivers, so will your tears flow. As their blood runs red upon the ground, so will your blood run; and the Great Glen will echo wie the mournful wailings of sorrow and ring wie the blows of the Grim Reaper's mighty sword.

"From the loins of the lion a golden tigress will spring. Dinna strike her down, though ye be fearful of her claws, for she alone will be thy salvation. Her blood will be your blood; and she will ride amongst ye unafraid, a tawny light wie black darkness by her side, for destruction will travel in her wake, and it must be borne! Yet as sorrow lingers, so joy will come, but only when ye hae turned full circle. When the stormy seas hae brought him who left ye home once more, two will kneel before their sovereign lord, who will lay his hands upon them and bless them for all time, as two were once blessed by another.

"Forgie. Forgie that a weary, troubled soul may rest in peace and walk no more amongst ye.

"So I, Grizel, do curse ye!"

Then suddenly, as though she had willed it, the flames blazed hotly; the smoke swirled high like a shroud about the harridan.

She grinned, and from the wide, gaping hole in her face a high, cackling sound of laughter split the night crazily with its echo, reverberating through the Great Glen. Then only the remains of charred ashes marked the place where she had stood. Like the village the hag was gone. Only the kirk rose untouched by the fire, its solitary spire glowing red, reflecting the blaze.

Those who had heard the old witch's words fell to their knees, crossing themselves fervently and bewailing their fate.

When, that year, the first of such children bearing the Carmichael eyes was born unto the Clan MacBeth, each side gazed upon the kirk overlooking the three castles and prayed for the salvation promised by the crone's cryptic words. When it did not come, the feud between them deepened into the fiercest and most bitter of Highland battles.

Neither faction lost any opportunity to do the other damage. Each raided the other's outlying crofts and villages, raping and pillaging, driving off cattle and sheep, and setting fire to that which could not be carried away. A Carmichael heir was brutally beaten and slain by the MacBeths of Glenkirk, who roped the dead youth's body to a battering ram and sent it slamming into the stout doors of a Carmichael keep. Two MacBeth children were starved to death in one of the towers of Bailekair and their bones, picked clean by rats, delivered to the MacBeths in a burlap bag. A Carmichael woman, taken prisoner and raped by several of the MacBeth men, threw herself from the high battlements of one of her enemies' holdings rather than face murder at their hands or the punishment her own clan would have meted out for her shame had she been ransomed. A MacBeth laird was tortured on the rack by the Carmichaels, then flung into the dungeons of Dùndereen to die of madness in the end.

The horrible stories of the feud were known by every Highland child. Many a young Carmichael or MacBeth bairn obeyed his elders under the threat that if he did not, the accursed enemy would snatch him away from his bed while he slept. As two of the Carmichael holdings, Abergorra and Glochlomond, were separated from the rest of the clan's estates by MacBeth land, there was ample opportunity for this to happen. More than one Carmichael or MacBeth disappeared while trespassing on the other's property, never to be seen again. More likely than not, they were cast into the deep Loch Ness, which carefully guarded all its dark secrets for all time.

But none of this was known to the child who was born at Bailekair that year of 1472, though it would be told to her from the time she was old enough to walk and talk. Nor did she know that at the exact moment of her birth a mountain lion screamed in the snow-covered hills, and a hush fell over the Highlands, which had been waiting, waiting nearly a hundred years for her arrival.

# Two

**Inverness, Scotland, 1477**

The pale grey mist that had cloaked the village earlier that morning had faded with the onslaught of the mellow summer sun. The river near the edge of town shone blue in the dappled light as it coursed its way to the still Loch Ness in the distance. The air rang with the loud cries of merchants hawking their wares, each trying to outdo the others as they shouted lustily to advertise the bargains available at their stands. The bolder ones stepped out in front of their carts, rudely thrusting their goods upon passersby, many of whom reluctantly gave the vendors a few coins just to be rid of them. The wind stirred faintly. The flute trilled; the lute twanged, and the harp sang along with the plaintively whispering breeze as wandering minstrels moved from corner to corner, passing their caps for small donations. Above all this was the hustle and bustle of the village people themselves as they crowded through the narrow streets of Inverness, pushing and elbowing their ways to the gaily colored tents that filled the square in the center of town and spilled into the twisting lanes. The fresh scents of hot bread, sweet tarts, and crisp apples seemed to mingle naturally with the smell of sweat from the many excited bodies abroad. In their jolly clamor, people rejoiced, thanking God for a good harvest; for today, August 1, in the Year of Our Lord 1477, was the festival of Lammas.

Hunched old men and young lads whose backs were already beginning to stoop from the heavy labor of plowing had tilled the soil earlier in the spring, readying it for the planting of the crops—the oats, wheat, and barley that were the mainstays of Scotland's people. The womenfolk, weathered and wrinkled from years of exposure to the sun and rain, old before their times, had followed in their men's footsteps, dropping the seeds of grain into the fertile ground; their children had covered the tiny kernels with mounds of earth. No bairn old enough to walk and talk had been spared the tiresome chores, the work that would continue until they had become so senile, aged, and withered that they would be allowed the small comfort of sitting before one of the squalid thatched huts, recalling memories of the days when they too had helped with the planting.

From the time the first green shoots had shown above the surface of the land the crops had been nurtured, tended, fertilized, and prayed over; for without them the poor serfs could not pay the *calpiches* due their overlords, much less feed the number of hungry mouths that seemed to grow larger with each passing year. If God had smiled upon them, if it had not rained too heavily, if the sun had not shone too hotly, if the weevils had not destroyed the young plants before they'd had a chance to grow, then the crofters had sighed with relief and begun the harvesting.

They'd trembled slightly when the bailiffs had come down from the manors of their overlords to count the number of bushels produced and carefully determine how many were to be paid to the lairds, for if it had been a bad year, there would be scarcely enough grain left for the serfs to survive the winter. But, ah, if the harvest had been good, then none would go hungry; and it would truly be a time for rejoicing throughout the land.

Aye, the Lord had, indeed, been good to them this year; the monies owed were paid, the bellies of the children filled; and this year the celebration of Lammas was especially wonderful, for a fair had come to town. Even those who could not spare a single penny (despite the good harvest) had flocked to Inverness for the occasion.

At one booth two women quarreled so furiously over a piece of bright cloth that the material gave way, splitting raggedly in half, much to its weaver's dismay. He shrieked helplessly as each woman scattered into the milling mass, clutching her hard-earned prize to her bosom. Then the cantankerous old man turned to rap the knuckles of an impish urchin attempting to steal a bolt of fabric from one corner of the peddler's cart. The weaver was still cursing loudly when he caned the lad away.

Farther on a vegetable bin was overturned as a group of careless young men raced past on horseback, clattering sharply over the cobblestones. One rogue paused to toss a handful of silver coins to the irate merchant, who shook her fist at him threateningly before she scurried to collect the half-crowns already being scooped up by a hoard of greedy, filthy children (who were cramming their pockets, in addition, with the beans, onions, and carrots that had tumbled from the crate). The woman screeched at the brats shrilly as they scampered off laughing, shouting derisive comments at her angry figure.

Down a lane a one-eyed barker promised a trinket to the first person who could successfully topple three stuffed dolls from the ledge at the back of his booth.

"The cost? Why, only a tuppence. Step this way, sir. A pretty necklace for the lady? Thank ye, sir."

Beyond a little girl and a young lad stood before a red-and-white-striped tent that advertised the gruesome sight of a two-headed monster for the price of a shilling, a day's wages for some.

Money, however, was not the reason the child hung back, for the *arascaid* she wore was richly woven wool, and even in the summer heat her feet were shod with soft leather boots, a luxury in the Highlands where most women and children went barefoot. She was frightened because she'd become separated from the rest of her family, and she did not want to view the promised freak inside the pavilion.

"I willna go in, Hugh, and ye canna make me." The girl's voice was shrill with fear as she glanced about anxiously for some sign of her brothers or even Nanna, her nurse, from whom she'd strayed earlier and who must even now be searching for her frantically. But none of these persons was in sight; she could catch not even a glimpse of the purple-and-blue *breacan* that marked her clan. Only her cousin Hugh was here.

"Och, Mary, you're the silliest wench I e'er did see." His brow was furrowed with rage. He gazed at her sulkily for a moment, noting the stubborn set of her jaw and trembling lips, then spoke again slyly, a taunting smile on his face. "Scaredy cat!"

"I amna!" Mary was indignant, for her father had taught her that even if she were afraid, she was never to let her fear show upon her face. She bit her lip, casting another timid glance at the striped tent.

"Well, then?" Hugh observed the indecision written plainly on her fair countenance and grabbed her arm before she had a chance to change her mind, dragging her up to the entrance as she began to struggle slightly. "Where's your shilling?"

Tears stung Mary's eyes as she reached into her knotted handkerchief to draw forth the proper coin; she brushed them away hastily, knowing her cousin would laugh spitefully if he saw. Her arm hurt where he'd gripped it so tightly, and the quick shove he gave her toward the now-open tent flap was none too gentle.

"God's teeth! You're nae only silly, but clumsy besides!"

"Well, I wouldna hae been if ye hadna pushed me!"

Hugh merely hissed under his breath as he pushed her again, propelling her rudely through the crowd of persons standing shoulder to shoulder inside the pavilion. The mass gave way easily, for even the most common among them realized the little girl and the young boy were of noble rank. Small as they were, the child only five and her cousin ten, the two already carried themselves with the arrogance of the privileged class.

Even before Mary's eyes adjusted to the darkness inside the tent, her nostrils were assaulted by the odor of perspiring bodies and the stench of something even more awful. Then she saw it. She longed to shut her eyes from the grotesque scene at once, but the morbid fascination of the thing was even more compelling, so Mary stared at the hideous monster, gasping aloud in shock. It had a human enough torso, but perched on its shoulders were two necks and two heads. One of them had the face of a toothless old witch, deeply engraved with lines, who smiled gapingly at the audience. But the other! 'Twas horrid! It had been the face of a woman once, too, but evidently it had recently died. The lifeless head lolled listlessly against its side of the shoulders, maggots eating away at the eye sockets, pieces of decaying flesh hanging in shreds and swaying slightly each time the torso moved. The putrefying skin was covered with masses of oozing sores.

Mary ran screaming from the pavilion, barely making it through the crowded onlookers to the outside before her knees buckled under her, and she retched spasmodically onto the ground. When she at last managed to glance up, Hugh stood before her, his fists clenched tightly by his sides, his feet spread wide apart. He grabbed her and shook her roughly.

"Ye stupid wee wench!"

"Stop it! Oh, stop it, please—"

"And what if I dinna? Are ye going to tell your father? Ye'd better nae, ye scrawny brat, or I'll smack ye proper—"

He winced with pain as Mary kicked out at him sharply, her small foot striking his shin a dull blow.

"Beast! Ye horrid beast!" she cried. "You're as crazy as your mad mother was—"

Hugh howled with rage as he jerked her back and forth again until Mary thought the teeth would rattle right out of her head. The joy she'd felt earlier this morning at her first glimpse of a *real* town (for up until now she'd been no farther in the world than the walls of her father's castle, Bailekair) vanished. Hugh had spoiled it for her, just as he always tried to ruin everything with his bullying meanness. She beat at him ineffectually with her tiny fists, miserably aware of the stares of passersby. But no one made a move to stop Hugh from mistreating her. No one would dare lay their hands on the children of lairds.

Nanna's face was pinched with worry as she hurriedly dragged the children, whose hands she held, behind her, searching the crowd frantically for some sign of the missing Mary.

"Drat the bairn!" She frowned at Alan, one of the men-at-arms who accompanied her. "Where can she hae gone?"

"I dinna ken, Mistress Flora," he replied, as anxious as she to find the little girl. "Lord knows, there'll be the devil to pay if something's happened to the Earl's bonnie lassie."

Mistress Flora (which was her real name and not "Nanna," as the children always called her) pressed her lips together grimly. Fortune had smiled upon her the day the Earl of Bailekair had come to the small hut she had shared with her family on the laird's holding. His new bride had been expecting a bairn, and a nurse had been needed to take care of the child after its birth. Flora, at fifteen years of age, had been a strapping wench with plain brown hair and sharp grey eyes that had missed very little. Someone had told the Earl she was a likely lass, knowledgeable in the plants and herbs of medicine, respected by the other serfs as a healer of ills. A midwife, she had delivered three babies just that year. The laird had raised her from her common status to a position of importance in his household.

For more than a decade now she'd resided in the castle of Bailekair, where she had never thought she'd set foot. The mighty fortress was a subject of reverence to the serfs who tilled its land, as awesome and overpowering as the laird who ruled it.

Flora had tended all of the Earl's bairns and done her job well, from Ian, who was twelve; Andrew and Harold, the twins, who were eleven; Gordon nine; and Charlie eight; to Mary, the only daughter and youngest of the lot. Flora had never, in all those years, lost a child, and she did not need Alan to remind her of the consequences of such a happening. Flora had seen the Earl when a rage was upon him, and she shivered slightly at the thought of that terrible anger being directed toward her. Why, Lord Magnus might even have her whipped, for bonnie Mary was his favorite bairn!

She forged ahead, setting the children skipping behind her to keep up with her rapid pace. They gazed at each other fearfully as they hurried along. None knew better than they the trouble Nanna would be in if Mary were not found, for two of them, Gordon and Charlie, had felt the sting of their father's riding crop across the seats of their *feile-begs* more than once. Joanna, a distant relative in training at Bailekair as a maid for the missing Mary, had been present upon four of these unpleasant occasions. Edward, the boys' cousin, had only heard tales of the Earl's anger, but even those were enough to frighten him out of his wits.

The three lads were blond, as were most of their family, for their people had come from England centuries ago and did not claim descendance from the Picts, the little dark persons who were thought to have first inhabited Scotland and who were even now confused with fairies and goblins. Gordon and Charlie had eyes of lavender lace; Edward's were a beautiful deep shade of blue. The two brothers were built sturdily, like their father, but their cousin was a slender youth, pale and sickly as a child, although he seemed well enough now.

Joanna's hair and eyes were a warm honey shade, though

no one knew how she had acquired this coloring. She was the bastard bairn of a young kinswoman of Lord Magnus, who, fearing her father's wrath upon learning her shamed state, had sought sanctuary at Bailekair and died giving Joanna life there. The name of the babe's father had gone with her mother to the grave.

All of the children had the straight noses and full, generous mouths that marked the members of their clan.

"Where do ye suppose she is?" Charlie ventured to ask after casting a discreet glance in Nanna's direction.

"Och, like as nae she wandered off after some trinket or toy. Ye know how the lassies are, Charlie," Gordon said with a gentle smile at the solemn Joanna. "Especially Mary. She's always liked bright, bonnie things. I doubt anything's really happened to her." His tone was doubtful, meant to reassure himself as much as his brother, for they both loved their little sister dearly.

"Nanna sure looks fierce." Charlie stole another peek at their nurse. "Do ye suppose father will put her in the stocks?"

"Nay, probably nae." Gordon shook his head. "He's always been fond of her. Besides, 'tisna just Nanna's fault."

"Nay, 'tisna," Edward piped up. "Alan is bound to get it as well."

The others agreed this was certainly the case, since Alan was the one in charge of the four men-at-arms who accompanied them. His responsibility was to see no harm befell any of the family in his care. They hated to think what would happen to dear old Alan if Mary had sustained some hurt. Why, just last week Lord Magnus had chopped off the hand of one of the serfs who'd stolen a loaf of bread from his neighbors! The punishment had seemed cruel to the two brothers and Joanna (for the entire household had been commanded to gather outside the castle walls to witness the penalty for theft), but the Earl had explained to them one loaf of bread to a serf might mean the difference between whether or not one of his children lived through the winter. Thus stealing, especially food, was a serious crime, indeed. Lord

Magnus had severed the man's left hand, which, he'd told the children, was a sign of mercy, for the serf was right-handed and would still be able to work the land to provide for his family, albeit with some difficulty.

Hugh was still shaking Mary when they spied her. Her *curraichd* of linen had been snatched from her head and trampled into the ground. Her light woolen *arascaid* was torn at the shoulders from his rough grasp. Her blond hair was tousled where Hugh had pulled it cruelly, and her bonnie face was puckered up dreadfully, although she was trying hard not to cry. Gordon and Charlie took one look, then yanked their hands free from Nanna's and ran to their sister's aid. They wrenched Hugh away from Mary, faces filled with a wrath that would have rivaled their father's.

"What in the hell do ye think you're doing, Hugh?" Charlie shouted angrily.

"Trying to knock some sense into—"

Charlie didn't wait for his cousin to answer. He punched Hugh in the jaw as hard as he could.

"Goddamn it, ye whoreson coward! I'll teach ye to lay your bloody hands on my sister! Daft! 'Tis daft, ye are!" he yelled as he rammed his head into his cousin's belly before Hugh could recover from the first blow. Charlie, like Mary earlier, had chosen the very words that would enrage and insult his cousin the greatest, for Hugh could not bear any thought connected with madness.

"'Daft,' is it?" Hugh snarled with narrowed eyes as he split open Charlie's lip. "I'll show ye daft, ye son of a —"

He growled as Charlie managed to black one of his cousin's eyes. Hugh grabbed him around the throat, attempting to choke him. Gordon, seeing his brother, who was not as old or as heavy as Hugh, was now getting the worst of it, jumped into the fracas to help Charlie. Mary stood by silently, biting her lower lip anxiously, although she was sure her brothers would win the battle.

"Here, ye lads! Stop this at once, do ye ken?"

Mary looked up to see Nanna standing over them all, her face a mask of severe disapproval, and Edward (Hugh's younger half brother) and Joanna watching the fight quietly, making no move to join in the *mêlée*. The boys scuffled on, paying no attention to Nanna as she turned imploringly to the men-at-arms for assistance. Alan cleared his thr t sympathetically, while the other four men shuffled their feet, but none was brave enough to touch the young lords, so the fight continued unchecked. There was a rending sound as Charlie's doublet burst open at the seam in one shoulder; all of the lads had lost their broad-bonnets, Hugh's having been squashed beneath the pack of flailing limbs; and Gordon's *feile-beg* had been ripped away from the leather belt that encircled it.

Finally Hugh, one eye badly blackened, his mouth bleeding, managed to scramble away from the other two and disappear down one of the twisting streets, shouting threatening curses and plans for retaliation as he ran.

"Ye crazy whoreson!" Charlie taunted back, still furious.

"Och, Charlie, let him go." Gordon grabbed his younger brother's arm as Charlie started after Hugh. "He got the worst of it after all." He brushed himself off, grimacing suddenly. "Christ! What is this stuff?" Gordon's hands came away from his doublet, fingers covered with a sticky yellowish green residue.

"Och, Gordie, I'm sorry. I was sick in the grass." Mary pointed contritely to the spot where the boys had fallen.

"Master Gordon, wipe yourself off"—Nanna handed the lad a square of linen—"and see Master Charlie does the same. 'Tis no doubt a whipping you'll both be getting when the Earl learns of this day's work." Her lips compressed together sternly. "And as for ye, Lady Mary—wandering off when I wasna looking—"

"I'm sorry, Nanna," Mary whispered, not daring to glance at her nurse's face and much upset at the thought of her father's anger when he was informed of the brawl. "I merely wished to hear the rest of the bard's song and followed him down the street. I dinna mean to lose ye; truly, I dinna! Hugh saw me, and he—he dragged me away and made me go in to see the mon—monster! I couldna help it because I threw up aft—afterward!" she wailed, bursting into tears at last.

"Is *that* what he was shaking ye for?" the hotheaded Charlie broke in, his rage renewed at the thought of his cousin laying hands on bonnie little Mary.

"Ayeeeee," she bawled. "And now ye and Gordie are co—covered wie vomit, and you'll both—both get a beating because of—of me—"

"Here," Nanna clucked, her face softening as the men-at-arms glanced at each other in distress. Lady Mary was a favorite with all of them and they hated to see her cry. "Dinna fash yourself, my wee bairn. You're spoiling your bonnie face. There was no harm done after all." Nanna felt relieved by the thought, and she knew Hugh was probably a worse monster than the one in the tent that seemed to have frightened the lass so terribly. "Blow your nose, and we'll speak no more of this matter."

Mary did as she was bid, slipping her coins into one tightly clenched fist as she unknotted her square of linen after retrieving it from the ground along with the trampled *curraichd*. Her face brightened considerably.

"Does that mean my brothers willna get a lashing?"

"Och." Nanna could never be strict with Lady Mary for long. "I said the matter was ended."

Everyone breathed a sigh of relief at this, recognizing from the nurse's statement that Nanna meant to hold her tongue and would not report the children's sad behavior to the Earl; she did not desire a reprimand from Lord Magnus for her own careless conduct any more than they did. The men-at-arms looked at each other in tacit agreement to keep quiet as well, for some of them had been clouted by the Earl in one of his tempers and had no wish to be punished so again.

"Let's go," Gordon said. "If we stay around here much longer, Hugh is bound to come back wie Ian and the twins."

Nanna decided this was probably the truth, Ian and the twins being much closer to Hugh than their own brothers and likely to seek revenge for their cousin's thrashing. She led her young charges away without another word of censure, wondering if she were getting soft and daft in her old age. Flora was but twenty-eight, but life at Bailekair, for all its comforts, had not been easy; already there were streaks of grey in her brown hair that accentuated the clearness of her eyes. She pushed a loose strand back into place, blushing as she caught Alan's admiring gaze upon her figure.

"I'll thank ye to keep your eyes on the road where they belong," she snapped tartly, although, as he turned away respectfully, a smile twitched about the corners of her lips.

Flora had never been married, for somehow during the long hours of service at Bailekair she'd never seemed to find the time for proper courting. Now she considered it highly unlikely she would ever wed. Still, her mind was plagued by thoughts of what she would do in a few years when Lady Mary was old enough to have Joanna begin maiding for her, for it appeared there would be no more bairns in Lord Magnus's household. His wife, Lady Margaret, had declared stoutly that Mary was the last of the lot and had installed a heavy iron bolt on her chamber door to insure this remained the case.

Nanna glanced at Alan covertly. He's nae a bad-looking mon, she thought, although his face is marked wie a few scars from battle; and the Earl thinks well of him, for more often than nae 'tis Alan he entrusts wie the care of Lady Mary. Aye, I could do a lot worse. 'Tis something to think aboot at least.

She did not protest when Alan took her arm to help her across the road.

"I'm *glad* they beat Hugh up, Mary," Edward confided passionately as they started down the street. "He shouldna hae touched ye."

Mary studied him thoughtfully, pondering how gentle and sweet Edward was, so different from his half brother, the despicable Hugh, whom she loathed.

Hugh's mother had been a dark wild Norman whom Mary's Uncle Thomas had brought back from France one year. The Carmichaels generally intermarried to further strengthen their close-knit ties; but Lord Magnus had announced that if his brother were happy, that was the end of the matter, so no one had dared say a word about Lord Thomas's bride. Still, many had prophesied privately that no good would come of his marriage to the strange black-haired wench.

Four years after her wedding, Celeste had at last given birth of a lusty son, whom she'd named Hugh. His hair was as black as his mother's; his eyes were so dark brown they seemed black as well. Celeste had appeared normal as she'd held the child in her arms, but as he'd grown older she'd begun to slip into her own fantasy world, wandering about the long halls of Thomas's holding, Dùndereen, at odd hours of the night, whispering secretly to herself or shrieking hoarsely at her husband and the servants. Several had fled the keep, declaring their lady mad, and finally Thomas had been forced to shut her up in her chamber, a heavy wooden bar across her door.

One night Celeste had somehow managed to obtain a lighted candle. She'd set her massive canopied bed on fire and been burned to death in the flames before the castle had awakened to the blaze.

About a year after he'd buried Celeste, Lord Thomas had then wed Lady Edwina Carmichael, a distant cousin who'd lived long enough to provide him with another small son before passing away quietly after some lingering disease. The laird, much grieved over the loss of both his wives, had never married again.

Now he and Edward, for Hugh had been fostered out this year, lived alone at Dùndereen, rambling about the empty keep with little company.

"Aye, Gordon and Charlie showed Hugh right enough," Mary answered her young cousin at last.

"Shall I—shall I buy ye a pastry to make up for it?" Edward asked haltingly; for, though he was three years older than she, he always felt a little awed by Mary's beauty.

Once when he and his tutor had been discussing Greek mythology, Master Elphinstone, thinking to cheer the lonely lad, had shown Edward an engraving of the piper, Pan, drawing a comparison between the classical Greek goatsman and the sensitive, serious student who also played the flute. Edward had been enraptured. In the picture had been a lovely golden-haired nymph rising out of a shaded summer pool to be enchanted by the piper's music.

"Och, sir. Will I hae a maid as bonnie as she?" The lonely child had glanced at the tutor longingly, his lip quivering slightly.

"Ahem." Master Elphinstone had cleared his throat hesitantly, for he'd felt that Edward, being such a solitary boy and a younger son, would more than likely enter the priesthood. Indeed the lad had already demonstrated a bent toward the religious in his studies. Still, there was no harm surely in a youthful fantasy. "Why, someday, Master Edward, to be sure."

Poor Master Elphinstone had kindled a spark in Edward, and though the boy had continued his preparatory courses for the ministry, he had come to think of Mary as the water nymph to his Pan. He made his offering of a sweet almost worshipfully.

"That would be nice," Mary said taking his hand. "Thou art always dear to me, Edward."

He blushed and did not speak again.

A tart stand was found—Nanna having given her permission for the treat—and Edward took his time selecting the best one of the lot, a plump cherry pie. Gordon bought one for Joanna, too, who waited for Nanna's quick nod of approval before accepting the pastry. Joanna, at seven years of age, recognized her station in life as a servant and knew better than to take for granted the privileges of the nobility. She savored the tart slowly, wanting to make the rare treat last as long as possible.

Before Edward could offer Mary hers, however, Charlie snatched it away from him impishly.

*"Nievie nievie nick-nack, which hand will ye tak? Gin ye're richt or gin ye're wrang. I'll beguile ye if I can."*

Mary smiled as she gazed at her brother, his hands behind his back, some of her excitement in the day being restored. Edward relaxed slightly, seeing that Charlie did not mean to eat the pie himself.

"Right hand," Mary guessed.

"Och," Charlie sighed. "You're a witch, Mary Carmichael."

He handed her the sweet, and she bit into it lustily, dribbling cherry juice down her chin. Edward grinned shyly at her pleasure, glad he'd thought of the tart.

Peace fell over the town as the sun sank lower in the blue sky, its golden rays turning to a pale pink blush on the western horizon. The tart stand owner and her daughter closed the doors on their cart, then hitched their tired nag up to the wagon. The vehicle rattled clumsily over the cobblestones as the mother wearily slapped the long harness against the back of the horse. The weaver folded his bolts of unsold material, covering them carefully in case of rain. The crone with the vegetables groaned as she heaved her bins into her wagon. As the last of the crowds started to drift out of the square the barkers began tearing down their gaily colored tents.

Mary quickly averted her eyes, her stomach churning, as she saw the two-headed monster being hustled off to a cage, but there was naught to fear now. Her brothers and Nanna were with her.

" 'Tis getting late," Nanna said noting the hour. "We must meet your parents at the edge of town."

The children sighed, sorry the day had ended, as they walked through the winding streets to the border of the village. They reached the outskirts at last, where a horde of men and women in the colors of the Clan Carmichael had already gathered. Amid the din nurses attempted to locate their young charges, and children were swapped hurriedly. Mary scarcely had time to thank Edward and bid him good-bye before his nanny bundled him off.

Someone helped her mount her small pony, and she tugged on the reins while searching for the rest of her immediate family. There were her brothers Ian and the twins kissing her mother's hand farewell. Ian was a page to Uncle Gilchrist of Leabaidh a' Nathair, where Hugh was also in service. Andrew and Harold, who'd had no wish to be parted from each other, were in training with Uncle Walter of Moy Heath. They no longer resided at Bailekair. Next year, when he was ten,

Gordon would be sent away for fostering at one of the other Carmichael holdings as well: Dùndereen, Càrnwick, Abergorra, or Glochlomond.

Hugh rode past, gazing at Mary spitefully, his eye almost swollen shut and his mouth caked over with blood. She pretended not to see him, although she shivered faintly when he had gone.

Because four households of the Clan Carmichael had met that day for the fair, there were fully one hundred men-at-arms present, in addition to the relatives; and the outskirts of town were a milling blaze of purple and blue, the Carmichael colors. Still there was one man who stood out from them all, a tall blond giant, the Chief and Captain of the clan. He wore a white shirt and the Chief's *breacan* of belted plaid; the long ends of the garment were draped over the left shoulder of his dark blue doublet and pinned in place with the clan's crest-badge. This was a circular brooch of silver, engraved with the Carmichael shield: *or a cross purpure* surmounted of a winged *or* unicorn *rampant argent, armed* and *crined or,* issuing from a cloud *azure,* the *dexter* foreleg bearing a broadsword *argent* and *or.* The unicorn, as befitting the man's rank, was crowned with a gold coronet. A dark blue broad-bonnet, with the clan's plant-badge of purple heather attached to the front, was upon his head. His broadsword hung at this left side; there was a dirk at his waist near his leather *sporran;* and his legs were encased in hose and high leather boots, the right one of which bore a *sgian-dubh.*

Mary's eyes picked him out of the crowd easily as she pressed her small pony forward.

"Father!"

He was busy shouting orders and did not hear her. She hauled on the pony's bridle, trying to get through the mass, ignoring Nanna's call for her to come back immediately. Someone came up close beside her. Mary only had time to see it was Ian, angry over what had befallen Hugh, before he slapped her mount sharply with his riding crop, cursing at her under his breath. The sudden blow startled the animal; it bolted, nearly tossing Mary from the saddle. She managed to remain seated by grasping the pommel, but dropped the reins in the process. The stubborn little beast, sensing its rider's loss of control, broke free of the other horses, galloping out over the sweeping terrain. Mary gritted her teeth, hanging on for dear life as the grassy moor seemed to rush toward her; her head spun dizzily, and all she could think about were her hands gripping the saddle horn tighter and tighter as she watched the bridle slip farther up along the bolting pony's neck, farther from her reach. Her heart pounded furiously in her breast. Hold on! she told herself, hold on! She heard shouting behind her and surmised correctly that someone had seen and given chase, but the pony was running wildly.

From the south of town the cage bearing the two-headed monster fumbled slowly out of the borders of Inverness; Mary saw, to her horror, that her uncontrollable mount was headed straight toward the hideous creature. She strained desperately for the reins, but they were just beyond her grasp. The animal swerved abruptly. The monster's keeper yelled furiously. Frightened, the pony shied, then bucked and reared, and Mary was thrown violently from the saddle. Before she hit the ground she caught one awful glimpse of the monster's live head cackling gleefully, then all was blackness.

# Three

The Countess of Bailekair, Lady Margaret, was in her early thirties. Her face was set in the grave lines that had come from too many years of struggle, too many years of childbearing, and too many years of watching the men of the Clan Carmichael ride off to battle, not knowing if they would return. Her pale blond hair was already streaked with grey; her cold, hooded eyes were the color of blue ice.

She turned from the fire to glance toward the long staircase in the main hall. Upstairs Mary lay struggling for survival, each breath the child drew a painful effort due to the ribs battered by the errant pony. Margaret could almost hear the ragged gasps that marked her only daughter's fight with death. The Countess smiled grimly to herself, for she despised Mary. Mary, the golden lass whom God had seen fit, in His wisdom, to send Margaret long after she'd thought her fruitful years ended and had turned the Earl out of her bed. God's and Magnus's last laugh; that's what Mary was.

Aye, God had sent the hated child; perhaps now He would take her away. Margaret prayed, but not for Mary.

The Countess was the bastard daughter of a Baron of Glochlomond long since dead. She'd been just fourteen when she'd married Magnus. Why the laird's eyes had settled on her, she'd never known; but she'd been pretty in her youth before the sour disposition of age had stolen her looks. And Magnus had always had a weakness for a bonnie face.

Her life at Glochlomond had not been a happy one. Her mother had been a lowly serf who'd passed away when the girl had been but two years old, and her father had had little interest in her other than as a tool for bargaining with the rest of the clan. The Baron's wife had not liked the child and had taken great delight in making her the constant butt of many cruel jokes. The maids of the household, observing their lady's hatred for Margaret, had done likewise; so the poor girl had been the victim of several sharp slaps, mean jests, and taunting remarks over the years. She'd been only too glad to marry Magnus—she would have wed a boar to get out of that household—and had been grateful for being raised to such a position of importance in the clan. Moreover, it had been flattering to be wanted by such a handsome, blond man.

But she'd been ill-prepared for marriage. She'd come to Magnus's bed on their wedding night frightened and with no inkling of the sexual act. Had Magnus been less drunk and less used to tumbling easy wenches, he might have suspected Margaret's fear and, having learned the reason for it, explained the ritual to her and used her gently. But instead he'd ripped the thin gown from her trembling body and forced himself upon her without another thought. Margaret, scared, dry, and unprepared, had felt herself torn asunder by his bruising entry. When his vigorous attack had ceased, and he'd lain sleeping by her side, she'd stared at him, horrified by the pain he'd wrought upon her flesh. In that moment she'd begun to despise him, to loathe the sight of his bonnie face and giant frame. When she'd discovered she was to undergo this terrible treatment nightly, she'd abhorred him all the more.

It had been some time before she'd found herself pregnant and, being incredibly ignorant, later than that when she'd realized the act she'd endured was what had gotten her with child. Magnus had been delighted at the thought of an heir; Margaret had been terrified! Women died in childbirth! Hadn't her own mother lost her life this way? Perhaps if she'd been able to discuss her fears with the women in her household, she might still have come to understand the function between a man and woman and the strange feeling of her own body burdened with the bairn. But because of her earlier treatment at Glochlomond by the Baroness's maids, Margaret had been unable to bring herself to discuss anything with her own women at Bailekair, so afraid had she been they would laugh at her stupidity.

Five sons. Five strong, healthy sons she'd borne Magnus Carmichael, with each birth growing more stern and dour, more determined to pay the despised Earl back for the pain his children had cost her. Then, with what little cold affection she'd been by then capable of feeling, Margaret had wooed Magnus's boys away from their father. From the time they'd first put their mouths to her laden breasts to suck the milk of life from them, she'd begun to undermine any sort of influence Lord Magnus might have had with his offspring. Through the years the Countess had fully succeeded with her eldest son, Ian, and the twins, Andrew and Harold. They were her lads, and it showed on their dour faces and in the fierce quarrels that often sprang up between them and the Earl whenever they were home.

Gordon and Charlie, Margaret merely tolerated. She'd

failed with them, perhaps because Magnus had finally realized her intentions, thwarting her schemes before they could take root. But his *heir* was hers, and that was what really counted. When the Earl was dead, Margaret would rule Bailekair through Ian. Bailekair! The grandest castle in all Scotland! 'Twould truly be hers then, hers alone! 'Twas a dream she would wait a lifetime if need be to see fulfilled.

For Magnus Carmichael, the rutting beast who'd assaulted her in such a disgusting fashion, filling her with the weight of his undesired sons, and for Mary, the product of his drunken usage one night two years after the Countess had ceased to share his bed, Margaret had no love at all. Mary was Magnus's child, as surely as Ian, Andrew, and Harold were hers.

Now an embittered, sharp-tongued woman, grown mean with her age and authority, Margaret was the spitting image of the now-dead Baroness of Glochlomond who'd despised her so heartily. She mistreated everyone and everything—with the exception of her three dear sons—to avenge the years of abuse, real and imagined, she'd suffered. Nothing escaped her sharp, prying eyes, not a speck of dust, not a single penny. She ruled her household with a spiteful, miserly fist, beating her maids and cheating her serfs at every opportunity.

She gazed across the room at Magnus, her husband. 'Twould hurt him deeply if he lost his only daughter. With her heart like a stone in her breast Margaret prayed for Mary's death.

Upstairs Mary Carmichael tossed fitfully in her sleep and cried out. Mistress Flora moved worriedly to soothe the unconscious lass, smoothing back the tangled strands of blond hair damp from the child's fever and rechecking the bandages that bound the fractured ribs and covered the deep cuts the pony's hooves had made.

"There, there, my lady. Nanna is here," Flora crooned softly.

The sound of her voice seemed to calm the bairn somewhat, and Mistress Flora settled back into her chair, though the anxious frown she'd worn ever since the accident was still upon her face.

She dared not give Mary any more of the mixture of herbs she'd brewed earlier. A larger dose might prove fatal for the girl.

"What is it, my bonnie wee bairn? What do ye see inside your mind that makes ye call oot wie such fright?" Flora asked quietly. "Och," she sighed. "Ye canna be telling me now; that I know. Still, I would ye rested easier."

The nurse sighed again, then arose to bank up the fire so the kettle of water hanging over the flames would produce more steam to aid the child's ragged breathing.

If Mary knew how desperately Flora fought to save her life, she gave no sign of it, for she lay locked in the hell of her own imaginings.

'Twas dark in her dream; the gray mist swirled around her so thickly she could scarcely see; the land through which she traveled appeared strangely twisted and unfamiliar. The steed she rode was coal black and high-strung. Mary could feel the wetness of the beast through the thin *arascaid* she wore and knew somehow its ebony coat was damp not from the mist, but lathered from wild flight. The animal's sides heaved as she paused and glanced back over one shoulder.

She heard crazy laughter in the darkness, and her heart pounded fiercely with fright. *It* was still chasing her, the horrible two-headed monster that had been following her for miles. She must get away! She laid her whip about the stallion's sides, pressing on frantically.

The hooves of the black steed clattered ominously over the rocky terrain, and the mountain toward which she rode loomed forbiddingly in the distance.

"Marrrrry. Marrrrry."

The whisper of her name was faint, but she would have known that voice anywhere. She breathed a sigh of relief.

"Father! I'm coming, father!"

Desperately she strove to reach him through the hellish shadows of the night. And then he was there before her, hanging from a cross at the side of the steep winding path she traveled. His head was severed, and blood flowed like a river from the mortal wound he bore.

Mary screamed.

Nanna turned quickly from the fire to restrain the distraught child, pressing a fresh, damp cloth upon the girl's forehead.

"Mistress Flora!" Magnus burst into the chamber. "I heard a cry. I—I couldna wait longer. Is she—"

"The lass is worse, my lord." Flora's eyes filled with tears as she gazed at the ravaged Earl before her. "I fear the fall has done something to her mind. The blow—when she hit her head—"

"My God! Is there naught we can do?"

"Nothing, my lord, except wait—and pray."

Mary yanked the black horse from the terrible sight before her, feeling the warm, sticky spray of the red blood fly up from the beast's hooves as it galloped. The blood that had once quickened in her father's veins spattered upon her face and hands, mingled with the mist in her cascading mass of blond hair. Tears streamed down her cheeks; she could taste the salt of them bittersweet upon her lips.

Branches slapped at her face as the steed raced recklessly on toward the mountain.

"Marrrrry. Marrrrry."

Her eyes strained in the darkness.

"Where are ye, Edward?"

"Here, Mary, here."

He rose up before her in the road.

"Oh, Edward—"

And then she saw the cross he carried in one outstretched hand.

"Nay!" She flung her hands up to hide her eyes.

The stallion reared and struck him down before her, but when she looked at him again, there was no mark upon him. His serene body sank into the ground beneath her until he was no more.

She heard the rattling of the two-headed monster's cage behind her, heard its keeper calling to her, drawing ever nearer.

"Help me, please! Somebody help me!"

But no one came, so Mary pressed on alone.

The black steed staggered up the mountain path, its legs moving ever more slowly, dragging now with each step.

"Faster! I know ye can go faster!" The girl beat the animal cruelly with her whip, but it was winded, tired. It could go no more.

Mary hung her head and wept.

"Dinna weep, child."

The lass raised her face at the sound of the cracked voice, staring with fear at the grizzled old woman who stood before her.

"Dinna be afraid," the crone said. "Ye called for help, and I am here to gie it to ye."

"Who—who are ye?"

"I am part of what once was and will be again. I come from before your time and hae waited many, many years for your arrival."

"How can ye help me?"

"By showing ye what few others hae e'er seen. Destiny!"

The hag flung her cape out from her withered body and was instantly surrounded by a mass of fire that burned hotter and hotter until she was enveloped in the flames.

"Do ye wish to see it, child?"

Mary trembled with fear, for 'twas bad luck to know one's future, but she could not seem to help herself.

"Aye." She nodded frozenly. "I want to see."

"Then, behold!"

The girl turned. The two-headed monster's cage was rumbling toward her, its keeper beckoning slyly to her with one hand. By the light of the blaze Mary could see it was her own mother enticing her toward the cage that contained the monster bearing the heads of her brother Ian and her cousin Hugh!

"They come for ye, child."

"But—'tis my own kin who seek me here." The lass felt oddly relieved.

"Och, then why did ye run from them?" the harridan cackled softly.

"I—I dinna know." Mary was genuinely puzzled by this. Hugh and Ian were bullies, true, but they were of her blood and meant her no harm surely! She had naught to fear from her own clansmen. Her eyes narrowed as she gave the woman a suspicious glance, wondering what spell the old witch wove.

"Look upward to yon mountain crag." The ancient seer gestured toward the peak in the distance.

From its crest rose the spire of a kirk, and in the swirling gray mist Mary spied a ghostly destrier upon which was mounted a shrouded figure. The girl shivered.

"Who is he?" she asked.

"Your mirror, child. Dinna ye see yourself reflected there in his eyes?"

"Nay!" she cried. "He is my enemy! I feel it!"

"Aye." The prophet grinned craftily. "But he waits for ye all the same, as do they." Her black eyes gleamed maliciously as she nodded toward Mary's family once more.

"Nay!" Mary screamed again. "He carries the scent of death upon his soul. Death! Dinna let him touch me! Cold. So cold. So many tears. So many graves. What does it mean?" Her voice rose to a shrill piercing. "What does it mean?"

But there was no one to answer. The grizzled witch had gone. The flames had taken her at last, and naught save ashes lay where once she'd been.

# Four

Mary Carmichael did not die, much to Lady Margaret's disgust. In time her fractured ribs mended; the deep, cutting wounds of the pony's hooves healed; and the memory of the accident faded from her mind. Even the terrible nightmare that had haunted her dreams that Lammas Eve mellowed until she could scarcely recall it. Indeed 'twas not until years later she would dredge it, with fearful detail, from the dark recesses of her mind; and, even then, she would not understand what the dream had meant.

She grew as other young lassies of the Highlands did, yet she was different from them as well. For Mary was her father's child, as Lady Margaret so often reminded her. She bore the stamp of his wild impetuousness, his brave-hearted spirit, and his just sense of honor deeply within her soul. No meek obedience, stoic endurance, or silent acceptance born of fear of a man's sharp word or stinging blow marked her. If she realized she lacked the gentler traits a more loving mother might have bestowed in preparation for a woman's lot in life, Mary did not regret their absence.

At fourteen years of age, she was a creature as wild and fey as those other animals that stalked the rich brown-and-green woods and roamed the gold-and-purple heaths of the Scottish Highlands, raw and untamed, like the land in which they struggled for survival.

Not beautiful in the usual way, Mary had an elusive and savage grace. She was like a forest nymph, beckoning to her lover, then slipping away before he could gather her in his arms, her haunting laughter rippling like the silver strands of the mountain streams.

Her heavy, shining mass of hair shimmered like a waterfall to her knees, the golden color of bracken in the sun; her skin was golden, too, like fresh sweet honey. She seemed to float when she walked, slender as a reed, with high round breasts and lithe limbs. Her nose was straight; her cheeks were tinged with rosy color; her jaw was as finely chiseled as the rest of her, meeting her long graceful neck in a delicate hollow.

She appeared, at first glance, as fragile as the broom on the Highland moors, as ethereal as the Scottish mist. Only her mouth and eyes belied the image. For her generous red lips promised passion, parting to show even white teeth. And her eyes—violet chasms they were, as purple as the heather she gathered on the Highland heaths—the glittering depths of amethyst crystal the Highland folk called "Carmichael eyes." Framed with golden brows and feathery golden lashes, they were eyes in whose depths a man could drown. A person could see them a thousand times and still be bewitched by their haunting purple shadows. They were the eyes of a changeling child, the Highland folk whispered; and there were more than a few who made the sign of the cross when Mary Carmichael passed by.

Truly she alone of all her siblings was the spawn of Bailekair and its heritage, proud and arrogant in her will, steadfast in her strength, stubborn in her desire. Mayhap 'twas this that made her Magnus's favorite, for the Earl loved Bailekair more than anything on earth, even his only daughter.

It was an impressive fortress, Mary's birthplace; and she worshiped it fervently. The castle was not beautiful; it was too ponderous, too powerful for that. But it was magnificent, awesome, compelling. Those who had once seen Bailekair never forgot the grand sight. It had no moat, but along its sides were deep crevices gouged out of the earth by the streams that rushed down from the top of the mountain during the spring thaw.

These were rapid, dangerous currents, especially when filled to overflowing as they were now, for spring came early to Bailekair that year of 1486, and the frozen ground gave way to the tiny green shoots of new awakening that pressed their arms to the surface. All across Scotland the still whiteness of winter's death disappeared with the bright colors of the earth coming to life again.

The Highlands were covered with the wide expanse of deer grass, upon which those majestic animals feasted; the crags of the mountains near the loch gave birth to the fir club moss that, seeking moisture, crept through the cracks and crevices of the rocks. The fragrant white flowers and aromatic berries of the bog-myrtle mingled headily with the scent of decaying peat in the deep stretches of mire; the red whortleberry bloomed. The handsome blossoms of the azaleas trailed upon the ground; the long, slender branches of the broom burst forth with yellow buds. The leaves of the laurel shone glossily in the sunlight; the purple heather and gilded bracken filled the sweeping moors and hillsides.

The oaks grew tall and sturdy, with dark acorns nestled among green leaves; the reddish brown nuts of the hazel played hide-and-seek among its rustling branches. The spire-shaped poplars bowed gently in the wind, their light wood glowing in the distance; the red hawthorn budded with bright fruit. The berries of the juniper flourished, plumply lush and purple, aching to be squeezed; the pink flowers of the crab apple tree fluttered delicately in the breeze. The tough mountain ash stood firm, unyielding; the green needles of the pines brought forth cones.

Wild boar foraged in the forests, grunting meanly when disturbed; wolves howled to their mates in the darkness of the night; startled does kept watch over spotted fawns; bears lumbered from their lairs of hibernation; mountain lions screamed in the hills.

The cruel, freezing winds of the Highland's dying season

lessened to the warm, gentle stirrings of the whispering breezes of the new spring with the appearance of the rich golden sun spreading its rays of melted butter across the bogs and glens, the moors and mountains of Scotland.

This was the promise of rebirth given to all God's creatures; how could they doubt it? How could they not believe such a fresh awakening as spring awaited them long after their bodies had turned to ashes and dust in the winters of their years? This was the hope that made them all look upward to the heavens and give thanks, the humility that made them lower their heads in prayer, the love that stood constant in their hearts. For *this* was life!

Bailekair rejoiced in the heady intoxication of the land. The frosty season had been brightened, of course, by the holidays: Samhain, Martinmas, St. Andrew's Day, Christmas, and Hogmany. But other than these there had been little to do in the winter except sit by the fire and embroider on some piece of linen.

Mary's fingers had grown stiff and clumsy on the delicate stitchery, earning her many reprimanding comments from her mother; her back had begun to ache from the long hours of perching on the edge of her hard chair, eyes straining to see the patterns of the tiny threads she normally sewed so beautifully. With the coming of spring there was work to do. Mary's days were busy as the great castle came to life with the rest of Scotland.

The soil must be tilled for the planting of crops. Livestock had to be driven back to their pastures for grazing and the outer ward of the fortress shoveled of their filth, the manure being saved for fertilizing the grains later on. The keep itself had to be cleaned and swept, old rushes bundled outside for burning, new ones laid upon the floors. Mattresses must be turned and aired, the wall tapestries beaten to relieve them of their winter dust. The larder had to be checked for low supplies, tallows poured to replace those used by the family, torches made for the iron holders that lined the halls of the keep. The huntsmen who supplied fresh game had to be instructed as to what was lacking in the way of meats; and salmon, the only readily available fish to the inlands, had to be replenished.

Mary helped with most of these chores, for it was Lady Margaret's duty to instruct her daughter in the arts of managing a huge household in preparation for the day the girl would wed and become a chatelaine in her own right. Following the Countess like a shadow, Mary marveled at the clink of the many keys that dangled from the huge ring at her mother's waist. The sound reminded her of Bailekair's grandeur and made her proud of her father for owning such a fortress.

As she and Lady Margaret entered the dark cool larder the retinue of servants that traveled in their wake scurried forward with candles to light the way and drive off the rats that pattered across the stone floor at the household's intrusion. Onions, lying in their bins, were plentiful enough, as were the crisp apples that had been dried and strung across the room. But the cheeses cured earlier were in low supply, as were the carrots and beans. These last items were noted in Lady Margaret's household book so they could be planted in the vegetable gardens later on.

"Write neatly, Mary Kathryn, and dinna let that candle drip upon the pages," the Countess chided sharply.

In the storeroom it was seen tallows were almost depleted. "New ones must be made to fill the empty bins after they hae been blessed on Candlemas," Lady Margaret told her servants. "They must be sweet and burn clearly, nae wasting away so rapidly they afford little light at all and nae so ill-made they smoke wie stench when lit."

The maids nodded their heads vigorously in unison, for they had all heard this same reminder every year, and many had suffered a sharp slap when all had not been done to the Countess's liking.

The torches, of course, always smelled; but that could not be helped, any more than the black soot that poured from them could be prevented. The castle walls, stained with the dark residue left from the oils in which the torches were dipped, could attest to that.

The mattresses were split open, stuffed with fresh ticking, then sewn back together, Lady Margaret smartly boxing the ears of one new maid who dared complain about the heavy chore. Some of the bedding was infested with lice. This had to be boiled in hot water laced with turpentine (made from the sap of pine trees), then scrubbed with lye soap—the household staff who'd slept in it done likewise. The male serfs of the keep were called to shovel out the rushes matted with rotten food, piss from men who'd been too drunk or lazy to seek a chamber pot, and the offal of the hounds that always accompanied Lord Magnus; then fresh reeds were laid down. The tapestries were whipped with stout sticks; the dust flew, making Mary sneeze heartily.

When these chores were done, there were lessons in reading, writing, ciphering, and languages (specifically English, French, and German) from the priest; sewing, soap- and perfume-making, dance, and etiquette from the maids; lute-, flute-, and harp-playing from the castle bard.

So the years of Mary's life had passed, one much like another, with only the changes she had expected from birth to mark their passage, changes made no less sorrowful by the knowledge of their coming.

She could still recall the bitter tears wept at six years of age when Gordon had been sent away to Dùndereen for fostering, the loneliness that had engulfed her the following year when Charlie had been dispatched to Càrnwick for the same purpose.

Fostering was an important custom in the Highlands. At ten years of age, the sons of the lairds and other family men were sent to this household or that for service. At first they acted as pages for the lords to whom they'd been fostered. They were taught humility and respect for their superiors; how to attend their masters; how to ride destriers, the highly trained war-horses used in battle; and how to employ their weapons. They joined in games that taught skill and strategy in combat. They played *Quintain*, a sport in which they jousted with dummies to glean the rudiments of tilting. They learned to hunt with hawks and falcons.

When they were fifteen, if they had accomplished these tasks well, they were given the title of *squire* and received a pennon, a small flag that bore their insignias and was attached to their lances. As they progressed through the advanced exercises of training points of the pennon were cut off for service until it became a banner. During this time they were allowed to fight in minor skirmishes, where they rode at their masters' sides, sometimes carrying their lairds' shields if, during their apprenticeship as squires, they had proven themselves worthy of this privilege. And always, even at the cost of their own lives, they protected their lords.

At twenty-one, the age of manhood, they were dubbed knights in a solemn ceremony. This could take place on the field of battle for great bravery in action, but was usually held during a time of peace. The night before the ritual the squire kept a sacred vigil over his armor and weapons; in the morning he donned a red-and-black cloak over a white tunic to make his vows. He knelt before the *parrain* (the laird who was knighting him) to receive the *accolade* (a touch on both shoulders from a sword held in the hands of the lord). If the newly created knight were not heir to some holding, he made his way in the world through battles and tourneys and in service to other men. Otherwise he returned home to learn how to manage his inheritance.

A man's foster brothers were as important to him as his own blood brothers, sometimes even more so. Often there were sworn oaths or pacts between them. Many times marriages and the fostering of their own sons grew out of these binding relationships. 'Twas not unusual for a man's younger brothers to reside in his household if the clan's holdings were not numerous enough for grants to be given to the lesser sons and for a man's foster brothers, if they had no holdings of their own, to live there as well. Thus families were often large and close-knit, overrun with men, women, and children.

The same year Charlie had gone to Cárnwick young Edward Carmichael had come to Bailekair to learn the ways of a warrior. A pale lad, however, he had seemed almost too thin, too frail to endure the rigors of training required for knighthood.

His slender hands were shaped not for swinging the heavy battle-axe but for playing the delicate flute from which he coaxed such beautiful melodies. His mind was not geared to devising war strategies but to formulating the poetry he penned upon scraps of parchment pages.

Still, in a time when even priests marched into battle, it had been necessary for him to persist in his endeavors.

"God's blood, 'tis hot," he moaned one day, wiping the sweat from his brow.

The ever-faithful Alan smiled. "Wait until you're weighted down wie armor, Master. You'll vow someone's placed ye in an oven."

"Marry-go-up! I canna ken that, sir. How can a mon move, encumbered wie such a burden?" Edward shook his head with disbelief.

"Some canna," Lord Magnus joined the little group. "'Tisna wise to let the metal-workers talk ye into the heavy plate they would fashion for ye, Edward, the better to enrich their purses. Many's the time I hae seen a knight so laden that when unhorsed, he couldna arise again and lay upon the ground like a turtle on its back. 'Twas much laughed at by those present, but a poor jest on the battlefield, for then he would be an easy target for a lance or battle-ax."

Edward nodded, storing this bit of information away carefully, knowing he had much to learn and remember, all of which he must do well if he were to distinguish himself in battle and win a holding of his own. For Edward was heir to no keep; his father's castle, Dùndereen, was the bold black Hugh's inheritance. Edward's goal was not born of greed, however. Indeed he would have been happier as a priest or wandering minstrel than as a powerful laird, for he was a dreamer, not a doer, born to a world for which he was ill-equipped to survive. But he had one burning desire in life, and to attain it he needed a title.

Edward loved Mary Carmichael, worshiped her feet and the ground they walked on with a secret, aching, all-consuming fever; and he knew the hand of the Chief's daughter would not be given unto a holy man or lowly knight.

Already he had seen Hugh, secure in the knowledge of his earldom and hungry for power, run his hot eyes possessively over the lass's ripening figure; and it sickened Edward to think of Mary lying in his half brother's arms. She was his, Edward's woman, his golden water nymph. Aye, she belonged to Pan, not Hades, the dark god of the underworld. She would pine away like Persephone in his half brother's keeping. Only he, Edward, stood between Mary and Hugh for there was no other clansman brave enough to thwart Hugh's plan to have her as his wife. Hugh was rising in the Carmichael ranks like the morning sun, fiery in his brilliance. Even Edward felt the bile choke in his throat at the thought of his half brother's rage upon losing such a prize, but Edward's desire for Mary was even greater than his fear of Hugh.

In moments of deepest reflection Edward realized Mary did not love him as he did her, but with his romantic nature, he brushed this thought aside, dreaming instead of how gratefully she would fling herself at his feet when he had saved her from his half brother and charmed her with the enchanted music of his pipes.

Mary herself adored Edward, just as she adored her brothers Gordon and Charlie. She had no idea of his or Hugh's plans for her. She never guessed that Edward loved her as a man does a woman.

Like these young men Mary had entered a new world at age ten. The much-loved Nanna had married Alan that summer, and Joanna had at last stepped into her station in life as Mary's maid. The makings of a woman had begun in earnest then.

Now, at fourteen, Mary Carmichael stood on the threshold of that womanhood, eager to explore more than just the Highland heaths of her birth, yet half-afraid to leave their familiar security. But leave she must, for she was to journey to Edinburgh, to Holyrood Place, where she would reside at Court for the next two years. It was an honor accorded her as the daughter of a powerful Highland chief. Afterward she would return home to marry the man her father chose for her.

But two years is a long time in the life of a young maiden,

so Mary had no thought of weddings upon her mind as she gazed out over the wide expanse of Bailekair's lands from a tower of the keep. Instead, like the two edges of a sword, excitement at the prospect of living at Court pricked her spirits, and sadness at leaving home pierced her heart.

In the distance she could see the grove of mountain ash trees where she had dreamt away her idle hours and where young Edward, playing Pan, had hidden with his flute; the vast, sweeping moors across which she and Joanna had ridden, unbound hair flying as they'd galloped headlong into the wind; the square fields and thatched huts of the crofters, some only blackened ruins, claimed by the enemy Clan MacBeth in its swift, sudden attacks upon Bailekair.

The stark patches of charred lands and desolate remains of shacks stood out prominently against the bright colors of the spring and the quiet village of the keep. Mary cursed the MacBeths silently under her breath, even though she knew that marauding Carmichaels visited such destruction upon MacBeth lands as well. *An eye for an eye. A tooth for a tooth.* So it had always been between the two clans.

The lass shivered, thinking of the nights she had watched the raids from the safety of the castle walls, heard the heathen war cries of her clan's enemies split the darkness with their savage fury. *A MacBeth! A MacBeth!* Seen the blaze of their red-and-green *breacans* by the light of the torches they had carried. Tended the wounded and buried the dead in the aftermath of their slaughter.

They were the thorns upon her rose, the worms in her apple. They trampled, looted, and burned the lands of Bailekair. And Bailekair was everything dear to her heart.

Someday she vowed to have her revenge upon them; but for now her mind was filled with thoughts of Edinburgh, and she had no time to waste upon the MacBeths. She was not a man to take up a sword and shield against them. Her armor was the low-cut Court gowns, not just *arascaids*, with which she and Joanna were outfitted for the trip, in spite of Lady Margaret's annoyance at the vast expense incurred. And Mary's weapon was her savage beauty, untouched by any man. If only she had known how well her accoutrements were to serve her!

But Mary did not. She had only a strange inkling of doom the day Edward came to her from the stables, leading the wild stallion he'd captured and trained in secrecy as a going-away present for her.

What a fine, spirited beast it was, with proud, flaring nostrils and strong, lithe limbs! But it chilled Mary to the bone the moment she saw it, for *it* was the coal black steed of her nightmare that Lammas Eve so many years past! She shrank from the horse, cold prickles of fey foreboding tingling up and down her spine. Her first impulse was to tell Edward to destroy the wicked animal at once!

Yet upon his boyish face his pride and joy mingled so touchingly with his eagerness for approval that the lass found she had not the heart to spoil his pleasure in giving her the steed. And so she kept it for her own, brushing aside her grave misgivings as she mounted the beast and rode out through the iron gate of Bailekair toward Edinburgh, her father and young Edward at her sides.

# *Five*

### Torra nam Sian Castle, Scotland, 1461

On a cold, bleak night in late February, gray rain shattered down from the massive clouds in the sky, glistening in the darkness as a flash of brilliant lightning lit the heavens. The tall, powerful towers of Torra nam Sian Castle, a stronghold of the Clan MacBeth, shone blackly against the horizon for a moment, the high battlements cutting a cruel, jagged edge across the sweep of the stormy background. Far below the fortress, which perched like a preying eagle upon a sheer cliff, the waves of the North Sea crashed against the rocks lining the coast, then thundered out again with a deafening roar.

Lady Laureen closed her eyes again, trying to shut out the sound. Her black hair straggled out, wet and unkempt, over her pillow, and the canopy of the huge bed seemed to close down on her in the darkness of the room. She was suffocating! She was used to a canopy of stars, the rustling of pines, not these heavy draperies at her sides that seemed to stifle her very being! Suffocating. I'm suffocating! she thought again. 'Twas only her mind playing tricks on her once more, however; she knew that. For, when she again opened wide her black eyes before another onslaught of pain, she saw the candles flickering eerily in the cool draft that swept in through the chamber. She breathed in the fresh air deeply.

"Push, my lady, push!"

Her hands gripped tightly the knotted sheets that had been tied to the bedposts. She strained and bore down, then her shrill screams pierced the night air again and again until the pain subsided and she panted raggedly. Someone wiped her brow with a damp cloth. The rain droned on; the waves roared against the coast below. The white glitter of the lightning split the sky and was answered by the booming echo of the thunder that bellowed from the clouds.

"Again, my lady, again!"

"God's blood! I'm going to die!" she moaned before another sharp burst of agony ripped through her body, and her high wail of torture knifed through the castle corridors once more.

Her mind wandered as the candles guttered in their sockets. Flames of firelight, aye, she could see the red yellow blaze of the campfire clearly now. She danced, lifting her arms teasingly; fluttering her hands. Her red skirt whirled out about her dark thighs; her legs flashed in the wavering light. She tossed her head, shaking her long black tresses away from her shoulders shining bare above the ruffles of her white blouse; her breasts strained against the thin material. Her white teeth gleamed as the crimson slash of her mouth parted in a feral snarl. She clapped her hands, stamped her feet.

"Bear down, my lady!"

She bore down in the darkness, lowering her parted thighs upon Ranald's heated pride. She moaned, fingers curling into little claws as she gripped his smooth back; her nails dug into his flesh, streaking blood from his broad shoulders to his narrow hips. Ah, Ranald, my love! His hands caressed her breasts, round and firm, as they slid proudly into his open palms; his wet mouth covered one lingeringly, tongue swirling about the nipple. It flushed to a stiff brown peak. Her naked body glistened like honey in the firelight. Ah, now, Ranald, now!

"Help us, my lady, you've got to help us!"

Her black eyes flew open again at the savage pain. The circle of worried faces blurred, cleared, then misted once more. She screamed. A stooped old woman hurried into the room. One cold hand rested on Laureen's belly; the other probed between her thighs.

"Fools!" the hag hissed to the other three women hovering around the bed. "The bairn is breeched. 'Tis no wonder the lass is in such misery."

"Then she will die," one sobbed, "and Sir Ranald will hae us put to death!"

"Silence!" The midwife's voice was sharp. "I know a way—"

She pushed her strong yellowed hands inside the dilated canal, ignoring the gasps of pain Laureen gave at the exploring assault. The beldam's fingers closed around the child, twisting rapidly. She muttered aloud to herself, ancient, chanting words of magic so that the bairn would not be strangled by the very cord that gave it life. Its small body turned with slow, piercing anguish. A violent cry tore from Laureen's lips.

"Any minute now, my lady," the hunched harridan whispered soothingly.

Down below, in the long hall, Sir Ranald's hand tightened convulsively on his chalice of wine, and his scared white face drew tight with worry. The smoking torches cast their shadows on the wall, and as he turned, the dancing images played across Sir Ranald's young visage.

" 'Tis taking too long"

Lord Duncan shifted uncomfortably in his chair. "The first time is often difficult, Ranald. Laureen's a strong lass."

"Christ! If she dies—"

"Old Bethia's upstairs now—"

"That medicine witch! That foul, evil—"

"The doctor canna come, Ranald. 'Tis the storm. The devil himself couldna find his way here tonight."

Ranald shivered. "All the same, that hag has the wicked eye. I wouldna hae a changeling child—God's breath! If my lassie should die—"

The Baron Torra nam Sian turned away from the anguish in the younger man's eyes as Sir Ranald set his cup of wine on the table and dropped his face to his hands in abject misery. Lord Duncan's chiseled countenance was hard in the firelight that sprang from the hearth as he thought of his young kinsman's wife upstairs. The Baron felt sorry for Ranald, but decided it would be best if Laureen passed on after all. The wench was a strange, wild, fey creature, a Romany gypsy; the marriage was most improper.

Ranald had come upon the girl's caravan camped on the moors one day, had fallen in love with the black-haired wench, and had wed her unbeknownst to anyone else at Torra nam Sian. Some claimed the gypsy had cast a spell on the lad; others swore she'd drugged his wine. Well, no matter how it had come about, when Ranald had returned to the fortress, Laureen had already been his bride and swollen with child, the bairn that even now was struggling to enter the world upstairs.


Laureen gasped.

"Just a little longer, my lady. 'Tis coming! 'Tis coming!"

The gypsy lass felt a wrenching tear as the baby's head forced its way through the passage, then the rest of its small body slithered from hers. There was a strange sensation of

57

calmness, of emptiness for a time, then another brief spasm of pain as the afterbirth was expelled. The cord was cut; the child gave a lusty cry. Laureen closed her eyes and slept. She never even heard Old Bethia crow triumphantly the bairn was a boy. Laureen was alive; that was all that mattered.

As the light began to fade the gray fog swept in from the North Sea, enveloping Torra nam Sian Castle with icy fingers. It prodded gently at first, as though feeling its way, then moved stealthily through the narrow slits of the windows, creeping inside the chambers of the fortress, advancing like cloudy breath. Fine droplets of moisture gathered on the stone walls, lingering there briefly before slipping to the floor to run in little rivulets along the seams between the rocks. Stains marked the cracks where the water had seeped and roughened surfaces where the stones had eroded away from centuries of such quiet assault.

Mistress Sybil moved hurriedly to the narrow shuttered windows to draw the heavy tapestries against the cold draft's invasion. She returned to the blaze of the bright fire at the hearth gratefully, holding her palms out to its warmth for a moment; then she picked up her cup of tea, blowing on the amber liquid to cool it slightly before taking a cautious sip. She licked her lips.

"I dinna e'er abide it here! So deathly still—especially when the fog sets in like this. 'Tis enough to make a body believe in ghosts, I always did say, what wie the wind moaning in the corridors and that mist sneaking aboot here like a cat—nasty animals, they are. I'll be glad to go, I will! Lord knows, I hae done my duty right enough; still, I'd hae washed my hands of the matter if the laird hadna made it worth my while." She lowered her voice. "This place has always gi'en me the shivers!"

"Why did ye stay on then, Mistress Sybil?" Mistress Winifred poured herself another cup of tea, then settled back into her chair, drawing her shawl more closely about her. "I mean, if ye hae ne'er liked the place? Surely the money—"

"Och, 'twasna just that, although I hae put away a tidy

sum." Sybil pursed her lips together smugly. "'Twas the lad, of course. But there, I'm forgetting you're newly come from Kildonen and nae likely to know of such matters." She leaned forward in her chair, fingers clutching at the arms, curling about the wood like talons. "The things I could tell ye—But then I hae ne'er been one to gossip."

"Och, do tell! What aboot the lad? Such a strange wee bairn he is," Winifred prompted obligingly.

Sybil glanced about rapidly to be sure they were alone. "Mind, this is for your ears alone, mistress." She paused until the other nodded vigorously, then continued, eager to let the woman know exactly what sort of household Torra nam Sian was! "'Twas nine years ago the puir laddie was born," she said with a sharp jerk of her head indicating the picture over the fireplace. "Lady Laureen—a gypsy wench, she was; Lord knows what possessed Sir Ranald to marry her—was haeing a difficult time of it. The bairn was breeched; there was a storm, and the doctor couldna get here, so they had to send for Old Bethia."

"The witch?"

"Aye." Sybil drew her chair closer to the other. "The villagers did find the devil's mark upon her body, burnt her up in her hut, they did; that old black ruin down by the creek is all that remains of it now. But, as I was saying, she came that night to deliver the child.

"There were three of us in the room besides that old crone: Mistress Alice, Mistress Dorcas, and me. I remember that right before Old Bethia got here the candles guttered in their sockets, and Mistress Alice, who left shortly afterward, lit fresh ones so the hag could see—her eyesight was failing puirly. Well, Old Bethia turned the bairn and brought it right enough, slapped it to bring the life to its body; and then— you'll ne'er guess what happened!"

"What?" Winifred asked excitedly, hanging on each word.

"A great gust of wind swept through the Lady's chamber and blew all the tallows oot, that's what!"

"The new ones?"

"Aye." Sybil nodded. "Mind, I'm nae saying 'tis the truth,

but they do swear that's when Old Bethia switched the bairns, that when the room was in blackness, she left a changeling child in place of Sir Ranald's son."

"Nay!" Winifred was suitably impressed.

"I dinna believe in such superstitious nonsense myself," Sybil sniffed. "'Tis my own thinking the old witch merely put a spell on the lad—if she dared! Lord knows, those gypsies hae their own kind of magic to ward off such evil tricks. Anyway, after we'd gotten the candles lit again, Mistress Dorcas, who's long since left the Baron's service as well, ran from the chamber, yelling the bairn wasna the same wee one brought into this world only a few moments before. Of course, I peeked at the boy, and he dinna look any different to me, but ye ne'er can tell." She shrugged her shoulders.

"Och, to be sure!"

"Well, whether or nae 'twas true, when Lady Laureen— who ne'er had any interest in the lad to begin wie—finally asked to see the child, she took one glimpse and started screaming her head off, claiming the bairn was cursed." Sybil leaned forward, whispering. "He *does* hae the Carmichael eyes, ye know, same as his grandfather, may *that* puir, accursed soul rest in peace."

Winifred inclined her head in assent, casting a discreet glance at the portrait over the hearth again. "Aye, I hae heard the legend. What happened then?"

"Och, two weeks later the Lady ran off from the castle and was ne'er seen again. Most folks aboot here think she went back to her own people, those Romany gypsies, to get a charm to take the spell off her son. Whether 'tis so or nae, she ne'er came back here—nae that she e'er really belonged at Torra nam Sian to begin wie. Everyone said the marriage was a disaster from the start." Sybil's lips compressed together with brief disapproval. "But ne'ertheless it broke Sir Ranald's heart. He wasna e'er quite right after she'd gone, moped aboot these long corridors—dingy things!—for months following the Lady's disappearance; then one night he went up to the northern tower and hanged himself!"

"Ye dinna say!"

"Aye." Sybil spoke darkly. "He was such a fine mon, too, more's the pity, nae like his father, Sir George. Aye, accursed, like the child, the *auld* mon was. They do say he went mad of it in the end, blinded his eyes wie the hot edge of a dirk before he drove the dagger into his heart."

"Nay!"

"Aye," the other repeated. "Puir Sir Ranald. His father and son both the devil's spawn. 'Tis no wonder the puir mon took his life like Sir George, followed him, unshriven, to the grave, for, of course, neither could be buried in consecrated ground."

"Och, to be sure!" Winifred exclaimed again. "And the bairn? What of him?"

"He's oot there." Sybil nodded toward the dark moors where the rain was falling now. "Somewhere, riding that ghostly horse of his. I hae done my best for him, puir, wee laddie; but he's a strange one after all, disappears into the fog at all sorts of odd hours like someone nae of this world. I dinna mind saying I'm half-afraid of the boy."

"Understandable, my dear Sybil," Winifred presumed upon the intimate conversation. "You'd think a body wouldna want to be ootside on a day like this!"

Sybil withdrew visibly at the presumption. "Aye, to be sure. But there, I dinna hold wie idle chatter, mistress. Mind ye hold your tongue aboot this conversation. The laird willna hear a word of this tale nowadays. Pities the child; I dinna hae doubts aboot that! And the bairn is peculiar enough wie'oot foolish twaddle prattled in his ear, do ye ken?"

"Dinna fash yourself, mistress." Winifred felt pleased that Sybil had entrusted her with the confidence, despite the other's reserved retreat, although Winifred was now having grave doubts about whether or not to remain in the castle. "The Baron willna learn a thing from *my* lips; ye can be certain of that!"

"Och, 'tis getting late, and I hae chores to be tending." Sybil paused a moment as she set her teacup down on a table, unbending slightly once more in light of the other woman's eager agreement and support. "As I hae said, the laird's paid me well enough to look after the lad all these years, but I'll be glad when he's sent away for fostering after all. Changeling or no, he's as fey as his wild mother was. There'll be trouble here one of these days if Hunter MacBeth returns to serve the Baron as the rest of his ilk hae served the Barons Torra nam Sian these many years past. Ye mark my words, mistress—there's gypsy blood in his veins; and, Lord knows, those Romanies are a pack of tramps and thieves! Why, even Lady Laureen—may the puir woman rest in peace—stole a solid gold necklace when she left here. It had been passed down to the brides of the accursed MacBeths since Sir George's time. Imagine! Aye, 'tis my belief the laird will live to rue the day he kept that odd boy on here, and I pity the keep that takes the puir child into training!"

High above the western shores of Loch Ness, set among the cliffs overlooking the deep chasm below it, as though it had been chiseled out of the rocky crags upon which it dwelt, rose Glenkirk Castle. 'Twas a beautiful fortress, perhaps the loveliest in all Scotland. Although its high walls were ten feet thick and built of heavy red sandstone, the keep was delicately fashioned, its tall towers reaching up to the white clouds in the azure sky, resembling the graceful spires of a church. There was no need for a moat, for there was only one way to gain access to the castle; that was a steeply graded road that wound its path through the rocks up to the iron portcullis of the gatehouse, making an assault on the fortress's defenses almost impossible.

Hunter MacBeth rolled over on his back. He came up here often to this little niche among the cliffs. For as long as he could remember he'd always needed a secret place of his own, a place to get away from those around him.

He liked the mountains of Scotland, for they were deceptive. They were not high, and, because they were rounded on the tops—not really peaked at all—they looked more like hills than rugged alps. 'Twas only when one began to climb them one realized one's mistake. They were filled with deep

62

chasms, gorges left from the time centuries ago when glaciers had covered the greater part of the Highlands; and they were hard, craggy. Little vegetation grew among the rocks, which were solid granite in some areas and the red sandstone of which Glenkirk had been built in others. Most of the time, even in the mellow summers, the summits of the ragged mountains were covered with white snow. Perhaps it was the gauzy clouds of mist that kept them so.

The man had come to Glenkirk fifteen years ago; he'd been ten years old then, a young lad alone, but not really lonely. He was used to being by himself. It had started in his childhood at Torra nam Sian when he'd had no one save Mistress Sybil to look after him; she'd been a sour old woman at best. Hunter suspected she'd been half-afraid of him as well. Well, who wouldn't have been, what with Lady Laureen's strange disappearance, Ranald's hanging himself, and George's self-mutilation before ending his own life, too?

Lord Duncan had been kind to Hunter, of course, but not much interested in anything the boy did. The Baron had treated the child nicely, primarily out of pity, and had been greatly relieved when the lad had become old enough to send away.

Encouraged by Lord Angus, Earl of Glenkirk, Hunter had worked hard at the chores put to his doing. Through the years he'd learned how to handle his broadsword and shield well, how to manipulate his lance so that his opponent could not unhorse him, and he was proficient in the use of a bow and arrows, one of the most deadly weapons employed by the Highland clans. His strong, muscular arms could swing a battle-ax or morningstar easily, and seldom did his dirk miss its mark. He'd learned these things gladly, knowing his skill in such matters would determine how well he would make his way in life through battles and tourneys, for Hunter was heir to no holding of his own.

Still, he remained an enigma to those around him. He mixed in well enough at Glenkirk, but only because it was necessary he do so, managing a lazy kind of charm that made him acceptable, even while he held himself aloof. And they did not press him, preferring his distance, for they all knew *that* branch of the MacBeths was cursed; and while they claimed their kin (they could scarcely ha✓e done otherwise, for the MacBeth features were plainly marked upon those arrogant, accursed faces), they could not help but view those of—and yet not of—their kind with the superstitious suspicion that had been firmly entrenched in their minds through the past.

Few people, except perhaps his foster brother, Cadman—whom he'd grown close to over the years—ever guessed what went on behind the silent, mocking mask Hunter MacBeth showed to the rest of the world; and only he knew what he'd suffered in his youth to make him so secretive, so elusive, so mysterious. He was a sensitive man, a solitary dreamer who'd been forced to build a hard shell around himself in order to struggle with the realities of life; and struggle he did. Desperately, coldly, jeeringly, for his pride would not allow him to be beaten; and even when he would have preferred to slip away into the crevices of his own mind, he fought on. If this were life, then, by God, he would make the best of it!

He gazed down at Loch Ness far below him, a strange, restless lake imprisoned between the two chains of cliffs that rose up steeply on either side, the Great Glen. Today the loch was still, silent; its clear blue waters lapped gently at the sandy shores that huddled at the bases of the tall jagged rocks which too had once been part of the massive, ice glaciers. Some believed the lake was bottomless, a dark, hellish, frightening pit with submarine passages that coursed out to sea. Some people claimed a monster lurked in the loch, finding its way in and out of the body of water through the deep, undersea fissures. Hunter had never seen it, of course, though he'd often searched for the animal along with the others who watched the lake and waited. Still, there *was* something eerie about Loch Ness. When the mist hung low and storms brewed on the horizon, the waves could shift with a roar, overflowing the banks for distances as great as thirty feet. He shivered. More than one person had drowned in that deceptive pool.

A passion stirred in the man as he stared intently out over the land. He loved it, och, how he loved it! The feel of the wind biting sharply against his face in the winter as he rode out over the hard, snow-laden ground. The smell of the rich, newly tilled soil in the spring; the sights of the stooped crofters as they walked behind their plows, taking care not to destroy the deep fresh furrows. The heat of the mellow, summer sun glinting golden over the sweeping acres of wheat, the prickly heads of the grain bowing like waves of a vast gilded sea in the distance. The whisper of the tall Scots pines rustling in the fall; the gaily colored *breacans* of the clans and the simple, homespun materials of the serfs as they danced their Highland flings at harvest time.

Such small pleasures, they were, yet without them Hunter could not have endured. He despised cruelty, though he himself was often cruel; and he hated the brutal world that forced him to be hard and unfeeling when he wanted more than anything to unleash the vital passions that flowed through his veins, eating him alive with their intensity. He wanted to live! God, how he wanted to live! Not just to rise each morning, put in the day's work, get drunk, and tumble an easy wench before falling into bed to sleep the night away. Day after day. Night after night. But to *live!* The other was merely existing, enduring; and the world had so much more to offer. There *had* to be more! He could not bear it otherwise. Ah, God, he wanted to go places, see what there was to see, touch the depths and heights of the burning emotions within himself yearning so desperately for release.

But he could not speak of these things to others. For they would not understand him, content as they were to fritter away their lives, to waste that God-given miracle of breath. Nay, they would look at him with puzzlement in their eyes if he were to say what he thought. Bread, wine, a roof that did not leak, a sensuous wench to dally with, and a proper wife to come home to, gold coins in one's purse. That was a good life according to most men. So why did he, Hunter, reach for something beyond that? Was not such a simple existence enough for him? Nay, 'twould never be enough!

Somewhere there was something, *someone* who would understand what he thought and had so much trouble putting into words. Somewhere there was a soul that burned as hotly with desire for life as his own, a soul that blazed with yearning, with an all-consuming passion that gave of itself over and over again until 'twas drained to the bitter dregs. He would find it. He must. He would have no rest, no peace of mind until he did.

Hunter sighed. Until then he would smile mockingly, amusedly, pityingly at the world, sorry for them because they did not know—would never know—the kind of emotions that raged within his soul. For such were beyond their comprehension. And sorry for himself because he could not be as they were, simple, easy to understand, without the complexities of the mind that plagued his dreams, the driving ambition that made him hunger for more than just mere survival, quiet contentment.

Och, would that he were a very old man so he could look back upon his life and know the right path to choose! But he was not; and so, as the young who have not the wisdom of age behind them, he reached for the stars, determined he would not come up empty-handed. With sudden insight the man realized the old were bitter with wisdom because they'd tried and failed; and he vowed he would not die with the sadness of wasted years behind him.

If there were to be sorrow, then let the tears come from the depths of his heart and soul; if there were to be happiness, then let it blaze with the heights of those things as well! But, oh, God, never let either one be just the fleeting, shallow emotion felt by those who thought: This is all there is; there can be nothing more!

Even before Cadman spoke his name Hunter heard the light tread of his foster brother's boots upon the summer ground, though Cadman, even as Hunter did, moved with the quiet stealth of a mountain cat. 'Twas a trait peculiar to them both and one that had served them well in battle. A less trained ear would not have caught the sound.

Hunter turned as his younger kinsman's shadow fell across him. Cadman's face was somber in the sunlight; his normally merry blue eyes were plagued with disquiet; his black hair was damp from the climb.

"Hunter, do I disturb ye?"

"Nay, Cadman. Come, sit beside me, and tell me what brings ye here to my mountain."

The smile Cadman gave his foster brother had melted many a bonnie lassie's heart. It hid the bitterness born of his bastardy that meant he would rise no further in life than his present knighthood unless, by some miracle or feat of bravery, he were honored by the King.

"I thought the mountains belonged to God, Hunter," he teased as he sank down upon a rock.

"To God and those strong enough to conquer them. Is that nae the way of all things?"

"Perhaps." Cadman reflected upon this for a moment. "But then your shield doesna bear the *bend sinister*."

"True," Hunter conceded softly. "But then I canna lay the ootward sign of *my* stigma aside after battle."

Cadman glanced into his foster brother's violet "Carmichael" eyes, and the younger man could have bitten his off tongue.

"Forgie me, sir. My words were heedless and born of self-pity. I gae no thought to your own misfortune."

"Dinna fash yourself, Cadman. I took no slight. Ah, we are a pair, are we nae? One a bastard, the other accursed! But come, ye wished to speak wie me and nae on the status of our ranks, I'll wager."

Cadman's visage grew even more sober at the thought of the news he'd come to impart to his kinsman. He said quietly, "A Royal messenger arrived today."

"Aye." Hunter nodded. "I saw the King's banner as he approached. It must be of import for ye to seek me oot, and your solemn countenance tells me the news is bad."

"The Queen is dead, God rest her soul."

Hunter thought briefly of Margaret, who had laughed and once given him her silk handkerchief to wear as a favor during a tourney. For a moment he was stirred to pity. Then his eyes narrowed as he thought of the possible political repercussions of her death.

To help pay for her dowry Margaret's father, Christian I of Denmark and Norway, had mortgaged the Islands of Orkney and Shetland to Scotland and canceled the annual rent Scotland paid for the Hebrides Islands and the Isle of Man. Hunter believed it highly unlikely Margaret's brother, Hans, who now ruled Denmark, would renege on the agreement, for 'twould mean war with Scotland, and he already had troubles enough in Scandanavia, but one never knew. In addition, Margaret's death meant Scotland's monarch, James III, was now free to marry again. What misalliance might be brought about by a king given to fanciful starts and fits of laziness, weakness of character and monetary greed? Hunter shuddered to think.

Cadman shifted upon his perch.

"Angus wishes us to attend him in Edinburgh. He must go to pay his respects to the King and find oot how matters stand at Court. We are to leave at dawn."

Hunter nodded again, wondering why a cloud suddenly chose that moment to pass over the sun and a mountain cat to scream in the snow-covered hills.

# Six

Lady Alinor Murray of Eadar Da Voe gazed at her new husband proudly. Despite the fact that she might have had her pick of Scotland's lairds or heirs and had chosen instead a man destined for knighthood, Alinor was pleased. She loved Charlie Carmichael, had loved him from the day she had first set eyes on him at Court; and she had hounded her father relentlessly until he had at last agreed to the match he considered beneath her.

She was fifteen years old, and oh! how lovely she was! Her long, shining hair was as red as flame, and her eyes glittered as greenly as the Carmichael emeralds Charlie had given her for a wedding present. She was bright and gay, laughing often to show even white teeth that sparkled merrily between her scarlet lips as she surveyed the guests assembled at Eadar Da Voe for her wedding. They had come from far and wide, and many were important, for the Clan Murray was one of the most powerful families in all Scotland.

Charlie's face, by her side, was flushed with wine and excitement. "You've made me verra happy, my lady," he whispered, "and my family as well. Your dowry was most generous."

Alinor pretended to pout. "Is that the only reason ye wed me, squire?"

"Nay." Charlie's eyes caressed her. "I would hae married ye had ye been but a beggarmaid."

And Alinor smiled once more, knowing he spoke the truth.

"Shall I ask your mother to dance? I swear she is already softening toward me." Charlie pondered this idea aloud.

"'Tis only because your father has flattered her all evening," Alinor giggled back. "Och, dinna despair, squire. He will win her to our cause, and she will love ye even as I do."

"Would your father did the same," Charlie grumbled.

"He gae his consent to our marriage, did he nae?"

"Aye, ye minx. Ye would hae driven him to his grave otherwise!" Charlie grinned, then sobered. "Och, Alinor, I swear ye will ne'er hae cause to regret this day. Sometimes I think I shall die of love for ye."

"And I, of love for ye, my lord," she breathed softly, eyes suddenly downcast with shyness as she dwelt upon the night to come.

Charlie guessed her thoughts, saying tenderly, "Hae no fear, my love, for I will be gentle as a lamb wie ye."

"I know."

They kissed each other with their eyes and smiled at the promise there.

Mary, watching the little exchange from across the room, felt an overwhelming sense of happiness for her brother and his glittering bride. She turned to young Edward by her side.

"Och, Edward, isna Charlie's bride as bonnie as he?" she sighed, glancing once more at the joyous couple.

"She is fair, 'tis true; but thou art the bonniest of them all, Mary." His eyes gazed at her with bashful appreciation. "Even that day at the fair so long ago, wie cherry juice running down your chin, ye were the prettiest lassie in all Scotland."

Mary blushed with pleasure, surprised he'd even remembered the incident.

"Och, flatterer," she teased. "You've always been dear as a brother to me, Edward."

A brother! Edward thought bitterly as he turned away to hide the yearning on his face. Can she nae see the longing in my eyes? Hear the language of love upon my lips? How can I show her how I feel? My tongue speaks, but I know the words are nae clever enough. Ah, sweet sorrow, this. What do I hae to offer the daughter of our Chief? She'll nae be wedded to such as me if Hugh has his way. Hugh is heir to Dùndereen, to an earldom, while my way lies in service to other men, to the priesthood. Och, Mary, Mary! I canna stand the thought of ye lying in my half brother's arms, his lips upon your sweet mouth, his hands upon your golden body, his— I hae loved and worshiped ye all these years. Canst thou nae spare some piece of your heart for me? Dinna treat me wie this brotherly affection when I yearn to kiss your pliant lips. Och, that I should be blessed wie that honor. I wouldst gie my life for it. Would Hugh? I will find a way to hae ye, to make ye love me as I do ye. I must!

But Edward did not speak these words aloud to Mary; he could not. Instead, he asked, "Are ye happy residing at Court?"

"Aye. But I've missed Bailekair." Mary's voice was tinged

with wistfulness. "'Tis good to see my family again, even if 'tis only for a few days."

"Do ye leave so soon then?" Edward hid his disappointment.

"I must. The Queen is unwell."

"When shall I see ye again?"

"I dinna know," Mary said and had no chance to speak further, for Hugh approached to claim her hand.

"Will ye dance wie me, cousin?" He bowed and did not wait for her reply, but caught her wrist in a grip of iron so that Mary had no choice but to allow him to lead her away.

She trembled slightly, for she loathed Hugh Carmichael.

"Cold?" His dark eyes raked her insolently.

"Aye, as though I had laid my hand upon the flesh of a reptile," Mary retorted.

Hugh stiffened, but the jeering smile he wore upon his visage never faltered. "How ye do hate me, Mary."

"'Tis no secret." She shrugged her shoulders indifferently as they executed the intricate steps of the dance. "Ye are a bully, Hugh."

She had not seen him for several months, and she studied him intently in the candlelight. How dark he was, his skin tanned brown from the sun, his thick black hair like ink. He had grown to resemble his wild Norman mother more and more as the years had passed. He was tall, like all of the Carmichael men, and powerful; his lean face looked hungry and cunning, with its contemptuous lips and the nose that had been broken when he'd been sparring without his helmet upon the practice field.

"I was like to be killed," he told Mary. "Or at least they thought so wie the amount of blood that spewed all o'er my face."

"How unfortunate ye were nae," she replied with mock sweetness.

Hugh only laughed, holding her tighter in his arms. "Ian did it, and 'twas an accident." His eyes narrowed as he looked at her. He spoke softly, "We are verra close, your brother and I."

71

There was a warning to the words; Mary shuddered involuntarily as the dance ended.

Hugh watched her walk away, his lip curling into an unpleasant leer. How he wanted that wench! Her intense dislike of him only made him desire her all the more. He could almost taste her full red mouth against his own, feel her writhing beneath him. How he would enjoy taming her, forcing her will to bend to his, punishing her for the words she had taunted him with that day at the Inverness fair. "Crazy," she had called him. Mad like his mother. His fists clenched whitely as he remembered. Well, she would pay, would Mary Carmichael! He determined to speak to her father—and soon. She of the lilting, scornful laugh would mock him no longer then!

Mary found Joanna's side in the crowd, accepting gratefully the cup of wine her kinswoman held out to her. She drank deeply to ease the dryness that had settled on her tongue at Hugh's menacing words, trying to still the trembling of her fingers upon the goblet.

*We are verra close, your brother and I.*

What had Hugh been implying?

Mary recalled her manners abruptly. "My thanks, Joanna. The wine is sweet, my throat thirsty."

"And the company sour?" Joanna said, watching Hugh's retreating figure with a slight frown.

"Aye." Mary's hand tightened upon the silver chalice. "There is a cruelty in him that somehow frightens me."

"Many men are cruel, Mary. He has become a mighty warrior and is much favored among the clan."

"Still I canna like him."

Joanna did not press the issue, for she too remembered the day of the Inverness fair and Hugh's childhood brutality.

"Your brother Gordon has grown most fair," she whispered to change the topic of conversation.

"Aye." Mary gave her maid a quick, searching glance, knowing Joanna had always favored Gordon. "He is dearest to my heart. Mayhap yours also?"

Joanna turned away without responding, but Mary noticed

the girl's eyes sought Gordon's in the crowd and that he did not seem averse to returning the lass's cool, solemn gaze.

The Queen was dead. So the Royal messenger who had interrupted the wedding last night had cried. 'Twas news that made the Carmichaels uneasy even while it saddened them, for though they were loyal to James, they were not unaware of his failings as a king, and Margaret had had a slight steadying influence on her Royal husband.

Mary, to her utter shame, had for one moment felt only a swift stab of resentment at the news that meant she must return to Court even earlier than she had planned before she too sorrowed for the Queen, who had been kind.

Now the girl rode toward Edinburgh with the rest of her family to pay her respects to the King, her depression echoing the melancholia of the day.

The gray sky was overcast with ominous, gloomy clouds and the air held the peculiar stillness that presages a thunderstorm. The cool breeze that touched the summer quiet was already damp with fine droplets of misted rain, and besplattered dust kicked up by the horses' hooves on the hard dirt road smote at Mary's eyes and filled her mouth with little bits of grit. She drew the many veils that fell in filmy folds from her steepled *hennin* more closely about her face. Despite the light current, she felt hot and sticky, stifled by the sweltering humidity, and she longed for the clean fresh scent of the mountain air. Only the sight of Lord Magnus's giant frame with its blond windswept lion's mane of hair, and young Edward traveling ahead of her brightened a morn as dark and dreary as the stern, set face of Lady Margaret who rode at her side.

The pace the Earl set toward Edinburgh was rapid, and because so many of his family traveled with him, there was naught to impede his progress. The thieves and bandits who might have attacked a smaller force pressed no onslaught against the Carmichaels or the hundred men-at-arms who accompanied them. At every stop the common folk hurried out from their taverns and inns to see to the clan's needs, driven to haste by their curiosity for news of the dead Queen, their honor at serving one of such rank as Lord Magnus, and their greed for the golden sovereigns he showered upon them. Each time Mary dismounted a little more stiffly, moving slowly to a water-trough to submerge her lace handkerchief, wring it out, then press it gratefully to her dust-streaked face and hands, wiping her neck and chest of the grime that had collected there, before she soothed her parched throat with a tankard of cool ale. She was not used to such rigorous travel and had a headache.

Only a little farther, she kept telling herself, and then ye can lie down wie a damp rag across your brow and eyes and rest. Rest! Oh, for the clean linen sheets of a bed, or even a hard pallet upon a floor—anywhere to close her eyes and sleep for just a little while so the pain in her head would go away. Soon we shall be in Stirling to pass the night. Only a wee bit farther now.

But the Clan Carmichael had not yet reached the boundaries of the city when the swift, summer storm broke upon them. The rain pelted the Carmichaels unmercifully, falling so heavily that they were blinded by its violent assault, able to see but a few scarce feet up the road. The once-well-ordered troops disintegrated into chaos as Lord Magnus strove even harder to reach the gates of the town.

The horses shied and whinnied, rearing and snorting with fear, adding to the general pandemonium. Mary's own high-strung steed, Desmond, strained against the wet reins, fighting her furiously for control. A jagged bolt of lightning struck a roadside tree with a loud crack that split above the roar of the storm and brought the pungent, burning smell of charred ashes to Mary's nostrils. Desmond bucked wildly, and at the sudden jolt she felt him gain the bit between his teeth. He tore out heedlessly over the rough terrain, plunging across the ditch that marked the road, galloping into the woods beyond.

Struggling to remain mounted in the saddle, she cursed Edward with a deep frightened rage for giving her the black stallion, and she pressed herself down low against its lathered neck to keep her own from being snapped in half by the branches that slapped at her face and yanked cruelly at the twisted, sodden gauze that had once so gaily adorned her cap.

She did not know how far they must have traveled thus, both of them choking with the blinding rain and fear, each of them struggling for mastery of the other until at last the beast was Mary's again. Winded, it could fight no more. She gave a cry of gladness as she saw they had halted in a small clearing with a huddled shack within its center. It was the hovel of some lowly folk, no doubt, but nevertheless a palace to Mary's eyes at the moment. She led the now-docile animal to the shelter of the overhanging branches of the grove, tying the horse firmly to the trunk of a stout tree, although its labored breathing and heaving sides gave indication of no further flight. She had no wish to become stranded at this place. Too weary to bother with the saddle, she half-slipped, half-staggered toward the thatched hut and pounded upon the door. It gave way easily under her frantic barrage, and Mary entered to find the shack long deserted, devoid of signs of recent human occupation.

She sank down upon the dirt floor, giving way at last to sobs of relief, for the memory of her runaway pony that day at Inverness had lain heavily upon her mind as she'd grappled with Edward's dark gift, knowing she must win the battle or be lost to blackness as she had been before. The muscles in her arms, shoulders, and back ached desperately from restraining the steed's wild flight, but already pride in her victory crept upon Mary and lessened the stiffening of her limbs. She shivered with sudden cold, for the storm had cooled the hot summer air quickly, and she was soaked through as well. She struggled from her wet garments until she was clad only in her shift, bemoaning the fact that she had naught with which to start a fire in the abandoned hut.

The steepled *hennin* was now scarcely recognizable as a hat; its many sheer veils were torn and strewn with twigs and leaves; its tall peak was bent and crushed beyond repair. Mary tossed it aside as she spread the silken damask folds of her surcoat and fine gown across the floor, brushing them out as best she could. A rueful smile crossed her lips for the effort wasted, for the clothes were ruined as well and would never be worn again. Still the furs and jewels with which they were trimmed might be salvaged, as could the material of some of the layered underskirts. Her girdle of gold mesh, with its many-gemmed dinner knife, was unharmed.

These tasks accomplished, Mary huddled upon the floor again, fingers pulling at the damp, tangled strands of her long blond hair as she wondered with forced calmness how long she would have to wait before her father's men came for her. At last she slept upon the crude, earthen floor.

Hunter MacBeth yanked hard on the reins of his powerful white destrier, Craigor, setting his gilded spurs to the horse's sides grimly. Silently he cursed himself for a fool for tarrying at the last tavern for a bit of dalliance with the serving maid who had winked at him so fetchingly. He knew he had only himself to blame for the slight delay that had separated him from Lord Angus and the rest of his clan, but the thought only further enraged him.

How their sides must split wie laughter, he fumed, warm and snug wie'in the walls of Stirling by now, wie food and ale in their bellies as they jest aboot my moment of folly and the price I must pay for it! *Jesù!* No doubt he looked like a drowned rat! If only he had heeded Cadman's warnings about the oncoming storm! But, nay, Hunter had only grinned, claiming Craigor could outrun the wind, and called he'd see Cadman in Stirling ere darkness fell.

Fool! Hunter thought again, eyes casting about in the steady downpour for some sort of shelter. For a moment he could not believe his good luck as he spied a thatched hut in a clearing some distance from the road; he made his way toward it hastily, glad of the coins in his leather *sporran* that would buy him a haven until the rain let up, and he could travel on to Stirling. His eyes narrowed as he neared the place and saw a black stallion standing restlessly in the grove, then he shrugged. No doubt some young page had been caught in the storm like himself, Hunter decided, for the mount was fine-boned, not the deep-chested destrier of a squire or knight; but nevertheless he laid his hand on the hilt of his sword warily as he unsaddled his own steed and tethered the beast nearby. Hunter noted with distaste that the other mount still bore its trappings. Were he its owner's master, he would have the lad flogged for such misuse of a fine animal. He determined to tell the boy so as he strode angrily toward the cottage, so lost in wrath he failed to notice 'twas the sidesaddle of a lady the black horse bore.

A lifetime seemed to pass between them in that first moment of their meeting. As though some unknown force had destined them for just such an instant in their lives, as though the years long past had been fraught with waiting for them both, a sudden, breathless hush fell upon them as their eyes met and locked across the room.

Hunter towered above her in the doorway as Mary awoke and leapt to her feet in fear at the sound of his abrupt intrusion, for the strength of his arms almost shattered the splintered wood of the frail door, and it banged back and forth on its hinges from the high wind and force of his entry. It clattered against one wall eerily, then Hunter slammed it shut, a slow, mocking smile spreading across his dark face. As ire drained from his limbs Hunter felt a new stirring in his loins at the sight of the golden wench before him.

Her damp shift outlined every rounded curve of her slender body. Her long blond hair lay tousled about her, as though a lover had caressed it, wrapping his strong hands amidst the cascading mass to draw her close. Her ripe breasts rose and fell rapidly beneath the thin material of her undergarment, and her trembling fingers clutched her riding whip, as though it might offer some protection against him.

Hunter wanted her, and his heartbeat quickened at the thought.

"Well, well." His eyes raked her boldly, appraisingly. "And here I had cursed my luck this day. What fool was I in my anger and haste, for God has smiled upon me after all."

Mary stared at the stranger before her, her earlier panic giving way to a slow, sickening dread that crept upon her like an icy death as she recognized the *breacan* she had hated and feared every day of her life. *A MacBeth!* Sweet *Jesù!* She was alone—trapped—with one of *them!* If he knew—dear God! He must not find out! She lowered her violet eyes quickly. He would know! The moment he saw their color he would know. The crofters did not call them "Carmichael eyes" for naught. He would rape her. Kidnap her. Slay her.

She studied him covertly from under half-closed lids. God's wounds! What should she do?

Tall and lithe despite his twenty-five years, he was sinewy, rippling with savage strength as he strode toward her from across the room. He wore a white shirt and a *breacan* of red and green, the plaid of the MacBeth whom Mary had watched burn, loot, and ravage the village and fields of Bailekair so often during her childhood. The long ends of the garment were draped over the left shoulder of his green doublet and encircled by the leather strap with buckle that proclaimed him as a clansman. His crest-badge shone silver against the belt, engraved with the MacBeth shield: *per pale gyronny or* and *sable,* and *or; the sinister* surmounted of a mountain cat *salient sable, inflamed proper,* the *sinister* foreleg bearing a Highland *targe,* the *dexter vert,* the *sinister gules, bordure sable.* Mary recalled the MacBeth motto with a shiver. Touch not the *catt bot* a *targe.*

His shoulders were broad; his waist was narrow, adorned by his leather *sporran,* dirk, and the broadsword that hung at his right side, marking him as the deadliest of foes: a left-handed fighter. The legs encased in the red hose and high black boots were muscular; the hilt of his *sgian-dubh* gleamed in the half-light from the top of his left boot.

He was swarthy, almost as dark as Hugh. Though his skin was rugged and weathered, he was handsome, his nose aquiline, bespeaking of the Romany blood in his ancestry. His lips were full, carnal, and the set of his jaw was hard and arrogant. Beneath the green broad-bonnet with the MacBeth plant-badge of a Scots pine tree upon it, his rainswept hair was the deep color of mahogany, the richest of browns to be found in the Highland forests.

But most compelling were his eyes. Set beneath thick ragged brows and lined with lashes so heavy and dark a woman would have envied them, Hunter's eyes were as unfathomable as the deep Loch Ness on a cloudy day. As purple as the mountain that shadowed the castle of Bailekair. As violet as Mary's own. A MacBeth with Carmichael eyes! Accursed by legend for all time . . .

*Dinna ye see yourself reflected there in his eyes?*

*Nay! He is my enemy!*

The words rose unbidden from the past as the nightmare of her childhood suddenly washed over Mary with stark reality. She knew then he was the shrouded figure who had haunted her dreams that Lammas Eve. Her enemy. The one with death upon his soul.

She was startled when he touched her, for she had not realized he had come so near; and Mary felt as though the devil himself had laid his hand upon her arm. Yet something she scarcely recognized rushed through her body at his touch, setting a fire in her blood so strong she believed for one moment she would faint from the searing heat of it.

*Here waits passion,* she thought suddenly, strangely. *Here waits love. . . .*

Nay! Nay! Of what am I thinking? With all her will Mary summoned up her anger. How dare a lowly MacBeth lay his hands upon her! Fury would drive the demon that haunted her from her burning flesh.

"Your clothes are silken, madam"—Hunter indicated the garments strewn over the dirt floor—"and the beast ootside no paltry creature, so I'll warrant this mean hovel isna your humble abode. Still ye are unaccompanied by men-at-arms, and I've nae seen the likes of ye at Court before, though I hae been absent from its halls these many months. Come, mistress." He shook his leather *sporran* so its contents jingled. "I hae a few gold coins wie which to buy your favors and while away the rain that brought us to this place."

Mary's downcast eyelashes fluttered like butterfly wings as a slow flush stole across her cheeks; she quivered in his grasp. Hunter smiled, mistaking her trembling for coyness, and thought how well she played the game, how well he was going to enjoy stripping away her false modesty to find the wanton wench that lay beneath.

"Five sovereigns then, mistress," he offered, "for, in truth, ye are most fair."

A *whore!* He thinks I'm a whore! Mary thought wrathfully as the rage that had engulfed her at his touch suddenly blazed into full force. With a strangled cry of outrage she brought her whip up, slashing viciously across the left corner of the smile that marked his mocking lips, cutting him upward in a scar he would wear always.

"God's blood!" Hunter swore at the swift, unexpected attack, grabbing her wrists with a cruel, twisting movement that made Mary wince even as she fought him, struggling wildly in his strong arms, kicking and clawing at him as they fell to the ground, and she felt the shock of his warm weight upon her own.

"Ye bitch!" he snarled. "Dinna tell me ye come so high my price was an insult!"

"An insult, indeed, sir!" Mary spat coldly. "For I sell myself to no mon, least of all a *MacBeth!*"

And Hunter gazed at last into the eyes that were mirrors of his own.

"*Jesù,*" he breathed. "A Carmichael woman."

"Aye." The word was proud, and in his moment of surprise Mary managed to free one hand, fingers curling tightly about the palm-sized stone she had seen lying upon the floor of the hut near her dirt-streaked face.

With a triumphant cry she struck Hunter MacBeth upon the temple, watching with satisfaction as his amethyst eyes closed, and he crumpled to the earth beside her.

She was halfway to Stirling when her father's men discovered her and wondered what had brought the smug, arrogant smile to her scarlet lips.

Dusk had long since fallen when Hunter at last opened his eyes. He was disoriented for a moment by the unfamiliar surroundings. A small fire blazed in the once-cold hearth, and the pitter-patter of the now-light rain beat a soothing tattoo upon the roof of the small shack. Aware he was not alone, Hunter attempted to stir, reached for his dirk, then fell back moaning at the excruciating pain in his head. Cadman crossed at once to his foster brother's side, kneeling to press a damp rag to Hunter's temple.

"Dinna try to move, brother," Cadman cautioned, his dark blue eyes filled with concern. "You've an ugly bruise there and some swelling as well."

"That I can believe," Hunter groaned, relieved at the sound of his foster brother's voice, "for it pains me like the devil." Then, ashamed at being found in such a helpless state, Hunter pushed his kinsman's ministering hand away irritably. "Still I dinna need to be cosseted like a bairn! Is there no brandy in this place?"

"Aye," Cadman replied as he tossed the unwanted compress aside and reached for his flask. "Mayhap 'twill sweeten your tongue and temper, though in truth it gladdens me to find ye are nae badly hurt after all."

Hunter coughed, then choked as the fiery liquid burned down his throat into his belly; then he leaned back against the wall, wincing at the pain the effort of sitting up had cost him, for he had refused his foster brother's outstretched arm.

Now he surveyed Cadman coldly, feeling very much a fool.

"Why are ye nae in Stirling wie the others? Didst grow fearful like a woman for me in my absence?" the older man asked sourly.

"'Tis well I did, sir, and that 'twas I, and nae another, who did find ye thusly; though had I known then the thanks I would receive, I would hae spared myself the trouble!" Cadman shot back.

The two men glared at each other angrily for a moment, then Hunter's eyes fell shamefacedly.

"Think me nae ungrateful, brother," he said more gently. "'Tis this wretched pain in my head and wrath at my own stupidity that makes my words so curt."

"I know." Cadman's face softened. "I meant no insult by my concern, Hunter, but when ye dinna arrive as promised, I feared ye had been set upon by our enemies, for the Carmichaels are in Stirling.''

"Aye." Hunter nodded. "I guessed as much, for 'twas, indeed, one of their own who did knock me unconscious and put this mark upon me." He touched his injured mouth, eyes narrowing as he thought of the afternoon past.

"Marry-go-up, sir!" Cadman gasped. "I did wonder what had befallen ye that ye came to such an end. 'Tisna like ye, brother, to be taken unawares, with your sword still sheathed in its scabbard." He noted the wicked blade by his kinsman's side. "Ye are lucky to be alive."

"Aye, more fool I," Hunter muttered darkly, then asked, "This wound, Cadman; how sets it upon my face?"

"'Tis a nasty gash, sir, and 'twill doubtless leave a scar. Still, methinks it nae unhandsome, Hunter, if 'tis your vanity that asks."

Hunter's fingers tightened on the flask of brandy he was holding. "My vanity be damned! 'Tis my pride that speaks, for I mislike carrying a reminder of my disgrace this day!"

Cadman shifted uncomfortably on his haunches. "'Tis a small price to pay for your life, brother. The blade might hae pierced your skull."

"'Twas no dagger's point, honorably wielded, which did put this mark upon me," Hunter laughed with bitter mockery. "*That* I could hae borne. But this—*this!* I was whipped, Cadman, whipped like a dog!"

"*Jesù*," the younger man breathed. "What whoreson Carmichael did stoop to such derision?"

"No mon, brother, more's my shame. 'Twas naught but a wench who bested me this day."

"God's body, Hunter!" Cadman was incredulous. "A woman?"

"Aye, a golden tigress whom I did mistake in my desire for a high-priced whore. Lord, how angry she was at the insult I offered in my ignorance! She struck me wie her riding crop, savage in her wrath; and I, in my own fury at being played the fool, did fight wie her and throw her to the ground. 'Twas then I saw her eyes. Och, Christ! Her eyes—even now they

**82**

haunt me, Cadman! As violet as the heather on the Highland heaths, they were, mirrors of my own accursed ones. *Carmichael eyes.*"

Hunter's voice hardened. "I would hae taken her then, my pleasure that much greater for it, knowing she was my enemy. But she scorned me as though I were naught save a lowly serf and hit me wie that stone ye see lying there."

"And left ye for dead, brother."

"Aye." The word was soft, but Cadman was not deceived. It rang with a dangerous sound that boded ill for the Carmichael woman, and Hunter's swarthy visage bore that peculiar, jeering smile.

"Hae care, sir," Cadman warned. "Let nae your folly at this wench's hands tempt ye to some reckless path."

"The lass stirred my blood," Hunter answered bluntly. "I would hae my way wie her and shame her as she has me. Aye, we will meet again, Lady Carmichael and I"—his fingers sought the wound upon his mouth once more—"and she shall learn indeed what it means to lay her brand upon Hunter MacBeth!"

# *Seven*

Nearly three months passed before Mary saw the MacBeth (as she had come to think of him) again, though he was often in her thoughts when she remembered that day of the summer storm and wondered if she had killed him. 'Twas hard to imagine him dead—he had been so passionately alive; and she recalled the magnetic shock of his touch with a strange mixture of hatred and excitement. Mary had told no one of their meeting, for she was at a loss to understand her conflicting emotions. The man was her sworn and hated enemy; she had left him for dead; and yet— *Jesù!* How he plagued her thoughts!

His dark brooding countenance, with its bold violet eyes, haunted the caverns of her mind more frequently than she cared to admit. The sound of his low, mocking voice teased her ears whisperingly. His jeering smile, white teeth flashing, appeared to taunt her at every turn. His hard, muscular body seemed to press against her own soft one in the darkness as she lay in her bed reliving the moment he had fallen upon her in the hut, his breath warm against her cheek. Then she would remember his small groan of pain just before he'd collapsed to the earth beside her, the tiny bit of blood trickling from his temple, and Mary would be filled with a strange, aching emptiness she could not explain. Och! If only he had not been so handsome!

The Queen had been entombed in her final resting place; and though mourned by those who'd loved her, Margaret's passing caused scarcely a ripple in the onrushing waters of life at Court. Whether the King missed the woman who had borne his three sons, Mary could not say; but James did not act as though he were a man bereft with grief. The Queen was hardly cold in her grave when he began considering proposals of marriage from other countries that thrust their Royal daughters at him like ewes before a ram. Still, there may have been some spark of caring for Margaret in him after all, for James rejected every offer and was never to marry again.

He was a bad king—his court frivolous and corrupt—but no more so than other courts, perhaps; and so the common folk still cheered him as they did that day he graced them with his presence at Grassmarket, the marketplace of Edinburgh. He looked resplendent dressed in the Royal *breacan* of the Stewarts, and the people sank to their knees at the sight of him as he rode abreast of them through the throng. Mary's own head was bowed low in respect and obeisance like the rest, for naught would lift their eyes until the King had passed.

Thus it was that her first glimpse of the destrier that clattered over the cobblestones some pace behind her sovereign lord was of its pale white hocks. Her breath caught in her throat as her heart lurched oddly within her breast, for she had seen such a beast only twice before: once in her dream that Lammas Eve long past and once at the poor thatched hovel that day of the summer storm. She knew then that the man who rode it lived.

She trembled as she rose to her feet, raising her eyes to meet those of the MacBeth, and, by the sudden tightening of his hands upon his stallion's reins, knew he had marked her face in the crowd. His violet gaze narrowed, glittering intently as it raked her, and the jeering grin she recalled so well lifted the corners of his mocking mouth, the mouth Mary saw she had scarred forever with her whip. She shivered. He would not forgive her that.

His insolent glance stripped her naked, bluntly evaluating her as though she had been but a slave upon a block. Mary felt a hot blush of indignation stain her cheeks crimson. Rage shook her body, along with something else she could not define; and she longed fervently to wipe the smile from his face as she had done once before. That smile challenged her. It was hateful and insulting, yet filled with desire at the same time; and it told Mary that for the MacBeth too a fire had ignited that day of the summer storm. He wanted her and meant to have her. She could see it in his eyes, and his lust and determination frightened Mary. She quivered. The very effrontery of the man! For him to presume even to kiss the hem of her gown was an outrage! Her lips curled with scorn, and with a deliberate provocation she did not feel Mary tossed her head and laughed.

Hunter went scarlet with fury, causing Craigor to prance and rear dangerously so he had to yank cruelly upon the steed's reins. The wench sneered at him, by God! Dared to taunt him with her laughter, remind him of her victory, make him feel like a fool! How he wanted to put his hands around her slender white throat and choke her until the mocking echo of her derision ceased! But even as Hunter set the gilded spurs of his knighthood to his destrier's sides to catch the King she tempted him all the same.

Mary saw Hunter several times again in the months that followed. Sometimes riding astride through the cobbled streets of Edinburgh upon that ghostly white stallion of his, he brazenly bowed low in the saddle if he chanced to see her, sweeping off his plumed broad-bonnet with a graceful flourish that somehow mocked her, even though the gesture was socially proper. Mary longed to box his ears for his impertinence, even while she grudgingly admired the dashing figure he cut. Almost as though he sensed her inner turmoil the MacBeth grinned impudently, touching his whip briefly to the corner of his scarred mouth before cantering past.

Sometimes she saw him strolling in the marketplace, pausing at this stall or that to examine a bolt of cloth or pluck an orange from a fruit stand, tossing a few coins carelessly to the waiting merchant. On these occasions Hunter lingered until he was sure he caught Mary's eyes, knowing, from the indignant blush that stained her cheeks, that she spied on him when she thought he did not see. He intrigued her, as he meant to, stalking and wooing her reluctant person as a mountain cat hunts down its prey.

Once when Mary hesitated uncertainly over a necklace of heavy gold metal at one of the displays, Hunter slid up beside her boldly, whispering intimately in her ear as though they had been lovers, his breath warm and sweet upon her flushed face.

"'Tis far too weighty for such a slender throat as yours, my lady," he murmured, while she glanced about frantically for some sign of Joanna and Gordon, who had lagged behind. Mary's heart lurched queerly at his nearness, and she found, to her dismay, that her hands trembled upon the jewelry.

"Get away from me!" she hissed.

He appraised her coolly; one eyebrow quirked upward with amusement as he caught her arm tightly when she would have flounced away.

"Hush, dearest," he cooed in a stage whisper, "or this peddler will o'erhear our quarrel."

"I dinna care who hears us!" Mary spat. "Take your hands off me!"

"Women!" The MacBeth rolled his eyes at the vendor, who nodded knowingly in return. "That fine-linked one there." Hunter pointed to a delicate filigreed chain. "The lady will take that one."

"Nay." Mary's voice was cold with disdain as she tried to yank free of him. "The lady will take this one." She paid for the heavier necklace defiantly, fuming silently at being forced to purchase the now-unwanted collar and damning the arrogance of the Romany knight, who had been right in his assessment of the two.

Hunter smiled smugly, guessing her thoughts. "The lady will regret it," he said before releasing her.

Mary suppressed the strong desire she had to slap his face, seizing her purchase from the cart, then practically running through the crowd to escape him.

That night the fine-linked chain was delivered to her chamber at the palace.

The arrogant cock! she raged. How does he dare? But still her fingers caressed the golden lace and felt the warmth of his touch leap from the delicate metal as she remembered the pressure of his hand upon her arm.

A fortnight later, in the King's long hall, he was even more daring in his manner. The courtiers and ladies were executing the intricate steps of a dance that moved in a circle, men on the outside, women on the inside. After each promenade around the ring everyone changed partners, each gentleman moving forward to escort a new maid, and so on, until all came full circle to stand before their original partners. Mary, caught up in the gaiety of the dance, did not see the MacBeth tap one of the *daoin'-uaisle* on the shoulder lightly and speak quietly in his ear. Sir Jardine raised his eyebrows quizzically at Hunter's request, but then shrugged carelessly, stepping aside so the Romany knight might take his place. 'Twas only when Mary glanced up once more that she saw, to her mortification, what had occurred and realized the next turn would bring her directly in front of the brash MacBeth. Her hands flew to her face in horror.

Godamercy! What can he be thinking of? she wondered,

shocked, for no Carmichael woman had danced with a MacBeth man in nearly a hundred years, nor vice versa. He will see us both dead, she thought, for there will be murder done here tonight if he persists. Dear Lord—

Mary prayed the ground would open up and swallow her, for she could not leave the floor. She was dancing with the King. She stumbled, treading on His Grace's foot.

"Och, forgie me, Sire. I dinna mean—"

"'Tis quite all right, Mary." James leered down at her. "Such a dainty foot, ye hae."

"Your Grace—" Mary tried desperately to distract his attention away from the bodice of her gown, for she was frantic to get away from the small circle before the next turn. "Perhaps the wine has unbalanced me. I will drink no more. Indeed, I do feel ill. Mayhap if I could lie down—" Her glance darted about the long hall worriedly.

Already people had begun to stare and whisper uneasily about the upcoming formation of the dance. Where was Mary's family? Och, any kinsman would do. Even the sight of Hugh Carmichael would be welcome at this moment! But the girl could discern no flash of her clan's purple-and-blue *breacan* among the crowd, for the Carmichaels seldom came to Court, and most had returned home after the Queen's burial.

"Nonsense, Mary!" His Grace was irritated by her request. "Ye must finish the round at least, or ye will upset the balance of the dance."

"Aye, of course, Sire. I dinna think. Ye are right, as always."

The King smiled smugly, his good humor restored, then moved forward to claim his next partner, while the MacBeth slipped quickly into James's place. Mary did not know what to do. It seemed as if all eyes in the hall were upon her as she stared at the Romany knight's amused, voilet eyes, her own shooting sparks of anger. She hesitated awkwardly.

"Lady Mary!" The King reprimanded her sharply in a voice loud enough to be overheard by all, too drunk to notice aught amiss. "Ye are holding up the dance. Begin again at once!"

"Aye, Your Grace. I'm sorry, Your Grace." She saw no choice but to curtsy to the MacBeth and take his hand.

Hunter grinned wickedly with delight. At that moment Mary caught sight of her cousins Adair and Balfour, two of Lord Dugald's sons. Her eyes begged them silently for aid, but 'twas obvious they knew no more than she what to do, although they glared wrathfully at the MacBeths present as Mary and Hunter went through the motions of the dance. Had they not been in the presence of their king and realized the two partners could scarcely have refused each other in light of James's harsh rebuke, things might have been different. As it was, the Carmichaels and MacBeths lounged against the walls of the main hall warily, hands upon the hilts of their dress-swords.

"Bastard!" Mary snapped as Hunter drew her tightly into his arms. "Dinna hold me so close. Ye will start a riot in the King's palace."

"'Twill be worth it, madam." He only laughed at her protests and pulled her nearer.

Mary saw Balfour half-draw his blade and Adair stay his brother's hand. Her mouth tasted like cotton. The pulse at the base of her throat fluttered wildly; her heart pounded. She just *knew* the Romany rogue could feel it, pressed up against his doublet as she was. She was certain of it moments later when Hunter breathed, "Is it anger or my charming self that makes your heart beat so fiercely, my lady?"

She longed once more to slap his face. Her hand tightened in his own. He smiled.

"How dare ye, whoreson?"

"I would dare many things for ye, madam." His eyes were suddenly hot with desire as they raked her slowly, hungrily.

Mary shivered in his arms.

"Ye flutter like a bird in the jaws of a cat, my lady," he noted. "Are ye so afraid of me?"

"'Tisna fear wie which I tremble, but loathing, sir!" came the sharp retort.

"Och, then ye hae nae wondered how my mouth would feel upon your own, how my hands would feel upon your flesh—"

"Silence! Cease your vulgar prattle, fool, else I tell my father of your familiarity—"

"And see him killed for his pains," Hunter broke in smoothly. "I'm deadly wie a broadsword or battle-ax, and the Lion is an aging warrior."

"There are many among my own who would champion me, MacBeth, and my father isna too old to dispatch the likes of ye to your maker."

"Ye think so, madam? Well, we will see."

"What—what do ye mean?" Mary gazed at him fearfully.

"Why, only that I intend to hae ye in the end, my lady. Och, dinna fight me, sweet. Ye will know pleasure in my arms, I promise ye." His voice was suddenly thick with passion.

"Ye dream—ye dare—" Mary sputtered, confused, indignant, unable to countenance what he was saying, for no man had ever spoken thusly to her before.

"Nay, I dinna dream," he whispered. "I know."

"Art daft, sir?"

"Aye, daft wie longing for ye, tigress. One day ye shall be mine, I swear it."

Why, 'tis—'Tis as though he courts me. Mary's heart beat fast once more. And he my enemy. She quivered as his strong arms gave her one final whirl upon the dance floor, then loosed her to move on.

Such incidents soon became commonplace. Like a shadow he harried her footsteps, teasing her, taunting her, pressing her against the wall in some darkened corridor or turning up the palm of her hand to kiss it lingeringly when he caught her alone.

"Yield to me, sweet. Yield," he would murmur huskily and bend his dark head as though to kiss her, yet his lips never once claimed her mouth.

The very fact that he held himself in check terrified Mary. What might he do once the savageness she knew lay beneath his cool façade was unleashed? She dare not write her father, for fear the two men would duel and Magnus, for all her boasting, be slain; so Mary suffered the MacBeth's attentions in silence, glad that at least she was lodged within the palace where, for all his boldness, the arrogant knight dare not force himself upon her.

*Ye will know pleasure in my arms,* he had said.

Mary trembled, remembering. To her exasperation she discovered he had begun to haunt her nights as well. Sun or moon he seemed to be with her, his jeering grin mocking her with its brazen challenge, filling her with hatred by the light of day as she raged at his insolence, consuming her with fear and a strange yearning in the darkness as she recalled his confident vow and wondered secretly what it would be like to be kissed by that sensuous, carnal mouth.

Wicked hussy! she chided herself angrily. Shameless wanton! Hae ye no pride or loyalty that ye ache for your enemy even whilst ye despise him? Och, if only he were nae so devilishly attractive! If only I were nae so confused. Why does he linger in my thoughts so?

Mary could not know that her desires and fantasies were natural for a young girl blossoming into womanhood, that the experienced MacBeth had cleverly piqued her interest, played upon her budding attraction to the cavaliers at court, heightened her very sexual awareness. She knew only that he filled her with a guilty longing she could not understand or combat.

To her mortification she found herself seeking him in the long halls of the palace. A queer tightness constricted her breathing when she saw his dark head bend near to some bonnie lass, his scarred lips brush a pale, slender hand. Her heart leapt if she caught sight of the MacBeth *breacan* in the marketplace, only to plummet if the wearer were not he. And yet if he approached her, she was icy in her manner, affronted and enraged by his daring.

She spent Christmas and Hogmany with her family at Bailekair cursing the MacBeth silently when his image intruded upon her holidays. Yet how often did her footsteps seek the ramparts of the keep? How frequently did she gaze across the loch to the castle whence he came? (She had heard spoken at Court he was knight to Lord Angus of Glenkirk, who was Chief of the Clan MacBeth and her father's longtime foe.) Her thoughts dwelt upon him in the darkness of her room late at night.

She could not forget him; some part deep within the recesses of her soul remembered and yearned for that magnetism of his touch, even while she, safe within the high walls of Bailekair, watched the MacBeths raid the village of her father's crofters that February, saw the silver blade of the man astride the white stallion flash cruelly in the winter sun, both sword and steed as blinding as the snow that lay upon the fallow ground.

"I hate ye, do ye ken?" Mary cried aloud, as though the Romany knight might hear her in the distance, and when, by some trick of fate, he happened to glance upward to where she stood, she whirled in anger from the ramparts of the castle.

She saw him touch his blade to the corner of his mouth mockingly and shuddered as she drew her cape more closely about her lithe body, thinking it might protect her from his hungry, violet eyes.

*Yield to me, sweet. Yield.*

Over and over his words rang in the chasms of her mind, taunting her with their bold, hushed urgency.

Mary returned to Court but a wraith of herself, grown pale and thin from her sleepless nights of worry, the torment of her dreams. And finally, in March, she knew she must rid herself of that accursed man once and for all!

'Twas nearly midnight and her birthday almost ended when a page brought one last gift to her chamber at the palace. The girl was surprised, for she had already opened all of the presents from her family and friends among the maids and *daoin'-uaisle* at Court; she could not guess what the package contained, nor who had sent it.

"'Tis from a secret admirer, Mary," Joanna teased with a smile.

"Pining away for love of ye." Alinor, who had joined them at the palace, pretended to swoon, clasping her hands to her breast in a sorrowful pose.

Mary grinned, shaking her head at their foolishness, for her courtiers had given her their gifts earlier that day: a poem from one much stricken by her beauty (or so he claimed); a song from another likening her to a graceful swan; and a damask rose, its silken petals cleverly fashioned from material stolen from the King's own coffers by a man braver than the rest.

Still the words of her kinswomen pricked her curiosity, and the lass opened the package with eager anticipation, tearing at the velvet folds of cloth and satin ribands that adorned the little box, lifting the lid to reveal that which lay within.

'Twas an oval of gold filigree lace with a slender handle at one end worked in the same intricate design. Mary picked it up, turning it over to reveal the looking glass that was set therein.

"Oh, Mary, how bonnie!" Alinor exclaimed.

"Look! There's a note!" Joanna cried. "What does it say? Who is it from?" she asked, knowing Mary, unlike most women of the day, could read.

Mary unfolded the little square of parchment carefully, giving a small gasp of shock upon seeing its contents. She should have known! In rakish letters fashioned with brazen strokes of pen, it said:

*For a golden tigress, whose eyes mirror those of one who doesna forget.*

It was signed with a large, scrawled *H*.

*Who is he?*

*Your mirror, child.*

The MacBeth knew! How could he know? 'Twas a childhood dream, nothing more. And yet he knew!

With a snarl of anger at herself and her enemy Mary flung the gilded reflector upon the hearth, where it smashed against the stones, splintered chasms cracking across the face of the glass.

"Och, Mary!" Joanna's voice was filled with dread even as she chided her kinswoman. "'Tis seven years' bad luck! Cross yourself quickly, and say a prayer for deliverance!"

"Aye," Alinor chimed in. "And 'twas such a lovely device

93

as well, more's the pity. What suitor is so ill-favored in your eyes that ye destroyed the gift he gae ye?''

"'Twas no love-struck courtier who did honor me thus!'' Mary's voice was sharp. "Nay! Dinna touch it!'' she spat as her brother's wife knelt to retrieve the broken ornate object. "For 'tis accursed like the one who sent it!''

Then, as though to prove this point, the girl snatched up the empty box with its velvet wrapping and gay satin ribands, and the note and threw them into the grate as well. The orange-and-yellow flames of the fire licked and smoldered, enveloping this new fuel in a translucent screen until only a charred scrap of the parchment note remained.

Mary gazed at it seethingly, for it seemed to her the scrawled signature laughed up at her mockingly from the hearth. She kicked it back into the fire, watching as the edges curled up in flames. How dare the MacBeth sign the initial of his Christian name as though they were lovers! *H.* Hunter . . .

She turned away, an icy shiver tingling down her spine; and though her kinswomen begged her to tell them what was wrong, the lass would say nothing more to the two women and sought the sanctuary of her bed shortly thereafter.

Mary dreamed again that night.

She dreamed she was in a strange castle, sitting upon a bed in an unfamiliar chamber, brushing the silken tresses of her long, blond hair. When she had finished, she picked up the mirror that lay upon the dressing table. Dazed, she noted with rising panic it was the one the MacBeth had given her, but still she could not seem to put it down. Mary stared at her reflection in the looking glass, mesmerized, until the image misted and became his dark mocking visage. She could see the scar plain upon the corner of his jeering mouth and the desire that blazed within the glittering pools of his violet eyes.

Against her will she drew closer, attracted by the magnetism that was his alone—savage, beckoning. With her breath like a fine, hazy cloud upon the polished mirror Mary placed her lips against the MacBeth's own. The silvery glass shattered into a thousand splintered shards at her kiss, countless prisms in which she saw his purple orbs reflected over and over again in endless echos of one another; and she wept, tasting the blood from his wound, bittersweet upon her tongue.

And when she awakened in the morning, the pillow was still damp with her tears.

Dreams. They are naught but dreams, she told herself. And the MacBeth is only a man. But still the visions came to her time and time again as the nights passed, as she tossed restlessly in her sleep and cried out in the darkness.

'Tis as though some madness has set upon me, Mary thought with fright as the days turned to weeks, or that accursed man bewitched me! Her eyes narrowed suddenly at the idea. Of course! It should have come to her before. The MacBeth had cast a spell upon her! No wonder he loomed like a demon in her mind! Did he not bear the Carmichael eyes? Was he not the spawn of the devil as many claimed? Aye, I must be rid of him, she decided, or else go mad from his wicked bane!

Still Mary shivered at the thought of what must be done and of the one she had heard would help her for a price.

The castle corridors were deserted at this late hour, chilly, with unearthly shadows cast from the flickering torches set along the palace walls. Mary drew her cloak more closely about her, glancing quickly over one shoulder as though expecting to stand any minute accused by the King's men, but there was no one. Heart pounding, she hurried on, footsteps echoing hollowly down the long hall.

Death! Death was the penalty she would pay for this night's work if discovered, a price far more dear than the gold sovereigns and few pieces of her jewelry it had already cost her. But she knew of no other way, so pressed on determinedly.

At last Mary stood before the chamber sought, rapping quietly upon the door. For one eternal, agonizing minute there was no response. Fists clenched tightly, half with relief at having been spared her ordeal and half with wrath at having been tricked out of her money, the girl turned to go. The door creaked open slowly on its hinges.

"You're late!" Lady Angelica Fleming hissed. She yanked Mary inside the room quickly, then poked her head through the entryway to give a swift look up and down the corridor. Satisfied no one lurked without, Lady Fleming closed the door. "What kept ye?"

"I—I feared to be followed," Mary responded nervously, "and had to wait until I was sure the others in my chamber slept soundly."

Angelica shrugged. "Doubtless they would only hae thought ye kept a lovers' tryst, but one ne'er knows. 'Tis wise ye took care. Ne'ertheless we must hurry now, for the moon has reached it peak."

She turned toward the fire to begin her preparations. Mary shivered slightly, for Angelica Fleming appeared like some unworldly spectre in the light of the licking flames. Her face was dead white, devoid of any rosy tinge of color. Her jet black eyebrows arched wickedly above wide, ebony eyes; and her coal black hair, parted in a widow's peak, hung freely to her knees. Mary noted the woman's hands, against the black shroud of a robe she wore, were stark white also. The lass jumped, startled, when Angelica clapped them together to summon a huge, black cat that snarled, teeth bared, before it rubbed against Lady Fleming's legs.

"My familiar, Sorcha."

Mary hastily suppressed the desire she felt to cross herself. She had paid for this night of necromancy; she would see it through.

"Hae ye no personal item of his?" Angelica queried. "No lock of hair, a fingernail, a scrap of clothing, or some piece of jewelry worn recently?"

"Nay." The girl shook her head. "Nothing."

"The spell willna be as strong then, but we must make do wie what we hae." She clapped her hands together once more. "We shall begin."

At Lady Fleming's last words an intense scent of headily mingled spices pervaded the entire chamber until Mary thought she would suffocate from the aroma. A strange silvery mist crept over the room. The crackling flames in the hearth blazed

96

higher, changing colors as the chanting Angelica threw some crystals upon them.

At the altar before the fire she knelt and motioned silently for Mary to do the same. Upon the low table lay a crude doll wrapped in the red-and-green *breacan* material of the Clan MacBeth. Lady Fleming raised it upward to the heavens. In an odd guttural voice she began to mutter in Latin, ancient incantations Mary could not understand. Only when she heard the words "Sir Hunter MacBeth" did the lass realize Angelica was naming the frightful image.

Mary watched, horrified, as Lady Fleming placed the doll upon the altar once more, sticking three pins through its heart. Then the cat howled ominously and leapt upon the evil thing.

Far and away Hunter MacBeth started fitfully in his sleep, throwing off the blankets that covered his feverishly burning body, for despite the cold, his upper lip was beaded with sweat.

He was dreaming.

Craigor pranced nervously beneath the pressure of Hunter's muscular legs. The steed's white coat gleamed ghostlike in the silvery spray of moonbeams from the heavens. The gray mist swirled about man and beast so thickly they could scarcely see. Still, Hunter knew the horse sensed something, for the animal shied again, whinnying shrilly in the night.

Then Hunter heard it—the soft pad of cat's feet moving stealthily through the darkness. He turned. It leapt upon him, claws striking his chest with a pain that seemed to pierce his very heart, bared teeth tearing at his throat. He was knocked from the saddle; he fell, hitting the frosted ground sharply.

In the pale haze of light he could see the beast now, a lithe golden tigress with glittering amethyst eyes.

*Mary!*

Even in his dreams she haunted him, taunting him in demon shapes, mocking him with her Carmichael eyes.

"I'll hae ye yet, bitch!" he snarled as the tigress sprang at him again. "I'll shame ye until ye scorn me no longer!"

He wrapped his strong hands aroung the cat's throat,

choking it slowly. . . . It struggled, whimpered, changed until it was Mary herself who writhed beneath him. His hands cupped her rounded breasts, parted her creamy thighs. She was his. His!

Mary felt the desire rise up within her so hotly she thought she would die from the shame of it. She lost all sense of time, of surroundings. She was locked in a place that was neither heaven, nor hell; a place where moments flew swiftly, like rain upon the wind, and only passion was fleet enough to catch them. She fainted from the searing ecstasy of it.

A high wail of pain brought her back to her senses, back to the spicy chamber of witchcraft, to things beyond all human understanding. Sorcha was dead—her neck broken. Angelica stroked the lifeless cat softly, moaning.

"What will come, will come," she droned at last in a toneless voice that sent chilling tingles chasing up Mary's spine. "The legend was written in the stars before my time. I canna help ye."

The legend! Deep from within the dark chasms of her mind Mary tried to dredge up the tales told to her in childhood, to recall the exact wording of the legend that had cursed the Clans Carmichael and MacBeth, that had spawned the demon-eyed children of her enemies. There was something . . . something about a tigress and—and destruction. Oh, God! There were many who called her thusly, daughter of the Lion that she was. *From the loins of the lion a golden tigress will spring.* Even the MacBeth had named her so! God's blood! 'Twas she! She, Mary, who would destroy her own family!

*Who—who are ye?*

*I am part of what once was and will be again. I come from before your time. . .*

The grizzled witch in Mary's dream that Lammas Eve so many years past had tried to warn her, and she hadn't listened! Now she was lost, lost to the MacBeth, and her family would be destroyed! Mary fled from the evil room as though the devil himself pursued her.

# Eight

In that late spring of 1487, the King decided to give a masquerade ball. How brightly the palace shone as Mary, Joanna, and Alinor descended the winding stairs to the long hall. Thousands of torches and candles blazed along the walls and in the sconces set upon the tables piled high to groaning with the feast. Whole boars and swans, trussed and roasted, lay amidst baked apples and slices of cheese; thick slabs of venison, beef, and mutton swam in pots of heavy, cream gravy, with onions, beans, and carrots; hundreds of little delicacies like hummingbirds and sweetmeats filled the lengths of the trenchers set row beside row.

At one end of the room musicians played gaily, the piping and plucking of their flutes and harps filling the air with sweet melody; at the other a group of acrobats and jugglers performed, walking on their hands and tossing bright globes of color into the air with dizzying rapidity. In one corner a crowd of ladies giggled and whispered, flirting with the young lairds who gathered round. In another a small knot of serious-looking men discussed affairs of state, casting discreet glances in the direction of their already-drunken monarch. Some couples twirled gracefully in the middle of the dance floor, while others sought the heavily laden tables, laughing raucously at some joke told by the King's droll Court jester. The Patch bowed with a dancing flourish before beginning an imitation of some lord.

And everywhere there were masks: plain velvet masks, embroidered satin masks, glittering jeweled masks, masks that covered the entire face, and masks that were held to one's eyes by means of a short stick. James's was of this latter, and he lowered it often to get a better look at his subjects.

Mary had chosen a violet sequined mask, with pointed tips, to match her plum-colored gown. Joanna's was of burnished gold satin that brought out the honeyed highlights of her hair most becomingly. Alinor had picked green velvet, the rich matte fabric seeming to contrast sharply with the glittering emerald of her eyes. The other Court ladies were similarly attired; but the *daoin'-uaisle*—och, how unfamiliar they appeared this night! For the King, perhaps with some perverse sense of humor, had prohibited the wearing of *breacans* that evening. Thus some of the most powerful lairds in Scotland were clothed only in shirts of the finest linen, brocaded doublets from whose belted waists jeweled dress-swords and daggers winked inscrutably in the candlelight, colored hose and silken slippers with toes that curled into points (the vain and frivolous having adorned these with bells that tinkled merrily when they walked), and plumed berets.

Without the plaids that marked the clans, the three lasses could not readily discern whether the cavaliers who addressed them were friends or foes, so wove their way through the mingling mass carefully, fingers intertwined so they would not lose one another in the crush.

One bold rogue grabbed Alinor about the waist, causing her to shriek indignantly before she realized 'twas none other than her husband, lately come from Càrnwick.

"Och, Charlie!" she chided with a smile. "What if it'd nae been I?"

"My love, no other lass in Scotland has those cat green eyes of yours. Ye canna imagine how many mask slits I hae peered through trying to find them!"

Then he kissed Mary and Joanna, but 'twas obvious Charlie hungered only for his bride. Mary, knowing how little time the newly wed couple had had together, told Alinor to go on. "'Tis plain my brother thinks nae of the King's ball this eve." She laughed somewhat ruefully, for she longed to hear news of her family, but realized her young sister-in-law would doubtless tell her everything later. Mary was rewarded by Alinor's grateful glance before the two lovers disappeared into the crowd.

"Well, Joanna," Mary said turning to her remaining kins-woman, "what say ye now?"

"'Tis rather unsettling, is it nae," Joanna understood at once, "nae knowing to whom one is speaking? Still"—her solemn face dimpled, thinking to lift Mary's spirits—"I'll warrant that's Sir Percy Chisholm who stares at ye so brazenly."

Mary's eyes narrowed as she caught sight of the young knight who had stolen the material for her birthday rose from James's own coffers.

"Aye, indeed." she nodded. "He *would* wear bells! Och, Joanna!" Mary suddenly clapped her hands together with a giggle. "Do let's go and tell him the Master of the Wardrobe has discovered the theft and wishes to see him at once!"

This suggestion found immediate favor with Joanna, and the two girls hurried toward the unsuspecting Sir Percy to carry out the impish plan.

At midnight, the hour of the unmasking, both lasses found themselves surrounded by a group of gay cavaliers, all of whom were seeking to reveal the girls' identities (which, of course, were already known by the courtiers). Each maid laughed as she slipped teasingly from the bonds of all-too-willing arms, shaking her head with mock playfulness as she deftly eluded all attempts at unmasking.

"Come, Mary," Sir Percy wheedled. "I know 'tis ye. Come. Let me remove that glittering disguise and win your kiss of favor."

Mary only smiled mysteriously, dancing out of his reach.

"Mistress Joanna, I shall pine away of sadness if 'tisna I who unties your mask to gain your sweet lips as my reward," Sir Henry Drummond mourned woefully. "Do step a wee bit nearer."

Mary and Joanna exchanged wickedly delighted glances at this flattering pleading; and suddenly as one they locked hands, running like fleet gazelles through the confusion of the unmasking, their bold, would-be-gallants in hot pursuit. Down the long corridors and out into the gardens they ran, breathless from laughter and the chase, then separated, hoping to throw the young men off the scent.

At another time Mary would have been glad to wander idly through the King's gardens, for the dizzying fragrance of the tall Scots pines and early-blooming flowers filled the night air; but the sound of pounding slippers upon the marble steps of the terrace warned her the hounds were not so easily outfoxed. Quickly she gathered up the long folds of her gown, pressing on into the darkness, as she cast about for a place to hide. Down the curved stone walkways she scurried, passing couples here and there in close embrace and cautious lords who'd chosen the cover of the unmasking to plot against the King. A merry squeal told of the capture of some young maid. Mary ducked into an arbor, wondering if it had been Joanna.

This part of the gardens was not lit with flaming torches as were the others, so it took a few moments for her eyes to adjust to the lack of light and for Mary to realize she was not alone.

"Percy?" she called hesitantly, somewhat alarmed for a minute.

The man in the shadows smiled wolfishly to himself. He had watched her all evening, waiting for a chance such as this.

"Aye, my lady," he replied softly.

Mary breathed a small sigh of relief. "How did ye manage to elude the others and find my hiding place?"

"Come here, and I'll tell ye."

"Are ye going to unmask me?" the girl teased (not at all averse to this now that the chase had ended), then gasped with shock as she came face-to-face with her cousin Hugh. "Ye!" she cried. "What are ye doing here?"

"Disappointed, my lady?" He leered at her unpleasantly, grabbing her wrist with a cruel yank.

"Let me go, Hugh! You're hurting me!"

"Ye were willing enough when ye thought me Sir Chisholm." He pulled her up next to him with a savage little shake.

Mary realized to resist would only inflame him further, so she soon stood passively in his arms.

"I—I was just surprised to see ye, that's all," she said on a calmer note. "I dinna know ye were at Court."

He gazed down at her inscrutably. "I only arrived this evening, and *I* dinna think to find that which is mine trysting in the King's gardens wie another."

"That—that which is yours?" Mary suddenly felt very cold at the pit of her belly with premonition. "What—what are ye saying, Hugh?"

"Och, Mary." He smiled unexpectedly, relaxing his tight grip upon her. "I was so eager to tell ye the happy news myself, and now I hae bungled it badly. Shall we nae start again?"

"What happy news, cousin?" Mary stared at him suspiciously, for 'twas most unlike Hugh to put himself forth graciously.

"Why, that your father betrothed ye to me two days ago."

If he had slapped her, Mary could not have been more stunned.

"Betrothed! Nay, my father wouldna hae done such a thing wie'oot telling me!"

"I hae his letter and a copy of the contracts right here." Hugh tapped the breast of his doublet. "He wanted to come himself, but I persuaded him to let me bring the good tidings instead."

"Ye lie!" Mary spat, but even as she spoke the words she knew the truth of the matter. Her cousin would not have been so self-assured otherwise.

"Come now, Mary," Hugh purred silkily. "Is this any way to behave toward your prospective husband?"

"I'll nae wed wie the likes of ye, Hugh Carmichael!" Mary snatched away from him, amethyst eyes flashing like jewels. "I canna ken what my father was aboot when he put his hand to this foul deed, knowing full well my dislike of ye!"

Hugh's face twisted with ugliness in the shadows. "'Twould be wise of ye to guard your tongue, madam," he snarled lowly, clasping her to him once more in a rough embrace. "For ye shall soon be mine to do wie as I please."

One hand traveled down her throat to her breasts, cupping them through the thin material of her gown, as though to accentuate this last. Mary struggled in his grasp, hating him for touching her, choking with fear and loathing at the thought of lying with him. Her pleasure in the evening was spoiled, just as Hugh had ruined that day at Inverness for her so long ago.

"Dinna make free wie me, Hugh!" she warned, wild-eyed with fright at what he might do to her alone there in the gardens. "I hae nae yet spoken the vows that will bind me to ye!"

"Nay," he muttered. "But I will hae a taste of what I will know!"

He jammed his mouth down on hers, bruising her lips and parting their resisting softness with his ravaging tongue until Mary thought she would die, for no man had ever used her so. His fingers twisted roughly in her golden hair, pulling it cruelly, hurting her. Then he sought the bodice of her dress again, tearing the violet silk in his crude haste, partially exposing Mary's heaving breasts.

"Unhand the maid!"

Mary and Hugh turned, startled, at the intrusion of a tall dark stranger wearing a black satin mask into the arbor. Mary trembled slightly as she pulled the ragged edges of her gown together with shaking fingers, for the intruder's jeering mouth was scarred in a manner that was all too familiar. The MacBeth! It could be none other. How ironic her enemy should save her from her clansman.

"Begone wie ye, sir!" Hugh snapped coldly, not knowing the man. "The wench is my betrothed and none of your affair."

"And unwillingly gi'en from the looks of her." Hunter's eyes took in Mary's scared face, her bruised, swollen lips, her torn garment. His jaw tightened with ill-concealed fury.

How frightened she must be of this man—a kinsman surely, for the Carmichaels generally intermarried—to keep silent about Hunter's identity rather than face being alone with her betrothed again. Her betrothed! Hunter's anger darkened. She was his—Hunter's! He had sworn to possess her. He would never let her belong to another. "I say again, release the maid, my lord."

"And if I refuse?" Hugh's black eyes narrowed as one hand dropped to the hilt of his sword threateningly.

The night air filled with tension. Mary could almost smell the odor of death that pervaded the King's gardens with its coldness.

*He carries the scent of death upon his soul. Death! Dinna let him touch me! Cold. So cold. So many tears. So many graves.*

Hunter laughed mockingly, breaking the pattern of her morbid thoughts. "I would be wary of forcing a quarrel in the King's gardens if I were ye, since ye dinna know whether I am friend or foe of His Grace."

Hugh's face flushed briefly with ire. His fingers tightened upon his weapon as he marked his adversary well. "Another time then," he snarled through clenched teeth, for he had no wish to be fined or thrown in the Tolbooth if the intruder were, indeed, one of James's favorites.

Hunter nodded, and once again Mary felt the chilliness of the grave sweep through her body. Then Hugh turned to her with a sneer.

"I shall wait on ye upon the morrow, madam, when ye hae no masked cavalier to defend ye."

She shuddered when he'd gone and stepped away warily from Hunter, feeling the force of her hate fighting desperately against the magnetism of the man.

"Why did ye champion me, MacBeth?" Her words shattered the silence lying heavily between them.

He swaggered toward her until she was pressed up against the trunk of a tree, placing his hands on either side of her body so she could not escape. His breath was warm upon her face, his voice husky in the darkness.

"Because ye are mine, and no mon will touch ye until I hae taken my fill of ye. I hae sworn as much. Do ye doubt it still?"

Mary's heart beat rapidly; a pulse fluttered at the hollow of her throat. But still she mustered her courage, saying tauntingly, "Your words are bold, sir, for one so easily bested."

"Aye, I wear your brand, 'tis true." Hunter touched the scar upon his mouth. "But I will hae ye all the same, and nae all of your spells will save ye."

Mary stared, petrified. How could he know what she had tried to do? His glittering, violet eyes seemed to pierce her very soul. 'Twas true! He *was* accursed! He laid his hand upon her throat, causing her to quiver violently.

"Ye would tear mine to shreds, would ye nae, tigress?"

"Take your hands off me!" She tried to yank away.

Surprisingly he did as she demanded.

"When are ye to be wed?" he asked abruptly.

"I—I dinna know," Mary replied truthfully, thrown off guard by the question. Her mouth tightened. "Hugh dinna seek to enlighten me."

Hunter caught the line of her jaw, tilting her face up to his own dark visage roughly. With one deft movement his fingers tore the plum-colored mask from her countenance.

"Ye hae bewitched me, Lady Carmichael," he breathed harshly before he brushed her lips roughly with his own. "I will kill him for ye, ye know."

And then he slipped away into the pines.

# Nine

The long field of Holyrood Palace was filled to overcrowding the day of the King's summer tourney. The brightly colored pavilions of the lords and knights who meant to participate in the tilting lined one complete side of the arena; their banners wafted gently in the breeze. Mary picked her father's tent out easily as she, Joanna, and Alinor settled onto the tiered benches provided for the audience along the other side of the stadium.

Lord Magnus had been at Court a week now, preparing for the annual event; and still his daughter had refused to seek him out, had turned away the messengers he'd sent pleadingly to her chamber at the palace.

"He's still your father, Mary," Joanna had chided gently, heartsick over the rift that had developed between two of the people she loved most in the world.

"Was he my father when he gae my hand unto Hugh Carmichael, wie the stench of wine foul upon his breath and so deep wie'in his cups he scarcely could sign his name to the documents that sealed my fate?" The sharp response had been bitter.

And Joanna had crept away quietly, recognizing it would have been useless to say more.

Now the maid noticed the direction of her lady's glance. "Lord Magnus would be honored, I know, to wear your favor in the tourney," she spoke softly, hoping.

Mary set her lips firmly, casting her regard elsewhere. Joanna sighed, and clasped her hands together helplessly in her lap. Mary, straight as a ramrod beside her, blinked rapidly to quell the tears that threatened just below the outwardly calm surface. The hurt of her father's betrayal ran deep; the wound would not be easily healed.

Well, she had asked for the truth; and she had heard it. She choked back the sobs of rage that rose in her throat as she remembered.

"I came as quickly as I could, Mary. I had thought to arrive before Hugh could tell ye the news himself. *Jesù!* How smug he must hae been, the strutting cock!"

Mary watched silently as her brother ran one hand carelessly through his ragged blond hair, a sign she knew from childhood bespoke his worry.

"Dinna blame yourself, Gordie," she said not unkindly. "'Twas just such a shock to me, that's all. I—I still dinna understand why father did this deed. He knows full well my dislike of Hugh Carmichael. Hae I angered our lord in some manner, brother, that he gies my hand unto one so contemptuous as my cousin?"

Gordon found he could not meet his sister's eyes. "Nay," he mumbled lowly.

"Then why, Gordie?"

"There are some things, lass, which are better left untold."

"Nay, brother. Dinna seek to spare me from the truth, for I would know if there isna some means of setting this unwanted marriage aside."

"Och, Mary, dear sister." Gordon flung himself to his knees before her. "The truth is a bitter vetch at times, and so 'twill be for ye—" His voice broke.

"Say on, brother!" Mary was suddenly alarmed. "Is father ill? Has he been beset by some madness? Oh, sweet Lord, has he lost our home and honor through some debt of which I know naught?"

"Nay." Gordon shook his head sadly. "I would that were my answer, for then gladly would my lips respond; but, God's wounds, sister! He was—he was merely drunk."

"Drunk!" The lass felt stunned, as though someone had dealt her a sharp blow. "Do ye mean my happiness was thrown away wie'oot a thought or care during a wine-steeped stupor?"

"Aye," Gordon answered bitterly. "'Tis sorry for it, I am, lass, but that was the way of the matter."

Mary stood up, walked slowly to the window of the chamber, feeling the sobs deep within her throat choke her. She stared sightlessly over the palace grounds, for her eyes were blinded by stinging tears.

Until this moment Magnus had been her God and Bailekair her heaven; she had basked in the warmth of her father's adoration as a maiden worships at the altar of a shrine.

No more! she told herself fiercely. No more! How could

Magnus have loved her so little that he bartered her hand away, to one she loathed, in the wee hours of a night filled with merry-making? And Bailekair. In some childish fantasy she had thought never to leave it, never wished to face the fact that someday she must. But Dùndereen would be her home when she left Court now, and Alinor would live within those very walls where Mary had hoped to reside forever.

Charlie and his bride came, still flushed from whatever lovemaking they had managed to find in some secluded corner of the castle; and Alinor was torn between trying to prevent her husband from beating Hugh senseless and her anguish for Mary.

"Nay, Charlie." Even through her pain Mary saw her kinswoman's plight. "I wouldna see the few days of freedom Lord Simon has granted ye wasted languishing in the Tolbooth. Only—only stand beside me when Hugh comes." She gave her brothers both a pleading glance. "Dinna let him touch me!"

And Joanna, who loved Gordon Carmichael, but knew he could not wed a baseborn maid such as she, shuddered at the thought of lying with some other man. She bent her head to her embroidery and, as though it had been her own, felt Mary's sorrow pierce her heart.

Mary came back to the tourney to meet her mother's cold, satisfied glance some rows away. She nodded to Lady Margaret, but it was merely civility at best, for she knew the Countess was well-pleased with the forthcoming wedding; and Mary could not bear the thought of her mother's smugness.

Margaret had always favored Hugh, for she knew him to be as unscrupulous as she and meant to make good use of his ambition. Between them Ian would rise to power, and she, Margaret, would reign at Bailekair. Hugh owed her that now. Had she not drugged Magnus's wine that night, knowing he would have rejected Hugh's suit even in a drunken stupor? Aye, she had done it, just as Hugh had asked her. He had won the golden bitch he so desired, and Margaret had gained his assurance he would help make Bailekair Ian's own. The

Countess smiled grimly. Mary was a fool. After the wedding Bailekair would be Margaret's, and she would be well-rid of both her daughter and husband.

She turned with malicious content to catch a glimpse of the King's latest mistress.

The purple-and-blue colors of the banners of the Clan Carmichael stood out proudly against the summer sky, despite the slight gray mist of the day. Mary saw Edward hurrying to aid her father, while Gordon assisted Uncle Thomas. Ian and Hugh clung for dear life to the bridle of the snorting destrier Uncle Gilchrist was attempting to mount; Andrew and Harold watched anxiously as Uncle Walter tried to bring his own prancing steed under control.

Shouts came from other tents as men scurried forward to assist their own lairds.

At a pavilion with an orange-and-yellow striped banner one lord was tossed into the air when his squire lost his grip on the bucking stallion the man was trying to calm. The laird hit the ground with a thud and promptly clouted the misfortunate squire upside the head. Farther down, before a tent bearing a brilliant wine-colored pennant, chaos reigned as two pages attempted to raise the visor on their laird's helmet. It was stuck, probably rusted shut from lack of care, and the poor lord ran about wildly as he tried to lift the metal plate from his face. In spite of herself, Mary laughed aloud at the sight.

At last the judges of the tournament gestured to the King all was ready, and James gave the command for the jousting to begin.

"The Earls of Huntly and Angus," the herald announced loudly over the din.

The opening tilt was merely a formality; and since everyone knew neither man would be unhorsed, very few in the audience paid any attention to the bout. The two men made three passes at each other along the wooden barrier that separated them, then retired from the field. The Earl of Huntly remained mounted, for he was the King's champion and would be called upon to joust against any who chose to challenge the Royal Stewart; but the Earl of Angus swung out of his saddle, took his helmet off, and walked briskly toward his tent.

As the tourney continued Mary and Joanna drew their shawls about them more closely to resist the cool breeze and damp mist that persisted. Alinor yawned.

"The Earl of Angus is close to the King's son, young Jamie, or so they say," Charlie's bride leaned over to whisper. She continued to impart bits of gossip about each of the contestants, all of which Mary ignored, being too wrapped up in her own misery to pay any attention.

"The Earl of Bailekair and Sir Gawain Campbell."

The Earl of Bailekair was in his early forties. A thoughtless, easygoing man, much like his youngest son, Charlie, Magnus stood well over six feet tall. His frame was giant, powerful; his head was thatched with golden hair, the thick, gilded mane that had earned him a name through all Scotland. "The Lion of Bailekair," he was called. His eyes were that intense shade of lavender that marked so many of the Clan Carmichael, and though fooled by many a bonnie maid, they were a good judge of a man's character. This was his saving grace, for the Earl did everything put to his hand openly, honestly. Sneaking down dark corridors to knife someone in the back was not his manner of fighting, and in a land where this was the easiest way for most lords to settle their quarrels 'twas only by his perception and the will of God that Magnus had managed to survive.

He was not intentionally cruel, but his strong sense of honor was deeply ingrained, and if justice told him a serf must be punished or a contemporary killed, then Magnus shrugged his shoulders and did the deed, saying that was the way of things. Those whom he disliked he ignored as long as they did not get in his way, and those he loved he showered with a careless haphazard warmth, much as he tossed his hounds the leavings of his supper once he had finished.

Well-liked by most men, respected by all as one who kept his word when he gave it, and a man who could be counted on to support his friends in time of need, the Earl was the first lord to raise an army and join his ruler if the King commanded his lairds to battle. Like the devil-may-care Charlie, he loved a good joust, whether it be a game or a fight to the death; and now he grinned broadly as he plummeted down the path toward his opponent, lance held in readiness.

On the second run Magnus unseated his foe, then looked proudly with expectation toward Mary's box. She did not join in the clapping, pointedly scorning her father's victory. The Earl turned away, crushed.

"That was a cruel thing to do, Mary," the usually quiet Joanna hissed angrily.

Mary did not answer, but had the grace to flush guiltily.

The herald called two more names.

Sir Hunter MacBeth swung lithely into the saddle, eyes narrowing as he watched the two men now upon the field. Neither one was any good, and he snorted derisively as each knight managed to unhorse the other through sheer clumsiness and lack of skill.

"Be ye a better jouster, brother, than *that* pathetic display?" Sir Cadman strolled over to his kinsman merrily, keeping a wary eye on Hunter's dancing destrier.

"I canna imagine how either one survived a battle to tilt here today," Hunter sneered.

"A small wager then, sir, since you're so sure of your skill."

"What is it this time, Cadman?"

"My winnings against yours that *I* crown the queen of the tourney."

"I knew it!" Hunter groaned. "Lord, nae again, brother. That last wench ye chose would hae passed for a sow in broad daylight, and the ladies insulted by your mockery so incensed their clansmen we barely escaped wie our lives!"

"How ye do exaggerate, Hunter. They merely pelted us wie rotten tomatoes."

"Aye, and ruined my best plaid, too!"

"Well, no matter." Cadman shrugged with a wicked grin. "Did I nae replace it? Come, sir. I promise to behave this time. What say ye to our wager?"

"I say ye will regret it when I relieve ye of your purse!" Hunter laughed before spurring Craigor onto the field.

Mary turned. Was it her imagination, or did the sky darken in that moment? Were her eyes playing tricks on her, or did the grey mist swirl suddenly like a gathering of clouds before a storm? Was it just some fleeting shadow cast from a wafting banner in the half-light or the spire of a ghostly kirk she saw there, upon the field, behind the mocking man who sat so proudly, so arrogantly upon the pale white steed at the end of of the arena?

She had wondered if he would come. As though he sensed her gaze upon him Hunter's eyes locked hers across the stadium. Mary had only a glimpse of their steely depths, caught only a flash of his sudden, jeering grin before he donned his helmet and bested his opponent on the field.

*I will kill him for ye, ye know.*

The words rang in her memory, and suddenly Mary was beset by an idea that would have done Lady Margaret proud. She would play them off against each other—the MacBeth and her cousin Hugh. They were well-matched, the two men; they would slay each other. And when it was ended, Mary would be well-rid of them both, the enemy who haunted her dreams and the betrothed who filled her with such loathing! She settled back much as her mother had done, a soft smile curving her lips.

At last the jousting was over; the names of the winners were called as they stepped forward to claim their prizes. Then it was announced Sir Hunter MacBeth, who had accumulated the most points of the day, had been awarded the honor of crowning the queen of the tournament, who would preside over the *mêlée* tomorrow at James's side. All of the maids in Mary's box tittered coyly at this as they leaned forth to display their charms, hoping to be the lucky girl selected. The herald droned on, explaining the bonnie sovereign lady was to be given a purseful of gold coins, in addition to the flower garland, and Sir MacBeth would receive a kiss from the lass he picked for the honor.

"Well, Hunter." Cadman rode up beside his kinsman, the younger man's chestnut steed prancing nervously at the close proximity to Hunter's white beast. "Ye hae bested me this day, I fear." He tossed his purseful of winnings over, a rueful smile upon his countenance.

Hunter caught the gold mesh bag easily with a laugh. "Perhaps my incentive to win was greater than yours, brother."

"How so? I saw no swooning maid gie ye a favor for luck, sir, though there are countless beauties present."

"Ah, but only one who takes my eye, Cadman."

"Point her oot to me, Hunter, that I may rest assured ye crown no ugly boar as I did in jest that day at Glasgow."

"No boar this, sir, but a golden tigress who doeth mock me wie her impudence."

A golden tigress . . .

"Nay, Hunter, ye fool!" But Cadman was too late.

Mary could not hear the words the two men spoke, but her heart thudded sickeningly in her breast as she watched the MacBeth's eyes sweep the arena, then saw his ghostly destrier begin to pace slowly down the field toward her box. All of a sudden she had a terrible premonition as to whom the lucky recipient of the flower garland was going to be. She panicked and would have fled had she been able, but as she was sitting in the front row and the other women had crowded forward, blocking the exit, she had no choice save to remain where she was. To sit there, her hands clutching the rail of the box desperately as she watched him ride toward her, his eyes fastening challengingly upon her face.

God's blood! Surely the mon wouldna dare! But even as the thought came to her Mary dismissed it. He would—and he did, drawing his white steed up next to the rail, tossing the wreath of blossoms in her lap.

She shut her eyes, feeling faint, as a cry of stunned surprise and glee rose up from the stadium onlookers, for all of Scotland knew of the hatred between the Carmichaels and MacBeths; and many present had witnessed the sight of Hunter and Mary dancing together that night at the King's palace as well. The buzz of voices rose in titillated speculation and curious anticipation. The Clan Carmichael stood staring, frozen with shock and outrage that an enemy had presumed—had dared—to lay claim to one of their own—and the daughter of their Chief as that! The Clan MacBeth muttered among themselves as to their kinsman's sanity, glancing uneasily at Lord Angus, who was white-lipped with anger. Even the King (sober for once) half-rose from his seat, uncertain, wary, and yet wryly amused. A deadly hush fell over the arena.

'Twas only when Mary caught a glimpse of Hugh's face, flushed with wrath, that she realized the MacBeth had handed her a golden opportunity to put her plan into action. Surely she could not be held to blame for the consequences! To refuse the garland—and thus the queen's place beside James at tomorrow's *mêlée*—would be an open insult to His Grace. Trembling, the lass arose from her seat, the circlet of flowers clenched tightly in her hands, eyes flashing with sparks of excitement at her *own* daring. With shaking fingers she pulled the steepled *hennin* from her head and put the tourney coronet in its place.

A wild cry of expectation rang out over the field.

"*Bravo*, my lady," Hunter said softly with approval before one hand caught the gilded strands that now wrapped about Mary's lissome body like a lover in the wind; the other grasped her jaw with a hard strength to take his reward, gauntlet pressing into Mary's tender flesh, tilting her honeyed face up to his own dark one before she became aware of his intent. She gasped as that scarred, jeering mouth parted inches from her own.

This was no quick, brushing caress like that of the night in the King's gardens. Nay, this kiss was rough, insistent against her lips as Hunter's tongue forced Mary's mouth open, pillaging the softness awaiting therein. The lass struggled frantically, for she had not meant it to go this far, but he was too strong for her. Soon her lips ached from his touch, ached with an unaccustomed, frightening excitement; burned, bruised, hungered for his mouth, the mouth that went on kissing her, in spite of the danger to himself. Her head spun dizzily. She could not seem to help herself; Mary's hands had a mind of their own as they crept up to fasten themselves in his rich mahogany hair, to draw this man, this enemy, even closer. She did not hear Hugh's howl of rage, Edward's cry of despair. There was no time for either of them. It ceased to exist in that moment when Mary surrendered to Hunter's encroaching, searing lips, moaning softly at the feelings he'd wakened in her flesh.

'Tis only a kiss! she thought wildly; but she knew instinctively no man would ever arouse her again like this one, take from the all-consuming passion he forced from her pliant mouth, stole from her beating heart, dragged from the depths of her very soul. They were trapped in a fire of their own creation, Hunter and the hunted. Mary stared into the violet pools of his eyes, so like her own, mesmerized, drowning in their depths; uncaring that the grey mist swirled around them like a shroud, a shadow of what was to come; uncaring that the Clans Carmichael and MacBeth drew closer to separate them, as they would always separate them.

She did not know in one fleeting moment of eternity she had set her heart on a rocky path from which there would be no turning back, no giving in until its last painful mile had been climbed, no peace of mind until she stood on the peak of its mountainous crag, still struggling to reach the sky. She only knew she wanted this man—this enemy—with the wild passion he'd awakened within her.

Until the day she died Hunter MacBeth would walk near her, lie beside her, live within her, a dark chasm of desire in the golden of her soul. Aye, if she never saw him again, he would still be with her, with her as long as she could remember the taste of his hard, demanding mouth against her own. She shivered violently in the mist. This man was her mortal foe! This man was the hell she had seen in her dream! She was damned! Damned to the eternal fires of her own blood!

"What hae I done? What hae I done?" she moaned gently.

"Sweet, sweet," Hunter whispered against her pale slender

throat hoarsely, hands still tangled in the heavy mass of golden hair before slowly he drew away, mouth still hungry for the taste of her lips, eyes still blazing with desire.

"Nay," Mary gasped softly, one hand pressed to her still-burning lips.

"Aye." The sound of his voice cut her like a whip. "Ye are mine now, tigress, fore'er. Thus 'tis written."

*The legend was written in the stars before my time.*

"Nay!" she denied him again.

And the glance of desire upon his visage darkened to fury at the scathing insult she delivered from her lips.

"A plague take ye, sir!" Mary cried. "Do ye dream, MacBeth?"

And then she flung the flowered crown into the dirt.

# *Ten*

*Disgrace!* The Carmichaels had been banished from Court in disgrace! No matter that the MacBeths had been told to get hence as well; 'twas the King's ire at the Carmichaels that counted, and Mary was to blame! Och, would she never forget the sound of her own voice shouting those dreadful words?

*A plague take ye, sir! Do ye dream, MacBeth?*

But what else was she to have done? She was a Carmichael, Hunter a MacBeth, and the two clans enemies for all time. Madness to remember the feel of those mocking lips against her own!

God's breath, but he had fought like a demon when the Carmichaels had attacked him; so had the other MacBeths present as well. Cowards they might have been upon a battlefield years ago, but no more. Only the intervention of the Royal Stewart men-at-arms had prevented killing in the bloody skirmish. The two clans had been ordered to relinquish their weapons; those who'd refused had been arrested and thrown in the Tolbooth. Even now Hugh and Ian were cooling their heels in James's gaol. How angry they must be!

Well, at least *that* part of Mary's plan had worked. Hugh would surely be hell-bent upon slaying the MacBeth now! Strange that knowledge brought her no joy, that her heart should cry out with longing for a man she scorned and despised.

And so Mary left Holyrood Palace, not as the proud and excited young maid who'd entered its halls with such high expectations of bedazzling gay cavaliers one and all, but as a rash, wanton woman who'd made a spectacle of herself at the King's tourney; who was even now being sung about by the traveling bards for her folly; whose name was being bandied about the taverns of the city; whose character was being gossiped and laughed about behind the fans of the Court ladies. No doubt James's jester had a bawdy joke to tell about her as well!

Mary set her small shoulders squarely as the gates of Edinburgh clanged shut loudly behind her, accentuating her misery. She vowed if she ever saw the MacBeth again, she would murder him herself!

"But ye *knew* she was a Carmichael woman!" Sir Cadman MacBeth stared at his foster brother with amazement as they rode toward home. "For Christ's sake, Hunter, the lass has bewitched yè, in truth! Surely ye knew her clansmen wouldna stand idly by while ye tasted her lips!"

Hunter shrugged his shoulders carelessly. "I told ye, the wench finds favor wie me. I would hae her if I could."

"Art daft, brother? 'Tis trouble enough you've caused us this day. We shall be lucky e'er to show our faces at Court again! Lord Angus will hae your head on a platter for this day's work, I promise ye!" Cadman prosphesied grimly. "And mine too for riding on wie ye when he distinctly ordered us to halt!"

"I can always return to Torra nam Sian," Hunter responded as though he couldn't care less what his laird did. "I tell ye, Cadman, I hae an ache in my loins that willna be eased until I hae that witch!"

"Christ's son, Hunter! Take your rutting lust to the taverns. There are willing enough lassies a'plenty in Scotland. This Carmichael woman is no different from the rest!"

"Nay, you're wrong, sir. You've nae seen her fair face, those violet eyes. Och, those eyes! How they do haunt me, brother! The golden tigress is a prize worthy of all Scotland."

Cadman felt a strange twinge of foreboding at his kinsman's words. " 'Tisna your loins that are addled, sir; 'tis your brain!" he snapped sharply. "And why do ye persist in calling her 'the golden tigress'? I—I like it nae."

"In truth, I dinna know. Why do ye ask?"

"Godamercy, sir! There are those who believe ye accursed among our own clan, who make the sign of the cross when ye pass by, and still ye think to question me! Ye know the legend as well as I do, Hunter; and she *is* the Lion's daughter, is she nae?"

*From the loins of the lion a golden tigress will spring.*

"Aye, but I will hae her all the same. If it kills me, I will make her mine, legend or no, for there is something between us that mustna, that *canna* be denied!"

"*Jesù*, brother," Cadman breathed softly, catching the sound of underlying pain in his clansman's voice. "Hae ye lost your heart to the girl?"

Hunter's violet eyes narrowed, and he made no reply to his foster brother's question.

"Thou art a fool," Cadman muttered. "No good will come of it."


The seasons passed. Summer ended, and the autumn that followed turned the trees of the Highlands into gold and flame. Then winter began to settle over Scotland with its cloudy white breath. The frost lay hard and thick upon the frozen ground, and the mountains were covered with powdered snow. The Carmichaels and MacBeths lay low in their castles,

**119**

waiting for the King's displeasure to subside as James found matters of more interest to occupy his mind. To keep their lands each clan had been commanded to pay a fine of 25,000 marks for the violence on the day of the tourney. For now, each family was more concerned with replenishing its purse than feuding. In the Edinburgh Tolbooth, Ian and Hugh diced and drank away their long evenings and plotted and planned.

'Twas St. Andrew's Day, the patron saint of Scotland. All week long Lady Margaret had been in a sour mood planning for the celebration, and more than one poor maid had burst into tears upon having her ears boxed smartly for some slight mistake.

In the cookhouse the servants had worked long hard hours preparing the *haggis* for the winter feast. Twenty cows and thirty sheep had been slain, their hearts and livers carefully drained of blood; then the carcasses had been boiled in huge vats, the windpipes of the animals being hung over the sides of the black kettles so the remaining impurities would run off. Afterward the two vital organs, plus parts of the intestines, had been trimmed of the skin around them, then minced into tiny bits of meat. These had been spread with a seasoning of oatmeal, salt, and pepper; then, together with suet and onions, they had been placed in the stomachs of the dead beasts and filled with gravy to make a thick stew. A little vinegar had been added for flavor, then the paunches of the animals had been sewn shut to be boiled slowly for hours. The cooks had been careful to use two casings for the mixture, because if a stomach had a thin spot in it, it would burst open during the boiling, thereby ruining the entire meal.

Het Pint had been made also from ale, whisky, sugar, and egg; and Heather Ale—a liquid boiled from heather shoots, then mixed with ginger, syrup, hops, and yeast—had been brewed, too. In addition there were several tuns of red wine.

The livestock had been turned out into the outer ward to make room in the stables for the many men-at-arms who would accompany the guests invited to Bailekair for the holiday. Vacant chambers upstairs in the keep had been opened up and aired for the more important visitors. Besides the usual household bards, minstrels had been summoned from Inverness to perform; Mary had watched some of them rehearsing outside in the bailey. There were jugglers and acrobats, dancers and jesters as well. Not a shilling had been spared on entertainment, Lady Margaret having opened her tight fist wide enough for more than a few coins to escape only because Ian and Hugh had at last been released from gaol and were to be at Bailekair for the celebration.

Mary sighed. Despite all this, the holiday was not a happy one. At the banquet that evening there was talk of rebellion against the throne. Both Hugh and Ian, who knew the latest news and were puffed up with their own importance because of it, vowed loudly that the King was attempting to secure the rich revenues of Coldingham, a holding of the Clan Home, for his own personal use. Morever, the two said, the notorious Hepburns had sided with the Homes, stirring up trouble in the Border Lands.

"Mark my words," Ian declared. "There'll be civil war next year—if nae sooner. The Clan Carmichael must decide on which side 'twill battle."

"Aye, and I say why should we fight for a king who banished us from court and locked Ian and me up in the Tolbooth?" Hugh asked angrily.

"Because he *is* our king, and we hae gi'en him our oath of fealty." Lord Thomas roused himself to give his eldest son a stern frown. "Besides, what do we owe the Border lords?"

"Nothing!" Lord Gilchrist snapped, for once at odds with his two favorite foster sons. "Godamercy! The Borderers call us Highlanders heathens and savages. One did speak such to my face in Edinburgh, although I took care of him well enough for the insult!"

"I say the Clan Carmichael has always been loyal to its kings," Lord Magnus put in slowly. "Why should this time be any different? I think we're all being a little too hasty in this matter. James has eyed holdings before this, and naught has come of it. Rebellion may ne'er arise at all."

"But, Magnus—"

Mary slipped away, not wanting to hear any more of their quarrel, shuddering faintly at the thought of war. For all that he had hurt her she did not want her father—or brothers—to die. Well, perhaps Magnus was right; perhaps there would be no trouble. Mayhap James would fall into one of his lazy moods again and forget about his lairds' holdings.

She made her way up to the ramparts of the castle, lashes blinking rapidly to dislodge the small droplets of grey mist that clung to them tenaciously. Far below she could see Alinor and Charlie chasing and teasing in the courtyard. Alinor's bright laughter floated up to her, somehow saddening her with its gaiety. There will be little enough such happiness in my own marriage, Mary thought. Oh, God, father! Why Hugh?

The bright stars in the sky were hazy outlines in the distance, as were the spires of Glenkirk when Mary turned her gaze to the keep across the loch. Unconsciously the girl pressed one hand to her lips. Even now they burned when she thought of the MacBeth's kiss; her heart pounded fiercely with the remembrance. I want him, she admitted bitterly to herself. He is my enemy, and still I want him! He has bewitched me, the arrogant devil! I should hae killed him when I had the chance!

"Mary?"

The lass turned. Edward was standing beside her; his deep blue eyes were kind; he had her cloak in his hands.

"I saw ye leave and thought ye might need this." He held forth the garment. "'Tis getting so cold these days."

"Aye." She took the cape from him gratefully. "There will be snow on the ground soon, as well as on the mountains." She held out one hand, catching the fine moisture inside her palm. "Already the mist is beginning to freeze."

Edward moved closer. Christ! How his heart ached for her! If only he could bring himself to say the words that tumbled to his lips, words of love, of despair, of hope he might somehow still prevent her marriage to his half brother, Hugh; but he found once more he could not speak to her of these things. For how could he tell her he loved her when she was betrothed to another? He had lost her before he'd ever even had a chance to lay claim to her. My golden-haired nymph, he thought sadly. Hugh will crush your spirit beyond repair. Edward sighed, helpless, and stood quietly by Mary's fair figure, longing, always longing.

No one stopped Mary as she rode out through the iron gate of Bailekair, and if they thought it strange she was unaccompanied by even a handful of men-at-arms, they did not seek to question her when, her violet eyes flashing like daggers, she commanded them curtly to open the portcullis. The keep was well-guarded; she would be safe as long as she did not stray too far from its walls, and in truth she had been known to ride out alone before. The sentries shrugged and closed the gate.

The cold wind whipped Mary mercilessly; the icy rain that had begun to fall stung her face sharply; but the shock of the elements felt good, and she wanted to ride! To get rid of some of the restless anxiety and desperation that tormented her body.

Candlemas! Her wedding date had been set for Candlemas! In three short months she would be the bride of Hugh Carmichael! Her father had told her so. Soon she no longer would be free to ride out over the frozen moors with her hair streaming out wildly behind her in the wind. She would be Hugh's wife, and Dùndereen, not Bailekair, would be her home. Mary shuddered, recalling the way Hugh's hot eyes had raked her body on St. Andrew's Day; how his sneering mouth had claimed hers possessively early this morning before he'd mounted to return to Leabaidh a' Nathair. Gordon and Charlie had stood by helplessly while her cousin had placed his betrothal ring upon her finger. Her brothers pitied her, and yet what could they do? Magnus had given her hand unto Hugh. They could not defy their father.

Oh, if only Mary had not turned her back so cruelly on the Earl, had not lost her temper this morning! Perhaps Magnus still might have listened when she had pleaded for release from her betrothal, still might have been persuaded against the match. But her father had been hurt by Mary's coldness, and her subsequent anger had only served to enrage him.

"Drunk! 'Twas drunk ye were when ye signed the contracts binding mè to Hugh Carmichael! Dinna seek to tell me now 'twas some strange lethargy that muddled your head so! Ye were in your cups, and ye gae me away wie'oot another thought or care!"

"Nay, daughter, that wasna the way of it—"

"Fie on ye, my lord! You're nae only a drunk, but a liar as well, do ye ken?"

"By God!" Magnus had roared, his face reddening with wrath at her impertinence. "This is what comes of me allowing ye to be tutored like your brothers! You've forgotten your place as a woman! I should hae kept ye to your needlework rather than listened to your cajolery. Well, no matter. I'll nae fash myself longer on your account, madam! Hugh will take ye in hand soon enough! Aye, I've gi'en my word—no matter the reason for it—and there's an end to it!"

Marry-go-up! He had called her "Madam," as though he had not known her. She would rather he had slapped her than to have referred to her so coldly, so impersonally. Och, to have quarreled with her father so! And over Hugh! Hugh, whom Mary could not love. Hugh, the cruel bully who had forced her into the monster's tent at the Inverness fair, the brute who had caused her to be sick upon the ground. Mary rubbed her face against Desmond's coal black mane to brush away the bitter tears that sparkled in her eyes like ice.

Two strong men topped the crest of a Highland hill, years of battle stamped deeply upon their hard, young faces. But for all this there was a gentleness about them both if one looked closely. The younger rode a beautiful chestnut steed with an ebony mane and tail. He was tall and slender, with a good deal of humor twinkling in his merry dark blue eyes, an engaging grin upon his mouth as he stroked his destrier's mane, black as his own unruly locks.

"God's wounds, Hunter! Think of it! Two whole months

of freedom and Christmas at Wynd Cheathaich!'' Cadman practically shouted with glee.

"Dinna forget we are to find oot how things stand at Court, brother,'' Hunter reminded him grimly. "'Tis only recently James lifted the ban against our presence there. Angus fears rebellion will arise, and we must know whether or nae the King is still angry wie us o'er the tourney.''

"Och.'' Cadman shrugged his shoulders indifferently. "'Tis a Highland feud, and no king has e'er put an end to it. James understands such things. Did we nae pay the fine he imposed? Aye, and now he seeks to gain the favor of those he insulted. Methinks he fears a dirk in his ribs; he has alienated so many of his lairds. At any rate, David will know the latest news. We need nae even bother going to Edinburgh unless affairs are worse than we thought.''

Hunter nodded, knowing David MacDonald could be trusted to tell them the truth. 'Twould not be wise anyway to ride into Edinburgh only to be arrested and thrown in gaol; and James was certainly dishonest enough to invite his banished subjects back to Court for just such a purpose. The King trusted few men these days, and more than one monarch had held onto his throne through the strange disappearances of those who would have opposed him. Hunter sighed.

"Well, we shallna let it spoil our holiday at least.'' He gave his foster brother a smile, knowing how much Cadman was looking forward to the season of festivities after months of confinement at Glenkirk—Angus's punishment for his having disobeyed a direct order of the Chief of the Clan MacBeth. Hunter himself had spent several weeks in the castle dungeon for his own wild conduct that day of the tourney—"to drive oot the demon that has possessed ye,'' Angus had said—and then been sent to collect each keep's share of the King's fine in person, much to his chagrin. It had not been pleasant to suffer his kinsmen's vile cursing or cold lecturing as they had delved into their *sporrans* to ante up the penalty; and Hunter had left each fortress with an uncomfortable sense of guilt and shame, which he had unscrupulously added to the ever-growing list for revenge against Mary

Carmichael. He'd been lucky Angus hadn't taken a whip to him besides!

"I'm told David lays oot a feast fit for a king at Wynd Cheathaich during Christmas," he continued absently.

"Marry-go-up! Who cares aboot food?" Cadman grinned again. "Just gie me a warm bed, an easy wench to tumble in it, and a bottle of wine to slake my thirst afterward!"

"Ale is more to my liking, and there's only one lass for me." Hunter frowned once more as he thought of the weeks he'd lain in some whore's embrace, dreaming of golden hair and eyes as violet as his own. God! Would he never be free of that wench?

"That bitch will be the death of ye!" Cadman snapped churlishly, his good humor fading with rapidity at his foster brother's remark. "Did ye learn nothing those weeks ye languished in Glenkirk's gaol? By God! Angus is right! Ye *hae* been beset by some madness, sir! Naught else could explain your obsession wie the girl! The witch nearly killed ye, and still ye disgraced us at Court to place that crown upon her head!"

Hunter made no reply to his clansman's accusations, for his gaze was riveted on the Highland moors stretching for miles before them. There in the midst of the sweeping terrain rode a solitary maid. His breath caught sharply in his throat, for even in the distance he recognized the long golden tresses flying out behind her in the wind, billowing about her slender caped figure like a sail upon the mast of a graceful ship. 'Twas almost as though he'd wished her there, and for a moment he could not believe she was real.

"Sweet *Jesù*," he breathed. "Is she daft? She rides wie'oot even a groom."

"Hunter, no!" Cadman called frantically, some inkling of impending doom invading his very being; but his foster brother had already set his heels to his stallion's white sides.

Afterward, until the day she died, Mary was never to recall just when she became aware of the two men on the crest of the hill that winter's morning. She remembered Desmond pausing, pawing the frozen ground and snorting as he danced, and an answering whinny coming from the knoll, followed by a wild, Highland battle cry.

"*A MacBeth! A MacBeth!*"

Mary recognized the savage yell at once. Her eyes strained afar, picking out the red-and-green *breacan* of the clan. Aye, her ears had heard a'right. Those blazing plaids belonged to the hated MacBeths, and they were coming toward her hard and fast. She swore softly as she discerned the sheer ghostly destrier, for there was only one like it in all Scotland, and she knew the man to whom it belonged. Mary glanced about anxiously, but she was totally alone. The high walls of Bailekair weren't even in sight. Godamercy! How had she come so far without realizing it? Why, she was nearly to Mheadhoin, the village of death. It seemed an ill-omen. For one fleeting moment the girl paused, recalling the MacBeth's kiss upon her mouth that day of the King's summer tourney. Desire flooded through her body like wildfire. Then some instinct born of years of hatred for her enemies forced her to wheel Desmond around abruptly, laying her whip hard about the palfrey's sides. There was no help for it. She would have to outrun them!

The powerful white steed surged forward rapidly under the pressure of Hunter's viselike muscular legs. By God, but Mary Carmichael was a braw lassie! She rode as well as a man, and that black horse of hers was as fast as his own Craigor. Still, he knew the smaller beast would soon be winded, for its delicate frame was built for speed, not distance, and Craigor was used to carrying a heavily armored man for many miles.

In no time at all, it seemed, Hunter's stallion was running neck-and-neck with Mary's own; so close she could feel the side of the lathered destrier pressed against her legs through the woolen material of her cape and *arascaid*; so close Hunter appeared to tower over her as he grabbed for Desmond's bridle. She sensed, rather than saw, his dark figure make the lunging movement, his white teeth gleaming, reminding her vaguely of Hugh, as he laughed mockingly by her side from sheer excitement of the chase. Her violet eyes flashed with rage and fear and something else Hunter could not define. She struck out at him furiously with her riding crop, but he caught her upraised hand in a cruel grip; and Mary knew her time of waiting had come to an end.

"Let me go, ye whoreson bastard!" she cried, struggling to free herself from his rough grasp. "Wouldst harm a defenseless woman?"

"Hardly defenseless, tigress," Hunter noted grimly as he pried the quirt from her gloved fingers. "Ye whipped me once, madam; ye willna do so again."

"Nay, this time I will slay ye, MacBeth, and make certain of the deed!"

Hunter stared hard at her, a smile playing about the corners of his mouth tightly, not quite reaching the glittering shards of his amethyst eyes. Aye, she was a fiery lassie all right. He'd known too many coy, simpering women in his day, women who had fallen easily at his feet when he'd commanded. But this one—no, she would not come easy. She scorned and sneered at him, threatened to kill him, even while her mouth trembled with fright. He would have to be on his guard, or like as not she would put a dagger between his shoulder blades the minute he turned his back! His hand tightened on Mary's wrist. He wanted her, and the lass shivered as she read what was written in his eyes.

*One day ye will be mine. I swear it.*

God's blood! He would take her now, this enemy, just as he had vowed, and Mary would be powerless to prevent it! Oh, to glimpse the secure, beckoning walls of Bailekair just beyond the horizon! Why had she ridden so far from their safe embrace? Mary bit her lower lip so hard she drew blood to stifle the sobs choking her throat. She was only dimly aware of the approach of another rider, only vaguely conscious of the MacBeth's release of her wrist as he turned to his kinsman. She rubbed the chafed place absently, knowing there would be a bruise there in the morning.

Cadman surveyed his foster brother coldly. Had the girl been anyone else, he would have delighted in his clansman's capture, shared in the rape of her, then ransomed her back without another thought. Such were the ways of the times. But this—this witch was different! She had possessed his kinsman's soul in some manner of which Cadman knew naught. He felt the strange tingle of foreboding run up his spine again. She ought to be burned at the stake, the devil's bride! Och, would that Hunter had never laid eyes on the bitch!

His displeasure plain upon his face as he gestured toward the girl, Cadman spoke curtly, "The wench is yours now and the consequences also. Let us ride, sir. We hae tarried o'erlong, and Bailekair is too near for my liking."

Mary glanced up with surprise at the sound of his harsh tone; Cadman's words of disapproval died upon his lips as he gazed upon her fair countenance at last. In spite of himself, his breath caught in his throat. Finally he understood Hunter's wild obsession with the lass. She *was* haunting, what with those wide violet eyes—like soft, shaded summer pools in her delicately boned face, they were; the generous scarlet mouth he warranted could smile prettily when she chose; and that mass of cascading spun-gold hair.

My God, she *is* a fit mate for him, the thought came unbidden to Cadman's mind. Like a preying eagle and a proud swan they are together, a wild stallion and an elusive unicorn, a mountain cat and his golden tigress. . . .

"God save us, brother," he whispered softly. "For the legend lives—in your accursed eyes and those of the tigress by your side. Och, Hunter. Loose the witch at once! She'll bring ye naught save sorrow, I promise ye."

Mary quivered. He thinks we are the two of whom the legend foretold. Accursed, both of us, the MacBeth and I, bound together for all time by the cryptic words of an old, malicious crone dead nearly a hundred years in her grave. Can it be true! Is this what draws me to my enemy, in spite of myself? Nay! It canna be! It mustna! I will fight my foe and this devil wie'in myself until they possess me no longer!

"He speaks of shadows, your kinsman," she sneered to the MacBeth. "Be he a simple fool? For naught will come but the men-at-arms of Bailekair to slay ye both where ye stand!"

Hunter wrapped the reins of Mary's bridle around the pommel on his saddle, eyes devouring her lithe figure.

"As your clansmen stole our ancestress from the walls of Glenkirk, so will we take ye from Bailekair, my golden tigress. Legend or no, I'll tame ye, wench, ere the sun's pale rays streak yon horizon."

"The golden tigress" he'd called her; and so she was, with her golden hair and face, like the rest of her flesh would be, Hunter knew, when he stripped the garments from her trembling body. Her ripe breasts rose and fell rapidly in her anger and fear of him; her red lips were parted with hatred and scorn. He found he ached to press his mouth against them once again; to force his tongue inside those soft, quivering borders of delight; to feel his lips traveling downward over that honeyed skin; to taste those round, young buds of womanhood; to caress that long blond hair, to have it wrapped around his throat.

"Whoreson coward!" Mary hissed, grabbing desperately for her bridle.

He twisted her hands away deftly. "I would hae killed a mon for that," he laughed unpleasantly. "But I'll take my revenge on ye another way, my lady." His eyes raked her slowly, leaving her no doubt as to his intentions. "And ye will find it sweet, indeed, as once I promised."

"God's wounds! Do ye dare, MacBeth? My father will hunt ye down and slay ye both by nightfall," Mary said tossing her head arrogantly, "and all of Scotland knows the MacBeths are nae noted for their fighting ability."

Hunter wanted to slap the sneer from her face, to grind his mouth down on hers until she begged for mercy, cried out with desire.

"Your tongue is sharp, and your manners are insolent, madam, but I will still them both soon enough," he vowed.

Mary shivered once more in the winter frost, but the chill she felt was not from the cold.

# *Eleven*

The white powdered snow lay thick upon the fallow ground in the twilight. The mountain ash trees, devoid of their leaves, stood like ranks of soldiers against the cloudy grey sky, branches uplifted as though in mourning at the slow death that had crept across the land. The blue streams that had sung so gaily were silent now, solid sheets of ice as crystal as panes of glass. Icicles encrusted the barren bushes and hung from the limbs of the trees, glittering like twinkling stars, yet as coldly sorrowful as a young maiden's tears.

Mary's teeth chattered slightly as she glanced once more at the hard face of the man who held her captive, who only an hour ago had given her his cloak for warmth, although she had tried to refuse it. She wished no comfort from her enemy.

He was not taking her to Glenkirk, as she had thought, nor any other MacBeth holding as far as she could determine; and any hope she'd had of being rescued from the fate he had planned for her had died in Mary's breast with that knowledge. They rode south, not west, and the rain that had turned to snow would have covered their tracks by now.

She grew more and more frightened, her brave front fading, as the snow flurried harder, and each mile they traveled carried her farther from Bailekair. Would he kill her, this man? Or would he only use her, then hold her for ransom? At least death would be honorable. The other—dear

131

God—the other! She would be shamed and disgraced for life! But, ah, sweet *Jesú!* How she wanted to live! She was only fifteen, and life was so precious. Was it to end before it had even begun?

Mary thought of her family. Surely they had missed her by now, had sent out search parties to look for her. Still, the snow was falling so heavily the tired horses staggered and slipped through its drifts; their hoofprints filled in again as quickly as they were made. The girl knew the Carmichaels' hunt would prove fruitless.

She thought of Joanna, no doubt huddled upon a three-legged stool before the fire in the main hall, attempting to embroider through the tears that must surely glisten in her eyes when the men-at-arms returned home without their lady. Of the past. Of Edward buying her the cherry tart at the Inverness fair. If she closed her eyes, Mary could almost feel the warm red juice trickle down her chin. Of Gordon trying to fix her doll after Andrew and Harold had pulled the stuffing out of it, and of Charlie holding out a bit of hard candy to chase away the tears that had threatened at the thought of poor Kirstin's insides lying there on the floor. Of Ian and Hugh locking her in one of the grain bins in the storage shed. Of her father laughing, swinging her high into the sky, safe within his strong arms. Of her mother marching sternly through the castle corridors, keys clinking at her waist. Of the glittering Alinor dancing with her new husband at Eadar Da Voe, and of Joanna running through Holyrood Palace the night of the King's masquerade ball.

Would Mary never see them again? Oh, why had she ridden so far from Bailekair without an escort? If only she hadn't been so upset with her father! Fool! Fool! she called herself for the hundredth time since her capture. At least Hugh was her kinsman, her cousin. The man who had her now was her hated enemy. And there would be no vows spoken to make his bedding of her rightful. Mary looked at him again. He *was* handsome; she had to admit that! At least she would be spared the humiliation of lying with some oafish clod! In fact, if the MacBeth weren't her enemy, she might—sweet Christ! What was she thinking of? Surely her brain was fatigued to the point of delusion!

"Where do ye take me, MacBeth?" she asked to stem the tide of her confusing thoughts and to break the silence that had lain heavily between them ever since the sharp words they'd exchanged over her acceptance of his cloak.

"I hae a gi'en name, lass." Hunter frowned at her darkly, not wishing to quarrel with her further, but determined to master her nevertheless. "I would ye would use it."

"I willna call ye as I would a friend, MacBeth." The girl bit her lip stubbornly. "Nor make ye free to name me thusly."

Hunter sighed. "Ye persist in needling me, wench."

"I hae a right to know where ye are taking me." Mary ignored his irritation.

"To Wynd Cheathaich. 'Tis a stronghold of the Clan MacDonald. Are ye satisfied now?"

Mary turned away without response. MacDonald. No refuge there, she decided with anguish, for the Carmichaels were not friendly with the MacDonalds, who were kin to the MacBeths.

He must be cold, Mary realized as her eyes flickered over her captor once more, but she saw no sign of it upon his face as she drew his cloak more closely about her, taking a perverse sense of delight in the clean male scent of its folds. Then she shuddered. Tonight his arms would be wrapped around her even as his cape was now; he had promised as much. Once again the girl wondered if there were not some means of escaping him and the uncertain destiny he had in store for her.

The castle, Wynd Cheathaich, seemed to glow like a halo as they approached it, for 'twas slate grey and shrouded in mist. The torches blazing along the ramparts glimmered with hazy flame, wavering in the steady snow. Mary was slightly relieved to see it looming before her, for she'd grown cramped and cold from the hours of being in Desmond's saddle and the long, hard ride. Still, she shivered with foreboding at the thought of what awaited her inside.

Cadman called their names to the sentry. The drawbridge was lowered and the portcullis raised so they could cross over the frozen moat into the outer ward of the fortress. Then they were passed through the second gatehouse into the inner bailey. Hunter lifted Mary from her saddle. She was so stiff she would have fallen had he not held her tightly, but still she drew away from him as though she had been stung by the shock of his touch. He laughed softly in the darkness.

"After tonight you'll welcome my embrace, madam," he promised softly.

The girl only shuddered, turning away from the hunger in his eyes.

Once inside the main hall of the keep they were approached by a serious-looking man with silver blond hair and blue eyes.

"Hunter, Cadman." The Earl of Wynd Cheathaich came forward, hands outstretched to welcome his guests. " 'Twas so late I dinna expect ye to arrive tonight. Ye should hae sheltered at an inn. There was no need to press on in this snow."

" 'Tis blowing hard oot there, David," Hunter explained as he clasped the MacDonald's arms warmly. "Cadman and I thought it best if we reached Wynd Cheathaich this eve, for 'twill doubtless be some time before travel is possible again if this weather keeps up."

"Aye, ye may well be right," David MacDonald replied with a frown as a gust of wind howled ominously through the main hall. The torches along the walls danced strangely at the sudden blast. He greeted Cadman, then turned once more to Hunter; one eyebrow lifted questioningly as his eyes fell at last upon Mary.

"This is Lady Mary Carmichael," Hunter said. "My—prisoner."

He must have known her first name, of course; nevertheless, Mary was surprised to hear it upon the MacBeth's lips, for Hunter had never called her by her given name. How melodiously it seemed to roll off his tongue. *Mary*. Och, if only it could have been a man who loved her, a man she loved, who spoke the word so musically!

"The Lion's daughter?" the MacDonald was asking as she came back to reality with a start.

"Some call my father that, my lord," she responded, setting her jaw in a proud line as he took in every detail of her bedraggled state of being. "I dinna apologize for my appearance, my lord," she said, her voice cool, "for 'tis no fault of my own. Your kinsmen took me captive early this morn, and the ride here was long and hard."

"I'm sure 'twas," David answered smoothly. "And I am ashamed of haeing kept ye standing in this drafty hall when doubtless ye are cold, tired, and hungry. Please, come this way."

He willna help me, Mary thought with anguish as she followed the Earl to another smaller chamber. I can see it in his eyes. He has accepted that I belong to the MacBeth by right of the ancient, unwritten laws governing Highland feuds, and he willna interfere. No mon would. Oh, God, what am I to do?

A fire blazed in the room, and the lass moved toward it gratefully, laying Hunter's cloak and her own upon a nearby chair, stripping off her gloves as she held out her hands to the inviting warmth.

"Edith," David called to his housekeeper. "Bring a light repast for our guests, some ale, and a bottle of brandy. Well," he said, turning once more to Hunter and Cadman, "sit down, sit down. How is Lord Angus?"

"Fine. He sends his regards." Hunter reached into his doublet for the messages entrusted to his care.

"And your sister Grace, Cadman? She is well?" the MacDonald queried as he took the sealed scrolls.

"Aye, more beautiful than e'er." Cadman flushed slightly as he stretched his booted legs out in front of himself, for David had once hoped to wed Grace MacBeth, and Cadman knew the Earl still loved her.

"I see you're planning to stay awhile." The MacDonald

lightly tapped the parchments he'd finished scanning, not wishing to make Cadman uncomfortable.

This easy banter went on for several more minutes as Edith returned with two other women to lay out the meal provided for the guests, supper being long since over at the keep. Mary huddled on a small stool by the fire, pretending to take no notice of the three men, although she studied them intently in the candlelight. The MacDonald must be a bachelor, she decided, or else his wife would hae joined us by now. Still, there was naught to give evidence of such, for the Earl's keep boasted neither speck of dust nor stinking torch. David MacDonald was a diligent and meticulous man.

Of medium height and build, he reminded Mary somewhat of Edward, though he had not her cousin's fragility. His cheeks were flat, with high bones; his nose was straight and sharply defined on the end; his lips were thin and purposeful. His blue eyes were clear—not dark like Cadman's, not deep like Edward's, not ice like Ian's—but clear, like the reflection of the sky in a still loch. Only the careless thatch of silver blond hair that fell over his forehead and that he constantly pushed out of his eyes belied the seriousness of the MacDonald's face.

He would make a good spy, Mary thought suddenly, and did not realize how close she had come to hitting on the truth of the matter.

He was twenty-four years old, the same age as Cadman, but looked older. Having come into his earldom at fifteen after his father had been killed in battle, David MacDonald had learned early the talents of survival, for there had been many within his own clan who had sought to wrest his inheritance from his grasp. The MacDonalds were a large and powerful family, and although the ties between them were strong against outsiders, within the clan dissension and greed ran rife. Still, his father's vassals had remained loyal to the lad, thwarting the attempts upon his life and lands. Through the years David had managed to ally himself strongly with the King, the better to enrich his purse and strengthen his defenses. He had spies and assassins throughout Scotland who reported his enemies' movements to him and eliminated the more dangerous of these when necessary. Nevertheless, in spite of his ruthlessness, he was honest with and faithful to the men he counted as friends. Hunter and Cadman MacBeth were two of these.

David frowned as his eyes fell upon the young girl Hunter had brought with him this evening. If the Earl's knowledge were correct, James would have little interest in reprimanding the MacBeths for her kidnapping should the Carmichaels bring the matter to the King's attention; but the Clan Carmichael itself would never let the deed pass without retaliation. Much as he liked Hunter and Cadman, the Earl hoped his friends were gone by the time the Lion of Bailekair discovered his daughter's whereabouts. Otherwise David would be forced to deliver the lass up or have his castle laid to siege. 'Twas not a decision he wanted to make.

Hunter's clansman, Cadman, was a devilishly good-looking man. Not handsome in the hard, masculine manner of his foster brother, but rather boyishly charming. His resemblance to Hunter was strongly marked, however, for he had the same square-cut jaw, the same carnal mouth. This latter was not framed by the deep lines that etched the sides of his kinsman's lips though, nor were his eyes drawn at the corners by the fine array of wrinkles that splayed Hunter's violet shards. Any scars of time Cadman bore had been put there by laughter, although deep within his eyes Mary thought she sometimes caught a glimpse of sorrow. He reminded her a little of her brother Charlie, though she suspected a sensitivity in him similar to Gordon's. Joanna would like him, she mused idly, then chided herself sharply for believing her maid would ever glance with favor upon an enemy.

Lastly there was Hunter, her captor. How like a restless mountain cat, symbol of the Clan MacBeth, he was! Lazy, prowling, dangerous. Aye, of the three men present he would be the most formidable opponent, because he would be the most unpredictable. The MacDonald, Mary felt, would handle his affairs by stealth of night, preferably in a dark corridor. Cadman, like Charlie, would rush headlong and thoughtlessly into open battle. But Hunter—Hunter would study his foe with an appalling and frightening thoroughness, striking at a fatal weakness when least expected.

Mary turned away and did not gaze at them again until Hunter arose to press a chalice of brandy into her hands.

"Come, and eat something," he coaxed softly.

"I'm nae hungry," the girl lied, for she had eaten nothing all day. But she accepted the liquor without protest.

He caught her hair, still damp from the snow, in his fingers, twisting her face up to his. "If ye displease me in front of our host, ye shall suffer for it later."

"Dinna touch me! I hate ye!" Mary spat, confused again by the tremor that once more coursed through her blood at his touch.

The corners of Hunter's mouth turned up sardonically in a mocking smile that did not quite reach his narrowed eyes.

"Ye would be wise to remember you're my prisoner," he warned. "Howe'er, it pleases me ye show some strong emotion toward me, even if 'tis only hatred. At least ye are nae indifferent to me. But then your kiss at the tourney told me that, tigress."

She gasped as his suddenly hot eyes raked her knowingly. He had guessed! He had known how his kiss had affected her! She bit her lip as her face flooded with shame. God! That he should have known how the desire had quickened in her body when his mouth had come down on hers that day! She could have died! What must he be thinking? That she actually wanted him? The horrible truth was that a part of her did! Some savage thing in her responded to him in a way she could not control. He laughed jeeringly at her distress.

"Aye, I felt your heart pound gainst my chest and your body tremble wie'in my embrace," he spoke cruelly. "As both shall once again tonight."

Mary's hands reached instinctively for the small dinner dagger she carried in her belt, fingers tightening convulsively upon its hilt.

"I will slay ye first!"

"Would ye?" Hunter queried slowly as he stared at the

tiny knife. "Aye, I believe ye would. In that case I shall gie orders to our host that if I am found dead in our bedchamber, he is to turn ye o'er to his men-at-arms for sport, then burn ye at the stake when they hae finished wie ye. 'Twill be a fit end for a witch who has cast her spell upon me," he snarled.

Hunter shrugged his shoulders indifferently, that smile curving upon his lips once more when she did not reply. Then he walked away.

Mary felt a cold clutch of fear grab her heart, wondering if he would indeed carry out this dastardly threat, then was sorry she'd refused his offer of food as her stomach growled noisily. 'Twas stupid to have rejected the meal. She could not starve and would need every ounce of her strength if she were to escape from him. Her chin thrust out defiantly, she went to sit beside the MacBeth at the table. Hunter said nothing as she settled into the chair, merely filling a plate and placing it before her. Mary pulled the knife from her belt and began to eat lustily.

She examined the tiny dagger closely as she cut a piece of hot meat, popping the morsel into her mouth quickly, licking the grease from her fingers. The girl pondered whether or not she really could stab her captor with this object and kill him, then sighed as she decided 'twas too small a blade to do any real damage. A wounded mountain cat is a dangerous animal, she shuddered at the thought. Almost as though he'd guessed her line of reasoning Mary saw Hunter's glimmering eyes on her speculatively. Her own fell before his piercing gaze.

"So James has forgi'en the incident at Court?" Cadman was asking.

"Aye," David nodded. " 'Twas merely an excuse to bleed his lairds of more money. I am told he found the entire episode highly amusing. 'Twill be a cold day in hell before *that* particular tourney is forgotten," he laughed, then sobered moments later. " 'Tis the King's damnable greed that has turned his thoughts from your feud and why you'll nae likely receive any censure from that quarter o'er taking the wench. 'Tis my belief James is headed on a path of self-destruction if he keeps on stealing from his lairds. The Borders already stir wie whispers and strange dealings late at night, and Patrick Hepburn is hungry for power. Beware, my friends, ye make no binding vows to the King, oaths that canna be broken if need be.''

"Honorable men dinna break vows," Mary sneered impetuously in the quiet that followed the MacDonald's warning. "But then we all know the MacBeths are nae honorable men."

Hunter's eyes narrowed as Cadman gasped aloud at her insult. David studied them all covertly.

"If they are clever, they word their oaths so they dinna hae to break them, my lady," Hunter drawled softly, but the lass was not deceived and wondered if the brandy had gone to her head to make her taunt him so. "If they are witless fools, like the Carmichaels," he continued, "they die for the binding words they hae thoughtlessly spoken, but, of course, wie honor."

"And ye—are ye clever, sir?" she mocked.

"To answer that, madam, ye need only ask yourself which one of us was taken captive this morning."

Mary pushed her plate away and put her dinner knife up, feeling suddenly very tired and overwrought. *She* was the prisoner. He could do whatever he liked with her, and she would be defenseless against him. Oh, why had she given into her wretched temper and teased him? What would he do to her? Would he beat her for her impudence? Nay, she knew how he would take his revenge upon her. The answer was there, in his desire-filled eyes, and promised from his carnal lips.

"Are ye quite finished, madam?" he questioned curtly.

She nodded, staring at her hands in her lap.

"Then I suggest ye retire for the evening. Ye hae half-an-hour, my lady."

David motioned to the two serving maids.

"This way, my lady," one of them said quietly, pity in her eyes. Faith, but men were monsters! Could they nae see how frightened the wee lass was? "Get on wie ye, Kirsty," the woman barked sharply to the other maid. "I'll take care of her ladyship. My name's Agnes," she said, turning to Mary kindly. "Come along now. A hot bath's just what you'll be needing."

Mary followed her slowly. Out in the main hall the girl saw with despair two armed men stood guard at the entrance of the keep. They snapped to attention when she appeared, warned earlier against allowing her to flee. There was no escape for her there. Feeling quite doomed, Mary trudged up the long, curving flight of stairs after Agnes, yearning for a swift, sudden death.

"Here we be." Agnes opened a door off the dark corridor. "Och, here now, my lady, dinna fash yourself so!" She stared, alarmed, at the tears that were slipping silently down Mary's cheeks. "I know you're here unwillingly, for I heard the talk below, but Sir MacBeth's a handsome devil, nae like to beat ye or share ye wie the others."

Mary gasped aloud at this last remark, for she had never thought of *that!*

"Oh, aye, my lady." Agnes correctly interpreted the girl's surprise. "There's some would do as much and more. Why, I heard tell of one puir lassie what was sold to Moorish pirates for a few pieces of silver. Chin up now. Sir MacBeth's quite taken wie ye. Oh, aye, I saw how he watched ye downstairs. If ye want my advice, my lady, you'll be soft and shy as a fawn wie him when he comes. You're a bonnie, wee thing. No doubt ye can twist him around your little finger easily enough—if ye ken my meaning. Mayhap he'll even wed ye when he's finished. 'Tis been known to happen."

"I—I am already betrothed, and, besides, he is my ene-my!"

"Aye, well, 'tis a pity then, for ye would be better off wie Sir MacBeth."

"What—what do ye mean?"

Agnes gazed at her compassionately. "Why, lass, surely you'll nae be thinking to return to your kin in disgrace, even if ye are ransomed. They'll nae be wanting ye unless some mon can be persuaded to o'erlook your shame and marry ye. Does your betrothed love ye enough for that?"

Mary shook her head. "Nay, he loves me nae at all."

"Aye, well then, there'll be a council called to decide your fate, or 'tisna the same in the Highlands as 'twas when I was a wee gel there. If some mon doesna come forward to wed ye, you'll be banished from your clan, and no holding of your family will offer ye food or drink or shelter. And if ye carry a bairn of Sir MacBeth's making, you'll most likely be slain."

"But—but I am the daughter of our Chief!"

Agnes studied her sadly. " 'Twill be even harder for ye then, my lady, for your father will be honor bound to deal wie ye more harshly, else your clan think him weak or partial and he lose his standing in their eyes."

Mary remembered suddenly the week before the Inverness fair during her childhood when she had stood and watched Magnus chop off the hand of one of the serfs for stealing.

"Aye, 'tis a sorrowful thing I do this day," Magnus had said. "For he was a good mon once, and I was proud to call him one of mine. But justice must be done, daughter. That is the way of things."

Mary shuddered. She had angered her father already over Hugh. Agnes was right! Magnus would not deal leniently with his daughter upon her return.

"Mother of God hae mercy," she whispered. "What am I to do?"

"Open your heart to Sir MacBeth," Agnes replied shrewdly. " 'Tis my belief he had already done as much for ye."

Then quietly she closed the door.

"Will the lady be wanting a bath, mistress?" Kirsty asked when Agnes entered the kitchen.

"Nay, lass. 'Tis best ye leave her alone for now."

Mary opened the shutters to the balcony after Agnes had gone, feeling the icy wind cut her like a sharp knife as she stepped out onto the terrace. Her head spun dizzily as she gaged the long drop down. She would surely be killed. Was it not best? What else was there?

As though in answer to her question Hunter entered the room softly, treading like a panther upon silent, booted feet.

For a moment his heart leapt to his throat as he surmised her intent.

"Is death really preferable to me, tigress?" He grinned with a forced laziness he did not feel, for he feared any moment she would jump. "I hadna thought ye such a coward."

The words stung, as they were meant to. Mary whirled; her chin came up defiantly.

"How dare ye call me thus? Ye wie the blood of your cur dog ancestors, who ran from the walls of Bailekair in shame, in your veins?"

"As ye would run from me, my lady?"

Mary had no response to that. As Hunter walked toward her she felt suddenly as though she had been waiting for this moment, waiting all her life for him to stalk toward her with that prowling, catlike grace, the shrouded figure of her dreams, the enemy of her reality.

I willna beg, she thought desperately, determinedly. I will be as brave as my father when he rides off to battle. I willna let this mon see how afraid I am.

"I—I will fight ye, sir!" she cried suddenly. "I must!"

But even as she spoke the words Mary knew they were futile. He was so tall, so strong; he would have his way with her in the end.

"Aye, tigress, I know," Hunter rejoined softly, a gentle understanding of her plight within his eyes.

He moved so swiftly Mary was unprepared when his left hand caught her wrist, twisting it roughly behind her back. When she struggled, he tightened his grip until she winced with pain and stood helpless against him, fearing he would break her arm. With his free hand Hunter unhooked her mesh girdle, tossing it aside with a clatter.

"I'm of no mind to feel the bite of your steel, madam," he noted the dinner knife sheathed in the gold filligree belt now upon the floor.

Then, grasping the material of her *arascaid* and shift at the shoulders, he ripped both garments in half with a single yank,

**143**

leaving her naked to the waist. Mary gasped, attempting to shield herself from his hungry stare as she turned to run, her long hair flying out behind her. Hunter grabbed the golden locks easily; the girl fell backward against him, staggering to her knees. They grappled on the floor until he pinioned her wrists above her head with one hand and, throwing a leg over her protesting thighs, bent to pull the boots from her slender calves with his other.

"Nay," Mary sobbed as his fingers moved upward, seeking the riband that tied her silken hose; but in moments the length of her body lay exposed to his gaze nevertheless.

Hunter's breath caught in his throat as his violet eyes raked her nakedness, more golden than he had imagined in the dancing candlelight and firelight. He loosed her to pull her to him. Mary clawed at him wildly, leaving bloody streaks along one side of his face and then his back as he threw her over his shoulder and carried her to the massive bed. She tried to rise, but he drew his dagger, pressing its point against the pulse throbbing at the hollow of her throat.

"Dinna make me use this, tigress," he warned.

Mary swallowed hard, feeling the tip of the dirk prick her flesh. She did not want to die! Even now, when she knew the MacBeth was within moments of taking his pleasure with her, some primitive instinct to survive kept her from that eternal darkness. He had won, her enemy. She was lost to him, as she had somehow always known she would be.

"Hae me then," she whispered bitterly. "And may God damn your accursed eyes to hell for it!"

Hunter studied her quietly in the glow of the candles as he divested himself of his garments, noting her trembling lips and the tears that threatened to slip from the corners of her amethyst eyes. God's blood! But she was bonnie! And so strangely vulnerable now that he had stripped her of her clothes and spirit. Well, he had wanted to shame her. But as he devoured the sight of her ripe, rounded breasts; the small flat belly; and the pale golden flanks, with their slightly darker mound of curls, Hunter found he could take no joy in the deed. He thought of her as first he'd seen her, so proud, so arrogant, in spite of her fear; like a wild filly she had been, like the golden tigress he'd named her. The sight of her now, quivering before him like a wounded fawn, sickened Hunter as much as the first stag he'd ever slain had done, gazing at him woefully from sad, frightened eyes before it had shuddered and lain still. He swore softly under his breath.

Here was a woman worth having. A woman who had fought him every step of the way with naught save her fierce pride and passion to defend her. Aye, here was a woman he could love for all time, and she wanted him not. Suddenly it became very important to Hunter she desire him as much as he did her. He slipped into bed beside her, all thoughts of a quick, brutal rape driven from his mind.

"I will be gentle wie ye, lass," he promised before his mouth found hers in the soft, shadowed light.

Mary was ashamed at the sudden desire that flooded her flesh at his kiss, the kiss she remembered so well from the tourney. His tongue teased the inside of her lips, taunting her, ravaging the inner sweetness of her mouth, on and on, until she felt dizzy from its hushed pressure, and a slow ache began to build between her thighs. And all the while the hard, masculine length of him pressed against her; his left hand caressed her, cupping her breasts, thumb flicking over the pale pink nipples until they flushed into stiff, excited peaks. The girl moaned deep within her throat. This was not the cruel, savage assault she had expected. What was he doing to her?

His mouth traveled to her breasts, tongue swirling over them, mouth sucking lightly at the hardened tips as his hand dropped to her thighs, opening the flanks that sought to defend themselves against his encroaching, searching fingers. He stroked rhythmically until Mary could feel the wetness of herself upon her flesh, the mounting flame of urgency his hand evoked between her thighs as he pulled gently at the soft curls and explored where no man had ever touched her before, caressing the sweet satin pulse of her, feeling it quiver beneath his strong, fondling fingers. She gave an odd gasp of shock and delight. Hunter brushed her breasts again; his tongue licked savoringly at the honeyed moistness his hand had left. Mary blushed, and her belly fluttered strangely as she closed her eyes and turned away from the intimacy of the moment.

He laughed softly, his fingers wrapping themselves amidst the strands of her long golden hair, tangling, drawing her back again as his lips found the place on her shoulder at the nape of her neck. Mary shivered, feeling little tingles of pleasure race through her blood as his tongue tickled that sensitive spot, sent tiny sparks of electric anticipation thrilling down her spine. And then his breath was hot in her ear as he blew gently there and whispered words in Romany she could not understand. He kissed her breasts once more, lingering over the rigid little buds that blossomed like cherries against the white-and-gold flowering of her chest. He moved on to her belly, his mouth fire against her skin, tracing patterns of petite circles along her sides and around her navel before sliding down the length of the gilded fluff that trailed a silken path to her womanhood. Mary felt ablaze from his searing lips, his restless, discovering fingers. His hands found the small hollows on the sides of her hips as he lowered his head to that soft nest between her thighs.

"Nay," she breathed. "Please dinna—"

But his tongue was already there, probing, eager as it tasted the clean, musky essence of the swell that trembled beneath his mouth. She knew she should strike him, claw at him again, anything to get him to stop this sweet, savage torture, but Mary found her hands would not move, could only curl up tightly in his own as they reached for him in the darkness, as she gloried in the writhing sensations he was producing in her body. She felt a series of quivering tremors begin, spread through her blood, building, heightening until she thought she would surely explode. And then she did! Over and over again as she panted raggedly from the wild crescendoes. And, still, he did not stop, but drove her on to even higher ecstasies as he drank the heady nectar of her deep rose mound, inhaled the fragrance of her exaltation.

"Yield to me, tigress!" He suddenly yanked away from

her, his violet eyes glittering as he bent his dark visage to kiss her lips once more. "Yield!" he muttered. "Say ye want me, or, by God, I will leave this bed to slake my lust upon another!"

He had aroused her to a frenzied pitch of desire, and he knew it. Mary ached to have him inside her. Instinctively she sought that final rapture, knowing she would not be sated until it came.

"Aye, damn ye! I *do* want ye! Ye hae made it so, ye accursed devil!" And then more gently, "I yield, aye, I yield."

She felt his hard shaft rub against her, find her in the dancing firelight. There was a sharp stab of pain as he entered her triumphantly, penetrating her with a swift plummet that left her breathless. She cried out.

"Hush, love, 'twillna hurt for long," he murmured huskily against her throat.

He lay still atop her until, as he'd said, the pain receded, and Mary relaxed in his strong embrace. Then he began to move within her, sliding in and out of her wet, velvet softness slowly at first, then harder and deeper as his desire grew, rhythmic plunges that aroused the tingling sensations in her flesh again. She wrapped her arms tightly around his back, feeling Hunter's muscles tense and ripple beneath her hands as he held himself above her with his powerful limbs. Her nails dug into his skin involuntarily as the spasms overtook her once more and some animal instinct forced her to arch her hips to receive his fiery, lunging blade. A thousand suns again burst within her, and a few moments later Mary felt the streaming jet of Hunter's life force fill her insides.

He kissed her face, her throat, her breasts, fingers entwining themselves in her golden hair, pulling the strands from beneath her body to wrap them around his throat. He buried his countenance deep within the tresses, sighing with pleasure.

Mary felt empty when he left her, but his dark body pressed against the side of hers in the candlelight as one arm went under her neck and the other rested across her belly. He had no need to ask, as most men do, whether or not it had been good for her. They were as one in that moment, and Hunter knew her as well as he knew himself. Mary lay silent in his caress, scarcely daring to breathe as she waited for the rapid pounding of her heart to slow to its normal pace. He had taken her virginity, this enemy, and in the end she had wanted him, perhaps had always wanted him. She blushed, crimson with shame, as she recalled the wild, wanton words with which she had urged him on, begged him to take her.

"Ye hae shamed me, sir," she whispered in the darkness, lips trembling now as she thought of the terrible consequences of this night's work.

"Would it hae been any less shameful if it had been your betrothed who took ye first?" Hunter gazed at her, eyes narrowed and veiled beneath half-closed lids.

"I—I dinna know."

"Ye dinna love him?"

"Nay." Mary was truthful.

"Did ye desire him?"

"Nay."

"But ye wanted me." His hand caught her jaw cruelly, twisting her face up so her dark, amethyst eyes met his in the half-light. "Did ye nae? For I heard the words ye cried out when I would hae left your side. Answer me, tigress." His fingers tightened into her flesh. Then he laughed lowly, mockingly when she refused to respond. He relaxed his grip. "Ye knew pleasure wie me, as I said ye would. There is no shame in that."

"Ye are my enemy!"

"Nay, Mary, I am your lover," he snarled thickly.

She could not fight him as he took her once more, this time roughly, hungrily by the dying light of the embers of the fire, as she found that lovemaking could also be violent and savage in its tender fury.

# Twelve

Mary stirred gently as the first pale streaks of the cold grey dawn touched the sky with icy fingers. She felt chilled to the bone and after some moments of slow awakening realized Hunter no longer lay beside her sharing his warmth. She drew the blankets more closely about her, nostrils breathing in the scent of his maleness that still lingered in the sheets, reminding her sharply of their lovemaking the night just past. He had been gentle with her, as he'd promised. This surprised Mary, for she had fully expected to be beaten and brutally raped. Her mind was filled with confusion at the thought of his tenderness.

How is it, she wondered, my enemy has used me wie much kindness and sent my body and soul spinning in his strong embrace? Has he some power, some charm of which I dinna know wie which he has indeed cast me under a spell? I would scorn him, hate him; and yet when he touched me, I grew dizzy wie desire. My body cried oot for him, and I couldna help its betrayal. God's blood! There is something animal in him to which I responded, something primitive and savage and yet curiously gentle that only he has wakened in me. 'Twas thus at the tourney and again yestereve. Och, why am I glad 'twas Hunter and nae Hugh who took me? There is pain in my heart as though—as though I were in love wie my enemy. Och! Christ hae mercy, for 'tis true! 'Tis true! I love him! I hae loved him since that day of the King's summer tourney and wouldna admit it!

Nay! Nay! He is my enemy! Dinna let my heart be gi'en where naught save sorrow waits! I am naught to him, naught but a captive wench he sought to shame wie rape. But he struck me nae once, though I fought him wildly and clawed him like the tigress he calls me. I hae seen men rape. Upon the ravaged fields of Bailekair I hae seen the marauders come and take the women of our village. 'Twas no tender act that lasted until the candles guttered in their sockets, but a quick and brutal deed. What manner of mon then is this who sought to gie me pleasure and ease my pain?

Oh, Hunter, Hunter! I know in my heart now I love ye, and 'tis all for naught! Why couldst ye nae leave me be?

With a strangled cry Mary pressed her face into the pillow, tears damp upon the linen material as she wept wrenching, muffled sobs.

She did not know Hunter had entered the room until he touched her gently on one shoulder. She turned, choking as she sat up and drew a sheet over herself to cover her nakedness. He smiled tenderly.

"I hae seen all ye would hide, lass." He pulled the cloth from her grasp, brushing her breasts softly as he smoothed the tangled mass of curls back from her face and bosom and caressed away the tears that stained her cheeks. "Is that why ye weep?"

"Is it nae enough?" Mary found she could not meet his eyes.

"Nay, tigress," he answered lowly. "I brought ye joy last night, just as ye did me."

"Nay, 'twas naught save sorrow I knew and why I weep this morn."

"Ah, Mary, dinna seek to deny me. Even now your silken breasts belie your words." Hunter cupped one ripe mound possessively, thumb teasing the rosy tip. "See how it hardens at my touch." He lowered his mouth to that soft place, tongue tracing tiny swirls about the nipple, lips sucking until Mary shivered with little tingles. "Aye," Hunter laughed winningly. "Ye canna lie to me, sweet. I feel how ye quiver when my mouth tastes ye there."

Mary blushed painfully. 'Twas bad enough he knew these things, but to speak of them openly embarrassed her dreadfully.

"Please dinna."

"Dinna what?" He went on stroking her, his eyes filled with amusement.

"Please, sir—"

"I hae a gi'en name, Mary, as well ye know. I want to hear ye say it. Now, tigress!" he commanded when she hesitated.

"Hunt—Hunter," she stammered self-consciously, for her use of his Christian name seemed to heighten the intimacy of his hands on her body.

"Aye, lass?"

Mary took a deep breath, for the thought of parting from him now tore at the strings of her heart like the clumsy fingers of an unskilled churl upon a delicate lute. Oh, my love! she wanted to cry out, but lowered her violet eyes quickly lest he guess her desire. He must not find out! He would only hurt her with the knowledge!

"My—my father will pay a goodly amount of gold for my return. Will ye nae send a message to Bailekair this day demanding my ransom?"

Hunter studied her speculatively for a moment. "Your father, Mary? But what of your betrothed?"

"I—I dinna think he will want me now." Mary twisted her hands nervously in her lap.

"He doesna love ye then, this mon?"

"He is hungry for power," the girl replied. "And the daughter of the Chief of the Clan Carmichael is no mean prize."

"I know," Hunter said softly. "Still, I couldna send a message in this blizzard, even if I wished to ransom ye."

Mary stared at him in horror. "Do ye—do ye mean to slay me then?" she cried with anguish.

"Nay! Nay!" He rose quickly to stand before her, his hands upon her shaking shoulders. "Oh, God! Ne'er look at

151

me like that again, Mary!'' he entreated earnestly, his eyes stricken with pain before he turned away, running one hand carelessly through his unruly locks. "Sweet *Jesú!*" he swore under his breath. "How I've wanted ye, wanted ye from the first moment I laid eyes upon ye that day of the summer storm, so proud, so arrogant, and yet so verra fragile. Like the heather on the Highland moors, ye were, blossoming into womanhood wie sweet, delicate buds so easily bruised or plucked, and yet wie roots that clung to the earth wie stubborn determination, bending, but ne'er breaking. Aye, how ye fought me and laid your brand upon my mouth, scorned and disgraced me for a fool and left me for dead.

"I wanted to kill ye then." His eyes met hers once more, seeming to plead for understanding. "To place my hands around your throat and choke ye until your mocking laughter ceased and your image haunted me no more. But more than this I wanted to revenge myself upon ye in the only way I knew would shame ye as ye had me. I wanted to feel your flesh beneath my own and hear your scarlet lips beg for mercy. But ye dinna beg. Though your mouth trembled wie fright, ye dinna beg," he repeated. "And the rage and hurt drained from my verra soul as though they had ne'er been, and there was naught wie'in me save desire and admiration for your courage.

"Last night—last night I took ye, Mary, as I would hae had ye been my bride; and the joy ye gae to me, willing or no, was the sweetest I hae found wie any wench. I—I canna let ye go, tigress. You're all I've e'er wanted in a woman.'' Hunter paused as for one brief moment he struggled with his pride. Would she mock him, laugh at him, play him for a fool again? It doesna matter, he told himself. She is mine, mine! And then his heart was in his eyes as he whispered passionately, "I love ye, Mary Carmichael. God help me, but I do.''

*I love ye.* Oh, how those three words echoed in Mary's heart! In strains of melodious mode they sang, trilled, and quavered to the beat of passion that played in that life-giving place. Could it be true? Oh, *aye!* He had used her tenderly because he loved her. And now he stood before her, his heart and pride laid bare, his eyes eager, searching, waiting, longing.

The years of battle and hatred between the Clans Carmichael and MacBeth faded as though their stain had never touched the two who gazed at one another with brilliant amethyst eyes and softly parted lips that winter's morn. There was nothing for them but each other as Mary flung herself joyously into his welcoming embrace, saying fiercely, "Then God help us both, my love!"

"Oh, Hunter. If ye hadna loved me—if ye hadna spoken— I—I would hae died of heartbreak."

"And I, also, had ye nae told me of your love for me in return, Mary." He stroked her golden tresses gently as they lay together, warmed by the soft afterglow of their lovemaking.

How sweetly feverish it had been! As though each had thought to suddenly awaken and find it had been naught but a dream. Only a dream. And they had clung to one another tightly as Mary had willingly received Hunter, abandoning herself to him so freely his breath had caught in his throat with joy at the depths of her passion. There had been no part of her he had not kissed, caressed, and loved.

"I—I'm afraid, so afraid, sir," Mary sobbed quietly now against his broad, furry chest. "My father and brothers will be honor-bound to come for me, though they banish me from my clan for my shame afterward. They'll—they'll slay ye and wie ye my heart also. I couldna live—oh, Hunter! I canna live wie'oot ye!"

"Nor I, ye. Hush, sweet. Hush," he murmured, holding her close, then made an attempt at a lighthearted jest. "Hae ye no faith in my fighting abilities? Och, methinks 'tis no tigress, but a timid rabbit wie which I hae saddled myself."

" 'Tisna funny, sir."

He sobered quickly. "Nay, I know. Do ye think the Clan MacBeth will welcome ye either? Nay, love. There is no place for us here in the Highlands, nae now, perhaps nae e'er. We must go away, to England or France mayhap." He tilted her face up to his. "Our life together will be hard, Mary, our burdens many; for this love of ours came swiftly, like the summer storm when first I touched ye, beset wie the winds of guilt, the fury of battle, and the blinding hatred that has lain between our clans these many years past. Nay, dinna deny it." He placed one hand against her lips gently as the girl sought to speak. "Our clan ties run as deep as our passion for one another, and the lessons of a lifetime are nae easily set aside. Though we are both proud, lass, ye are the daughter of a chief. I am but a puir landless knight, wie naught save my sword to defend ye, my shield to protect ye. I canna offer ye the finer things to which ye are accustomed. I—I canna even wed ye, Mary, for ye are bound legally to another. But I swear I will love ye as no mon has e'er loved a woman, and ye shall be as my wife in my heart and soul, though no priest may gie us his blessing. Is it—is it enough, tigress?"

Mary thought of her family. She would never see them again. And Bailekair, so tall, so majestic, cast in the shadow of the purple snowcapped mountain. That too was lost to her now. Even if she returned to its massive, beckoning walls, there would be nothing for her there. If another man had taken her, some clansman might have been bribed to overlook her soiled state and wed her; but no Carmichael would accept a woman who had lain with a MacBeth. Certainly not Hugh. Hugh, who, as her betrothed, would have the right to choose the punishment for her disgrace. Hugh, who would scorn her and spit in her face, cast her out to become a whore or worse! Hugh, who, if she carried Hunter's child, would surely kill her! Such was the fate of a Carmichael woman sullied by the seed of a MacBeth. So it had always been. Agnes was right. It doesna matter, Mary thought. I hae Hunter. Hunter, who loves me enough to gie up e'erything he has e'er known and cherished. Can I do any less? Nay. If we are to share our lives together, I must meet him halfway. This love of ours is a fragile cloth, woven of silken threads, rent wie flaws from its beginning, as Hunter has said. It must hae time to flourish and grow strong, stronger than the hatred that will destroy us both otherwise.

Aye, I am Lady Mary Carmichael, daughter of the Lion of Bailekair, no longer. From this day forward I am the wife of Sir Hunter MacBeth in all but name. Mary touched the scar that marked the corner of her lover's mouth.

"Aye, my love," she answered him at last. " 'Tis more than enough."

And when Hunter's lips claimed hers, Mary vowed fervently to make it true.

Some time later Hunter sent for Agnes and Kirsty to assist Mary with her toilette. They filled the tub of hammered brass in one corner of the room with buckets of steaming water, Kirsty eyeing Mary curiously all the while, Agnes with a barely suppressed smile as Mary, singing happily, stepped into the hot bath. She allowed the maids to lathe her body vigorously with heather-scented soap, grateful for the experienced massage that helped ease the soreness in her muscles still stiff from the long, hard ride to Wynd Cheathaich and Hunter's lovemaking.

Downstairs Hunter smiled softly to himself at the sound of her voice.

" 'Tis a nightingale I've caged and no mistake."

Cadman frowned darkly. "No good will come of this, Hunter, I promise ye."

"Marry-go-up, sir!" Hunter swore. "Ye hae warned me thusly once too often, mon! I'll nae listen to any more of your dire predictions. I love her, I tell ye; and she loves me. I mean to take her away from Scotland wie me as soon as this snow lets up."

"Och, Hunter! Where will ye go? Think, mon! The lass isna used to such hardships as your life has to offer her, and you'll nae hae your family to turn to in times of trouble."

"I hae my sword and shield. We shall manage well enough," Hunter retorted in a firm tone that brooked no argument. "And if ye love me as a brother, Cadman, you'll say no more aboot this matter. I hae nae asked ye to share my exile, and if ye canna find it in yourself to accept my lady and love her as I do, then begone wie ye, sir!"

The two men glared at each other angrily for a moment, then Cadman lowered his eyes repentantly.

"Forgie me, brother, for I know ye wouldna turn against me were our positions reversed. I do love ye and shall try to love your lady for your sake; and though ye dinna ask it of me, I shall come wie ye on your journey, for there is naught in Scotland for me."

Hunter clasped his foster brother's arms warmly. "I thank ye, Cadman, for in truth I would welcome another sword and shield at my side."

"Then 'tis settled."

"I would like to be of help to ye also, Hunter." David MacDonald entered the room. "Is there anything I can do?"

"Well, if you've materials in your storeroom, I would purchase some from ye, for Mary is wie'oot even a change of clothes."

David smiled. "I will do better than that for her if Cadman has no objection. Come wie me."

And so by the time Mary had finished soaking, Hunter had returned to their chamber, bearing a coffer filled with garments. The girl gasped as she saw the rich brocades and satins, silks and furs, all of which looked as though they had been designed especially for her, so appropriate were their colors.

"Oh, Hunter, they're beautiful! Howe'er did ye manage—"

"'Tis a long story, sweet, and nae a verra pleasant one," he explained as the maids began lifting the gowns from the chest for Mary to make her choice. "They belonged to David's sister, Janet; they were to hae been her trousseau."

"Were?"

"Aye, she was to hae married Cadman. My foster brother is—baseborn, but Janet loved him, and since David thought naught of Cadman's bastardy, only of Janet's happiness, the Earl agreed to the match. Shortly before the wedding David held a hunting party to begin the week of festivities. During the hunt we were set upon by the Fraziers, whose feud wie the MacDonalds is no less famous than that between the

Carmichaels and MacBeths. God's blood! It happened so quickly, Mary, and we were drunk wie ale and the fever of the chase, for the hounds had flushed a boar that day. Many were killed. Janet was taken prisoner.

"David wanted to lay siege to the castle wherein she was held captive at once, but Cadman feared she would be slain. He loved her, lass. He begged David to pay the ransom and promised to wed Janet the moment she was freed. It mattered nae to him she would no longer be a virgin. Finally David acquiesced to my kinsman's demands, and Janet was returned to us. She was heavily veiled and spoke to no one, locking herself in her room, where neither food nor drink passed her lips. Cadman pleaded wie her to marry him, but Janet refused to see him and sent away his messages unread. Even David couldna reason wie her. A few days later we found her body in the courtyard. She had thrown herself from the balcony.

"We—we couldna understand why until Cadman stripped the veils from her face to kiss the cold lips of his beloved one last time. What the Fraziers had done to her—God's wounds!" Hunter smote one fist into the open palm of his other hand, causing Mary and the maids to flinch at his anger. "She was blond and bonnie like ye, love, but after they'd raped her those whoresons had taken their dirks and cut her face up beyond all recognition."

Mary gasped. "That's horrible!"

"Aye, as was the revenge David took for her. The morning dew lies sweet upon many a Frazier grave now. But that's nae the end of it. David was to hae wed Cadman's half sister, Grace, as well, as part of the bargain between our two clans. But Lord Torquil, Cadman's and Grace's father, blamed David for Janet's death; and so he annulled Grace's contracts wie the Earl and betrothed her instead to Lord Angus's youngest son, Francis. David has ne'er married, and Grace awaits her wedding day wie much unhappiness.

"'Twas a feud that took Janet's life, my lady, and left three others miserable. Dinna let such come between us."

"Nay, sir." Mary understood his fear. "Will it nae cause them pain, David and Cadman, to see me in Janet's gowns?"

"Time has dulled their grief, Mary, if nae their love for her. I think nae."

Only a few minor alterations were necessary to fit the dress Mary chose, and these were quickly accomplished. The gown was of blue silk, styled much in the manner of a Court dress, cut low across the bodice, with wide puffed sleeves and a slight train. The skirt was narrow, but draped gracefully. Mary's gold filigree girdle, with its jeweled dinner knife, encircled her waist. Her own soft leather boots adorned her feet. The dark blue of the gown's material made her violet eyes shine even more dramatically in her pale golden face; her blond hair shimmered, unbound, in the winter light as she descended the stairs on Hunter's arm. A blue riband wound around her slender throat, since she had no jewels to wear, but this simple ornament proved more beautiful than gems, drawing attention to the curve of her ripe breasts and the shadowed hollow between them as no other necklace would have done.

Mary blushed slightly as Cadman and David came forward to kiss her hand, remembering how curt she had been with them the night just past. But they did not remark upon it, treating her instead with the courtesy they would have shown her had she been Hunter's wife, and she guessed her beloved Romany knight had spoken to his kinsmen of their love for each other.

And when Cadman knelt before her, saying, "As I love Hunter like a brother, so shall I love and honor his lady like my sister, and my sword and shield will be e'er at her side," Mary's cup was filled to overflowing.

God smiled upon them. Surely He did! For the snow fell and fell, enveloping the castle, Wynd Cheathaich, in a white cocoon of satin; frosted flakes spun with crystal ice from which there was no leaving for the lovers, nor entrance for their clans. All across Scotland the world stood still, the roads stretched empty, and the marketplaces remained bare. Mary and Hunter reveled in one another, safe for a time from the feud of hatred that shadowed their lives and lay heavily upon their guilt-ridden souls.

"I am Mary, sir, a lowly beggarmaid."

"And I am Hunter, mistress, a Romany gypsy."

"Then I shall be wary of ye, sir, for I hae heard tales of gypsy thievery and hae naught save the meager coppers I beg for in the streets of town. Wouldst take them from me?"

"Nay, mistress, 'tisna your coins, but your heart I would steal, and, once mine, it will be my most treasured possession, I promise ye."

"Then I shall gie it gladly, sir, and pray ye dinna break it."

This game they played, and others, as the fire died slowly with the night, and they lay locked in one another's arms. It was easier to love that way, easier to forget each was the sworn enemy of the other. But their pasts were still much a part of them both and crept in often, in spite of their attempts to avoid the subject. Mary talked of Bailekair and her family, of her love for her father, Gordon, and Charlie. She spoke of Edward and Joanna, of the glittering Alinor, and of the despicable Hugh.

"How can I leave, Hunter, knowing how deeply I hurt my father and how badly we quarreled o'er Hugh Carmichael? Hugh!"

"Ye must, my love. I'm sure, in his heart, the Earl has already forgi'en ye."

"If only I could send word to him—"

"Nay, Mary. We must make a clean break if we are to be free of the past. There must be no trail left for our clans to trace us by, for we shall become broken men by our leaving and will be slain if they find us."

"I know, I know," she moaned miserably as she buried her face against his chest and clung to him more tightly.

He told her of his father's death. Hunter spoke of how he had found the gypsies of his mother's band only to learn Laureen had died of childbed fever after reaching her family.

"I rode wie them often, for I was lonely as a lad, and they taught me the ways of the Romany. My grandmother was verra highly regarded by my mother's people; I was proud to bear her blood, to feel I belonged somewhere. One night grandmama read the Tarot cards for me and told me I would be a prince among my own. The others fell back in awe as I danced a Highland fling before the fire, certain I was to be King of the gypsies, that I had found my destiny at last. When I had finished, I fell before grandmama for her approval. Her eyes were sad, Mary, so verra sad. And she said, 'My grandson, that was no dance of the gypsies, but of the Scots. Your path lies not among us. Go now, and do not come here again.'

"I was hurt and bitter wie anger as I spurred my steed off into the night, for the gypsies were the only friends I had e'er known, grandmama the only real family I had. Days later I went back, but the caravan had gone. I ne'er saw them again. Shortly afterward I was sent to Glenkirk to learn the ways of knighthood.

"For a long time I waited for the truth of grandmama's prophecy to come to me. 'Twas only when I grew to monhood I understood 'twas naught but an old woman trying to please a young bairn.''

"Nay, Hunter," Mary spoke quietly. "Ye *are* a prince, *my* prince, and your fate is here, in the arms of a Scotswoman."

And then she made love with him feverishly, as though she could somehow make up for all the loneliness he had suffered as a child.

Hunter taught her to speak the Romany language and how to play chess and dice in the evenings they shared together. One night he laced her rich, red wine with brandy, the sweet nectar of the gods and nobility, he told her; and Mary drank until she was drunk with the liquor, the laughter, and her lover. At supper she learned much about the politics of Scotland by listening to Hunter, Cadman, and David discuss the mechanisms and intrigues of the government. Later she helped to decorate the keep for Christmas and sewed fine linen shirts as gifts for the three men, embroidering Hunter's with delicate designs to set it apart from the others.

Life was an unreal dream those days. Years later Mary was

to wonder if they had ever been at all; and whenever she thought of them, it would be with a hazy kind of happiness tinged with the grey mist of foreboding.

The passion she'd had for Bailekair she now gave to her lover those nights they lay together in the darkness; and if there were clouds on her horizon, Mary chose not to see them. Her world was a snow-covered castle wherein Hunter filled her sweet flesh with his own until the wee hours of the morning. Beyond its walls she dare not venture.

# *Thirteen*

The snow had ceased. The winter stillness that had lain over Bailekair was broken now by the sound of horses' hooves thudding over the cobblestones that lay buried beneath the soft, white drifts in the outer bailey of the keep.

Moments later Lord Magnus turned from the window of his chamber, where he had watched the arrival of the small party of men, to receive two of his nephews, Will and Geordie. They were his brother Walter of Moy Heath's sons, fostered out across the Minch to Abergorra and Glochlomond. He was surprised to see them, for passage over the channel that separated Scotland from the Islands of Hebrides was dangerous this time of year; and, moreover, they were armored as though for a raid. Nevertheless, he shook hands with both warmly as they knelt before him.

"Will, Geordie. Ye lads are a long way from home. What brings ye to Bailekair?" the Earl questioned as he motioned for them to be seated, offering each a tankard of ale.

"My lord, forgie our intrusion," Will, the eldest, apologized as he drained his draught, "and our coming to your chamber armored and besplattered wie the stains of travel.

But our business is urgent, and we thought it best nae to wait for a bath and meal.''

"Say on." Magnus nodded his approval.

"Will and I spent Christmas at Moy Heath," Geordie continued the story. "Och, we knew 'twould be a rough crossing upon our return to the Islands, but mother was set on us coming, and we couldna disappoint her. We'd nae seen our family in months. We stayed for the holiday, then five days ago began our ride back to Abergorra and Glochlomond. Our journey was slow, for this damned snow has made travel nearly impossible, but we pressed on anyway, for Lords Dugald and Owen desired our return to the Hebrides by Hogmany."

"Finally we managed to reach the Minch," Will broke in, picking up the tale. "At its shores we were set upon by the cowardly MacBeths of Faoghail. We were unprepared for the attack. Marry-go-up! We'd nae seen a single soul upon the roads since leaving our father's house, uncle! We had no thought of ambush! 'Twas a terrible battle, my lord, for we were all frozen wie the cold that chilled our armor like ice. But Geordie and I managed to get away with some of our men and one prisoner."

"Ye took a captive?" One eyebrow quirked upward on the Earl's frowning face.

"Aye, my lord," Geordie rejoined. "We would hae slain him, but—begging your pardon, uncle—'tis Lord Angus's heir, young Stephen. We thought him too valuable a prisoner to decide his fate ourselves. His whoreson kinsmen had burned our boats at the channel, so there was no way for us to cross. We determined 'twas best to come here. I—I hope we did the right thing, uncle."

For the first time in weeks Magnus's heart soared. Angus's son! Angus's *heir* was a captive of the Clan Carmichael!

The Earl's thoughts went back to that grey day in November when a young goatherd had come to Bailekair to give a horrified and tearful report of Mary's abduction by two men, one of whom had ridden a steed as white as the driven snow.

"I—I seen 'em from the hills, m'lord, where I tends me

goats, but 'twerena nothin' I could do." The lad's lower lip had trembled defensively with fright. "I dinna know who they were, 'ceptin' they wore the MacBeth *breacan*, and one o' 'em rode a horse so white it 'boot blinded me. They chased her down, our lady, and took her wie 'em, m'lord. Where, I canna say, for they headed south. I—I would hae blowed me horn, m'lord, but—but I feared for our lady if'n I gae warnin', for they looked fierce, those clansmen, and the one on the white horse were rough wie her, he were!"

Mary! Oh, dear God, not Mary! Not his bonnie lassie! But she was gone, and the flurrying snow had driven Magnus and his men-at-arms back to Bailekair, leaving the Earl's daughter unto the hands of Sir Hunter MacBeth and his kinsman.

"I should hae slain that whoreson bastard at the King's tourney!" Magnus had sworn with rage and fear and wept when he thought of what his daughter must suffer at the hands of that arrogant Romany MacBeth who rode the blinding white steed.

The Earl had waited in vain for the ransom demand, realizing finally it could not come, that no messenger could travel during the winter storm; and he had berated himself a thousand times for the harsh words with which he had belittled the girl that morning, the words that had sent her from the walls of Bailekair so heedlessly. For in spite of all that had passed between them, Magnus loved Mary still.

Was she dead now, his brave, bonnie lassie? Or had those cowardly curs merely used her savagely, again and again, until her spirit had been broken? Magnus had to know!

"Ye did the right thing, laddies, and I'll nae be forgetting it," he said.

Then, his mouth set in a grim, determined line, the Earl reached for his pen and a piece of parchment paper.

Lord Angus, Earl of Glenkirk, unfolded the scroll in his hands carefully after breaking the seal stamped boldly with his enemy's coat of arms. Magnus, Lion of Bailekair. What did Magnus want of him? Angus's face paled as he read the words therein.

*Bailekair Castle, Scotland, January, 1488*
*To Lord Angus MacBeth, Earl of Glenkirk,*
*Greetings.*
*I am holding your heir, Stephen, hostage*
*in exchange for my daughter, Mary, whom*
*your knight, Sir Hunter, did abduct from*
*Bailekair these two months past.*

*I would suggest the exchange take place*
*ootside of Mheadhoin on neutral territory.*

*I shall await your reply.*

> *Lord Magnus Carmichael*
> *Earl of Bailekair*

"Sir Neil! Sir Callum! Sir Roderick!" Angus called hoarsely.

The three men who had been dicing in one corner of the main hall sprang up in alarm at the tone of their laird's voice.

"Aye, my lord," they answered as one.

"I've a message for Sir Hunter at Wynd Cheathaich and a month's wages for the mon who gets it there first."

As grim-faced as his old foe, Angus watched as his men rode off into the night.

One hundred of them there were, assembled that pale grey dawn to the north of Mheadhoin, perhaps upon that very spot where years before but one had stood. Upon the cliff overlooking their three castles and the dark crystalline waters of the cold Loch Ness, their destriers pranced and snorted, blowing little white clouds of frost from steaming nostrils; and wary men-at-arms shifted and shivered on leather saddles that creaked like new in the chill of the winter air.

Mary Carmichael looked at them, but did not see them.

She saw only Hunter's face as it had been at Wynd Cheathaich, a face tortured by torment and despair. Where before there had been joy such as radiates from a house filled with naught save laughter, now there was a bleakness to equal it in kind upon his ravaged countenance as he walked toward her, hands fingering the scroll of parchment he held as though he would tear it to bits and be done with it. She recognized the MacBeth shield upon its seal and trembled slightly as she waited for him to speak, knowing somehow their snow cocoon had been ripped asunder by whatever message lay within those pages her lover crushed between the hands that had caressed her so gently late into the wintery evenings.

"I dinna know what to do," he said simply.

Mary's heart lurched queerly at the words, for if one pities the weak, the frail, how much more is one sorrowed by the downfall of the strong, the virile?

"What—what is it, my love?" she asked haltingly, dreading his reply.

"Your father's men hae taken Lord Angus's heir, Stephen, prisoner."

There was hatred and bitterness in his heart when Hunter spoke; the lass was reminded sharply of just how fragile their love was, how deep and volatile their passions of the past.

"Is he dead?"

"Nay, but I would to God he were!" came the outburst, followed by a hasty crossing of his darkly bronzed chest. "He's alive and being held in exchange for ye." Hunter paused. A log upon the hearth sparked and broke in the silence as Mary considered the import of his words. Then he continued, "I love ye, tigress, God knows, I do! I would gie anything to throw this scroll upon the fire and leave the Highlands as we had planned. But Angus is my lord, Mary. I hae sworn allegiance to him. He demands ye be brought to Glenkirk at once for the exchange, and my honor commands me to obey."

Ah, what a knife of resentment twisted in Mary's heart at that!

"Damn your honor!" she cried passionately, stung by the thought that she was less than such in his eyes, that his worldly commitments should take precedence over his personal vows, though so it has been for most men since time immemorial. "What of me? What of our lives together? Forget their cursed feud! Soon we shall be free of them fore'er!"

"Shall we?" His voice was low, scornful, as though he mocked himself, laughed at himself for daring to dream what could not be. "And at what price, my love? Wouldst hae me deny my sacred oath to my lord, to live fore'er wie the stain of shame upon my honor?"

"Nay, but neither would I hae ye leave me!"

"Nor would I! Canst thou nae see how torn I am? For God's sake, Mary! If I dinna take ye back, some part of me will be destroyed; for to be a mon wie'oot honor is to be no mon at all! But to live wie'oot ye—to know I may send ye to your death—is to die also. I—I canna bear that upon my soul. Tell me! Tell me, my dearest love, what to do."

The lass swallowed hard. Aye, the choice was hers and rightly so, for his decision would determine her fate, mayhap her final destiny. What should she say? She had only to ask, Mary knew, and he would take her away from the Highlands as they had planned; but at what price? God's blood, what price? The man she left Scotland with would not be the man she loved, but only a shell of his former self.

She laid her hand gently upon his arm. She loved him, and only a fool destroys that which he loves.

"I love no shadow of a mon, sir, and canna. Dinna fear I go to my death, for I carry no bairn of your making. 'Tis but to certain banishment from my clan ye return me, and perhaps 'tis best that way, for then I shall be freed fore'er from the chains of my past. Och, Hunter! Love me! Love as though 'twere the last time!" She cast herself feverishly into his arms.

"Dinna say that! Ne'er say that! 'Tis bad luck. I will wait for ye to come to me, then naught shall e'er part us again, I swear it!"

Oh, my love! My love! Shall I e'er see ye again? Mary thought as she glanced across the wide expanse of white terrain to where her family awaited. For one fleeting moment she had a sudden wild urge to flee them all as though the devil himself pursued her. Hunter felt the swift pounding of her heart as though it had been his own. He laid a restraining hand upon the bridle of her coal black steed.

"My maiden gold," he whispered softly. "My beloved tigress, my own. No matter how long it takes, I will wait for ye here, in Mheadhoin."

And then she was galloping over the snow-swept cliff toward Lord Angus's son, the tears frozen on her cheeks. Halfway across, as Stephen passed her in the exchange, Mary yanked Desmond to a halt. She could not part without a single word! The stallion pawed the frozen ground, then reared slightly, dancingly. Through the hush of the morning stillness the girl's voice rang out clearly across the crystal field.

*"Nunquam obliviscar!"* she cried. *"Nunquam obliviscar!"*

'Twas the Carmichael motto, but there was only one man upon the cliff that winter's dawn who understood the true message of her words.

*I will ne'er forget,* she had said. *I will ne'er forget.*

*I will wait for ye here, in Mheadhoin.*

Those words were Mary's talisman, her armor as her betrothed spat in her face and called her the whore of the MacBeth. Her hand shook as she wiped Hugh's spittle from the lips her lover had kissed with such fierce tenderness, as she lowered her eyes from her cousin's burning, hate-filled glance.

*I wasna his whore!* she longed to scream, to deny Hugh's shameful accusations against her. *Even now he waits for me, loves me!*

But she did not say these things, of course, for her betrothed would kill her. Already the flesh encircling one of her violet eyes puffed and swelled, darkened to match the color of her iris where he had struck her. Her! Mary Carmichael, daughter of a Highland chief, to whom no man had ever dared raise a hand—no man, except for Hugh.

"The contracts must be annulled. I'll nae take to wife the whore of a MacBeth!" Hugh's mouth twisted with ugliness as he sneered the words again.

The high and mighty bitch! Scorned him, did she? Loathed him, did she? Laughed at him, did she? Well, she would beg him for mercy before it was all through; and after he'd done with her, banished her from all Carmichael holdings, he would seek her out, and she would give him that which he had thought to wed her for and be glad to do it!

"I hae agreed to the annulment," Magnus sighed sadly as the clan council, assembled in the main hall of Bailekair for Mary's hearing, stirred uneasily. "But banishment, Hugh! Surely ye wouldna be so cruel! The lass dinna ask to be kidnapped and raped. Och, she is ruined for *ye,* heir to an earldom as ye are, to be sure; but there must be *some* place for her." The Earl sought to save the daughter he loved, the daughter whose eyes he could not meet. "Perhaps some other mon—" He searched the chamber eagerly, hopefully.

"Look at her!" Hugh laughed wolfishly. "God knows how many of the bastards fucked her! What Carmichael worthy of the name would take a MacBeth's leavings?"

Mary cringed at the ugly words. Nay! Nay! 'Twas never like that! She drew herself up painfully, pulling together the ragged edges of her dignity and pride.

"I am no virgin, 'tis true," she said. "But I wasna treated ill, nor shared among the others."

"Ha!" Hugh pounced on her like a cat upon a rat. "Ye pleased him then, this arrogant Romany, that he kept his kinsmen from ye? Tell us, whore! Tell us how ye pleased him wie your whore's tricks! How ye spread your legs for him—"

"Stop it! Stop it!" Mary screamed to hear her love defiled so.

Hugh slapped her hard. The girl crumpled to the floor, whimpering, but no man made a move to halt her cousin's onslaught. He stared at the others gathered in the main hall, a triumphant smirk upon his dark jeering visage.

"Look at her, I say!" he commanded with a leer. "I ask again: What mon here would hae her now?"

And in the silence that followed, with love and pity mingled plainly upon his pale thin face, young Edward Carmichael at last found the courage to speak.

# BOOK TWO

*Weep Thy Sad Lament*

# Fourteen

**Bailekair Castle, Scotland, 1488**

As long as Mary lived she was never to forget the sound of Edward's feverish words echoing dumbly in the main hall of her father's keep or the sight of Hugh's dark face twisted with black searing rage as he stared at his half brother menacingly. The earth rocked under the lass's feet in the uneasy silence that fell with shrouded hush over the assembly as Edward, pale and oddly defiant, returned Hugh's gaze waveringly.

"This I canna countenance, *brother!*" Hugh snarled in the deadly quiet. "Hae ye no more pride than to wed wie a whore?"

"She isna a whore!" Edward's voice rang shrilly, childishly as his fists clenched angrily by his sides, "and ye willna call her thusly again, Hugh. 'Twas no fault of her own that her maidenhead was lost to the whoreson Romany; and if she carries nae his bastard bairn, we shall be wed on Candlemas."

"Ye are a fool then, *brother!*" Hugh sneered the last word again. "But mayhap 'tis to be expected from one who spends more time piping and penning than warring and wenching. Aye, mayhap your flute and poetry has made ye less than a mon, *brother,* that ye need take a whore to wife. Och! Ye'd best pray the MacBeth *did* pump a bastard brat into her belly, for I doubt you're up to getting a child on the bitch!"

The hall gasped as one. Hands flew to sword hilts. Edward swallowed hard. If he defended himself against the slur on his manhood, Hugh would surely slay him, and Mary would be cast out to a fate worse than death. Mary, his golden-haired nymph, banished to a life of scorn and ridicule, starvation and deprivation. Edward could not risk that! Nay, if he were to save her, Edward knew he must live.

"Ye—ye are my brother, Hugh, and I want no quarrel wie ye, so I shall forget your hasty remarks. I know they were spoken in anger and that ye will apologize when your rage has cooled. By your leave, my lord." He turned to Magnus as the council began to mutter among themselves, numbed and outraged by Edward's cowardice. "Mary and I hae much to do in the scant time before Candlemas, so I know ye will forgie us if we go now to begin our preparations."

"Aye, lad, aye." The Earl nodded, embarrassed for and ashamed of his foster son; for though Edward had saved his daughter from disgrace, Magnus could not respect a man who had refused to defend his own honor.

The laird looked away, calling rather too heartily for ale to be brought to celebrate his daughter's upcoming nuptials.

"Och, Edward! Edward! What hae ye done? What hae ye done?" Mary moaned as she stumbled blindly after her now-betrothed, still suffering from the shock his words of salvation had brought her. "Ye hae lowered yourself for me and slunk like a whipped dog from Hugh's insults. There's naught in the clan will respect ye for it. Oh, God, why? Why? Why could ye nae leave me be?"

"I—I love ye, Mary. I hae always loved ye." He blushed as he stammered the confession, suddenly unsure of himself, for Mary had not flung herself at his feet in joy as he had expected. "Hugh would hae killed me—I saw in his eyes he meant as much—and ye would hae been banished as he desired. I—I couldna let ye suffer so, lass. Oh, Mary, I would do anything for ye!" He glowed passionately. "I dinna care what they think."

"But—but your honor—oh, Edward! To be a mon wie'oot honor—" Hunter's words haunted her briefly.

"I dinna care," Edward repeated stubbornly. "Mayhap Hugh is right. I hae ne'er joyed in war—no, nor wenching either. 'Tis a simple, peaceful mon, I am; and ye hae always held my heart, my lady."

"Oh, Edward, ye canna know what ye hae done! What of your studies for the priesthood?"

"The life of a monk isna for me, nae when ye need me, Mary."

"Oh, Edward! Surely some madness has come upon ye. Go back, quickly, and tell them ye were moonstruck—"

"Moonstruck? Nay, lass. 'Tis naught save love for ye wie which I am possessed."

"God's wounds, Edward! I—I know ye meant well, but—but—"

"Och, Mary. There is no need for ye to worry. This is the happiest day of my life."

"How can ye speak so? We are disgraced, both of us now! My father willna hae us here—no, nor Sir Thomas at Dùndereen either! Did ye nae see the scorn upon their faces when ye walked away from Hugh's black words? Och! Where shall we go? What shall we do?"

"Hae no fear, my lady. We shall go to Court. The King is fond of musicians, and, aye, in truth, I would be far more content wie a flute in my hand instead of a sword. Aye, that is what we shall do, lass, for I'll nae see ye mocked here by our own, and there are many who will spit upon ye, in spite of my taking ye to wife. As for my own shame..." He shrugged his shoulders. "It matters nae. Dùndereen was ne'er meant for me, and I wouldna hae wanted it if it had been. Go now, and make ready for our wedding."

Mary gazed at him pityingly, still stunned by his actions, hurt and angered by his interference in her life. He dinna know! she told herself. He meant it for the best—

"Oh, Edward!" She burst into tears at last as the full realization of his salvation hit her like a sharp blow. "Ye dinna know what ye hae done!"

Then she fled from him blindly, her heart shattering into a million pieces.

And so Mary Carmichael was wed; not to Hunter, her beloved, nor to Hugh, whom she despised, but to Edward; pale gentle Edward, whose worship of her she cursed each time his adoring, blue eyes gazed at her with love and admiration shining from their depths. It was too cruel! She could not bear it! A terrible pain tore at her heart every hour, every minute, every *second* of each passing day as she thought of Hunter waiting for her at Mheadhoin, so near and yet so far.

Oh, beloved! Beloved! I canna come to ye, can ne'er come—

The sobs choked in her throat, suffocating her. She could not breathe. Mary was frantic with despair, consumed with longing, sick with heartache. She did not even know how to send Hunter word of her plight, for whom could she trust with the knowledge of her forbidden and dangerous love? And she herself would not be allowed to ride out again until after the wedding, when they were certain she carried no child of the MacBeth's making. Oh, God! Hunter would think she had forsaken him, would turn from her in anger, his love grow to hate, believing she had played him for a fool again.

Oh, Hunter! Hunter! May God damn your pride! Your *honor!* For I am to wed a mon who has done what I couldna ask of ye, and each stitch in my bridal gown nas seen a needle in my heart at the thought of parting from ye. I sewed so slowly, my love, hoping ye would come for me, but ye dinna; and now my shroud is finished. Aye, shroud, Hunter, for ye hae ruined me for all other men. 'Tis ye I'll love until my dying hour, though your honor was my death, in spirit if nae in flesh!

It should hae been black, Mary thought as she stared at herself in the polished mirror. The deep, purple folds of her wedding dress enveloped her like the Scottish mist upon the moors, for she had outdone herself in its creation, determined she would not go like a lamb to slaughter, but with the steely pride that was her backbone. There were many who might snigger at her disgrace and think Edward a fool, but her head would be held high, Mary vowed, and their laughter fall on deaf ears. She would not give them the satisfaction of seeing her, the daughter of a Highland chief, humbled and humiliated on her wedding day.

She entered the chapel like a queen, regally, looking neither right nor left as she walked slowly down the aisle to where Edward awaited shyly, eagerly. And for one hushed moment there was not a clansman present who would not have traded his soul to stand in Edward Carmichael's place, so breathtaking was Mary's beauty.

The rich, violet satin of her gown flowed like rippling clouds across a harvest moon, shimmering in its depth of color, making her eyes stand out even more dramatically in her pale face. Around the hem *rampant* white unicorns with golden wings, horns, manes, tails, and hooves marched in bold, embroidered design. Spun-gold lace edged the borders of the material that swept upon the ground, the full, hanging sleeves, and the low-cut bodice. A long purple satin train, trimmed with ermine fur and lined with gold brocade, fastened at each shoulder with a gold rosette. From the folds of the trailing outer sleeves, inner sleeves of the same gold lining peeped as Mary clutched her Bible, rosary, and bridal bouquet of hard-gotten thistle tightly. Her long golden hair had been woven into two thick plaits that curled into braided buns over either ear, for she could not wear her locks down, as tradition dictated, to indicate her virginity. Violet satin ribands and the same flowers of her bouquet intertwined each shining mass. Soft, white, leather boots tread whisperingly as she moved slowly down the aisle. A solid gold crucifix hung at her slender, pulsating throat.

At long last she knelt at Edward's feet.

He gazed down at her joyously before he bent to take her hand. Together they faced the priest and repeated their vows, and then it was over, and he was kissing her gently; a cousin's kiss, a brother's kiss, a husband's kiss; but never that of a lover. Mary bit her lip and saw there was a drop of blood upon one finger where the thistles of her bridal bouquet had pricked her ruthlessly, just as a thorn of sorrow had pierced her heart.

There was no celebration following the small, private ceremony, no tables ladened to groaning for the bridal feast, no red wine drunk to toast the newlyweds, no gay skirling of bagpipes and shouts of laughter, no Highland flings danced late into the night. There was only Edward's chamber, where Mary lay in her husband's massive canopied bed and waited and wished she were dead.

Mary Carmichael paced the stone ramparts of Bailekair restlessly, a lone figure of a girl as strikingly solitary against the grey mist of the morning sky as one of the circular watchtowers set in strategic points along the high, machicolated walls of the fortress. She sighed, for she could see nothing, then damned silently the fog that clouded the Highlands. How many? How many of the Carmichael men would return home safe this day? She gazed off into the distance again, brushing away impatiently the fine drops of rain that clung to her eyelashes. God's wounds! Would they never come? She thought of Edward's fair face when last she'd seen him. Edward. Her husband. And the gnawing worry deepened inside her.

She placed her hands upon her belly, round and full, where her husband's child lay safe within. Would it ever know its father, this bairn conceived upon Mary's wedding night? Forever a reminder of that shameful Candlemas Eve. The lass bit her lip at the thought of it. The quiet, hasty ceremony; Edward's small room she was now to share; lying cold and rigid upon the freezing sheets as she waited for him to come to her; his shy, eager fumbling in the darkness; her desperate, heart-wrenching cry.

"Dinna touch me!"

He drew back and lit a candle, shivering slightly, for the chamber was chilly from the draft that crept in from the corridors and the small wooden shutters of the one narrow window. He studied her quietly in the dim light, his face hurt and puzzled.

"Dinna touch ye? When I hae longed and prayed for this night e'eryday of my life?"

"I—I canna bear it if ye do," Mary choked out softly.

Some dawning of what he thought was understanding flickered in Edward's deep blue eyes.

He cursed himself silently. "I—I should hae realized— Oh, my poor lamb! I know you've been hurt and—and used, but it doesna hae to be like that. Let me show ye. I shall heal those places the whoreson MacBeth bruised, for I will be gentle wie ye, lass."

*I will be gentle wie ye, lass.*

It seemed as though a lifetime had passed since Hunter had spoken those very words. Oh, Hunter! Hunter! Did ye wait for me, beloved? I canna come, can ne'er come to ye now.

Pain, dark and sorrowful, ripped at Mary's heart. She looked at the man whose adoration for her had spared her from banishment, kept her from her heart's desire. She did not hate him; she could not. Oh, Hunter!

"Nay, Edward. Ye—ye dinna understand." The words came with difficulty. "Ye should ne'er hae married me. Ye hae lost much standing in our clan for it and all for naught, I fear."

"I dinna care what they think, I told ye! I—I love ye, Mary. I hae always loved ye. I care naught for my own disgrace in wedding ye, nor your shame at being taken by another against your will."

"Ye hae been duped and deceived, cousin, for I amna the woman ye think me. I am only a shell, Edward, an empty shell. I hae no love to gie ye in return for yours, though your sacrifice was noble, your deed pure in heart."

"I hae waited all my life for ye," he answered gently. "I can wait a little longer. I shallna press ye. In time ye will grow to love me as I do ye."

"Nay, dear Edward, though I would 'twere true, for I wouldna gie ye pain when ye hae been so kind to me, sweetest cousin. But I hae no heart left wie which to love another, and a seed grows nae in fallow ground."

"I—I dinna understand, Mary—" Had he not saved her from Hugh, whom she loathed? And from, mayhap, a fate worse than death? This was not how he had imagined her response.

She looked at him as a serf does a calf before its slaughter. He felt confused and frustrated by the pity and shame upon her face.

"I—I canna love ye, Edward, though thou art dear as a brother to me as e'er. I—I love another, and I'll go on loving him until the day I die, though my lips ne'er taste the sweetness of his kiss again."

His mouth twisted. He was stunned. He could not believe her words, for there could only be one man to whom she referred—the Romany MacBeth! Who else could it be? Who else had kissed her pliant mouth, held her in a warm embrace, made love to her in the darkness of a chamber? Anger set in. It could not be! She was his, Edward's golden-haired nymph! He had made himself a laughingstock for her, thrown away a lifetime of preparation for the ministry! And she, who should have fallen at his feet with gratefulness and adoration, scorned and pitied him instead! Edward could not bear it! For the first time in his life he was consumed by rage. He grabbed Mary and shook her roughly.

"Nay! Nay! 'Tisna true! I canna—willna accept it! Dinna tell me ye love this—this whoreson coward nae fit to wash your feet! Nay! How—how could ye? An enemy of our clan who wrested ye from its ranks and shamed ye for all time! Dinna tell me he had willingly that which ye now refuse me, your husband—your master!"

"Aye, I'm sorry, so verra sorry, dearest Edward. But, aye, that is my sin, and now I am punished for it, for I shall ne'er see my beloved again. Please, leave me be now."

Fury shook him, drove him beyond the bounds of control.

"Leave ye be? Nay, madam. My brother was right! Ye *are* a whore! Ye gae yourself to our enemy. Ye shall do no less for me!"

'Twas then Edward raped her, brutally, violently, with a savagery that shocked and appalled them both. Mary lay rigid beneath him, not believing the cruelty of her childhood friend as he tore the shift from her body, pinioned her wrists above her head, and forced his way into her viciously. Tears streaked her face in mourning for the base defilement of that which she had shared so freely with her beloved.

Afterward Edward withdrew from her in disillusionment, not just physically, but mentally as well. For he was never the same after that night. 'Twas as though some light had darkened in his soul. His mind could not accept the shattering of the dream he had cherished through the years. He was not strong enough, not realistic enough; and because of his weaknesses, his failings as a human being, he became that saddest of creatures: a man bereft of dreams. For Edward's was a megalomaniac fervor, crushed by Mary's confession and rejection of him, never to be fanned to flame again by aught else. 'Twas as though he now moved in a world of his own, a place where no other man dared tread, and Mary could not reach him. Too late she tried to talk to him, to find something to be had from their pathetic marriage; but as Edward himself was frail, so was his dream fragile, his character tragic. He had loved and lost. The cruelty of it overwhelmed him. He might never have known Mary at all, such a stranger did he become to her. Sometimes he looked at her, but he did not see her, and Mary knew he had retreated from the living to that hell of his own making in his mind.

He took to wearing a hair shirt beneath his belted plaid. He pored over his Bible in the evenings. He kept a constant, silent vigil in the chapel of Bailekair, praying and meditating with Father Matthew, the castle priest. His rosary never left his hands, except when he managed to force himself to continue his training for the knighthood.

He stared at Mary as his lips moved voicelessly, counting off the decades of his beads. She knew he despised her.

"Go on! Tell me ye hate me!" she cried. "I dinna blame ye for it!"

But 'twas as though he had not heard.

'Tis myself I hate, myself I blame! he wanted to reply; the dream was mine, nae yours—ne'er yours. Why could I nae see that? Och, Mary, what hae I done? What hae I done, indeed? Forgie me. Forgie me.

But the words stuck in Edward's throat, and the distance between him and Mary widened irreparably. He was sickened unto to death by his rape of her. He, who loved beauty and grace, kindness and compassion, had committed an atrocity of the lowest sort. He had called Mary a whore and degraded her in the vilest manner a man can hurt and humiliate a woman; and he despised himself for it. And though he was not brave enough to seek it out, Edward waited for death to come to him, prayed it would come to take away the pain and bitter remorse that filled his heart, cleanse his guilt-ridden soul of that horrible, animalistic deed. His eyes glittered with a strange expectancy that frightened Mary when she saw it. He never touched her again.

But his child grew within her, a constant reminder of the futility of their marriage and their lives.

Mary did not hate the child. How could she, when she herself had been the victim of just such a maternal viciousness? But it was not the child of the man she loved, and that she could not forget. Och, it should have been Hunter's bairn that filled her belly, Hunter's name she bore!

Night after night Mary lay beside the man who was her husband and longed for one who was not—and never could be. She was sick with yearning for Hunter and knew what it meant to die and go on living.

She turned her violet eyes toward the castle across the loch. Glenkirk. Hunter. Oh, why were they so tantalizingly near and yet so far? Had he waited for her as he'd promised? Was he waiting for her still? What had he thought when she had not come to him? Did he too despise her now? Such was too painful to even consider. Mary pushed it from her mind as the sudden sobs rose up in her throat.

I must think of Edward. Edward, my husband.

Would he never come? Oh, he was made for gentle laughter, for coaxing sweet notes of music from his wooden flute, not for war. Not for the death to which Mary believed she had driven him, for now she understood that strange glitter in Edward's eyes, for she saw it in her own each time she looked into a mirror and remembered her beloved. Oh,

Edward was too pale, too fragile, too poetic for the rigors of battle; not like the black Hugh, who welcomed the sights of hostility, who jeered cruelly before smiting down the enemy with either his cutting tongue or flashing sword. Mary could almost hear her dark cousin shouting the Carmichael war cry: *Buaidh no Bàs*, Victory or Death! She prayed if one of them were dead, it would be Hugh. Hugh, whose black eyes still raked her body with desire, in spite of the fact that he'd spurned her. Hugh, whose white teeth had gleamed maliciously when he'd sworn to spread her legs and have her like the whore she was. Mary shivered in the cool grey air, recalling. How angry he had been when Edward had married her, saved her from banishment and disgrace. How Hugh had waited to get her alone, put his hands on her, and promised to take her, husband or no.

Aye, let it be Hugh's lifeless form the Carmichael men carried home to mourn if any, not Edward's, pray God, not Edward's.

For her father and five brothers Mary had little worry. They would protect each other as always, fighting close to each other's sides so that if one of them faltered, another would be there to take his place, defend him until he steadied again. She hoped they would do as much for the man she'd married, the man she'd loved like a brother until fate's cruel jest.

I will make it right, she vowed with the wild fervor of the desperate. Just let Edward come home, and I will make it right! Gi'en time—

They'd had so little of it before the shadow of civil war had fallen over Scotland like a swooping hawk; no time to seek a place at Court; no time to bridge the chasm of their marriage. The King's feud with the Homes and Hepburns over the rich revenues of Coldingham had broken into open rebellion over the throne as the unruly Border lords had risen up in arms against James. His Grace had had the outlaws put to the horn as traitors, then fled north for safety, where the Earls of Huntly, Buchan, Errol, and Crawford, and the Archbishop of St. Andrews, and the Bishop of Aberdeen were loyal to him. The Lion of Bailekair had rallied three thousand men to the

King's cause, and Mary had been forced to stand by helplessly, while her husband of a few scant months had ridden off with the Clan Carmichael to war. And the parting had been doubly painful, for she had known somewhere Hunter MacBeth galloped southeastward toward the battle as well—but not for James.

The rebels had grown stronger in numbers, more powerful throughout Scotland. They'd captured Dunbar and at Stirling taken the King's son, young Jamie, Duke of Rothesay and heir to the throne, captive. A valuable and dangerous pawn. The boy was only fifteen, a moody and impressionable lad. Would he need much persuading to turn his eyes to the crown and join the rebels' cause?

And so the messages had come, day after day, apprising the women of Bailekair of their men's movements. But today there had been naught save silence.

Mary scanned the vast, empty moors anxiously; but dusk fell, and still there was no word.

That night she sought her lonely chamber to dream of troubled battlefields and Hunter MacBeth astride his pale white steed, silver sword flashing, like some dark and shining god in the midst of the bloody *mêlée*.

'Twas just south of Stirling, on June 11th, upon a field known as Sauchieburn the battle had taken place. The stakes had been high: a kingdom and a crown. All day long, beneath the brightness of the summer sun, the fighting had been brave and fierce; the blood had flowed like red foam upon the golden sea of the broom-swept heath; the tortured screams of the dying had pierced the air with agony. But now the clash of sword upon sword, battle-ax upon shield, morningstar upon armor rang no more. The blood caked hard upon the ground; the dead lay still and silent. Here and there looters robbed and plundered, snatching at a coin-filled purse, cutting off the finger of a corpse to steal a ruby ring.

At last Hunter MacBeth sheathed his mighty weapon, smiled, and claimed the honor of being one of the many men who crowded round young Jamie, lately Duke of Rothesay, to lift him to their shoulders in glorious victory and call him "King."

The fifteen-year-old lad shouted and laughed, head spinning with the excitement that surrounded him. Red wine trickled from his lips as he raised his flask high to drench himself with the sweet malmsey. The moment was unreal, the gaiety unnatural, an aftermath of the frenzied slaughter that would soon be replaced with sickness and shame; but the boy did not see that, caught up in the head-swelling thrill of triumph that was his.

"King!" they called him and knelt at his feet to do him homage.

Far away the youth's defeated father fled desperately from the field of Sauchieburn, his crown and kingdom lost, his very life forfeit if he did not escape. He beat his mount cruelly with his whip, urging the steed on. He had never ridden well. The horse stumbled, and James was thrown. Moaning, he staggered to his feet, shards of pain shooting through his body. He moved a hand to staunch the blood that dripped from a searing wound.

In the distance a place to shelter beckoned to him softly, inviting smile wrapped about a deceit the fallen King's misted eyes could not clearly see. Weary, numb in flesh and mind, he limped toward the safe haven gratefully, relief filling up his bones. Just outside the doorway he sprawled facedown into the dirt. The wooden paddles of Beaton's Mill churned on without interruption, slapping softly as they cut the waters of the stream that turned them. The miller's wife finished tossing the last of her corn to the chickens that strutted upon the yard. She brushed her hands off efficiently, then bent to pick up the basket of eggs that lay at her feet. She turned.

"Godamercy! Godamercy! Husband, come quickly! Quickly, do ye ken?"

Miller Beaton rushed from the small shed in which he had been sacking flour in burlap bags to be marketed that coming Saturday. His apron flew, sending up a fine cloud of grain dust as he ran toward the body over which his wife now knelt.

"Is he dead?"

"Nay," the wife answered grimly. "But like to be—and soon. Help me get him into the house."

The miller glanced around uneasily. "I like it nae, wife. We are puir common folk, and the mon is a rich laird by the look of him. If he dies—"

"Then 'twould be better for us if we had gi'en him aid. 'Twould go ill indeed if 'twere discovered we had left the puir mon lying here."

The husband nodded and bent to help her lift the heavy body. Together they managed to get James into their meager house, where they laid him upon their bed. The wife bustled about worriedly, wringing out a wet rag to lay across the dying man's forehead, bringing a cup of cool water for him to drink. He lifted his head weakly at her efforts, trying to smile his thanks.

"I'm—dying," the defeated King groaned slowly. "Nay, my lord." The miller's wife sought to comfort him in his darkest hour. "My husband will fetch a doctor, and all will be well."

"Nay—" James gasped, sitting bolt upright in bed as he clutched feverishly at her arm. The woman shrank back in alarm. "A priest! Hae your husband fetch a priest!"

"Wife, we are but puir folk," the miller began again nervously.

His Grace fumbled at his leather belt, loosened his *sporran*. His hand trembled. The purse fell upon the floor, opened; gold sovereigns scattered heedlessly with a clatter. The miller and his wife stared, awed and afraid.

"A priest," the dying man rasped hoarsely once more. "I mustna die unshriven. For God's sake, mon! This morn I was your king!"

"Holy Mary, pray for us." Miller Beaton sidled away apprehensively.

The wife rose from the bed where she had been sitting, hands twitching anxiously at her skirt as she gazed, numb with terror, at the bloodied stranger.

"My God! My God! A priest! A priest!" She ran screaming from her humble abode, arms waving to flag down a group of horsemen thundering past upon the road.

One of them broke away from the others, dismounting to follow the shaking woman into the house. He was armored, the miller's wife noted idly, but the woolen robe he wore was drab and brown. He looked down cruelly into the ashen face of the man who had once commanded him. James's eyes flickered open briefly. For one heart-stopping moment they leapt with mortal fear. Then the "priest" drew his dagger, swiftly plunging it into the dying King's breast.

"I'm sorry; this mon is dead." David MacDonald turned toward the miller and wife, then strode purposefully from the hut. The succession was secure now.

The woman's hands quivered as she placed them to her open mouth to stifle the horrified screams that threatened from her throat.

"Dear Lord, hae mercy upon us," she whispered, grabbing for the miller's arm to keep from falling. "Husband, that was no priest—"

"Hush, woman! 'Twas murder done here today. Go now, and lock the door. Think ye that men who would kill a king wouldna slay us like flies in a barnyard?"

Shrinking with fear, the miller's wife scurried to do as she was bid.

Far away Hunter MacBeth and Patrick Hepburn helped young Jamie to bed to sleep off his drunken stupor.

Word had come at last. James had attacked the rebels at Sauchieburn, near Stirling, without waiting for the Northern loyalists who were on their way to join him. Now Mary waited silently to know the outcome of the battle.

It was that—the waiting and watching—that made her prowl the stone ramparts of Bailekair like a caged tigress once again. The other women of the household were down below in the long hall, embroidering a tapestry, warmed by the blaze of the small fire lit to dispel the cool damp summer mist that filled the air. But Lady Margaret had made it plain that Mary was not welcome there, so she had sought the walkways of the castle, alone in her misery.

For the past two nights Mary had dreamed. Her beloved was safe; she was sure of it, for had she not seen as much in the dreadful scenes of battle that had painted themselves so vividly across her mind as she'd slept? Aye, she need have no fear for Hunter. But something else was wrong, something she could not quite fathom. It had hung like a shroud on the borders of her dreams, hovering forebodingly, but never drawing close enough for Mary to see it clearly. Mayhap her love for Hunter had obscured it. Perhaps it was Edward—

Nay—pray God, the girl thought again as her eyes searched the horizon of the Highlands, 'tis Hugh who doesna return alive! Nae Edward! Then, with a snarled oath, Mary drew her cloak more closely about her, whirling toward the tower. She would wait no longer to know her fate. She would ride out to meet it.

Those who had fought for their rightful king scattered homeward hurriedly, certain to be put to the horn as traitors by nightfall. They intended to be barricaded behind the high walls of their castle keeps when retribution came, not swinging from the gallow's rope or beheaded on the chopping block for a crime they'd not committed. More than likely they would be stripped of their lands and titles and thrown into the Tolbooth. At very best there would be the penalty of a heavy fine to pay.

Those who'd supported young Jamie's and the rebels' cause rode homeward also, but not in fear. They rode with the triumphant thrill of victory and the expectation of rich rewards for their brave deeds in battle.

But Mary's clan was not of this latter, and she knew it instinctively before she reached them. David MacDonald had foreseen the future clearly when he'd warned Hunter against binding himself to James III. Her eyes raked the beaten group frantically, counting rapidly. How many were there? Edward, her husband, first, shaken and more pale than ever, but alive, thank God, alive! Quiet Gordon and bonnie Charlie, looking worried and stricken for some reason, shouting at her to get away, to go back to Bailekair. Her fath— *Where was her father?* Mary drew Desmond to a halt, her heart fluttering strangely within her breast as she understood then why her brothers had not wished her presence on the hillside. She slid slowly from her saddle, walked stiffly toward the body hanging over the Earl's bay steed.

"Fath—fath—father?"

But Mary knew, even before she managed to choke out the word, he could not answer, would never answer her again. The mighty Lion of Bailekair was dead.

It has begun, the girl thought with queer detachment, like one who has received a stunning blow, but does not realize it. The final curse of the legend has begun. The grizzled witch foretold of such and warned me in a dream, but I wouldn' listen. We sinned, Hunter and I, and hae brought the wrath of God upon us all. Accursed. Both of us accursed!

*Thy sorrows will be many for the sadness ye hae wrought, spire for spire, kirk for kirk. As 'twas in the beginning, so will it be again. . . . And the Great Glen will echo wie the mournful wailings of sorrow and ring wie the blows of the Grim Reaper's mighty sword.*

Oh, God, forgie me!

"Dinna, Mary." Gordon was somehow at her side, holding her up as her knees buckled beneath her. "Dinna look at him, please."

Mary did not hear him. "I hae to know," she said.

She pulled away the blanket they had covered her father with and almost swooned at the sight. Magnus Carmichael's head had been cleaved into; a bloody pulp was all that remained of his once-handsome face; the gold hair was matted with splinters of bone and brain; the nose was on one side of the jagged thing, no longer the straight, arrogant mark of the Clan Carmichael; the lavender eye was torn from its socket on the other, dangling uselessly from the empty hollow.

"Aaa—eee—iii—"

Mary stepped away, wailing, her eyes blinded by tears from

the shock. It was Gordon who caught her when she fell and Charlie who quickly covered the thing again, hiding the mess from her stricken face. She gagged, vomiting green bile onto the ground, retching until there was nothing left to come up, and she knelt trembling in her brother's arms from the aftermath. Edward came to wipe her face with a rag as the rest of the Carmichael men shifted uncomfortably in their saddles. She was like a broken bird, this woman Edward had once thought to love and cherish; and her plight stirred him to pity, touched him at last through the ravaged walls of his distance breached two days ago by the bloody horrors of war and the agonized screams of the dying.

"Ye shouldna hae come, Mary. Ye shouldna hae looked at the body." He spoke gently, hands cleansing away the traces of heaving from her mouth. "Ye must think of the bairn."

Mary clung to him passionately, with haunted violet eyes, eyes he could have drowned in once.

"Oh, Edward, Edward, how did it happen?" Her tears came freely now as she buried her face in his chest, scarcely feeling the bite of his armor against her cheek, forgetting, for the moment, their strained and bitter marriage.

"I dinna know." He shook his head sadly. "I dinna know. I lunged forward to protect him from an enemy lance, and when I turned again, he was gone. Hugh was wie him when he fell."

*Hugh was wie him when he fell.*

The words drummed in Mary's head, beating inside like a senseless refrain as she stared at her dark cousin.

*Hugh was wie him when he fell.*

"How did it happen?" she asked again.

"An enemy blade got him," Hugh replied. "My horse slipped. I couldna save him."

He was lying. Mary knew it, knew it as surely as she knew the sun would rise over Bailekair in the morning. Hugh, who could cleave a man into with either his mighty broadsword or battle-ax; he was lying. But why? Was it Edward for whom he'd meant the fatal blow—Edward, who'd lunged forward at the last minute to fend off an enemy lance? The ax, once set into motion, could not be halted. Had it taken her father's life by mistake?

Nay, Hugh had murdered her father! Aye, how easy it would have been in the heat of battle; so easy for Mary's dark cousin to ride at her father's side under the guise of protecting him; so easy for Hugh to bring his blade down upon the Earl's head when no one was looking, claiming the enemy had done it. Who was to say how the unsuspecting laird had died? Many men died in battle. Horses slipped on bloody ground. No one save Mary would doubt Hugh Carmichael's story.

But Mary knew, knew when she met his eyes that Hugh had wielded the blade that had chopped her father's life in half; knew when she saw the naked desire upon Hugh's dark visage as he watched her in Edward's arms that he had cut her father down like a dog on the battlefield. But why?

*I was drugged, lass, drugged, I tell ye!*

Her father's words haunted her in that moment, and Mary was filled with shame and guilt as the truth of them struck her. The Earl had *not* been in his right mind when he'd given her to Hugh; and Hugh had known it. Had Magnus somehow discovered the deed for certain? Had Hugh killed him for the knowledge?

Mary moved toward her black cousin, so close she was almost touching him, so close no one save Hugh heard the words she snarled so softly in his face.

"Ye whoreson murderer!"

His black eyes narrowed, and then he smiled mockingly. Mary lost her temper then, tears ceasing, her rage in full force as she slapped him hard across the mouth. He never batted an eyelash, but she knew one day Hugh would make her pay for that blow, make her pay because he could not take her then and there, drag her down into the mud and force her to beg for mercy as he so longed to do.

"For God's sake, Mary! 'Twasna Hugh's fault!" Gordon and Charlie dragged her away from her cousin hastily.

She gave them a wry, pitying glance. "Who? Who did ride at my father's other side?"

"Why, 'twas Ian." Charlie wondered what the lass was driving at.

"Ian." Mary stared at her oldest brother coldly.

Aye, it would have been Ian. She knew full well the love between the two foster brothers. Ian, whom Hugh's fatal blow had handed an earldom.

*We are verra close, your brother and I.*

How well Mary remembered those words! She shivered violently in the mist. Her heart beat sickeningly in her breast. They had plotted together to slay her father! From this day forward she must be on her guard against their ambitions and desires. They had killed her father. What might they do next?

Edward. She must never let Edward out of her sight again! Without Edward she would be defenseless against them, for Ian would be her guardian; Ian, who had little love for his sister. He would give her to Hugh—a whore for his foster brother's using, just as Hugh wanted. Dear God—

Mary turned to her husband shakily, placing an unsteady hand upon his arm.

"Edward, wouldst ride wie me to the castle?"

"Aye, my lady, I will."

She turned and mounted Desmond then, spurring the steed away from them all bitterly with Edward by her side. Mary did not want them to see she still wept. Not the crystal tears of sadness that had fallen earlier, but violent, choking sobs of fury at being a woman—a woman helpless and desperate against Hugh and Ian Carmichael.

Hugh watched them ride away, then pulled his stallion up alongside of Ian's.

"She knows."

"Did ye think she wouldna, cousin?" Ian gave him a sharp glance. "She isna a fool."

"Nay, I guess nae. Still, I would the bitch dinna hate me so much," Hugh replied, his jaw set. "She may babble to the others."

"Dinna worry," Ian laughed shortly. "She'll keep it to herself, for none would believe her now that she has fallen from her state of grace. As for her dislike of ye"—he shrugged his shoulders indifferently—" 'twill matter little once ye hae her in your bed. Take my word for it, cousin, the fawning whores are all the same. Once you've spread their legs they come begging back for more.''

Hugh looked at his foster brother speculatively.

"I wonder who 'tis, Ian, that pleads as much from ye?"

"There are some things, Hugh, that are better left unknown."

'Twas a night for death. The mist stalked the castle of Bailekair like the Grim Reaper, the grey clouds of his scythe finding their way into the keep with icy stealth. In the long hall where they'd laid the Earl's body the torches flickered eerily, casting their dancing shadows on the stone walls like ghosts who'd come to fetch the Lion of Bailekair home to his cold, earthy grave. Mary stripped her father's corpse of the metal armor to wash the putrefying flesh, cleansing every inch of his soiled skin of the blood and dirt that encrusted it. She paused to wring the rag out again, the drops of the splashing water tinkling like chimes in the basin that ran red with the liquid of life that had once flowed so strongly, so vitally through her father's veins. She pushed her hair away from her face, sniffing to hold back her tears.

Joanna came with the Earl's formal belted plaid, and together they dressed him carefully, lovingly in the torchlight, each haunted by her own thoughts.

"And there's my brave, bonnie lassie," Lord Magnus swung his daughter into the air, laughing roaringly. "Did ye miss me, Mary?"

"Och! I'd nae be forgetting my best lass now, would I? Look into that *sporran*, daughter, and see if there isna a bonnie bauble for my bairn."

"Why a wee angel did come down from heaven and whisper in my ear that Joanna longed for a golden harp for her birthday. Do ye like it, lassie?"

"Joanna, ask her again. I wasna in my right mind, I tell ye. I wouldna hae gi'en her to Hugh otherwise."

The two girls folded the earl's arms across his broad chest, their hands meeting, entwining tightly over his body. Violet eyes met brown ones, and there were tears in each for the man they had both loved and shared.

"I loved him. I shouldna hae let him ride away wie'oot a word, but I—I ne'er thought—" Mary's voice broke.

"He forgae ye, my lady," Joanna said quietly. "In his heart he did, or he wouldna hae pleaded wie the council to spare ye from banishment. He is at peace now, where'er he is. Forgie and forget, Mary, that he may rest easy in his grave."

"Oh, father, I do! I do!"

Mary must have jolted the table in her passionate outburst, for one of the Earl's hands slid from his breast to rest upon her own slender fingers. She clutched his strong limb silently and eased the sorrow in her heart.

Oh, never again to see his handsome blond figure come riding up to the iron portcullis of Bailekair upon the giant bay steed he'd loved so well. Never again to hear his roaring laughter ring out over the bailey upon learning some new jest. Never again to lay her head upon his lap by the fire in the evenings, while Joanna sat sewing quietly in the corner.

The two girls glanced up expectantly at the sound of footsteps descending the stairs into the main hall. 'Twas Alinor, who had come to Bailekair to be with her husband's people at the beginning of the civil war, when Court had not been safe.

Charlie's wife was not happy at the great castle. Oh, 'twas not the keep itself that depressed her, for her own home, Eadar Da Voe, was even more damp and oppressive, set on the coast as it was. No, it was the atmosphere of Bailekair that stifled her very being. She did not like Lady Margaret, whom she shrewdly guessed was an unscrupulous tyrant whose ego knew no bounds. The Countess's dour, unfeeling façade did not fool the glittering Alinor. Charlie's wife suspected that beneath Margaret's cold exterior beat the fiery heart of a fervent fanatic. The Countess terrorized her maids, and Alinor stood alone in her outright defiance of the lady of Bailekair. Charlie's bride was a Murray, and she made certain Margaret was reminded of it—and often. Alinor's tongue could be sharper than the Countess's own upon occasion, and the mistress of Bailekair stood in awe of her youngest son's powerful wife.

Sly, like a fox, she is, wie that red hair and those green eyes, Lady Margaret told herself. The vixen! She trod warily in Alinor's presence lest she arouse the sleeping beast that was the infamous Murray temper.

'Twas Alinor who made life bearable for Mary and Joanna, for she did not hold them in contempt as the others of the household did. Without her they would have been cruelly treated, for those who had once loved them both now kept their distance lest the Countess's wrath at any kindness shown to "that whore and her tart" (as she now referred to Mary and Joanna) fall upon them with a vengeance.

Alinor wept when she saw the Earl, who had danced with her at her wedding and flirted with her mother so outrageously.

"He was a good mon," she said, "far better than that wailing hypocrite upstairs deserved."

"How dare she presume to cry when she wouldna even prepare him for his funeral?" Mary asked bitterly.

"Mayhap she sheds but tears of joy," Joanna spoke.

Alinor's eyes darkened to deep emerald. "She will live to rue this day, will Lady Margaret. Are ye ready for the others now?"

"Aye."

*Hugh was wie him when he fell.*

Mary wanted to scream as she pressed her clenched fists against her temples for the hundredth time, trying to shut out the dreadful sound of Edward's words; but she could not. Even over the loud, mournful keening of the women who had gathered in the long hall she could hear them.

*HUGH WAS WIE HIM WHEN HE FELL!*

The bagpipes droned plaintively as the Clan Carmichael carried the corpse of their Chief and Captain to the cemetery set in the hills overlooking Bailekair; the men in their mourning belted plaids, the women in black *arascaids*, unrelieved save for the tartans over their shoulders, the *tonnags* held in place with silver brooches engraved with the Carmichael coats of arms: Bailekair, Dùndereen, Leabaidh a' Nathair, Moy Heath, Càrnwick, Abergorra, and Glochlomond. The list of earls, barons, sirs, lairds, and ladies was endless as the Carmichaels streamed to the fresh grave to pay their respects to the late Earl and lay bunches of sweet heather and bracken, thistle and broom upon the mound of earth. Representatives from the neighboring clans came as well, just as the Carmichaels had sent a few men to the funerals of other families. The Murrays had delegates, the Flemings, the Douglases, the Campbells, the MacDougalls, the Hamiltons, the Lindsays, the Gordons, the Duffs, and the Chisholms, to help bury Magnus. Women wept and wailed; men danced the funeral rituals. Mary leaned heavily on Joanna's arm with Edward by her side. Joanna, who listened long into the evenings as Mary poured the grief from her heart, and she did the same. For only another woman can know the terrible sorrow a maid feels at the death of a man she has loved.

Retribution from King James IV was forgotten for a time. Young Jamie was grieving, too. Now that he held the throne secure he mourned the death of his greedy, lazy father; his father, whom Jamie's men had murdered at Beaton's Mill. All of Scotland seemed paralyzed by sorrow, although messengers came and went, and furtive conversations were held in the main hall of Bailekair long after supper had ended, and the women had retired for the evening.

Mary was grateful for the time of quiet, for it gave her a small respite from fate, and from Hugh and Ian, who eyed her rounding belly speculatively and waited.

# Fifteen

Hunter MacBeth stood at the narrow slit of the window in his room at Glenkirk, gazing out across Loch Ness to the castle in the distance. Bailekair. He studied the towers of the impressive keep speculatively, the thin openings along the high, machicolated battlements, the sweeping ramparts. Was she there, within those massive walls she'd loved so dearly? Had her betrothed wanted her after all? Or had Hunter sent his beloved to her death at the hands of Hugh Carmichael? Och, why had she not come to him? A thousand questions plagued Hunter's tormented soul.

*I waited, Mary, my love. I waited so long at Mheadhoin, but ye dinna come to me. Why? Why? Oh, God, beloved! Did ye nae love me after all, or are ye even now lying in some cold, dark grave? Curse my honor! Damn my pride! Ye were worth them both, and, still, I wouldna see it. And now—now when 'tis too late— Oh, Mary!*

His eyes searched for her ceaselessly, the solitary figure on the coal black steed, but there was naught upon the Highland moors save the sweeping bracken, gold as her silken hair.

*Bailekair. Tell me if my love is there.*

Over and over the senseless, little refrain echoed in Hunter's heart, but there was no answer.

Strange how he had always seemed to look through the regal keep before, knowing it was there, in the distance, just as the purple mountain that rose up majestically behind it was there, but never really noticing the tall towers reaching upward to the sky. Now he longed to imprint each detail of the fortress upon his mind, just as he could recall every aspect of Mary Carmichael's haunting face: the violet eyes, the gilded hair, the yielding mouth. Her image was branded in Hunter's very soul! If he closed his eyes and tried very hard, he could still taste her sweet, pliant lips quivering beneath his own, smell the scent of heather that lingered on her golden body, feel her trembling breasts pressed against his bronzed chest, hear her gentle cry of surrender as he drove into that soft place between her thighs. Oh, Mary! Why did ye nae come to me, beloved?

Hunter *had* to know. He turned his attention once more to the Royal missive that lay upon his desk.

It had come to Glenkirk just that morning, causing a stir in the entire household with the shield stamped upon its seal—the King's coat of arms. Young Jamie, it would seem, did not intend to forget those who'd served him—and served him well—in battle. Hunter was to make whatever request he desired, and it would be fulfilled. He knew, from the wording on the parchment, Jamie had granted him a special favor by allowing him to choose his own boon. And he knew, too, the reason why.

When Jamie's staff-bearer had fallen in battle, Hunter had caught up the banner the man had carried before it had been able to touch the ground, waving it aloft again. For if the young King's colors had been trampled into the bloody earth, his army would have thought their leader dead, their cause ended, and fled the battlefield. His Grace's father might have won that fateful day, might still be seated upon the throne of Scotland, instead of having met his final end at Beaton's Mill.

Hunter had fought on, in spite of the heavy burden, hanging on to the staff with one hand, holding his sword in the other, clenching his reins between his teeth. Thank God, Craigor was a worthy and well-trained destrier! Otherwise Hunter might not have been able to manage. The act had not gone unnoticed by the King, and the reward for his bravery was now Hunter's for the asking.

His eyes turned once more to the window, to Bailekair standing so proudly in the distance. Then he picked up his pen to answer the Royal favor. There was only one thing in all Scotland he desired.

"Marry, but the King is sure to reward Hunter well," Francis, youngest of the MacBeths of Glenkirk, exclaimed excitedly. "I wonder what he'll ask for."

"A holding of his own, no doubt," Blair, his older brother, mused.

"Nay, I think nae, cousin." Cadman frowned, his usually gay countenance troubled by what he feared Hunter was upstairs even now requesting. Kidnap of the wench was one thing in the eyes of the Clan MacBeth, but *marriage!* Well, *that* was another thing entirely! Neither side would countenance the match. At least an uneasy peace lay over the Highlands right now. Cadman hated to think what would happen if it were to be broken. And yet, he thought to himself, I would do as much for the woman I loved; and he found his heart still ached upon remembering Janet MacDonald, dead in her grave these many years past. I dinna blame ye, brother.

"Art daft, Cadman?" Lady Euphemia interrupted his musings irritably. "Hunter would be a fool nae to take advantage of such a promise of riches!"

"I'm sure he had no thought of gold when he salvaged Jamie's colors," Lady Grace, Cadman's half sister, spoke gently in defense of her cousin.

"There, I'm sure 'tis Hunter's business after all," Lady Sophia, Countess of Glenkirk, noted smoothly, aware of the animosity between her daughter and niece and fearing a quarrel brewed just beneath the surface of the conversation. " 'Tis like as nae he'll tell us what he's decided, and you'll all be wrong. The lad was e'er one for the unexpected." She shook her head, smiling slightly. Hunter had always been a favorite with Lady Sophia.

Cadman groaned inwardly. Unexpected was right!

"Quite so," Lord Angus, Earl of Glenkirk, agreed, shifting his wounded leg to a more comfortable position.

Grace noticed at once the grimace of pain that shot across her uncle's face.

"Shall I dress your wound again, Uncle Angus? 'Twillna do for it to become stiff and fester."

"Aye, child, your touch is gentle," the Bear of Glenkirk responded. "Though I fear from these red streaks an infection has set in, in spite of your care. Och, I'm getting too auld to ride into battle, I guess. Better to hae gone oot in a blaze of glory like my auld enemy, Magnus, than to rot away bit by bit." He frowned sadly. " 'Twillna be the same, nae haeing the Lion to harry from my cave.' '

"There's always the young cub, Ian," Grace said comfortingly. "Now let me see that gash." She unwrapped the bandages slowly, eyes widening with alarm as she saw her uncle was right. Ugly, red marks shot out from around the sore; to her dismay it had grown a yellowish green color and puffed since last she'd dressed it.

"Cadman, the mixture of mud and cobwebs in my room, would ye fetch it please? Aunt Sophia, some brandy. Blair, I shall need your help and yours too, Francis. I'm sorry, uncle," the girl apologized, "but I fear this will hurt."

Lord Angus waved his hand airily. "It can pain no more than it already does, Grace. Dinna bother your bonnie head aboot me, lass."

She bit her lip, nodding. "Francis, stoke up the fire a wee bit. The knife must be verra hot," she explained as Blair drew his dirk from his belt, understanding what needed to be done.

The bitch! Euphemia thought nastily. She does but open her mouth, and my family runs to do her bidding. What do they see in her, the whey-faced whore? Daughter of an earl she may be, but *I* am the daughter of the Chief and Captain of the Clan MacBeth! How dare they hold her in such reverence when such is *my* due and mine alone? Well, she has been brought down—from David MacDonald to my brother, Francis. Francis! A puny lad two years younger than herself. Och, how I laughed to hear it! Serves her right, the conniving witch, for the MacDonald should hae been mine, *would* hae been mine had Grace nae wormed her way into his heart!

That this was not true did not bother Effie, for she saw only what she wanted to see. Even when David MacDonald had spurned her coldly, she had flung herself at his feet, crying that Grace had bewitched him and that he was not in his right mind.

Och, no matter, Euphemia decided. I hae found a prince to replace him. Aye, a prince, and together we shall rule the Highlands. My family willna scorn me then!

She was not pretty. The features that made her clansmen handsome looked plain and harsh in the face of Euphemia MacBeth. Still none would have likened her to a sow had she not worn a perpetually sour grimace upon her countenance, a scowl born out of her jealousy and greed. Effie liked the finer things in life and could never get enough of them, in spite of the fact that her coffers were crammed with silken gowns and damask surcoats, and her jewelry boxes held treasures even a queen would have envied.

Even more than this she coveted the attention of men. Any man would do. From the lowliest stable lad to dukes of the realm Effie parlayed her meager charms in a grasping, fawning manner. That most of the objects of her worship held her in disgusted contempt escaped her. She was not an astute woman, although, like a sly, dumb beast, she was cunning and shrewd. Effie fancied herself a gracious beauty, only dimly realizing she was, in truth, pitied and despised by those who knew her. She had no friends, and until recently she had comforted herself in her lack of a husband by believing all women so jealous of her they could not risk exposing their menfolk to her person for fear of being left upon the shelf themselves.

There was only one fly in Effie's preening ointment, and

that was Grace. Grace, whose gentle mother had been killed when Lord Torquil, Angus's brother, had insisted his timid wife ride a palfrey much too hard-mouthed and high-strung for her to handle. The steed had bolted; the Countess had been found with her slender neck broken. This, coming hard on the heels of Grace's broken engagement to the MacDonald, whom she loved quietly and dearly still, had been too much for the young girl. She had pined away until her enraged father had packed her off to Glenkirk in hopes her half brother, Cadman, might be able to raise her spirits and Francis, her now-betrothed, woo her thoughts from the Earl of Wynd Cheathaich.

The former of these expectations had been met, for with the exception of her half brother, Grace was an only child, and she worshiped Cadman greatly. The latter had only moderate success, however, for Francis had not his affections engaged by any woman and had accepted Grace simply because he'd liked her and known he had to marry someone. A lengthy conversation with his father over the considerable amount of Grace's dowry had persuaded the youngest son easily of the advantages of the match; and while Francis was pleased with and fond of the gentle, biddable Grace, he treated her with the careless callousness of youth that did little toward alleviating the pain in the heart of one so aptly named.

From the day Grace had come to Glenkirk, Euphemia had despised the sweet, cloying wench. She had no desire to see her brother marry the girl—although Effie thought Francis a silly twit—simply because she could not bear to have any man around her who was not enamored of herself. Well, Francis would be gone soon enough, as would Blair. Her eldest brother, Stephen, had already returned with Lord Lachlan, another of her father's brothers, to Faoghail, where he was in service. Next week Francis would be off to Oir Uisge and Blair to Rath na Mara. They had already lingered overlong at Glenkirk.

Euphemia gave Grace another hateful stare. Someday, she vowed silently, I'll get rid of that bitch! Would to God her father had ne'er sent her here!

Then, with the sly smile of someone who has a secret, but

will not tell, unnoticed by the others, Euphemia slipped quietly from the hall.

"I've been waiting for ye, Effie."

"I'm sorry. I couldna come before this," she explained as she dropped from her saddle, hurrying to the arms of the tall blond man who stood impatiently in the shadows of the grove, the mellow sun playing upon his dour face through the branches of the trees.

He kissed her eager mouth, fingers fumbling with her *arascaid* as he pulled her down onto his cloak, already spread across the dewey grass. In a moment they were both naked, flesh pressed against flesh as he jammed his maleness deep inside her waiting thighs. Her long nails dug into the muscles of his back, clawing tiny furrows down the smooth skin.

"Aye, oh, aye!" she cried, groaning with pleasure at each sharp thrust.

When it was over, they lay spent in each other's arms, satisfied smiles on each of their faces. The man stroked Euphemia's pointed breasts idly, thinking again how small, how firm they were. They appealed to him because he was so miserly, loathing waste of any kind. They filled his mouth as he devoured them greedily for a minute, and he deemed them large enough.

Then he raised his head.

"I so seldom get to see ye. Why were ye late?" he demanded, his hand between her thighs.

"Ah," she moaned, grabbing his probing fingers, helping him with the motion. "I ne'er get enough of ye."

"Answer me, Effie, or I'll stop."

She pouted prettily, or so she thought.

"A Royal messenger came for Hunter today to grant him the King's boon. The household was in such an uproar I had difficulty getting away. 'Twould hae seemed odd had I nae shared in their excitement."

"Aye, curse him! Who knows what the ootcome of the battle might hae been had that Romany devil nae rescued Jamie's banner!"

"Och, who cares?" Euphemia did not want to talk of war. She had heard enough of that at home, what with her brothers continually reliving the battle and her father complaining of his wound. "Do ye love me? Oh, tell me ye do!"

"Aye, though I'm damned for it, I do," Ian Carmichael grunted, for in his own peculiar way, he really did care for the wench. "And in time, now that my father is dead, I shall find a way for us to be together always, Effie."

How he wanted her, longed to flaunt her before his mother, Lady Margaret, who bullied and frightened him even while she teased him unnaturally with a promise she would not, could not honor, the bitch!.

Euphemia licked her lips, pleased by his response.

"Aye, 'twas a lucky thing for us, his getting killed. Imagine, the auld Lion dead! Would the auld Bear were, too! Och, Ian. If only ye could win the King's favor as well, then none might gainsay us! We would be a power to reckon wie in the Highlands, ye and I." She traced his swelling manhood idly. "Sometimes I think of the legend and feel we are the two of whom it spoke."

"Are ye calling me the spawn of the devil, wench?" Ian smirked wolfishly at the thought, for it gave him pleasure. Indeed, it must have been a demon who enticed his mother to bed, the cold-bodied whore!

"Wasna Judas such? Aye, we are betrayers, ye and I. But we shallna be damned for it, love. Nay," Euphemia's eyes glowed with hunger. "We shall rule the Highlands as one, and even sovereign lords will bless us and beg our favor. Aye, 'tis coming, Ian! I feel it in my bones! And naught will e'er mock us again!"

"Aye, the time ripens as summer wheat, and we shall reap a harvest of gold and glory, love; for we were born to it, ye and I. Ye are a bonnie lass, Effie." Ian kissed her lightly, for when she talked to him like this, he felt powerful and deserving of the riches each so desperately craved, as though together they could make the promise real. Aye, he'd show his mother, the cow who laughed at him, called him a puny weakling, bullied him into doing her will, shuddered if he so much as touched her even while she bared her juglike breasts before him, reminding him 'twas she who had given him life and that his duty lay with her, who had suckled him from those pendulous udders. Not like Effie, who begged him to take her and made him feel like a man. "Shall I buy ye a new dress, a bonnie bauble? What would ye like, Euphemia?" he queried.

And Effie, grasping Effie, for once replied, "Ye, my lord, only ye."

Ian mounted her again in response to her desires, twisting her head up cruelly to meet his mouth in the manner he knew aroused her so well, hammering into her white flanks violently. Aye, she was a match for him, was Euphemia MacBeth! She enjoyed being abused by his lovemaking, and Ian enjoyed doing it to her. He squeezed her breasts hard as she bit down upon his lip, remembering the first time he'd come upon her in the grove.

She'd been a virgin then, who'd fought tooth and nail against his assault, fearing the consequences to herself were her ruin to be complete and discovered. He'd had no other thought at first than to rape a maid alone in the woods. But once Ian had penetrated her she'd seemed to give into him, liking the brutal way he'd treated her. Upon discovering she was no less than Lady Euphemia MacBeth, who'd somehow gotten separated from the rest of her hunting party (upon whom Ian had been spying) he'd been smart enough to see the advantages such a relationship could have. He had recognized in her a kindred spirit, and rather than taking her prisoner for a ransom that only would have enriched the coffers of his father, Ian had asked her to meet him again, somehow knowing she would. Bit by bit he'd gained her love and confidence, turned her against her family, nurtured the seeds of hatred and want embedded in her soul.

Through her he learned information that was valuable to him, helping him time his raids upon the MacBeth holdings and earning him much respect as a warrior within the ranks of his own clan. If there were those who wondered at Ian's uncanny knack of knowing just where and when to strike, they kept their suspicions to themselves.

Aye, the bitch was as vicious and perverted in her desires as he, and Ian had taught her all manners of ways of pleasing them both, things even the lowliest of whores would have been repulsed by. She had won his love, grudging though it might be, because of her willingness to do anything he asked of her; and she had gone to him time and time again because she could not get enough of him. They had become a drug to each other, and now their addiction knew no bounds. Ian needed her because no other woman would have borne the humiliation and degradation it was necessary that he inflict in order to be truly sated. And Effie—well, Ian was a man, and although she did not consciously realize it, he was the only man who'd never scorned her because of what she was.

"Do it to me, Ian," she whispered throatily. "Do it to me hard."

## Sixteen

"What's next?" His Grace, King James IV of Scotland, dipped a strawberry into a bowl of curdled cream, twirling it about several times to be sure it was thoroughly coated before he rolled it in a silver tray of sugar, then popped it into his mouth. The treat eaten, he sighed and reached for another plump, juicy, red morsel.

The Earl of Angus, the King's guardian, watched the young Stewart thoughtfully as Lord Patrick Hepburn, newly created Earl of Bothwell, smiled.

"The reply from Sir Hunter MacBeth, Your Grace." Patrick handed Jamie the letter.

"Well, what does he want?" the young monarch asked rather sourly, for the strawberry had been rotten. He spat it out upon the floor, causing the Earl of Angus to jump nervously at the motion. "If 'tis Fleming's estates, he canna hae those, because I hae decided to pardon his lordship."

"Nay, Sire, 'tisna lands he requests." The Hepburn grinned even more broadly now, not in the least bit disturbed as he accidentally stepped upon his sovereign lord's rejected treat. " 'Tis a wench."

"A wench, Patrick?" Jamie glanced up from the serious matter of his strawberries in surprise, then his eyes narrowed dangerously, reminding the other two men sharply for a moment of the King's late father. "Is she rich, important, her holdings of military value? By the Virgin Mary, Patrick, what is so funny?"

"I'm sorry, Your Grace. 'Tis only that it seems Your Grace's Court abounds wie men a'mooning after women who dinna want them."

"Ye refer to yourself and my cousin, of course." Jamie recalled well the infamous marriage contract he'd had drawn up for the Hepburn, stating Patrick might choose to wed whichever of the two Gordon sisters pleased him best.

Although all of Scotland knew 'twas the King's cousin Jane whom Lord Bothwell favored, she had scorned him pointedly; and so the mischievous Hepburn had persuaded his monarch to the wretched deed in order to insult and anger Patrick's intended bride. The courtiers swore Jane Gordon's cry of rage had been heard throughout the palace halls.

"Hae no fear, Patrick," His Grace continued with a chuckle. "She will come aboot in the end. They always do, ye know; and Jane knows full well 'tisna her sister ye mean to hae. So, tell me, who is it the MacBeth desires that would spurn him as my cousin does ye?"

"Lady Mary Carmichael of Bailekair, Sire."

"Isna that the lass Sir Hunter attempted to crown queen of the summer tournament last year, the one who caused such a furor by throwing the garland into the dirt?" The Earl of Angus glanced up in surprise, feeling obliged to join in the conversation.

"Aye." The young King frowned. " 'The golden tigress,' some call her, spawn of the Lion of Bailekair. There is a feud between the two clans."

"Ye are well-informed, as always, Your Grace," Patrick claimed as Jamie nodded, pleased by the compliment. "I believe it began many years ago when one of the Carmichaels kidnapped a MacBeth woman."

James sighed once more. "Och, 'tis bound to cause trouble if I consent to the match then. Christ's son! Dinna I hae enough problems as 'tis wie'oot war between the clans?"

He glared at the two men, and they hastened to agree with him.

The Earl of Bothwell cleared his throat tactfully. "Still, the boon *is* Sir Hunter's for the choosing, Sire. If I may say so, dinna the Carmichaels oppose ye in battle?" He hesitated to mention the late rebellion.

"Quite so, Patrick, quite so." The young sovereign was angered by the thought. "The Earl of Bailekair was killed in the engagement. His son now holds the fortress. Ah, what was the name of that wench again, the one they call 'the golden tigress?' "

"Lady Mary, Your Grace," the Earl of Angus replied.

"Well, send her a letter informing her she is to deliver herself up to Sir Hunter MacBeth at once, and fine the Carmichaels 150,000 marks. *That* should keep them busy for awhile! God's teeth! They should consider themselves lucky I dinna strip them of all their lands and titles. I believe their holdings are quite numerous."

"Aye, Sire." The Earl of Angus glanced at the Hepburn, nodding with satisfaction. It seemed Jamie did not intend to wreak more havoc on the land by hanging or disowning the lairds who'd fought against him in the recent rebellion. The two men considered this a prudent course of action.

" 'Twill be a fit penalty for them to pay, Your Grace," Lord Bothwell added. "And may produce some amount of peace between the two clans. A wise decision."

The King smiled. "I like ye, Patrick, even if ye do flatter me outrageously."

"Sire—" the Hepburn started to protest.

"Hae a strawberry, Patrick." James pushed the bowl toward his subject. "Then tell my fool secretary we'll do no more work today. Wie all this talk of wenches I've a mind to go a'hunting."

"Aye, Your Grace." Patrick grinned broadly once more, then helped himself to a cream-and-sugar-coated treat.

To say Mary's hands shook as she unrolled the message from the King was an understatement. They trembled so badly she dropped the scroll on the floor and collided with the Royal messenger who bent to retrieve it as quickly and horrifiedly as she. What could James possibly want of her? Was it retribution for that terrible day at the tourney? But surely that was long past!

The girl was not a coward; still, even the bravest of men had been known to quail before a king's wrath. Her eyes covered the parchment page rapidly. The page, who waited expectantly for a reply, did not realize it, but she was so stunned she read the words written therein twice to be sure she understood them correctly. She turned and laid the scroll on the table unseeingly, her shaking hands going to her cheeks, which were now suffused hotly with color.

"Godamercy!" she breathed, her heart pounding strangely. "He doesna know I am already wed."

Whether she referred to His Grace or Sir Hunter, the messenger could not be sure (for rumor of the contents of the letter entrusted to his care had reached his young ears in the palace corridors), but he caught enough of her whispered outburst to understand she could not obey the King's order.

"My lady," he bowed respectfully, "is that your reply to His Grace?"

"Nay!" Mary cried, recovering masterfully. "Do ye go to the cookhouse and be fed, lad." She suddenly remembered her manners and that this young man had no doubt traveled far without resting to deliver the King's command. "I shall need time to compose a letter to His Grace."

"Aye, my lady." He bowed himself out of the room, glad to escape her troubled presence.

Mary collapsed upon a chair after he'd gone, a sharp, tearing pain knifing through her chest, an ache born of grief that time would dull, but never heal. Tears of joy and sorrow mingled, trickled slowly down her cheeks. Hunter loved her! After all this time he wanted her still. Of all in Scotland he might have had he had chosen her.

"Oh, my love, my love—" Her voice broke softly in the stillness of the empty chamber as she wept.

A terrible loneliness engulfed her as it had not done since she had ridden across the snow-covered cliff at Mheadhoin to her family's cold embrace. She thought of the nights she'd lain awake, her heart as though it had been ripped asunder within her breast, her tears wet upon her cheeks in the darkness as she had racked the caverns of her mind to find some way of getting a message to her beloved; of the overwhelming emptiness that had come when there had seemed no path to follow; and the mountain had been steep indeed; of the gradual acceptance of her lot in life; of the misery that smote her heart each time she stood upon the ramparts of Bailekair, gazing out over the loch to Glenkirk, so near and yet so far; of the ache in her flesh each time Edward lay, untouching, a stranger beside her in the night.

"Oh, better ye were dead in battle like my father, Hunter, than to offer me this hope where none can be!" She smote her fist upon the table. "Damn ye! Damn ye for loving me and me for loving ye!" The words were wrenched from her in rage and pain and echoed hollowly in the empty room. "Nay, I'm sorry, sir, sorry, my love, for that which we knew and can hae no more. If only I hadna known what love could be, I might hae been happy wie Edward. I—oh, love, love! Dinna haunt my heart like this!"

With hands that trembled still Mary reached for pen and paper to write the words that came with such difficulty, such longing, such bitterness before the blur of her violet orbs.

*Bailekair Castle, Scotland, September, 1488*

*To His Grace, King James IV of Scotland,*

*Greetings.*

*Your Grace, I am in receipt of your message commanding me to marry Sir Hunter MacBeth. I regret to inform ye that, loyal subject though I am, 'tisna wie' in my power to comply wie your request, as my cousin, Edward Carmichael of Dùndereen and I were wed on Candlemas Day of this year. We are expecting our first bairn.*

*The ceremony was quiet, because of the unrest of the times, and mayhap that is why few hae learned of it.*

*I most humbly beg your pardon for being unable to fulfill your command, Sire, and hope my marriage doesna displease ye.*

*May I offer my sincerest wishes for your continued good health and a prosperous reign as our True and Sovereign Lord and King of all Scotland.*

*I remain your faithful, humble, and obedient servant.*

> *Lady Mary Kathryn Carmichael*
> *Of Bailekair*

This done, she sealed the parchment with wax, pressing her shield ring into the molten liquid. Then she picked up the King's letter and threw it into the fire, for Mary wanted naught in the household to know its contents. They might pry and speculate, but they would never learn for certain what it had contained. She shuddered to think what might happen if they did. Mayhap they would kill her, guessing she had gone willingly to Hunter's arms; for Edward, though he for some strange reason had remained silent on the matter, knew of Mary's love for the MacBeth and might be persuaded to speak against her, to rid himself of the woman who had become the stranger he called "wife."

Thank God, Alan, who had loved her as a child and loved her still, had had the presence of mind to usher the Royal messenger quietly upstairs to Mary's small chamber. If aught were asked of her, she decided to say the King had sent his condolences on her father's death as a simple courtesy to a former lady-in-waiting of the Court.

It was not until the girl turned to descend the stairs to the main hall below that the first spasms of pain tore through her belly. She nearly fell, grabbing the table for support, her reply to James still clutched between her fingers.

"Dear Virgin Mary," the lass prayed fervently through gritted teeth. " 'Tisna yet time. 'Tis too soon! Too soon!"

Twelve hours later Mary Carmichael was delivered of her husband's tiny, premature son. She named him "Geoffrey" and gave thanks he was plainly Edward's bairn.

One week afterward Sir Hunter MacBeth received his reply from King James IV of Scotland. Upon reading its contents he damned Edward Carmichael and himself and sorrowed for the woman he loved but could not have.

Och, Mary! Mary! May God curse my honor! Damn my pride! If nae for those, ye would be wie me still, beloved. . . .

"Choose another boon," Jamie had said. Hunter's response to His Grace was curt and bitter. He wrote briefly: *There is naught else I would hae.*

## Seventeen

Fall lingered late that year of 1488, so in October the Clan Carmichael chose to celebrate the holiday of Samhain by holding the games that would determine the new Chief and Captain of its family, for this position was earned, not hereditary, and had been postponed after Magnus's death due to the upheaval caused by the civil war. The games were to be followed by the final hunt of the season to prepare for the coming winter.

The main event in the contest was the hurtling of the *cabar*, a twenty-foot pole weighing eighty-four pounds. It took a great deal of strength to lift this log waist-high, balance the main body of the pole against one shoulder, then fling it end-over-end. The distance the missile went was not what counted, but rather the accuracy of the throw. There was also wrestling, in which two participants each hooked one hand around the other's neck, then spun about, attempting to force the other to the ground. In addition, the competitors had to perform the tossing of the sheaf, a sixteen-pound burlap bag of hay. This had to be propelled over a crossbar with a pitchfork; the barrier was inched higher as the day went on to weed out the less worthy opponents.

After one man had succeeded in winning the games, thereby gaining the title of Chief and Captain of the clan, the family elected its second in command, the *Tanist,* by voting.

Mary did not want to see the games. Her father had won his rank in the Clan Carmichael the year of his knighthood, so she could not remember a time when Magnus had not been head of her family. She would not be missed, she knew.

But Lady Margaret was in a fine fettle as those from Bailekair set out toward Leabaidh a' Nathair, where the contest was to be held. Magnus was dead; her daughter had been reduced to the position of a nonentity; and she, Margaret, had high hopes Ian might win the games, in spite of the fact that Lord Gilchrist was the man favored. Even though she had Bailekair to herself, through her eldest son, the Countess discovered 'twas not enough. She had forgotten her husband's demise would reduce her own state of rank and power within the clan. Aye, it must be regained, and Ian must do it!

After they'd gone, Mary took her young bairn, who was

thriving well, in spite of his smallness, and sought out Joanna. The two women desired to call on some of the crofters who were ailing. Lady Margaret, in her newfound authority, could not be bothered with such trivialities, and Nanna, who once more looked after her people as she had of old, was with child, a difficult burden at her age, being her first bairn. The Countess had begrudgingly allowed Mary to assume the task of caring for the common folk only because Ian, in a rare disagreement with his mother, had told her to.

"The people still love the bitch, regardless of her shame," he'd said, shrugging his shoulders. "It can do no harm."

But Mary realized her brother had gotten his way over this small point only because he needed the good will of the commoners she helped to maintain, for she seemed to them some final link with Lord Magnus and the old ways.

The burden of taking over the massive castle of Bailekair had not been an easy one for Ian. He was little liked by the serfs. His dour disposition did not command the respect of his crofters as his father's roaring laughter and honesty had done. Ian was too sour, too petty in his dealings with the serfs and vassals for that. They were sullen in their work now as a result, shiftless whenever possible. They tilled the soil, planted the seeds, and harvested the crops out of fear of starvation and fear of Ian, not love as they had once farmed the land. They hid their produce so the bailiff had difficulty determining just how many *calpiches* were owed. They stole from the castle keep and from each other as well, a rare occurrence in the old laird's day.

Ian had not the wisdom of his father nor the generosity the late and just Earl had shown to his people. Nay, Ian was a skinflint, a pinch-penny like his mother. He squeezed every last farthing out of the crofters, then demanded more. He imposed extremely harsh and cruel punishments on those who opposed him. He refused to listen to reason when a few of the truly loyal men-at-arms, such as Alan, attempted to counsel him, sluffing off the old retainers in favor of the more rash, hotheaded, and brutal men among them. He was slowly but surely destroying Bailekair.

Mary hated her brother for it and aided him only out of love for the proud, regal fortress.

Lady Margaret was given a free rein in the household, and her conceit and meanness knew few bounds. In the olden days the bonnie Lion of Bailekair had restrained her sharp tongue and temper; the serfs had known they had some recourse if they were unfairly treated. Now they trod warily in the keep and fields, taking care to stay out of Margaret's way whenever possible, for Ian usually agreed with his mother on every turn. The servants stood no chance against the both of them.

'Twas only Mary, Joanna, and Alinor that the Countess left alone. The three women had banded together in the miserable household, doing the best they could to ease the heavy burdens of the servants. They took pains to be always in each other's company so Margaret never got an opportunity to catch one of them alone. In this Alinor was a godsend, Mary thought, for Charlie's wife was one of those rare women whose sense of fun and flirtatiousness had not reduced her to an insensitive gladpie. She seemed to comprehend without asking the way matters stood in the keep and took what measures she could to make things better for them all. In fact, Mary suspected that, like the deep and still Joanna, there was a good deal more to the lovely, glittering Alinor Murray Carmichael than met the eye.

Mary's sister-in-law was happier at Bailekair, too, for shortly before Samhain Gordon, Charlie, and the twins had come home to the great keep for good. Everyone had been much surprised by their arrival, because although Andrew and Harold had been knighted and were free to go where they pleased, Gordon had one more year to serve at Dùndereen and Charlie two at Càrnwick. However, as they made themselves agreeable to the crofters, managing to stave off the rebellion all had felt brewing for weeks, Mary soon understood why Ian had sent for them. To have the serfs rise up in arms against him because of his own mismanagement and stupidity could not be a very gratifying experience. Ian had avoided it cleverly, but Mary alone guessed it did not increase his fondness for the two younger brothers, both of whom were much better liked than Ian.

Yet it was not of these things Mary spoke as she and Joanna made their way to Mistress Flora's cottage to pick up the necessary herbal remedies prepared by Mary's old nurse for the crofters. Mary talked of Edward's rejection of their young son, whom she held cradled in her arms, for Edward could not bear the sight of the child who was forever a reminder of his base, bestial behavior that Candlemas Eve.

" 'Tis as if he despises our bairn, Joanna." The lass sighed as an autumn leaf brushed her hair.

"Has Edward said aught to ye of why, Mary?"

"Nay." She shook her head. "Though mayhap I can guess the reason. Things hae—hae nae been well for us from the beginning. Now—we—we seldom speak with each other. Still, I wouldna see my babe suffer for sins that are nae his own."

"My lady—my friend—I dinna know what is wrong in your marriage, but your unhappiness is plain to see. Let me talk to Edward. We were close of auld, and I may of some help to ye both," Joanna said impulsively.

"I—I dinna know," Mary faltered, thinking of the things Edward might reveal. "He has grown so reticent of late—"

"We all change, Mary. We play the cards fate has dealt us, and sometimes we must make the best of a bad hand."

"Aye, how well I know it! Och, I am to blame if anyone. Your life is none the easier for me either, Joanna. If only—if only—"

"What's done is done, my lady. I hae loved and served ye always. Naught has changed that. Please, let me speak wie Edward."

"I owe him much and hae paid in bad coin." Mary's words were bitter. "Aye, ye must comfort him for me, Joanna, for I canna. And—and whate'er he says I pray ye dinna turn from me in loathing."

The maid's cool brown eyes met Mary's own violet ones steadily. "There is naught ye could hae done, dear friend, to earn my disgust."

"Ye dinna know!" Mary burst out violently, causing little Geoffrey to fret irritably at her vehemence.

"Do I nae?" Joanna's gaze sought the castle, Glenkirk, across the loch thoughtfully, wryly. "We canna help where we love, Mary," she spoke gently, "for the heart knows no rules."

Mary stared, blushing with confusion and apprehension.

"Nay! How—how—"

"Hae no fear, my lady, for I am sure none other has guessed your guilty secret."

"Then how—"

"Och, Mary, ye sorrow for your father, 'tis true; but ye hae a lifetime of happy memories to ease that sad pain. Only a taste of the love between a mon and a woman, so bittersweet, then gone, could cause the kind of grief I know is in your heart; and I hae seen your eyes stray oft to the castle across the loch."

What a relief to break her dam of silence, to allow the depths of her emotions to come flooding forth! In a tide of passion Mary's story came pouring out, while Joanna listened quietly.

"He is my enemy," Mary sobbed at last. " 'Tis wrong of me to long for him so, and, oh, how bitter is my punishment!"

Joanna was silent for a moment. When she spoke again, her words were wise beyond her years.

"I believe when true love comes, my lady, there is no right or wrong; aye, and no pride either, for we become shameless in our passions, our desires. 'Love bears all, conquers all, endures all,' " she quoted softly. "It wounds us wie its wild crescendoes, its heart-wrenching plummets; and sometimes it destroys us. But still we seek it oot. Still we seek it oot," she repeated, "and our lives are empty wie'oot it."

"Oh, Joanna." Mary's heart jerked queerly in understanding. "Ye love someone even as I do."

"Aye, but he isna for me, anymore than the MacBeth is for ye." Her face was shuttered once more, and Mary found she could not ask the question that rose to her lips.

The two girls walked on in silence, heart aching in each breast.

The howling of the dogs in the woods of Leabaidh a' Nathair had reached a feverish pitch. Hugh Carmichael knew from their excited yaps that a boar had been flushed from its lair. He heard the angry squeals and grunts the beast gave as it ran through the forest, crashing loudly amidst the brush, the hounds in hot pursuit.

The hunting party whooped with delight, the gold and silver spurs of the men digging into the sides of their mounts sharply as they pressed forward eagerly, their women close behind.

At last they saw it, a huge wild creature with angry red eyes and snorting nostrils. It had turned to make a stand in a small clearing, but for some reason had failed to protect itself. The dogs were on all sides of it, teasing, nipping, barking.

The men dismounted rapidly, lances in hands, hunting knives ready as they edged toward the pig, taunting it, jabbing at it with their pointed shafts. The animal rushed forth briefly, catching one of the hounds in the side. There was a wild yelp of pain as the dog's intestines spilled from the fatal slash; then it trembled and lay still. The pungent smell of blood further excited both the boar and the rest of the hounds, which closed in, snarling. The men backed off, giving the beast room to make its next move, positioning themselves strategically around the clearing, the pommels of their lances jammed against the ground to absorb the shock of the creature's blow should one of them be lucky enough to spear the pig.

The animal shook its massive head, its little eyes filled with heated rage, its deadly tusks lowered as it suddenly charged forward again. Hugh surged forth to meet the assault, bold as always, stabbing at the boar furiously. The blow slipped as the beast turned aside at the last moment, the tip of the shaft merely puncturing the creature's bristly back, then sliding off the thick rough skin. Hugh drew his dagger hurriedly, but the pig was already past him. One of the hounds ran up, slashing at the animal's hindquarters. It grunted meanly, turning its ferocious gaze on the dog, lowering its head as it attacked once more. The hound caught the full force of the ivory tusks in the chest. The boar sent the dog flying into the brush, then continued its onslaught.

Lord Thomas rushed ahead, his lance ready, calling to the beast. The creature snorted, pawing the ground, then pounded toward the old laird. The blow was badly aimed, striking the pig in the shoulder just above the chest. Mayhap when the lance had been forged, the metal had been weak, for the length of shining steel shattered on impact. The wild animal came on before Thomas had time to draw his dirk, the deadly tusks gouging a long tear in his belly before the boar rushed on past, then turned to assault again.

Ian was closest to the elderly man. He could have saved him, pulled him out of the mindless path of the enraged beast; but he moved slowly, deliberately, as though hypnotized by shock. The creature caught Thomas, shaking the frail laird's body on its skewering tusks. And then Lord Gilchrist, the new Chief and Captain of the Clan Carmichael, was there, his dagger driving home into the thick neck of the pig. Its shrill cry of wrath sounded horribly once more before it toppled, crushing Thomas beneath its enormous weight. The blood spattered. For one unbelieving eternity the hunting party stood, stunned with helplessness and horror at the quickness of the incident. Then they moved forward as one to lift the massive, dead animal from the elderly lord's crippled legs and lower extremities. Thomas moaned faintly, as though by some miraculous feat of strength and willpower he could manage to keep his blood and guts from spilling out in a slippery mass upon the ground. And, indeed, perhaps it was that same faith that kept him alive at that moment.

"Uncle Thomas." Ian knelt before the old man. "I'm sorry. I should hae diverted the boar, helped ye—" His voice broke, but the eyes he had downcast in mock shame and repentance were sly.

"Nay, Ian. 'Twas—naught ye—could hae—done," Thomas managed to gasp weakly.

"Aye, dinna blame yourself, lad." Gilchrist clapped his foster son upon the shoulder, gazing at his dying brother. " 'Twas an unfortunate accident."

"Our Chief speaks truly, brother." Hugh gave Ian, who had won the coveted position of *Tanist*, a cool glance. " 'Twas an accident."

Ian met his cousin's narrowed stare levelly. *As ye slew my father and gae me an earldom, so hae I done as much for ye,* his ice blue eyes said silently.

*Aye, but 'twas I who wie'drew my name from the running so ye might be* Tanist, Hugh's black eyes replied.

*My father was much loved. 'Twas oot of respect for his memory I was chosen and would hae been regardless, brother.*

*Mayhap, but ye are little liked, Ian; and my charm has a winning way.*

*I will gie ye my sister for it.*

The darker man suddenly grinned wickedly, wolfishly, speculatively.

And so, though no actual words had passed between them, each knew Ian's debt to Hugh Carmichael had been paid. Moments later the new Earl of Dùndereen raised his hunting horn to his lips to sound the *mort*.

# *Eighteen*

One by one the links of the chain to Mary's past were breaking away. Her father was gone, dead and buried beneath the frozen earth she dug at with her hands, as though by clawing at the snow-covered ground she could bring him back again, bring back the time when she had been just a wee lass, and the laughing Lion of Bailekair's strong broad shoulders had borne all of her responsibilities, her happiness, her pain. But she was alone; Magnus would never be her shield again. Lord Thomas was dead, too; an accident, all had said. But Mary knew the mark of Hugh and Ian lay upon the deed as surely as their hands were in the slaying of her father. Poor old harmless Thomas, who had stood between his eldest son and earldom, as only Edward stood between Mary and Hugh.

The girl shuddered, recalling how Ian had come to her chamber after Lord Thomas's funeral, slyly suggesting the favors she might reap by becoming the whore of Hugh Carmichael now that he was the powerful Earl of Dùndereen. Though Ian had hesitated to come right out and say it, his implication had been plain, his threat clear. Mary was to spread her legs for her dark cousin whenever he desired, or Ian would make her life very unpleasant, indeed.

"I—I canna believe ye intend what you imply, Ian," she said, afraid, though her voice was cold.

"Aye, ye take my meaning well enough!" he retorted, eyes roaming over her figure lasciviously, as though appraising her worth and the price she might bring him. "Hugh wants ye still, and ye would do well to treat him wie compliance. Ye hae whored for the Romany and for Edward too, for ye love him nae, though ye wedded him in bargain to save yourself from banishment. Aye, ye sold yourself to Edward; ye can do as much for his half brother, my lady, or you'll find yourself wie'oot a roof o'er your head after all."

"Edward—Edward will gain a place for us in Court, Ian. Dinna seek to threaten me!"

"That puling pup!" her brother snorted derisively. "He is a dreamer, nae a doer. He has resigned himself to his lot wie'in the clan, and Hugh will bring him to heel like a smart bitch dog if he thinks to stray!"

"Perhaps, Ian." Mary conceded this point, for she knew 'twas true. Then she flung her head up proudly. "But if 'tis whore I am to be, then I'll spread my legs for no less than the King himself, for they say Jamie is oft taken wie a bonnie face. Dinna force my hand, my lord, or it may be ye who is wie'oot a roof!"

Ian hissed sharply, seeing she meant the words, the bitch! Aye, she *would* run to Jamie, the lustful King, and he would be only to happy to take her into his bed. If she gained his favor, he would deny her naught, for Jamie had proven himself a generous ruler.

"Think ye I would let ye leave here to cast yourself into the King's arms?" Ian snapped. "I am your lord, sister; ye answer to me."

"Nay, Ian, I answer only to Edward, my husband, and ye are a fool if ye believe I canna persuade him to my cause, in spite of ye and Hugh," Mary lied desperately.

Ian drew himself up angrily. "Verra well then. I shall gie Hugh your answer, madam, but ye will regret it, I promise ye!"

The words haunted Mary, for she had been safe with Hugh at Leabaidh a' Nathair where he had had Lord Gilchrist's service to occupy his time. Now that he was laird of Dùndereen he gave orders instead of taking them, and his time was his own. He came often to Bailekair, always hoping to catch Mary alone.

So frightened did the girl grow of him and Ian that she sought out Alan and cajoled him in to teaching her in secrecy those things learned by a young squire or knight: how to wield a dirk or broadsword with deadly accuracy, how to aim a lance and hit her mark from Desmond's back, how to shoot a bow and arrows, how to swing the heavy mace. If Alan questioned her motives in learning such things, he said naught, but did as he was bid. He even had the blacksmith forge special lighter weapons for Mary's use. She soon became surprisingly adept at all her lessons, but 'twas the dirk with which she really excelled. Now the piercing silver blade hung always at her side. She would not face Hugh Carmichael defenseless when he came.

She crept around furtively at Bailekair, never knowing when he might be lurking in some dark corridor or lounging jeeringly in the main hall, his dark head bent close to Ian's and Lady Margaret's blond ones.

The Countess's face soured daily, like milk that spoils

when left, forgotten, without the coolness of the larder. Deep lines etched their marks upon the skin she sought so vainly to keep youthful, and not all of her powders and creams could spare the onslaught of the wrinkles born of her hate and greed. Mary thought 'twas sickening the way Margaret flirted with her son and nephew, as though she were a young lass and they her lovers.

To Mary, Bailekair's household became a place of unhappiness from which she escaped whenever she could. Oftimes she sought her father's grave, as she had done today, for she seemed to feel the nearness of his presence there and find some measure of peace in her saddened life. For the dull ache in her heart was with her always, though she had become accustomed to it. She longed for her beloved more fervently with each passing day and knew it was a yearning time would not rid her of, though nearly a year of parting lay between them. Her eyes searched the horizon ceaselessly for a tall dark man upon a pale white steed, but she might as well have looked for a ghost.

Her son, Geoffrey, was her only small comfort. He grew rapidly, in spite of his premature birth, and she felt a mother's pride each time he suckled at her milk-laden breasts. He had Edward's deep blue eyes, and for that the lass was grateful, for she did not think she could have borne the sight of eyes as violet as her own and Hunter's accursed ones. But Geoffrey's mouth was hers, showing the promise of her arrogance and pride, and some of the fear that he might not survive lessened when she heard the angry, stubborn squall that rose from his lips each time his tiny will was thwarted. She was glad he had not his father's frailty, for her son would need to grow strong if he were to make his way in the world.

Sighing, the girl laid the few naked branches, fallen from the mountain-ash trees, she'd gathered earlier upon the mound of frost that was her father's grave, traced the words chiseled upon the cold, granite stone at his head, then walked away. She felt restless, for the peace she had thought to find had not come to her that day. And suddenly she realized for the first time since her father's death and the birth of her child that she was alone. *Jesù!* How many other such precious opportunities had she wasted, wrapped up in her grief, motherhood, and fear as she had been?

Did she ride that way knowing? Mary never knew. But she was drawn there all the same, to the cliff overlooking the loch, where 'twas said an old crone had once delivered a curse that even now shrouded Mary's life in shadows, reached out to embrace her from the grave. To Mheadhoin, village of death, she rode.

It started to snow once more. The crystal flakes clung to Mary's hair and eyelashes like the grey Scottish mist and played hide-and-seek among the black strands of Desmond's wild mane. She shivered. Why had she come here?

Up ahead, set on a small hill a little way above the village, the girl could see the rock walls of the kirk, its high steeple topped by a solid stone cross reaching upward to the heavens. It looked grey and forbidding; the colors of the stained-glass windows had been dulled by time and now the white flurry of cold powder that crept in through the many now-broken panes. Mary was drawn to it like steel to a magnet.

She dismounted, pushed the heavy wooden doors open. They creaked on rusty hinges, protesting loudly her violation of the kirk's solitude. It was empty, deserted inside, dead, just like the village. Snow drifts covered the rotted oak floor, a floor Mary realized must have once gleamed with loving pride and care; the soft whiteness was banked against the few pews that still survived, in spite of the ravages of time.

It was cold, unearthly, a desolate, depressing scene. Even the cobwebs, remnants of the spiders' summer toil, strung across the dark corners and interlacing the rafters, glistened with the stark frost. Aye, death lay over the kirk with its silent stillness as surely as it touched her father's grave. Mary turned to go.

He stood there, lounging idly against the doorjamb, waiting for her as he had waited nearly a year. And Mary knew, when she looked into his violet eyes, naught had changed between them. With a cry of joy she flung herself into Hunter

MacBeth's outstretched arms, kissed fervently that mouth she had branded as her own.

There were so many words to say, and yet they did not need them. There would be time later to wash away the pain that lay between them, the guilt that haunted them still. Their need for one another overwhelmed them in that moment. Without speaking they sought a sheltered place within the kirk.

Mary had no thought of Edward, her husband, as her beloved spread his great cloak for them upon the raised dais of the altar, for though she and her childhood friend were bound by the ancient vows of marriage, Hunter held her heart—had always held it—and the words of love they had spoken between them were to Mary no less honorable. Indeed they were more dear, for they had been given freely, not bought with a band of gold. Nor did she think of Geoffrey, for no bairn, no matter how loved by its mother, can ever take the place of her own heart's desire. Nor did Mary think of the sin, of the eternal damnation that was surely hers for the crime of adultery. It seemed no sacrilege, the love she and Hunter shared. Fate had charted the course of Mary's life, not she. Edward was a stranger to her now; only Hunter was real, made her feel alive again! Surely God was kind, merciful, and understanding. Surely He would not condemn such a love as theirs, a love they sought so eagerly beneath the roof of His blessed house!

Hunter crushed his mouth down on hers, forcing her to his cloak, his hands wrapped in the masses of her long gold hair. His tongue teased, taunted her, driving in and out of her lips with a savageness that set Mary's heart to beating, fluttering within her breast, and her head to spinning dizzily.

It had been so long—so long since a man had touched her—so long since her *love* had touched her! She needed no urging, no slow awakening to respond, for she was as ready as he. Her arms crept up and locked around his lithe back, feeling the muscles, powerful from years of battle, ripple beneath her cold palms. She shivered, trembled in his rough embrace, knowing how hard he fought to restrain himself, to take her gently as was his way. And then she warmed by the blazing fire that swept through her at his touch as he stripped her naked, tearing her woolen *arascaid* in his haste, feasting his violet eyes upon her golden flesh as though he could not get his fill of her. Golden, as he had remembered, as though bathed in the resplendent, glorious radiance of a mellow Scottish summer sun. How Hunter had wanted her, had longed for her! He cast away his garments, revealing every line of his hard dark body to Mary's loving, eager glance, every nuance, every scar that marked him as a Highland warrior. He knelt over her, kissed her breasts; the flushed nipples stiffened beneath his lips, his hands.

"'Tis sweet torture, this. Take me now! Now!" Mary whispered hoarsely, fiercely, brokenly, shameless and wanton in her passion.

But Hunter only smiled and went on kissing her forever: the pulse beating rapidly at the hollow of her throat, that soft place upon her shoulder. He kissed her mouth, lips melting across one scarlet corner to her cheek, her hair. He wrapped those golden strands around his throat, murmuring husky words against the silky tresses, against sweet lips that parted for him as though they had a will of their own.

Mary held him tightly, pressed herself against every part of him, felt the wetness of his masculinity upon her thighs. Her fingers traced the outline of his mouth before she kissed it. Her body slid down his; her cheek brushed the softness of the dark mat of hair across his chest, then touched the even darker bush lower still. Her lips caressed him lightly there, teasing, before she took him in her mouth, tongue whirling, fluttering, loving, traveling the length of his manhood, while he moaned with pleasure.

"Oh, God, Mary! Mary!" he breathed, his fingers entwining the cascading mass of her silken tresses as he pulled her to him, then gently pushed her away, afraid he might end their lovemaking far too quickly.

He stroked her flesh, her belly, her thighs, found the soft curls he loved so well. The lass quivered in response to his searching fingers. Hunter took her hand so Mary might feel him touch her there in an intimacy that made her swoon as though the earth had dropped out from beneath her feet. She gave a small, jerking sigh. He heard it and was pleased. He caught her other hand, held it fast as he lowered his head and put his mouth upon that trembling place, kissing the slender fingers intermingled in her honeyed moisture, while he tongued her slowly until she ached for him inside her. He sensed her yearning and eased it momentarily with one hand as he continued his tender onslaught into her senses until he felt the tremors that came to her again and again, and she tingled feverishly, her mind reeling from the explosions.

Mary cried out for him, tried to pull him to her, but he teased her still.

"Tell me, tell me what ye want," he spoke lowly, thickly. "I want to hear ye say it. Tell me."

She was shy with him. The words did not come as easily to her lips as the brazen things he whispered so boldly in her ear. He coaxed her. Desire made her speak. She told him.

He raised himself, towering above her upon his knees, his passion-darkened eyes raking slowly the length of her satin flesh spread before him. That gentle smile touched his lips again. His violet eyes were filled with tender triumph as he lowered himself over her body to kiss her breasts once more, and Mary felt his hard maleness pressed against the damp curls between her golden flanks. He reached for her hand, placed it upon his shaft that she might guide his flaming sword to her velvet sheath.

He entered her swiftly then, the jarring shock making her gasp aloud with sharp desire.

He pulled away to see her face, kiss her mouth, caress the sight of their joining with his eyes. Mary shivered at the intimacy of his gaze, longed fleetingly for darkness that he might not watch them thusly, seeking her response, forcing her passion to break through the walls she kept between them out of shyness and fear of being hurt. He wanted to be close to her, to explore the darkest chasms of her soul where even

Mary dared not venture, to believe she was his in a way she would never belong to another man, to know he had conquered her in every manner, possessed her always as his own.

Hunter did not speak these thoughts aloud to her, but Mary read them in his eyes and understood. It was the way of a man, the ultimate, primitive challenge that brought him to her, demanded her surrender, even while he loved her. It was cruel; it frightened her, made her vulnerable to him; but still she understood and could not deny the very essence of his manhood that commanded her response. Hunter loved her spirit—he wanted no clinging vine, no mating of his heart and soul with a woman who was not his equal—but his pride and arrogance were even greater than her own; and in this he was as liable as she. He needed her surrender to feel secure in his masculinity; and she needed to risk all and find he would not hurt her to trust him always as a man who would love, cherish, and protect her as her womanhood required. She would be his—and only his—until the moment he betrayed that precious trust; and then she would never truly belong to him again.

Somehow this age-old relationship was communicated between them without words, relayed by the triumph in Hunter's darkened amethyst eyes as he took her, the demand of his mouth against Mary's own, the force of his driving maleness inside of her, the flutter of Mary's downcast lashes when she could no longer meet his purple shards, the parting of her lips in gentle obedience, the arch of her hips as she received him. Aye, she was his, and he knew it when she gave a low cry of surrender, of wanting, of needing, and pulled him to her once again.

God! How he played upon the strings of her heart and body, her very soul! Like a skilled musician he aroused her with an all-consuming melody until she clung to him, her nails digging into his back with desire, her legs wrapping around his to draw him closer; until she rose and crescendoed against him, body singing like a rapturous lute, chords crashing, trilling, echoing to the rafters of the barren kirk again and again. He knew the moment of her sweet pleasure and gloried in it before he found his own, loving her until Mary lay sobbing in his arms from the joy and pain of the ecstasy he tore from her, gave back to her, shared with her.

Ah, she was a woman made for loving, was Mary Carmichael! She felt as though she were dying, as though Hunter had taken a part of her and yet left something of himself behind in return. She felt fulfilled to overflowing and marveled with wonder for the man who had made her thus. Softly he kissed the tears from her cheeks, her eyelashes, pulled her into the cradle of his strong arms, her head upon his bronzed chest that she might hear the furious pounding of his heart. Mary's happiness was complete. He had not turned from her in haste or indifference now that he knew her to be his. He held her still, kissed her still, wanted her still, loved her still.

And there was only the quiet mingling of their breathing to break the winter silence of the snow-enveloped kirk wherein two lovers lay.

They talked at last, and reality crept in harshly; like children who have just been told they cannot attend a party they have looked forward to for so long they were crushed, smothered by its chilly embrace, colder than the kirk now that their fiery lovemaking warmed them no longer with its glow.

"I thought no mon would take ye." Hunter's words echoed bitterly in the emptiness. "I waited for ye here, as I promised, but ye ne'er came. I lived through hell, fearing I had sent ye to your death after all. And when the King's letter arrived, telling me—"

"Dinna blame yourself, sir. I knew naught of Edward's love for me, for he had ne'er spoken. Och, Hunter! My heart ached for ye! I knew no way to send ye word of my plight, beloved, and my hours were empty wie longing for ye! Too many things happened so quickly: the war, my father's death—"

"And your marriage?"

"Aye—aye, that also, sir. Oh, Hunter, Edward loved me— canna ye understand? He—he thought to save me from banishment. He dinna know I—I had naught to—to gie him in return, that I longed to be sent from my clan that I might seek your arms. I hurt him deeply, and he cares for me no longer.''

"Then come away wie me, now! We'll leave here as we had planned and—''

"I—I canna, my beloved, though my heart yearns to follow yours, where'er it may lead me. Do ye forget I hae a wee bairn now?''

That wounded him; she could see it in his eyes and the quick jealousy that flared there also at the thought that another man had known her.

'' 'Twas against my will, he took me, Hunter. I would ne'er hae welcomed another mon into my bed. Surely ye know that!''

"It should hae been *my* bairn that filled your belly!'' he breathed fiercely, and Mary was frightened by his vehemence. "*Me* who stood beside ye at the altar! To think of ye lying in another's embrace—''

"Dinna tell me ye hae lived like a monk since our parting!'' The girl's voice was sharp with fear he would turn from her in his jealous rage.

He understood; his face softened.

"They meant naught to me, love. I did but use them and parted wie'oot care. Oh, sweet, I hae cursed my honor a thousand times since the day I lost ye!''

The lass suppressed the dull ache that invaded her heart at his first confession, feeling for the first time in her life the beginnings of the wound a man can inflict upon a woman. Ah, too much to hope he had been faithful all this time, true to a memory, a love so wild with passion it might have been only a dream.

"Ye hae nae lost me, my love,'' she answered quietly. "I am here now and wie ye always in spirit.''

Oh, tell me! Tell me ye love me! her heart cried silently, and take away this pain that tears at me inside. Tell me there is no other for ye, nor e'er will be!

Was there ever such a man who understood a woman's

228

needs so well? Who drew her close within the shelter of his strong arms and truly meant the words he spoke?

"Dinna fash yourself, lass. I thought ne'er to see ye again, or I wouldna hae touched another. Ye hae my heart, Mary, and now that I hae ye back I shallna sully our love by sharing that which we know by lying wie aught else. 'Twould be a poor substitute, indeed, for the love and joy I find wie ye. Och! Come away wie me, beloved! Bring the bairn. I hae love enough for two."

Och, would that she could! But even as her heart leapt at the thought Mary knew she could not do it. 'Twould be a certain death sentence for them all if they were to be caught, and Geoffrey was so young—she could not expose him to such a danger.

"Aye, I understand." Hunter laughed with bitter mockery when she told him of her fears. "Is this all there is to be for us then? Moments stolen together until we're discovered and slain, or is that risk too much for ye, too? Och, damn my pride!"

"That was unfair, sir." Mary felt his torment and despair as deeply as her own, felt him tremble with wrath at his own helplessness, saw the muscle that worked in his jaw as he struggled with himself for control. "I would rather die than live wie'oot ye again." Her voice was clear, like a bell now in the emptiness of the kirk, with no quiver of fright in its echo.

"My brave, bonnie lassie," he whispered. " 'Tis ashamed, I am, of my harsh words."

And Mary thought of her father, who had called her his lassie, and for a moment she was cold and sick with dread for the future. Then Hunter kissed her softly, and the shadows lightened.

"I love ye," Hunter breathed against her throat, as though aware of her thoughts again and longing to dispell them once more. "I shall always love ye, aye, and no doubt hurt ye, too. 'Tis the way of a mon toward a woman, else we would be slaves to ye all, so great is our passion for ye. Forgie me

229

that, and come here again to Mheadhoin, to me. I shall watch the Highland heaths for ye, as I hae done these many months past, and I shall be waiting, always waiting.''

'Twas madness, of course. The Clans Carmichael and MacBeth would kill them both if they knew. But still Mary could not hold back her fervent reply.

"Aye, I will come again, my love. There is naught could stop me!"

*I will come again*, she had said.

But Christmas came and went, and there was no time for her to slip away unseen to that place in the hills that beckoned to her heart.

The yule log burned brightly on the hearth in the long hall of Bailekair. Hugh gave Mary a Court gown of crimson velvet cut shockingly low—a whore's costume, a King's whore! And once more her fear of him rose to haunt her like a specter, for she knew he mocked her and sought to have her still. She gave the dress away, and if the lowly wench so favored questioned her lady's generosity, she did not show it as she clutched the frock greedily to her breasts with filthy hands. From Edward came a verse written by the castle bard and inscribed stiffly with a small message for Mary in her husband's delicate hand. She never read it, for she knew the words therein were penned without emotion, and their sad formality would only serve to remind her of the childhood closeness they'd shared and lost. Joanna had embroidered her a new tapestry for her small chamber; Gordon gave her bright ribands for her hair; Alinor and Charlie presented her with a warm woolen shawl the former had sewn. These gifts Mary accepted gratefully and used. From Lady Margaret and Ian the girl received nothing.

Hogmany passed. Three weeks later Mary rode out alone through the iron portcullis of Bailekair.

He was there, as she had known he would be, his tall dark figure hidden in the shadows of the kirk. She paused in the doorway to push the hood of her cloak back from her face, shaking her golden hair free from the confines of the woolen material. Hunter stepped forward, one hand outstretched to her, thinking again how beautiful she really was.

"Ye came."

"My days hae been years wie'oot ye." Mary's voice throbbed with passion before she flew to his open, waiting arms.

Slowly the tension drained from Hunter's body as he bent his dark head to kiss her eagerly, finding her warm moist lips in the grey half-light of the kirk.

"Tigress, tigress," he murmured. "Ye dinna know the hell I've been through thinking ye wouldna be able to return to me."

He had built a small fire on the altar because the kirk was so cold, and it was near this he led her, spreading his cloak upon the dais as he had done before, then laying the girl's own atop that. She trembled with wanting as he gazed at her. Hunter drew her to him, holding her close, warming her with the heat of his body and the fire.

"How I need ye," he said, stroking her shimmering hair softly.

"Show me. Show me how much ye need me, love."

And gently, fiercely, he did.

Afterward Mary gave him the bracelet she had braided for him for Christmas from the long, silken strands of her golden hair. He fastened the little gilt catch, interwoven in the tresses, around his wrist.

"I shall wear it always," he spoke gravely. "As ye must wear this."

He hooked a gold locket around her neck. Mary sprung the clasp. Inside lay a lock of his mahogany hair.

"Now we are truly *bound* to one another." She smiled at her small jest, but there was a sadness in her eyes all the same.

They lived in fear through those months that followed, torn between the Clans Carmichael and MacBeth, afraid one or both would discover their clandestine trysts and slay them; and indeed it was a miracle neither did. But in spite of this and the sadness that touched her at each parting, there was a happiness on Mary's face that had never been there before. Alinor thought it was a mother's pride in her son, for Mary spent a great deal of time with Geoffrey at the keep. Hugh thought it was because she managed to avoid him deftly on every possible occasion. Only Edward and Joanna suspected the truth, and they said nothing—Edward because he knew he had driven Mary from his side with his brutal rape of her and Joanna because she too shared a love and moments stolen such as Mary's.

Mary loved Hunter, och, how she loved him! And he, her! But they were only human after all, with human weaknesses, human failings; and though their passion for and excitement in one another remained intense from their forced separation, there was also a terrible, constant strain between them that frayed slowly from the guilt that haunted each and that, with the coming of spring, threatened to snap the fragile threads of their relationship.

For now that Scotland lay at peace once more, and the rushing mountain streams of the spring thaw marked the beginning of the warmer season, the clans were restless in their keeps. Like bears from slumbering hibernation they ventured forth; and, as with all animals, those among them who could not slake the lust that stirred their loins at the sight of the budding green shoots that marked the mating season turned to battle as a means of cooling the blood.

Hunter did not want to go. How could he? How could he lay to torch all his tigress held so dear? But how could he refuse? What reason could he give?

Nay, my Lord Angus. I canna make war upon the castle that spawned my beloved, burn the fields her dainty feet hae trodden, steal the cattle that would fill her small belly, rape the women she calls friends, slay the men she loves. I couldna face her afterward wie such guilt in my eyes and blood on my hands. Bailekair blood, Carmichael blood. She would turn from me in loathing.

Oh, love, love! Forgive me, for I must hurt ye once again.

High upon the machicolated ramparts of Bailekair Mary stood and watched the raiders, as she had watched them so many times in the past; only this time it was different, for this time she loved the marauder who stood out among the rest upon his pale white steed, his silver sword flashing as she remembered it of old; and her pain was that much greater for it. *How could he?* Each blow of his shining blade smote her heart with piercing sorrow.

The vast, fertile fields, once a sea of green beneath the gold of the spring sun, now blazed where the plunderers had set them afire, belching great clouds of black smoke that sullied the sweep of the clean, endless azure sky. The freshly tilled furrows of those acres as yet unplanted crumbled as the riders trod upon and galloped over the dark earth that the serfs had toiled so long and so hard to plow. The cattle lowed fearfully as they were driven off; the sheep stumbled and bleated as they followed mindlessly behind. Everywhere the blood ran red, and the dying sprawled, pitiful and ugly, where they had been cut down by the treacherous hands of the enemy.

Mary clenched her fists helplessly at her sides. It was not to be borne! Och, that her heart had been given to one who ruined the heaths of Bailekair! And yet even as the thought came she watched Hunter beat off an attack by Ian's men-at-arms and gasped in fear her beloved would be slain. She ran from the ramparts in tears, unable to remain, knowing if she were asked to choose between the two, her traitorous heart would claim Hunter nonetheless.

"Of course I was there." Hunter's defensiveness made him angry as Mary hurled her accusations at him defiantly in the kirk. "I canna refuse to raid Carmichael lands. The MacBeths would gie me no peace until they discovered the reason for it. What am I to say? That I love ye? Godamercy! There are many who *still* wonder what did pass between us at Wynd

233

Cheathaich, though Cadman backed my lies to the hilt! Wouldst see me hanged? And seventeen men, women, and children lie dead at Rath na Mara from a Carmichael attack!''

''Ye burn our crops, steal our cattle, rape our women—''

''I've touched no woman save ye since first I took ye here!'' His arm swept the kirk.

''Nanna's bairn was killed!'' The girl's stricken eyes filled with tears. ''He was only two months old, and she and Alan may ne'er be able to hae another child. Her delivery was difficult; she isna a young lass.'' Mary thought of Mistress Flora's screams the night of the birth.

She had not worried greatly over Nanna's pregnancy. Nanna was a crofter after all, strong and healthy from the years of hard work that were the lot of a serf. The villagers dropped their babes like sheep and were up and about again the next day, not like the nobility, who remained abed and were waited on hand-and-foot afterward. And if a serf died— Well, 'twas God's will and certainly no fault of the long hours of toil and meager sustenance that were the life of a crofter.

''I'm sorry,'' Hunter apologized bitterly. ''What else can I tell ye to ease your pain? So it has always been. Ye know that.''

''Aye, and so 'twill always be. We are fools, ye and I! Fools, do ye ken? We hae always been enemies, the Carmichaels and MacBeths, and so shall we always be such! We are fools to think otherwise!''

''Nay, nae ye and I, Mary. We are lovers. Lovers!'' Hunter snarled before he pressed her to the ground. ''Why canst thou nae accept that?''

His tongue pillaged the inside of her mouth, turning, twisting, seeking. She tried to fight him off in her rage, but he flung the weight of his body down over hers, pinioning her to the floor.

''We were fated for each other, sweet,'' he murmured, staring hard into her violet eyes. ''Ye canna fight the stars, any more than ye can fight me. Ye felt it yourself the first time I took ye, and ye gae yourself to me as ye always will.''

"Nay." She turned her face away from his gaze wrathfully. "I am a woman. I hae needs, just as a mon does. Ye fill them, but only for now, only for now!''

"Ha!" he laughed cruelly. "If that is the only reason ye come to me, why dinna ye let Hugh take Edward's place in your bed?''

"I despise Hugh—''

"And call me your enemy!" His hand swept over her breast, baring it to his touch. "Do ye want me to leave ye alone, to go and ne'er return here, is that it?''

"Why do ye torment me like this?''

"Ye torture yourself, tigress," he whispered. "I love ye. I would wed ye tomorrow if ye were free and raise your son as though he were my own. Why willna ye accept that?''

"Because Edward stands between us; the clans stand between us; nearly a hundred years of hatred and battle stand between us!''

"Nay, there is only your guilt, beloved. Guilt that I hae brought ye happiness. I, a mon your heart and body covet, but your mind seeks to deny!''

"Hae I no right to feel guilty? Ye are my mortal foe. So I hae been taught from the time I was auld enough to walk and talk. And I betray myself, my clan, and my husband and bairn each time I come to ye! Christ's son! I am ashamed to sit in kirk each Sunday!''

"Your husband," he sneered. "A mon who raped ye and then turned ye oot of his bed! And kirk—sweet *Jesù*, Mary! Ye commit this—this 'crime,' as ye call it, beneath God's verra roof!''

Hunter was, by this time, yelling at her, so afraid was he of losing her again. Mary could not help herself. She burst into tears. He was distressed by the sight and sounds of her weeping, appalled at his behavior.

"Hush, hush crying, sweet," he said more gently. "Dinna allow them to tear us apart like this.''

"Oh, Hunter. I love ye so much. Why do I feel this way then?"

"Because ye are decent and honorable. Do ye think I feel nae the same, that I would take ye as my mistress if I could hae ye to wife, that I dinna know there are those who would call ye whore and spit upon all that is precious between us? It kills me, I tell ye! And I blame myself and curse my clan for it, but it doesna change the way things are."

"Nay, you're right, of course. Och, Hunter! Hold me! Make love to me! I can forget—in your arms—I can forget e'erything save ye!"

"Nothing will e'er keep me from ye, I swear it," he vowed before he lost himself in her silken flesh and healed her tormented soul.

The torches blazed and hissed stealthily, like spitting cats, against the long walls of the main hall of Bailekair as the rain that marked the beginning of the April showers seeped down in little rivulets from the seams of the massive eaves, tracing the patterns of the weathered mortar that joined the great hulking stones of the grey keep. The flickering shadows arched and jumped feyly over the faces of the serving wenches who hurried to and from the cookhouse, heavily laden with ewers and platters, eyes blinking to dislodge the fine spray of moisture that clung to their lashes.

In Lord Magnus's day this room would have echoed with the raucous gaiety of the evening supper, in spite of the ravages of the weather outside. The dripping men-at-arms would have ribbed each other good-naturedly as they tousled each other's wet heads and offered lewdly to towel-dry the prettier serving maids. But naught tonight dispelled the somber atmosphere of the long hall, as though the miserable eve had somehow found its way inside the regal fortress. The men-at-arms ate sullenly. The wenches served hurriedly, glad to escape the unpleasant, sober chamber.

Mary felt a momentary pang of sadness and longing for days gone by as she slipped into her place at the table silently,

236

knowing she was late for yet another meal and hoping to be overlooked. Alinor gave her a worried, inquiring glance, but Mary turned away from the glittering, questioning eyes of her brother's wife. Perhaps Alinor guessed all, but she revealed little. Joanna, as always, looked at her sharply, but said nothing. Edward merely stared at his trencher.

The pounding of Mary's heart lessened slightly. Mayhap none would remark upon her tardy entrance after all. But, alas, this expectation was crushed as quickly as it arose.

" 'Tis late, Mary, as are ye," Ian said from the head of the table, his ice blue eyes lowered as he jabbed his fingers into the butter and smeared the yellow cream onto a thick slab of bread.

The agitated fluttering in the girl's breast resumed. Och! Why must she be late tonight of all nights? She cursed her foolishness as she realized suddenly that Hugh Carmichael sat at her brother's side. One pale, one dark, and yet how alike they were, the foster brothers whose greed and ambition had brought them both earldoms sooner than if they had had no hand in the matter. 'Twas for Hugh's benefit Ian chided her, for normally Mary was beneath her eldest brother's notice. Hugh, who took a cruel delight in seeing his once-betrothed persecuted in any manner, no matter how small or petty.

"I'm sorry, my lord," the girl murmured, popping a piece of hot meat into her mouth. It burned her tongue; hurriedly she reached for her wine chalice, upending the vessel so it hid the expression on her face.

"What? No explanation, my lady?" The Earl of Bailekair raised one eyebrow mockingly as he sneered the last words.

"I hae been to the cemetery to visit my father's grave," Mary replied, shrugging her shoulders as though the matter were of little importance. " 'Tis of no interest to ye, my lord, I'm sure."

"Oh, but 'tis, Mary," Ian answered slyly, while the others began to shift uncomfortably upon their benches, and Hugh smirked openly, as though waiting to see the lass squirm like a bug on a pin. "I am curious as to why ye feel compelled to seek the cemetery so often and why ye remain there until ye are late to supper and return long after dusk has settled on the land, especially on such a miserable eve.''

'' 'Tis peaceful there, my lord.'' Mary was careful to show her brother no disrespect, knowing how quickly his temper would flare in front of Hugh. ''I find the solitude restful and dinna notice the hour. As for the rain''—she shrugged again—'' 'tis sweet and cleansing, like the spring itself. Hae I no right to tend my father's grave?''

''But, of course, Mary.'' Ian spread his hands charmingly in a gesture much reminiscent of Hugh, putting the girl further on the defensive as he smiled at her in Lady Margaret's sour manner. ''I merely worry aboot ye, as I do all the members of my household. 'Tis unsafe for ye to ride oot alone and so often. Ye might be kidnapped and raped— again.'' He spoke the final word blandly as Joanna gave a small gasp, and the Countess sniggered mirthlessly.

Mary choked on her wine, longing to scream that the only danger to herself lay with him and Hugh, who watched her covetously from beneath half-closed black lashes; but she didn't dare to speak so with Edward sitting across from her like a stone, refusing to meet her silent pleas for help.

''I ride only on Carmichael lands, my lord,'' she managed to say calmly, ''as I am accustomed to doing from past. In my father's day 'twas safe enough. Is it nae still thus?'' she challenged him.

''The MacBeths grow bolder, more daring in their raids,'' he responded. ''I think it best if ye dinna venture oot alone again.''

Mary stared at his sly, smiling face, hating him, rage filling her breast, clawing its way up to gag in her throat. Hugh had done this surely! Spoken with Ian, told him to forbid her rides as punishment for her refusal of Hugh's crude offer. For Ian had feared Mary enough never to have troubled with her on his own since the day she had threatened to seek the King's bed. Mary cast her cousin a look of utter loathing. Hugh wanted to imprison her in the castle keep; to drive her mad with longing for the open moors, the feel of the wind against her face; to force her to acquiesce to his desires by making her beg him to take her like the whore he thought she was or face ever-diminishing freedom until she became little more than a slave in her own home. Och, how well the lass understood his warped mind, his clever, sadistic plan! A word here, a word there to Ian, and soon her life would become an unbearable living hell that only he, Hugh Carmichael, could ease. Hugh still held such sway over Ian. Mary could have wept with frustration and despair. She would never see Hunter again!

God's blood! She would go insane with yearning if she did not have that special fulfillment, that heady rapture, that drug of passion that made her forget her ruined marriage and her shamed state—if only for a little time. The balm that gave her the fleeting moments of happiness she lived for now.

Aye, Hunter loved her, wanted her, needed her; had made her feel alive again; had taken her to the heights of ecstasy, the depths of despair; filled her with joy, tormented her with guilt and grief. She could not, *would not* let that go without a struggle!

She swallowed hard, opened her mouth to protest—

"Mary is *my* wife, Ian." She was stunned beyond belief to hear Edward speak, to hear him acknowledge her in some manner. "And I dinna forbid her rides."

Mary gazed at her husband; he met her glance briefly, then looked away. He knows! she thought, and suddenly she knew without a doubt 'twas true. Edward knew she had a lover, had guessed who it was, and did not care—had even kept her secret and defended her against Ian and Hugh. Why? Why?

Of course. He was a dreamer, a romantic. The plight of two star-crossed lovers could not help but appeal to his imagination. The brave and charitable husband; the beautiful, passionate wife; the bold, gallant lover. How many times did such a scenario grace the pages of history? Edward would know and have read them all. 'Twas the old Arthurian triangle, and having lost the role of Knight Bedwyr, Edward would have settled for the wronged and gentle King. Aye, he would protect her guilty secret because he had loved her once—mayhap still. Och! How Mary suffered for that knowledge and the hurt she had done him. But she blinked away her tears and shot Ian and Hugh a smug, triumphant stare, tossing her head proudly.

Ian scowled blackly as Hugh's eyes narrowed with anger. The former tried a different line of attack.

"May I also assume ye dinna forbid her Confession?"

"Confession?" Edward's face filled with confusion as Mary felt her hands tremble.

"Father John informs me Mary hasna been to Confession for o'er four months," Ian spat. "And, in spite of this, she still continues to receive Communion at Mass!"

The entire table gasped, then fell silent at this remark, the very idea of such a sacrilege too terrible for them to comprehend.

"Well, Mary?" her brother jeered.

"I—I found Father John too—too set in his ways for my taste." She faltered lamely over the lie. "Father Matthew has been my Confessor since childhood. He hears my sins and prayers when I visit the cemetery. I—I saw no harm in that, my lord." She crossed herself mentally for telling so many untruths in one breath.

Ian glared at her suspiciously for a minute, then settled back upon his bench, shrugging as though it were unimportant.

"Father John was concerned for your soul, Mary. He feared ye condemned to eternal damnation. I shall tell him he worried in vain, although I'm sure he'll be disappointed ye preferred Father Matthew."

"A good priest is understanding, my lord." Mary smiled glibly, determined not to fall into the trap he had set for her.

She did not trust Father John, the new priest her brother had brought to Bailekair after Lord Magnus's death, claiming Father Matthew had grown too old and addled for his duties and relegating the elder man to the position of caretaker of the graveyard. Father John's eyes were sly and his penances far too strict for the small sins Mary had confessed to him in the past. She felt a seething hatred in him for all women, and twice he had accused her of flaunting herself before the men-at-arms of Bailekair, taunting them to wicked thoughts and behavior.

Moreover, the lass knew he did not keep confessions to himself as he was honor bound by his vows to do, for once Hugh had let slip a remark to her she had made in the privacy of the Confessional booth; and Mary had realized after reflection that he could only have heard it from the priest. Nay, she could not confess to that fanatical Father, could not tell him of her adulterous affair, the forbidden release she had found for her traitorous, young heart and body. He would label her a whore, a harlot, a temptress, and would lose no time in informing Ian and Hugh of her trespasses.

Still, she should have recognized the priest would remark upon her absence from Confession and wonder why Mary still continued to receive Communion. She would *have* to be more careful! When Mary received the Holy Sacrament on Sundays, she would spit it out into her handkerchief when she thought no one was looking. It grieved her deeply to commit this atrocity, but she could not swallow the wafer when she had not made a full confession of her sins. She would have been mortally damned for certain. Bad enough to carry the burden of guilt on her conscience for the betrayal of her marriage vows, with a man who was an enemy of her clan, without making a mockery of the Holy Eucharist as well.

Sweet *Jesù*. Mayhap someone *had* seen her perform this act at Mass. She must be more careful!

As for Father Matthew, he really was senile as Ian had claimed, and their questions, should Mary's brother and Hugh seek to interrogate him, would doubtless only confuse the old priest. Mary could not, in reality, confess herself to the elderly man, for he had known her since childhood and would have been hurt and shocked by her revelations.

She pushed her bench back from the table.

" 'Tis late," she said, reiterating Ian's first words, "and my bairn will be hungry."

She left the hall hurriedly, feeling Hugh's black eyes bore into her back with hatred—and desire—all the way.

'Twas in the shadowed corridor leading to the small chamber she shared with Edward and their child that Hugh caught her, pressing her up against the wall, leering into her face so she could smell the soured stench of ale upon his breath when he laughed cruelly at her distress.

"So ye mourn the auld bastard, do ye?" he gripped her arms tightly, bruising her tender flesh with his callousness.

Mary was frightened, but she daren't show it, for there was no telling what he might do in his drunken state.

And so her words rang bravely, challengingly in the dark hall.

"Aye, I mourn my father, Hugh; my father, whom ye slew. And each time I kneel upon his grave I swear his death willna go unavenged. One day I will hae my recompense, and I shallna even need to wield the sword that will cut ye down as ye did him!"

"Witch!" Hugh rasped hoarsely, and for a moment there was panic in his black eyes. Mary seized upon it quickly, knowing her bravado would soon desert her otherwise.

"Aye, 'witch,' the crofters call me, my lord, and there are many who make the sign against me. Ye should hae thought of that before ye killed my father!"

He shook her roughly.

"Cease this prattle, bitch!" he hissed. "Satan's tricks—pah! Naught are ye save mortal whore. Whore!" he spat, and before the girl realized his intent he was tearing at the bodice of her gown, fingers groping down the hollow between her breasts.

Mary thought she must die of shame as she struggled with him frantically, clawing at him like some wild beast until he seized her wrists, jamming his carnal mouth down hard upon her own screaming one. His tongue shot deeply between her lips, making her gag. She kicked out at him with one booted foot, catching him sharply on the shin.

"Whore!" he growled again. "You'll pay for that."

She saw then he meant to strike her, tried to raise her arms to shield her face from the cruel blow.

"Let her go, Hugh." Edward's voice echoed softly in the corridor.

Hugh stepped away from Mary, laying one hand warily on the hilt of his sword. "The bitch led me on," he lied. "Begged me to take her. 'Tis a whore you've wed, brother, and no mistake!"

"You're drunk, Hugh," Edward spoke. "And I've no wish to quarrel wie ye, so let's just forget this ugly episode."

After one tense moment Hugh laughed. "The coward again, brother? Verra well then. I hae no wish to dirty my blade wie the blood of a faint-heart!"

And then he was gone. Mary pulled the edges of her bodice together raggedly, fingers shaking.

"Thank ye, my husband."

For one wild eternity she thought Edward meant to finish what Hugh had started, for he gazed at her heaving, ripe breasts with hungry, ravaged eyes; Mary shrank away from him, startled and appalled. He saw her cringe and grimaced bitterly.

"You've naught to fear from me, madam." The words were curt. "Get ye to your bairn; I shallna touch ye! Aye, get ye to Geoffrey, madam, that ye may teach him the ways of the Highlands so he mightna grow into a frail poet of a dreamer such as myself, but a bold, valiant warrior such as your lover! Aye, your lover, madam! Think ye I dinna know the reason for your lonely sojourns upon the moors? Well, get ye to the MacBeth if he is mon enough for ye, for I shall ne'er be; and raise your son in *his* image that Geoffrey might win many a battle and a keep of his own in the bargain. Nay, nae Dùndereen." He glimpsed the unspoken question in Mary's wide violet eyes. "Nae Dùndereen, where Hugh has sat in my father's chair, supped from my father's silver plates, bedded my father's women. My father! Whom Hugh and Ian slew! Oh, aye, I guessed the way of it, for I was there, remember? *I was there,* and I did nothing. Oh, God, forgie me for my weaknesses!"

A racking cough took hold of him; he put one hand to the wall for support, his body heaving from the painful rasps.

"Edward! Are ye ill?" Mary asked as she tried to help him get his breath.

"Nay!" he shoved her away irritably. " 'Tis naught but this miserable, damp weather—a chill has settled on my chest. I shall be all right, madam. Dinna think to run freely to your lover so quickly!"

And then he too was gone. Mary stood alone in the darkened hall, tears of self-pity streaking her face.

Dreams came to Mary again that night, troubled dreams, horrible dreams. Dreams in which she stood beside Hugh Carmichael in the wedding gown she had worn during her marriage to Edward and spoke those same eternal vows with her black-eyed cousin, instead. Felt him seize her lips with his own brutal ones to seal her fate forever. And then he was tearing at her clothes, forcing himself upon her, inside her— She cried out, awakening in a cold, trembling sweat only to find Edward sitting by the fire, gazing at her with pity in his deep blue eyes.

"My lord. 'Tis nearly dawn." Mary was alarmed. "Didst I waken ye wie my nightmare, or hae ye nae slept this eve?"

"I couldna rest easy," he said, but when the lass would have arisen to comfort him, he waved her away.

"Nay," he gasped. "What I want from ye, wench, ye canna gie; and brute and fool was I to try to take it. Leave me be. There is no worldly cure for that which ails me."

And so they waited in silence for the first pale streaks of dawn to touch the sky. Not ten feet of distance lay between them, but it might as well have been an eternity, so far apart were they.

Hunter swore when he saw the bruises Hugh had made upon Mary's arms.

"Goddamn that bastard! I *will* kill him!" he raged, reminding her of that night they three had stood within the shadows of the King's gardens at Holyrood Palace, and she had smelled the scent of death upon his flesh. "He'll nae hae ye, tigress; that I promise ye! I'll slay him first or be dead myself ere he touches ye!"

"Oh, love, love! What are we to do?"

244

"Shhhhh," he whispered gently, kissing the strands of her golden hair. "This is our world, now and here in this barren little kirk. And for today naught can mar our lives; we are alone save for each other. Ah, come love me, Mary."

Blind with passion, she moved into his arms, turned her face up to his, felt his mouth, warm and seeking, caress her own softly before it became harder, more urgent, demanding in its hunger. Mary trembled in his strong embrace, marveling that he only needed to touch her to make her quiver with longing, ache with desire.

"He willna hae ye!" Hunter's face darkened again as he thought of Hugh Carmichael, and his voice thickened with anger and passion. "Ye are mine! Mine! Oh, God, I love ye." He pressed her to the floor, raining searing kisses upon her temples, brushing outward onto her golden hair, burying his lips, his nose, his eyes, his face into the shimmering, cascading mass. His hands gathered great bunches of it, soft and silky as he breathed in its heady fragrance. Heather, always heather, Mary used; and he would always associate that sweet, dizzying scent with her now. "I love ye like no mon has e'er loved a woman, I swear it. In truth, ye are a witch, Mary Carmichael, for ye hae cast a spell upon me from which I shall ne'er be free, nae as long as I live. Oh, tigress!"

He tore at her *arascaid,* impatient in his haste and yearning for her, fingers rough against her satin skin. Mary shivered as he stripped her naked, then scattered his own garments heedlessly, the massive muscles flexing in his arms and back. She felt a thrill of excitement shoot through her at the sight, mingled with a tiny twinge of fear as well. How many men had that powerful body slain? And yet he cradled her as tenderly as a bairn. 'Twas an awesome feeling, knowing the hands that caressed her so gently might just as easily have snapped her neck with a single sharp movement. Aye, this is why we are defenseless against them in the end, Mary thought, why a woman trembles so violently wie desire when a mon such as this takes her in his arms. 'Tis the awesome power of them that overwhelms us and the knowledge that though we hae gentled it for a time, 'tis always there, just beneath the surface, ready to spring like a panther upon its prey. 'Tis brutal; and for all their inner strength women are fragile creatures, needing to be cherished and loved.

*Jesù!* To be loved by such a mon as this! If we are discovered today, this hour, this moment, and killed, 'twill hae all been worth it. Aye, worth it just to know I hae seen his violet eyes darken wie passion, as they are now, when he gazes upon me, worth it to know I hae been woman enough to tempt this mon, to tame that awesome power—if only for a little while—to feel it wrapped around me, within me. . . .

"Make love to me, Hunter." Mary's voice was soft and slurred with passion and lust. "For I hunger for ye."

He needed no urging. His mouth closed over hers violently, bruising her crimson lips, lips that parted for his tongue eagerly. She met them with her own, as savage as he in her desire until they were both gasping for breath. He pulled away to kiss her cheeks, her earlobes, her temples, her eyelids, muttering her name, describing boldly, brazenly, the things he was going to do to her. Mary shuddered with wanting, blushed shyly at his intimate words, wishing his raking eyes did not seek hers to ferret out her thoughts, as though to claim her soul as well as her body. He laughed when she turned away from his hungry stare, for her silent denial of his right to probe the chasms of her mind told him more eloquently than words how close he was to making that elusive essence of her being his very own.

"Aye," he breathed. "I will hae that too, beloved. In the end there will be no part of ye that isna part of me as well."

"Ye would take a great deal, sir."

"I would gie a great deal in return. Trust me."

What magic did he weave as his teeth sank lightly into her shoulder, his hands cupping her breasts as he pressed the length of himself against her? His mouth teased the pulse beating rapidly at the base of her slender throat, then moved lower to suck gently at the swollen pink nipples, like two sweet, ripening cherries upon her blossoming breasts, and then sank lower still to the soft curls that twined between the thighs that opened for him of their own accord, aching, wanting. Mary felt dazed and lethargic and yet vitally alive and excited all at the same time, as though she could have lain there forever thusly, his tongue tracing the quivering swell of her womanhood urgently.

She moaned and writhed as the quicksilver tremors began to course through her flesh; her blood burned like waves of flame, searing in their ecstasy, building until her hips rose up wildly to meet his caressing lips. He yanked away in triumph as she cried out, his hot and ready maleness melting into her with a savage surge of power, pirouetting down into the depths of her being furiously, like a whirling maelstrom, intoxicating in its vertigo. Mary breathed raggedly against him, clung to him feverishly, her body exploding beneath his.

He panted in her ear heavily as he drove harder and harder into the sweet, silken nectar of her flesh.

"Christ! Oh, sweet Christ!" he groaned.

Their hearts beat frantically against each other as they lay still together in that moment after blind satiation. Mary could feel little rivulets of sweat pouring down her sides. Hunter moved from her, smiling at her glistening nakedness.

"There is a leak in the roof, tigress, for we hae been rained upon this last hour."

A slight flush stole across Mary's cheeks.

"Rogue." She grinned, a dimple peeping at one corner of her mouth. "And yet I'll warrant ye speak verily, sir, for in truth I did hear the roar of thunder in my ears and felt the rush of lightning spark my veins."

"Wench!" Hunter gasped, laughter choking him. "Ye will be the death of me!" he said, then sobered all too quickly. "Nay! Nay! I spoke in jest, lass." He was horrified by the sudden tears that started in Mary's eyes. "I dinna mean—"

"I know, I know," she sobbed as he pulled her close, and she laid her head upon his chest. "Oh, Goddamn their bitter feud! 'Tis tearing me apart inside. I want to be wie ye always, to wake in the mornings and see your dark head lying next to mine. I hate them!''

"Hush, sweet, hush. We canna change the ways of the Highlands. Och, Mary. Be glad we hae moments even as these, no matter our guilt and shame for them.''

"I am, God knows, I am, but—''

"Aye, I would hae ye to wife honorably, nae that of another mon taken in deceit and forbidden rapture, but if that is the only way for me to hae ye, then so be it, for hae ye I will, lass, and no mon will gainsay me!''

"Oh, Hunter! 'Tis tempting fate to love so much, to want ye so badly I dinna even care I am wed to another! We shall be punished for our sins.''

"Nay. There is no crime in loving, Mary.''

"I want to believe ye,'' she said fervently. "I want so much to believe ye!''

"Then believe,'' Hunter implored before he took her in his arms once more.

But this time there was a different kind of urgency to their lovemaking, as though they would never see one another again and were trying to imprint each detail of the other upon their memories so they would have those if nothing else; and they were sick at heart at their parting.

That day, when Mary left him, a great storm blew up. The sky turned dark and angry, and the rain that shattered from the giant, black clouds beat upon her fiercely, nearly blinding her with its sharp, biting sting. Desmond snorted wildly, whinnied high with fear, his eyes rolling so the girl could see their frightened whiteness at the corners.

Vast Loch Ness far below heaved and washed upon the shore, waves roaring, tumbling, seeming to grow taller with each thundering thrust of the undercurrent; and each swirling gust of wind grabbed at the whitecaps as though to pluck them from their peaks and hurl them along its wild rush.

Mary was terrified, for although she had never seen the like, she knew from stories sung of old that the crashing surf could spew over its banks, flooding the entire terrain beyond.

She laid her whip to Desmond's sides, trying to outrun the engulfing tide.

'Twas then she saw it, a hulking mass in the midst of the whirling waters. Like some Scylla or Charybdis it rose from the grey depths, its head and neck the length of a python or more and similar in its snaky appearance, the slender stretch too small, it seemed, to belong to the huge, rounded hump of its body. It was as an elephant or camel swimming might have looked, save for the horrendous size of the creature.

Sad, Mary thought it, lonely and forlorn, forsaken by all others of its kind if such had ever existed, monster to the fey folk of the Highlands, shrouded in their superstitions even as Scotland lay shadowed in mist.

Its sorrowful call rang above the high wind of the storm, tearing at her heart even as parting from Hunter had done.

Aye, weep for me! Mary gazed at the beast wistfully. Weep thy sad lament, thy keen of sorrow, monster, for my heart is too full of its own anguish to gie way to tears, else they flow like a river, ne'er ending. Aye, weep for me and mine, but let it nae be a dirge of mourning, a requiem for me and my beloved.

The monster seemed to understand, for it glided away as silently as it had come, back to the depths of the turbulent Loch Ness. Still it frightened Mary, as the unknown does always; and she fled from the dark beast of myth and omen, filled with foreboding for the future.

# Nineteen

The sun shone orange and yellow in the blue summer sky. A hint of breeze swept over the wide expanse of deer grass, which rippled across the open terrain and whispered gently to the leaves of the birch trees that formed a small grove at the edge of the bracken-filled moors.

Joanna Carmichael sighed, a sound as plaintive as the wind, and stretched her lithe, naked body languidly, soaking up the warmth of the sun's hot rays as they caressed her honeyed skin even as her lover had done moments just past. The quiet, leonine man beside her frowned briefly, his eyes filled with sudden pain.

"Art thou sorry, dearest fawn?" he questioned hesitantly.

The girl smiled reassuringly. "Hae ye nae asked me that upon each occasion of our lovemaking, and hae I nae replied 'nay' each time also?"

"Aye." Gordon Carmichael nodded. "But—och, Joanna! I wouldna bring shame upon ye, and I know in your heart there is sorrow for what we hae done."

"Nay! Nay!" She pressed her fingers against his lips. "Dinna speak so—'tisna true."

"If only I could make ye my wife—"

"Nay, love." She embraced him gently, knowing how much the thought tormented him. "Ye canna wed a baseborn maid such as I—I, who know nae the name of my father and hae no dowry wie which to enrich the Carmichael coffers."

"I care naught for that."

"Aye, I know, but your family does. I'll nae see ye lose your rightful place wie'in the clan for the likes of me. I amna good enough for ye, Gordie, bastard wench that I am."

"Ye will drive me to distraction, lass." Gordon made a poor attempt at playfulness, for his eyes were sober, in spite of his smile. "Ye are worth a thousand kingdoms; so soft, so gentle, so fine, as the sweetest fawn in the forest so like are ye. Dinna hold yourself so cheap."

"I am what I am, my love, and naught can change that. I am happy for whate'er moments we share together. Dinna ask for more."

"'Tis ye who are too good for me, lass," he breathed before he pressed her down upon the sweet green summer grass once more.

Mary was to go again to Edinburgh, to Holyrood Palace, whose narrow corridors she had thought never to step foot in again. Alinor had found a place for herself, Mary, and Joanna at Court for the summer, for young Jamie had taken a mistress, pretty Mariot Boyd, and needed ladies to attend her. Ah, how thrilled was Mary their bonnie King had given his approval of their service. She, who had been shamed and disgraced, brought down from her proud rank as daughter of the Chief of the Clan Carmichael to dishonored wife of a second son and knight—she would hold her head up high again, daring her clan to mock her now. For when Jamie received her the stigma of her disgrace might be removed. Who would dare chastise her if the King glanced at her with favor? And Mary meant to make certain he did!

She prepared herself for the journey ahead with a smug triumph, for Hugh and Ian had trod warily in her presence since the summons from Scotland's ruler, no doubt wondering if Mary intended to make good her threat against them and seek young Jamie's bed.

Her joy increased a thousand-fold when she learned Hunter was to be in Edinburgh also, for her heart had been sore pressed to think of parting from him, even though he had bade her go when she'd told him Alinor's news.

"Aye, lass." He swung her into his arms, whirling her about like a madman in his happiness. "The whole summer will be ours, for Angus's leg still pains him like the devil, and he'll nae travel to the tourney. Besides, rumor whispers that more plots abound against the throne, and I've a need to see David to confirm the truth of the matter."

He was honest in his words, Mary knew, for only some months before there had been trouble at Methven when some of the lairds had attempted to rise up against young Jamie. Och, will it ne'er cease? the girl wondered. For all its power and glory, a crown would weigh heavily upon one's head.

The summer sun was glorious in its radiance when the small retinue from Bailekair set out toward the gates of Edinburgh. Flowers bloomed in riotous color upon the moors;

the more fragile of these huddled at the bases of the gorse that sprang up here and there in clusters of green amidst the gold-and-purple sweep of the heaths.

They spent four wonderful days upon the road to Edinburgh, talking and laughing as they traveled, drinking and dancing each night they passed at some wayside inn; for neither Lady Margaret, nor Ian accompanied them, and the shadow those two cast receded.

Mary had almost forgotten how huge Edinburgh was, and she drank in the sights as they clattered through the city streets.

Edinburgh lay in a valley that sprawled gently with curving slopes to the harbor of Leith, a few miles to the northeast; the glen itself, however, was wild and rough. Great random crags thrust upward from the land. Some of the peaks were actually extinct volcanoes. The vast swells of the hillsides were ridged and broken, for here too, as in the Highlands, wide expanses of ice glaciers had once dominated the earth. When storms raged upon the North Sea, the high winds moaned with untamed lament through the towering cliffs and down Edinburgh's narrow twisting alleys to the moor beyond.

High upon sheer basalt bluffs Edinburgh Castle surveyed its domain regally, gazing down toward the cluster of houses and buildings that lined the crest below and formed the main bulk of the town. The spur of rock upon which the edifices huddled linked the old keep to Holyrood Palace at the east edge of the village walls. To the south, at the foot of the hard, castle crags, Grassmarket, the town marketplace, sat in a patch of green from which trees grew up in neat little rows.

Here and there cathedral and chapel spires rose upward to the heavens, stone crosses stark against the azure sky.

Like the flowers upon the moors the city was a blaze of color. The Royal *breacan* of the Stewarts, the *breacans* of the clans: the Murrays, the Canmores, the Irvines, the Davidsons, the Ruthvens, the Boyds, the Sinclairs, the Ramsays, and countless others, mingled with the simple homespun garments of the common folk and the district *breacans* of the Edinburgh middle class that belonged to no clan. The black robes of the monks and magistrates were the only somber notes in all the city's glitter.

Dogs barked incessantly. With stout sticks gangs of young lads batted barrel hoops through the narrow wynds of the town, laughing as they raced down the steep stone steps of the alleys, dodging past the older inhabitants of the village, who sometimes smiled at them in delight, remembering the days when they too had skipped and run carelessly through the cobbled streets; or frowned at the boys, calling sharply for them to have care, or shaking an angry fist, muttering sullenly to themselves about the lack of law and order within the town.

Mary heard snatches of conversation as she rode along also.

"That's two more shillin's ye're owin' me, Master Seaton, and nae another drop of whisky will ye be gettin' until 'tis paid!"

"I beg to disagree wie ye, sir. 'Tisna a question of man, but of God!"

"Do ye go to MacDuff's house then? Fine. I shall see ye there this eve. Mark ye mind your manners, for the Earl has three bonnie daughters, and his wife, Lady Claire, has a powerful sharp tongue upon occasion!"

"Here, ye lad. Here's a penny for ye if ye watch my horse while I'm in Master Robertson's shop, and another if you're still here when I come oot again."

Och. How well Mary had begun to recall it all, and never was her excitement greater than when she entered the long, whispering corridors of Holyrood Palace to kneel again before a king.

Was there ever such a man as Scotland's sovereign lord? At sixteen he was but a year younger than Mary, and already weighed down by the burdens of monarchy. Though he was gay and boisterous, there was a serious dignity about young Jamie that commanded respect. He had the Stewart charm, which his father had so lacked, and the foresighted nobles among the land flocked to his side to beg his favor, for Jamie cared little for the base musicians and architects (or "fiddlers and masons," as some had called them) that had been his sire's downfall. Mayhap the sight of Rogers's and Cochrane's slaughter before the boy's eyes had etched itself too deeply in the memory of the man; but the King had no favorites such as his father had had. James grieved always for his part in his father's death and wore a heavy iron belt around his waist to remind him of the deed and as penance for his sin until the day he died.

All this Mary, with her deep sensitivity, saw when she raised her eyes to look upon her sovereign lord.

"Arise, Lady Mary," he said resonantly, "and let me see if ye really are the tigress I hae heard ye called."

The lass blushed, hot and crimson at his words, for 'twas Hunter's name for her the King used, and for one horrible moment she thought James must know all and intend to expose her before the Court as an adulteress. Then she recovered, for, indeed, she was the Lion's daughter, and there were many who called her by the name. She smiled, reminding herself Jamie was, in addition to being the King, a young and lusty man whose favor she desired. Her eyelashes fluttered delicately as she flirted oh-so-gently with His Grace.

"And am I, Sire?"

"If you've a tongue and temper like my cousin Lady Jane Gordon, my lady, then I must say 'aye.' " He glanced toward the Earl of Huntly's sister.

Mary looked warily at that which Patrick Hepburn coveted. Lady Jane was as golden as Mary herself, perhaps more so, for even her eyes were of a tawny shade. Mary had heard, of course, of the infamous marriage contract and knew the bride-to-be (although he had not yet said so) of the mighty Earl of Bothwell was a power to be reckoned with at Court. Still, Sir Hunter MacBeth was a favorite of the King as well. Mary took the lady's measure and swept her a slight curtsy, for though Lady Jane was cousin to young Jamie, Mary was still the daughter of an earl and the lady's equal.

"We Highland women are nae meekly raised, Your Grace." Mary chose her words carefully. "For 'tis we who must bear the mighty warriors who defend Scotland's borders and her King and we who must battle for our salvation when those same men hae failed in their cause of duty.''

She saw Jane Gordon's eyes flash with surprise and quick approval and knew she had gained a friend, for Jane's brother George had fought for James III and been exiled for a year for his part in the late rebellion.

Jamie's eyes narrowed, and for a moment Mary trembled in fear of his wrath at her impertinance; then he smiled, and she knew she was home free.

''Aye, ye hae a tart tongue, my lady, and a temper too, I'll wager. The heart of the Lion as well, for 'tisna many in your place who would hae spoken thusly to me, but your father was e'er a mon for truth and honor. Would my own had been as much. Ye are audacious as a Stewart in your boldness.''

''If so, 'tis due nae to my upbringing, Sire, but to the Stewart blood that runs in my veins,'' Mary said, reminding the King that, distant though the connection was, the Carmichaels were also kin to His Grace.

''Aye, I had forgotten, my lady, but am delighted to recall the relation.'' Then abruptly he changed the subject. ''We hae heard rumors in Court, Lady Mary, that my father's tourney wasna the last of your adventures.''

Mary was mortified he would mention such a thing to her and before the courtiers as well, but then doubtless all knew of her disgrace anyway, for news of such events traveled like wildfire through Scotland where one's very life might depend on knowing who was feuding with whom.

''Nay, Sire. 'Twasna,'' she managed to choke out.

''Dinna distress yourself, my lady.'' His Grace was kind as he cast a stern eye over his Court to be sure they marked his words. ''No doubt ye braved your ordeal as brazenly as any Stewart''—he stressed the name—''for we are nae gi'en to letting our trials get the best of us.''

Mary realized suddenly the King was offering her a piece of wise advice, telling her to hold her head high at Court and smoothing the way for her by making light of her kidnap and reinforcing the bond of kinsmanship between them. None would dare cut her now, for to do so would be to insult His Grace.

"Thank ye, Sire." Her violet eyes spoke volumes when she looked at him again.

"Ye are well-married too, are ye nae?" James continued, seeing she had heeded his silent warning.

"To Edward Carmichael, Your Grace."

" 'Tis well, for otherwise your bonnie beauty would certainly cause havoc in my palace." He laughed loudly at his observation; the others present joined in his mirth and approval, not wishing to be remarked upon by the King if they did not. Then James lowered his voice so his words reached Mary's ears alone. "I denied a boon for it, my lady. There was naught else the MacBeth would hae."

Mary had not known this, for Hunter had never told her of it. She was touched in a way she could never have been otherwise to know her beloved had held all Scotland at his feet and had requested only her. She had assumed he'd taken something else in her place—gold, land. But, nay, he had wanted only her. In that moment Mary's heart was in her eyes. She could not help it. And she knew the King saw it, for 'twas his business to know the hearts and minds of men.

"Sire—"

He cut her short with a wave of one hand, raising his voice once more so the Court could hear.

"We are well-pleased wie ye, Lady Mary," he toned most royally. "Ye will be as an amethyst among our jewels here at Court."

And smiling at his jest about her violet eyes, His Grace held forth one many-gemmed hand for Mary to kiss by way of concluding his audience with her. 'Twas only when she rose once more to take her leave that James said softly,

"Wie'oot his mind mon wouldna rule the world, lass, but 'tis the heart wherein his true happiness lies."

Mary hesitated for a moment, then nodded bravely, realizing the King had given his silent approval for any relationship she might have with Sir Hunter MacBeth. Then young Jamie, her sovereign lord, in all his dignified grace, winked at her before she turned away.

How happy Mary was that summer! Filled with laughter and gaiety such as she had not known since her childhood, for she was Lady Mary Carmichael once more, daughter of the once-Chief of the Clan Carmichael, who had died most honorably on the field of battle. James had made it so, and those who might have spurned Mary and wondered about her sojourn with Sir Hunter MacBeth forgot their idle gossip and speculation as they followed the King's example. Indeed, in reality, Mary's mind had exaggerated the matter because of her family's treatment of her, for there was scarcely a clan in Scotland that had not suffered some such like, since feuds were fierce and many in their day.

Except for Geoffrey, whom Mary had brought with her, she might have been a young, single maid again. She danced and flirted with the courtiers and clasped the secret of her lover to her breast as delightedly as any foolish girl, basking in the absence of Lady Margaret's sour face, Ian's pompousness, and Hugh's dark desire, for they would not arrive until a week before the summer tourney. Gordon had attained his knighthood at last, and, free to travel as he wished, had chosen to accompany the girls to Court. Ian had given Charlie also leave to come, only because Alinor's father, the powerful Earl of Eadar Da Voe, had persuaded him to do so. Edward had remained behind.

They were a gay party, the five, and if at times Mary felt the lack of a partner, 'twas only because Hunter could not be at her side, for there were many who escorted her and sought her favor, despite her being wed.

There was only one for her, however, and there were many nights she waited for the women in her chamber to sleep soundly so she might creep from the bed she shared with Joanna and Geoffrey to slip silently through the palace corridors to her lover's eager, waiting arms.

They made love feverishly, as though each time were to be

the last, and gloried in each other's nearness, for scarcely a day went by that they did not pass each other in some winding hallway or chance a lingering glance across the main chamber of the palace.

They hunted with the King and daringly lost themselves from the rest of James's party, their cries of ecstasy mingling with those of the hounds baying in the distance.

Indeed, it seemed as though their sovereign lord were a party to their affair, for he asked for them often: "Patrick." He would catch Lord Bothwell. "I should be pleased if Lady Jane and Lady Mary would accompany us this afternoon. And Sir Hunter, also. I find much to favor in that mon."

And if the powerful Earl suspected the reason behind His Grace's penchant for Lady Mary and Sir Hunter, he kept his tongue in his head, knowing Lady Jane's presence would be removed from these little excursions if he blabbed his thoughts about the palace halls.

Mariot Boyd, young Jamie's pretty mistress, was older than His Grace and wise for her years. She recognized her status at Court depended on her sovereign's favor and was not a demanding woman. Instinctively she knew the things that pleased the King, and a pompous display of one's own importance was not one of these. The ladies of her circle came and went as they desired, for Mariot was not one to have her women forever at her beck and call. Thus Mary's freedom was greatly unhampered, and her opportunities for being with Hunter were almost unlimited in number.

They grew much together that summer, Hunter and she. On early mornings before the dawn lit the sky, when Mary must hurry back to her own chamber, he tickled her like a mischievous lad until she boxed his ears and threw herself upon him, begging for mercy. Hunter shopped often in the market, bringing Mary pretty trinkets such as a ring or fan; and she chided him for spending his hard-earned sovereigns on such nonsense, but was pleased all the same. She mended his clothes, adding a fine bit of trim here and there, which she had purchased over *his* protests, longing to robe him in silk and velvet as rich as any laird's.

" 'Tis but a puir knight I am," Hunter mocked her when Mary said as much. "As I've warned ye oft enough. I hae nae the likes wie which to deck myself oot in, lass."

Mary only laughed at his protests.

"Ye should hae asked Jamie for lands and a title, instead of wasting your boon on the likes of me," she teased.

"Och, tigress. What were the use of gold trappings wie'oot a jewel for their setting?"

He smiled, but the serious intensity of his eyes gave truth to the words. Mary sighed and thought no two had ever loved more than they.

The summer tourney came and with it Lady Margaret, Ian, and Hugh. Mary smirked to herself at their obvious discomfiture and anger at finding her so solidly installed at Court. Oh, she was riding high once more! Secure in her position and forgetting "pride goeth before a fall." Only when she learned Edward had not accompanied them did the first inklings of doom trouble her.

"He refused to come," was all Ian would say. "And I had no need of him anyway."

This worried Mary, and the more she thought about it, the more she decided 'twas best if she returned to Bailekair, despite her happiness at Court. Edward was, after all, her husband, and she owed him something for the hurt she had caused him, albeit through no real fault of her own.

"Dinna go," Hunter pleaded with her that night as she lay safely within his arms. "Dinna go. I—I feel in my bones naught will e'er by the same if ye leave me now."

Mary laughed gently. "Och, is this the mon who has always jested at my foolish fears?"

"Mayhap I was wrong, beloved."

"Nay. Ye told me to believe, sir, and so I do. After the tourney I shall return to Edward for a time, for I am sore worried aboot him. But I will come back to ye, my love, hae no doubt."

But the King's summer tourney was to be a turning point in Mary's life, setting off a chain of events none could have foreseen and would not have believed had they known.

The tourney began well enough, for the day was blue and orange in its mellow radiance, not overcast with shadows as the first tourney the girl had attended had been. She was in a fine fettle as well, because Alinor, Joanna, and she had been invited to sit in the King's box. Mary could not help but cast a smug, triumphant glance at her mother, who was seated among the benches reserved for the lesser royalty. How reversed their roles were that day.

The opening joust began, and things proceeded smoothly for several hours. None clapped louder than Mary when Gordon, in his first major tourney, won his bout on the third run. And though she could not openly do so, her heart applauded silently when her beloved also unseated his man, then retired from the field, lips caressing gently the violet scarf favor Mary had tied about his arm that early morn.

'Twas near dusk tragedy struck, though the lass could not share in the grief it caused. Such a senseless death, it was, brought about by the careless laziness of an idle squire who had dawdled with a serving wench rather than see to his master's armor—not just once, which might have allowed the laird to escape unscathed, but many times. The metal had weakened from lack of vigilance in its care, for the steel must be constantly cleansed and oiled to keep it strong and free of rust. How the lord did not notice it Mary could not tell, but 'twas said afterward he was a busy and heedless man. It cost him his life that day, for his armor plate did not hold, but shattered on impact with his opponent's well-aimed lance. Moments later Lord Torquil, Earl of Rath na Mara and Cadman's father, lay dead upon the field.

Hunter was not overly grieved either, for he had thought his foster brother's father a hard and vain man; but he shared his kinsman's pain and ached for Cadman's sorrow.

" 'Twill go hard on him, Mary," he told her with a troubled frown. "What wie Cadman's bastardy he'll nae inherit, and although he knows it, 'twill be a bitter blow to him all the same. Though he ne'er speaks of it, I know he feels his lack of rank most keenly."

"He has a place wie Lord Angus surely."

"Aye, but the auld Bear sickens, lass, and his time of death draws near. Grace couldna save his leg. They had to cut it off at the knee, and I fear it still rots."

Mary shuddered, suddenly glad her father had died gloriously on the battlefield.

"And what of ye when Lord Angus dies?" she questioned anxiously.

"I dinna know, lass. I dinna know. Stephen is young and untried. In truth, I couldna serve him wie respect as I hae served the auld Bear."

And so, once more, the uncertain future loomed gloomily before them. Their sleep was troubled, and in the middle of the night Hunter suddenly sprang from bed, his sword held wickedly in his left hand, pressed against some intruder's throat.

"Hold, mon," Mary heard him growl.

And then, "Hunter, 'tis I, Cadman. Put away that blade before ye kill me!"

There was hesitation in the air. Mary could feel her lover stiffen with tension beside her.

"Light a candle, lass," he commanded softly.

She did as bid with trembling hands, wondering at his strange mood; the wick caught, and Cadman's face showed clearly in the flame. Still Hunter did not withdraw the point of his silvery weapon.

"Swear, Cadman," he hissed, his voice deadly, causing Mary to stare at him as though he had gone quite mad to speak so violently to his grieving and obviously drunken kinsman. "Swear ye still love and honor my lady as your sister, that your sword and shield will be e'er at her side, and that naught of this eve will e'er pass your lips upon pain of death. Swear it, sir, on your father's grave!"

"The witch!" Cadman spat. "There has been naught save trouble for us all from the time ye first laid eyes on her! And now my lord is dead. Dead!" he sobbed, hiccuping slightly. "And who do ye think will rule at Rath na Mara? Nae me! 'Twill be Blair who gains that holding. Blair! The young pup!

And what of me, nameless bastard that I am? When Angus is gone, I shall hae nothing, nothing, do ye ken? Och, Hunter. Hae pity on me. Forget this—this bride of the devil, and come away wie me to England or France, where we may seek our fortunes as we had planned of auld. There's naught in all Scotland for us," he whined.

Mary understood Hunter's caution then; relief coursed through her at his foresight.

"Cease your blubbering, mon, and swear." Hunter jabbed the point of his sword gently into his foster brother's flesh. A small drop of blood formed at the tiny wound. "Hae ye no pride, sir," he continued cruelly, "that ye need must come staggering to my chamber in a drunken stupor, weeping like a woman? 'Tis no shame to be a knight. Ye could hae done worse, Cadman, and there's few in Scotland who can touch ye wie a sword or battle-ax."

"I dinna know what has come o'er me. I'm bewitched. Aye, that wench of yours has cast a spell upon me to rid me from your side!"

"Stop your mewling!" Hunter warned him again, thinking suddenly of the many women who had been burned at the stake in Edinburgh as witches. "Mary has treated ye as a brother, and ye repay her wie slander and lies. Swear to me now, sir, or I'll nae be responsible for my actions!"

At last Cadman repeated Hunter's vow, and the tension between them eased as the younger man fell at his clansman's feet, crying with drunken grief. Finally Cadman slept, drained and weary from his loss and the torment that had poured from him. Hunter covered him lightly with a sheet and placed a small pillow under his head.

"His bones will ache in the morning, I'll wager, from sleeping on the floor; and no doubt his head will split, wie all the ale he has consumed. Lord! He fairly reeks of it!"

"Oh, Hunter! The things he said—"

"He dinna mean them, Mary," her beloved broke in quickly. " 'Twas his bastardy eating away on him again that made him speak so hatefully. Ye see, lass, Lord Torquil might hae acknowledged Cadman as his heir, haeing no other sons to inherit, but for some reason—whether 'twas because Cadman's mother, Mistress Elizabeth, ran off wie another mon or simple spite or malice, I dinna know—he ne'er liked Cadman. 'The whore's brat,' he called my foster brother and wouldna sign the documents naming Cadman as his successor, although he taunted and tempted my puir kinsman often enough wie the promise. Torquil was a cruel mon, and I believe his pride was sore injured when the Mistress Elizabeth left him for the Duke of Logie. At any rate, the Earl treated Cadman most harshly. Try nae to blame my foster brother too unkindly for his words, for he will be greatly ashamed in the morning, I'm sure. Go now, tigress. He'll nae want to wake and find ye here after such a tirade. 'Twould embarrass him deeply. Do ye leave Edinburgh this morn?''

"Aye."

"God be wie ye then." Hunter kissed Mary slowly, longingly, reluctant to part with her so soon. "Until we meet again in Mheadhoin.''

# *Twenty*

But Mary was not to see her Romany knight in Mheadhoin. Nay, not until years later would she meet her beloved once again in that deserted, hallowed kirk where they had lain and loved. For she returned to Bailekair to find her husband ill unto death. "The lung tisk," the doctor said; and by the time Mary reached Edward's side he was coughing blood, and she knew there was no hope for him. How long had he been so? Had she been too uncaring to notice? God, how she blamed and hated herself, felt her soul eaten up with guilt. And still she held his wasted hands in hers and thought of Hunter, who waited for her at Mheadhoin.

Edward's eyes were closed; he breathed raggedly. His nostrils had that faint, pinched look of the dying.

"Joanna," Mary called softly, not wanting to waken him. "Ye must ride to Mheadhoin for me."

The maid's doe eyes widened in surprise and fear. "Hae ye lost your wits, Mary? There's naught would go there, for the scourge of the Black Plague still lingers in that place and would strike them down wie its foul disease."

"Nay, 'tis but a fool's tale, for I hae been wie'in its borders many times these past months and lived to tell of it to ye. Ye must go. Sir Hunter awaits me there, and I must send word to him of my plight."

Joanna's eyes shuttered against Mary.

"I've asked naught of ye, Joanna, save this. You've been as my dear and cherished sister all these years, though serving maid ye are. Dinna deny me this one request, I beg of ye!"

And so Joanna rode to Mheadhoin to meet the enemy who was her lady's lover.

He was tall—she had not realized how much so—and he laid one hand on the hilt of his sword warily at her approach. He knew who she was before Joanna ever introduced herself, and though he made her a slight bow, she swept him no curtsy. She saw his violet eyes glint with mockery at the gesture, then fill with concern as he asked if aught had happened to Mary.

"Nay, she is well, sir, and bid me tell ye so. 'Tis Edward who is ill. He willna live the night."

Joanna turned away from the sudden hope she witnessed upon the MacBeth's face.

"Take no joy in his death, sir," she warned lowly, "else it be marred by that much measure."

How well Hunter was to remember those soft sharp words!

"Ma—ry."

"Dinna—dinna try to talk, Edward."

"Nay, I must—" He paused, coughing great rasps of blood once more. Mary wiped the red foam from his face. "I must tell ye— I loved ye always—from the time we—we were but bairns."

"I know."

"I—I thought to wed ye. I knew ye dinna—dinna favor Hugh. But ye loved—my enemy. I couldna accept it. I forced—forced myself on ye, lass, thinking to—to make ye love me."

"Edward, please."

"Nay! I'll nae die wie such on my soul! I—I turned from ye. 'Twas wrong of me. I know that now—now when 'tis too late for us. Mayhap 'twas always too—too late for us. Ye dinna love me as I did ye. Nay, dinna deny it, lass."

"I should hae tried. Oh, Edward. I'm sorry, so verra sorry."

"Dinna be, Mary. 'Twas the MacBeth who held your heart. Ye couldna help that—anymore than—than I could help loving ye. I forgie ye for it, lass, I forgie ye all. I wanted to—to protect ye. Hugh and Ian—"

"I know."

"Nay! They're—they're murderers, lass. I—I couldna tell ye before. Hugh—"

"I know," the girl repeated, alarmed by Edward's agitated breathing. "Please—"

"He slew your father."

"Aye, I guessed as much. Lie quietly now, my husband."

"Oh, God! The pain!" he suddenly cried out. "The pain! I canna bear it!"

"What can I do? Edward, what can I do?" Mary felt his misery as deeply as her own, hating to see him suffer. His face was drawn and grey, like ash. She buried her own in her hands, weeping.

"Help me. Help me, lass. Put me oot of my sorrow. 'Tis glad I am to go."

"Godamercy! Ye dinna know what ye are saying! Ye are oot of your head wie pain! I—I canna!"

"Please, do it, lass. 'Tis what I ask of ye. 'Tis all I'll e'er ask of ye—now. I—I let ye go to him. I kept your secret. I loved ye so much—I would hae done anything for ye—"

265

His deep blue eyes pleaded with her, and suddenly Mary thought of him as he had been that day at the fair at Inverness, so young, so vulnerable as he had stood by and watched Hugh bully her, gazing helplessly as Charlie had snatched the cherry pie from his hands, smiling at her gently as she'd bitten into the treat. Edward had always worshiped her and yet been too weak to defend her. Mary had been the strong one.

Oh, God. God, forgie me what I do, she prayed silently as she picked up a small pillow from the bed where her husband lay so pitifully, gasping, coughing, the blood spitting up from his lungs in great hunks now. Edward's begging eyes never left her own violet ones as he watched her slow, dazed movements. A light seemed to glow from within their blue depths, a radiance, a joy as she hovered over him, afraid and uncertain.

"Ye—ye can do—do it, lass," he rasped hoarsely.

Mary looked at him anxiously, sadly, the tears streaming down her cheeks like rain, falling onto his face.

"Why do ye weep, Mary? Dinna ye hear the music? So sweet. So sweet. 'Tis angel harps, I'll warrant."

"Nay—nay, Edward. 'Tis Pan—'tis the pipes of Pan. Aye." She saw his face brighten wonderously. "Pan has come, Edward. See," the girl lied, remembering Edward's childhood game of pretense. "Ye must get your flute, aye, quickly, young Edward, go quickly. If ye hurry, ye may catch him . . ."

Slowly as she talked Mary pressed the pillow down over his serene, wasted face. Harder, harder, harder . . .

And *when she looked at him again, there was no mark upon him.*

# BOOK THREE

*Of Passion's Woes*

# *Twenty-one*

**Glenkirk Castle, Scotland, 1490**

Grace MacBeth was happy, so happy she thought she must die of it, her soul sprout wings and take flight unto the heavens. Today! Today she was to marry David MacDonald. For with her father's death Cadman had become her guardian and, wishing to see his sister joyfully wed, had annulled her marriage contracts to young Francis, betrothing her instead to the man Grace so dearly loved,

A year had passed since her father's death, for 'twould have been unseemly to have held her wedding so soon after Lord Torquil had died. But Grace had not grieved for her father, whose stern will and quick temper had been the cause, she was sure, of her mother's mortal accident. Instead Grace had waited impatiently for the time she might become David MacDonald's wife.

She was truly beautiful as she descended the long stairs of Glenkirk to the main hall where David awaited. Her blue black hair glistened like a raven's wing, hanging unbound to her knees as tradition dictated. Her dark blue gown made her skin seem even whiter, like untouched snow, except where the warm blush of her maidenly modesty and love for David flushed her cheeks like the red roses that intertwined her hair and that she carried in her trembling hands.

"How long I hae waited for this day, my sweet, gentle dove," David said as his eyes caressed her.

Together they walked slowly to the chapel, unaware Euphemia watched them evilly, a hateful glare glowing wickedly upon her jealous countenance.

"I mean to wed her, Ian, and you'll nae stop me!" Gordon's face was flushed with ire. "She carries my child, and I love her, besides. I care naught for her bastardy or the fact that she'll nae enrich the Carmichael coffers!"

"You'll nae be bound to me if ye do, Gordon. I'm warning ye," Ian hissed. "There'll be no place for either of ye here at Bailekair."

"Aye, no place for ye anywhere wie'in our ranks, cousin," Hugh added slyly. "We hae the ear of Lord Gilchrist, our Chief; dinna forget that!"

"Nay, I dinna forget!" Gordon spat bitterly, seeing the two men did not mean to make things easy for him. "Nor do I forget how each of ye came by your earldoms!"

"Just what do you mean by that, cousin?" Hugh's black eyes narrowed dangerously.

"Dinna seek to play me for a fool, Hugh!" Gordon lashed out. "Edward told me of his suspicions, just before he died, fearing your intentions toward Mary. I hae no doubt he was right, too, for I hae seen how ye leer at her, Hugh, longing to make a whore oot of her, and ye aiding and abetting him, Ian. Ye, her own brother! 'Tis well she sought the haven of Court and James's protection after Edward's death, else ye would hae succeeded in your plot by now! Aye, ye guard her bairn, Hugh, nae because he is your heir, but because ye would force Mary to come to ye. Well, my sister knows ye dare nae harm wee Geoffrey. There hae been too many deaths already laid at your door. Aye, dinna tell me 'twasna your hand that didst slay my father, nor yours, Ian, which did Hugh such favor in kind. Murderers, the both of ye! And though I hae no proof, there's many would listen to me wie'in our clan, for I'm nae the only suspicious one among us!"

Hugh glanced around the deserted moors speculatively. For

miles on end the purple heather and golden broom stretched ceaselessly. No human spirit marred the unbroken sweep of terrain. Only a single doe grazed warily nearby. Hugh laughed jeeringly.

"Thou art a fool, Gordon. I dinna take kindly to your threats."

And before Gordon became aware of his intention Hugh pulled the dagger at his waist, grabbing his cousin about the neck with one arm, stabbing the younger man swiftly in the back. Gordon crumpled, blood spurting from the fatal wound. Startled, the doe stood paralyzed for a moment, then took flight across the heaths.

"Marry-go-up, Hugh! Did ye hae to kill him?" Ian stared at his brother's body, aghast.

"Dinna be stupid!" Hugh retorted sharply. "He meant to expose us, and unfortunately Gordon was right. There are indeed those who wonder at our good fortunes, and Gilchrist doesna love us enough to countenance the murder of two of his brothers! Och, mon! 'Twould hae taken only a few to speak against us, to accuse us openly of the deeds, and the whole world would hae crumbled down aboot us! And dinna forget Mary has the King's ear!"

Ian groaned glumly. "Still what are we to do?"

"Think, brother! Think!" Hugh snapped.

" 'Tis what ye should hae done before ye slew him," Ian snorted in answer.

"For God's sake, mon! Cease your mewling. We must get rid of the body in some way that willna connect us to his death. Ye owe me, Ian!" Hugh's dark visage was suddenly very nasty as he grabbed his foster brother's shoulders roughly. " 'Twas I who wie'drew my name from the running so ye might be *Tanist* of our clan and get your mother off our backs! Ye promised me Mary too, and I hae yet to get her into my bed!"

"Dinna toy wie me, Hugh. I know full well ye mean to be rid of Gilchrist and claim the Chief's place as your own!"

The two men gazed at each other angrily for a moment. Finally Hugh smiled benignly.

"Come, Ian. 'Twill do no good to quarrel, and each of us stands to lose much by it." He forced himself to relax. "We can hae no falling oot between us if we're to keep what we've gained."

"Aye, 'tis right, ye are," Ian admitted grudgingly. "I've thought of a plan that might save us, but you're to keep your trap shut aboot it!" He glanced at his murdered brother. "Put him on his horse. He'll hae to be moved from here."

Together they put Gordon's body on his horse and carried him to a small clearing at the edge of Glenkirk's border. Hugh was highly curious as to why Ian knew his way so well in MacBeth woods, but kept silent, fearing to begin their argument once more.

"Here, 'tis far enough. Throw him o'er there, facedown." Ian motioned, then removed a small mirror from his doublet.

He tested it briefly until it caught the sun's rays, then aimed it directly at one window high in Glenkirk's keep. Minutes later an answering flash lit the grove. Hugh's eyebrows raised speculatively, but still he said nothing. Thirty minutes later Euphemia MacBeth raced recklessly from the trees, her mare lathered from the flight. She drew rein shortly upon the sight before her, eyes filling with fear and dismay. She cried out softly.

"Easy, lass," Ian crooned soothingly. "'Tis no harm we mean ye."

He helped her dismount, then made her known to Hugh.

"My pleasure, Lady MacBeth." Hugh swept Effie a mocking bow; the girl shrank against Ian for protection, her animal brain sensing danger and evil in the man before her.

"You'll nae treat her like that, Hugh," Ian warned. "I mean it! I'll nae tolerate your disrespect toward Effie."

"God's blood, Ian! Let us nae stand here quarreling o'er the wench. Tell her what needs to be done, and let's get on wie it!"

"Effie, lass, ride back to Glenkirk, and fetch one of your kinsman's daggers. Hugh, here, has slain my brother, and the deed mustna fall at our door. Do ye understand me, love?"

She nodded, quick and shrewd as always.

*As they are betrayed, so will ye be betrayed.*

"There's a good girl."

When she had gone, Hugh sneered lowly, "I underestimated ye, brother. How long hae ye been fucking that bitch? Wench," he corrected hastily at Ian's glare.

" 'Tis none of your concern."

"Long enough, I'll wager, to hae learned a good deal aboot the MacBeths' habits and weaknesses. Long enough to hae earned the respect of our clan for the astuteness of your raids." Hugh whistled softly. "No wonder ye know when to strike so well. The wench tells ye."

"Aye, she tells me what I wish to know, does Effie. When I—we—gain control of the clan, Hugh, I mean to hae her to wife. She deserves no less, and I hae promised her as much." Ian was somewhat defensive.

Hugh laughed shortly. "I care nae if ye wed the lass." His eyes were half-closed in cunning. "But my silence has a price, brother, and ye know what 'tis."

"I've said ye could hae her, Hugh. 'Tisna my fault Mary has run to the King for protection."

" 'Tis your duty to get her back and into my bed, Ian!"

"Aye, there is a way, of course. But nae to whore, Hugh. As ye said, she has the King's favor now. Ye must take her to wife if ye mean to hae her."

"That little slut!"

"Och, think, Hugh. I swear for one so smart you're inordinately stupid at times. If ye wed the bitch, she'll legally be your property, to do wie as ye please. Nae even the King will interfere, unless ye wind up killing her. But, of course, ye dinna want Mary dead, do ye Hugh? Ye wish to make her suffer, do ye nae? Tell me, what has she done that ye hate her so? In truth the rape of her by the Romany is just a wee part of it, is it nae?"

"Aye," Hugh conceded irritably. "As for the rest, 'tis something she said once, years ago. I hae ne'er forgotten, nor forgi'en it, and I mean to make her pay for those ugly words!"

"Then wed her." Ian shrugged, wonderingly privately if

his cousin were daft to have harbored such a silly grudge for so long, but not really caring one way or the other. "Ye are an earl now. Ye are powerful enough to wed whom ye choose wie'oot comment."

There was silence between the two men for a moment. Then slowly Hugh smiled.

"Done," he said curtly.

Euphemia crept quietly up the stairs from the main hall of Glenkirk to the private chambers of her family. Her brothers' rooms, of course, were empty, just as she had known they would be, and devoid of any of their weapons. Lord! 'Twas just like Ian to put her in such a fix! Just where did he think she was going to get a dagger? All the men-at-arms carried theirs upon their persons, and the idea of trying to snatch one from its sheath did not appeal to Effie. Any man-at-arms worth his salt would feel the slightest touch upon his blade, and Effie did not relish trying to explain an attempt to steal a man's most prized possession. And the weapons not normally in use were kept locked up in the armory. She fingered her own dinner-dirk absently as she slunk through the hallway. 'Twas too bad it was too small for the purpose Ian and his cousin had in mind. His cousin, Hugh—Effie shivered just thinking about the dark Norman. He was evil; she could feel it. And to have stabbed his own cousin in the back! Effie's heart beat fast at just the thought of the gaping wound she had seen in the dead man's body. She did not want to face Hugh Carmichael's wrath if she did not accomplish her mission—and soon! Every second the Carmichaels lingered on MacBeth land was dangerous. Ian might be caught and slain; she couldn't bear that! Quickly she began checking the remaining rooms.

Cadman's chamber was empty as well, for he was in the courtyard training the young squires in the arts of battle under the direction of Lord Angus, whose leg had grown steadily worse. It had had to be amputated again, this time at the hip. Effie knew her father had not long to live. In many ways this disturbed her, not because she cared about her father, but because after his death her brother Stephen would rule at Glenkirk. Stephen was an untried lad in several respects and would be greatly influenced by his mother, Lady Sophia, whose saintly demeanor hid a backbone of steel. Effie shuddered slightly. Her mother would not ignore her odd comings and goings as had her father, who seldom paid his only daughter any attention. In addition Effie suspected neither Cadman nor Hunter, her father's right-hand men, relished the prospect of serving Stephen. In fact Hunter had been spending more and more time at Court recently. As he was a favorite of the King, Angus had no objection to this, but Effie conjectured that after her father's death Hunter would become Jamie's man rather than swear an oath of fealty to her brother.

Hunter! She should have thought of him before. He was home and had asked earlier for water to be brought to his room so he might cleanse himself of the stains of travel. The girl hied herself to his chamber, pushing the door open just a crack. From beyond the screen that sheltered him she could hear the slight splash of water as her kinsman bathed himself. Stealthily she sneaked into the room, tiptoeing to the massive bed where his clothes and armor lay. Quick as a lithe little cat Effie snatched up his dagger and ran from the room, hugging it closely to her pounding breast.

'Twas four hours after Gordon's horse wandered up to the iron portcullis of Bailekair that Ian's men-at-arms brought his brother's body home. They had taken Gordon's great Palomino steed with them when they'd first set out to search, and now he lay over the beast's back, a jeweled dagger protruding from between his shoulder blades.

Murdered! Gordon had been murdered in the foulest manner possible! Only a whoreson coward of the lowest order would have had so little honor as to stab an unwary man in the back!

In a tense, peculiar silence Joanna walked slowly toward her lover's corpse. She could not breathe. There was a weight on her chest so heavy she thought it must crush her as the sobs rose up in her throat; huge tears filled her doe brown eyes, penciled the soft blush of her tender cheeks. The shock was too much for her. She could not believe the man who only last night had lain so vitally alive in her arms now hung so coldly still over the back of his beautiful gold destrier, the gilded manes of both bonnie creatures stained with the blood that had dripped from the mortal wound.

"Oh, Gordie, Gordie!" she cried and did not know she wailed aloud until Charlie and Alinor came to comfort her.

She clung to her lover's dead body hysterically, uncaring that all were staring at her as though she'd gone quite mad. Joanna grabbed Gordon's bright head and kissed his cold face repeatedly, as though the touch of her warm mouth might somehow breathe life back into him.

They dragged her away, still screaming, as she watched the steed plod quietly over the cobblestones to the doorway of the keep where they would lay Gordon out in the main hall, just as they had done his father two years ago.

And then suddenly the lass crumpled at Alinor's feet, blood staining her gown, as it had soiled the horse and her lover's body, and soaking into the ground beneath her as she lost the child that would have been Gordon Carmichael's bairn.

Mary knew Gordon was dead long before Alinor's sorrowful message reached her at the palace, for she had dreamed and in her dream had seen her dear brother's body laid out in the main hall, his arms folded peacefully across his breast, the torches dancing ghostily around his serene corpse. And though Mary had never admitted it to herself because it frightened her, she knew now she had what the common folk called "the Sight" and so knew too her brother was dead.

Still she prayed it was not true, prayed until the moment the messenger from Bailekair pressed the scroll sealed with Alinor's coat of arms into her trembling hands. Had it been Hugh or Ian's shield emblazoned in the wax, Mary would have thought it merely a ruse to entice her back to Bailekair, and they had known as much. But Alinor would never have been a party to such a cruel trick, and Mary knew the horrible thing she'd feared was a reality.

Oh, Gordon, why? How did it happen, dear brother, to you who gave no cause to be hated by any man? A thousand questions plagued Mary's tormented soul as she rode out in a state of shock through the iron gates of Edinburgh toward Bailekair. She wished fervently Hunter were there beside her to share her grief, for she did not think she could bear alone the terrible agony that welled up in her breast. But Hunter had returned to Glenkirk a week past, for Lord Angus had had to have more of his wounded leg amputated, and 'twas feared the gangrene that was slowly eating up the old laird's body could not be halted.

It had been nearly a year since Mary had seen the home she so dearly loved. She shuddered, recalling the horror and pain of the fateful day she had left Bailekair, vowing never to return.

Edward lay dead and by her hand, though the girl realized she had but put an end to his dreadful, heart-wrenching suffering, the deepest kindness she could have shown him at the last. She had seen the lung tisk before; it was a fearsome way to die. At least Mary had spared her husband its final agony; the blood filling up the lungs until they swelled and burst, drowning the choked and gasping victim unmercifully in his own internal fluids. No, Mary felt no guilt or remorse at having been the instrument that had saved Edward from *that!* Only a deep sense of sadness, of having failed someone she'd loved pervaded her very soul as she looked down at him lying so peacefully on the bed they had shared.

Oh, Edward! We are what we are, and we all hae our weaknesses. I wish I could hae been the woman ye desired, but ye asked for a goddess, and I was but a wench who loved another. I couldna, canna help loving him, any more than ye could help loving me.

They buried him at Dùndereen. It was a simple ceremony, as he would have wanted. Mary's heart ached as the first clods of dirt fell upon his coffin and the beautiful, haunting notes of the flutist she'd had play died away; the sweet sad melody still echoed in her ears as she walked slowly toward the castle.

The earth lay yet fresh upon Edward's grave when Hugh and Ian sought her out.

"Hae ye no mercy that ye canna leave me alone to mourn my husband?" she lashed out at them as they confronted her in a small room off the main hall.

"Dinna seek to play me for the fool wie your false tears for my half brother, madam," Hugh rejoined coldly. "For ye bartered yourself to him to escape banishment from our clan, as we both well know. There was no love in your heart for Edward."

"That's nae true!" Mary cried. "I couldna hae loved him more if he had been my own brother."

"Mayhap," her dark cousin conceded. "But 'twas no wife ye were to him, at least in the manner he wished, for I know the puir bastard e'er had a weakness for ye. Aye, 'twas his misfortune he loved ye as a mon does a woman, and your affection for him was but sisterly. No doubt ye found cold comfort in his bed, madam. Well, no matter. 'Twill make ye more eager for me, for I'll wager ye are a lusty slut." His black eyes raked her meaningfully; a tight grin lurked about the corners of his leering mouth.

Mary feared him, but she could not let him know it. She tossed her head, laughing shortly.

"I hae the proof of Edward's monhood in my arms, Hugh," she said, indicating her son proudly, determined not to let her cousin learn of Edward's failure as a husband. "What need hae I of yours pray tell?"

Hugh scowled ominously. "Do ye dare to mock me, woman?"

"Marry-go-up, my lord, I hae no need of that either. 'Tis ye who make a fool of yourself. Ye dinna need my help."

"By God, ye bitch! We shall see who laughs last." He strode toward her angrily, yanking Geoffrey from her grasp.

The little lad began to wail, frightened by this rough treatment.

"What are ye doing?" Mary ran after her cousin as he started to the main hall. "Gie me my bairn! Ye hae no right to take him!"

"Dinna I? Edward is dead, madam. His son is my heir now. Ah, I see ye begin to understand me. Oh, aye, Mary. I hae e'ery right to take him. Weep all ye wish. There's nae a mon here who will gainsay me."

Mary struck out at him blindly, tears streaming down her cheeks as she clutched frantically for her child, heedless of Hugh's satisfied smirk.

"Ma—ma! Ma—ma!" Geoffrey bawled.

Hugh shook the boy, then flung Mary to the floor harshly.

"Hear me, whore, and hear me well," he hissed. "Ye will come to my bed wie'in the hour, or you'll see your babe no more. Do I make myself clear?"

Miserably Mary nodded, shoulders shaking piteously as she collapsed in a wretched heap, her son's screams ringing in her ears as Hugh carried him off.

"Get up!" Ian spat coldly. "Ye are a disgrace to the Carmichael name. 'Tis a marvel Hugh still wants ye. Get ye hence to make ready for him. Ye hae played the whore before. I trust ye will please him wie your charms, else your son will suffer for it!"

Mary tried to pull herself together. "The King will learn of this, Ian, I promise ye!"

Her brother sniggered. "Aye, well, 'twill be too late for James to help ye, madam, for by then ye will be Hugh's wife and swollen wie his bairn."

"Wife!"

"Why, Mary. Surely ye dinna think Hugh would risk the King's wrath for ye. Nay, all will be legal, madam, for we know too well Jamie's sense of honor and your own favor in his eyes. We are nae fools, my lady, for all ye would like to believe such."

"I—I am a widow, Ian. Ye canna force me to wed that whoreson. 'Tis the law! I hae a right to choose my own husband now."

Ian snorted contemptuously. "Why do ye think Hugh hastens to get ye to bed, little bitch? Even James will gie his consent to the match if your belly is big wie Hugh's child!"

"Oh, God," Mary moaned, realizing her brother spoke the

279

truth. There had been more than one reluctant widow brought to the altar by such means.

She staggered to her feet. She could not do it; not even for Geoffrey, her son, could she allow Hugh Carmichael to put his hands on her and sully that which she and Hunter had shared. Aye, and all for naught, for she could not prevent Hugh from taking her child, no matter what she did. He was right. The law of the Highlands was on his side, for 'twas a man's privilege and duty to guard and keep his heir safe. And—and surely he would not harm the lad! He would be made to answer for that! His heir's death. Even Hugh would not be able to escape responsibility for that when he held Geoffrey in his care certainly!

Mary began to breathe a little easier. Nay, 'twas merely a ruse to get her into Hugh's bed. Sooner or later she would have been parted from her son anyway. 'Twas the way of the times. Still, her heart cried out in anguish for her bairn as she ran dimly from the keep, mounting her black stallion and riding wildly from the castle walls. She prayed desperately her child would understand and forgive her when he reached manhood. Then Mary cruelly shoved all thoughts of Geoffrey from her mind. She must not, could not think of him if she were to escape. She would weaken, falter; Hugh would rape her and take her to wife. Oh, Geoffrey! Geoffrey! I will punish him for this, too, I promise ye!

Bailekair loomed ahead in the distance now. Bailekair! From which Mary drew her strength, her life. She hardened her resolve, shored up her determination. She *had* to reach the safety of Holyrood Palace where the King would protect her. Alan would help her, he and a few of her father's loyal men who loved her still. Even in her desperation Mary was wise enough to realize the folly of believing she could attain Edinburgh on her own, a woman alone. She would be set upon on the road by God only knew what kind of evil men: cutthroats, thieves, ravishing marauders!

"Alan! Barry! Godfrey! Ninian!" She reined her horse up sharply. The steed reared, pranced dangerously as Mary fought for control of the beast. "To me! To me, do ye ken?

The King! I must reach the King! 'Tis a matter of life or death! *Buaidh no Bàs! Buaidh no Bàs!''*

The men scurried to the outer ward of the bailey at her clamor, mounting their destriers rapidly in a manner born to those who must struggle for survival, who must be quick and deadly with a blade, swift and sure upon a stallion.

"The King," the serfs began to mutter among themselves. "Is the King ill?"

"Dying," one vowed solemnly, a tear tricking from her eye. " 'A matter of life or death,' our lady said."

"Jamie is dying!" another took up the incoherent cry. "Our puir Jamie."

"The King is dead!" another proclaimed. "May God rest his soul," and crossed herself hastily.

Confusion reigned in the courtyard. Mary rode out through the iron portcullis of Bailekair as suddenly as she had arrived amidst the shouts and keening. Her ploy had worked. No one even saw her leave in the scatter of the madding crowd, and Ian would not be able to punish the men who accompanied her upon their return, for they could claim themselves duped, misled as the rest had been.

Once out of sight of the grand castle Mary pulled Desmond to a halt, telling Alan quickly what had befallen her. He listened quietly, his face grave. The wrath darkened upon the countenances of the other men as she concluded her tale. Mary had chosen her saviors wisely.

"We'll get ye safe to Edinburgh, Lady Mary," the brash Barry vowed. "For Lord Ian isna the mon your father was. We'll cut him down if need be!"

"Aye, hae no fear for us, Lady Mary," the gentle Godfrey put in reassuringly. "Your brother dare nae raise a hand against us, for there's many who would rise up against him should he seek to punish loyal men."

"And we *are* loyal men, Lady Mary." The knavish Ninian flashed her a broad grin. "Loyal to the Lion and his tigress."

"Thank ye. Thank ye, all." Mary turned away, tears stinging her eyes once more.

"There, there." Alan cleared his throat gruffly. "We canna

stand here all day, my lady, if we're to reach the King and soon, for Ian and Hugh will no doubt send their men after us once they hae learned of your trick.''

"Aye, Alan." Mary stiffened her spine determinedly. "Let us ride at once!''

It was well over an hour before Hugh and Ian, smug in their victory and secure in their position, realized they had been duped and set out to search for her. By then Mary had eluded all attempts at capture.

Three days later she knelt before the King.

James welcomed her warmly, for he favored her much; and though she knew he would have taken her had Mary been willing, the young sovereign recognized Sir Hunter MacBeth held her heart. James made no move to touch her when she burst in upon him feverishly, begging for mercy.

"My dear Lady Mary!" His Grace waved away the men who sought to restrain her as she fell sobbing at his feet. "Whate'er is the meaning of this? My puir lass, are ye ill? Ye look as though some madness has beset ye.''

The courtiers sidled away somewhat apprehensively at this.

"Nay, Sire," Mary managed to get out more calmly. "I am well and in my right mind, I assure ye, although I'm certain I dinna appear so. Indeed I must look a fright.'' She glanced suddenly at her travel-stained *arascaid* and tried to smooth out her tangled locks raggedly with one hand.

"Ye are as bonnie as always," the King stated graciously, giving his men a stern frown.

"Your Grace, please." Mary bit her lip timidly, unsure of herself now that she actually knelt before the King. "Send your men away that I may speak wie ye in privacy.''

The courtiers nudged each other secretly, smiling slyly at this. 'Twas but a ruse! The Lady Mary had tricked them, seeking to connive her way into James's bed. Lord! Was there nothing a woman hoping for the King's favor wouldn't do?

James noted their prattling angrily. "Cease tittering, knaves!'' he ordered sharply, remembering the scandal of Mary's kidnap by the MacBeth that still clung to her skirts. The young monarch did not want *that* dredged up again! "The Lady

Mary is a virtuous woman. 'Twasna my bed that brought her so boldly to my chamber; of that I can assure ye. She suffered once at the hands of a rogue. Do ye think her a fool to seek oot another?''

"Nay, Your Grace," they mumbled repentantly.

The King's mouth twitched. "Are ye calling me a 'rogue' then?"

"Nay, Your Grace," they hastened to reply.

"Och, then Lady Mary is a fool, I see."

"Nay, Your Grace," the courtiers repeated a third time.

"The Patch has more sense than ye do!" James snapped, but his eyes still crinkled with amusement. "Either I'm a rogue, or Lady Mary is a fool. Now which is it to be?"

The men stared sheepishly at the floor, not knowing how to answer, recognizing they would err one way or the other. The King's Court jester danced a merry little fling about the room before bowing low to Mary and His Grace.

"Tut! Tut!" The malicious dwarf cocked his head mischievously to one side. "I thought them all so clever, and yet they canna respond to the simplest of riddles."

"Perhaps ye will enlighten us then, Patch"—James's lips quirked humorously once more—"if ye can solve the puzzle."

"Why, 'tis, indeed, an easy feat, Sire." The jester gave the courtiers a triumphant smirk. "If ye are nae a rogue, then neither can the Lady Mary be a fool; for if she were a fool, she would hae sought a rogue; and since she is no fool, ye, Sire, are no rogue. The lady is wise and has sought a king, instead."

"Well done, Patch!" James crowed with delight as the jester bowed low with a flourish again, then proceeded to jig around the room once more. The King turned to his courtiers. "Dullards!" he announced arrogantly. "Now ye know why ye are dismissed from my presence!"

The men slunk from the chamber stupidly, feeling somehow there was something not quite right about either James's or the Patch's reasoning, but unable to figure out just exactly what it was.

When they had gone, the young ruler gazed at Mary with some concern. "Are ye quite recovered now, my lady?" he asked.

"Your Grace is kind." A tear trembled upon Mary's eyelash, for James's ploy had sent the courtiers away feeling too foolish and worrying too greatly about the King's wrath to remark upon her strange and emotional conduct. She brushed the droplet away hastily. "I am quite composed, Sire, and ready to behave more sensibly than your men." She managed a tremulous smile.

She told the sovereign as much as she thought was wise about her position. His mouth tightened grimly at her words. He sighed.

"For all that I am a king, lass, I canna wrest your bairn from your cousin's stronghold. 'Tis, indeed, the Earl of Dùndereen's right to hold his heir in safekeeping. I canna risk dissension by failing to uphold the laws of the land. But dinna fash yourself, Mary. Hugh has no right to *ye,* and ye willna leave my Court unless 'tis willingly ye go."

He smiled gently at her as she curtsyed gracefully, then took her leave. After she'd gone James sent a messenger to Glenkirk, ordering Sir Hunter MacBeth to Edinburgh. He could not prevent Mary's grief over losing her child, but the dark and savage knight might ease her pain a little.

Although she had brought nothing with her from Bailekair, Mary did not suffer at Court, for James opened his purse and coffers to her generously; and though this gave the courtiers much cause for speculation, 'twas Mariot Boyd who still stood at the King's side, not Mary Carmichael, and the gossip soon focused on more interesting matters, seeing no entertainment in the offing from Lady Carmichael's quarters. Lady Jane Gordon too had proven herself a true friend to Mary, for she had insisted Mary lodge in the chamber she shared with her sister at the palace and was forever parting with some small nicety she knew the Carmichael lass lacked, for James still had much to learn about the needs of a woman.

"*Jesù,* this fan," Jane would begin, handing Mary the trinket for inspection. "I dinna know what possessed me to buy it, for it suits this dress nae. Ye take it, Mary. 'Twill go nicely wie your gown, I'll warrant.'' Or, ''Here, Mary. That fool weaver has sent twice as many handkerchiefs as I ordered. I shall hae his head on a platter if he seeks my gold for his mistake; but even so I canna possibly use them all. Choose a few for yourself, my lady, else they will fall pray to moths wie'in the fortnight.'' Or, ''Christ's son, the Hepburn! Does he think to buy me like some whore? Och. 'Tis such a bonnie flacon, too; 'tis a shame to waste it. Isna heather *your* fragrance, Mary?''

Jane's sister, whose name was the same as Mary's, although spelled differently, also proved to be quite kind.

''Och.'' She smiled softly, for she was not bold and brazen like Jane, but shy and gentle-spoken. ''Whate'er will Jane do wie myself being 'Mary Katherine' and ye being 'Mary Kathryn?' We shall be fore'er stumbling o'er one another when she calls.''

''Marry, Kate.'' Jane grinned mischievously at her small play on the girls' first names. ''Ye hae always favored your middle name, sister, as well ye know. Ye will answer to 'Katherine' or 'Kate,' of course, and Mary to 'Mary.' ''

This settled, the three women proceeded together smoothly.

The two sisters helped to alleviate much of Mary's pain, for she confided a part of her story to them, and they knew how dearly she grieved for her son, in spite of her efforts at gaiety. Indeed, had it not been for the loss of her bairn, Mary would have thought her life perfect the day Hunter arrived.

She was in the King's gardens, dressed in lavender silk and looking as beautiful as an amethyst jewel as she strolled amidst the potted beds of flowers, twirling one bright blossom idly in her hands, when he came. She had not known he was coming, for James had sought to surprise her, and for one moment Mary could not believe she had heard her softly spoken name a'right.

''Oh, Hunter!'' She turned, flying to the warm embrace of his strong bronzed arms. ''Hugh took my child! He took my child!''

And then she was sobbing fiercely against the cradle of his

285

broad chest, the sorrow she'd kept bottled up inside her pouring forth in a torrent of passion. He held her tenderly, allowing her to get it all out, stroking her gold hair gently, kissing and crooning to her sweetly as she cried.

"Hush, love," he said. "We will find a way to get the lad back, I promise ye."

She gazed into his violet eyes tearfully and believed him. Relief invaded her very being. He had come to her. He loved her. He would help her, against the King's wishes if need be; and James would turn a blind eye to their deeds, for had the young monarch not sent for Hunter with just such a thought in mind? Aye, Mary felt in her heart 'twas true.

Hunter led her to a more secluded spot in the gardens, pressing her down upon the fresh summer grass smelling of the crisp autumn that already approached.

"What are ye doing, sir?" She glanced at him dreamily as she sipped the wine he offered from his flask.

"Making love to ye."

He freed her breasts from the bodice of her gown, kissing each flushed and rosy nipple slowly, tongue teasing each hardened tip as his lips sucked gently, his hands caressing the ripe mounds tingling beneath his mouth and palms. Mary moaned, then suddenly, remembering where they were, pushed at him frantically.

"Nay, tigress," he laughed huskily deep within his throat. "James is near wie Mariot Boyd. Hear? Listen!" From the depths of the gardens came pretty Mariot's high giggle, followed by the King's lower one. "Aye, he is trysting wie his bonnie wench and has sent the others from this place."

"Then we must be gone from here as well," Mary gasped, struggling to pull her gown into some semblance of order.

"Nay, lass. 'Twas but a ruse on Jamie's part to gie us a few moments of privacy. Come, sweet. Ye are wasting what little time we may hae."

Deftly he bared her breasts again, then shoved her skirts up around her thighs. Mary shivered as his violet eyes darkened with passion to deepest purple, almost black in their desire.

Beneath the tangle of her rumpled gown he knelt between her golden flanks. She could not see him then, but she could feel him, feel his tongue dart with quick urgency to the heat and moistness of herself, feel the little sparks that began as he teased that soft place faster and faster until she quivered all over, hips straining upward against his tongue, hastening him on, fingers digging into the ground beside her as she panted raggedly, then felt the sudden rush that pervaded her maddened blood like the fire of a brandy. She cried out quietly, breathing unevenly as Hunter raised himself, freeing his shaft from its constraints, hard and ready.

With careful deliberation he plummeted into her all at once, sliding down the sweet, velvet length of her, feeling her hot wetness close over his manhood tightly, snugly, enveloping his maleness sensuously, like silk, as he buried himself deep within her. Unhurriedly he withdrew from her, taunting her unmercifully with the tip of his searing lance. Again he thrust into her and again withdrew.

"Dinna," she begged. "Dinna torment me like this."

He laughed softly, muscles flexing in his arms as he poised himself above her, staring hungrily down into her golden face, wild and naked with desire. Mary's hands came up like little claws to drag him down upon her once more. Her hips arched to attain that which he withheld so tantalizingly near. She wrapped her legs around his back to pull him to her. Hunter hurled into her then, aroused to a feverish pitch of excitement. Mary felt his heart hammer against her own, as loud as the hooves of a galloping stallion over a hard dirt road. Incoherently she urged him on, feeling the tension of his muscles as they rippled sinuously in his shoulders, his back, his hips, his buttocks as he gyrated into her quicker and quicker, heard her sob his name, felt the contractions that shook her dizzily before his own came, swift and sweet, in a long, shuddering sigh of rapture and triumph.

For nearly a year they had loved, bold but secret in their forbidden desire for one another. Hunter had begged Mary to wed him, and James would have given his approval to the match, in spite of the feud between the two clans; but Mary had feared for the safety of her bairn at Hugh's hands had she undertaken such a step.

"Hugh would kill him," she told Hunter sadly. "And even the King mightna be able to stop him, nor prove 'twas by Hugh's hand my son died. My cousin is clever. He could arrange an—an accident. Geoffrey is but a bairn. I—I dinna think Hugh will harm the lad as long as he sees the child as a means to bringing me to bed, but if the boy no longer serves that purpose— Godamercy! I fear to think— Nay, Hunter, as much as I love ye I canna come to ye as your wife until I hae my babe by my side once more."

They thought of kidnapping the bairn, but Hugh and Ian must have suspected Mary would attempt as much, for they kept the little lad closely guarded day and night; and Hunter and Mary saw no opportunity to take the child without great risk to themselves.

"Let it be, my love, for I wouldna lose ye, too," Mary said.

"Christ's son, tigress!" Hunter slammed one fist onto the hunting table in his chamber. "How long can we go on like this? I want ye for my wife! I want to shout my love for ye from the rooftops of Edinburgh, and still ye say me nay!"

"Do ye nae think it hurts me, too? How can ye be so cruel? Ye canna ask me to obtain my happiness at the death of my son! 'Tis too high a price to pay!"

"Look, we'll hae James send Hugh away, on a mission to England or France—"

"He's nae such a fool, my cousin. He would take Geoffrey wie him, and James has no reason to stop him. The child *is* Hugh's heir."

"I canna take this any longer." Hunter's voice was grim and deadly, his jaw set determinedly.

"Where are ye going?" Mary ran to his side as he started for the door.

"To slay me a Carmichael."

"Nay! Och, love, you'll be killed, I know it! Dinna leave me!"

His face softened momentarily. "I must see aboot Angus, lass, for the leg rot has worsened, and I owe it to my liege to hold his castle fast for Stephen if Angus dies. I'll do naught rash, I promise ye. But I shall get your wee bairn, Mary, or come to ye no more, for it hurts me too badly inside. 'Tis tearing me apart—this wanting and knowing ye can ne'er truly be mine."

He kissed her briefly, hungrily, longingly before he tore himself from her side; but Mary sobbed bitterly late into the night after he'd gone, fearing one way or another she had lost him for all time. Mary came back to the present with a start. Now Gordon, whom she held most dear unto her heart, lay dead. Dead! Dead at the hands of her lover's family. First Magnus, then Edward, and now her brother. The curse of the legend hovered dark as a shadow over Mary's troubled, grieving soul as she rode toward Bailekair.

'Tis I who hae destroyed them, she thought sadly, I and my lust for Hunter MacBeth! I knew, oh, God, I knew, oh, God, I knew the many sorrows my love for the Romany knight would bring, and still I hae ached for him, lain wie him, loved him—and love him still. I shall be damned for it, I know, and yet I wouldst love him even in hell.


Mary stared at the dagger Joanna had handed her and that now lay evilly in her shaking, unbelieving hands.

"'Tis a MacBeth blade," Joanna's voice quivered. "See, 'tis a mountain cat carved into the hilt. That—that is how we—we knew— And they found him at the edge of Glenkirk's forest. Och, Mary! Why? Why?"

Mary could not respond, for her heart had constricted painfully in her chest, pushing its way up into her throat, choking her. She knew that dagger. Oh, God, she knew it! A thousand times it had cut up her meat at supper; sliced chunks of cheese for her; hunks of good rich bread; cored a winter apple; or peeled a sweet summer peach. Oh, God, no! She felt sick to the pit of her belly. He had sworn to her! Sworn to her upon his honor never to harm one who was dear to her heart! Slowly she turned the dirk over in her hands, saw the initials engraved upon the other side of the wicked, silver blade: *HGM. Hunter George MacBeth!*

*Where are ye going?*

*To slay me a Carmichael....I shall get your wee bairn, Mary, or come to ye no more....*

*TO SLAY ME A CARMICHAEL!*

"Nay! Nay! 'Tisna true! 'Tisna true!"

Oh, sweet *Jesù.* Thank the Lord, the others in the main hall of Bailekair thought she cried out for her brother. Only Joanna suddenly knew differently. Joanna, whose doe brown eyes turned upon Mary's own violet ones accusingly.

"Your brother!" she spat so lowly that naught save Mary and Alinor, who stood close by, could hear. "He slew your brother! 'Twas your lover's hand that wielded that blade! Your lover! Sir Hunter MacBeth! Our enemy! Dinna deny it, Mary! Oh, dear Christ! Why? Why? I hae loved ye like a sister! May God damn ye to hell for it, Mary Carmichael!"

Then Joanna ran from the room, sobbing as though she would never cease.

Alinor gazed at Mary speculatively. "She is ill, lass. She carried your brother's child and lost it at the shock of his death. I fear the fever of the miscarriage is still upon her. She shouldna be oot of bed. Dinna blame her o'ermuch."

"Nay, I shallna," Mary moaned blindly, "for she isna to blame. Oh, God, forgie me, Gordie!"

Then she too ran weeping from the hall.


"I want to leave here, Charlie." Alinor's voice was firm, her mind made up. "We'll go to Eadar Da Voe. My father will take ye on or find a place for ye at Court."

"Why, sweetheart." He glanced up in surprise. "What-e'er—"

"I'll hae no argument aboot it, sir. 'Tisna safe here for ye. I feel it in my bones. There's something strange aboot Gordon's death, something we dinna know."

"He was murdered by that whoreson who kidnapped and

raped my sister. That arrogant, Romany devil! What is so strange aboot that? Mary has said she recognized the blade from the time she spent wie him at Wynd Cheathaich and sworn to hae her revenge upon him.''

''Charlie, I—I dinna wish ye to think ill of Mary, nor do I want to tell secrets that are nae mine to speak of, but I love ye, dearest. Ye are the most important thing in my life, so I dare nae keep my suspicions to myself. But promise me you'll say naught of this to anyone else. Promise!''

''All right.'' He nodded slowly, confused by her manner.

''Sir Hunter MacBeth is Mary's lover,'' Alinor blurted in a rush. ''Aye, 'tis true! I heard Joanna accuse her of it, and she made no attempt to deny it.''

''Alinor! Shut your mouth, woman! Ye dinna know what ye are saying! I canna believe—''

''Wait, hear me oot, sir.'' Alinor trembled slightly, for Charlie had never spoken thusly to her, then she summoned her Murray temper to the surface. ''It matters nae if ye believe me or nae—dinna ye see? He loves her; I'm sure of it now, though I had only guessed before. 'Twas even rumored at Court he asked the King to order a marriage between them, but Mary was already wed to Edward. Nan Chisholm, Percy's sister, did write to me of it at the time, but I dismissed it as idle gossip. Ye know how the courtiers are. But dinna ye see? If 'twere true, and he loved her enough to marry her, he would ne'er hae harmed her brother, especially one he must hae known was as dear to her heart as Gordon was, for to do so would hae turned her against him. Whate'er else he is, Charlie, Hunter MacBeth is no fool!''

''What are ye saying, Alinor?'' Her husband's eyes narrowed.

''I think—'' She took a deep breath, fearing to enrage him further. ''I think Hugh and Ian were behind your brother's death. I dinna know how they managed it, but somehow, someway— Och, Charlie, 'tisna safe here for ye,'' she repeated urgently. ''They've no scruples, none whatsoe'er. Dinna ye think it odd how they came into their earldoms? Godamercy, sir, ye may be next on their list!''

Charlie was silent for a moment, then said, "I do believe 'twas strange how they came to inherit and admit I did wonder aboot my father's death after Mary's ootburst that day we brought his body home. Lord Thomas's demise, also, was curious, for ne'er hae I known Ian to stand stupidly by in the face of danger. Ne'ertheless, there is no proof of any foul play, Alinor, and besides, what reason would they hae to murder Gordon? My brother was no threat to either one."

"Unless *he* had the proof we lack, Charlie," Alinor reminded him grimly. "And whilst Joanna lay ill from her miscarriage, she cried oot deliriously many times, begging Gordon nae to confront those two, vowing to leave Bailekair before the bairn came, insisting Ian would ne'er consent to Gordon marrying her."

"Marriage!"

"Aye, sir. Your brother was a most honorable mon. It must have grieved him sorely nae to be able to make Joanna his bride, for ye know a nameless bastard wie no dowry wouldna hae gained Ian's approval as your brother's wife. For shame, dearest! Ye hae seen what a miser Ian is! He has near ruined Bailekair. 'Twas why he brought ye home in the first place. Och! Your father would rise up from the grave to haunt that whoreson if he could see his once-proud castle now!"

"Aye, *that,* at least, is true. Aye, and Gordon didst always hae a soft place in his heart for Joanna from the time we were but bairns. But, marry-go-up, Alinor. I canna countenance these theories of yours, my love. To think Hugh and Ian would—would hae slain their fathers and my brother! Och, sweetheart! 'Tis too evil a thought to be borne! Why, if I thought that—"

"Ye would be murdered for your pains, just as Gordon was!"

"Oh, Alinor! And Mary and the MacBeth! Surely my sister wouldna be so lacking in honor!"

"Charlie, she *was* different after he took her," Alinor insisted.

"What woman wouldna hae been?" he snorted.

"Nay, nae like ye mean. She dinna wish to wed Edward.

292

'Twas as if she *wanted* to be banished! And those rides of hers—to the cemetery, or so she said—och! If e'er there was a woman who still smoldered wie passion upon her return! 'Twas there she must hae met him, for some days her mouth was still bruised from his kisses, I swear! I tell ye, 'tis true, whether ye believe it or nae. I couldna countenance it at first myself, but the more I watched, the more I was sure she had a lover. And he was there at Court too, Charlie, that summer. Oh, dearest, there were nights she left our chamber and dinna come back until dawn! Even then I dinna want to face the truth of the matter. I knew Edward was ill. I dinna think she would—''

"She wasna happy wie Edward,'' Charlie stated, feeling sick himself. "Even I could see that. And mayhap she dinna know he was so puirly. She couldna be so cruel. Why, it hurt Mary even to see her doll when Andrew and Harold pulled the stuffing oot of it during our childhood! Still we Carmichaels are a passionate clan, and when we love, we love beyond all reason; but the MacBeth!''

"Dinna blame her, Charlie. Ye dinna know what ye might hae done in her place. Suppose my father hadna gi'en his consent to our marriage?'' Alinor's eyes were pleading, for she had come to love Mary as a sister and did not wish for Charlie to turn against the lass.

"We are nae enemies of your clan!''

"Nay, but what if we had been?''

"I wouldna hae taken ye upon your father's grave; that's for sure!''

"Well, mayhap 'twasna the cemetery where they met,'' Alinor put in hastily. "I dinna know for certain. I might be wrong. Indeed I canna see Sir Hunter doing such a thing either now that I think aboot it.''

"Even so—''

"Even so, if we had been enemies, sir, and ye had loved me as much as ye claim to now,'' Alinor persisted.

Charlie Carmichael was a good man, a fair man, despite his recklessness and hotheaded temper. He smiled and spread his hands helplessly in sudden understanding.

"Ye should hae been a magistrate, minx, for I would hae loved ye all the same, aye, and taken ye, in spite of the obstacles in my path."

Alinor breathed a small sigh of relief. She had not wanted him to hate Mary and had feared he would. In addition, she knew, liked, and respected Sir Hunter MacBeth, for the Murrays had no quarrel with his clan; indeed, she wished the lovers well, wanting everyone to be as happy as herself.

"There's one thing wrong wie your entire line of reasoning, howe'er." Charlie was sober once again.

"What?"

"The dagger, lass. 'Twas the Romany's dirk; Mary has said so. I dinna see how even Hugh and Ian could hae accomplished that."

Alinor bit her lip worriedly, for in truth, neither did she.

"I dinna know how they did it, Charlie, but somehow they did; I just have a feeling in my bones."

"Woman's intuition, love?"

"Call it what ye like. I only know we must leave here at once! Ye hae attained your knighthood now, sir. Ian has no right to hold ye here. Promise me we'll leave here tomorrow morn!"

"Ah, little cat, ye know I can deny ye nothing." He pulled her into his lap and kissed her lightly.

"Or are ye thinking of, sweetheart?" she asked quietly a few minutes later.

"Puir Edward."

"I know. He knew Mary loved another. There was a—a sadness in his eyes that wouldna hae been there otherwise."

"He loved her, ye know, from the time we were but children, just as Gordon loved Joanna; but somehow Edward's heart was—was ne'er really in it, Alinor." Charlie struggled for the words to explain. "'Twas as though he were nae of this world. Och, I dinna know what I'm trying to say. He should hae been a Greek scholar, or a musician at a court such as King Arthur's of England must hae been, or a monk. Aye, he was to hae gone into the priesthood, but wed Mary, instead. Och. He ought to hae taken his vows as he'd planned. He dinna belong ootside a monastery.''

"You're right, my love. He wasna happy in our world. Where'er he is now, I know he has at last found the peace for which he searched. For, in truth, I believe he sought an angel, and Mary was and is still but a mortal woman.''

"As are ye.'' Charlie grinned, the shadow of Edward's life and death lifting as suddenly as it had come. "Come to me, Alinor, for I hae need of a worldly wench such as ye.''

"Dinna go, Alinor, please. You're all the friend I hae left here now.'' Mary bit her lip pleadingly. "For Joanna hates me—I know she does—and I dinna blame her. She hasna spoken to me since—since—''

"Dinna regard it, Mary. Mayhap she is still fevered from her illness. I know she wouldna turn against ye, dear as ye hae been to one another.''

"Aye, she would! She despises me for my part in Gordon's death and rightly so,'' Mary said, for she knew it had been useless to try to hide the truth from Alinor's sharp, glittering green eyes. "Och, Alinor, dinna tell me ye loathe me, too!''

"Nay, I'll always be your dear friend and sister, Mary. Dinna think otherwise.'' Alinor hugged her kindly. "''Tisna because of ye we are leaving. 'Tis because 'tisna safe here for Charlie.''

"Nae safe? What do ye mean?''

"Och, look into your heart, Mary, for ye know the answer far better than I. Here.'' She twisted a small emerald ring, which had been part of Charlie's bridal gift to her, from her fourth finger. "Take this, for 'tis dear to me, and I want ye to hae it. If e'er you've need of me, send it. I vow I will come wie the King's army if necessary.'' Her voice was suddenly as steely as her powerful father's was.

Then she hugged Mary swiftly again and was gone. Only the fragrance of her heady perfume lingered where she had been.

*'Tisna safe here for Charlie.* What had Alinor meant by

those cryptically spoken words? Gordon had been slain by the MacBeths—Hunter MacBeth, Mary's lover! With a sob Mary rushed upstairs to her chamber, barely making it to the heavy glazed pot therein before she vomited again and again.

Euphemia laid down her pen, smiling secretly to herself, sealing the missive she'd just finished writing before pressing her shield-ring into the hot wax. Francis. It *must* be Francis, the puling wretch! If he had not been such a mewling weakling, letting Cadman annul the marriage contracts with Grace, Grace would not now be the Countess of Wynd Cheathaich, wife to the earl that she, Effie, should have wed. 'Twas all Lord Torquil's fault anyway. Euphemia eased her guilty conscience. Not having been content with sending his daughter to Glenkirk to ruin Effie's life, he had had the bad manners to get himself killed as well, leaving Cadman as Grace's guardian. Well, Effie had gotten even with Cadman, too, for his part in her misery. She had given Ian Hunter's dagger that day. And although Effie had not planned it that way, the blond bitch Hunter had kidnapped and raped once had identified the dirk as his. Sooner or later the Carmichaels would slay Effie's accursed kinsman. Lord, 'twould destroy Cadman when he learned of his foster brother's death, for the two could not have loved one another more had they been brothers by blood.

But first Francis must die.

*As their blood runs red upon the ground, so will your blood run.*

"Choose one whom ye hate, Effie," Ian had told her, "for the twins are quite grisly wie their daggers."

And so she had chosen Francis. And when he came to meet her, spurred on by the distress contained in her letter, she would not be there. 'Twould be Andrew and Harold Carmichael who awaited Francis. But he would not live to accuse her of the trap, and the Carmichaels would have their immediate revenge on the MacBeths for Gordon's death.

Effie was disappointed Hunter was not to be their victim,

but Ian had decided against the idea when she'd suggested her accursed kinsman's name.

"Nay, Effie, we'll get the Romany in the end; hae no fear of that. But he is much in favor wie the King right now, and we dare nae risk it. Pick someone else."

And she had thought of Francis.

Of course, Andrew and Harold Carmichael knew naught of the plot either. Ian planned to send them scouting in the area, knowing they would find Francis on their own and kill him. Ian could not afford to have anyone else find out about Effie until they were ready to be married. 'Twas bad enough Hugh knew. Effie understood. Hugh Carmichael gave her the shivers!

She went downstairs, handing the message to a page for delivery to Oir Uisge. She need have no fear he would speak of his journey to her Uncle Farquhar's keep afterward, for she had instructed Francis, in her letter, to slay the lad. Francis, the fool, was a loyal MacBeth. He would do the deed, and she, Effie, would be safe. Ian was not the only clever one!

# Twenty-two

In vain did Hunter wait at Mheadhoin, for Mary came no more. And though he had not expected her for a time after her brother's death (of which he had learned from the crofters, who had their own ways of knowing everything that occurred in the Highlands), he could not understand why she did not seek him out now. Surely she knew he waited for her! She could not blame him for Gordon's slaying; after all, he'd had naught to do with it. And the Carmichaels had taken their revenge and well, Hunter shuddered, remembering the sight of poor Francis's brutally maimed and mutilated body. There was something strange about his kinsman's death, but Hunter could not quite put his finger on what was wrong.

Suddenly his ears pricked up hopefully as they caught the sound of muffled hoofbeats outside the kirk; all thoughts of young Francis driven from his mind, he started eagerly toward the door.

"Nay, Hunter." Cadman filled the frame, his face pitying. " 'Tisna the one for whom ye wait, and she'll come to ye no more."

"What—what are ye saying, Cadman?"

"The Lady Mary is to be wed. I heard the news at a tavern in Inverness."

"Wed? To whom? Surely ye jest, brother!" Hunter could not credit this piece of information.

"Nay. She's to marry her cousin Hugh wie'in the fortnight."

"Och, Cadman." Hunter relaxed slightly. "Ye hae been the victim of a drunken joke, for she loathes that whoreson."

"Nay, brother. 'Tis no fool's tale, I promise ye, for minstrels, dancers, acrobats, and jugglers hae been retained already from the city to perform."

"You're lying, sir!"

Cadman stiffened visibly.

"I shall forgie ye that remark, sir, for I know ye hae cause to believe me a false friend to your lady e'er since that night of my father's death when I didst speak so viciously against her in my grief and drunken stupor; but I swear 'tis the truth I tell ye now."

"She's being forced into the match then! I canna believe otherwise. Dear God! I must find a way to aid her—"

"Nay, Hunter. She has ridden openly and alone, as she did of auld. She has had e'ery opportunity to escape as she did before, and still she hasna. Instead she has gone to Dùndereen to o'ersee the preparations for her marriage. I am told the King even sent the Hepburn to inquire into her well-being, and she bade Patrick return to Court, saying naught was amiss, that she awaited her wedding day wie much joy.''

"Nay!'' Hunter exclaimed furiously. " 'Tisna so! 'Tis me she loves—''

"I'm sorry, brother. I dinna know what passed between ye at court to bring ye home to Glenkirk, but mayhap your lady believed ye cared for her no longer.''

"Oh, Cadman, we had quarreled, 'tis true, and she—she *was* crying when I left, but surely she knew I meant to return to her, in spite of the angry words I spoke at our parting. 'Twas but my love and longing for her that wrenched them from my lips. I dinna intend to hurt her. Oh, Lord! I ne'er dreamed—marry-go-up! I said I would come to her no more! Och, what fool was I—I must go to her at once, try to explain—I dinna mean it! I dinna mean it!''

"I am at your side, brother, if ye need me, for in truth I dinna fancy seeing her wed to the Carmichael either. I hae heard many a dark tale aboot his bedroom manner and fear for your lady deeply should he succeed in taking her to wife.''

But Hunter was not to stop Mary from her course of action, for by the time he and Cadman had thought of a plan to reach her it was too late.

Mary was to wed Hugh Carmichael. She did not care. She had been like a dead woman ever since Hunter had slain Gordon. She had gone through the motions of living, but she might as well have joined her father, husband, and brother in the grave. He had brought her naught save sorrow, had the MacBeth. He had used her body, made a mockery of her love, and betrayed her trust. She tried not to think of him. She went no more to Mheadhoin. She convinced herself she hated him. She had misjudged him, just as she had been wrong about Hugh; Hugh, who had been most kind to her since Gordon's death. Not once had he tried to touch her or force himself on her; and Mary was too filled with grief to connect this with the King's favor and Hugh's uneasiness at guessing James had heard the girl's entire tale of woe. God only knew what she had accused him of. He had to placate her, to win her over.

He brought her son to Bailekair. He knelt at her feet most honorably, begged her forgiveness for his past treatment of her, and swore to love her if only she would consent to becoming his wife.

"I love ye, Mary! I hae loved ye always. 'Tis like a madness that bewitches me, this love for ye. It nearly drove me oot of my mind when the MacBeth took ye as his. That is why I treated ye so harshly. I couldna bear the torment of knowing the things he must hae done to ye. I couldna even look upon ye wie'oot wanting to kill him and ye, so pitiful was your shame. I dinna wish ye to be exposed to the cruelty of the others, knowing how they would make mock of ye, so I tried to hae ye banished. I would hae come for ye, lass, I swear it. I wouldna hae turned ye oot to fend for yourself. But Edward—Edward spoke up and married ye, instead. Oh, God, I canna tell ye how ashamed I was of my own coward- ice that he had dared what I couldna. And then he died, and still ye wouldna hae me. Och, Mary! Mary! Dinna deny me again. I want so much to love and protect ye, to hae us all together as one happy family." He ruffled Geoffrey's hair gently. "The lad needs a father—and a mother. Say ye will marry me, lass. I would gie anything to hear ye say it," Hugh ended passionately.

Mary felt so helpless. She wanted her child desperately. Perhaps Hugh *had* changed, or perhaps she had been wrong about him all along. What difference did it make? Hunter did not love her; he had slain her brother. There was nothing left for her. Hugh was a Carmichael. He was of her blood. He was little Geoffrey's uncle. He would take care of them. She laid her hand on her dark cousin's arm.

"I want my son, and for his sake I shall try to forgie ye and love ye as ye claim to love me."

Mary's misery was complete.

The castle of Dùndereen was small, built of hard stone so pale in color the fortress seemed almost white in the early morning light and ghostly when the mist settled over the land at dusk. Set in the sweeping hollow of a Highland hillside it was surrounded by a muddy-watered moat fully ten feet wide and as many deep into which various amounts of refuse had been dumped over the years, causing the murky depths to ooze with a foul smell when the wind blew just right. The circular towers were short, since no cliffs hid the view from the keep, and like stout squat friars surveyed the land from the square-cut, machicolated battlements. Although the walls looked easy enough to overcome, the moat made it almost impossible to climb the barriers that guarded the castle, and Dùndereen had withstood numerous sieges throughout the years. A clever, agile man or two might have managed to attain the battlements, but not an entire army.

To this stronghold Hugh brought Mary to be wed, for he had no wish to be married at Bailekair, where she had spoken her vows with Edward. The autumn air was filled with the crisp clean scent of the coming winter, and all the land was ablaze with the red-and-gold beauty of the fall. There could not have been a lovelier day for a wedding. Why, then, did the girl feel the season mocked her?

She wore the same gown she'd worn at her ceremony with Edward. Hugh did not notice or gave no sign of it if he did. And, again, she looked as regal as any queen when she descended the stairs of Dùndereen to take her cousin's arm; but her voice trembled as she spoke her vows in the chapel, and her lips were as cold as ice when Hugh kissed them fiercely, possessively.

'Twas only when he set her away from him, whispering so lowly that naught save Mary heard his terrible words, that the lass seemed to rouse herself from her state of shock; and the full import of what she had done dawned upon her most harshly.

"Ye hae played the game well, madam." Hugh smiled down into her suddenly frightened eyes wolfishly, and his voice sent shivers down Mary's spine. "But I know ye for what ye are, and your whore's tricks hae nae fooled me."

"What—what are ye talking aboot, Hugh? I hae tried to

like ye for wee Geoffrey's sake. I hae vowed to love and obey ye. I hae promised to come willingly to your arms—''

"Och, I hae no doubt aboot *that*, madam! For ye are as lustful as any bitch in heat, I'll wager." He licked his lips, appraising her coolly. "But let us hae no pretense of love between us. I know ye hae played the adoring bride-to-be these many weeks past because ye hae finally come to your senses and realized ye wouldna get your son back any other way. And I hae e'er lusted for ye, Mary. Aye, I do admit it; and I could hae ye no other way, curse ye and Jamie! But, ye are mine now, and nae even the King can say me nay."

"But ye said—said ye loved—loved me—''

"Och, what a fool ye are, madam. Aye, fool, for love is but a fool's notion; and 'tis certainly nae what I desire from ye. But hae no fear, dear wife, I care naught for your wit or brain. 'Tis that between your legs that had best please me."

Mary shuddered at his crude words. Dear God! What had she done? What had she done? She should have seen him for what he really was, recognized he had not changed as she had thought. Och! If only her misery and grief had not blinded her so insensibly. If only she had not seen her child, ached to have him near her once again. Oh, how cleverly Hugh had used her son, bringing the lad with him each time he'd called upon her at Bailekair. How she had clung to little Geoffrey, and he to her, and known she would never have him again unless she agreed to Hugh's proposal. And with Hunter gone, turned from her so cruelly, her bairn was all she'd had left. Sweet *Jesù!* She should have realized the ruse for what it had been. Mary stiffened her spine. She could not let Hugh see how afraid she was. He would prey upon her fear, and she would be powerless against him.

"Aye, I love my babe; and ye took him from me, Hugh, knowing there was naught I could do to prevent ye. Ye hae caused me great pain for it, oh, aye, great pain, Hugh; I gie ye the satisfaction of knowing that! But ye will pay for it, I promise ye; for since we are telling truths, I shall tell ye I know ye for the murderer ye are and remind ye I hae sworn to

hae my revenge upon ye for my father's death. Aye''—
Mary's violet eyes flashed dangerously, for she was fighting
for herself and her son now—"I shall share your bed,
whoreson, because I must, but ye will find no joy in the
taking of me. And some day, I vow it, I will hae my
vengeance upon ye, and it will be sweet, indeed.''

"Ye think so, madam?'' he drawled insolently. "Do ye
mean to take up arms and fight me like a mon?''

"Nay, Hugh, I hae no need of *worldly* weapons," Mary
narrowed her eyes slyly, knowing the thought of witchcraft
frightened Hugh nearly as much as the thought of madness.
"Aye, Hugh, I hae the Sight; did ye nae guess it?'' she
continued wickedly. "It comes on me in dreams. And I hae
dreamed of ye, dark cousin," she lied brazenly. "I hae seen
ye lying dead in a pool of blood—''

"Shut your mouth, bitch!'' Hugh hissed sharply. "I'll nae
listen to your lies, bride of Satan!''

"I am that, Hugh, for ye made me so today.''

He moved as thought to strike her, then recovered himself
masterfully, recalling the guests present at their wedding.

"'Satan,' ye call me, madam? Well, then, I will show ye
what a devil I can be—tonight, when I hae ye at my mercy in
bed!''

And Mary could not cease her trembling as he escorted her
from the chapel.

Oh, was there ever such a wedding feast as theirs? Hugh
Carmichael, Earl of Dùndereen, had outdone himself in
order to impress his guests with his rank and wealth. Twenty
cows and sheep apiece had been slaughtered and half as many
stags hunted down and killed. There were five roast boar and
half-a-dozen trussed swans; vegetables, tarts, and breads too
many to mention. Three huge pies were wheeled in on carts;
the red wine ran freely, and the ale flowed like the mountain
streams' spring thaw.

Still Mary ate little, drinking more than she was wont, as
though trying to calm the furious pounding of her heart and
the shaking of her hands. She wanted nothing more than to go

and lie down; her head ached badly as the day wore on into the evening, and the revelry continued. She was like a person in a daze.

What hae I done? What hae I done? she asked herself for the thousandth time that day. I hae wed my father's murderer and willingly. *Willingly!* I shall go mad! she thought wildly. 'Twill be my final revenge on Hugh Carmichael, married to a half-wit, just as his father was! Aye, I shall go mad, for insanity frightens him even more than witchcraft.

Mary, who had not smiled once all day, suddenly tittered aloud at the thought. People gazed at her oddly, for her laughter was high and strained, unnatural; and even the drunkest among them began to mutter to one another. Here and there a few made the sign against her. "Half-wit," the girl imagined them saying, nodding to each other for confirmation. "Puir Hugh, puir laddie, wed to a madwoman, just as his puir father was, may the *auld* laird rest in peace." Mary giggled again.

"What is so funny, madam?" Hugh inquired coldly. "Will ye nae share your mirth wie us all?"

"My friends." Mary lurched unsteadily to her feet, peering at the guests unfocusedly through the mist that seemed to be clouding her eyes. "My husband wishes to hear a tale of jest. Clear the table, lads and lassies!" She waved her hands about wildly, then pulled the pins from her hair, sending them scattering as she loosed the cascading mass of gold, her laughter rippling like a challenge from deep within her throat. "Begone, ye jugglers and acrobats! Ye dancing girls and mocking fools! For I myself will entertain this eve!"

Great cheers arose, ringing the very rafters of the hall, at this, for the Lady Mary, who had a bonnie voice and wit, had not once performed since her father's death. The serving wenches hastened to shove the platters and trenchers from the long table upon the dais, while the men-at-arms seized Mary, hoisting her to their shoulders. They carried her about the room raucously before depositing her on the top of the now-empty table. She cocked her head slyly, then danced a few skipping steps much reminiscent of the King's Patch along the length of her improvised stage.

"Music! Music!" she cried.

"What would ye hae, Lady Mary?" came the reply.

She knelt briefly, whispering something into the ear of one of the men. Moments later the minstrels began to play. Hugh settled back upon his bench, arms folded across his chest as he watched with grudging admiration.

Och, she was wild and savage, beautiful and alive that night! As though she poured every emotion from her heart, draining it to the bitter dregs so none might guess the wrenching sorrow it contained; so Hugh, when he took her, would find her naught save an empty shell, more devoid of feeling than even Edward had known, for there had at least been caring in Mary for Edward, despite her love for Hunter, and there was nothing at all in her for Hugh. Nothing but hatred.

Drunkenly Mary hitched up her skirts, kicking off her leather boots as she continued to dance, faster and faster, a wild Highland fling, while the men and women present stamped their feet and clapped their hands, urging her on with their hoots and whistles and shouts of approval. The noise reverberated through the main hall, filtering out into the bailey, snaking its way along the walls of the keep to the moat beyond.

"My God!" Cadman MacBeth stared at the castle fearfully. "What can be going on in there?"

"I dinna know," Hunter responded grimly as he shook the length of coiled rope in his hands, freeing one end upon which swung a great, iron hook. "But I thank the Lord for it, for none shall hear us o'er the revelry."

"We shall be killed! Killed, I tell ye! Marry-go-up! I was in my cups, to be sure, when I agreed to this mad plan of yours!"

"Nay, brother, ye were sober as a priest." Hunter flashed him a devilish grin.

"More fool I then." Cadman groaned. "Och, Hunter, surely there must be some other way."

"Nay." Hunter swung the rope. The heavy metal claw flew into the sky and fell short of its objective. "Damn!"

" 'Tis too steep, brother, I'm telling ye."

"Nay, 'tisna. The wall is no more than twenty-five feet high at most, and we are angled a good ten feet away from its side. 'Twill catch, I tell ye."

"Oh, Lord," Cadman moaned as the minutes crept by, and still their goal remained elusively just out of reach after half-a-dozen tries. "We shall be killed! Marry! I feel it in my bones!"

"Hush, o' ye of little faith," Hunter hissed victoriously as the iron hook clattered at last upon the ramparts of Dùndereen. He drew the rope toward himself slowly, carefully. The metal prongs pressed against the battlements. The claws held. He breathed a sigh of relief. "See?" He gave his foster brother another wicked grin.

"Satan take ye for his henchman, Hunter!" Cadman snapped. "For we shallna escape here alive this night."

"Bah! Two MacBeths are more than a match for a thousand Carmichaels."

"Ye are mad! Mad, I say!"

"Aye, but 'tis a fine madness all the same."

And then, securing a good hold upon the rope, Hunter swung himself over the castle moat, striking the wall of the keep with a sharp blow that pained his shoulder blades. The keen edges of the stones scraped along his back, tearing at the skin. He grunted, then began to hoist himself hand-over-hand along the length of the rope. After what seemed like ages he gained the ramparts of the fortress, pulling himself over the jagged battlements. He paused, breathing raggedly for a moment. Then he yanked the rope up until he held the free end. This he tied about a weight he carried inside his doublet for just such a purpose. Then he lowered the rope once more approximately halfway down the wall, giving it a good swing. The weighted end flew out over the moat. On the third try Cadman managed to catch it at last. He followed his foster brother to the ramparts. Hunter assisted him over the edge. Cadman too was panting; his face glistened with sweat in the moonlight.

"If—if the Carmichaels dinna—dinna slay ye, brother, I will," he gasped. "The flesh on my back was near bitten off by those stones!"

"I—ah—meant to warn ye aboot that."

"By God, Hunter!"

"Shhhhh! Someone's coming!"

The two men melted away into the shadows. The sentry never even had a chance. Hunter silenced the guard quickly with a swift slicing of his dirk across the man's throat. Together Hunter and Cadman dragged the body to the battlements. With a heave, for the corpse was heavy, they rolled the dead sentry over the edge of the wall so he might not be found and an alarm raised to warn the keep of its assault. Far below they heard the muffled splash as the guard hit the waters of the moat. Then they moved as one toward the main hall. Five murdered watchmen later, they stood silently in an alcove off the great chamber, staring at the drunken, dancing figure of Hunter's beloved upon the long table setting on the dais at one end of the room.

"Take a good look, brother," Cadman said softly, "for *that* is the wench for which ye hae risked our lives this night!"

"And too late! 'Tis a bridal feast, Cadman. She has already wed!" Hunter groaned in despair. "But I will hae her all the same."

"Art daft, fool?" Cadman was startled by his kinsman's move toward the hall. "Ye canna go in there!"

"Can I nae? Nay, dinna try to stop me, brother! She is mine, and I will hae her, I tell ye!"

"Hunter, please!"

"Look, get ye to Lord Gilchrist at that far end, and put your dirk to his throat. None shall dare restrain us then." Hunter's violet eyes were narrowed with cunning at the thought of outwitting his enemies within their very keep and shadowed with pain at Mary's wedding.

Cadman glanced at his clansman's grim, forbidding face and knew further argument would prove useless.

"Verra well then, sir, but I hope ye willna be sorry for your folly!"

By this time Hugh, to Mary's surprise, had joined her upon the table, dancing as well as she, his black eyes snapping with a strange approval for her courage, for he guessed the fear her brazen behavior hid. His white teeth flashed with a quick leer as she matched him step for step, each more difficult than the last.

"By the Virgin Mary, ye are a braw lassie!" he shouted over the roar of the hall, oddly intrigued by her boldness, as he had always been. She would fight him tonight—he was sure of it! And his pleasure would be that much greater because of it, for Hugh took joy in a woman struggling against him. "I might change my mind and learn to love ye yet! What say ye to that, witch?"

Mary glanced at him slyly, past caring about what he might do to her. In reply to his question she began to sing a taunting, slurring ditty about a woman who had poisoned her husband:

> *Och, she was fair, was Lady Cat,*
> *But her tongue was sharper than keenest knife.*
> *She told proud Keith she'd hae none of him,*
> *And, still, he swore he would hae her to wife.*
>
> *Deep he drunk of their wedding cup,*
> *Wie leering jest sought marriage bed.*
> *But 'twas the Lady Cat laughed last*
> *When they laid him in his coffin, instead!*

What Hugh would have done for her impudence Mary never knew, for just then, over the revelry of the great chamber, a voice rang out the girl would have known anywhere. Abruptly the music ceased; the men and women who had been gaily clapping, stamping, and dancing faltered; the laughter died. Gasps of mortification, outrage, and anger swept the vast hall at the sight of the tall, dark man who swaggered at its fore and his younger version who held a dirk to Lord Gilchrist's throat. None dared make a move upon them, lest the Chief of the Clan Carmichael be slain where he stood. Mary was ill. She was sure of it, for the room kept spinning long after she'd stopped dancing, and Hunter MacBeth stared at her insolently each time she opened her eyes. It couldn't be! It just couldn't be!

"Ye! What are ye doing here?"

Hunter gazed at her, suddenly unsure of himself, for she had not run to him in joy, as he'd expected, when she saw the risk he'd taken to lay claim to her. Then it dawned on him that, of course, she could not do so, for she would condemn herself in the eyes of her family by her very actions if she did.

He grinned and drawled lazily, "Why, I hae come to cage a tigress, as I did before. Didst think I would let ye go so easily, my lady?"

"Ye dare—ye dare, ye accursed defiler of women, ye whoreson murderer, to show your face here? Be damned to ye, sir! Slay him, Hugh, slay him where he stands." Mary turned to her husband wildly. "I shall forgie ye all! I shall do whate'er ye ask! Draw your sword, husband, and revenge my honor and that of my brother—now! Now!"

Hunter couldn't believe his ears. God's wounds! 'Twas as though—as though the wench hated him! What was she babbling about?

"The first mon who moves will be responsible for the death of your chief," he stated grimly, staring at Mary as though he'd never really looked at her before.

"For God's sake! No one lift a hand against them!" Gilchrist ordered frantically.

The men-at-arms settled back upon their benches warily. Hugh, who had started forward at Mary's words, felt his fingers tighten and then relax upon the hilt of his blade.

The silence in the main hall was deafening. Mary could not stand it. 'Twas like some horrible nightmare, only it was real!

"Play!" she gestured to the musicians irrationally. " 'Tis my wedding day! Play, ye whoresons!"

Confused and terrified, they began, of all things, the Dance of the Swords. Hunter smiled again, this time a tight, jeering grin that didn't quite reach his narrowed violet eyes, as though Mary had somehow challenged him, and he were sweeping up the gauntlet she proffered.

He crossed to Cadman's side and, as though daring the crowd to prevent him, drew the blade from his foster brother's scabbard, then walked to the center of the room, where he laid his own upon the other so they formed a wicked, silver *X* upon the oaken floor. His eyes fastened on Mary's face alone, Hunter MacBeth began to dance.

Och, how he danced! And for her alone! The man she thought the murderer of her brother. His booted feet never once touched a shining sword as the pipes continued to wail. How dared he? How dared he look at her with the love and lust mingled plainly on his handsome countenance as he executed the intricate steps? She had forsworn him! She hated him! She would slay him herself! And yet, in her heart, Mary knew she loved him still. For when love comes such as it had to her, in a rush of passion so strong and torrid everything else must be swept away before its roaring tide, it can never be denied, no matter the consequences. 'Twas for this last, more than anything, she cursed him, because he held her heart and soul, and she would never be free of him, not as long as she lived!

He finished the dance, sweeping a low bow before her.

"Ye were mine first, Mary Carmichael," his voice echoed softly to the rafters of the great chamber. "And mine ye will remain, for I will hae ye yet again, tigress; and ye, my lord"—he turned to Hugh—"will be powerless to prevent it. Aye," he laughed low, mockingly. "Look ye upon her bonnie face, Carmichael, and know this day ye wed the woman of Sir Hunter *MacBeth*, that I hae held her beneath me and branded her as my own. What I hold I keep, my lord, and will slay ye for, I promise ye."

Hugh's black eyes flashed.

"Let us see then, ye Romany bastard! Fight me now. If ye

win, ye can take the wench and leave here unharmed. I vow it."

"Hugh—" Mary gasped.

He glanced at her coolly. "I am more than a match for that strutting cock, madam, I assure ye."

"Maybe so," Hunter jeered. "But the oath of a Carmichael is a worthless thing, and ye insult me by gieing it. Nay, whoreson, we shall duel, hae no fear, but nae wie your men in attendance to harry my heels and stab me in the back. Alone, wie only the wench as witness to your death, my lord, the wench I will hae, while your blood lies fresh upon the ground."

Then, seizing Mary's hand, Hunter yanked her from the table, wrapped his fingers in her golden hair, twisted her face up to his, and ground his mouth down hard upon her own. She would have swooned had his arm not supported her, for her knees buckled as she felt the old familiar flame of desire flicker in her loins and spread its aching fire through her veins like hot coals.

"Like this, whoreson, I will hae her"—Hunter glanced upward to where Hugh stood seething—"and more." Then he snarled two words in Mary's ear before releasing her, and she wondered he asked them; he, who knew the answer far better than she! He, who'd lain with her, used her, and then slain her brother. He had said, "Why, Mary?"

She broke away from him, hating him, tears blinding her eyes, eyes that flashed violet sparks of shame and anger.

"I would kill myself before I e'er let ye touch me again, bastard!" she hissed, then slapped him hard across the face.

Och! How his own accursed amethyst shards glittered like steel at that!

"We shall see, tigress," he breathed menacingly. "We shall see. Cadman!" he turned on his heel.

Cadman pressed the point of his dirk gently into Lord Gilchrist's throat. "Move," the younger MacBeth commanded with a soft growl.

Then the two men were gone as swiftly and silently as they

had come, dragging the Chief of the Clan Carmichael with them as hostage for their safe exit.

Hugh leapt slowly to the floor from the table, advanced stealthily toward Mary.

"So, ye *did* please the Romany wie your whore's tricks, madam!" he accused her quietly before he dealt her a ringing blow. "After them! After them, cowards!" he yelled to his men. "*Buaidh no Bàs! Buaidh no Bàs!*"

"*Buaidh no Bàs!*" The others took up the cry as they rushed to follow Hugh in a frenzied fever for revenge.

'Twas dark. Mary lay in her chamber at Dùndereen, where her women had carried her, unsure of what had awakened her from her stupor. Then she felt the gentle prick of a dagger at her throat once more. She swallowed hard. 'Tis Hugh, she thought. He means to kill me.

"Dinna cry oot, lass," Hunter warned lowly.

Mary was ashamed at the sudden relief that flooded her very being at the sound of her lover's voice, knowing 'twas not her husband who loomed over her so menacingly in the shadowed light. The moon passed from behind the clouds that had enveloped it, and she saw his face, his twisted, scarred mouth in the silvery haze that streamed in through one narrow window. There was wrath in his violet eyes, dark and fearsome, and yet a strange puzzlement as well, an odd vulnerability, a sense of helplessness and confusion that lurked also within those amethyst depths. He withdrew his blade and made no further move to touch her.

"Why, tigress?"

"What are ye doing here?" She shrank back in alarm at the glimpse of his forbidding countenance.

He swore softly. "I hae ne'er left the keep, of course. Cadman and I hid in an alcove, while your husband's men rode oot through the gate, thinking we had left the fortress, the fools! Surely ye dinna believe I would leave wie'oot some explanation from your lips. Why hae ye wed him, Mary? I know we had quarrelled, but, before God, I meant to return to ye, to find some way to get your bairn and come back to ye.

And even if I hadna gotten the child, I would hae returned. I spoke in haste, in anger. Surely ye knew that! I could ne'er hae left ye, though it destroyed me in the end. I love ye too much. Oh, God, Mary, why? Why?''

The girl stared at him in disbelief. She trembled slightly, with hurt or rage, he could not tell.

"Ye dare—ye dare to ask me that, whoreson? Get ye gone afore I scream this castle down aboot your ears!''

Hunter studied her quietly, a muscle working in his jaw.

"Scream then. There's none who shall come to your aid, madam. That bastard ye hae wed has them all oot burning MacBeth villages to the ground in search of me. 'Twill be a month or more before he gains control of them again; he has so inflamed them wie his own burning fever for revenge. But even so, if I knew a hundred of my enemies would come charging through that door at your cry, I wouldna leave here wie'oot learning the reason for your hatred of me. And, by God, I will discover it, Mary, if I hae to kill ye for it!''

"As ye slew my brother? Would ye like me to roll o'er, sir, so ye may stab *me* in the back as ye did him? Ye whoreson coward! Nay, dinna seek to deny it, for I knew 'twas your weapon the moment I saw it! Did ye think I wouldna?''

He grabbed her and shook her roughly. "What are ye blathering aboot, wench? Your brother? What has he to do wie us? I had no hand in that, I promise ye!''

"Dinna lie to me! 'Twas your blade! Oh, God! 'Twas *your* dirk they pulled from Gordon's back! Why? Why? Ye swore to me upon your honor—''

"Aye, I gae ye my word, madam, and I hae kept it!'' Hunter hissed, understanding now. Oh, how it hurt him, cut him to the quick to think she had loved him so little, trusted him so little she had not even had the courtesy to confront him with her accusations, to give him a chance to explain before turning against him. "It might verra well hae been my blade that did end your brother's life; I dinna deny that, tigress. But 'twasna my hand that wielded it. My dagger has been lost to me these many weeks past; I know nae when or how, but 'tis the truth, I vow it!''

Mary could not, *would* not believe him. Her head ached from the wine she'd consumed and Hugh's blow. Dazed, she could not think clearly.

"Liar! Liar!" she screamed. "What MacBeth would hae done such a thing, and why? For what purpose would he hae taken your dirk to use in a manner for which his own would hae brought him much reward and recognition from your clan? By the Virgin Mary, dinna seek to play me for the fool again, sir. I hae been the butt of your jests and lies for the last time! I loved ye, betrayed my clan for ye. 'Believe,' ye said. 'Trust me,' ye said; and ye hae repaid my faith and trust wie the murder of my brother! I hate ye, do ye ken? Ye hae destroyed all we e'er shared, and I am ashamed of e'er loving ye! Oh, God, the verra thought of knowing I hae lain wie ye sickens me!"

Christ, how she wounded him with her bitter words. Hunter felt ill unto death; the pit of his belly heaved. His mouth tightened; the scar curled up derisively as he stared at her, feeling his love for her tear at his heart until he thought he would die of it; then the emotion began to sour, to spoil slowly like bad milk, for he could not have kept his sanity otherwise, so great was his passion for her. The moment of her painful rejection of him, her denial of their love was too sharp, too intense, too real; the blow too sudden, too stunning, too harsh. He reacted instinctively in self-defense, lashing out at her, wanting to hurt her as badly as she had done him, as he would have slain his own foster brother had Cadman suddenly wielded a sword against him.

"'Tisna I who hae destroyed our love, madam." His voice was curt, his laughter mocking, jeering. "For there was no love between us. If ye had come to me in love as ye vowed, madam, ye *would* hae trusted me, wouldna hae doubted me and my promise. Nay, ne'er call it loving, bitch! 'Twas naught save lust we shared, the lust between a mon and his whore! *Whore!*" he lied cruelly, knowing just how to wound her the worst, as only two lovers can do. "By all that is holy, ye will rue the day ye loved and trusted me so little, I swear it!"

Abruptly he stood and began to divest himself of his garments. Mary gazed up at him, wild-eyed with fright.

"What do ye think you're doing, sir?"

Hunter laughed shortly, harshly once more.

"This *is* your wedding night, is it nae? And since 'tis lust ye desire, then 'tis lust ye shall hae!"

"Dinna touch me! Bastard!"

Hunter caught her gown at the neck, tearing the filmy nightdress easily, the shift that should have been for Hugh.

"Once I sought to rape ye, madam." His violet eyes were deadly with intent in the moonlight. "Tonight I will show ye how 'twould hae been."

He threw himself upon Mary's naked body, pinioning her arms cruelly when she tried to fight him off, to claw at him like the tigress he called her.

"Bitch!" he growled.

He caught her jaw between his fingers, crushing the tender flesh as he forced her lips up to his, bruising her mouth with his rough, searing kisses, shooting his tongue inside like a fiery sword, scarcely allowing her to breathe as he pillaged her resisting softness. One hand moved to her breasts, fondling carelessly, pinching her nipples gently until they ached and tingled with the slight pain he caused. Pain that soon mingled with pleasure as, to her horror, Mary felt herself begin to respond to his violent lovemaking. Her body betrayed her, for he knew well how to arouse her, even when he did it with the brutal savageness of which she had known him capable, but never thought to have directed toward herself.

He was bullying her, breaking her, for she seemed little more than a rag doll in his arms, boneless and limp, with fear and surrender and wanting all mixed up inside her as he towered over her, wrapped his arms around her, and forced her to acquiesce to his desires by sheer strength alone. She was helpless in his crushing embrace—and she did not care.

"There is no love in this," he whispered hoarsely.

"Oh, God, Hunter, nae like this, please," Mary moaned, begged.

Dimly he heard her pleas for mercy, knew somewhere,

somehow, in the dark recesses of his mind, she was sorry; but he could not seem to stop what he had started. She had touched him on the raw, and as with all passionate men, his emotions ran deep and furious. Mary had unleashed his hate as violently as she had captured his heart. She had taunted a mountain cat, brought it to its most bestial peak. He was beyond all reason.

He spread her thighs, plundering her as though she were nothing, a chattel, a vessel, a thing to be used and then discarded when his seed was spent, his lust slaked, his fury abated. Mary climaxed quickly from the hard, rapid assault, and almost immediately Hunter's own release followed.

Silently he rose and dressed, barely glancing at her quivering, sobbing figure upon the soiled sheets. Mary bit her knuckles to stifle the choking gasps that came wrenching from her throat.

"I'll nae forgie ye this! Ne'er! Ne'er, do ye ken?"

His violet eyes raked the length of her slowly, and there was no sorrow in them for his deed.

"Ye are mine, tigress, first, last, and always; in love or lust, aye, lust—I dinna care. Ye hae ruined me, bitch! Ruined me for all other women, and ye must pay the price for it! Ye hae one hour to be at Mheadhoin. I'll tarry no longer for ye than that. Aye, ye will come to me willingly, Mary, in spite of all that has just passed between us, for ye know in your heart 'tis me ye want, me you'll always want, just as I want ye, even if it kills us both! For we are mates, Mary Carmichael, in the truest sense of the word; ye are as savage in your passions as I, as once I told ye. Ye would trod on any other mon and trample him into the ground," Hunter laughed. "Oh, aye, ye need me, tigress; ye need me because I'm the only mon wie a shoulder strong enough for ye to lean on, strong enough to master ye and yet gentle enough to love ye wie'oot breaking your spirit, secure enough wie myself to love ye as ye are, proud and arrogant, soft and vulnerable; fire and earth and wind and rain all mixed up into one passionate, realistic, elusive romantic of a woman. Oh, aye, lass, ye need me because I'm the only mon who knows how to conquer them all wie'oot destroying them. One hour, Mary Carmichael, or ye will regret it e'ery second of e'ery day ye live!"

Sweet Christ! The very arrogance of the whoreson! To think she had loved him! Every chord rang true, and still Mary denied him, hated him for knowing her down to her very bones.

"Get ye to hell, bastard of Satan!" she cried.

"Even there I will hae ye, witch!"

Then, with a searing kiss that would live forever in her memories, he was gone.

Fearing she would have a stroke if the pounding in her head did not cease, Mary arose, robed herself, and walked with feverish intent to Hugh's desk in one corner of the room. Grabbing a quill and a scrap of parchment paper, she scrawled five words across the sheet and, in doing so, signed Hunter MacBeth's death warrant.

*The Romany waits in Mheadhoin,* she had written.

Then she yanked open the chamber door, calling for a man-at-arms.

"Collie, take this to my husband at once," she ordered coldly to the young page who answered her fearsome cry. "Tell him to hurry!"

Then Mary flung herself onto the bed, where Hunter had made love to her so brutally, and wept for the bitter ruins of her life.


Oh, Mheadhoin! How it lay entangled in their lives, the Carmichaels and MacBeths. The kirk loomed up in the blackness of the night, beckoning to Hugh's men like a guiding light, stark and steady against the torch-dotted sky that signaled their coming. Like Christmas luminaries they lined the winding path leading up to the west border of the village, descending rapidly like hawks upon prey in the darkness, *breacans* flapping in the wind, effectively cutting off Hunter's escape back to Glenkirk. To the east lay Bailekair and Dùndereen, and no help would he find there. To the north were the cliff and the great, rushing waters of Loch

Ness. 'Twas southward, then, he must flee. Hunter mounted Craigor swiftly, flying like the devil as he cursed Mary Carmichael silently under his breath, for he knew 'twas his own beloved who had sent her husband and the Carmichael men-at-arms in hot pursuit of him.

He had a good head start, and he paced his white destrier evenly, realizing he would have a long, hard ride to Edinburgh. For, although Oir Uisge, Wynd Cheathaich, and Eadar Da Voe lay nearer, Hunter could not be sure of his welcome at the first, not knowing how soon word of his escapade this evening might reach his kinsmen; and he had no wish to bring the revenge-mad Carmichaels down upon David MacDonald or Alinor's Clan Murray. 'Twas for the King's palace he rode. Jamie owed him.

# Twenty-three

Nearly a month after their disastrous wedding day Mary's husband returned to her with the stink of wine and whores upon him still as he burst through their chamber door, a triumphant smirk upon his brutal lips. She had known he had arrived, of course, for the watchmen in the towers had long since heralded his coming; still she had not thought he would seek her until dusk, and she faced him fearfully, veiled terror shining from her amethyst jewels. He ordered the maids curtly to get out, then laughed cruelly at Mary's obvious distress.

"Rejoice, madam." He danced a few pantherish, graceful steps across the room, and Mary realized the headiness of liquor was with him still. "For I hae avenged your ravished honor and Gordon's slaying. The Romany MacBeth is dead!"

"Dead?" Mary went numb with shock, for though she had

wished it and sent that fatal message to her husband, some part of herself had still hoped Hunter would escape. Dead! How could it be? The Sight had not come to her to apprise her of Hunter's demise. Surely it would have! Sweet *Jesù!* Mayhap in cutting her beloved from her heart she had closed her subconscious mind to him as well! Oh, God! God! Dinna let it be true! Please, dinna let it be true! I'm sorry! Sorry! Oh, God! I dinna mean it!

"Aye, dead," Hugh chortled. "You should hae seen him, the boasting cock!" He began to reenact the fatal duel, thrusting his sword devilishly as he lunged at an imaginary opponent. "Still I'll warrant I taught him a thing or two before he died! Ha! By the time I'd finished wie him he was so weak he could scarcely lift his shield. I got him in the shoulder first, a clean hit, and told him to bind it, that I was of no mind to slip on his blood. He bound the wound, then tried to fend me off, but I beat him back. Lord, ye ought to hae been there, Mary! And then"—he feinted as Mary struggled to keep from screaming at the horrible pictures painted in her mind—"Ah! I skewered him like a stuck pig—right through the belly!"

Sick, I'm going to be sick, Mary thought as she fought to keep from retching.

*He'll nae hae ye, tigress; that I promise ye! I'll slay him first or be dead myself ere he touches ye!*

Oh, Hunter! Beloved! What hae I done? Nae your death, too, upon my soul!

Mary would have wept with grief had not Hugh grabbed her then, jamming his mouth down on hers painfully, tearing at her *arascaid* with deft rough fingers. She steeled herself for his rape, knowing it was his right as her lord and master, and was suddenly relieved to get it over with so quickly, for she needed Hugh's seed inside her desperately. Her monthly flow was two weeks late. In his savage assault upon her on her wedding night Hunter MacBeth had at last left Mary with child.

Naked and frightened, she stood in her husband's muscled arms as his hands roamed maliciously over her shrinking flesh, for in spite of her need of him, Hugh's touch repelled the girl violently as it always had. He yanked her hair back brutally, forcing her to look at his leering grin as he pinched her breasts hurtfully.

"Fight me, damn ye! Fight me!" he growled.

"There—there is no need for—for it to be like this, Hugh," Mary pleaded with him, afraid. "I hae said I would come willingly to your bed."

"Oh, aye, I can see ye are just pining away for me, ye eager slut!" he sneered sarcastically. "I know ye hate me. Why don't ye fight me, bitch? By God, I'll make ye fight me!" With a swift, sudden movement he kicked Mary's legs apart and pushed his fingers up inside her. "Dry as a drought! Is *that* how ye pleased the Romany? Come, come, you'll hae to do better than that, whore," he chuckled. "What, no answer? Well, no matter. 'Tis tight as a maid ye are, soiled though ye may be. Och, was nae the MacBeth or my half brother mon enough for ye, madam? Aye, that's it. Come on. Fight me, bitch. I'll show ye what a *real* mon is like."

Mary could stand it no longer.

"A *real* mon, Hugh?" she jeered. "Do ye mean a mon who murders unsuspecting lairds and abuses and humiliates defenseless women? A *real* mon? Ye make me sick!"

She clawed at him wildly, leaving bloody streaks down one side of his face as he tried to grab her flailing limbs. She could not seem to stop herself, even though she knew it was what he wanted. Aye, he *wanted* her to struggle. He wanted to hurt her. He was grinning. I dinna care, Mary thought. I dinna care if he kills me. I *will* fight him. I'll— She slapped his dark smirking visage again and again as he attempted to restrain her. Her fingers tore at his black unruly hair.

"You're insane," Mary hissed. "Insane."

Too late she realized her mistake. She had pushed him too far. My God! He really *is* going to slay me—

Hugh pulled his leather clan-belt from his chest, advancing toward her quivering figure slowly, an evil, forbidding look upon his countenance.

"You'll pay for that, whore," he said. "I've waited a long time to make ye pay."

What happened next would always be a horrible blur in Mary's memory. She only knew she raised her arms protectively before the first of the cruel blows came as the lash descended upon her furiously, cutting deeply into her pale satin skin, biting and tearing at her naked flesh. The third stroke knocked her to the floor. She curled up, trying to cover her belly as she heard the whistle of the leather, felt the terrible sting of the belt as it fell again and again upon her trembling body. Angry red weals blotched her goldenness. Welts she knew would be a mass of purplish blue bruises in the morning. Hugh towered above her, demon-eyed in his in rage. He *is* mad. He's going to kill me, Mary thought before the black void of unconsciousness swirled up to engulf her.

She awakened to find herself lying in the massive canopied bed. Her wrists had been bound to one of the four posts. Hugh had stripped and was moving toward her once more. Mary groaned. There was no part of her that did not ache throbbingly with pain.

"Please—" she pleaded hoarsely, for he had half-choked her in his rage, and her lips were swollen twice their normal size.

Hugh only laughed. "Ye look like the village idiot," he mocked. "Aye, my wee half-wit. I thought you'd ne'er come to. But now that ye hae—"

God's breath! He actually strutted to where she lay mute and horrified, parading himself before her. Mary moaned and bit her lip. He was so big; he would rip her asunder, and still she could not tear her eyes from his manhood, hard and pulsating as he watched her. He caressed it gently with one hand.

"Aye." He noted her terror at its size. "I'll warrant 'tis more than enough for ye. Well, bitch, spread your legs so I may get an heir upon ye. Goddamn it!" he yanked at Mary's locked thighs, forcing them apart with his fingers. "I told ye to open your legs, whore!" His knees joined his hands as he fell upon her, pried at her, holding her in readiness. His shaft stabbed between her flanks.

"No!" Mary sobbed, but he was already hammering into her violently.

She gasped aloud at each painful piercing, and he delighted in her misery, muttering oaths and obscenities she'd never heard before, breathing heavily upon her throat, her face, her hair.

This wasn't happening! It couldn't be happening to her, Mary Carmichael, daughter of a Highland chief! It was too horrid! Too unreal! But it was happening all the same. Without even consciously realizing it Mary divorced her soul from her body; it was but a shell that received Hugh, while the essence of Mary's being floated somewhere above to gaze on with strange detachment.

This—this was rape! For there was no caring in Hugh for her at all. Even when Edward and Hunter had used her thusly, there had at least been love mingled with the hurt and anger in their glazed eyes when they'd taken her. But Hugh—Hugh brutalized her with an impersonal violence that dehumanized her utterly; and she felt nothing—nothing but shame and an odd sense of relief when he finally shuddered atop her and lay still. He did not even care the girl had not responded to him. It had not been Hugh's intent to give her pleasure. He rolled off her stricken form, laughing crudely as he rubbed his darkly matted chest.

"Och, there's naught like an unwilling lass, maidenhood or no."

Mary made no reply, for she was beyond being wounded by his cutting remarks. She only wanted him to go away so she might wash the filth of his seed from her thighs and aching womanhood. She would never be clean again. Not as long as she lived! *I willna think aboot it—e'er! I'll go crazy if I do—*

"Still," Hugh continued as though speaking to himself, "I'll wager I've nae been cheated of your *other* virgin places."

Mary stiffened beside him apprehensively, not understanding what he meant, and realized he had grown big and hard once more.

"Aye," he sniggered when he saw where her haunted eyes strayed. "There's naught can rise again to the occasion as quickly as Hugh Carmichael!" He crowed loudly. "Turn o'er, whore, I'm nae through wie ye yet."

When he finally released and left her, Mary would have done anything Hugh commanded of her, so sadistically had he broken her body and spirit. She staggered from the bed to retch horribly into the chamber pot, over and over again until there was nothing left to come up, and still she heaved, shaking with the aftermath of the violence done to her that night. She tried to rise, to crawl to the window bench, for she could not bear the bed, and sprawled upon the floor.

The screams began then, clawing their way out of her throat hysterically. She could not stop them. Scream after scream they came. The last thing she remembered was Joanna's sweet, solemn face bending over her; Joanna, who had not spoken to her since Gordon's funeral and who had come to Dùndereen as Geoffrey's nurse only to fill the void left by the loss of her own child; Joanna's shocked-beyond-belief voice crying with revulsion and pity,

"My God, Mary! What has he done to ye? What has he done?"

# *Twenty-four*

Hugh had left Hunter for dead, so gloating in his under-handed triumph that he, to Hunter's fortune, had failed to make certain of the deed. Hunter knew Hugh's vanity was his weakness then, for had Hunter been in Hugh's place, he would have slit his enemy's throat before leaving that spot outside of Stirling where the duel between the two men had taken place. But Hugh Carmichael was not Hunter MacBeth and so the Romany knight lived, lived because Cadman had followed his foster brother and the Carmichaels those many long days when Hugh and his men-at-arms had run Hunter down like a dog.

The young MacBeth stanched the flow of blood quickly, covering the gaping wound in his clansman's belly with mud and cobwebs as Grace had taught him, after cleansing the injury with some brandy from his flask. Then he tore Hunter's *breacan* into strips, binding his kinsman's abdomen to keep the dressing in place, and carried him, unconscious, to Wynd Cheathaich, fearing all the while Hunter would not survive the journey. Still Cadman dared not seek a nearby village, not knowing if the Carmichaels would return to Dùndereen or linger in the area.

"Christ's son, Cadman! What happened?" David ran to the MacBeth's aid as Cadman staggered into the main hall of the castle with his foster brother's body. "Grace! Grace, come quickly! Agnes! Edith! Kirsty!"

"I'll explain later," Cadman responded grimly as they struggled with Hunter's inert form.

"Oh, my God!" Grace appeared, one hand held to her stricken face before she moved to help the two men. "Girls, prepare a room upstairs. Hurry! Oh, my God, Cadman! How did this happen?"

"Later," her brother repeated,

The three maids scurried to pull down the blankets upon the bed in the chamber normally used by Hunter at Wynd Cheathaich, then set about heating water and fetching Grace's herbal medicines without being told. Grace nearly swooned when she eased away the makeshift bandage Cadman had managed.

"Sweet *Jesù*!" she breathed. "How can he still be alive?"

"Will he live, Grace?" Cadman inquired anxiously.

She shook her head sadly. "I dinna know, brother. I dinna know. 'Tis a miracle he has survived this long. Oh, Cadman! He needs a doctor. How long has he been like this?"

"Nearly three days."

"My God! how far hae ye come, brother? Why dinna ye take him to the closest village?"

"I couldna risk it, sister. The Carmichaels were after him. There must hae been fifty at least, and they were determined to see him slain. Hunter had a good head start. He would hae reached the King, but the cowardly curs broke up into shifts to chase him down. He had no time to eat or sleep. God's blood, they wearied him so and ran him to ground just ootside of Stirling. He dueled wie the leader, the Earl of Dùndereen—the whoresons gae him that chance at least. Ha! 'Twas a yellow dog's fight, I tell ye. Hunter was so tired and weak he could barely stand, and the laird's bastards ringed around the two men, jeering, laughing. They threw a rope o'er a nearby tree so that Hunter knew they meant to hang him if he won, that he was going to die anyway. I had to bring him here, Grace. I had no way of knowing if the Carmichaels would return—"

"Dear Lord. David, send someone for the physician at once. I canna trust my skill wie this—"

"Grace, we canna wait! He may die!" Cadman exclaimed.

"I can see that!" Grace interjected more sharply than she'd intended, wringing her hands worriedly. She probed gently at the inflamed area. "I canna tell what damage has been done. I must clean him up. Thank God, he's unconscious. David! Dinna stand there like a daft mon! Get the physician! I will do what I can in the meantime."

That anyone would speak thusly to David MacDonald made Cadman's jaw drop open, especially when it was his shy sister, Grace. His amazement only grew when the Earl of Wynd Cheathaich turned silently to do his wife's bidding.

"Cadman, fetch a bottle of whiskey, the strongest ye can find! Hae ye lost your wits as well, fool?" She rounded on him angrily when he did not stir.

"Nay, nay." He shuffled off quickly.

Tears filled Grace's eyes as she gazed at the gaunt, unshaven man who lay upon the bed before her. This wasn't Hunter! Surely it couldn't be! Hunter was so vital, so alive! Hastily she brushed away the fine droplets that splashed upon her cheeks, then set her deft fingers to cleansing the ugly wound, not realizing she was holding her breath until she suddenly expelled it in a huge sigh upon seeing at last that the gash looked much worse than it actually was. Still it would have killed Hunter had Cadman not been there to stop the loss of blood, which had been tremendous. Grace dabbed gingerly at the caked mass, relieved to see her brother had kept the dressing moist as she had warned him when instructing him in the care of battle injuries. His heed of her words had prevented Hunter's exposed organs from drying out and putrefying. A part of the intestines had been sliced through, but Grace did not believe the damage would be mortal if the maimed section could be tied off and cut out and the remaining good ends rejoined. Och! If only the doctor would hurry! A portion of the now-naked muscle was mangled as well, but Grace knew it would mend on its own, given rest and care. The torn flesh itself would have to be sewn together and would leave a horrible scar.

She glanced briefly at Hunter's mouth. Her own lips tightened. He was too handsome a man to be disfigured so. Och, 'twas the price of being a mighty warrior and the way of all men. God only knew why they found joy in the destruction of one another.

After doing all she knew for his belly Grace turned her attention to the lesser wound in her kinsman's shoulder. It was neat and clean and, thank the Holy Virgin, not life-threatening.

Master MacTavish came at last, a skilled and learned physician who had, as a youth, studied with the knowledge-able doctors of the Ottoman Empire. The physician performed the necessary surgery upon Hunter quickly, confidently, and efficiently, and the Romany knight's life was spared. But it took Hunter nearly a year to recover from the crippling injury, a year in which Master MacTavish and Grace nursed him patiently and diligently. Hunter was not able to get up at all for the first three months, for the damaged muscle and organs would not tolerate the strain of movement; but he was too weak to even care. Once he lapsed into a fever and knew no one, which frightened Grace dreadfully, for she feared that an infection had set in that would rot her clansman's life away as surely as Lord Angus's leg was slowly ending her uncle's existence. But it was a bout of the sweating sickness brought on by Hunter's poor condition and lack of resistance to disease. Grace tended him lovingly, pouring gallons of cool water down his throat to replace the fluids lost from his haggard body. 'Twas for this reason Hunter survived, for most healers of the day would have bled him and given him naught to drink; but Master MacTavish reasoned logically that liquid sweated out of the body must be put back in and so saved his patient, where another doctor, looking for a more complex answer to a simple problem, would have failed.

When Hunter was finally able to stand, he found he could barely walk.

"Dinna push yourself, brother." Cadman hastened to grab his arm before he fell. "I hae sent word to Glenkirk of your fate, and though Angus misses us sorely, he doesna wish ye to be up and aboot until ye are ready."

"How—how is he?" Hunter grimaced as he sank back down upon the bed.

"He willna last another year, I fear."

"Och, Cadman, 'tis our duty to hold Glenkirk safe until Stephen is mon enough to manage his inheritance."

"Aye, and what good will ye be to the lad in your condition? Rest, I tell ye, and get well."

"Cadman—" Hunter held a restraining hand out as his foster brother turned to go. "Hae ye—hae ye heard aught of—of Mary?"

Cadman's blue eyes darkened. "Nay, brother. Forget that accursed witch! 'Twas she who brought ye to this."

"She thought I slew her brother. Marry-go-up, sir. 'Twas my dirk in Gordon's back. *Mine!* Och, Cadman, how could it be? How could it be? Who would hae taken my dagger—and why?"

"I dinna know, Hunter." The younger man shook his head. "It doesna make sense. Och, forget her, brother! I hae said naught of what brought the Carmichaels down upon ye, else our clan turn against ye for your foolishness and betrayal. Leave her be now. 'Tis o'er! She wants ye nae!''

"Nay." Hunter's scarred lips twisted. " 'Twillna be ended until I hae my revenge upon her. Oh, God, I loved her so! And she—she cared for me so little in return she dinna even gie me a chance to explain aboot my dirk. Nay, Cadman, hae no fear I shall seek her love again." He saw the unspoken worry in his foster brother's troubled eyes. "I mean to kill her. Only then shall I be free of her fore'er!''

He became obsessed with the idea. Each day as he slowly regained his strength Hunter thought of Mary Carmichael's shimmering golden hair; her haunting violet eyes; her lilting silver laughter; and she spurred him on to recovery. His shoulder healed quickly, although it would never again be able to sustain the heavy blows of his shield slamming against it that it had once borne; but it would serve him well enough. It was his belly that pained and worried him. When he thought it stabilized, Hunter began a torturous routine of exercise to make it hard and taut as a bow string once more.

That early summer of 1491, he and Cadman returned home to Glenkirk. By this time physically Hunter was well, though he would wear an ugly, jagged scar across his abdomen for the rest of his days; but mentally he was dazed and ill. He still could not fathom the accusations Mary had hurled at him so cruelly or the denial of her love and trust. The agony in his heart and soul festered like a pus-filled wound, eating at him with grinding torment until he knew he would have no peace of mind until he had won vengeance against her for her perfidy.

He stood often at his window, gazing out over Loch Ness and the wide sweep of terrain that rushed toward the purple mountain in the distance whence Bailekair stared back at him so regally. And Mary's violet eyes haunted him time and time again before he remembered she was at Dùndereen with the man she had chosen over him. Och, how Hunter's pride suffered over that! And still he stood and scanned that far horizon for some sign of her.

I will slay her, he told himself over and over and began to imagine various slow and horrible ways in which he would accomplish this. Sometimes he tied her to a stake in his mind and burned her for a witch. Sometimes he stabbed her repeatedly in her·flat white belly, touching the searing scar that marked the length of his groin at the thought. Sometimes he placed his strong hands around her slender throat, snapping her neck in half. And always before each one of these fantasies of death he stripped her naked, bathed her ritually, massaged her with perfumed oils, and made love to her slowly, sweetly, violently, savagely before he killed her.

Och, Mary, Mary! Bitch and betrayer! Lady and lover! She was all mixed up in his mind, part maiden, part whore. He sought out women to ease the ache in his loins and cursed them when they did him no good, yelling at them drunkenly before throwing a few gold coins at their hastily retreating figures and shouting at them to get out of his sight. The villagers thought him daft, more accursed than ever, and made the sign against him openly when he rode by upon his ghostly white stallion, grim and forbidding in his newfound hardness. Those men brave enough to force a quarrel on him did not live to regret it, for Hunter showed them no mercy, no quarter. If he had been respected and deferred to before, he was feared and dreaded now. He was a driven man with a single goal to which his window was the key. His window, where he stood and watched and waited.

'Twas for this reason Hunter saw, one day, the flash of Ian Carmichael's mirror as the Earl of Bailekair signaled to Euphemia, though the Romany knight did not then realize what it was. Hunter watched his kinswoman's answering gleam and moments later glimpsed her hurrying across the courtyard. Curiosity pricked his being, and he followed her to learn at last who had taken his dagger, and why.

He was sickened by the sight of them coupling in the grove, vicious in their lovemaking as no normal mating should have been; and he burned with a slow, furious rage to think those two—animals!—had destroyed all that had been precious and beautiful between him and Mary Carmichael, for Hunter knew now it had been Effie who'd stolen his dirk, Effie who'd taken his dagger to hide Ian's murder of Gordon Carmichael. Oh, God! Hunter wanted to kill them both, those two who moaned and panted in the grove, biting, slapping, and clawing one another, oblivious to his presence. How easy it would be to end their lives this very moment! He had only to slip from behind the tree that served as his cover and cut them down with his broadsword. They wouldn't stand a chance. But he could not do it. His honor and his vow to Lord Angus wouldn't let him.

Instead Hunter cornered Euphemia in her chamber upon her return to Glenkirk. She was his liege's daughter. Hunter would do her the courtesy of facing her with his accusations, giving her a chance to explain, the chance that had been denied him; but he did it for the dying Angus's sake, not for Euphemia MacBeth.

She dared to flirt with him when he entered! With the stench of Ian Carmichael upon her still she put her arms around Hunter's neck and sought to kiss him. He shoved her away roughly in disgust, then slapped her hard across the face.

"My God, ye would spread your legs for any mon, Effie, like a bitch in heat, and I hae nae even offered ye an invitation! How can ye be so shameless ye would even *think* of lying wie me wie the stink of your lover's seed fresh upon your thighs?"

Euphemia faltered; her eyes widened with fright and then narrowed with sudden sly cunning. She had been found out! Christ's son! And by Hunter. Hunter, who was frighteningly crazed these days. The man could almost see the wheels clicking in her head as she determined how best to deal with him. She decided. She laughed brightly, tossing her thin mane of dark hair.

"I'm sure I dinna know what ye are talking aboot, Hunter. What else was I to think when ye came so brazenly to my room?"

"Dinna play me for a fool, bitch! I spied ye wie Ian Carmichael, eagerly spreading your legs for him like the

whore ye are! How long? How long, slut, hae ye been lying
wie him?''

Effie backed away from the wrath within those accursed
violet eyes.

"Spawn of the devil!" she hissed. "Get oot! Get oot now
afore I call my father!"

Hunter caught her arm, twisting it cruelly.

"Lower your voice, bitch! Would ye kill Angus wie the
shock of the shame ye hae brought upon us, coupling wie that
dour-faced whoreson?''

"Ye dare," she shot back, white-lipped, "ye dare to speak
to me of shame when 'twas ye who caused our banishment
from Court wie your lust for Ian's sister? Two months ye
spent wie her at Wynd Cheathaich, and God knows what *really*
happened there! She has bewitched ye, the bitch! And ye hae
brought us to the brink of ruin for her still! Well," Effie
snorted derisively. "She wants ye nae. Och, what puir sport
in bed ye must be, kinsman, that she wed a spineless lad such
as Edward Carmichael to salvage her honor. Aye, and *he*
got a child on her, and now she is to bear his half brother's
brat as well! Such fertile soil, Hunter," she taunted heedlessly,
"and yet *your* seed dinna take root in it! Are ye less than a
mon, ye demon-eyed—''

"Dinna say it, Effie," Hunter warned silkily.

"I'll say what I damned well please!" she retorted. "Even
father has said ye are daft. Och, I know too what brought
Hugh Carmichael's rage down upon ye, ye puir fool—''

"Shut up! Ye—''

"Nay, why should I? How dare ye accuse me when ye are
guilty of the same crime, for ye love Ian's sister even as I
love him, do ye nae?''

"Love?" he purred softly, menacingly. "Whate'er love
there was between Mary and me, ye and Ian killed wie yours.
Aye, 'twas ye who stole my dagger, Effie, was it nae? Ye
took my dirk that Ian's murder of his brother might nae be
discovered.''

" 'Twasna Ian who slew him; 'twas Hugh!'' Euphemia
burst out, too late realizing she had incriminated herself. She

plunged on, uncaring. "But Ian was wie him when it happened, and I couldna let any shadow of blame fall upon him. I love him, do ye ken? Love him as ye lust for that bitch he calls his sister. I mean to wed him and be quit of this place. What other chance do I hae? Do ye think I dinna know how I am talked aboot among my own? God's foot, mon! I'll nae be the laughingstock of the Clan MacBeth!"

"Ye puir fool." Hunter began dimly to understand what had driven her to Ian Carmichael's arms. "He's used ye, Effie. He'll nae wed wie ye."

"He will! He will! Ye dinna know him as I do!"

"Nay, but all the same, he willna hae ye, bitch," Hunter's voice hardened once more. "For I mean to slay ye."

"I've done naught to warrant such!" she spat. "Bring me up before the clan council. I'll deny e'ery word, and ye hae no proof—"

"I hae no need of proof of your perfidy, for 'twas ye who sent young Francis to his death, was it nae?"

It was a shot in the dark, but Euphemia did not know that. She blanched sickeningly.

"I had to, oh, God, I had to— Dinna ye see? Ian *had* to hae revenge for Gordon's death. 'An eye for an eye. A tooth for a tooth.' And I'm nae sorry!" She flung her head back proudly. "My only regret is that 'twasna ye the Carmichaels slew! Still"—her eyes narrowed shrewdly again as she licked her lips—"you've nae evidence of that either."

"Oh, aye, Euphemia, he does, he does."

Hunter and Effie turned to see Lady Sophia standing in the doorway, a handkerchief held with trembling hands to her tearstained, horror-stricken face.

"Oh, God, Euphemia! Francis! My baby! How could ye?"

"Mother—mother—" Effie held out her hands pleadingly. "I had to do it; I just *had* to!"

"My son. My son! Your brother, Euphemia! Nay, dinna touch me!" the Countess's voice had suddenly gone very cold. "I could hae borne anything—anything, but this. Oh, God, 'twill kill Angus. 'Twill kill him, do ye ken?"

"Mother, I'm sorry—"

"Sorry? Sorry! Ye hae murdered my son Francis as surely as though ye wielded the dirks that took his young life. Oh, may God curse the macabre day of your wretched birth, Euphemia MacBeth! Get oot of my sight, ye wicked wench! Surely ye hae been visited by the devil to hae aspired to such an evil deed! Get hence! Get hence from Glenkirk, do ye ken?"

"Lady Sophia, 'tisna your place to decide your daughter's fate. 'Tis a matter for the clan council," Hunter reminded the Countess quietly, his heart aching for her.

"Nay! Nay, Hunter! No one must know of her vile betrayal. 'Twill be the death of my husband, I tell ye, and he—he doesna hae much time left—"

Hunter nodded. "Verra well then. I will gie her one hour to be gone, my lady, and then I will kill her."

The Countess drew the edges of her dignity together raggedly, placing one hand on Hunter's arm. Tears filled her soft eyes.

"Be swift, Hunter, and merciful. She is still my daughter. Regardless of what she has done, she is still my daughter."

"I promise ye that, my lady. I—"

"Nay, I dinna want to know how 'tis done."

Silently Sophia left the chamber, closing the door behind her, ignoring Effie's desperate, begging cry. Only when the Countess had reached her own room did she allow the wrenching sobs to come pouring from her throat.

*As their tears flow like rivers, so will your tears flow.*

Euphemia's heart pounded queerly. One hour. She had one hour to escape from the certain death to which her mother had condemned her at the hands of Hunter MacBeth. She threw open the lids to her coffers hurriedly, frantically yanking her gowns from their neatly folded states. She put on as many as she could, then made two big heaps of all her other favorites, almost weeping with despair as she saw how many still remained. Hastily she added four more to the two piles; she just couldn't bear to leave them behind! Then she dumped the contents of her jewelry boxes, one after another, on top of the clothes. An old string of pearls broke at the rough treatment, sending the soft white globes scattering. With a small cry Effie bent to retrieve them, grabbing up as many of the beads as possible.

Casting a quick glance at the hourglass, through which sand was slipping rapidly, she hoisted her bundles from the bed, lugging them downstairs stealthily. They were heavy, but she refused to part with them. She dragged them to the stables, uncaring that the men-at-arms and some of the serving wenches in the courtyard were staring at her curiously, whispering behind her back.

"Sean," she called to one of the grooms. "Saddle my mare, and help me load these things upon her."

The lad, who was sixteen and big for his age, cupped Euphemia's buttocks with one hand, giving them a gentle, possessive sqeeze.

"Here. What's this now? Marry, but ye look like a cow in all those clothes, Effie! Big as Maddie Craddock when she was wie child!" He laughed and slapped his knee. "I thought for a moment there ye were ready to whelp yourself!"

"Save your stupid remarks, Sean, and do as I ordered ye."

"Here. What's your hurry now that ye ainna got time for auld Sean?"

"If ye must know, I'm running away. 'Tis a matter of life or death!"

"Och, Effie. Ye surely do try a mon's patience."

"No worse than you're trying mine at the moment. Now hurry up!"

"Well—" He cocked his head to one side slyly as she tapped her foot impatiently, slapping his exploring fingers away rudely. "Mayhap I shall, and mayhap I shallna. It all depends."

"Depends on what? For God's sake, Sean, I'm desperate, I told ye!"

"Now you're right aboot that; that's a fact. I ainna e'er seen anyone as desperate as ye were the other day. Just aching to get at it, were ye nae? Aye, I guess you're just aboot the hottest little piece I've had in a long time. Well, I'll tell ye what, ye sweet slut, ye just pull them skirts up around your bonnie thighs and make auld Sean as happy as he was the last time. I ainna enjoyed bedding a wench like I did ye since I had ye. Come on, Effie. Ye do that for me, huh, and auld Sean'll hae your mare saddled and loaded in no time, no time at all.'' He caught her in his arms and gave her a wet kiss.

"Nay, Sean, nay,'' Euphemia protested weakly, but his fingers were already fumbling at the bodices of her garments, pushing them aside to fondle her small, swelling breasts.

"Shut up, Effie.'' He shoved her toward a pile of hay. "You've spread your legs for me afore now, and I've always gi'en it to ye hard and good.''

He pushed the skirts of her clothes up around her thighs awkwardly and yanked her hose down before reaching for the fastenings on his codpiece. Moments later he was rutting away merrily between her flanks, while Effie moaned and strained beneath him. It was over as quickly as it had begun.

"How was it?'' he asked eagerly. "Hot and sweet just like I promised, huh?'' he bragged.

"Fine. 'Twas just fine, Sean, just like always. You're the best, ye know it? You're going to break my puir auld heart one of these days,'' Effie flattered and gave him a coy smile. She straightened her garments and brushed a bit of straw from her hair. "Now saddle my mare, please, Sean, and put those things on her back.''

"Anything ye say, my lady.'' He smirked and blushed. "Anything ye say.''

He was whistling smugly as he went about his chores. Euphemia could have screamed with exasperation. He was so damned dumb and slow. What had she ever seen in him? After he'd finished up and helped her into the saddle she looked down at him coldly.

"Ye know what, Sean?''

"Nay, what?''

"Yours is the worst cock I've e'er had in my life. I'd rather bed a board than ye, ye oafish lout!''

And then she kicked him in the chest and lashed her mare quickly out of the stable. The horse lumbered through the postern gate of Glenkirk, stumbling now and again under the heavy burden it bore upon its back. Effie swore under her breath, sawing at the bit and laying her whip smartly across the animal's rump. After she'd gotten up some speed she threw back her head and laughed. She hoped that stupid churl never got it up again! It would serve him right! Wasting her valuable time like that! She sobered at the thought. She just *had* to reach Bailekair. Bailekair, where Ian would take care of her. Ian wouldn't let anything happen to her, and he'd have to marry her at last too!

"Faster! Faster!" She beat her horse cruelly and began to breathe a little easier when the beast lengthened its strides.

It willna be long now, Effie thought, and then I'll be safe. Safe in Ian's arms.

"To hell wie ye, Glenkirk." She made an obscene gesture at the slowly diminishing keep, then smiled once more as she looked toward Bailekair in the distance.

She had reached the cliff outside of Mheadhoin overlooking Loch Ness when the crazy, morbid cackling started. It echoed through the Great Glen and rang horribly in Effie's ears. 'Tis only the wind moaning, she told herself sternly, or perhaps 'tis Hunter— She glanced back worriedly over one shoulder, but could see nothing. The girl began to whip her mare furiously once more.

"Oh, nay!" Effie cried as her bundles suddenly slipped from the horse's back, breaking open and sending her clothes and jewelry scattering. The garments fluttered and rolled this way and that, blowing away with the breeze.

Euphemia reined her mount up sharply, dropped from the saddle, and ran toward the flapping gowns, trying to catch them. Tears stung her eyes. She would never be able to retrieve them all, and she'd already had to leave so many behind at Glenkirk! It just wasn't fair! It just wasn't fair at all! Oh, Goddamn that stupid Sean for not tying her things on more securely! If she could get her hands on him this minute, Effie vowed silently she'd—she'd castrate that bragging cock!

"'Tis no use, Effie. You'll hae no need of fancy gowns and jewels where you'll be going."

Euphemia looked at the black leather boots a few feet from

336

her face. She shivered. Her eyes traveled upward to see Hunter towering over her, his white destrier standing like a specter in the distance. The scar upon her kinsman's mouth was twisted unpleasantly, reminding the lass chillingly of a devil. She backed away from him, one hand going to her throat, her eyes widening with terror as he walked toward her stealthily. She gave a small sob of dismay and turned to run. He grabbed her swiftly.

"Ye hae made Grace miserable. Ye hae lied and cheated. Ye hae betrayed our clan and brought shame upon us all. And ye sent young Francis to a grisly death." Hunter spoke softly, coldly. "But more than this, Effie, ye hae destroyed my woman's love for me wie your greed and lust and placed her in God only knows what kind of peril. I'm going to kill ye, Effie. I'm going to kill ye so your evil sickness can harm naught else."

"Do it quickly—" Effie pleaded as his hands came up around her throat, began to tighten cruelly. Dear God. He was laughing, laughing! But his lips weren't moving. And still the laughter went on and on, jeering at her, high and shrill in its maliciousness. His scarred mouth was closed in a terrible grimace as his strong fingers dug into her flesh. And that laughter—that wicked laughter—Effie could still hear it. "I'll see ye in hell, Hunter," she managed to choke out, and then, "Iaaaaan!" before Hunter snapped her neck and sent her body hurtling over the edge of the cliff.

He glanced downward to where she lay far below upon the rocky beach, the waves of the cold Loch Ness slapping gently at her broken corpse as they washed upon the sand, then drifted out again.

# Twenty-five

For the rest of her life Mary Carmichael was to have little recollection of that past year, for she had become half-crazed after the unspeakable things Hugh had done to her that evil, gloating afternoon he had come to their chamber at Dùndereen to tell her of Hunter's death and to force himself upon her. Oh, God, those things he had done! Things he had continued to do, as though he had taken some strange, perverted joy in Mary's horror. He had lain beside her at night and described those things to her in great detail before he'd actually done them, and somehow the macabreness of his meticulous explanations had been even more frightening than the actual deeds.

To protect herself Mary had pretended to be mad, and gradually during those dark days of the past year she had become so, unable to distinguish between what was real and unreal in the nightmare of her life.

The horrible jest of which she had thought that day of her wedding had come true. Half-witted, she was; and she did not need to hear the whispers of the servants to confirm it.

Joanna was her only frail link with sanity. Joanna, whose lover Mary's own had slain. Somedays she knelt beside Mary after tending her cuts and bruises and wept grievously.

"Forgie me, Mary. Please, God, forgie me, and get well. I dinna mean the things I said to ye before. I know Gordon's death was nae your fault. I spoke in haste and anger and hurt. Oh, sweet *Jesù*, forgie me, Mary! Say something! Anything!''

And though Mary heard her sweet, pleading voice, saw Joanna's gentle face twisted with agony, she could not speak. 'Twas as though her lips had been paralyzed by the shock of Hugh's brutality.

Other days Joanna would bring Geoffrey to Mary's chamber; Geoffrey, Mary's son, whom Joanna raised as she would have reared her own had she not miscarried. Geoffrey was two-and-a-half years old now.

"See, Mary. See how fast he's growing," Joanna would say. "He walks and talks so well. Speak to your mother, Geoffrey Edward. Tell her how much ye love her.''

And Mary's child would run to Joanna, kiss her, and say, "I love ye, mama.''

Mary realized he did not know who she was, and her heart ached with sadness at the thought that perhaps it was better that way.

"Oh, Mary.'' Joanna would bite her lip. "He needs *ye*, nae me. Willna ye even try, for his sake at least?''

Why? Mary longed to scream. What good am I to him? I'm filth! Filth! And I'll ne'er be clean again. Ne'er!

But, oh, how she attempted to cleanse herself of her husband's touch and seed, Sometimes she would bathe half-a-dozen times a day. But nothing could erase the purplish blue bruises that continuously blotched her once-golden skin, nor blot out the horror in her mind.

And so it had continued until Mary's belly had become too swollen with the bairn she carried for Hugh to bed her easily. That night, when he'd found he could not penetrate her, he'd left the room in a rage only to return twenty minutes later with a twelve-year-old child. The girl had been a young crofter, a virgin, thin, shaking, and petrified. Hugh had bound Mary's wrists to one of the bedposts and forced her to lie beside them and watch as he'd raped the lass repeatedly in various ways. Mary could still hear the child's screams mingled with her own. The horrible ghastliness of that wicked, perverted travesty had brought on Mary's labor. It had been time for it anyway, but, thank God, none had known. They had assumed the bairn's birth was premature, just as Geoffrey's had been.

He was a lusty lad, Mary's bairn, dark as a gypsy, with a swatch of thick mahogany hair. Joanna had taken one look and known immediately whose child he really was; but mercifully Hugh had not questioned the child's parentage and had, in rare good humor, accepted the name Mary had managed to utter when Mistress Flora, who'd delivered the bairn, had asked the girl's preference. "Ranald Thomas," Mary had said. *Ranald* for Hunter's father and *Thomas* for the old Earl of Dùndereen. After all, Hugh's father had been a good man. Mary had wanted someone to remember the elderly laird whom her brother had refused to help that day at Leabaidh a' Nathair.

Nanna had not failed to notice Mary's listless state or the bruises that marked her battered flesh either.

"Dinna try to beguile me wie that tale of Mary falling down the stairs, Hugh," she'd warned. "I am no fool and hae known ye since ye were in swaddling britches. Ye were a bully then and are a bully now. Ye hae beaten the lass and driven her to the brink of madness. If ye persist, if ye dinna gie her a year at least to recover her strength, I promise ye she'll ne'er bear ye another wee bairn and will surely die. Young Jamie willna be lenient wie ye for that, Hugh Carmichael!"

And Hugh, who'd wanted Mary to live and suffer, had turned away from Mistress Flora's piercing gaze with a muttered oath after acceding to her threatening demands. He would have liked to strangle the old witch, for she did indeed know him only too well, but he'd had a healthy respect for Alan's sword-arm and had realized the old knight would cause a great deal of trouble if aught happened to Mary or Nanna.

After that Mary had been moved into Joanna's room. Hugh's beastly crimes upon his wife's body and soul had ceased for the time being. And somehow, in her heart, when

Mary had looked at Ranald, she'd felt Hunter's presence and been glad her lover had cheated Hugh of his wedding night and son, too and had begun to live again.

Mary regained much of her health, strength, pride, and sanity in those months that followed Ranald's birth. Joanna nursed her tenderly, as though Mary had been but a bairn herself; and Mary knew the lass was truly grieved she had added to her lady's pain. Of Hugh they spoke little, but always the shadow of his wicked presence clouded what small happiness they found, though they managed to be cheerful for the sake of Mary's sons. In the evenings they spent together in Joanna's chamber Mary's elder boy became less of a stranger to her and quickly, to her delight, learned to distinguish between "mama" and "Cousin Jo." He would draw close to Mary and watch shyly as Ranald suckled contentedly at her breast and, if someone aided him, would hold the wee bundle that was his half brother, cooing and giggling with pleasure. Mary was glad of this, for she did not want her children to grow up enemies as Hugh and Edward had been.

In fact, only two things marred Mary's newfound peaceful existence. Shortly before Ranald's birth Ian had begun drinking steadily. No one knew the reason for it, but he was now an alcoholic and seemed to have lost all interest in living. Lady Margaret was running Bailekair, and the castle Mary loved so dearly was slowly being ruined by the Countess's management of it, for Margaret lacked even Ian's good sense in trying to win the crofters to her cause. It saddened Mary to see her father's once-proud heritage crumbling slowly before her eyes.

The other thing that troubled the lass happened so gradually it appeared to have occurred in a single day. One moment Ranald's eyes had been the deep blue of the dead young Edward's, and the next they were the accursed violet of Mary's own. She saw in her child a miniature of Hunter MacBeth that would haunt her until the day she died and thereafter lit a candle for his soul each Sunday following Mass.

Another summer was upon them, and the good clean scent of the Lammas harvest that year of 1492 filled the air with its sweetness as Mary walked upon the stubbled ground. She breathed in deeply, rejoicing in the fragrance of the land. It hardly seemed possible that she was twenty years old and had borne two children. 'Twas quiet, for most of the household and village of Dùndereen had gone to Inverness for the Lammas festival. Only Mary had stayed behind, the childhood memory of the last August 1st she had spent with Hugh Carmichael still too sharp and painful in her mind. Where had those fifteen years gone? she wondered.

She reveled in the solitude, gathering great bunches of wild flowers before she sought the cemetery where Edward lay, placing the bouquets on his grave, idly pulling a few weeds from the plot. She touched the chiseled headstone, cool in the shade beneath the pine tree under which her first husband rested. Silently Mary read the words upon the marker, simple words as Edward would have wished:

LORD EDWARD ALAN CARMICHAEL

Beloved son of Lord Thomas Hugh and Lady Edwina Alana
Carmichael
Earl and Countess of Dùndereen

Half brother to Lord Hugh St. Clair Carmichael
Earl of Dùndereen

Husband to Lady Mary Kathryn Carmichael
of Bailekair

1469-1489

R.I.P

He had been just twenty years old when he'd died, the same age as Mary was now.

*Cold. So cold. So many tears. So many graves.*

Oh, Edward! Mary laid her head upon the granite stone and wept.

"Well, well. Dinna tell me ye prefer a dead husband to a live one?"

Mary glanced up through her tears to find Hugh glowering over her. She looked around rapidly, but they were totally alone in the cemetery.

"What do ye want, Hugh?" she asked quietly. "Why are ye nae in Inverness wie the others?"

"I missed your company." He grinned slowly, wickedly. " 'Tis been nigh on a year since I bedded ye, bitch. Nay, dinna seek to tell me ye are nae well, for I know ye are. Take off that dress, whore, and spread your legs."

It was as though the past year had never been. All Mary's horror came flooding back in an instant. She saw him reach for his leather clan-belt.

"Nay! Nae here, Hugh! Please, nae here!"

But he only laughed as he sent her sprawling across young Edward's grave.

"Geoffrey! Geoffrey!" Joanna cried frantically, pushing through the milling mass of the Inverness Lammas festival fearfully. "Geoffrey, where are ye?"

God's body, but the child had held her hand a moment past! Where could he gave gone? She shifted the weight of little Ranald to her other arm.

"Ranald, child, canna ye walk wie Cousin Jo?" She bit her lip as she gazed at the wee lad.

"Nay! Nay walk!" the boy replied stubbornly, for he already had a mind of his own, though he was barely a year old.

"Mistress Joanna! Wait up!" Connall, Hugh's chief man-at-arms, called anxiously, but the girl did not hear him over the gaiety and laughter of the rabble that surrounded her, and soon Connall and the rest of his men realized they had lost her in the crowd.

"God's toenail!" Connall swore. "Lord Hugh will hae my head for this!"

"Och, the laird doesna like the wench anyway," another man returned. "Blame it on the lass, Connall. The Earl willna care."

"Damned if I willna!" the other answered. " 'Twas but Squire Edward's brat that disappeared, and the laird doesna gie a hang aboot him either! The girl should hae stayed wie us, or gi'en us the Earl's wee bairn. The stupid wench! He'll flay her alive if aught happens to his heir!"

"Afore he's used her awhile, of course," a third man sniggered.

"Dinna look so glum, Connall." The second man clapped his comrade rudely on the back. "Mayhap the laird will share her wie ye."

"Och!" Connall spit in the dust. "I'm for some ale, lads. The lass will know where to find us when she's ready; I hae no doubt aboot that!"

Joanna did not realize she was unaccompanied by the men-at-arms until a lewd stranger accosted her, grabbing at her with hairy palms, trying to force one hand down the bodice of her *arascaid*.

"Leave me be!" she snarled, slapping at him wrathfully before she stumbled on down the street. "Geoffrey!"

At last she saw the child standing near the corner of a market stall. He seemed to be conversing with someone, which did not surprise Joanna, for the boy would talk to a fence post; but she couldn't see who it was, for the person was shielded from her view by the booth.

"Geoffrey!" She raised her voice in anger, intending to give him a smart spanking for scaring her out of her wits. 'Tis just how Mistress Flora must hae felt fifteen years past, she thought as she hurried across the road, her mouth a grim line of rage.

"Geoffrey Carmichael!" She gave the lad a small shake. "I told ye nae to be wandering off in this crowd, did I nae? Do you know the trouble you've caused me this day?"

"Nay, I'm sure he doesna." A tall dark man stepped out from around the corner of the market stall.

Joanna gasped. He was as lithe as a whipcord, hard, and muscular. His unruly black locks ruffled gently in the slight breeze. His blue eyes glittered as he raked her body slowly. A smile tugged at the corners of his carnal mouth. He laid his hand on her arm, his grip like steel. Joanna felt it like a searing brand through the thin material of her *arascaid*. The blood rushed through her veins in a way it had not done since Gordon's death. Her doe brown orbs widened with fright as she stared at his red-and-green *breacan*. She tried to yank away.

"Mother of God!" she breathed. "A MacBeth! Oh, Geoffrey! How could ye?"

"Is he a bad mon, Jo? I dinna know; truly, I dinna." Geoffrey turned his suddenly fearful eyes up to ones as blue as his own. "Ye willna hurt my cousin, sir, will ye? Oh, please, sir. She's a good lass, she is."

Cadman stared at Mary's son, and his face softened momentarily. Then he remembered that two years ago Hunter had nearly died at the hands of this boy's uncle, had been betrayed by the lad's mother, and had yet to be revenged for it. His dark visage hardened once more. Geoffrey wasn't Mary, but he *was* Mary's child. Cadman glanced at the other bairn, turned the boy's face up to his own as Joanna tried to protect the lad, saw the child's violet eyes. His heartbeat quickened.

"This one—this one is Mary's bairn, too, is he nae? Answer me, wench!" The pressure of his fingers tightened on Joanna's arm. "Is this one the son of Mary and Hugh Carmichael?"

"Aye," Joanna lied, for she could not bring herself to betray Mary's guilty secret.

"Then I will take them both wie me." His eyes roamed lingeringly over Joanna's trembling figure. His loins ached at the sight of her. "And ye also, mistress," he said more softly, fingers cupping her breast, thumb flicking gently at the nipple that lay beneath the light cloth of her *arascaid*. Her lip quivered slightly.

"Please, nae before the bairns." She indicated Geoffrey's confused and frightened eyes. Even Ranald by this time sensed something amiss.

Cadman withdrew his hand. "I can wait, mistress," he promised, and the girl felt her heart sink. "Come on now, and if ye cry oot one time, I'll slay both ye and the brats where ye stand, do ye ken?'' He pressed the tip of his dirk into her side to emphasize this point, and Joanna nodded dumbly. ''Good.''

He escorted them down a twisting alley to where his chestnut destrier awaited patiently at one end.

''Up wie ye, lad.'' He tossed Geoffrey upon the saddle, grabbing a quick hold of the reins as Logie snorted and pranced dangerously. ''Easy, Logie, easy,'' Cadman crooned to the beast. Obediently the horse calmed itself. ''Now ye, mistress.'' He turned to Joanna, the quicksilver wanting in his groin deepening as he wrapped his hands about her waist to lift her to the saddle.

*Jesù*, her eyes! They weren't even violet, but honey brown, and still they beckoned to him, aroused his desire to a flaming pitch. Oh, sweet Christ! What was it about Carmichael eyes?

''Sir, you're hurting me,'' Joanna whispered as his fingers dug into her flesh, her heart pounding again at the way he looked at her.

He loosened his grip, swung her and Ranald upward until they sat firmly behind Geoffrey; then Cadman mounted his steed, arms encircling them all as he reached for the reins and kicked his golden spurs sharply into Logie sides.

''Are ye a witch as well?'' he muttered in Joanna's ear as he realized suddenly he could no longer recall Janet MacDonald's sweet, lovely face.


''We dinna know where she is, my lord.'' Connall quaked in his boots before his laird's wrath. ''One minute she was there, and the next she was gone. She took the two lads and disappeared into the crowd before we could catch her. Is that nae right, boys?''

The others nodded in agreement.

''The bitch!'' Hugh swore. ''The bloody bitch! This is *your* doing, Mary!'' He whirled upon his frightened wife. ''Ye bade that bitch of yours hide my nephew and son. What did ye think to gain by it, woman? Your freedom? Bah! So help me, God, I'll beat ye wie'in an inch of your life if ye dinna tell me where they are and now!''

"I dinna know, Hugh; truly, I dinna." Mary held one hand to her fluttering throat. "I swear to ye upon my father's grave. For God's sake, Hugh, send your men oot to look for them at once. Something terrible has happened to them. I just know it! I had no hand in this, I swear it!''

His black eyes narrowed dangerously for a moment, but finally he believed her and went cold at the thought of what might have occurred.

"If you're lying to me, whore—" He turned to give the orders to his men-at-arms.

Mary shuddered convulsively. Dear God. What had happened to Joanna and Mary's sons? For hours the girl waited for some word, but none came; and at last she went upstairs to bed, leaving Hugh alone in the main hall. When sleep came Mary tossed restlessly and dreamed. . . .

# Twenty-six

"Sweet *Jesù!*" Mary awakened with a muttered start. "Cadman has them—my God! Cadman has them! He'll slay them, my bairns, and Joanna—"

Hurriedly she threw back the covers and arose. What should she do? What should she do? She paced the room restlessly, trying to decide. Should she call Hugh, inform her husband of what she had seen in her dream? Nay, for then she would have to tell him the true reason Cadman had kidnapped Joanna and the children and why he would kill them rather than hold them for ranson. He wanted revenge for Hunter's death, Hunter, whose own lover had betrayed him. Oh, God, what should she do? Slowly a desperate plan began to form in her mind. Quickly, before her courage could fail her, Mary ran to her chamber door, opening it just a crack.

"Collie," she called softly to the young page who slept without. "Collie."

He stirred, yawning and wiping the sleep from his eyes. "I'm sorry, my lady." He suddenly snapped wide awake. "I must hae just dozed off."

"'Tis all right, Collie." She held one finger to her lips, indicating he was to be silent. "Come here. I need ye."

Timidly the lad approached. Her ladyship's behavior was very odd, and he was a little frightened. Maybe she really *was* crazy as some had claimed. Why, it was nearly midnight, too! Nevertheless, he did as she bid, afraid of losing his post otherwise. After all, she was still the Countess of Dùndereen.

"I'm verra sorry to hae to do this, Collie," Mary said once he'd entered her room, "but Hugh would punish ye severely otherwise."

And with that she smashed a small vase over his head. The youth crumpled to the floor, groaning. Rapidly Mary stripped him. He was about her size, and his clothes fit her very well after she'd gotten them on. She stuffed her long hair up inside the boy's plumed broad-bonnet, then jammed it on her head. She looked approvingly in the polished mirror. No one would guess I'm a lass and nae a young page. She smiled and ran her tongue over her lips with excitement. She felt alive! For the first time since Hunter's death she felt alive! She was going to rescue her sons and Joanna, and no one was going to stop her! She paused only briefly to take Hunter's dirk from the coffer where she'd kept it since Gordon's death to remind her of her beloved's betrayal. She fingered it lightly, and it strengthened her resolve. She would trade her life for her sons' and Joanna's lives tonight. Let Cadman slay her with Hunter's dagger in their stead. Surely it would be revenge enough for him! Desperately, feverishly, Mary prayed that it would be as she tiptoed quietly down the long corridor and winding stairs to the main hall and let herself out into the night.

"Saddle Desmond, and be quick aboot it," she told the groom at the stables, giving what she thought was a very passable imitation of young Collie. She held the boy's cape close about her and remained half-hidden in the shadows so the groom would not become too suspicious of her slender figure, for the page was a wee bit stocky. "The Countess is ill and bade me fetch Mistress Flora to attend her. My lady said I was to take her horse as it's the swiftest in the stables."

"All right, Collie, all right," the groom grumbled good-naturedly, not paying much attention to the boy. "Her ladyship's crazy. We all know that. I dinna think ye were trying to steal her steed, lad."

Mary jumped lithely into the saddle, gathered up the reins, then trotted slowly toward the postern gate, where the same story opened the wrought-iron spikes that barred her path. She wrenched a torch from its socket upon the stone wall at the side of the exit, then cantered out into the darkness.

The night was black; *the grey mist swirled around her so thickly she could scarcely see, and the land through which she traveled appeared strangely twisted and unfamiliar.* The wind whipped at her cloak, whirling it about her fair form like a raven's wings. Mary could feel the wetness of Desmond's winded sides through the thin material of her clothing. *The hooves of the black steed clattered ominously over the rocky terrain, and the mountain toward which she rode loomed forbiddingly in the distance.* As dark as the craggy chasm from which Glenkirk arose it was and so like Mary's dream that Lammas Eve these fifteen years past she felt she must still be caught in the grips of its terror. Her torch blazed eerily and sputtered in the wind.

*...and she will ride amongst ye unafraid, a tawny light wie black darkness by her side...*

On and on up the steep, winding, mountain path she rode until at last she stood before the great, iron portcullis of the keep that was her enemies' stronghold, until she stood before the very gate of hell, asking, nay *demanding* entrance.

349

Joanna stood very still in the middle of Cadman's bed-chamber, her honey brown eyes clear and unwavering.

" 'Tis no frightened virgin ye seek to rape, sir," she said quietly to the handsome knight before her. "For I hae loved and lain wie a mon and would hae gi'en him a child had I nae miscarried it."

Cadman's blue eyes gazed down at her briefly; his jaw set. "Ye are wed, mistress?" he asked, feeling jealousy surge through his veins hotly at the idea.

"Nay, sir."

" 'Twould hae been a bastard brat then, mistress," he snarled. " 'Tis best it wasna born!" The vehemence of his tone surprised her. "Do ye know what 'tis like to be a bastard, wench?"

"Aye," she answered him steadily, "for I am such myself, sir."

Cadman caught his breath. So she was like him, was she? His blue orbs raked her slowly once more, taking in the thick gold brown hair, the solemn eyes, the pulse fluttering rapidly at the base of her throat, the swell of her tanned creamy breasts above the bodice of her *arascaid*, the small waist, the finely tapered legs.

"I hae killed a mon for ye," he stated bluntly, for upon their arrival at Glenkirk one of the men-at-arms had sought to share her with his fellow knights, and Cadman had slain the man, claiming she belonged to her captor alone and daring the others to challenge his sole right to her.

Joanna nodded. "I am grateful ye kept the others from me."

"Then ye had best please me, wench, for I mean to hae ye," he breathed before he bent his head to kiss her.

Joanna struggled in his arms, for no man had touched her save Gordon Carmichael. Cadman's tongue teased between her lips, taunted her, driving in and out with a delicious swirling that made her heart beat faster, in spite of herself. Nay! Joanna thought desperately. I'll nae respond to him! I wilna! But still she could not stop the tide of passion that flooded her body, the burning ache that pulsed deep within

350

her womanhood and spread like wildfire to her belly and breasts. Is this how Mary felt, swept away by her MacBeth even as I am now by this one? Oh, God! Joanna shuddered. Cadman felt her tremble, felt her nipples harden with a will of their own against his chest.

"Dinna fight me, lass," he murmured. "I will make it good for ye." He pulled her heavy hair from the pins that constrained it, sending them scattering as he tilted her face up to his own dark one, as he wrapped one hand in the glowing burnished mass. He swore, "Goddamn ye, witch! What is it aboot ye Carmichael women that drives us MacBeth men to the edge of madness?"

Then with another snarled oath he swept her off her feet and carried her to her waiting bed.

"Nay!" she cried out. "Gordon, oh, Gordon!"

"My name is Cadman," he muttered against her throat. "Cadman," he repeated as he knelt over her in the shadowed light, as she gazed into his dark blue eyes and felt the memory of Gordon's lavender ones slip from her grasp to fade into the recesses of her mind forever.

"Open the gate!" Mary called loudly to the sentries who stared down at her from the main watchtowers of Glenkirk. "I hae a message for Sir Cadman MacBeth from Lord Hugh Carmichael, Earl of Dùndereen. My lord knows Sir Cadman holds his son and nephew and also his wife's maid, the Mistress Joanna, captive inside these walls. We hae received no message concerning their welfare. My lord wishes to know the terms for their ransom."

"Ransom? Ha! Tell your whoreson laird he will get his answer in the morning—in a burlap bag!" The guardsman laughed.

Mary's blood went cold. 'Twas just as she'd feared. Dear God! Her bairns might already be dead!

"I must see Sir Cadman!" she cried. "My lord will punish me severely if I dinna deliver the message entrusted to my care."

"Get ye hence, lad!" The sentry spat down at her. "Sir Cadman's busy—if ye ken my meaning."

Mary understood only all too well. Sweet *Jesù!* Puir Joanna. Och, Jo! Jo! I'm sorry! So verra sorry!

"And tell your bastard laird," another guard hollered down, "nae to send a lad to do a mon's job next time!"

"Are ye *men* afraid of a mere *lad* then?" Mary shot back desperately, hoping to goad them into opening the gate.

"Och, be off wie ye, boy, and thank the Lord ye are nae wie'in these walls, or we'd gie ye a sound beating for your insolence!"

"Cowards!" Mary flung up as a last resort. "We all know who was beaten at Bailekair. Ye ran from the Carmichaels like whipped dogs, wie your tails betwixt your legs!"

Slowly the wooden doors swung open wide on their hinges, for the impudence of this insult the MacBeths could not endure. Mary rode through to be yanked from her saddle and searched roughly for concealed weapons. One man snatched Hunter's dagger from her waist where she had strapped it on at Dùndereen.

His eyes narrowed. "Why, 'tis Sir Hunter's blade and no mistake. Who are ye, lad, and where did ye get this? Answer me, quickly, brat, before I beat it oot of ye!"

"I told ye—" she began, then cried out in alarm as he grabbed the plumed broad-bonnet from her head to get a better look at her face. Her violet eyes blazed up at him in the wavering torchlight. Her golden hair cascaded down her back.

"A Carmichael wench! By God, 'tis a Carmichael *wench!*"

"A Carmichael wench!" The others took up the cry and started to pass her from man to man, pawing at her crudely, tearing at her clothes, their earlier rage turned to lust at the realization of her sex.

Tears stung her amethyst jewels as Mary fought them, struggled against them, demanding to be taken to Sir Cadman MacBeth, but they paid no heed until a tall dark man strode angrily across the courtyard, authoritatively commanding them to cease their rowdy behavior and explain the cause of it.

With a startled, disbelieving sob Mary turned to look at the man she'd love and lain with and thought dead. Nay! It couldn't be! It couldn't be! But it was! It was Hunter! Hunter, who stared at her as though he were seeing a ghost, the flickering flames of the torches dancing eerily across his shadowed countenance, the bronzed visage twisted with shock and hatred. Oh, God, he lived! Lived and hated her! She could see it in his eyes. He was going to kill her. He reached for her in the wavering half-light, and Mary fainted at his feet.

"God's blood!" Hunter swore. "Mary! Mary!" he knelt and shook her gently, but there was no response. His mouth tightened into a grim line as he lifted her up into his arms. The MacBeth men stepped back silently, warily, afraid. The one who had started it all moved forward shamefacedly. He held Hunter's dirk out in one hand.

"She had this wie her, sir; 'tis yours," he said; then more boldly, "She—she's just a Carmichael wench after all, sir—" He broke off quickly at the ugly look in the Romany knight's accursed violet eyes.

Hunter took the dagger without a word, then walked toward the keep, leaving the others confused and shaken and glad to escape his wicked temper. They gave an odd sigh of relief that he had not turned on them with his sword as Cadman had done earlier, then began to chatter speculatively about the wench he'd taken inside.

Mary regained consciousness slowly. She was lying in a bed in a very masculine chamber, and someone was pouring brandy down her throat. She choked. The flask was taken away as she opened her wide purple eyes, trying to focus them confusedly.

"What are ye doing here?"

She stared at Hunter, mesmerized. For two years she had thought him dead and tried to drive the demon of his memory from the caverns of her mind, the chasms of her soul; and now he stood before her, arrogant as always, his muscular legs spread in the swaggered stance she recalled so well, his violet orbs raking her insultingly with that same hot hunger, his mouth curled jeeringly in that same insolent, mocking grin. She glanced down at herself. Her garments were torn open where the men-at-arms in the courtyard of Glenkirk had manhandled her while they'd taunted her with their lewd remarks. Her rapidly heaving breasts were partially exposed beneath the damaged doublet. But she was unharmed—and now she knew why. Hunter MacBeth lived—lived to take his revenge upon her and her sons. Mary shivered at the thought, for she knew what he had planned for her, and there would be no love in the deed. Oh, God, she could not bear it! Not after Hugh—

She cursed herself a thousand times for a fool. Why had she come here alone? Why had she slipped away from Dùndereen without her husband and his men-at-arms? Why had she gone from her bed without even a word left to someone of her destination? Had she known, deep in her heart, Hunter MacBeth still lived? Oh, God, just the nearness of him still had the power to make her tremble! Mary was ashamed of her weakness and wanting him. It would never be the same for them. He would only beat her now and use her as Hugh had done. There would be no tenderness in his touch, only cruel cold callousness. She drew the edges of her clothes together, trying not to let her fingers shake at the thought. And still there was silence between them, a heavy stillness that fraught the air with crackling tension.

"What are ye doing here?" he asked again. "Well, madam?" He raised one devilish eyebrow inquisitively, and his voice was icily cold. Mary's heart sank. She was right. He did not mean to be gentle with her. Well, why should he be? She was naught to him now, naught but a captive wench who had betrayed him and nearly cost him his life. "They tell me ye came alone," he continued.

Mary did not know what to say or do. She was at his mercy, his utter, horrible whim. And so, though her rank by birth was greater than his, she rose and swept him a deep curtsy, remained kneeling at his feet.

"Ye are alive," she spoke.

"Obviously," he replied dryly.

"I—I— Cadman took Joanna and my sons. I saw it in a dream this eve. Ye know I hae the Sight, sir. I—I came to—to trade my life for theirs," she offered softly, hesitantly, "for I knew your kinsman dinna mean to ransom them, but to slay them, instead, to take his revenge upon me for your death; or so I thought. I—I hadna guessed I would find ye here."

"God's wounds! I'll wager nae!" He laughed shortly.

The faint fragrance of her perfume—heather, always heather—wafted sweetly to Hunter's nostrils. The ache in his loins that had begun when first he'd seen her in the bailey hardened, grew stronger. He stared at the shining mass of shimmering gold that hung like a curtain around her lithe body as she knelt before him, her head actually touching the floor in her obeisance. Well, he had wanted to see her groveling at his feet, hear her beg for mercy from his wrath. But now that she was in reality before him he found 'twas difficult to turn his heart from the tender plea in her violet eyes, upon her honeyed lips.

He yanked her suddenly to her feet, his purple eyes boring into hers, taking a strange joy in frightening her, upon letting her see she was helpless before him, his for the taking and powerless to prevent it.

" 'Twas dead, ye believed me, was it nae?"

She nodded dumbly, the sight of him still a shock to her senses.

"And so I would hae been hadna Cadman and Grace saved my life. Look ye, madam, look upon the scar your lack of faith in me and your betrayal left upon my flesh." He pulled his *breacan* open so she might see the ugly, jagged wound across his belly. Mary's eyes widened with horror. Sweet *Jesù!* How had he survived? "Aye, madam, your husband rode me down like a dog, and when I could barely stand, he laid my belly open wie his sword."

"Ye slew my brother—"

"Nay, madam." His voice was hard; his eyes were glittering and deadly. "Nay, madam, I dinna. I gae ye my word of honor. How could ye think I would break it? 'Twas your own husband and your brother Ian who murdered Gordon in so foul and cowardly a manner!"

355

"Nay—"

"Aye, madam, though you'll nae believe it. Ian had been lying wie my cousin, Euphemia. 'Twas she who stole my dagger and helped your kinsmen blame me for the evil deed, betrayed one of her own. But she has paid for her crime." His dark visage was murderous, and Mary shuddered to think what must have been Euphemia MacBeth's fate in Hunter's strong lethal grip.

"I'm sorry!" She buried her face in her hands and wept, recognizing at last he spoke the truth. She should have known. Hugh and Ian had slain her father and uncle. Why would they not have done as much to her brother Gordon? "So verra sorry. I dinna know, sir. I dinna know. 'Twas your dagger they pulled from Gordon's back. What else was I to hae thought?"

"Ye could hae had faith in me, Mary. 'Twas what our love was built upon, but ye destroyed it because ye couldna trust me, because ye couldna forget I was your enemy, because ye couldna believe in my love for ye or yours for me."

"I will make it up to ye, sir. I swear I will! If only you'll forgie me—"

"Forgie ye, bitch! Ye would ask that of me?"

"Aye, oh, Hunter, if e'er ye loved me, let me take Joanna and my sons and leave here in peace. God has punished me enough already for my sins against ye. Ye canna know how well he has punished me—"

"Nay, madam, I canna. Ye are too late, Mary. Whate'er there was between us is finished, dead. Ye killed it. Even now Joanna lies in Cadman's arms; and tomorrow morning your sons will die a slow and painful death, and ye will stand by and watch it before I place my hands around your throat like this"—he demonstrated, but Mary did not flinch as his fingers tightened cruelly in her flesh—"and send ye to your grave."

"Slay me then, but spare my sons," she begged. "Ye canna hae forgotten what we knew together. Ye canna! If only for that, spare my sons! My son— Hae ye seen my sons, sir? Geoffrey is three now. He has the blond hair and blue eyes of his father, Edward. And Ranald." She paused, waiting to see what effect her youngest son's name would have upon Hunter. "Ranald is his father's miniature also. He has his father's mahogany hair; his father's accursed violet eyes; his father's dark Romany flesh—''

"What are ye saying, bitch?" Hunter shook her roughly.

"Ranald is *your* son, Hunter. Yours!"

"Nay, ye lying whore! 'Tis but a ruse! Ye would say anything to save him!"

"Nay. He *is* your bairn, Hunter! Your seed grew wie'in me before Hugh Carmichael e'er touched me. Send for the children. Look upon Ranald's face, sir, and then tell me he isna your babe if ye can! God's body! Do ye think I would hae called him after your father if he were nae your child?"

She lied to him, surely she did! And yet— He stared at her flashing amethyst jewels briefly, then strode angrily to the chamber door, hauling it open with suppressed fury.

"Ye, Michael! Gavin! Bring the Lady Mary's bairns here at once!" He turned back to the quivering girl. "If you're lying to me, Mary—'' He did not finish the threat, but moved to the hunting table to pour himself a tankard of ale. "Will ye hae wine, madam?"

"Aye." Mary went to stand beside him, gazing up at him imploringly. He looked down at her implacably, his eyes diamond-hard. She bit her lip.

The arrival of her children interrupted whatever she might have said.

"Mama! Mama!" they cried and flung themselves into her arms.

"Oh, my precious lambs! My sons!" She drew them to her closely, fiercely, relieved they were as yet merely frightened, but not harmed. She glanced up at Hunter again.

The child was his; he could not doubt it as he stared down at the small mirror of himself that was his son. Ranald. *His son!* He raised his eyes wonderingly to Mary's own, searching, seeking, waiting, and suddenly longing. He turned to the two young pages who served him.

"Take the boys back to their quarters. See no harm comes to either of them."

Mary began to breathe a little easier. Her heart leapt with sudden hope.

"Do ye deny him, Hunter? Do ye deny he is your son?" she questioned quietly after her children had parted from her reluctantly, Mary kissing them both and assuring them she would see them in the morning.

"Nay, I canna," Hunter answered.

"Ye will—ye will spare him then?"

"Aye."

"And—and the bairn of the man I betrayed for ye, Hunter?"

"Aye."

Mary expelled a small sigh of relief and sent a quick prayer of thanks to the heavens.

"And—and Joanna?"

"She belongs to Cadman. I can do naught for her."

Mary swallowed. "I—I understand. Thank ye, sir."

He was silent for a moment and then, "Well?"

"Well, what, sir?"

"Ye dinna ask aught for yourself, Mary?"

"Nay, Hunter. Do wie me as ye will."

He looked at her from across the room, pulled his dirk slowly from its sheath at his waist. He walked toward her stealthily, with that peculiar, catlike grace she remembered so well. I willna cry out, she thought. 'Tis enough my sons are spared. And then suddenly his hand was wrapped in her mass of golden hair as he tilted her face up to his, pressed the point of his dagger against her throat.

"Once before I held ye thusly, lass," he murmured lowly. "Do ye recall it?"

"Aye." Mary nodded. " 'Twas the—the first time e'er I lay wie ye."

His violet eyes darkened. "I ought to slay ye, but I canna!" He swore and flung the dirk aside. Then for the first and only time in his life Hunter struck her, backhanding her across her pale gilded countenance. "Goddamn ye to hell for a witch, Mary Carmichael! I love ye still!" he breathed before his mouth came down on hers, hard. Mary's heart pounded. So, he had *not* been able to forget, to drive her out of his heart and mind, however hard he had tried! "Oh, God, tigress." His mouth slashed across her cheeks to her earlobes, the thick tresses of her hair as his fingers tangled hurtfully in the shimmering cascade to draw her close. "Oh, God, beloved." His lips found hers once more, his tongue shooting deeply between her quivering borders as they parted gently, trembling, for his ravaging assault. He swept her up into his arms, carrying her to the bed.

He towered over her in the half-light, his passion-darkened orbs almost black as they raked her slowly, lovingly. His hands moved to undress her. Mary began to shake violently. She could not stop herself. He would rape her, beat her, hurt her.

"Nay," she sobbed and tried to pull away.

He mistook her pleas for shyness, her shivering for desire.

"Nay, sweet, ye canna say me nay, nae now, when I hae hungered so long for ye," he muttered against her throat, growing half-angry as she continued to struggle against him, for he could not comprehend her fighting him.

With a snarled oath he pinioned her wrists above her head and stripped the garments from her body, in spite of her protests. He gasped sharply. Horrible purplish blue bruises marred her golden flesh, marks put there just that afternoon by Hugh Carmichael when he'd taken Mary so brutally upon young Edward's grave. Hunter drew back. His heart ached for her. Tears stung his eyes, for he knew now what had been done to her and why she feared him so.

"Oh, God, beloved. Mary, Mary, look at me, sweetheart." He attempted to turn her face up to his once more, but she denied him, tears streaking her cheeks.

"Nay. Dinna. Dinna, please," she pleaded. "How can ye bear to look at me? I'm nothing. Nothing! Nothing but filth! Please—"

"Dinna say that!" he commanded sharply. "Oh, God, beloved. Whate'er ye hae done ye hae paid for it a thousand times o'er. Ye dinna deserve this. What has he done to ye, the bastard? Oh, God. I'll kill him, the whoreson! I'll kill him for this if 'tis the last thing I e'er do! Oh, sweetheart, please, look at me. I willna hurt ye. I promise ye that. I love ye. I love ye, do ye ken?"

"How—how could ye?" she lashed out at him. "Ye can—can see what I am, what he's made me!"

"Aye, I can see. I can see you're a bonnie, desirable woman who's been shamefully treated and abused by a mon who doesna deserve the name! Only an animal of the lowest sort would hae done this to ye, Mary. 'Twasna your fault, beloved. 'Twasna your fault! Look at me. Ye are no less in my eyes for it. I swear it. I love ye. Oh, God, tigress, please, look at me, and let me love ye again as ye were meant to be." He tried to reason with her, fearing in his heart Hugh Carmichael had destroyed all the love and passion that had been Mary's for all time.

"Oh, Hunter," she moaned. "Whye'er did I turn against ye? Ye are so good, so good to me. Ye dinna know what he has—has done to me—the things he—he made me do. Oh, God, horrible things, ugly things—"

"Hush. Hush! Dinna think aboot it now. 'Tis o'er now and best forgotten. 'Twas your body he used, beloved; he ne'er touched your soul, that part of ye that makes ye what ye truly are. Ye are nae to blame for what he did. *And ye are no less in my eyes for it,*" he repeated slowly. "Do ye understand that, beloved?"

"How can I? Sweet *Jesù,* how can I?"

"I will show ye."

"Nay, dinna touch me! I dinna want your pity!"

"'Tis my love and myself I offer, lass."

"How can ye? How can ye still—still want me after—after—"

"I *do* want ye! Naught could e'er prevent me from wanting ye, stop me from needing ye, do ye ken? I love ye. I will wipe the horror of that whoreson bastard's touch from your mind and make ye whole again, beloved."

"Oh, Hunter! Help me! Please, help me—" She reached for him blindly in the shadowed light and wept as he cradled her tenderly in his arms.

"There has ne'er been aught but thee and me," he whispered

over and over again. "There has ne'er been aught but thee and me."

He was so gentle with her, so kind. How could she not love him, not respond to him? For everything a man should ever be with a woman, to a woman, Hunter was with and to Mary that night.

He kissed her slowly, deeply, holding her, talking quietly to her, stroking her, caressing her until gradually her violent trembling began to cease. He kissed her mouth, the tip of her nose, her eyelids, her temples, her cheeks, her hair, her throat, her shoulders, her breasts, her belly, her womanhood, her hands, her thighs, her feet. He told her over and over again how much he loved her, wanted her, needed her. He whispered it to her in Gaelic, in Romany, in English, in French, in German. His tongue pleasured her in a thousand different ways, pilliaging the inner sweetness of her mouth, swirling, darting in and out between her lips, tracing them softly before he kissed them again, lingeringly, savoringly, lovingly, searingly, cleansing her, wiping away the horror of Hugh's touch as he had promised.

His hands moved upon her breasts, cupping them, molding them, feeling their softness swell against his fingers, his chest. He played with the rosy flushed nipples, bringing them to excited peaks as he teased them, stroked them, brushed them lightly with his fingertips, arousing them with his tenderness. He smiled at her, lowered his mouth to the little buds that strained against his tongue eagerly, hard and beckoning. They quivered beneath his whirling, sucking motions, his gently demanding ardor. He buried his face between them, relishing first one and then the other, his hands warm and strong as he pressed his fingers into the ripe mounds, caressed them longingly beneath his moist, covetous mouth, urgently making his desire known to them. He murmured softly against her throat, found the place that tingled upon her shoulders when he kissed her there, biting her tenderly, nibbling at that inviting spot, feeling the electric sparks that tingled through her veins as she shuddered with wanting. He stroked her hair, enveloping himself in its softness, its silky golden strands, reaching for one satin tress to draw her close, wrapping the gilded threads around his throat, binding her to him. He nuzzled at one ear, breathing huskily in that graceful shell, speaking thickly as he licked her there, tracing the pattern of the delicate curves, teeth nipping at the lobe, sending tickles of delight racing through her blood.

His head sank to her breasts again and then to her belly, where he teased the flower of her birth, tongue circling the pretty navel, then sliding down her sides to lap its way back up once more as she gasped aloud at the thrilling sensation.

He spread her thighs, fingers trailing down the insides to her knees, then returning to twine sweetly in the dark gold curls before he repeated the design over and over until she ached to have him touch her there, on that throbbing swell of her womanhood. His hand danced upward along her flanks again to fondle that enticing mound of gilt, dally with the warm moistness that bespoke her readiness to receive him. How he cherished that trembling place, explored it, fingers flirting rhythmically, moving up and down the length of its wetness slowly and then faster and faster until she arched her hips against his hand, feeling it slip inside her as his mouth took its place, tongue probing, wooing, adoring, idolizing, tasting the honeyed nectar of her pulsating being.

"Oh, now, Hunter! Now!" she sobbed, pulling at his rich mahogany hair, yearning for him.

He smiled above her, his dark glittering eyes splintering like shards as he gazed at her, passion melting from their very depths.

"Aye, now beloved." He buried his bronzed visage against her throat, against her golden hair, breathing in the sweet, heather fragrance of her as she reached for his shaft, guiding it to her hot molten core. He plunged down the fiery length of her as she closed over him; drowned in the vital, quickening waves of her as she wrapped her legs around his back; dug her fingers into his taut buttocks to pull him even nearer, as though she could make them one and the same. And she did. They fused in perfect unison, moved in perfect harmony as his hard, throbbing maleness immersed itself in her, then withdrew, only to submerge itself again and again, as though it could not get enough of her, wanted to go on surging down into her, to be engulfed by the blazing velvetness that surrounded it, lured it, sucked it down like a furling eddy, tightened upon it, then released it, only to bring it spiraling back like a flame once more.

Mary wanted it to go on and on, wanted to feel him driving in and out of her forever, cleansing away the stain of Hugh's brutal touch, replacing it with Hunter's own burning brand that would mark her always as his own, his woman, to be loved, cherished, and protected by him, whatever the price to them both. For *this* was love! When he worshiped her as though she were some goddess on a pedestal, then dragged her down to the earth so she might see the stars that filled their universe and know only Hunter could show them to her as he made her his. The spheres glowed like conflagrating gold, shooting sparks of white-hot silver as they exploded within her body and soul, as for one moment she actually stopped breathing, caught upon a precipice, fell, and for one fleeting eternity soared in mid-air with the incendiary cosmos, hearing Hunter's own sweet trill of joy as he experienced the lightning flash that lit the galaxies and beyond.

Time ceased like a black void, and they were timeless too, spinning through a darkness to that elusive center of all things, again and again, forever bound to one another, silent together, one at last.

"My God," Hunter breathed, "my God." He gazed at her, enraptured; one hand rested lightly on her throat, tightened gently. "I will be your master, beloved, else I shall become your slave."

Mary's lips parted softly; her violet eyes widened.

"Ye are my lord, my love," she whispered. "There is naught for me, but ye."

His visage darkened. "If e'er ye play me false again, I'll kill ye."

"I know," Mary said quietly before his mouth claimed hers possessively, and she felt the awesome power of him unleashed within her savagely once more.

'Twas not yet dawn when they left Glenkirk. The pale haze of the summer moon still lit the silvery blackness of the sky, but the grey, morning mist that was already sneaking up like a catspaw warned them that they did not have much time. They left furtively, by the postern gate, for they were fugitives now, men, women, and children who had broken with their clans. In a day or less they would be outlawed as traitors to their own—by their own—and death would be their fate if they were caught by either the Carmichaels or MacBeths. They did not fool themselves into thinking the end would be merciful.

Mary held Ranald tightly in her arms as the horses picked their ways carefully down the hard, craggy path of the treacherous mountain chasm from which the castle sprang, and she shuddered to think of the lad's dark head lying bloodied beside his small body.

Slowly they reached the foothills at the base of the towering peak, and gradually the rocky trail thinned to the flat open savannahs of the Highland moors. The broom and heather rippled with a hushed whisper where the little group passed, closing up behind them like the parting and meeting again of a sea, and Mary had some inkling of what Moses must have felt during his flight from Egypt's Pharaoh. Here and there the gorse thickened, and the woodlands lay just beyond; but they rode clear of the forests, for speed was imperative.

Ranald whimpered softly. Mary shushed him as best she could, for the plaintive cry carried like a bell across the heath. But Geoffrey, riding before Hunter in Craigor's saddle, needed no warning to be silent. He was as still as a grave, seeming instinctively to understand the tension that enveloped them. Once Mary glanced at Joanna, mounted pillion behind Cadman upon Logie, his chestnut steed, but the girl's solemn face was as impassive as ever, and Mary could not guess what thoughts must be chasing through the mind behind that smooth mask. Joanna's arms clung to Cadman's waist like ivy to a tree, but Mary did not know if the lass were only afraid of falling off and being left behind or if Cadman had touched her with the same MacBeth magic that haunted Mary. Once or twice Cadman caressed Joanna's hand, and Mary thought she saw her maid's fingers tighten upon Hunter's kinsman's in response.

They made for Perth, for though Dumbarton and Glasgow were closer, both lay near Oir Uisge, a stronghold of the MacBeths, and the fugitives could not risk being seen there. Wynd Cheathaich was ahead of them this way; they counted on the MacDonald to offer them refuge if they needed it.

Dawn was just breaking over the eastern horizon when they reached Mheadhoin, having come roughly fifteen miles. The red glow of the burning ball that was the sun fired the heavens until it seemed the whole world was ablaze. The cross-topped steeple of the kirk stood out starkly against the fiery sky. For a brief moment, Mary recalled lying in Hunter's arms there. She looked into his eyes, as they halted the horses for a brief respite, and saw her thoughts mirrored. There too the memory of the legend shadowed them with its prophecy. Mary felt the presence of Grizel strongly. The lass shivered as the lifting mist touched her face with chilly fingers.

"Let us be gone from this place," she said.

The others needed no urging. 'Twas as though they too had sensed the witch's warning reach out from the ground of her resting place to mock them. They pressed on hurriedly, and for a time the heavy silence lay again upon them.

At midmorning they stopped once more, this time at the near bank of the River Spey. Mary dismounted stiffly, seeking the sheltering shade of a birch tree. She sat down to rest, back against its trunk, as Hunter and Cadman went to make arrangements with the ferry master for their crossing and to fetch tankards of cool ale with which to wash down the chunks of cheese and hard bread they had brought with them. Ranald laid his head upon Mary's lap and slept, but her eldest son gazed about him curiously, wide-eyed at their adventure. Presently Joanna came to sit beside her lady. There was a constrained awkwardness between the two women. At last the maid spoke.

"They are our enemies, Mary."

"Once 'twas true, Joanna, and I grieved for loving where I dinna dare to tread. But that time has passed now. The auld ways are gone. We canna turn back. In a short while we shall be exiles from our homeland, and those two men will be all that stand between us and death—or worse.''

''I—I dinna love Cadman as ye do Hunter. I hae nae such strength to sustain me. Och, Mary! Mary! Can ye forget so quickly how they murdered your brother?''

''Nay, Joanna. There is naught to forget,'' Mary answered and told her maid of Hugh's and Ian's treachery.

''And ye believe this?'' Joanna asked when Mary had finished her story.

''Ye ask me that after knowing my husband?'' Mary's voice was sharp.

''Nay, then. But—''

''Cadman is a good mon, for all he is a MacBeth.'' Mary indicated Hunter's kinsman as he came out of the ferry master's hut. ''Gordon was my brother, and I loved him dearly, but he's dead, Joanna. Dead! And naught will e'er bring him back. Life is for the living. Dinna turn so quickly from one who would defend ye wie his sword.''

''And attack me wie another!''

''Was it—was it so verra bad?''

Joanna had the grace to blush furiously. Her hands twisted in her lap. ''Nay,'' she replied softly, ''and for that alone I canna forgie him!''

The maid sprang to her feet, fairly running along the riverbank to the place where the ferry awaited, her small shoulders squared with pride and anger. Cadman watched her speculatively for a moment, then went to stand beside her. Mary could not hear the words that passed between them, but when he caught Joanna's arms and spun her to him roughly, Mary saw upon Cadman's dark visage that same fierce look of rage and longing that had marked Hunter's face before he'd come to love her; and she knew in the end Cadman would have Joanna's heart even as she now held his, unbeknownst to them both.

The sight of Hunter, carrying the tankards of ale in his hands and Geoffrey upon his shoulders drew Mary away from her maid and Cadman. How the bairn clings to him, she thought as she watched her child with her beloved. Already Geoffrey has begun to love him. It gladdened Mary's heart to know her son would not grow up without the steadying influence of a good father after all, for she recognized in that moment Hunter would give of himself to Edward's bairn what he would give unto his own. Mary had never loved him more than she did when Hunter handed her the ale, then swung her child, who was laughing with delight, to the ground, ruffling the boy's gold hair. Hunter offered his cup first to Mary's son, fingers steadying the heavy chalice so Geoffrey might drink more easily. Mary slaked her own thirst slowly, dipping pieces of the hard bread into the ale to soften them before giving a bite to Ranald, who had awakened confused, as he would be for many weeks hence, by his strange surroundings. He fretted irritably as he chewed and rubbed his eyes crossly.

"I will take him, Mary," Hunter offered somewhat shyly.

Mary knew her lover's conscience smote him sorely at the thought that he might have slain his own child, and awkwardness and awe filled him, too, at the knowledge that he had a son.

"But, sir," Geoffrey protested. "There willna be room for us all upon your steed."

Hunter appeared to ponder this thoughtfully.

"Aye," he rejoined at last, head cocked to one side as though still musing. "That's true, lad. And then, too, your mother would hae no mon to help her wie her own mount, although I do admit Ranald is a might wee yet for the job."

Geoffrey tilted his head in much the same manner as Hunter had done, his face screwed up with concentration as he studied on this. Mary turned away to hide her smile as he swaggered slightly.

"I could help her, sir." Geoffrey's eyes sparkled at the challenge. "I could guide Desmond and—and fight off bandits, too, if need be." He blurted out this last rather less confidently, reaching for the small dirk at his waist as though to reassure himself of its presence.

Hunter considered this with a very serious expression. "Aye." He nodded finally. "All right then, 'tis settled. Ye will ride wie your mother and protect her even as I would and will.''

Geoffrey's cheerful countenance clouded suddenly as Hunter moved to help Mary to her feet.

"Sir." He tugged anxiously at the older man's *breacan*.

"Aye, Geoffrey?"

"Sir," the boy began again, taking a deep breath before plunging on, "you're nae a bad mon, are ye?"

Hunter was almost undone by this. "Why, nay, lad," he responded, startled. "Why would ye ask such a thing?"

"Because—because my Uncle Hugh was a bad mon," the child stammered in a rush. "He hurt my mama, and she wasna happy for a long time, and I—I dinna want ye to hurt her, too, and make her unhappy again."

Mary's eyes met Hunter's own pitying ones over the boy's head. She had not thought, had not even considered how Hugh's brutality might have affected Geoffrey, and his sudden distraught outburst unnerved her. Hunter hunkered down quickly by the child's side, his hands on Geoffrey's shoulders.

"Ye listen to me, lad." His tone was grave but kind. "I love your mother verra much. I hae always loved her and would hae married her had your father nae wed her first. I wouldna e'er do anything I thought might hurt her if I could help it. Do ye understand me, lad?"

"Aye. Sir?"

"Aye, lad?"

"Was my—was my father a bad mon?"

Pain flashed across Hunter's countenance, but he hid it instantly. "I—I dinna know your father, Geoffrey." He chose his words carefully. "But he loved your mother in his own way as much as I do, and he—he did what he thought was right for her always, even when—when—" His voice broke. "Someday I—I shall tell you aboot your father, lad, for he was a verra good mon—the best."

Geoffrey's face brightened like a Christmas morn. "Oh, thank ye, sir. Thank ye e'er so much!" he shouted before running to inform Joanna of his news.

"And I thank ye too, my love," Mary said, reaching for Hunter's hand, gripping it tightly as the tears started in her eyes.

For one fleeting instant Mary felt the shadow of Edward pass between them, then it was gone, and she knew the ghost of the gentle, poetic youth who had once been her husband would never haunt them again. Somehow she could almost see Edward smiling in that soft, shy way of his and knew he had given them his blessing.

"A penny for them."

"I was thinking Edward would be proud to hae ye raise his son."

Hunter was touched. "If our lives had been different, I might hae called him my friend. I will guide the lad as my own and teach him those things his father treasured also. I willna let Geoffrey forget Edward Carmichael," Hunter vowed fervently. "This I swear by all that is holy."

Somewhere a lark trilled sweetly, like a mellow flute, as they walked to the ferry.

Four hours later the small party crossed the River Tay in the same fashion and were in Perth shortly thereafter. There they booked passage on a ship bound for France. They all stood at the rail as the vessel pulled slowly out to sea and watched until their homeland faded from sight, each of them trying to imprint its last details upon their memories. The majestic purple mountains; the sweep of the golden moors; the glitter of Jamie's Court; the cry of a sea gull that echoed clearly over the grey green waves, its high, piercing call the last thing they were to carry with them. It seemed fitting—the sad, plaintive, dying note—for none of them ever expected to see Scotland again.

# BOOK FOUR

## *And Wildest Hearts*

# Twenty-seven

**The North Sea, 1492**

The mist did not cling upon the waters in a swirl of grey haze as it was wont to do in the mountains of Scotland, but came down like a ghostly blanket over a bairn, thick and nearly white in the blackness of the nights the fugitives passed upon the North Sea. Above the restless, shifting waves the moon shimmered in and out of the clouds and touched the fog with silver fingers so the fine spray of the ocean seemed as alive as a mass of shooting stars. And once, before they crossed the English Channel, a storm broke over them from the heavens, sending an eerie blaze of green fire skipping along the lines from which the wind-fraught sails billowed and strained upon the creaking timbers of the masts. White horses danced before the ship as its bow plunged ever forward through the peaks rising up like horns of unicorns, rearing and prancing upon the turbulent, grey green depths of the fathomless mystery that was their field.

Far below in the hold Craigor, Desmond, and Logie (who traveled with their masters, for a knight without a destrier can serve no man) whinnied as though in response to the call of their pale washed cousins.

Mary, standing at the rail after her initial seasickness had passed, felt, for the first time in her life, small and insignificant as she gazed out over the vast, madding waters.

The party landed at Rouen, France, the city that had once held the jewel-encrusted court of the Normandy kingdom whence William the Bastard had sprung to conquer all England nearly five hundred years past. From there they bought passage on a barge to Paris, where Hunter and Cadman hoped to attach themselves as knights to the French Court or some lord.

They reached the city a few days later. On the side of the Seine known as the *Rive Droit,* or Right Bank, the grand *Jardin des Tuileries* bloomed in bright bursts of multicolored flowers, and the great *Palais du Louvre* rose up at the river's edge in all its radiant splendor, the residence of the King, the key to the city's western walls and defenses. Geoffrey and Ranald were not the only two who stared at the gardens and French fortress in awe, for its brilliance far outshone the now-seemingly austere Holyrood Palace in Edinburgh. The French structure had originally been built by King Phillippe-Auguste in 1220, upon the site where the Vikings had camped during their vain attempt to lay siege to Paris in 885. Through the years various French monarchs had added their own wings to the construction until it had become the huge, many-roomed palace to which Hunter and the rest sought entry.

They chose Mary to present their letters of introduction, for she was a distant cousin of King James IV of Scotland. Presumptuously, she had made more of the relationship than it merited, knowing Jamie would forgive her. Because of this, two small chambers were found for them in an obscure portion of the castle.

Once comfortably lodged the six set out to explore the city to fill the time that would lapse before Charles VIII received them. They shopped in *Les Halles,* the marketplace of Paris, agog and gaping at the vast display of wares set out upon the many stalls cramming the square. They bought nothing, however, except a gift for the King, for their funds were strictly limited. The knowledge that she could only look, but not purchase, brought home to Mary more sharply than anything else the poverty and hardship she would face in the new life she had chosen.

"Nay, Geoffrey, dinna touch," she chided as her son reached out toward a ripe peach.

"But, mama, we always had them at home," he protested.

"And ye will hae one now and Ranald too," Hunter intervened swiftly. *'Tis hard enough for the bairns*, his eyes said to Mary. *This one time canna hurt.*

And as though he understood their straitened circumstances, Geoffrey offered part of his peach to the others. Touched by his thoughtful generosity, they refused, finding joy, instead, in his pleasure.

They visited the *Bastille,* but the sight depressed them all. They left quickly, turning to the *Menagerie* at the *Jardin des Plantes* to lift their spirits. There they saw wild beasts that prowled in cages upon restless feet; great cats that snarled warningly, showing daggerlike teeth; bright-plumed tropical birds that cawed loudly and perched with gnarled feet curled tight around branches; chattering monkeys that swung from bar to bar, pausing now and then to groom one another.

One week later word came that the King would see the Scots.

The Valois monarch was but twenty-one years old, built of less than medium height for his age, and ill-shaped. Though his face was a pleasant oval, and his liquid brown eyes were large and set beneath delicate brows, his nose was too big, hooking out over a thin, firm upper lip and a fleshy lower lip that bespoke a lustful nature. His chin was square and deeply clefted. Brown hair hung straight and stringy to his jaws. His nervous habit of twitching his hands unnerved those who suffered his presence, either by irritating them beyond all patience or making them ill-at-ease themselves. He sat upon a dais beneath which lay an intricately worked tapestry and above which hung a velvet canopy embroidered with gold *fleurs-de-lys.* Beside him sat Anne of Brittany, whom Charles was shortly to marry.

At sixteen Anne was a small slight girl, too thin in body for the fat face that squatted upon her neck. She had dark wide eyes; a bulbous nose; and a pouting cupid's bow mouth. She limped when she walked, and she clung to the King with a jealousy that far outstripped reason, guarding his moments greedily, for fear he would stray from her.

Two long benches ran against the walls on either side of the room; upon these lounged the Princes by blood and resident prelates who composed Charles's privy council. At the end of the chamber opposite the dais another bench rested. It was here the King motioned for Mary, Hunter, and Cadman to be seated after they had knelt and made their introductions (Joanna had stayed behind in their chambers to look after Geoffrey and Ranald).

Hunter acted as spokesman for the little group, and though Charles seemed pleased with the golf club they gave him (for he was overly fond of sports), he made no promises, dismissing them somewhat curtly when Anne of Brittany leaned over to whisper slyly in his ear. The would-be Queen Consort gave Mary a hard look as the Scots bowed and exited from the room; Mary knew the King's intended bride would not long tolerate their presence at Court. The lass's heart sank, for it meant they would have to move on.

She laid her hand upon Hunter's arm as the doors closed behind them, speaking in rapid Gaelic so she would not be understood if accidentally overheard.

"The Breton bitch was jealous of the King's attention to me. If *she* has *her* way, Charles will find himself surrounded wie naught save cows!"

"Dinna fash yourself, sweet." Hunter's eyes narrowed. "I dinna care for the way the King leered at ye myself."

"Nor did I; ye may be sure of that!" Mary snapped back tartly, for indeed Charles's glance had strayed to her bodice more than once during the interview, and a bit of spittle had actually drooled from one corner of his open lips (the monarch's mouth was never fully closed). She shuddered.

"He thinks to stave off the Romans by taking the Breton to wife," Cadman said, "for they will gain control of Brittany if they can, and Charles seeks that duchy for his own."

Hunter made an impatient motion with his hand. "He is a

fool then, for he broke off his betrothal to Maximilian's daughter to make the match, and Anne was already wed by proxy to Maximilian himself. I dinna see how either the Pope or the Emperor will stand for it. Charles will hae the Holy Roman Empire breathing down his neck for this insolent bungling of brides; ye mark my words.''

Cadman grinned. ''Then mayhap we should attach ourselves to the Austrian court, brother. They may hae need of men-at-arms.''

''That arrogant Hapsburg!'' Hunter dismissed Maximilian I. ''They are a stuffy lot, those Germans.''

''Ne'ertheless, sir, we are beggars and canna afford to be choosy. We could do worse than exile at Emperor Maximilian's palace.''

''Aye.'' Hunter nodded. ''Let us begone from here then. I dinna care to hae Mary living under that lecher's roof anyway.'' He gave a quick jerk of his thumb toward Charles VIII's hall.

''Nor I, Joanna. 'Tis just as well she remained wie the bairns.'' Cadman's face was suddenly hot with jealousy.

Mary found she was blushing. She wondered if all the MacBeths were as passionately possessive of their women as these two and whether or not Cadman fired Joanna's blood as Hunter did her own.

The Scots made their way overland through Burgundy to the border of Switzerland, where the Alps towered higher than their own Highland mountains. Their voices echoed strangely from crag to crag when they spoke, and they derived a great deal of amusement by shouting out ridiculous things to one another and then waiting to hear the statements repeated over and over and over. . . . It was the only laughter they shared, for otherwise the Alps were deadly.

The lines of strain upon Hunter's face deepened grimly at the sight; Cadman too looked older, harder, and Joanna shivered slightly at the chill that now lurked deep within his once-merry blue eyes. Thus far he had been kind to her, although he took her nightly with a hunger that would not be denied; but he said naught of loving her as he lay atop her in the darkness, and she feared he might set her aside if he tired of her physically. This apprehensiveness melted her cold manner toward him somewhat.

"I am a burden to ye." Her honeyed eyes sought his blue ones upon the border of the Alps.

He studied her speculatively for a moment. "An unwilling maid is always trouble."

"Ye knew I was unwilling when ye took me, sir."

"And now, Joanna—what of now?"

Her cheeks stained with color at his boldness; she could not meet his piercing gaze. But she did not turn away when his lips brushed hers roughly. Cadman helped her remount Logie with a secret, knowing smile.

If there were a way for them to pass through the massive mountains, the Scots were not privy to it; disheartened, they were forced to retrace their steps back into Burgundy and from there journeyed through a place that was then part of Austria until they reached the point where the lands of Württemberg (of the German kingdom) and Bavaria joined.

By this time autumn lay with red-and-gold ripeness upon them, and winter nipped at their heels.

Mary had heard tales of the great and mighty warriors of the Teutons and the Huns, men who traveled through promontories and threw spears or swung battle-axes like lightning or the thunder of hammers upon anvils. She had no cause to doubt the validity of these stories as the six made their way through the Germanic strongholds. 'Twas truly a country of giants. Giant Alps rose up along the banks of the rivers that had cut deeply into the jagged, towering rocks through the endless centuries, creating breathtaking gorges that made one's head swoon dizzily at the long steep drops from the edges of the cliffs. Giant forested flatlands swept into palegreen valleys that stretched awesomely where the ragged peaks did not sit like great blue-and-purple gods upon the land. Giant spires atop churches soared to caress the heavens from their perches above the hamlets nestled in the hills.

They crossed the magnificent River Rhine by ferry and sailed again by barge up the graceful River Danube, as blue and shining as the snow-covered crags.

Fall burst around them in an undreamed-of splendor. Dense black woods were patched with flaming orange and glittering yellow, as though an artist had stood back from his easel to fling the colors of his bright paints against the canvas. Red deer and pied deer scampered in startled parade to break the still hush of the countryside with rippling crash through clustered bushes. Wolves stalked the twisted pathways of the grandly cloaked trees, their yellow eyes shining in the dark nights that came down upon the land with ebon witch's stealth to shroud glade and heath with great cape.

The adults had no need to caution the children against straying. Geoffrey hung close by Hunter's side or sought his mother's skirts; Ranald, who was learning to walk, toddled no farther than the length of Mary's or Joanna's arms.

The fine cloud of winter's breath hovered near when the Alps at last gave way to the vast Pannonian Basin of eastern Europe and Vienna, where Roman troops had once marched through narrow winding streets and Richard the Lion-Hearted of England had been held for ransom.

After disembarking from the barge the Scots rode past the church of St. Ruprecht, turning onto the cobbled road of *Tuchlauben*. Here, set back from the street, was the palace *Am Hof*, house of the earlier dukes of Babenberg, who had originally ruled Austria. Farther on, at the end of *Kohlmarkt* street, which angled to the west of the city, sprawled the *Hofburg*, palace of the mighty Hapsburgs, in all its magnificence, for the now-ruling family of Austria had scorned the *Am Hof* and had built their majestic home south of the old castle. Like the *Louvre* in France various monarchs had added wings to the *Hofburg* through the centuries, and the fortress spun out haphazardly along the edge of the trade center.

Once again Mary's presumption upon her kinsmanship to King James IV of Scotland gained them chambers at the palace. After stabling the three horses and unpacking their meager possessions the small party sought the marketplace off *Wollzeile* street to buy a gift for the Emperor.

Here the towers of St. Stephen's Cathedral rose up in the distance, gutted by fire in the Thirteenth Century. Reconstruction had begun on the Romanesque structure at the opening of the Fourteenth Century, however, and was almost ended. The west front, with its massive Portal of the Giants and two Pagans' Towers, had been preserved in its original design, and behind this had been built a long Gothic addition. The completed south tower of this wing jutted spirelike into the sky; the north tower had not yet been finished and stood forlornly desolate opposite its companion. The great, rounded roof gleamed with glazed colored tile in the sunlight.

Nearby the chapel and chapter house of the Order of Teutonic Knights, dating from the time of the Crusades, sat like guard-dogs posted before a gate.

Mary, drawn to the cathedral, broke away from the others to enter the hushed stillness of the church. There she knelt briefly in prayer.

"Holy Mary, Mother of God," she prayed softly, "grant unto me and mine thy blessing, and forgie our many sins. Look down upon us wie favor, and guide us in this strange land so far from our home."

She paused, uncertain of how to continue, and then Hunter was kneeling there beside her, head bowed low. He clasped her folded hands gently.

"Oh, God in heaven," his voice whispered in the silence. "We are not worthy of being thy servants, for this love of ours has brought much pain to those we cherish and wouldna hae hurt had there been any other way for us to be as one. Forgie us our selfishness; hae mercy upon us whose love for one another came as swiftly as a summer storm and grew wie passing time as a seed from rain-washed ground. We are husband and wife in heart, if nae in name, and no truer love hath mon for woman than Hunter MacBeth for Mary Carmichael. Before God, I pledge my love and life unto her."

"And I, mine unto thee." She turned to him fiercely.

Hunter kissed her then and placed a gold sovereign in the alms box as they left the church quietly.

"So much?" Mary murmured anxiously, guessing at the state of their meager funds.

"For thee, I would hae laid a King's ransom there."

" 'Tisna right to love so strongly; we hae been punished for it."

"Nae, Mary, we hae been tried and stood constant in our hearts. Wie'oot that there is no love worth haeing."

"That arrogant Hapsburg," as Hunter had called him, kept the Scots waiting nearly a fortnight before he received them. The brilliance of the palace wherein Maximilian I, Emperor of the Holy Roman Empire, reigned was beyond comparison with the court of Edinburgh. Never had Mary seen such a diamond-studded gathering as that which encrusted the long reception hall of the Hapsburg. Statesmen from Bohemia, Moravia, Bavaria, Croatia, Serbia, Hungary, and as far away as Prussia, Poland, and Russia flocked to the Emperor's Court. A shrewd and vain man, Maximilian was a powerful warrior and an ambitious ruler, for he had a burning desire to unite all of western Europe as it had once been under Charlemagne. He spoke only French or *Wienerisch,* distaining the *Hochdeutsch* of the neighboring countries, much as his ancestors had scorned the palace of their predecessors.

Mary trembled when she knelt before him, for his hard face was stern and selfish. His eyebrows arched arrogantly over cold, hooded eyes. His great, jutting nose humped out broadly over purposeful lips given to thinning in anger. His heavy jowls were marked with deep creases. His light hair hung like a bowl before fluffing out into a smooth, puffed wave around his ears.

The Scots felt awkward and out-of-place in the richly bedecked hall, for the Holy Roman Empire was not on as familiar terms with Scotland as France generally was. Their plain *breacans* and Mary's *arascaid* stood out like sore thumbs among the silks and satins, the brocades and damasks of the cavaliers and Court women. The Scots had little money and represented a country that was of no importance to the Emperor. He took no note of them. Certainly he had no need of them with the wealth of countries and men-at-arms already at his disposal.

Bedraggled and discouraged, the Scots moved on amid the first flurries of winter snow. The River Danube, once as blue as a sapphire beneath the flaming autumn sun, froze to a marble whiteness. The six were forced to abandon the barge when it could no longer make its way through the cakes of floating crystalline ice and finally the solid glazed sheet the waters had become.

Blinded by the stark white drifts, cold beyond belief, they plodded through the falling snow, grateful for the fur coats for which they had bartered their precious coins before leaving the Austrian court. They slept in stables when there were no inns available, huddling together amidst the winter hay for warmth.

Geoffrey and Ranald sickened and flushed with fever, coughing raggedly as Mary forced spoonfuls of medicine bought from a hamlet doctor down their throats. It seemed to help, but she worried to the point where she fell ill herself, and nearly a month was lost in a small village where Hunter insisted they take shelter until she and the children were recovered. He nursed them with shadowed eyes; Cadman and Joanna crept softly in his presence, afraid of the half-madness that settled upon him, for Hunter blamed and cursed himself for Mary's and the children's sickness.

"I shouldna hae taken her and the bairns from Scotland. They are nae used to this bitter weather."

"Nor are we," Cadman pointed out. "They hae the strength of the Highlands in their blood. They will get well."

"I am accursed," Hunter moaned. " 'Tis all my fault."

"Nay, sir." Joanna knelt and laid one hand upon his own. "Ye are blinded by love and crazed wie guilt. Mary has forsaken all she knew for ye; dinna fail her now."

Renewed, Hunter sought their chamber at the inn, kissing

Mary's sleeping face fiercely, as though by force alone he could make her better. Slowly her eyes fluttered open.

"Ye hae come, Prince Charming," she whispered with a faint smile.

He saw her fever had broken at last. Relief swept through him like rushing waters through a crumbling dam. Nearby Geoffrey and Ranald stirred irritably, then asked for some supper. Hunter knelt, gathering his small family in his arms. Tears pricked his eyes; a muscle worked tensely in the side of his jaw; his hand trembled when it reached for Mary's own.

"Oh, lassie," he breathed. "Dinna stray from me again. I canna live wie'oot ye."

And then there was silence until Geoffrey squirmed like a little fish in Hunter's tight grasp and demanded his dinner. With laughter on the verge of tears Hunter ordered up the best meal the inn had to offer.

They left the hamlet a few days later, Mary insisting she was well enough to travel and Geoffrey and Ranald obviously (from their rough-and-tumble play with one another) themselves again.

The Scots lay under the crystal stars, which looked like snowflakes in the black sky that night, with only the flames of their campfire to break the dark void of the evening as it settled upon them with stilled hush. But for all this they were warm enough, for the sharp, piercing wind was muffled by the denseness of the trees wherein they sought shelter.

Hunter shifted uneasily on his haunches by the blaze, for the quiet of the forest reminded him of the deathly peace that hung with grim foreboding over a field before battle. He caught Cadman's blue eyes, bright in the twilight, and knew the same eerie thought had occurred to his kinsman.

"I like it nae," he murmured in Cadman's ear.

"Nor do I, brother, nor do I. 'Tis too still, and too many shadowed trees abound for men to lurk behind."

"Get the women and bairns together by the fire, for we shall not sleep this night."

Mary and Joanna huddled close together in the darkness;

Geoffrey and Ranald breathed easily and deeply between the two women, eyes closed peacefully. Finally the girls, too, dozed, Mary, caught in the terrifying throes of a nightmare, awakened shortly thereafter with a start.

"Hunter! Hunter!"

His dark figure melted toward her out of the blackness; Cadman appeared just as swiftly from the other side of the camp

"What is it, tigress?" her lover whispered as he knelt beside her.

"A dream—a horrible dream—men—"

"Quickly, lass, how many?"

"Five—I think there were five—"

"From what direction did they come?"

"South. They came out of the south like vultures to prey upon us in the night. Outlaws. There was a fight. I heard Joanna screaming. I was screaming. The bairns—oh, my bairns." She clutched her sleeping sons to her frantically.

"Douse the fire, Cadman," Hunter ordered sharply. "Get ye to that far tree there. They'll outnumber us, but we shall hae the element of surprise on our side." Cadman stared at his kinsman and then Mary fearfully, stunned wonder and suspicion plain upon his face. "She has the Sight." Hunter's words were clipped. "I hae known it for some time. It comes upon her in dreams. Mother of God, mon! Dinna stand there like an addle-wit! 'Tis no time for your ignorant dread; save your superstitions for later!"

Cadman nodded dumbly, but in the dying embers of the snow-drenched flames Mary saw him make the ancient pagan sign against evil against her stealthily with his hands. She shivered uncontrollably as she bent to awaken Joanna.

"Mary, what is it?"

"Men are coming, outlaws. We must get the bairns to safety."

Joanna asked no questions, but lifted Geoffrey in her arms, knowing Mary was not yet fully recovered from her recent illness. Ranald's weight was like a feather as Mary carried him to a cluster of bushes. He stirred fretfully, but his eyes did not open. She and Joanna crouched beside the sleeping boys in the denseness of the thickets and waited. Once a stag crashed through the forest, nearly scaring them to death; after that there was only the slight rustle of the leaves upon the wind and the nervous whinnying of the horses as they pawed restlessly upon the frozen earth with their tethered hooves.

Then they heard it, a muffled soughing in the underbrush and a mutter of whispers that might only have been the gentle sighing of the plaintive breeze. The skin crawled on the nape of Mary's neck; prickles of fear shot up and down her spine.

There were five of them, as Mary had foretold; outlaws, they towered suddenly in the darkness like macabre demons. She felt a scream rise in her throat, but the sound that split the night was not her voice, but those of Hunter and Cadman as the MacBeth battle cry rang out sharply over the terrain.

"A MacBeth! A MacBeth!"

Whether it was the element of surprise, the jeering call to arms, or the appearance of the *breacaned* warriors melting with ferocity from the shadows of the trees, Mary did not know. But the two kinsmen were able to slay two of the renegades swiftly and now dueled with two more. The third remaining man paid little attention to the ongoing battle, moving like a caged panther through the confines that had been the camp. A slow smile suddenly lit his wicked face as he stared at the tracks in the snow. With a grunt of satisfaction he discovered the women's hiding place. They screamed wildly, piercingly, shrill cries of fear that cut the night like knives as he yanked them forward. The children woke, sobbing in confusion at the turmoil that surrounded them. The Scotswomen fought, not only for their own lives, but for those of the bairns they protected like a tigress her cubs. The man tore at Joanna's *arascaid*, exposing her breasts, honeyed and pale beneath the silver, slivered, winter moon. With a jerk Mary remembered the dirk at her waist and tore it from her girdle. She was not her father's daughter for naught after all. The blade plunged deep and true into the outlaw's gullet as he threw his head back in laughter at Joanna's horrified disgust. The smirk choked into a strangled gurgling, the wind whistling through his throat as he crumpled to the ground, surprise upon his face. He twitched once and then lay still.

Nearby the men battled furiously. Hunter's strong sword-arm parried an evil thrust, muscles rippling, the veins along his limb standing out like cords from the strain of wielding the heavy weapon. His opponent was larger than he, a heavyset brute with a scraggly beard and gap-toothed leer. The lout's red gold hair hung down in a wild mane as he roared and rushed again. Hunter's shield caught the full force of the blow, but the charge of the metal against his bad shoulder and forearm numbed the limb and sent waves of pain searing up along its length. He staggered; Mary gasped. Geoffrey and Ranald quivered with stifled sobs behind her skirts. Joanna had disappeared.

Hunter regained his balance quickly, but he feinted in a ruse to make his opponent believe he was unable to fend off another assault. The trick would not have worked in daylight, but the night was dark and the outlaw made stupid by his blinding lust for slaughter. The man lunged forward with another bearlike growl, head lowered like a charging bull. Hunter waited until his attacker was almost upon him before stepping, sudden as a leaping cat, to one side, bringing his broadsword down in a rapid slice that severed the man's head cleanly from its thick neck. Blood spurted like water from a fountain, gushing over the snow, foaming red. The head rolled off toward a bush, staring up lopsidedly from sightless eyes. Mary's knees gave out from underneath her. The ground was cold and wet where she knelt, gathering her sons to her breast so they might not see the gruesome thing.

From the far side of the small clearing came a startled cry. Cadman had tripped upon the root of some tree in the darkness. He fell awkwardly. His sword flew from his fingers as though it had suddenly been given wings. Defenseless, he bunched instinctively, intending to roll to one side as his opponent loomed over him like a giant in the shadowed light for the final thrust. It never came; for out of the undergrowth Joanna cantered like some avenging angel, an Amazon of half-mad fury born of fear, breasts bare and glistening moistly with the sweat of terror, nipples hardened from the cold. She clung like a burr to Logie's naked back, legs astride the savage beast, one arm swinging Cadman's heavy mace with a force she had not known she possessed. The spiked morningstar drove into the side of the outlaw's head, smashing against his helmet with a sickening blow that echoed like a hammer upon an anvil across the clearing. The steel hood split with a rending grind, brains splattering pulplike in all directions as the marauder fell.

She canna control the steed, Cadman realized suddenly as he saw the mace fly out in a wide arc from Joanna's hand at the force of the impact. The powerful chestnut destrier reared, then lunged as the spinning ball-and-chain whipped past its nose. Joanna strained desperately upon the reins, but the horse plunged forward into the forest depths, branches of the parting trees slapping wildly at her face.

To Cadman's knowledge no man save Hunter had ever ridden the ghostly Craigor who snorted cloudy breaths of white and shied at the edge of the underbrush; but in moments, the younger MacBeth was astride the white steed's bare back, yanking hard upon the reins as he set his spurs to the horse's sides. The stallion bucked and reared, twisting and turning this way and that; but his fear gave him strength, and Cadman mastered the beast quickly before setting out after Joanna.

In moments he was riding neck-and-neck with her, weaving in and out of the woods with the skill learned during his childhood training when, as a young squire, he'd been taught to race a spiked obstacle course in preparation for the swords, battle-axes, and maces he would later have to outwit upon horseback on a battlefield. He grabbed for Logie's bridle. It was nearly a quarter-of-a-mile before he managed to halt the heedlessly galloping beast, but at last the stallion slowed, sides heaving, blown. Joanna slipped from the animal's back in a dead faint.

"Jo! Jo!" Cadman called hoarsely as he ran to kneel beside her.

With relief he saw she was still breathing. He cradled her

in his arms, slapping her face lightly with cold snow until she stirred and moaned. Her eyes flew open.

"Nay, ye are safe now," he said gently as she struggled against him. She recognized his voiced and quieted. "Thank God, ye are safe."

He stroked her hair lightly, drawing the bodice of her *arascaid* closed as she noted her nakedness with a shy blush. His fingers lingered over a small bruise from the outlaw's rough grasp. Tenderly he kissed the mark.

"Ye saved my life, lass."

She nodded, eyes closing once more as she laid her head against his shoulder, secure in his warm embrace.

"Why? Ye would hae been free of me otherwise."

"And ravaged by that animal who would hae taken your place!"

"Ah, then I was preferable to the outlaw, eh?"

"N—Nay."

"Nay, Jo?" Cadman raised one eyebrow inquisitively as he suppressed a quick smile. "Ye must ne'er lie to your lord, lass. Do ye love me nae at all?" His voice was thick and hushed.

"I—I care for ye a—a little," the maid replied at last.

Her feelings for him went much deeper than that now, Cadman knew; but she was proud. He did not press her further.

"Well?" Joanna waited expectantly.

"Well, what, lass?" He turned away so she would not see the secret love and amusement lurking in his dark blue eyes.

"Having forced such an admission from my lips, hae ye naught to say to me, sir?"

"What is it ye would wish me to say, lass?"

Joanna bit her lip. "Sir—Cadman—" She stumbled over his Christian name, for she had not called him by it before. "I—I know there was another whom ye didst love once. Mary has told me of her."

"Aye, Jo, that is true, just as your heart once belonged to Gordon Carmichael, but they are dead, lass, and we are alive."

"I canna—canna take her place, though, anymore than ye can Gordie's"

"Nay, but there are many ways of loving, Jo, if that's what you're driving at."

Joanna blushed again. "I dinna say that, sir."

"Then perhaps ye tell me what ye mean."

The girl drew a deep breath. "We shallna see Scotland again, sir."

"Most likely nae," he agreed.

"We are exiles in a foreign land. 'Twould be easy for ye, sir, to set me aside for another of your rank, for ye are an able and willing knight; ye might even snare a well-dowried bride for your prowess on the battlefield. I know I am naught save a captive maid to ye, Cadman; but I was gently bred and raised. 'Twouldna be so simple for me here in this strange country to find such a man with rank as would take me to wife. In Scotland, at least, I would hae wed some lowly knight. But here—I hae no maidenhead, no dowry, and I am a bastard, sir."

"As am I, Jo," Cadman said softly. "Ye know that. I say again, mistress, what is it you're asking?"

"I'm asking—I'm asking," Joanna went on in a sudden rush, "if ye care for me at all, as I hae admitted I care for ye—if ye—if ye care enough to—to wed me?" She could not meet his eyes. "I will be a good wife to ye, I promise ye that. And in time I might come to love ye in my heart as well as—as well as—the—the other." She flushed with embarrassment at her reference to their lovemaking. "I wouldna ask, but I think I am wie child, Cadman, and I wouldna hae my bairn's shield bear the *bend sinister* like your own."

Cadman's breath hissed with sharp intake. "So. Once again Carmichael and MacBeth blood are to mingle as one. Verra well, lass. I do care for ye and will take ye to wife since that is your desire, for I wouldna sire a bastard child either. But I too hae a promise for ye, mistress." Joanna glanced at him warily. His face was grim in the shadowed moonlight. "I shallna touch ye again, madam. That is my promise.

"Ye will be my wife in e'ery way, Jo," he said, answering the unspoken question in her surprise-filled eyes. "But nae until the day ye come to me willingly, wie love in your heart for me and me alone. For I willna fight a ghost, any more than I would expect ye to. Mine has been laid to rest. Yours has nae. Until that day I willna lie wie ye as a mon does his wife, nor will ye take another to your bed in my absence, for I will slay ye if ye do. This I swear, Joanna."

"And if I ne'er seek ye oot?"

"Och, ye will, madam; dinna doubt it. Ye hae known two men, and your body has felt the joys lovemaking brings. Ye will grow lonely in your empty bed and ache for the feel of me between your thighs. Ye will come to me in the end."

"Ye are so sure?" Joanna whispered.

"Aye, I am sure," Cadman breathed before his mouth claimed hers fiercely in the night.

They walked the horses back to camp in silence.

The Scots had no wish to linger in the evil place, so as soon as Cadman returned with Joanna they set out once more upon their journey. 'Twas nearly morning anyway, and the slivered moon lighted their way well enough. They managed to ride amost twenty-five miles before halting at an inn to break their fast. There, at a hamlet church, Joanna and Cadman knelt before an Austrian priest in the little village to speak the vows that proclaimed them man and wife. It was a somber ceremony; she in her torn *arascaid;* he in his blood-stained *breacan.* But the old Father saw naught amiss as he blessed the two; life was hard; the times were uncertain. A battle-marked warrior was a common enough sight to his failing eyes. Hunter and Mary watched the rites solemnly, pain upon their faces that they could not kneel before the elderly priest in joyful union.

A short distance from the village the small party happened upon a recent avalanche. They knew it was fresh, for the snow had not yet had time to harden into a solid frozen mass, but was as soft as the blanket of a wee bairn. They moved closer to examine the fallen drift, seeking some means of passage through the white cascade.

"Oh, look, sir," Geoffrey said to Hunter as the child neared the place where the snow bunched in tumbled silence. There, near the spot where the flakes flattened onto the terrain, fluttered a small bird. Its wing was broken, and 'twas near frozen from the cold. " 'Tis hurt." The lad knelt beside the wounded creature, looking so much like his father in that moment that Mary had to turn away to hide the tears that glistened in her eyes. Oh, Edward! He is so like ye, she thought. "It canna fly," the boy continued.

Hunter too glimpsed some of what he guessed must have been Edward's sensitive nature in the child.

"Let me see, son," He bent to cradle the bird in his strong hands. "Aye, ye are right, lad. But I believe the damage can be mended."

"Really, sir?" Geoffrey brightened at this.

"Aye, shall we nae try?"

The boy nodded vigorously. So Hunter set the broken wing with a splint fashioned from a tree branch as best he could, then tucked the wounded animal away inside his *breacan* for warmth.

"In the spring, when the wing has mended, and the bird is well again, we shall set it free," he told the lad, not wanting Geoffrey to become too attached to the small creature.

But the child looked up at Hunter with understanding in his deep blue eyes.

"Of course, sir," he said. " 'Tis a wild thing, nae meant to be caged. 'Twouldna be right to keep it."

At the boy's words the sun burst over the eastern horizon, radiant in its glory, as though God had seen and smiled upon them all.

# Twenty-eight

The bird brought them luck; they were sure of it, for they
encounted no more difficulties on their journey; and Christmas Eve they reached the twin cities of Buda and Pest on the
banks of the River Danube in Hungary. Gateways between the
East and the West they were, those cities. Set at the center of
the Carpathian Basin linking the Great Hungarian Plain with
northern Transdanubia, Buda sprawled over the gentle slopes
of the Buda Hills that swept down to the western banks of the
river. Buda Castle, the Royal palace built by King Béla IV
in the years following the Mongol invasion of 1241, surveyed
the vast terrain of the twin cities regally from its perch high
upon Castle Hill. Opposite Buda, Pest squatted upon a seemingly
endless flat plain devoid of significant features, for its twin
contained most of the gardens and forest area of the two
cities. To the north Óbuda situated itself between Buda and
Pest, the original site of civilization, where the Romans had
once sheltered.

Filled with every form of vile, depraved wickedness and
every kind of exciting, foreign enchantment as well, the cities
surpassed any the Scots had seen during their long travels.
Here minarets mingled with cross-topped steeples, Turkish
coins with German francs, Anatolian carpets with French
tapestries, Chinese silks with Indian brocades, Russian vodka

with Greek ouzo. For these two cities had become the major trade center joining Asia and Europe.

The six picked their path carefully through the milling mass of market stalls and foreigners; and once again Mary's ruse found chambers for them at the Royal palace.

Unlike Charles VIII of France and Maximilian I of Austria, Ulászló II (Vladislav Jagiello), King of Hungary, did not keep the small party waiting for his reception. They were welcomed warmly into his presence the day following their arrival in the twin cities. Although he had signed the Treaty of Pressburg last year and was no longer at war with the Emperor of the Holy Roman Empire, his city, Belgrade, on the outskirts of the Hungarian borders, had been attacked by the ruler of the Ottoman Empire, Bayezid II, called Adlî (meaning The Just), and the King of Hungary was in need of men-at-arms to drive off the Turks. Although he had many soldiers at his disposal, Ulászló had heard tales of Scottish prowess on the battlefield with a bow and arrows and was interested in having his army, which was not proficient in the use of this mighty weapon, trained in its employ. So Christmas Day Hunter and Cadman became soldiers of fortune for the Hungarian monarch.

The Scots celebrated the holidays with much laughter and many presents bought with the money the King had advanced to the two men; and although they were sorry to leave the twin cities so quickly, they were glad of employment.

The Danube carried them by barge to the outskirts of the city of Belgrade in a comfort they had not known since leaving Scotland. Built on the site of an ancient fortress of the Celts on the Kalemegdan headland, Belgrade was located at the point of convergence of the Rivers Danube and Sava to the southwest of the Transylvanian Alps. Destroyed by the Huns in 442, it had been ruled by many people over the centuries: the Sarmatians, Goths, Gepidae, Franks, Bulgars, Serbians, and the Turks, who had laid siege to it in 1440, lost it during the intervening fifty-two years, and now sought to take it once again.

At the Hungarian camp about twenty-five miles north of the city Hunter and Cadman found the captain of the troops and presented their orders from the King.

"I am glad to have you," the Hungarian officer said grimly. "For our ranks have dwindled alarmingly since the ascent of King 'Dobre' to the throne."

"'Dobre?'" Hunter questioned, one eyebrow raised.

"It means 'all right' in your language, I believe," Captain Ivan Tisza said, translating the Hungarian word into French, which was something of a universal language at the time.

"Please, continue," the MacBeth urged, wanting to find out exactly what the Scots had let themselves in for.

"After the death of Matthias Corvinus, the old King," Captain Tisza explained, "the magnates gained much power and chose Ulászló of Bohemia to rule them. He is a weak monarch who tends to agree with the magnates on every turn. Thus the name 'Dobre.' At any rate, he has allowed the disbanding of the Black Army, which numbered some 30,000 mercenaries under Corvinus. This pathetic, little group"—the Hungarian indicated his troops with a wave of his hand— "is all that remains of it. Five thousand men against six times as many." His voice was bitter.

If Hunter and Cadman were alarmed by the odds, they did not show it.

"There are men in Belgrade, surely," Cadman said, joining the conversation.

"Maybe a thousand or more roughly," Captain Tisza replied. "When the Turks could not take the walls by force, they withdrew to lay siege to the city. For nearly three months now they have besieged Belgrade, hoping the city's supplies will run out and force its inhabitants to open the gates. The infidels do not know we are camped here. We have been waiting also to see if they will become discouraged and give up their siege, for they are a devilish lot, these Turks. They attack in hordes and seem to have no concept of loss of life or limb. One man is beaten off, and then more rise to take his place. We thought with the onslaught of winter they would return home, but they have rotated their troops, instead, sending in reinforcements to take the place of those who can no longer tolerate the freezing conditions. For my own men, of course, there has been no such relief. A fortnight ago the sappers began digging.''

"The sappers?" Mary asked.

Captain Tisza turned to her courteously. He had ignored the women previously, for his curiosity concerning them had not been aroused. There were many such who followed their men into battle, wives, mistresses. It was to be expected. Now he answered tiredly, his face drawn as a man who recognizes defeat, but can do nothing to prevent it.

"Yes, my lady. The men who will dig vast tunnels under the ground to the city's walls, then set them afire. The scorching heat beneath the surface of land will 'sap' the strength of the earth, drawing it downward, thus causing the collapse of Belgrade's defenses. It will be much the same as though an earthquake had crumbled the walls. 'Tis a time-consuming process, one that can take years to accomplish; before then, of course, the inhabitants will be starved into throwing open the city's gates if we can get no supplies to them. I do not believe Belgrade can hold out much longer. Six to eight weeks at the most, perhaps.''

"And then?"

"And then we shall be forced to attack, my lady. But enough of this. Come this way, and I'll show you where you may lodge.''

Six to eight weeks! Mary glanced at Hunter's sternly set face anxiously. Six to eight weeks in which to train a largely unskilled group in the use of a bow and arrows. 'Twas an impossible task!

Indeed, it seemed as much as the days passed. The Hungarians were bitterly cold and hungry, for rations were short. They did not look forward to the coming battle, but longed instead for their homes and families in Buda and Pest. Surly and reluctant, they learned sullenly. Many would not have learned at all had not Captain Tisza ridden up and down the ranks of men, wielding a snakelike whip with which he lashed the more resentful among them into shape.

"Ye will order yourself in lines of fifty men." Hunter gazed out over the hostile troops warily, while Captain Tisza translated. "A squad will consist of two lines each, approximately six feet apart in distance. Each squad will be twenty-five feet apart. We hae relatively few men, so there will be no unnecessary risks taken." The men appeared to thaw a little toward the Scots knight at this, and Hunter continued with more confidence. "The front lines will kneel, the back lines stand. Those men standing will shoot first, aiming their bows so their arrows fire into a high arc in the sky. This will bring the shafts raining down upon the infidels' heads."

"But, Sir MacBeth," one soldier protested, "will the Turks not simply put up their shields to guard themselves from above?"

"I fully expect them to." Hunter permitted himself a grim smile. "That is when the lines of kneeling men will fire. They will shoot directly into the infidel troops, who will then have no shields blocking them from a frontal attack. They will then, if all goes right, lower their shields once more, and we will repeat the same process."

The men saw his reasoning at last, turning to one another to discuss it quietly as they listened. Sparks of hope began to light their eyes.

"When the first squad has loosed all its arrows," Hunter went on, "it will split in the middle, retreating in two columns to the rear. The second squad will then take its place, and so on. The latter squads will dip their arrows in pitch, since by then the Turks will most likely be close enough that the distance the weighted shafts will hae to travel willna matter."

And so it went. In the evenings Hunter and Cadman would drop wearily to the ground inside the tent that sheltered them from the cold, creeping close to the fire in the center of the small pavilion to warm their numbed hands and chapped faces. Mary and Joanna would pull the boots from the men's frozen feet, rubbing their limbs vigorously to restore circulation. The two knights would ravenously wolf down the meager meal prepared for them by the women before falling into the deep sleep of exhaustion.

Day after day the Scots knights drilled the Hungarian troops. Night after night they staggered to the tent, too tired even for lovemaking. And always, in the distance, the sound of the sappers' hammers chipping away at the frozen earth rang ceaselessly in their ears.

Geoffrey and Ranald grew unnaturally subdued and clung to the women's skirts as though to let go would be to lose them forever. Mary worried over her children's quietness and took to telling them tales by the firelight and singing them to sleep at night, spending as much time as she was able with her frightened sons. Joanna's body rounded with the child she carried, and she fretted for its well-being.

As the days turned into weeks, and the relentless blows of the sappers' hammers continued their steady drone, the reality of the coming battle sank into Mary's bones with a cruelty she had not known before: a psychological cruelty. Always in the past she had been safe behind castle walls; now she recognized she had naught save Hunter's sword and shield to protect her here. Not only she, but her sons as well, would be exposed to the danger of the infidels' attack. The worry gnawed at her. Daily she began to search for a place in the hills wherein they might find a secure haven from the Turks if the Hungarians were to lose the battle. At last she discovered a cave nestled high in the knolls that she thought might serve her purpose. She cleaned it thoroughly, stocked it with what small supplies she could carry, secreted in her garments, from the camp. Then she dragged what brush was available on the barren terrain to hide its entrance from prying eyes.

Hunter watched her preparations, but said nothing, glad of her foresight, for he did not delude himself about the outcome of the fight. If the Hungarians won,'twould be a miracle. Rather than undermining his confidence, Mary's task lightened Hunter's burden by relieving his anxious conscience about what his small family would do were he to be taken captive or killed on that plain outside of Belgrade.

He strolled through the camp in better spirits. He stepped aside to allow some of the heavy wagons passage, lost in thought. Then suddenly his head snapped up abruptly.

"Wait!" he called to the soldiers.

They stared at him, but continued with their chore, not understanding him. Realization dawned on Hunter.

"Captain Tisza! Captain Tisza!"

"Yes, Sir MacBeth?" The officer rode up briskly at the sound of Hunter's voice

"Tell your men to stop what they are doing, and come here at once!"

Captain Tisza eyed him curiously, but translated the order without question, for over the weeks he had come to respect and admire the two Scots and to recognize their military expertise.

"Look here," Hunter began when the troops had gathered round. "I want these wagons disassembled. Cut them in half, like so"—he demonstrated—"and move the axles toward the back of each section so they resemble Roman chariots. Then build the sides of the walls up so men may stand inside wie'oot fear of falling oot."

"Yes, but what are you driving at, sir?" Captain Tisza queried. "We need these wagons to carry supplies."

"They'll be worthless for that purpose if we dinna win this fight." Hunter lifted one eyebrow coolly. "They will serve us far better in the manner I intend. I want your men to forge some short spikelike blades to attach to the wheels on either side. Then we'll drive the vehicles through the infidels and mow them down like grass."

"Ah, now I see." The Hungarian officer began to smile slowly. "And the men inside will be able to defend the wagons from being taken and used against us."

"Quite so," Hunter responded dryly.

"Ingenious, Sir MacBeth."

"Nay, Captain, 'twas a device of the Romans. I dinna know what made me think of it."

"A sense of *déjà vu*, perhaps." Captain Tisza shrugged his shoulders noncommittally. "This was once the sight of the

Roman city, Singidunum. You men get busy on Sir MacBeth's modifications for the wagons.''

One corner of Hunter's mouth quirked downward sardonically as he pivoted on his heel and caught Cadman standing behind him, making the pagan sign. The younger man blushed, abashed.

''Well, it canna hurt.'' Cadman smiled sheepishly.

Hunter threw him a curt frown before striding off.

The preparations for the battle continued. Winter melted into spring, and still the city of Belgrade managed to withstand the siege. The frozen earth thawed rapidly as the sun's rays began to warm once more. The sound of the sappers' hammers increased furiously as the ground softened. Here and there great patches of terrain began to show through the slushy snow and buds to force their way to the surface of the land.

Then one day in early March that year of 1493, the dawn padded over the horizon, unnerving in its silence. The ring of the sappers' hammers had ceased. Mary sought Hunter's side anxiously, the skin crawling with fear on the nape of her neck.

''What does it mean?'' She gazed out over the sweep of countryside apprehensively.

He shook his head as his eyes narrowed toward the city in the distance.

''I dinna know. I canna believe they hae reached the walls of Belgrade.''

''They have not.'' Captain Tisza joined the two Scots. ''The people of the city have thrown open the gates as I feared. We must attack at once!''

Hunter moved swiftly to obey, pausing only to kiss Mary roughly before he set her aside, eyes meeting hers as though to memorize every last detail of her golden face.

''Get Joanna and the bairns to the cave,'' he said. ''I shall come for ye there.''

She nodded without speaking, for sobs choked her slender throat. She held out one pale hand to him, but he had already turned away.

The Turks, secure in what they thought was their victory, moved slowly to take Belgrade, unaware of the force that massed upon the hillside to the north. Thus the infidels were unprepared for the troops that streamed downward from the far side of the knoll. The Hungarians did not swarm forward in droves as was their usual style of battle, but held back as Hunter had directed, forming into squads of one row of kneeling foot-soldiers behind which stood the second row of men, and so on, alternating down the lines. The standing archers loosed their arrows first, shooting high into the sky so that the shafts arced, then flew straight down into the Turkish troops. The infidels, surprised, did not react quickly, and several hundred of their men were lost in the first barrage.

After several rounds of fire they began to catch on as Hunter had hoped. Sprawled out upon the flat plain below Belgrade they squatted, raising their shields above their heads to form an almost solid roof of metal. The Hungarians laughed, a horrible sound. Now the kneeling row of their countrymen loosed their shafts. The arrows shot straight and true into the unprotected chests of the infidels. Many more staggered and went down.

Belgrade, finally realizing it had reinforcements, closed the city gates and began its own resistance from the ramparts of the walls. Great pots of pitch were poured upon those Turks seeking entrance. The flaming bodies fell away from the machicolated battlements with piercing screams of anguish.

Confused, the foot-soldiers of the Turks did not now know what to do with their shields. If they held them above, they were certain to receive a frontal attack. If they held them naturally, they would be assaulted from the sky. Seeking some sort of compromise, they inched forth across the vast sweep of terrain, alternating the placement of their shields. It was a haphazard device at best; more and more of the infidels fell prey to the clumsy archery of the Hungarians. Seeing the confusion of the Turks, Captain Tisza ordered the restructured wagons brought forward.

At his command the vehicles raced toward the infidels, cutting a wide swath between the rows of ordered troops, then withdrew as the Turks retreated to regroup their scattered forces. Once more the archers loosed their arrows and were followed by the onslaught of the wagons.

Again and again this formula was repeated with success as the Turks marched, a seemingly endless supply of men. They trampled over the bodies of their own without compunction, like a horde of ants eating up the countryside. As the infidels drew closer the Hungarian archers began to dip their arrows in hot pitch, sending the flaming shafts spinning through the sky like shooting stars, leaving trails of black smoke along the way.

And through it all Hunter and Cadman rode like two young gods, invincible, awe-inspiring.

Far and away Mary, Joanna, and the boys huddled inside the cave, but even there the screams of the dying soldiers reached them. The pungent odor of burning flesh wafted sickeningly to their nostrils, mingled with the fresh scent of blood. Joanna moved quietly to retch in one corner of their hiding place. Mary stood up to go to her kinswoman's aid, but before she could take a single step a horrible buzzing started in her ears, growing louder by the minute until it rang with as much clarity as the hammers of the sappers had done. The world seemed to darken before her eyes, whirl as though she saw it from a drunken stupor. Mary put her hands to her ears and closed her eyes, trying to shut out the whirring sound, the spinning earth. With a terror greater than any she had ever known she felt a wrenching pull, as though her soul were being yanked from her very body, snatched from the center of her forehead. Gasping, she fought against the fearsome power, resisted it with all her might. Dying! 'Tis dying, I am! she thought. This is what it feels like! She groped frantically at nothing, hands waving spastically as she grabbed at the thin air. She was losing. She knew it. She could feel the helplessness that engulfed her as control of her body slipped from her grasp. Then she was floating, a sheer veil of mist. She saw her body lying upon the floor of the cave, Joanna and the lads bent over her worriedly. Then the picture faded as the sight of the battlefield far below played itself out before her. It was so vivid! So very real! She could actually hear the cries of the soldiers, smell the charred and bloody bodies. Her eyes watered from the smoke. Her mouth thirsted.

She saw Hunter astride his ghostly destrier, shouting ordes, sword-arm flashing as his blade rose and fell again and again, clearing a path through the rows of infidel cavalry. A dark Turk bore down upon him on the field. Behind ye! Mary called a silent warning. Behind ye, my love! But Hunter did not hear. Moments later the girl watched as a swarm of infidels enveloped his tall dark figure. It was the last thing she remembered.

"Mary! Mary!"

It seemed as though hours had passed when she awakened, but Mary saw from the still-bright sun that not more than a few minutes at most had elapsed. Joanna was chafing her lady's hands anxiously. Mary withdrew them from her maid's clutching grip, rising unsteadily to her feet. Her head ached furiously, and her heart was still pounding violently.

"Mary, what is it? Please, tell me what's wrong!" Joanna pleaded.

" 'Twas the—the Sight. The Sight come upon me so strong and sudden, like ne'er before! A waking vision—oh, God, hae mercy—"

But even as she spoke the words Mary knew in her heart Hunter MacBeth would not return to her that day.

Twenty-five thousand Turks lay dead or wounded. The Hungarians, thanks to Hunter and Cadman, suffered only minor casualties in comparison. The infidels retreated and sent a white-flag-bearing messenger to talk terms of surrender and peace with Captain Tisza, who spoke Arabic.

Three days later Mary rode down to the plain before Belgrade to meet Bayezid II and discover what ransom was demanded for Hunter MacBeth's safe return.

"My lady," Captain Tisza pleaded trying to dissuade her from going. "I beg you to remain in camp! These infidels are not to be trusted!"

But Mary only shook her head, and even Cadman, who'd been the sad bringer of the news of Hunter's capture, could not reason with her.

"He is my lord," she said softly. "The father of my child. He would lay down his life for me. I can do no less for my beloved."

She did, however, accede to Captain Tisza's wishes that she veil herself heavily, for she had no desire to be spirited away to some harem, and the Hungarian officer's tales of such frightened her more than Mary cared to admit.

Bayezid II, the Sultan of the Ottoman Empire, was a handsome man. At forty-six years of age he was tall and massively built. He had beautiful dark almond-shaped eyes set under brows that were almost too delicately arched for a man. His nose was long and straight. His lips were small and thin, given to pursing, as though he lusted for and was accustomed to the finer things in life. His brownish black hair was cropped close to his head; and a mustache and beard covered most of his face. He wore a huge white turban and a silk tunic that hung to his booted feet and was belted at his waist with a girdle of braided gold. His surcoat was of paisley brocade lined with rich velvet.

His eyes flickered mutely over Mary's concealed figure standing straight and proud between Cadman and Captain Tisza. They knelt before him, then he motioned for them to be seated on the satin cushions that covered a greater part of the lovely rugs lying on the sand in his pavilion. Refreshments were served by scantily clad maidens in halter tops and harem pants, who moved silently and unobtrusively on naked feet. In one corner of the tent musicians played softly upon instruments with which Mary was not familiar.

At last the Sultan spoke, and Captain Tisza translated so Mary and Cadman could understand.

"You have come to bargain for the life of the Scots knight, have you not?"

The girl nodded, but did not speak.

"He is a fine warrior," the Sultan continued, "worth his

weight in gold." He raised one eyebrow, glancing at Mary's veiled form again speculatively.

She gave a small gasp, and her heart sank. Between all of them the Scots could not raise such an amount of money.

Bayezid was silent for a moment, then went on. "If you have not such a sum, my lady, do not fear. Our slaves are well-treated, and the Princess Shelomith"—he indicated a sultry woman curled up regally on a pile of satin cushions a few feet away, fanning herself idly— "has taken a fancy to your lord. I assure you he will not suffer."

Mary's hands clenched tightly by her sides as the Princess gave her a slow, languid smile. She willna hae him! Mary thought furiously. Hunter belongs to me! Frantically she wracked her brain for some means of obtaining her beloved's release. Her eyes fell on a small, jeweled casket setting at the Sultan's feet. Slowly an idea began to take shape in her mind.

"Ye are a rich mon, my lord," she stated. "Ye hae much wealth and many jewels and treasures. Ye hae no need of a knight's weight in gold coins. I offer ye something in exchange for him much finer, instead. Gie me that chest there"— she pointed to the casket— "and before sundown I will return it to ye filled wie spun-gold as pure and fine as silk."

"My lady—" Captain Tisza stared at her aghast, while Cadman's eyes narrowed inscrutably. 'Twas a trick, the MacBeth knew, but he did not care. If Mary had thought of some ruse to get Hunter back, Cadman did not mean to interfere with her plans. He leaned forward.

"Translate what she has said, Captain Tisza."

The Hungarian officer swore under his breath, but did as Cadman bade him.

Bayezid's dark eyes fluttered once with interest as he considered the words. He was intrigued, as Mary had known he would be. The Princess snapped her fan shut with an angry toss of her head and proceeded to glare at Mary evilly.

"Spun-gold, my lady?" The Sultan pondered wonderingly. "Many have tried to attain as much, but have always failed. Have you learned some ancient secret, I wonder? Well,

well. How very interesting. Very well then. If you can deliver to me what you have promised, your lord will be returned to you. Otherwise"—his eyes strayed to the pouting Princess—"Shelomith will be a very happy woman. Sundown, my lady. Pray—do not keep me waiting."

"Spun-gold! Spun-gold!" Captain Tisza paced the camp restlessly and wrung his hands worriedly. "Whatever possessed you to say such a thing? Why, there's naught of such to be found upon this earth! Spun-gold! Oh, my lady, how could you? Whatever were you thinking of? Where will you get such a thing?"

Mary smiled as she removed the heavy veils from herself one by one. With fingers that trembled slighty she took the jeweled dagger from her waist, handing the silver blade to Cadman. Then she reached for the pins in her hair, pulled them free, and shook the shining gilded mass until it cascaded down her back, hanging to the ground.

"Cut it off at my waist," she said.

# Twenty-nine

They rode into the twin cities of Buda and Pest like conquering heros, the Scots and the two thousand Hungarian troops that accompanied them (the rest having remained behind to be garrisoned at Belgrade); and they were welcomed just as warmly. "Saviors," called the people who crowded the streets as the cavalcade passed in grand parade amid the joyous shouts and gaiety. "Belgrade is saved!" the cries rang out. "The southern border of Hungary is secure!" Red May roses were strewn and flung before the soldiers. Bold women ran forth to rain kisses upon the men's mouths and hands. The church bells pealed merrily, and chalices of wine were passed from one person to another as the common folk lifted their cups to salute the troops and celebrate the Hungarian victory. There was a special cheer for Hunter and Mary, and romantic maids wept at the sight of the young girl who had shorn her golden locks to ransom her lord. Hunter gazed at his beloved tenderly as he recalled how bravely she had knelt before the Sultan and raised the lid of the jeweled casket to reveal her ruse. For one horrible, heart-stopping moment the Romany knight had thought they would all be slain, their bowed heads sliced with swift retaliation from their necks by the silver scimitars of the Turkish guards. For an eternity Bayezid had stared at the gilded tresses, then suddenly, to all's surprise, had thrown back his head and laughed.

"Spun-gold, you promised, my lady, and spun-gold you have delivered," he'd said, and Hunter had been freed.

There was naught in Hungary who had not learned of the touching tale; and they opened their hearts to the Scots couple whose love for one another had inspired such courage and noble sacrifice.

"A health! A health unto the lovers!" The people toasted Hunter and Mary and showered them with rose petals amid shouts and laughter as they paid tribute to the two.

It was a wondrous moment of triumph, and the Scots who had lost so much gloried in the head-swelling homage done to them by the twin cities that claimed the foreigners as their own. Mary smiled at Hunter as they mounted the steps to the King's Royal residence and knew they had found a place to love and be safe at last.

In the days that followed their victorious return people flocked to the palace to see the Scots, and throngs of young men joined the growing ranks of the Black Army, in which Hunter and Cadman had been awarded positions of command. Daily the two men drilled the units of soldiers until they marched in perfect precision and mastered the weapons and techniques of battle, while Mary and Joanna shopped in the marketplace, made giddy by the knowledge that they could purchase whatever they chose without fear of starving for it afterward. Geoffrey and Ranald regained the boisterous normality of two small boys, and their mother had not the heart to stifle their exuberance. Life was grand, and they reveled in its beauty. They set Geoffrey's bird, whose wing had mended, free, watching as it tested its limbs from a balcony of the palace, fluttering slightly before it gained control and soared gracefully into the azure sky. Their hearts lifted at the sight and filled to overflowing for the tiny creature of God that had brought them luck and joy. It flew unfettered in the distance, a small dark speck against the white clouds until finally it disappeared, as wild and free as the young gypsy who came to the Scots' chambers at the palace that same night. Like an omen, Mary was to think later.

He was tall and slender, with a swarthiness that reminded her of Hunter, and she knew, somehow, even before he spoke, he was gypsy. He addressed her in Romany and seemed surprised she replied in the same language, admitting him into Hunter's presence. The youth knelt before her beloved silently.

"Rise, lad," Hunter said softly. "Ye need nae bow before me."

"You are the knight from Scotland, the one who led the Hungarian soldiers to victory at Belgrade, the one of whom all Buda and Pest speak?"

"Aye," Hunter nodded. "Do ye wish to join the Black Army, lad? If so, ye must seek out Captain Tisza—"

"Nay, sir, I am no fighting man. Is it true ye are of the Romany blood? But, of course, you are—I need not ask. I can see with my own eyes you are one of us, and both you and your lady speak our language. You learned it of old, sir, in Scotland?"

"Aye," Hunter replied. "My grandmother taught me the ancient tongue and ways."

"Then you are the one whom I seek, sir, and it is right I kneel before you. I bear a message from the Queen of the Romanies, sir, inviting you and your family to our humble camp outside of Óbuda. She asks that you join her tomorrow evening for the night repast, sir, and bade me tell you she would be honored by your acceptance."

Hunter glanced at Mary questioningly.

"But, of course, we must go," she cried.

"Tell the Queen of the Romanies 'tis she who honors us by her invitation," Hunter replied to the lad gravely. "We would be happy to join her tomorrow as she requests."

Just outside of Óbuda the gay tinkle of laughter and the wild, haunting fury of a melodious stringed instrument accompanied by a dull-sounding drum and the ringing clash of brass upon brass reached the ears of the Scots. Then the magnificent splendor of a brightly colored, vitally alive gypsy camp burst upon them in its full glory with its painted caravans set upon high, rimmed wheels and closed with ruffled curtains. Mary could not suppress her quick gasp of delight as Aziz, their messenger the previous evening, led them through the maze of wagons and dark-skinned gypsies in a riotous blaze of multicolored peasant dress. The Romanies eyed the Scots curiously, and those who had been dancing fell back to let them pass in sudden silence, kneeling and touching their heads to the ground as Hunter wove his way through the throng.

Mary caught his eye inquisitively, but he shook his head in reply to her unvoiced question, for he knew no more than she why the gypsies bowed before him.

Finally, at the far end of the camp, the Scots caught sight of the Queen of the Romanies. She was ancient and yet timeless, regal in her bearing as she studied them with dark glittering eyes. Her skin was like brown cream. Her nose was aquiline, her mough full and sensuous, sultry beneath her slanting eyes. Her shining silver hair hung straight and freely to her waist, and a circlet of gold sat upon her head. She was dressed in a bright brocade tunic of flowing damask; hordes of sparkling jewels and gilded bangles adorned her ears, neck, arms, wrists, fingers, and ankles. At first glance she seemed tiny and frail, but as she arose to welcome her guests

Mary saw that the huge gold-leafed throne with red velvet cushions upon which she'd been ensconced had made her appear so. She was tall, majestic, almost overpowering. The scent of her musky perfume wafted to Mary's nostrils as the Queen of the gypsies held out her hands to the Scots in greeting.

Hunter took one look, then whispered hoarsely, "Grandmama?" before he flung himself into the old woman's arms.


"Well, my grandson, you are a long way from Scotland," Ashiyah, Queen of the Romanies said after the initial shock of her appearance and relationship to Hunter had begun to wear off. They had all settled themselves on the ground beside her and been served ale, wine, and a meal of various meats, cheeses, fruits, and hard bread.

"Aye, grandmama, as are ye. It dinna occur to me 'twas *your* band here in Hungary, else I would hae guessed, of course, the reason I was so deferred to by the messenger and then the others this evening."

Ashiyah laughed. "I warned Aziz I'd have his head on a platter if he spoiled my surprise." Her eyes twinkled as merrily as Cadman's. "And then naturally I could not really be sure 'twas you, though from the rumors that reached our ears I felt certain it could be none other. So. Let me look at you. Ah, how proud Laureen would have been to see what a fine man you have become, such a mighty warrior. Aye, even here, in our humble camp, stories of your brave deeds in battle have been told us. How you kept Belgrade from falling to the 'infidels,' as the Hungarians call the Turks. They're all infidels if you ask me, for the true religion is the Romany one; however"—she shrugged with another smile—"that is neither here nor there. Aye, you saved a city, and a lass saved you, Hunter."

"Aye, grandmama. This is Mary, my lady."

"I guessed as much. Such bonnie golden hair. You must love my grandson very much to have parted with it, child."

"Aye, madam."

"And these—these are your children?"

"Aye, madam. Geoffrey is the son of my first husband. Ranald is Hunter's bairn."

"Ranald. Laureen would have liked that. Ah, they are fine lads. How glad I am I have lived to see my great-grandson."

"And this my foster brother Cadman and his wife, Joanna," Hunter completed the introductions. "Now, grandmama, ye must tell me why ye left the Highlands and how ye came to be in Hungary."

"Why, I left Scotland, Hunter, because you needed me no longer, so my task there was completed. I returned here because Óbuda was my birthplace. Ah, you did not know that, Hunter. Aye, Hungary is my homeland, and I missed it as much I am sure you miss the Highlands. You are exiles." It was a statement, not a question.

"Aye, madam, but how did you know?"

"Mary's eyes, grandson. She bears the Carmichael eyes, as do you. One does not love an enemy and survive in Scotland."

"Nay, madam." Hunter's voice was bitter. "We hae discovered that."

"Then you have broken with your clans, the MacBeths and the Carmichaels?"

"Aye, madam, 'twas no longer safe for us in the Highlands. I wouldna see Mary or my son dead."

"Nor I, Joanna or the bairn she is to bear me," Cadman put in.

"Ah," the Queen suddenly cackled slyly. "Your clans were twice betrayed then?"

"More than that, grandmama." Hunter went on to explain about Ian and Euphemia.

"Well, it certainly sounds like quite a pretty tangle," Ashiyah said when he had finished. "So now you are in Hungary. Well, well. How very interesting. And now 'tis getting late. I am an old woman and fear I tire easily. Hunter, you must visit me again, and bring your family. I have quite enjoyed the evening."

"Of course, grandmama. I'm sure I speak for us all when I

**410**

say we hae been entertained as well," he was on his feet in an instant, helping the elderly Queen from her throne.

"Good night." Ashiyah inclined her head to the Scots gracefully, then melted into the shadows toward her brightly painted wagon.

Time flew by so swiftly that summer—too swiftly, as though it were rushing to outrun itself. Mary had never been so happy, and yet she felt as though her life had become like a carousel at a carnival gone mad, spinning and spiraling toward some unforeseen vortex of doom; and she lived each day to its fullest, as though it were to be her last.

If she were not a gypsy by blood, she was one at least in spirit. She made gypsy costumes for herself and learned to dance, and none was more wild and unrestrained than Mary those nights the Scots gathered round the fire of the gypsy camp to drink and sing and dance with the others. She learned to play the tambourine, the oud (the strange stringed instrument she'd heard the first time they'd visited the Romanies), the doumbek (the dull-sounding drum), and the zils (the brass cymbals used by the gypsies). Within three months she had mastered the basic, rudimentary skills of the sensuous oriental movements of the dance and could give a passable demonstration of her talents, although Ashiyah said it would take years for her to become a true expert.

Mary and the Queen became close friends during those passing summer months, and the young lass poured out much of her heart and soul to the elderly woman, while Ashiyah listened gravely and thoughtfully to the sad, romantic tale, sometimes offering advice, other times comfort when the story became too difficult to tell, and tears streaked the girl's cheeks.

"Oh, madam," Mary wept. "I love Hunter so much. I ne'er dreamed there could be such passion in me and for my enemy at that. Has it been wrong of us to love so deeply, so selfishly, wie'oot regard for any but ourselves? This love of ours has brought much pain and death to the Highlands, and now we are exiles because of it."

"Nay, Mary." The old Queen patted the lass's hand gently. "It was something ordained before your birth, and you cannot change your destiny."

"Oh, madam, do ye know something aboot the legend? Please, tell me if ye do! I dinna know the entire tale, only what was told to me during my childhood. Perhaps if I knew more of the story—"

"Aye, I know a great deal about the legend. Mind you, no one will ever know the whole truth of the matter, for those who gave birth to it are long dead now. But I believe I know more than anyone else alive about the legend that cursed the Carmichaels and MacBeths, for I too have a small part in its drama. Aye, Mary, I will tell you what I know, but only on two conditions."

"Oh, anything, madam!"

"The first is that you will marry Hunter."

"But—but, madam!" the girl protested. "I am already wed to another!"

"Bah!" The Queen waved this away as though it were unimportant. "I do not recognize your marriage. There can be no true wedding in my eyes except that of a Romany ceremony such as my daughter, Laureen, and her husband, Ranald, had. Ah, we shall have a fine celebration—the finest in all Hungary. Please, Mary, I ask it only for myself. I know it will not be legal under the laws of Scotland, but it would please me to see my grandson wed before I die, and the match will be sanctified as far as I am concerned."

"As ye wish then, madam," Mary said, nodding at last. "And the other request?"

"That I cannot tell you now. You must trust me, and give me your word you will carry it out after I have told you what I know of the legend. Is that agreed?"

Mary looked into the old woman's dark eyes. "All right, madam," she said finally. "I shall gie ye my word and trust your judgment in this matter."

Ashiyah leaned back abruptly, closing her intense, glittering eyes. "It is done then," she sighed. "I shall arange for the ceremony to be held after Joanna's child is born. Do not fail me in this, Mary.''

In August Joanna gave birth to twins, a boy and a girl. There could not have been a prouder father than Cadman as he gazed at the tiny infants lying small and snug in his tired wife's arms.

''I hae waited to name them, sir,'' the maid spoke as she looked up at her husband. ''I thought—I thought 'twould please ye to choose such.''

Cadman knelt before his wife's bed and took her hand. ''Aye, lass. I would like to name the girl 'Janet.' ''

''And your son, sir. What of him?''

''My son I would call 'Gordon,' my lady. Does that please ye?''

''Aye, Cadman,'' Joanna replied softly, her eyes filling with tears. ''It pleases me verra much.'' And in that moment she knew she loved the MacBeth knight who had taken her captive and made her his bride.

Hunter and Mary stood as godparents to the beautiful twins and in September began the preparations for the forthcoming wedding, Ashiyah having also gained her grandson's approval for the ritual.

Cheeses were cured; wild game was shot and skinned; fresh fruit was picked; and the wine barrels were filled in gay anticipation of the ceremony. Mary helped with it all. She strung necklaces of glass beads, helped the Queen card wool for weaving in the looms, and sewed the beautiful outfit she planned to wear for her marriage. It was a silky green print with birds whose vivid plumage of orange, red, gold, blue, and violet created an all-over pattern. The bodice of the dress was cut low, with billowing sleeves that reached to Mary's elbows, and had a full, ruffled skirt. Over this she would wear a surcoat of red satin. Her own gilded girdle and jeweled dirk would adorn her waist. She would wear sandals upon her feet, like the gypsies, and flowers would twine amidst her golden hair.

At last the night of the wedding arrived. Mary dressed

carefully in her gown, brushing her hair until the sparks flew as she prepared herself nervously in the wagon that had been given her and Hunter for the ceremony, a marriage gift from Ashiyah. On Mary's ears were giant gold hoop earrings that dangled against her shoulders when she tossed her head; strand upon strand of glass beads encircled her throat; gilded bangles slid and tinkled upon her wrists as she ran through the bouquet-strewn paths of the camp, the gypsy men laughing, teasing, and chasing her all the way until finally she knelt beside Hunter before the Queen.

How handsome Mary's beloved looked! The girl's heart swelled with pride as she glanced at him, and he took her hand in his. He had grown even darker and more swarthy under the Hungarian sun, so that the scar on his twisted lips gleamed whitely. He wore a white linen shirt and black hose. There was a wide red sash at his waist that matched the embroidered, red and black bolero over his shirt. His black boots gleamed in the firelight as Ashiyah began to speak the ancient words of the gypsy ritual. The couple repeated their vow softly but firmly, each one wishing fervently this was indeed their true marriage; for they were still too bound by the ways of Scotland to think the ritual real in their minds. They shared the traditional meal and chalice of wine, then finally Hunter kissed Mary, and the ouds struck up an enchanting melody.

The girl moved from her lord's side to begin the wedding dance. Her violet eyes were half-closed as she curved her lips into an inviting smile, arms raised as she swayed to the beat of the music and clapped her zils together with a resounding ring. Beads of sweat formed in the hollow between her breasts. She spun around until she stood before Hunter, her hips shaking, belly undulating, legs flashing as she whirled teasingly, caressingly, flaunting herself before him, her body throbbing sensuously to the haunting rhythm. Her skirt flew up around her pale thighs as her cheeks flushed, and her mouth parted slightly, beckoningly. She danced wildly, passionately, tauntingly, her naked shoulders gleaming in the firelight as she tossed her thick mane of hair, and it showered like a blaze of hot gold sparks. For Hunter alone she danced, pouring her heart and soul into the ancient, enticing movements, each one beautifully filled with every ounce of love she possessed for him. She closed her purple eyes; the gypsy camp faded; there was nothing for Mary but the pulsating sound of the strange, lovely music and Hunter—always Hunter—forever Hunter.

She did not see him grab a whip from one of the gypsy men, uncoiling its length, tossing it out behind him. It was not until the lass heard the sharp crack and faint hiss it made as it swept by her body, so close she could feel the slight breeze it stirred that she realized her lover was in the center of the circle with her, an odd, triumphant smile on his face as he wielded the black lash. Her eyes flew open abruptly at the sight. She had forgotten this part of the ceremony where the husband proved he would master the woman he possessed according to the gypsy tradition in which Ashiyah had instructed them both. Mary must not be afraid, she remembered. To do so would shame Hunter before the eyes of the gypsy men. He had learned to handle the whip as a child. He would not hurt her. Mary drew strength from the knowledge as she continued to dance. The gypsies roared in approval. Time and again the coil snaked by her, but never touched her, for one stroke would have marred her golden flesh irreparably. Her lips curled. Her laughter rippled from deep within her throat like silver strands.

Finally, with a soft, snarled oath, Hunter sent the lethal lash spinning, wrapping it about Mary's waist. She did not even feel the slight twinge of pain as the whip wound about her, cutting into the material of her dress and barely biting into her skin. She tried to pull away from the snaking coil, but Hunter tugged on it hard, yanking her to him amidst the encouraging cries of the gypsies. One hand tangled roughly into her mass of flowing hair before he twisted her face up to his and ground his mouth down onto hers searingly. Mary reveled in his crude embrace as he pressed the length of his body up next to hers, almost breaking her back as he forced her over, only his supportive grip keeping her from falling.

Her head spun dizzily as he kissed her, his hard, demanding mouth causing a blind hot sensation in her mind and limbs as she weakened against him, as he drained the very life from her body and poured it back in again. From somewhere she heard a strange animalistic cry, then realized dimly it came from her own throat. Hunter's eyes blazed into hers victoriously as he released her to a startling round of cheering and applause only to grab her once more and fling her violently over his shoulder before he strode from the circle to their waiting wagon, the others showering them both with flowers before he slammed the door to shut them out.

Mary shivered as Hunter loomed over her in the darkness of the caravan after throwing her down upon the bed. His fingers ripped at the bodice of her gown.

"You'll tear my dress," she whispered.

"Then take it off, tigress, for I lust for thee."

He stepped away, pouring himself a drink as Mary shuddered with excitement beneath his bold, admiring gaze. Slowly she loosed the brightly colored folds of cloth; the gown dropped to the floor about her feet.

"That too, beloved." Hunter motioned toward her shift.

For the barest instant of time he didn't even breathe as he stared at her naked flesh and saw the faint flush on her cheeks as she cast her eyes downward to avoid his piercing, desire-filled glance. He finished his ale, then walked toward her, reminding Mary of some lithe, dangerous, catlike animal, his cool veneer scarcely hiding the violence she knew always lay just beneath the surface of him. Momentarily her hand went protectively to her slender throat.

"Sometimes ye frighten me," she murmured.

"Do I?"

"Aye, ye are so savage, so intense."

"'Tis the lust ye arouse in me, tigress. Sometimes I believe I love ye beyond all reason."

He tasted of ale when he kissed her, his lips burning slowly across her mouth, his tongue seeking, plundering, ravishing as his hands cupped her rosy breasts to stimulate the pink nipples, then traveled down over her belly and hips. She quivered at the strange tingle of desire that soared through her body at his touch, as she felt his hard manhood pressed against her. He was like finely tempered steel, his body strong and muscular as he carried her to the bed and laid her upon the soft mattress. He towered over her briefly as he removed his clothing, then slid in beside her, muttering softly under his breath. She heard him breathe ''witch'' before he parted her thighs and entered her, easing the ache that spread through her loins as he thrust deeply into her being, neither one of them wanting or needing any foreplay.

Mary had been dreaming. She must have been, for she had fallen asleep with Hunter still a part of her, and now she could feel his flesh swelling inside her again. How long had she slept, her head dizzy with the red wine she'd drunk and his lovemaking? She did not know. She stirred, gave a soft cry he silenced easily with his lips. The moonlight streamed in through the windows of the caravan brightly, casting the contents of the wagon in an odd shroud of shimmering silver. Mary could see her lover's hard, arrogant profile in the darkness; the glittering violet eyes; the aquiline nose; the square-cut jaw; and the white twisted scar that marked the corner of his carnal mouth as his gaze raked her. The slow rise and fall of his chest sounded huskily in the half-light. She stared back at him, hypnotized by the expression on his face. The pulse at the hollow of her throat beat rapidly. She found she couldn't move, didn't want to move. She lay with her limbs sprawled out over the bed as he drove between her golden flanks, his hands under her back, arching her hips to receive him.

''I love ye.''

Was that really her voice, so soft and slurred, that had spoken? He laughed gently in her ear, a silky, rippling noise like the purring of a cat. She was drowsy with passion as he kissed her throat and shoulders and breasts, as she felt wave after wave of slow, languid ecstasy wash over her.

"Ye are mine Mary Carmichael, always mine."

"There will ne'er be anyone for me but thee," she vowed feverishly before she gave herself up to his hot wild embrace.

Hunter tossed in his sleep and reached out one hand to draw Mary close once more. Damn! His violet eyes flew open with a start as he realized the bed was empty. She was gone. He rose and dressed.

Geoffrey jumped up from the stoop of the wagon as Hunter appeared in the doorway.

"Good morning, sir," the lad said shyly.

"Why, hello, Geoffrey." Hunter ruffled the boy's blond hair fondly. The older man scanned the camp quickly, but could see no sign of Mary. He would have gone on to look for her, but something in her child's face stopped him. He bent to sit upon the step. "What are ye doing up and aboot so early, son?" he asked.

"I wanted to talk to ye, sir, that is, if ye hae time."

"Of course I hae time," Hunter replied kindly, drawing the boy down beside him. "Now, what is it ye wished to speak wie me aboot?"

"Well, I dinna really know how to explain it to ye, sir—"

"Do the best ye can, lad. I know 'tis difficult to find the words sometimes to say what's in your heart, but try anyway." He studied the child's serious expression thoughtfully.

"Well, sir, 'tis like this. I dinna really hae a father—"

"Of course ye do, Geoffrey."

"But he's dead, sir, and 'tisna really the same."

"Nay, I guess nae," Hunter agreed. "My father is dead, too."

"Oh? Then ye know how I feel, sir."

"Aye, son, I think I do."

"Well, ye see, sir, for a time I had my Uncle Hugh, but he really wasn't my father; he was my uncle and he was a bad mon, besides. I ne'er really liked him, and I dinna think he liked me. He ne'er hardly spoke to me, except right before he married mother. Then he used to pat my head like ye, sir, only he gae me the shivers when he did it. I dinna know why really. There was just something aboot him—''

"I understand, Geoffrey.''

The child looked relieved at this. "Well, anyway, I was glad when Cadman came and took us away; only at first I thought he was a bad mon, too, except he wasna.'' Geoffrey paused. "He's *nae* a bad mon, is he, sir?''

"Nay, lad.'' Hunter shook his head. How to explain a highland feud to a five-year-old bairn?

"I dinna think so,'' the boy spoke gravely. "I knew Jo wouldna hae married him otherwise. It all seems so strange, sir. I dinna quite understand what happened to my Uncle Hugh, but I'm nae sorry we dinna live wie him any longer. He hurt my mother. And ye, sir, ye hae made her happy again. Och, ye should hae heard her this morning, sir! She was singing like the bird whose wing ye mended. Remember, sir?''

"Aye.'' Hunter felt a queer tightening in his throat.

"Well, that's how she sounded. And she gae me and Ranald a piece of sweet bread too, sir, afore she left and told me to be sure and tell ye she'd gone for a walk and that I mustn't forget to let ye know. And I dinna, did I, sir?'' He beamed at Hunter proudly.

"Nay, Geoffrey.''

"Well, anyway, sir, what I wanted to ask was—since you're married to my mother now—I mean, that sort of makes ye my father, doesna it, sir? And I was wondering whether or nae I could call ye such, sir? Och, I know I'm nae truly your son, but Ranald calls ye father, sir, and 'twould be e'er so nice if I might too. That is, if ye dinna think my real father—the one who's dead—would mind and if ye would care to hae me call ye that, sir,'' the child ended in a breathless rush.

Hunter's heart gave an odd jerk of pain. Oh, Edward, ye would hae been so proud of him! And how do I explain his mother and I are nae really wed?

"I—I—'' Hunter's voice broke. He turned away so Geoffrey

might not see the quick tears that started in his eyes. He cleared his throat. "I would be honored to hae ye call me father, Geoffrey," he managed to answer at last.

"Oh, thank ye, sir—I mean—father." The lad smiled timidly, then gave Hunter a brief hard hug.

The older man clasped the child to himself tightly. "I dinna e'er want ye to forget your real father, Geoffrey," he said. "For he was the best of men, and he would be so proud of ye if he had lived."

The boy's face brightened quickly at this. "Do ye really think so? Och, I shallna forget him. I promise ye that. Ye see?" He held up his dirk for Hunter's inspection. "Mother has gi'en me his dagger to remember him by and told me how brave he was in battle when he fought in the civil war."

"Aye, son, he was verra brave, and he had a—a sense of grace, an outlook on the beauty of life— Do ye understand what I'm saying, lad?"

"Aye. Mother said he wrote lovely poetry and played the flute. Do ye think I might hae one—a flute, I mean. 'Twould help me to be close to him. I canna even recall his face."

"Of course, Geoffrey. We shall buy one in Óbuda tomorrow. As for his face, why, ye need only look in a mirror. Ye are his verra image, son."

"Do ye think so? Oh, thank ye. Thank ye e'er so much—father," he cried before scampering off to tell Ranald the good news.

Hunter sat on the stoop of the caravan for a long time afterward before he at last arose and went to look for Mary.

She was standing on the crest of a small rise outside of the camp overlooking Óbuda. Hunter's breath caught in his throat at the sight of her. I shall ne'er tire of her, no matter how many times I gaze upon her lovely countenance, he thought. 'Tis as though she grows more beautiful with each passing day. Her solitary figure turned, caught sight of him. She smiled, running with bare feet through the fall-touched grass to his arms. She kissed him, then laid her head upon his chest as he held her close.

"A penny for them." Her violet eyes were filled with love as she looked up at him.

"I was thinking how beautiful ye are. Seven years, Mary. Has it really been seven years since I first laid eyes upon ye? And six years since I first made love to ye? It doesna seem possible. Where has the time gone?"

"I dinna know, beloved."

"Och, if it had been a hundred years, I would love ye still. What are ye doing up here alone? I reached for ye this morn, but ye had gone."

"Looking out o'er Óbuda, Buda, and Pest. 'Tis a strange land, this Hungary that has welcomed us wie open arms."

"And so verra far from home, is it nae? Ye are happy here, Mary?"

"I am happy where'er ye are, beloved."

"But your heart pines for the Highlands. Nay, dinna deny it, tigress. I can see it in your eyes as I see the same longing in my own when I gaze into a mirror. We are Scots, my love. The wild call of the Highlands is in our blood. We shall ne'er truly be free of it."

"Nay, I guess nae. Even now I can see Bailekair so clearly, as though it were only yesterday I stood upon the cliff at Mheadhoin to gaze at my father's castle rising up so proudly from the purple mountain in the distance. 'Tis etched upon my mind fore'er. I hae that much at least. I dinna ask for more, Hunter. If I had it all to do o'er again, I would still gie it up for thee. Thou art my life, and I would but exist like an empty shell wie'oot ye. Ye hae made me whole. I feel but half-alive when we are parted."

"As do I, my dearest love. Och, would that our wedding last night had been a true one! I would hae gi'en anything to stand beside ye this morn and call ye wife.' "

"As would I hae to call ye husband. Oh, Hunter, it doesna matter. Ye are all that fills my heart e'ery hour of e'ery day, forever, my love."

"And ye are the sun that lights my darkness. Wie'oot ye I would be as an endless night, cold and void, wie'oot planet, moon, or star to fill my hollow being. Wie ye the wine in my chalice flows ne'er-ending, no matter how many times I drain it to the bitter dregs. Even your children—our children— touch my heart. Do ye know this morning Geoffrey asked if he might call me father?''

Mary's face brightened, and she smiled. "And ye, beloved, what did ye say to that?''

"I told him I would be proud to bear the name and promised him a flute to remind him always of Edward, besides.''

"Ye are so kind to Edward's bairn. I thank ye for that, Hunter.''

"Come, my love. There is a place in the woods I would show ye and chase away the clouds that darken your horizon.''

Then he led her to a sheltered grove and pressed her down upon the dying summer grass.

The night was still and black. Somewhere in the darkness the plaintive cry of a solitary bird echoed softly upon the gentle wind that barely rustled the flame-and-gold leaves that had begun to color the as yet half-green trees. The fire danced like a sensuous gypsy in the silence of the sleeping camp of the Romanies. Ashiyah drained her goblet, then leaned back in her throne, closing her dark glittering eyes for a moment. She sighed, then glanced toward the Scots, who sat at her feet. Finally she spoke.

"It is time. I feel in my bones it is time at last for me to tell you what I know of the legend.'' She paused, studying her waiting audience, then continued, satisfied by what she had seen. "Many, many years ago my grandmother was the Queen of the gypsies. Her name was Grizel, and she was a great prophetess, possessed of all the ancient powers that have been handed down to the Queens of the Romanies from time immemorial. One night she had a dream. In it she stood upon a cliff, outside the ruins of an old village, overlooking a vast body of dark grey green water that was imprisoned between two great chans of jagged rocks. It was night, but the night was not black, for a full moon shone silver against the crooked sky, and a shroud of mist lay upon the land so everything shimmered as though it were unreal. In the distance, through the wispy haze, Grizel could see three castles rising up in grand silhouette against the sweep of the horizon. One was of a pale white stone that glistened ghostily in the half-light. One was of grey granite, massive and overpowering. The last, which lay across the lake from the others, was red like blood; its graceful towers resembled the spire of the kirk that stood alone upon the crest of a small rise just above the old, ruined village.

As Grizel watched, the swirling waves of the lake below suddenly tossed and heaved, and there appeared before her eyes a black monster that glided up silently from the whirling vortex of the whitecaps. It beckoned to her and cried softly in the night, a strange weeping lament. It was indeed a keen of sorrow, a funeral dirge, for the waters parted once more, and ghosts danced sadly, like pale white shadows, upon the ripples of the grey green lake. One, a young maiden with long black hair and midnight blue eyes, stood out from the rest. She came to the edge of the shore and floated across the golden sands that were the beach to kneel before the cliff, her arms held out pleadingly toward my grandmother.

"Grizel awakened then, and in the morning told the others of her dream, insisting she must find the place of her vision that had called to her so strongly. She relinquished her throne to my mother, Nejat, and set off to search for the grey green lake that lay shrouded in mist. Why Grizel was chosen for such a mission, I do not know, except that, as I have said, she knew the secrets of the ancient mysteries and had great powers. She traveled many, many miles across the continent to strange lands never before seen by the Romanies, but nowhere could she discover a trace of that place for which she searched. Finally she journeyed across the North Sea to Scotland, and there, in the Highlands, came at last upon Loch Ness, which was the odd, mysterious lake she had seen in her dream.

"At the red castle, Glenkirk, a child had just been born to Lord Kevin MacBeth. The bairn was a girl, and when Grizel

423

learned of the news in Glenkirk's village, she knew it was the young maiden who had knelt before her on the golden sands of Loch Ness. My grandmother presented herself at the keep and told the Earl of Glenkirk her story. I do not know why, but he allowed her to raise his daughter, perhaps believing Grizel might somehow save the child from the fate my grandmother had seen for her in the vision. The girl's name was Anne, and Grizel came to love her fiercely.

"Now it happened there was a feud between the MacBeths and the Carmichaels, who lived across the lake. No one knows how it really started, for though it is said now the deep hatred between the two clans began with Anne MacBeth's kidnapping by the Carmichaels, the feud had actually arisen many years before that. One night, when Anne was fifteen, the violet-eyed Earl of Bailekair, James Carmichael, and his brother Robert of Dùndereen raided the village of Glenkirk and took Anne captive. How this was accomplished was never known, for there was never an assault upon the keep itself, and Anne had been safely ensconced behind the walls of her father's fortress. Some claimed James had changed himself into a great bird and plucked Anne from the ramparts of the castle, for how else could he have violated the impregnable battlements to snatch her from her home? Whether or not it was true, the fact remained that Anne had been spirited away by the bold Carmichaels and was held for ransom at Bailekair.

"Kevin MacBeth laid siege to the mighty fortress upon the purple mountain, but Bailekair stood fast, and the MacBeths returned to Glenkirk in shame because they had not rescued their lady. Anne was never seen again. Now, many tales are told about her fate, but this is the true one. During that battle between the Carmichaels and MacBeths, which took place in the summer of 1397, James had a falling out with his brother Robert. The two men dueled on the ramparts of Bailekair, and James slew Robert with his mighty claymore and flung his brother's body foom the battlements of the keep. Afterward Anne rode out through the iron portcullis of the castle to disappear into the Highland mist forever. No one knows why

James fought with Robert, or why the Earl released Anne after having taken her prisoner—if he did, indeed, set her free following his brother's death. Perhaps the two men quarreled over her, for she was a bonnie wench, and James's conscience smote him afterward so he could not bear the sight of her; I do not know. I only know Anne escaped, because her white mare was found later upon the sandy shores of Loch Ness, where it is said she now dances ghostlike upon the grey green waters.

"Following Anne's disappearance my grandmother wrote to me, telling me this story. Grizel was an old woman by this time, and the Grim Reaper hovered like a black angel just beyond her horizon. She told me of the curse she intended to leave upon the two clans as her revenge for Anne's death, for Grizel was certain her bonnie lady was dead, and bade me journey to the Highlands to watch for a MacBeth child with Carmichael eyes that would signal the beginning of the curse.

"My mother had been killed earlier by some drunken soldiers who'd raided our camp, and I was Queen of the Romanies. I was frightened for my people's safety, and had no wish to linger in a place that held unhappy memories for me; so I traveled to Scotland with my band of gypsies. Some months later we arrived in the Highlands, and I learned that a child who bore the Carmichael eyes had been born to the MacBeths far to the north. It was Sir George, your grandfather, Hunter. He grew to manhood and in time married a distant kinswoman, who died in childbed giving birth to your father, Ranald. Ranald did not have the Carmichael eyes, and Sir George went crazy, thinking himself the sole accursed MacBeth. He put out his eyes and killed himself in the end.

"Some years later Ranald happened upon our camp outside of Torra Nam Sian. He fell in love with my daughter, your mother, Laureen. They were married in the Romany tradition, then wed by a priest as well, for Ranald followed the ways of Scotland and had no wish for anyone to be able to set his gypsy bride aside, as Lord Duncan, the Baron Torra nam Sian, most certainly would have tried to do. In due time you were born, Hunter. Laureen loved you and feared for you deeply because you bore the Carmichael eyes, and she knew the power of the curse from the tales I had told her. She rose from bed, still weak and ill from your birth, and sought me out to prepare a talisman for you to protect you from the curse. As you know, she was flushed with fever when she reached me and died shortly thereafter. I could not save her.

"But she left me this." Ashiyah pulled a heavy gold necklace from the jeweled casket that lay upon her lap. It was a beautiful chain, its links intricately woven, like the fragments of a puzzle, the passages of a maze. Two gold keys, one large and one small, dangled from the gilded strand. "It originally belonged to Sir George, who gave it to his wife, just as Ranald gave it to Laureen. I give it now to you, Hunter, so that you may give it to Mary, your bride. That is why I insisted on the Romany wedding ceremony. I could not, in good conscience, part with it had you two not been bound in my eyes by gypsy tradition at least, for I believe these keys to be the means of lifting the curse that has haunted the MacBeths and Carmichaels these many years past and do not know what powers they contain. I have never worn the necklace myself and could not let Mary risk it either unless she were to be a MacBeth in the Romany way, for Grizel's knowledge of the ancient secrets was vast and her curse a Romany curse. Put it on now, Mary, so that if aught happens I might try and protect you, though my powers are not equal to those of my grandmother."

Shivering, Mary placed the heavy gold chain around her neck. For one eternal, agonizing minute she scarcely dared breath, for fear the gilded links would choke her; but naught occurred. She gave a sigh of relief.

Ashiyah closed her dark eyes briefly. "It is done. You are safe. You are a Romany by marriage, and Grizel will let no harm come to her own. And now, Mary, I will tell you the second of my conditions for relating this story to you all. Come spring you must return to the Highlands of Scotland. It was there the legend began, and there it must end. You may stay until your bairn is born, but then you must go home. You are Scots, and your paths lie not among the gypsies."

426

"My—my bairn?" Mary asked.

"Aye, the child you conceived on your Romany wedding night will be born in May. I know this because I have the ancient power. You gave me your word, Mary, as the daughter of the Lion. My part in the legend is finished. You alone may bring it to a close. Do not fail me in this request, or the great dark monster of Loch Ness will forever mourn the dead of Scotland who lie beneath the grey green waves of the mist-shrouded lake, and Anne MacBeth will walk upon its sands of gold, a restless ghost for all eternity."

# Thirty

That spring, as Ashiyah had predicted, Mary's child was born. He was a handsome bairn, and the two lovers named the boy "Magnus Hunter" after his father and the bonnie Lion of Bailekair who would never see his grandson.

When Mary was well enough to travel, the Scots said good-bye to Ulászló, King of Hungary, who was sorry to lose his two best commanders; but with the easygoing indifference that had earned him the nickname "Dobre" he shrugged his shoulders and said, "all right," when they insisted they must leave the Royal palace. The King saluted the two MacBeth men smartly, then hugged them both before the Scots departed with the escort of Hungarian outriders Ulászló had ordered. The parting from Ashiyah, Queen of the Romanies, was even harder. Mary wept unashamedly, as did Joanna, and even Hunter and Cadman found their throats choked as they took their leave of the Queen.

"Courage, child." Ashiyah lifted Mary's face to her own. "The blood of the Lion runs in your veins. Remember that."

"I dinna forget, madam. 'Tis only that we hae been happy here, and Scotland holds naught for us now."

"Nay, Mary, that is not true, for I have seen you upon the hill overlooking Óbuda and known your heart was at the cliff at Mheadhoin. That is where you belong. You will find a way, I promise you that. When the time is ripe, the necklace will show you the path back to the Highlands forever. Believe, Mary, as you have had faith in my grandson's love for you, and you will not fail. Believe, and you will not fail."

The Scots journeyed across Europe in the caravan that had been Ashiyah's wedding present to Hunter and Mary, the two destriers and Desmond tied behind, the wagon being pulled by a team of stout horses. It made the going easier, for Mary was but recently recovered from childbed, and she was able to lie inside upon the bed she'd shared with Hunter and rest whenever she felt the need without slowing the others down. Then too the caravan offered them all some protection against the torrential spring rains that poured down from the heavens, turning the rolling hills and plains of Europe a lush clean green.

They did not press themselves hard, for there was no need for urgency, and, thanks to Ulászló, they had plenty of money. They could afford to travel slowly and with some modicum of style. Months later they reached the shores of France, from where the Scots sailed by ship across the English Channel and up along the beaches of Britain to the North Sea. Finally the small party landed at the port of Leith on the Scottish sands of an inlet known as the Firth of Forth in the county of Midlothian. They were home at last!

But 'twas a home that had no welcome for the exiles, for they dared not venture into the Highlands, where death awaited them all, nor even to Court, lest any of their clansmen be in residence. For even Jamie's roof would not offer them protection from a dirk in a dark corridor, nor could the King prevent Mary's husband from demanding and forcibly obtaining her return to Dùndereen should Hugh discover his fugitive wife's whereabouts. It was a dismal homecoming for the

Scots who had risked so much to set foot on their native soil again. They were as homeless now as they had been when they'd left.

Not knowing what else to do, they traveled just south to Edinburgh, for 'twas easy to lose one's self in the big city if one did not wish to be found; and Hunter intended to lodge, unbeknownst to his old laird, in Lord Duncan's town house, where they might find some measure of safety.

The house was closed, of course, as the MacBeths had expected, for Lord Duncan had not, with the exception of the time of Queen Margaret's death, been in Edinburgh in years. The old Baron was happy and secure in his great, northern domain of Torra nam Sian and had no desire to become involved in the many intrigues that ran rife at Court. Hunter broke a window and climbed over the sill to unlock the door for the rest, having no fear of arousing the servants, for Lord Duncan kept none in Edinburgh.

"Good Lord!" Mary wrinkled her nose with distaste as she entered the musty house, for it stank from disuse. "How long since this place was cleaned, sir?"

Hunter grinned. "Knowing the Baron, years at least. I fear his wife was the tidy one, nae he, and since her demise he has cared little for housekeeping. I wonder he even keeps this place, but no doubt he has his reasons for it."

Mary and Joanna stared at the furniture shrouded in dust-covered sheets; the floor was matted with layers of old rushes that had been piled one tier over the other; the fireplaces were three to four inches thick with black soot; the tapestries hung buried in grime. The two women grimaced at one another ruefully. Mary turned to Hunter with a stern frown.

"This place is uninhabitable and will remain so unless Joanna and I get some help to clean it up. Ye surely canna mean for us to undertake these heavy tasks alone, Hunter! We shall need at least three maids, a cook, and a serving wench, two men to do the more burdensome chores and gardening and stable-work, and two or three lads to assist us in general. I warn ye, sir, nae a finger shall either I or Joanna lift until the staff I hae requested arrives, and dinna tell me ye are but a puir knight, Hunter, for I know full well Ulászló rewarded both ye and Cadman handsomely for your services to him!"

"Christ's son, it ne'er fails! Gie a woman a house of her own, and immediately even the most loving of them turns into a vile-tongued shrew! Verra well, my ladies," Hunter said, acknowledging the equally set-faced Joanna. "Come, Cadman, let us begone afore we are assaulted wie pots and brooms and put to work like lackeys ourselves, for I assure ye a fate worse than death awaits us if we dinna escape and soon." The Romany knight laughed uproariously, impervious to Mary's scowl. "We shall be bedecked in aprons and accosted by our fellow knights, in their ignorance, in the marketplace. Oh, la, sir!" Hunter hid his face and fluttered his eyelashes coyly. "'Tis a good gel, I am, sir, but, lud! How the sight of two sovereigns do tempt me!" he continued, while Cadman made as though to draw a shawl about himself shyly and simpered in one corner.

"Oot! Oot! The both of ye!" Mary cried, barely able to contain her laughter. Even Joanna smiled at the sight of her husband flirting outrageously with an imaginary knight. "'Twould hae to be a mon desperate indeed to approach ye two 'gels,'" Mary snorted. "Just make certain ye dinna proposition any yourselves, or 'twill be a fate worse than death for ye when ye come home and no mistake!"

The men only sniggered as they curtsyed to one another and left the room, moving the gypsy caravan into the walled garden behind the house and stabling the horses before they went off in search of the servants Mary had demanded.

The moment of silliness helped to lighten the girls's moods, and, regardless of Mary's threat to Hunter, they set about cleaning the house and had a good start by the time the first of the employees Hunter and Cadman had engaged arrived. By the end of the week they had a complete staff, and Lord Duncan's town house was nearly in order. Hunter had also hired a tutor for Geoffrey and Ranald, so the boys no longer needed Mary to instruct them; there was also a bard to teach the oldest lad how to play the flute Hunter had purchased for him in Óbuda.

In the weeks that followed the close-knit group settled into a routine of sorts, with Hunter and Cadman or the servants doing most of those things that required someone to be abroad in Edinburgh and Mary and Joanna remaining in the house or garden. The women protested this at first, but the men were adamant about the two girls not venturing out where they might be recognized and kidnapped or slain by the MacBeths or Carmichaels. It was dangerous enough for themselves, the knights pointed out, and both men had grown heavy beards and mustaches in an attempt to disguise themselves. Neither appeared in the red-and-green *breacan* of the MacBeths, but wore the uniforms of Hungarian officers, instead.

"Remember, Jo," Cadman warned his wife sharply. "Even if the clans are nae after us for being broken men, Hugh Carmichael will doubtless stop at nothing to get Mary back into his clutches. Ye hae been associated wie your lady since childhood. Even a village idiot could spy ye and guess Mary wasna far off. Do ye want to endanger your lady?"

"Nay." The lass's doe brown eyes were wide with alarm, for she had not thought of this when she'd asked if she might at least be allowed to do the marketing, for the men did not know ripe vegetables from bad ones and often brought home spoiled goods.

"Send Cook if ye canna trust our *rotten* judgment." Cadman grinned, then he sobered once more. "But dinna go oot yourself, Jo. Mary's safety depends upon it, and I've no desire to face Hunter if we somehow cause his lady's capture through our own carelessness."

Joanna sighed and did as he bade her, wishing they were not forced to live like outlaws. Cook, she was sure, cheated them in the marketplace, for all the staff were, of necessity, from rather low backgrounds, men and women who would have no reason to know the MacBeths or ask questions about their strange manner of living. Indeed from the way some of the servants behaved Joanna had no doubt they were escaped convicts or otherwise wanted by the law. It frightened her to think of herself, Mary, and the bairns consorting with thieves or possible murderers, but there was no help for it. Thank God, the servants were awed and afraid of Hunter and Cadman and greedy for the sovereigns the MacBeths paid them to remain in the town house and keep their mouths shut about their employers. Still Joanna had more than once caught one or another of the rough hired churls eyeing herself or Mary with lewd speculation and shuddered to imagine what would happen to the two women without the protection of their strong, fiercely possessive knights.

But if the Scots' lives were furtive and seemingly without cheering prospect, they still tried hard to be gay. Two weeks before Christmas Hunter and Cadman felled a large Scots pine tree outside the city limits of Edinburgh and dragged it to the town house. With much difficulty and shouts of encouragement from the women and children they managed to erect it in the main hall. Then everyone gathered round to trim the tree. They had strings of cranberries, raisins, and paper chains. There were gingerbreadmen; candy canes; candles; and a huge, silver star for the top. When that was finished, each member of the family hung his or her presents on the bedecked pine boughs, and the larger ones they stacked underneath. Then the yule log was brought in and lit in the fireplace, where it would burn until Christmas Day had ended. They sang carols, and Mary wept as she heard her favorite from childhood in the Highlands:

> I saw a sweet, a seemly sight,
> A blissful bird, a blossom bright,
> That morning made and mirth among:
> A maiden mother meek and mild
> In cradle keep a knave child
> That softly slept; she sat and sung:
> Lullay, lulla, balow,
> My bairn, sleep softly now.

Hunter cradled her head softly against his chest, brushing away the tears that stained her cheeks, not understanding why she cried.

"Come, beloved," he spoke gently. "'Tis no time for sadness. 'Tis the season to make merry. Why, then, do ye weep, tigress?"

"I'm sorry." She tried to smile up at him. "'Tis only that—that my father used to sing that song to me at Christmas. 'Twas my favorite carol. He would hold me on his lap by the fire, recite the story of the Christ child to me, and then sing, 'Lullay, lulla, balow,/My bairn, sleep softly now.' Oh, Hunter, so many of my loved ones are gone fore'er from me. Must I lose the Highlands, too?"

His arm tightened around her. "I dinna know, beloved. I dinna know."

"Och, forgie me, sir. I know we promised we wouldna speak of the Highlands. I'm sorry. I hae become sentimental and maudlin wie the season. Forgie me, dearest. I am happy where'er ye are."

But despite her denials, he knew that one small part of her heart that was not his, but Bailekair's, longed for the castle of her birth that was lost to her now for all time; and he was troubled by her words all the same. Och, Mary, Mary! I wouldna see ye sorrow so, but what else can I do? Och, beloved, once I alone was enough to fill your heart. Is it nae still thas? And yet, sweet *Jesù*, how can I blame ye? This isna the life I would hae gi'en ye, fraught wie fear and hiding. Nay, I would hae offered ye a kingdom had it been wie'in my power. Oh, my love! 'Tis ye who should forgie me—

Christmas came at last. They drank wassail made of ale, roasted apples, eggs, sugar, nutmeg, cloves, and ginger, and ate plum porridge and mince pie. The house was filled with the aroma of holly and rosemary, which had not yet begun to flower. The men chased the women around with many shouts and much laughter as they attempted to lure the girls under the mistletoe, and the children clapped their hands and giggled at the sight. Then they opened their gifts, the adults trying hard not to recall Christmas in the Highlands and how different it would have been. Hunter's heart was heavy because he could not give Mary that for which she yearned most of all, and he vowed silently to find a way to ease the pain he sometimes glimpsed deep within the violet pools of her haunting Carmichael eyes.

Hogmany passed, and early in January the men began to grow restless, chafing at the restraints put on their freedom by their self-imposed hiding. Hunter was also burdened by the thought that he had taken Mary away from the Highlands and that, although she said nothing further, she secretly pined for Bailekair. He had thought it would be enough for them to be in Scotland once again, but he realized now this was not so. He himself felt the wild lure of the gold-and-purple moors calling him home and knew the Highlands were forever in his blood even as they were in Mary's. He determined to find some way to get into Court to see the King, believing Jamie might be able to help them in some way.

"Still I dinna see how we can manage it, Hunter," Cadman argued one evening before the fire. "There are guards posted e'erywhere in the palace, and even if we were to bribe one, what excuse could we gie for wanting to see Jamie in privacy? They would think us spies or assassins and throw us in the Tolbooth! 'Tis too chancey. We canna risk it, brother. If we were to be seen and recognized—"

"We *must* find a way, Cadman! We are loyal men to Jamie, and he has doubtless worried aboot us these past years, for ye know we left wie'oot his leave—"

"We were nae bound to him, sir, but to Angus."

"Aye, and we left wie'oot his leave, too!"

"There was no other way, Hunter; ye know that."

"Aye, I know, I know. Still, I grow weary of this life, brother. 'Tisna pleasant feeling like a trapped beast; and Mary isna happy living like this. I know she isna, despite her protests to the contrary. I would find some way to set matters a'right if I could."

"As would I, brother, for in truth methinks Joanna grows more like a startled doe e'eryday; and I wouldna raise my bairns to fear the slightest shadow. But what can we do, Hunter?"

The older man grinned, a rare, devilish smile. "I hae thought of a plan, brother, but I doubt you'll favor it."

"I doubt so, too, from that gleam in your accursed eyes. Well, what is it, brother?"

"Do ye remember our jest the day we arrived here at the town house?"

"Aye. Oh, nay, Hunter! Ye canna be serious?"

"Och, 'tis perfect, Cadman. Come, dinna take offense. We'll dress ye up like a woman, and I can pose as a newly landed officer or emissary from Hungary on a secret mission of grave and delicate importance, or some such matter. I can offer ye as a mistress to the King as a token of my country's good will and friendly intent toward Jamie, for all of Europe knows our young ruler has an eye for the ladies. We can surely then bribe one of the guards to smuggle us up to his Grace's chamber wie'oot being seen on the pretext of nae wanting an enemy to learn of our presence in Scotland and, in addition, nae desiring to offend or anger any of the King's current maids wie our 'gesture of benevolence.'"

"I knew I wouldna like it. Why in the hell do I hae to be the woman, Hunter?"

"Because you're so verra bonnie." The elder MacBeth clapped his kinsman rudely on the back.

Cadman managed a rueful smile. "Well, you're nae so bad yourself, mon." he returned.

This set the two men off into gales of laughter, and presently Mary and Joanna appeared to learn what was so funny. They did not think their knights' plan nearly as hysterical, but offered to do what they could to help, realizing they could not persuade the foster brothers against the idea.

Cadman went to shave himself, while Joanna hunted through the house trying to find something that would fit her husband. Mary cleaned and brushed Hunter's Hungarian uniform until it shone like new, while her Romany lover sat down at the table to forge a letter of introduction to Jamie from the King of Hungary. When Hunter had finished this task, he sanded the parchment paper to dry the ink, then blew upon it lightly after shaking the grains from the scroll. This done, he sealed the document with a ring the Hungarian monarch had once given him as a token of appreciation.

"'Tisna Ulászló's seal, of course, but 'tis unlikely any of Jamie's Court will know that," he said encouragingly as Mary looked worriedly over his shoulder at his work. "Tomorrow I'll go to the palace to see aboot bribing one of the guards."

The next morning he set off toward the old monastery, while Mary and Joanna spent a greater part of the day attempting to instruct Cadman on the arts of being a wench, much to the amusement of the children and staff.

"No, no, Cadman! Ye must take smaller steps, and sway your hips like so." Mary demonstrated.

"Christ's son, lass! I can scarcely walk as 'tis. This dress is too tight, I'm telling ye. God's wounds! I'm near to bursting it oot at the seams!

"Hunch your shoulders in, sir." Joanna covered her mouth with one hand to hide a smile at the sight of her husband, for his appearance was comical to say the least.

"I'll hae no chest then if I do! Lord!"

"Well, ye are nae a soldier on the battlefield who must stand ramrod against the enemy."

"Better that than this, Jo!" He gazed down at himself indignantly.

The girls had discovered an old coffer in the attic filled with Court gowns that had apparently once belonged to Lord Duncan's wife. From all indications the late Baroness had been a tall and rather stout woman, for her dresses were overly large, but even so her garments were strained on Cadman's muscular figure. The tight sleeves of the dress hit him just below the elbow, while the hem line fell inches short of the tops of his boots. The low-cut bodice was drawn oddly across his broad breast. The women had draped a fichu of lace around his neck to hang in concealing folds over the dark mat of hair that showed above the scooped material. The surcoat refused to meet in the front and trailed awkwardly down either side, instead, its gold clasps jingling with a merry little tinkle each time Cadman moved, as though to mock him. The hooded cape the lasses had draped over the entire ensemble had fallen prey to moths, and tiny holes raveled here and there amidst the woolen fabric.

"*Jesù*! I was in my cups to be sure last evening when I agreed to this sorry idea of Hunter's. I'll kill him. I hae gone along wie many a mad scheme of his, but this time he has gone too far! Mistress, indeed! I look worse than a gutter-snipe! Marry-go-up—" Cadman shouted as he tripped upon the skirt of the binding gown and fell face-down upon the floor.

"Och, kinsman, now ye truly are a *fallen woman*," Mary howled, one hand held to her side to ease the stitch that started there at her laughter.

Even Joanna went into a fit of the giggles at this, while the bairns whooped with glee and ran to pummel Cadman good-naturedly as they'd sometimes seen the street urchins of Edinburgh prey upon drunken sots.

"This—this is too much!" the much mortified Cadman managed to huff.

"Och, get up, my love." Joanna bent to help her husband after shooing away the children.

"He'll ne'er do," Mary sighed. "Mayhap one of us should go in your place, sir."

"Nay, 'tis too dangerous." Cadman brushed himself off. "I'll just hae to keep trying. Now, show me that walk once more."

By the time Hunter arrived home the girls had decided they had done the best they could with what they had to work with.

"Well?" Cadman looked up at his kinsman sourly, his dark blue eyes just daring Hunter to make some crack. "Is e'erything set, or hae I wasted an entire day making a fool oot of myself?"

"Hae no fear of that, brother." Hunter tried hard not to

smirk at his clansman's odd appearance. " 'Tis all arranged. Lord! 'Twas Sir Percy Chisholm I bribed into the deed, and he ne'er even recognized me! I even managed to talk him into sending a coach-and-four for us," he chortled delightedly, pleased with his success. "So you'll nae hae to ride sidesaddle, sir."

"Sidesaddle! Christ's son! I hadna thought of that! Thank God I am to be spared one indignity at least!" Cadman sputtered.

"Why, hae ye had a trying time today, brother? Ye dinna look it. Indeed, methinks ye quite—fetching, Cadman." Hunter smothered a choked laugh.

"Hunter, I'm warning ye, this is absolutely the last time I intend to be made the butt of one of your jests!"

"Och, but ye always do it so well, brother," Hunter said with mock pity, his face pursed up ridiculously before he ducked quickly to dodge the blow Cadman threw at him.

Moments later the two men were wrestling upon the floor as they had not done together since their teens.

"Stop! Stop!" Cadman cried at last. "You're tearing my dress!"

This sent them both into fresh gales of laughter, and it was all Mary and Joanna could do to restrain them from starting up again.

"Marry! I dinna know why I even bothered," Hunter teased as he got to his feet. "Ye dinna hold a candle to the Carmichael women."

Cadman moved to a mirror to straighten his ensemble and grinned. "That's the truth! Lord! Jamie will take one look at me and toss us both into the Tolbooth for the insult!"

"We must pray he is in his cups when he receives us," Hunter rejoined with false solemnness. "For I fear he wouldna gie a ha'penny for ye otherwise."

"Take that for your impertinance, sir." Cadman boxed his foster brother's ears soundly. Then with a sweep of his skirts he turned and muttered, "Vulgar churl! Dinna take up with that brute, ladies. A ha'penny, indeed," he sniffed.

"Shhhhh," Mary hissed with a smile, her violet eyes

twinkling with amusement. "The bairns will hear ye, and I'm afraid we hae already said enough to set their young minds a'wondering this day."

"Och, no doubt you're right, lass. Come, Jo, help me oot of this stuff before this brigand"—he indicated Hunter with a wink—"accosts me again."

"Cadman!" Joanna frowned, glancing to where the children were quietly building a fortress with wooden blocks.

"All right. All right," her husband said, cringing playfully. "I'll save my lewd remarks for later."

"Oh, Cadman!" Joanna reiterated with a shy blush as he slapped her gently on the bottom.

"Hurry up, my lady, before this gown begins to show curves where it shouldna!"

Night closed around Edinburgh with bitterly cold darkness. The wind had changed and stung sharply as it blew in off the coast, sending the soft, white powdery snow flurrying up in little eddies from where it lay blanketed upon the paving blocks of High Street just outside the town house. The thick grey mist shimmered in the glow of the coach's lanterns and the light of the pale silver moon that was just beginning its slow ascent into the heavens. That odd, charred smell of smoke from the fires lit within the houses which lined the street to dispell the winter chill filled the night air with acrid fragrance.

The door banged shut loudly behind Hunter and Cadman as they entered the carriage. The horses stamped nervously in the darkness, champing at the bit, impatient to be moving briskly along the road once more. The footman climbed upon the box and seated himself next to the driver, who cracked his whip with a rippling snap that broke the stillness of the night like a pistol shot. The animals jumped and shied, then started down the street with a jolt, hooves clattering with a hollow echo over the cobblestones as the vehicle lumbered down the hill toward Holyrood Palace, swaying on the leather straps upon which it was hung. The miserable night reached out with icy fingers to batter at the coach as it bounced precariously over the snow-covered streets, beneath which lay a fine sheet of dangerous ice. Little shards of sleet pelted the sides of the carriage unmercifully, as well as the driver and footman seated upon the box. One of them swore furiously, but the sound was masked by the dull thud of the horses' hooves and the rattle of the high, reeling wheels of the vehicle as it floundered through the night.

"Lord, I feel like a fool," Cadman growled as he stretched his booted feet out in front of him and huddled down onto the soft seat inside the coach, drawing the cape Joanna had given him more closely about himself. He shivered. " 'Tis a bitter night, this, to be masquerading aboot as a wench. I dinna know how the puir creatures stand it. I shall certainly buy Jo an ermine-lined cloak tomorrow, even if her low rank forbids her to wear it!"

Hunter made no reply to this, for just then the carriage tottered dangerously around a firewood peddler's cart. The driver hauled on the reins, his heart pounding with fright at the near miss, for the accident, had it occurred, would have been treacherous. Hunter rapped sharply on the bottom of the box and called loudly for the man to have care. The vehicle sped on down the hill, still a mile from its final destination.

At last Holyrood Palace loomed before them. The coach turned into the outer bailey, then passed into the inner ward of the fortress. Hunter and Cadman alighted in silence to be ushered swiftly up a private staircase to the King's chambers.

"Wait for us," Hunter ordered the departing footman, then opened the door that would admit him and his kinsman into Jamie's presence.

The King was not alone. He and five of his most trusted advisors were bent over a table in the center of the room, examining various pages of parchment paper. Their voices, as they discussed the documents, were low and heated. Jamie looked up, and the hushed, angry argument ceased. Hunter searched the curious faces quickly, wondering which of those present might give him and Cadman away should their disguise fail. Lord Bothwell? The Earl of Angus? Alinor's father, the powerful laird of Eadar Da Voe? Who were the other two men standing in the shadows? Would they recognize him or Cadman? Nay, he and his foster brother had had little to do in the past with Darnley or Maitland. Hunter permitted himself a grim sigh of relief. It had been a shock, finding the King was not alone as he'd expected.

The Earl of Angus stepped forward. "Captain Tisza?"

"Aye," Hunter lied.

"We hae been expecting ye, sir. Allow me to present ye to His Grace."

Hunter bowed low before the King. Cadman managed a clumsy curtsy. Patrick Hepburn glanced at the overly tall woman sharply, for the younger MacBeth, despite all Joanna's strict admonishments, had forgotten to stoop slightly. Lord Bothwell's cool eyes narrowed with sudden suspicion, for his wits and instinct for survival had been honed to a keen edge by the meeting with the King and his advisors that evening. After all, a plot to overthrow a government was a serious and deadly business. Had English spies somehow managed to infiltrate Jamie's chamber attendants? Had vital secret correspondence been intercepted? Hungarians. What were Hungarians doing in Scotland? Something was wrong. What if these men (for by this time the Hepburn was convinced the "woman" was really a badly disguised male) were paid assassins sent by Henry Tudor to rid himself of his enemy ruler to the north? The murder of Scotland's monarch would throw the country into chaos. Was England planning to invade again? Hungarians. God's foot! The man who'd spoken did not sound foreign!

"Sire, 'twas my understanding we were to see ye in privacy," Hunter was saying as Lord Bothwell moved forward to stand warily and protectively beside the Scots King.

"Your pardon, Your Grace," Patrick interrupted the conversation abruptly before James had a chance to speak. "Ye there! Aye, ye, *wench*," he sneered slightly. "Remove your cape if ye please. The King likes to inspect his gifts before transacting business so he may learn how highly he is valued by those who would enter into an agreement wie him."

Cadman stiffened and shot a quick, questioning look at Hunter. They had not counted on this. One hand moved stealthily to the dagger the younger MacBeth carried concealed beneath the folds of the cape. The Hepburn noted the small gesture.

"They're imposters! Seize them! Seize them!" Lord Bothwell cried and flung himself upon Jamie, knocking the King to the floor as Patrick attempted to shield his sovereign from whatever danger threatened.

"For God's sake! Put up your blades!" Hunter hissed frantically as the King's men surrounded him and Cadman, pinioning the two struggling kinsmen against one wall. "Christ's son, Patrick! Call them off before they slay us, do ye ken? 'Tis Hunter and Cadman MacBeth!"

"Hold, men!" Jamie commanded as he craned his head out from beneath the Hepburn's bulk, straining to see the two imposters in the candlelight. "God's blood!" he swore, irritated. "Cadman, you're the ugliest wench I e'er did see. 'Tis no wonder Patrick suspected ye. Leave them be," he told his men. "Marry-go-up, Patrick, but ye weigh a ton! Get up, mon, afore ye crush me!"

"'Tis I who am crushed." Cadman grinned as he yanked off the offending, moth-eaten cape after the King's men had released him and Hunter. "Hunter said I was right bonnie."

"Well, you're nae!" Jamie grimaced sourly as he rose to his feet. "I wouldna hae gi'en ye a tuppence in some waterfront tavern."

"Well, that's slightly more than Hunter offered at least."

Lord Bothwell brushed the King off hastily, apologizing for having knocked the young monarch down.

"Och, cease your blathering, Patrick. I know ye did but mean to protect me." After a moment in which he glared at everyone in the chamber Jamie began to laugh. He laughed until the tears ràn down his face. "Lord! Only ye two would hae thought of such a ruse." He hugged the MacBeths warmly. "By God, but 'tis good to see ye both! I hae been sore worried aboot ye and missed ye here at Court. Where hae ye been these past three years wie'oot so much as a by-your-leave to me?''

"Forgie us, Sire." Hunter sat down as the King called for ale to be brought, and Cadman pulled off the gown he was wearing, which had split open down the back in the struggle. "But we had our reasons. Before I explain, Your Grace, I must hae your word this tale will go no further than this room.''

"Ye hae it, mon." James glanced sharply at the others to be sure they understood this. "Now, say on."

It was fully one hour later when Hunter and Cadman had finished their story. The King studied them thoughtfully for a time afterward.

"Aye, now I can see why ye went to such drastic lengths to speak wie me in privacy. Marry, but 'tis a pity we canna jest of it at Court, Cadman. I'll warrant ye'd receive a dozen bouquets at least from the courtiers!" Everyone laughed loudly at this, then the young ruler sobered once more. "So Hunter has two sons by the Lady Mary, and ye, Cadman, hae wed her maid. Well, well. Let me tell ye what has happened in your absence. The auld Bear died the day ye disappeared. He ne'er knew ye had left the Highlands." The two MacBeths were saddened to learn of Lord Angus's death, but gladdened he had not known of their betrayal. "After 'twas discovered at Glenkirk ye had fled," Jamie continued, "Lady Sophia wrote to me, explaining as much as she knew or guessed aboot the situation and asking me to intercede on your behalves. She must love ye both dearly, for she realized ye had broken wie the MacBeths and sought to aid ye anyway. I had Patrick put it aboot ye were both away on a secret mission for me. I dinna know how many of your own believed it. I'm sure some knew the truth, despite my tale, and others may hae learned of it. 'Twould be wise of ye both to continue your precautions, and think of yourselves as broken men until we can discover some way oot of this sad mess for ye. I can gie ye my protection, of course, but even that willna save ye from a dirk in some dark corridor if any of your clansmen are determined on your deaths. Nor, in any case, can I prevent Hugh Carmichael from forcing Mary to return to Dùndereen as he most assuredly will if he learns of her whereaboots. She is still his wife.''

"Aye,'' the laird of Eadar Da Voe put in gravely. ''He has claimed she went mad, escaped from him, and kidnapped the bairns; and he has offered a reward of 25,000 marks for their return.''

"I see,'' Hunter said slowly.

"Och, dinna fash yourself, lad,'' the Earl went on. ''Few believed Lord Dùndereen's story, for many know of his brutal manner and assumed the lass could bear no more and fled him. Certainly my daughter, Alinor, and her husband, Mary's brother Charlie, were nae deceived by the tale. They did, however, fear Mary dead and hae been sore a'grieved by the thought. They made subtle inquiries, but could learn naught. 'Twill be a great joy to them to find they were mistaken. Nay, Hunter, dinna be afraid they will gie ye and Mary away. Alinor suspected Hugh and Ian Carmichael of Gordon's death from the beginning and guessed much of the rest of the affair. She confided in Charlie, for she was worried he might be his kinsmen's next victim. Mary's brother was, of course, enraged at first by what he considered his sister's betrayal; but he's a young hothead and nae to be blamed for it. Alinor has a way wie him,'' Lord Eadar Da Voe laughed somewhat ruefully, ''as methinks she does most of her men, me included. Och, well, the gist of the matter is that Charlie no longer condemns his sister for whate'er she has done. Ye may rest easy on that. He has sworn that if he finds her alive, he will forgie her and countenance her love for ye, Hunter. He was like to slay Hugh Carmichael when the lass disappeared, but I couldna let him risk it. He is young yet, and Lord Dùndereen is a vicious mon. A spell in my dungeon cooled Charlie off soon enough.''

"My thanks to ye, my lord,'' Hunter spoke. ''For doubtless he would only hae gotten himself killed, and I dinna think Mary could hae borne his loss. She was half-crazed o'er Gordon's death. Let Alinor and Charlie know of my lady's well-being, then, but warn them nae to speak of it to others, nor to try and contact us. Hugh may hae surmised Mary would go to them for help and had them watched. We canna be too careful if we are to keep my lady safe. I will deal wie the Earl of Dùndereen in my own way and time." His voice was grim and deadly with intent.

"I am certain ye will, Hunter." Jamie gave him a piercing stare. "But unfortunately I must insist ye put your plans aside for the time being." The King indicated the documents upon the table with a sweep of his hand. "We are hatching a plot to harry King Henry of England, and I can use both ye and Cadman, so 'tis glad I am ye are here. Since ye must go abroad in secrecy anyway, and since I hae said ye were doing so in my name, then 'twill be best if that is the case, for it may help to convince your clansmen of the truth of my words. Richard III may be dead, but Henry's hold on the throne is still shaky, even if he has wed Edward's daughter Elizabeth. Edward's sons, both of whom stood before his brother Richard in the line of succession, hae disappeared. No doubt the puir laddies were murdered in the Tower by either their uncle or the upstart conqueror Henry Tudor, but if so, it has yet to be proven." Jamie smiled slyly. "I am in possession of a young mon who is no doubt a Plantagenet bastard, possibly even of Edward IV's begetting. His true name is Perkin Warbeck, but he claims to be young Richard, one of the supposedly murdered Princes, who managed to escape from the Tower and is the true heir to the crown of England. I mean to support him in this contention. He is to wed Lady Mary Katherine Gordon to lend credence to his story of noble birth and then set sail for England. Hunter, I would like ye and Cadman to escort him to his—native land. While there ye will act as spies for me, and report back anything ye feel might be of importance or might be used against our auld enemy to the south. The fact that ye hae both been abroad in Europe posing as exiles will help to strengthen your defense if ye are caught, for ye willna be as highly suspected of treachery when 'tis discovered ye hae been homeless for the past three years. Thus though Henry may guess Scotland's fine hand has been behind the matter, he willna learn of it for sure. I am sorry to send ye away again so soon, but ye hae both served me well in the past. I know ye willna fail me in this. I shall do what I can to aid ye in your own plight in the meantime. That is all.''

Hunter's scarred mouth tightened into a forbidding line. How could the King even think of sending him away from Mary after all they'd been through together? It was too cruel! And for Mary and the bairns to be left alone, unprotected—it was unthinkable! The Romany knight would have made some protest, begged at least to be allowed to dispose of Hugh Carmichael before leaving Scotland again, but realized Jamie's mind was made up. Hunter's own plans would have to wait. He could not bear it, but it would have to be borne. His jaw set, he and Cadman bowed low before the King, then strode out into the pale dawn light that was just breaking over the eastern horizon. It had been a long night.

"Hunter, wait!" Patrick Hepburn hurried down James's private staircase after the two MacBeths. "Wait!" he called once more.

Hunter turned impatiently from the coach he was about to enter. "Aye, Patrick?"

"I'm sorry, mon." Lord Bothwell gazed into the Romany knight's hard violet eyes. "I know ye are angry and upset o'er being forced to leave your lady, but Jamie is your liege, and your and Cadman's circumstances are such that ye *are* the best men to send to England. We had quarreled for hours o'er who should go. Your arrival and your situation were like a gift from God. Your duty to Scotland *must* take precedence o'er your own personal concerns. 'Tis fate, mon!''

Aye, Hunter thought achingly, but at what price? He remembered placing his commitment to Lord Angus above Mary and losing her because of it. God's blood! Was the world always to come between them? Oh, sweet *Jesù*, beloved. I should ne'er hae sought the palace this eve. May God damn my accursed honor once again—

"Always the King's mon, eh, Patrick? Well, hae no fear I shallna keep my word to Jamie." Hunter was curt.

"Nay, I dinna." The Hepburn's face softened momentarily. "'Tis your lady, I know, for whom ye are concerned. Ye wouldna hesitate to undertake this mission otherwise. Och, send her to her brother, sir. Lord Charlie would guard her wie his life."

"Aye, and I fear that's what it would cost him, too! Then nae only would Mary be in her husband's clutches once more, but her brother would lie dead, besides. She has borne enough for me. I wouldna ask that sorrow of her as well!"

Hunter thought briefly of asking Lord Bothwell to take Mary under his protection during his absence, for the Hepburn was a power to be reckoned with in Scotland and a mighty warrior, in addition. But then the Romany knight realized the Earl would refuse such a request. Hiding a man's fugitive wife was a crime, even if she had been shamefully abused at her husband's hands. After all, a woman was a man's property. That was the law of Scotland; even the King must bow before it, and Patrick was Jamie's man above all else.

Lord Bothwell must have guessed the MacBeth's desperate, silent search for some answer to the tangle that confronted him, for the Earl repeated, "I'm sorry, mon."

"Aye, so am I," Hunter replied bitterly, then swung into the carriage, his cloak whirling about his dark figure like a shroud in the mist, his heart breaking at the thought of parting from Mary Carmichael once again.

# Thirty-one

"Thieves! Robbers! Blackguards! Scoundrels! I shall hae the law on ye, I will! Breaking into a mon's house! By God, no less than the King himself will hear of this, I promise ye! 'Tis a fine day indeed when the streets of Edinburgh are nae safe and rogues such as the likes of ye dare to make yourselves at home in a mon's own town house! 'Tis a good thing I sent Humphrey on business in the city, and he warned me of your presence here, else I should hae been robbed blind! By God, I'll haul the lot of ye up before a magistrate this instant, do ye ken?"

"Marry-go-up! What is going on down there?" Mary was rudely and abruptly awakened by the terrible commotion downstairs.

Hunter was already up and dressed and buckling on his sword. "I dinna know, sweet, but I mean to find oot," he growled before taking the stairs down two at a time.

Mary rose hurriedly to clothe herself and follow as Cadman too bounded loudly past her chamber, and Joanna appeared after him in the hallway, still in her nightdress, one hand held to her slender throat.

"Mary, what is it?"

"I dinna know." The girl shook her head as the two women glanced at one another fearfully, the same horrifying thought occurring to them both. They had been discovered by either the MacBeths or the Carmichaels! They would all be slain! With a gasp of terror they crept silently down the hall just far enough to hear without being seen. Mary's hand closed purposefully over her dirk. She would not allow herself or her bairns to be taken without a fight!

"Lord Duncan!" they heard Hunter cry, and their worst fears were realized.

Quickly they ran to the chamber where their children still slept soundly, Joanna pausing only long enough to snatch up her garments before the lasses bolted the door behind them, then moved to further barricade the entrance with a heavy coffer as Hunter and Cadman had instructed them in an emergency. Joanna dressed herself hastily, then the two maids sat down upon the massive chest, weapons ready, hearts pounding, to wait.

Below the old baron looked hard at the young bearded and mustached man approaching him. His watery red-rimmed eyes narrowed.

"Hunter? Hunter MacBeth? Is that ye, lad? Why, I wouldna hae known ye, son, such a mon ye hae become. Nay, nay, Humphrey, ye fool! Canna ye see this is my kinsman, and those are his servants? Turn that wench loose. Thieves in my town house, indeed! Ye twit! Ye got me all worked up o'er naught, and ye know the doctor said I mustna become too excited; and ye had us make a damned long, hard journey in the cold and snow for nothing, besides. Hmph! Robbers indeed! By God, Humphrey! I swear if I drop dead this minute, 'twill be on your head, mon, I promise ye!"

"I'm sorry, my lord, verra sorry," the Baron's man-at-arms apologized hastily, bowing and scraping profusely, "but I dinna know; truly, I dinna. They dinna wear the MacBeth *breacan*. What else was I to think—"

"Och, I ought to hae known ye were nae capable of the task!" Lord Duncan bellowed. "For God's sake, stop blithering like the idiot ye are!" He waved the knight away irritably. "My blood is just boiling; I can feel it! We shall all be lucky if I dinna keel o'er dead this second! Well, Hunter, dinna stand there gaping like an addle-wit, or I shall think ye as daft as Humphrey! Fetch me a chair and a tankard of ale, then sit down and explain your reasons for breaking into my house, young mon! I'm verra displeased wie ye, verra displeased indeed. The glass in that window came all the way from France, I'll hae ye know. 'Twill be a costly thing to replace, I tell ye. Why, who's that wie ye? Torquil's bastard? Dinna glare at me, lad, for that's who and what ye are. My eyes are nae that bad yet! Cadman, isna it? Well, ye sit down, too. I want some answers right now from the both of ye, do ye ken? What's the meaning of this? Damned disrespectful curs. I dinna know what the world is coming to these days. I ought to hae ye flogged, impudent pups! Ye young men nowadays just dinna hae any respect at all! No respect for your elders. No respect for other people's property. If you'd just written me ye needed the house, I would hae sent ye the key. There was no need to destroy a fine window like that so wantonly, ye reckless rogues. I dare say ye thought 'twas naught. Well, you'll pay for the damage, I promise ye that! All the way from France that glass came, and a pretty penny it cost me too! I just dinna know—''

"Lord Duncan. Lord Duncan. We'll replace the window," Hunter broke in after discerning the Baron obviously did not intend to slay them and somewhat astounded and slightly overcome by this tirade. "I hae already ordered the glass, but these things take time—"

"Of course, they take time, ye insolent whelp!" Lord Duncan roared. "What do ye take me for, a fool?"

"Nay, my lord, certainly nae."

"Hmph!" the elderly man snorted again, but was somewhat mollified. "Well, what are ye doing here and oot of *breacan*, besides? 'Tis no wonder Humphrey thought ye thieves. I heard ye were dead or some such nonsense. Or was that Angus? Aye, it must be the auld Bear who's dead, since you're obviously alive and well. 'Tis lucky for ye and Cadman ye were nae the robbers I suspected ye of being. I'd hae had ye up before the King by now. James III mightna be able to sit a horse, but, by God, he knows the law!"

"Lord—Lord Duncan, James III is dead," Cadman spoke

gently, his face a trifle pitying as he began to realize how badly the laird had declined in his later years and forgiving the Baron for his earlier harsh, blunt remark on Cadman's lineage. "His son is the King of Scotland now."

"James dead? Young Jamie, Duke of Rothesay, King? Well, imagine that! Just goes to show ye how cut off from news I am up north. Has there been a plague? Seems like e'erybody I know is dead."

"Nay, my lord." Hunter too was sorrowed to see how senile his elderly kinsman had grown over the years. "There was a war, a civil war. James III was murdered at Beaton's Mill during the *mêlée*."

"Oh, aye, does seem like I recall something aboot that now. Well, no matter. I'm too auld to ride into battle anyway. Well, explain yourselves, lads! What do ye mean by breaking into my house?"

"We're sorry, Lord Duncan," Hunter apologized. "But we're on private business for the King and needed a hiding place," he informed the Baron, which was the truth, albeit somewhat twisted. "Scotland's welfare is at stake"—which was not quite the truth, but would serve—"which is why we're nae in *breacan*. We dinna wish to be recognized. I must ask ye therefore, my lord, nae to reveal your knowledge of my and Cadman's whereaboots," he finished, feeling slightly guilty at preying upon the old laird's dotage to deceive him.

"Hmmm. Secret mission, eh? Well, I shallna press ye further then, even though I guess I'm loyal enough to keep my trap shut when matters warrant. Well, if there's aught I can do to help ye, lads, just let me know. Otherwise I'll start back for Torra nam Sian in the morning. Canna abide Edinburgh; damned noisy city! Too much of a strain on me, the doctor says. Hae to hae peace and quiet."

An idea began to take shape in Hunter's mind at Lord Duncan's words, a daring, risky scheme, but then the Romany knight was desperate. For nearly a fortnight he had pondered how to keep Mary safe during his absence, racked his brain feverishly for some plan to his liking, but had failed to come up with one. Now he thought furiously, weighing the dangers in his mind. Torra nam Sian was far to the north of Scotland and quite isolated. Few persons ever went there, even members of the Clan MacBeth. The forbidding castle was too desolate. And it was obvious, besides, the Baron had become very eccentric in his old age and knew little of what was happening in the rest of the world outside his keep. Certainly he was not aware Hunter and Cadman were broken men, or he would have attempted to kill them by now, in spite of his infirmities. Just witness the manner in which he had ridden to Edinburgh to defend his town house! And Hunter was willing to wager the Baron hadn't left Torra nam Sian in years. Still the Romany knight's decision might well bring about the deaths of Mary, Joanna, and the bairns if it went awry, for Lord Duncan *was* a loyal MacBeth, no matter how aged. Och, what to do? If the women and children were left alone in Edinburgh, they might be seen, recognized, and taken captive in Hunter's and Cadman's absence, for the MacBeths could not trust the servants not to run off once the two men were gone; or worse yet the street ruffians they'd hired might do some harm to the women themselves. Aye, the lasses and bairns would fare far better if the Baron were to agree to take them to Torra nam Sian, even if it were a stronghold of the MacBeths. Indeed, amidst the enemy was probably the last place anyone would think to look for the girls; the move was so brazen. But if Lord Duncan himself discovered the maids' true identities—

Hunter gave Cadman a quick, inquiring glance, knowing the same thoughts must be chasing through his foster brother's mind, for they had argued for days about what was best for their families. Cadman's dark blue eyes were veiled as though he too were considering the risks involved. At last the younger man gave a small, almost imperceptible nod in response to his kinsman's searching gaze. Hunter drew a breath.

"As a matter of fact, there *is* something ye can do for us, my lord, if ye would," he addressed the old laird.

"What's that, Hunter? Ye just name it, lad." The Baron's

rheumy eyes lit up with anticipation at this. Truth to tell, he *would* enjoy a wee bit of excitement, in spite of his doctor's orders! Why, he hadn't felt so alive since he fought against the Turks in '44. . . .

"Well, my lord, 'tis like this. Cadman and I hae our wives and families here. We'd feel more comfortable, I know, if we knew they were being well-guarded from danger during our absence, for we must leave Scotland shortly and hae acquired many enemies during our—mission." Again Hunter felt a small twinge of guilt at taking advantage of the Baron's decrepitude with his lies, but plunged on anyway. "Would ye mind taking them to Torra nam Sian wie ye, my lord, and protecting them for us? I understand 'tis a formidable chore." He made an attempt to ease his culpability by telling himself 'twould make the elderly man feel important and useful once more to be needed by someone, for Hunter felt certain Lord Duncan was lonely with naught but his memories of past glories to sustain him during his waning years. "But I know ye would hold them safe for us, my lord. Even now your prowess on the battle field hasna been forgotten."

"I'll wager nae!" the grey-haired laird blustered indignantly, but was pleased by the flattering thought that the bravery of his youth was remembered all the same. "Of course I'll see to your wives and bairns. Ye can count on that! Where are they now?"

"Mary! Joanna!" Hunter called, praying the Baron was so nearsighted he would not discern the violet color of Mary's eyes, for they were a dead giveaway as to her identity. " 'Tis all right. Ye can come oot now, and bring the babes wie ye."

The two women and children walked quietly down the stairs, Mary holding little Magnus in her arms. The maids had managed to hear enough of the conversation through the barred door to know the elderly man meant them no harm, but even so they remained wary, for they too realized the haunting purple of Mary's eyes might prove their death warrants.

"Lord Duncan, this is my wife, Mary," Hunter stated, warning her with his eyes not to try and explain the strange tangle of their relationship.

The Baron stared at the young woman before him sharply, his watery blue gaze seeming to pierce momentarily her very soul. She faltered in her step forward, and Hunter laid one hand uneasily on the hilt of his sword, startled. Had he misjudged his failing kinsman after all? Nay. The brief, tense minute passed as Lord Duncan held out his hand for Mary's kiss.

"How do ye do, my lady." He nodded politely.

"My lord." Mary swept the Baron a low curtsy.

Is he blind? the lass wondered, that he canna see the color of my accursed, Carmichael eyes? Or is he but biding his time, waiting for his chance to take Joanna and me and the bairns from the protection of Hunter's and Cadman's sword-arms? Oh, beloved, I hope ye hae nae erred in this.

"And these are my sons," Hunter continued with more assurance than he felt. "Geoffrey, who'll be seven this year. Ranald, who's almost four. And Magnus, barely nine months, my lord."

If the Baron thought it strange Hunter's youngest boy bore the name of the MacBeths' old enemy, the Lion of Bailekair, he gave no indication of such.

"Ah, they are fine-looking lads, Hunter. Ye must be verra proud of them." Lord Duncan actually beamed as the two older youths made their bows and very nicely too. "They've been well-trained." Again he glanced at Mary assessingly.

"Thank ye, my lord." She accepted the compliment graciously, although she was thrembling inside.

"And this is my wife, Joanna." Cadman motioned toward the solemn maid. "And our twins, Gordon and Janet, my lord, nearly a year-and-a half."

"My lady, children," the Baron said, acknowledging the remaining introductions. "Well, I shall be verra pleased to hae ye all entrusted to my care and hope ye will find your stay at Torra nam Sian entertaining." Lord Duncan sounded a trifle doubtful at this last as he gazed at the bairns, suddenly recalling there was little to do at the massive fortress far to the north of Scotland. "We—we are a wee bit cut off from the rest of the world. I hope—"

"Please, dinna worry aboot us, my lord," Mary reassured him. "We too find the crowds of Edinburgh disruptive and shall be glad of a place where the babes may play freely."

"Why, that's fine then." The Baron smiled, and Mary's heart began to warm toward him as she dismissed her earlier suspicions that he might have guessed her true identity. He'd been just naturally curious about Hunter's wife; that was all. No doubt since he had raised the Romany knight from childhood, he had wanted to make certain his protégé had done well for himself and was a credit to the MacBeth name. "I'm sure we shall all get along splendidly. Well, then, whene'er ye wish to depart, I shall be ready," Lord Duncan went on. "Now, if ye dinna mind, I would like my chamber prepared. I confess I amna as young a mon as I used to be and am quite tired oot from the rigorous journey into which Humphrey hoaxed me."

"My lord—" the man-at-arms started to protest.

"Och, 'twas just as well, Humphrey," the old laird cut in, silencing him, suddenly wearied and overwrought as Joanna led him away kindly. Lord Duncan turned at the doorway momentarily, his eyes twinkling once more. "My kinsmen mayna be thieves, but they're scoundrels all the same!" He managed to get the last word after all and left the others feeling decidedly uneasy again.

"Oh, Hunter, are ye certain this is wise?" Mary queried softly when the Baron and his entourage had been taken care of. "Why dinna ye let us go to my brother? Charlie and Alinor would welcome us, I know."

"Aye, but Hugh may hae set a watch on them, Mary, and ye know how oft ye hae told me what a hothead Charlie is. I dinna like to think of him getting killed o'er ye, and that is a real possibility. Ye couldna live wie that on your conscience, beloved. Ye hae borne too much already. I believe you'll be safe wie Lord Duncan. He doesna seem to recognize ye, and I doubt Hugh would think of looking for ye at Torra nam Sian. Aye, 'tis the only way, sweet." He stroked her golden hair lightly. "I dare nae leave ye in Edinburgh wie'oot Cadman or myself to attend ye. I dinna hae any other choice. The brigands on our staff might set upon ye or any number of other unpleasant happenings might occur if I leave ye here in the city to fend yourselves."

"Och, Hunter, I am sore worried aboot this mad plan of Jamie's. Is it verra dangerous?"

"I'll nae lie to ye, lass. I dinna know. We are to escort the Pretender to England and act as spies for Scotland. I dinna think the risk to ourselves will be great, for I dinna believe King Henry VII is a stupid mon who willna see the ruse as an attempt by Jamie to annoy him, despite our sovereign's ideas on the matter. I doubt the Tudor will place us in any position to learn anything of importance even if we do manage to infiltrate his defenses. We are Scots after all, exiles or no. Most likely the worst thing that will happen is that the puir impostor will be thrown into the Tower, and the rest of us will be sent home wie our tails between our legs!"

"I'm frightened, my love." Mary's face was grave and pleading as she looked at him. "Suppose the Baron finds oot we are nae truly wed, that Joanna and I are Carmichaels? He isna so senile he canna remember who his enemies are! Och, damn Jamie!"

"There will be little chance of Lord Duncan learning much, I think," Hunter responded. "The worst moment was today, and it has passed. Ye will just hae to be on your guard, Mary. Alan has trained ye well, better than some young squires even, and Joanna isna afraid of battle either. Trust no one, no one, lass. And if ye fear Lord Duncan has discovered your lineage, slay him, and get oot while ye can. Go to Jane Gordon at Bothwell if ye become truly desperate. She has wed the Hepburn and is a power to be reckoned wie in Scotland, as ye know full well. Aye, go to Jane, nae your brother, Mary. Remember that."

"Och, so Patrick got her at last." Mary smiled mischievously for a moment, wondering how the arrogant Lord Bothwell was liking marriage to the hot-tempered Jane Gordon. Mayhap they would be glad of company, the girl thought, then sobered upon recalling why she might need their aid. "Do ye think 'twould be wise, Hunter? Patrick is the King's mon and nae gi'en to breaking the law."

"Unless it suits him," Hunter answered dryly. "I dinna know. For all I like him I canna trust the Hepburn. He is an enigma and unpredictable. Still were it nae for him we wouldna be in this fix, for he might hae persuaded Jamie against the idea. He has much influence wie our young King. But he dinna speak up for me or Cadman, for our circumstances suited his purposes. Still if ye are truly in need of help, I dinna believe he will turn ye away. I dinna think his conscience would permit that, especially if 'tis Jane doing the talking!"

"All right. We shall go wie Lord Duncan then, and if aught amiss happens, we shall seek Bothwell in the Border Lands," she said, but her voice quivered.

"Come, where is that tigress I love so well? My brave, bonnie lassie. Dinna let me leave Scotland wie the thought of tears in your violet eyes on my mind, or I'll nae be able to go at all, and Jamie will hae me put to the horn as an ootlaw." He attempted to smile, but Mary felt that old prickle of fey foreboding run tingling up her spine and wondered if this parting were to be their last.

A fortnight later Mary was bouncing along in Lord Duncan's coach toward Torra nam Sian with the Baron, Joanna, and the children. The MacBeths had let their own staff go, but Lord Duncan's servants brought up the rear in three wagons laden with coffers, jewel caskets, and other possessions with which the two women had refused to part. The old laird's few knights galloped alongside the small cavalcade. Joanna chatted pleasantly with the elderly man, but Mary, who'd joined in the conversation earlier only out of politeness, was not aware of the others now.

She closed her eyes and for one bittersweet moment was back at the townhouse on High Street in Edinburgh, lying next to Hunter in the darkness of their chamber.

He turned and reached for her, drawing her close within the

shelter of his strong arms as he kissed her deeply, lingeringly, passionately.

"Nay, beloved," she murmured against his lips. "Tonight I will make love to ye. Lie back, and let me pleasure ye."

He was surprised, but did as she requested, a glimmer of interest and excitement flickering within the depths of his purple eyes. The barest hint of a smile touched his scarred mouth.

Mary twined her fingers in his rich mahogany hair as she bent to kiss the lips she had branded years ago as her own. She traced the outline of their carnal borders with her tongue, parted them gently, exploring the inside of his sweet mouth. He tasted of ale, fresh and clean, like the clear sparkling waters of a mountain stream; and she slaked her thirst for him as her tongue teased his softly, quick and darting as she swirled it about his own in delicious ravishment. She moved on to his cheeks, his earlobes, breathing huskily there as she whispered words of love against his ear, purring silkily in Romany, the language that would forever remind them of the time they had spent together in wild abandon in the gay gypsy camp of Hungary. She kissed his nose and then his eyelids and temples. She smiled and pressed her face up against his to flutter her eyelashes coyly against his dark visage in imitation of a butterfly's wings. He laughed at the tickling of the feathery fringe upon his cheeks. Mary laughed, too, and buried her face into his hair, breathing in the fragrance of his maleness mingled headily with the sandalwood scent he always used. She slid down his throat, nibbling at his shoulders as she rubbed one hand caressingly over the satin fur of his darkly matted chest. She kissed him there, mimicking the movements he always employed to arouse her own ripe mounds, and found his broad chest could respond in a manner similar to her own pale golden breasts. She glanced up at him in delight at the knowledge.

"Aye, love, I hae feeling there, too," he confirmed.

She ran her fingers lightly up and down the long, jagged scar that marred his belly. Tears started when she remembered how he had received it. She placed her mouth upon it

458

tenderly, feeling the muscles of his firm, flat groin tauten as he also recalled.

"'Tis but a scar, lass," he whispered gently. "And its shadow no longer lies between us."

"Ye are too kind to me, my love."

She put her hands on his sides. His waist was so narrow; his hips too were slender as her fingers brushed the hollows on either side, then slipped beneath his hard, powerful body to tighten upon his buttocks before moving down his steely legs. Mary kissed his feet, his calves, his thighs, on and on, taunting him, raising his desire to a feverish pitch before she at last found his manhood. Her lips glided along the engorged shaft lightly, strayed to the dark hair from which it sprang, then traveled to the rounded globes beneath it, where her tongue licked with hushed fervor before flitting its way back up the length of him once more. She encompassed the tip of his searing blade, tongue whirling round and round before she took him into her mouth, enclosing him deep within her throat, then releasing him only to repeat the pattern again and again as her fingers tightened on the base of him and stroked the spheres just beneath in gentle torment.

Hunter gasped and moaned, wrapping his hands in the golden mass of her cascading hair that spilled out over his belly and thighs.

"Sweet," he panted. "I canna take much more."

She smiled up at him again, her eyes dancing dark with passion as she pulled herself up and placed her knees on either side of him. She grasped his fiery sword firmly, piercing herself with it as she lowered the sweet sheath of her womanhood and engulfed him with her very being. She slid slowly down, down, then just as languidly raised herself once more, muscles contracting to keep him within her. Her flanks sank upon his again and then again as he dug his fingers into her flesh to help her remain astride his lithe, whipcord body. She laid herself upon him, breasts pressing into his chest as she rode him faster and faster. Her gilded tresses billowed about his face, smothering him in a cloud of wet golden softness as the sweat of her trickled down the silky strands to drip upon his countenance, his throat, his shoulders, his chest. He gloried in the heather dewiness of her satin skin, arched his hips to meet her own, felt the moisture of her honeyed being like a bolt of velvet furling around him in glistening folds as he came into her, crying out in his passion.

Triumphantly Mary raised herself, flung her head back, the waterfall of her locks flying out like the sparks of a hot, molten gold fountain as she clasped her fingers into his sides, her naked breasts shimmering before him, as though she had been some wild, wanton goddess luring him on with her siren's song. She parted her mouth, ran her tongue lightly over the damp sheen of her lips once before her voice rang out in a pure trill of joy, tears streaking the luster of her cheeks like rain.

Hunter pulled her to him with a thick, hoarse moan.

"Oh, God, Mary. Oh, God," he breathed.

"I—I dinna want ye to forget me, my love, my life. 'Tis my farewell to ye. It seems we are fore'er parting, and I ne'er know when each time might be the last. Oh, God be wie ye, Hunter, on the morrow."

"Hush, hush, dinna weep, tigress. I will return, I promise ye that. I will always return to ye. Oh, Mary, my maiden gold, to part wie ye is to lose half of my heart and soul. I love ye. I love ye more than life itself. I will return, I swear it! When the heather blooms purple on the Highland moors, I will come for ye, beloved."

# BOOK FIVE

*Where Legends Remain*

# *Thirty-two*

### The Highlands, Scotland, 1495

The snow flurried down, white, hard, and relentless as the small cavalcade wound its way from the Lowlands to the Highlands of Scotland. Progress was slow. Many times the procession was forced to halt while the men-at-arms held their gloved hands over the noses of the horses to warm the fine openings from which the beasts snorted and blew clouds of pale white frost into the dull grey winter air. Otherwise the nostrils of the animals would have frozen shut, and they would have smothered and died where they stood. The men themselves drew their heavy cloaks about them closely and tried hard not to curse Duncan MacBeth for undertaking such a journey in the dead of winter, when the roads were nearly impassable. Humphrey they ignored completely, blaming him for the entire wild-goose chase.

The inhabitants of the Baron's carriage huddled together for warmth, but seldom spoke, for their teeth chattered uncontrollably. Mary gazed out one window for a time, but was soon compelled to shutter it once more against the stinging sleet and crystal flakes that whipped and eddied about the coach without pity. Winter was cruel that year.

The drifts lay blanketed as high as six feet in some places.

The trees stood rigid and naked, stark silhouettes against the barely visible horizon. Great, pointed icicles hung like daggers from the barren branches. Night fell early, enveloping the land with a soft black shroud that gave one the deceptive feeling of being wrapped in a safe, secure haven from which one could not see out, nor others in. Only the foolish were lulled into sleep; they would not live to gaze upon the strange lightless dawn that followed. Oddly silver and hostile in its brilliance, it blinded the eyes like the blade of a steely sword when turned to catch the rays of the glittering sun.

If one of the vehicles floundered in the snow, its inhabitants had to get out and walk, while the men-at-arms struggled to free the high, rimmed wheels from the clinging whiteness.

Perhaps of them all Mary and Joanna fared the best, for they had survived that horrible winter in the Alps, and the Scottish weather seemed almost mild in comparison.

The party stopped only once unnecessarily—upon the cliff outside of Mheadhoin. Mary saw the cross-topped spire of the kirk in the distance as they neared it and bade the carriage halt when they reached it. She alighted and stood alone upon that place where years ago Grizel had laid her curse upon them all. A solitary figure against the sweep of the jagged sky, Mary ignored the freezing snow and sleet that pricked her face unmercifully and mingled with the tears that traced a bittersweet path down her cheeks. Almost four years. It had been almost four years since Mary had seen the Highlands of her birth, the kirk where she had lain and loved with Hunter. Glenkirk, whence he had come, bold, dark, and handsome, to wrap her in his strong arms and make her his. Dùndereen, where gentle Edward lay buried beneath the cold hard ground, and Hugh, her husband, still reigned supreme. And Bailekair. Ah, Bailekair, her life, her strength. It glistened hard and silvery in the half-light, like a single brilliant diamond, from its perch upon the forbidding, purple mountain that still hovered doomlike over her home. Her home. Mary would never think of any place but Bailekair as home. Bailekair, which called to her heart and did not know she could not answer. Bailekair! Oh, Bailekair! Lost to her forever!

Mary stood upon the cliff and wept.

"Come away, Mary." Joanna was suddenly at her side, her arms about Mary's sorrowing figure comfortingly. "The others will begin to wonder, and 'tis dangerous for us to linger in this place. Please, come away."

Mary did as her maid bid, realizing the lass spoke the truth. Mary did not wish to endanger Joanna or the bairns by arousing Lord Duncan's suspicions or to chance being seen and recognized by any of the inhabitants of the three castles. She squared her small shoulders at last and did not look back as they drove away.

The weeks at Torra nam Sian slipped by, one much like another, endless and empty because Hunter was not there to share them with Mary. She filled her hours by taking charge of the great fortress, which, like the town house, had fallen into a state of disrepair. She tended her bairns, loving them all the more fiercely in their father's absence. In the evenings she played chess with Lord Duncan, a pastime that never failed to delight the old laird. Often she stood with Joanna upon the ramparts of the keep, watching and waiting for some word of her beloved. But Mary received no letter from Hunter; she had not really expected any, though she had hoped in heart and known 'twas in vain. It would have been too dangerous for him to write her, not knowing into what hands their correspondence might fall.

Oh, beloved, how I miss ye, long for ye. My days are barren wie'oot ye to fill them. The girl tossed restlessly in her sleep at night, arms outstretched to draw Hunter close to her only to awaken to remember he did not lie beside her sharing his warmth. She yearned for the feel of his hands upon her silken golden flesh, and even in the coldness of the bitter winter nights her sheets were damp from the heat of her flushed body as she dreamed of him towering over her in the darkness, his scarred lips kissing her feverishly, his bronzed chest pressed against her soft breasts, his maleness throbbing deep within that part of her that ached for him alone. Oh, Hunter! Hunter! Damn Jamie for sending ye from me! Do ye long for me, my love? Do ye dream of me as I do thee? Och, hurry home, beloved! Hurry home to me!

Spring came, and the cruel, sharp wind of the harsh winter softened to a gentle sigh of its former self. Patches of earth began to peep through the now-soft, slushy snow that melted until at last it was no more. The sun fought its way through the thick grey clouds of winter mist to awaken the land with the first touch of warmth that grew stronger with each passing day. Little green shoots sprouted from the spongy, yielding ground, gradually blossoming like lovers when kissed and wooed by the waxing, orange-and-yellow rays. Soon the heather began to bud upon the Highland moors. Mary waited and waited, but Hunter did not come.

Instead one day that early spring a peddler appeared at the gate of the old castle. He drove a rickety wagon that had been fashioned to resemble (unintentionally) the caravans of the gypsies. It was brightly painted and had the same high, rimmed wheels with contrasting spokes of color; gay ruffled curtains were at the windows. Inside were all manner of pots and pans, pins and needles, bolts of cloth, cakes of soap, flacons of perfume, hair combs, every little nicety a woman might crave. The wenches of the household gathered round with shouts of laughter, chattering eagerly to one another as the man opened the doors on the cart and began to spread his wares upon the ground so they might make their choices. Many of the usual items that the maids could just as easily have made themselves, such as candles or scent, seemed precious and desirable when displayed by the tinker, for some had come all the way from France (or so he claimed). Few of the peasants could resist this exotic lure, and soon the peddler's purse jingled with coins. He was a clever man and knew just how to flatter subtly and many a common lass foolishly went away with a piece of bright red satin or a rhinestone-studded comb when a new cooking skillet, teakettle, or other kitchen utensil would have served her far better.

Mary and Joanna gazed on from one window of the keep longingly, yearning to join the others, but hesitant to do so.

"Och, Joanna, do let's go down." Mary's heart ached as she watched the little crowd and spied the merry wagon, remembering the time she and Hunter had spent so happily together in the gypsy camp.

Joanna shook her head reluctantly. "'Tis dangerous for more than Lord Duncan's folk to know we are here."

"Och, he's only a simple peddler. He'll nae recognize us. We wear the MacBeth colors," Mary wheeled, for indeed both maids had changed the pattern of their garments upon leaving Scotland with Hunter and Cadman. "He'll nae know we dinna live here. The tinkers are a solitary lot, nae gi'en to mixing, but to minding their own business. Och, please. Come, Joanna. He might hae news of Edinburgh and mayhap somehow of our knights."

'Twas this last that finally persuaded Mary's maid, against her better judgment, to leave the fortress. Eagerly the girls pushed their way through the crush of clamoring women, as excited as the rest.

The peddler could not help but notice the golden-haired wench with violet eyes who stood out among the other women. Lord, but she was bonnie! He felt a twinge of desire chase through his loins and thought he would give a month's pay at least to possess her. He was curious about her, for she was obviously not a servant. She must be one of the auld laird's bastards, he decided, or the whore of one of his knights. He stepped forth admiringly as she and Joanna made their way to his side.

"What news, Master Peddler, what news?" Mary cried, hoping for some word of the expedition into England and thereby of Hunter and Cadman. "What news hae ye for us this fine day?"

He held up a pair of combs for her inspection, studying her with unconcealed appreciation. "What is it ye would hear, mistress?"

Mary gave a small sigh of relief. The man was something of a dandy and a flirt, besides, not reticent and needing to be coaxed like most of his trade. 'Twill be like picking apples off the ground, the lass thought, getting information from this would-be gallant, for she had not missed his interest in her. She flashed him a brilliant smile.

"Why, whate'er ye would tell, mon."

He unrolled a bolt of purple satin. "Then I would tell ye your eyes are the color of this cloth, and your beauty is bonnie enough to win a king." He gazed at her invitingly. Common or no, perhaps he could persuade her to come lie with him.

"Do ye think so?" Mary cocked her head slyly, pretending to be all a'flustered. "Oh, la, Master Peddler, ye would turn a puir maid's head wie such flattery. I vow I could swoon this minute! What chance would I, an ignorant, country gel, hae to catch the eye of young Jamie? No doubt he is besieged by bonnie ladies." She sighed a little woefully, laughing to herself and longing briefly to tell the tinker she had, indeed, won the King's heart once, though she and James had both known she would never take it.

"Well, they do say he is quite taken wie Maggie Drummon, but 'tis a shy maid she is and leading him a merry dance. I'll warrant he'd leave her in a minute could he but catch a glimpse of ye. I know I would." The peddler moved a little closer.

Och, puir Mariot. How fleeting the love of a king. And Maggie engaged to young Crief, or so I thought. Mary pondered this piece of information for a moment.

"Och, ye hae a silver tongue, mon," she bantered back minutes later, "finer than a courtier's, I'll wager, clever enough to rival even young Jamie's." The tinker smiled, pleased, and wondered if he dared take her hand. Perhaps he had been wrong in his earlier assessment of the wench, for she seemed willing enough. Mayhap she was but the by-blow of some common slut after all, for her manner was almost brazen.

" 'Tis ye who hae a bonnie wit, mistress," he cooed.

Once again Mary did not correct his manner of address. 'Twas safer if he did not learn she was titled. "Methinks ye plot to steal my heart, mon. Ye must be a master of intrigue, for I thought it well-guarded until now," she lilted archly.

How badly he wanted to impress her. Mayhap he *could* talk her into stealing away with him for awhile. He could just feel the length of her pressed up against him in some field.

"Well, as to that, mistress," he said, lowering his voice conspiratorily, "I did chance to be involved, in a small way, of course, in one of the King's schemes."

"Really? Och, do tell!" Mary widened her eyes with excitement, as though hanging on each word (which, indeed, she was at that instant).

"Oh, aye, mistress. Richard Plantagenet, one of Edward IV's young bairns, wasna murdered as thought, but escaped from the Tower of England and was right here in Scotland!"

"Nay!"

"Aye, 'tis true, I swear it. And who do ye think he rode wie, in disguise, of course, as far as Perth—for he had sailed to Ireland and from there to here—one evening?"

"Oh, nay, Master Peddler, truly?"

"Aye, mistress. Right up there on the seat of my cart he rode."

"Where is he now?" Mary's heart beat so fast she thought surely the man must hear it.

"Och, he seeks to regain the throne his uncle stole and lost to Henry Tudor. 'Tis said Jamie has sent ships and men to aid the lad, but I hear tell they were blown off course, which has delayed the invasion. There are those who say the two vessels hae been sighted as far north as Cleves and as far south as Braganza, so who can tell? Personally I believe the story that claims they hae landed in Burgundy, for young Richard has powerful relatives there."

"Well! How verra exciting to be sure! Ye must be proud to hae been part of such an adventure. Thank ye, Master Peddler." Mary's heart danced secretly, for she had learned all she wished to know. With a toss of her head she paid for the cheap, tawdry combs and the material, thinking their outrageous price a bargain for the precious information she had just received.

"Mistress!" The tinker suddenly became emboldened and seized her hand. "I was wondering—"

Mary snatched it away abruptly. "La, I must run. My lord awaits me," she called over one shoulder, trying hard not to laugh at the woebegone expression on the poor man's face as she and Joanna, who had bought nothing, ran toward the keep.

The tinker ruefully watched them go, then turned to the likely lassies surrounding him, wishing they had not suddenly paled in comparison to the bonnie golden wench with eyes like amethyst jewels. Damn! He would have given a month's pay for even a kiss!

The peddler moved on, and Mary forgot him, wrapped up in the knowledge that for the time being at least Hunter was safe and had been prevented from coming to her only because an ill-wind had chosen to interfere with his mission, driving his ship off course. She hugged the thought of his well-being to her breast with delight and kept faith he would return to her soon. She put the hair combs away in her jewelry box, the purple satin in her coffer, and gave the man who'd sold them both to her not another thought.

The tinker, on the other hand, found himself haunted by Mary's face and wished he had dared ask her to slip away to the tall broom upon the Highland heaths with him for just a little while. Och! To have tumbled such a wench as she had been would have been a feather in his cap, indeed!

"I should hae asked her." He stared glumly at his tankard of ale, his words slurred with drunkedness. "She might hae agreed; ye ne'er know. Och, what am I thinking of? She was too fine for the likes of me."

"That's the trouble—hic—wie women." A man sitting next to the peddler raised his head off the bar. "Always think they're too good for ye. Well, they're—hic—nae!"

The tinker was pleased to have found an ear willing to

listen to his tale of woe. "Och, ye should hae seen her, mon," he sighed. "Hair as gold as bracken in the sun, and her eyes—Lord, her eyes. I ne'er seen the like before. Like amethysts, they were. Do ye know what amethysts are, mon? They're purple jewels. I seen 'em once on some auld bawd in Edinburgh. My friend, Davey, was wie me at the time. A pickpocket, he were, but he ne'er took anything off me, mind. He were a true friend, a true friend, indeed. Well, he turns to me and says, 'Would ye look at them gems, Finn.' Finn—that's my name. He says, 'Them's what ye call amethysts, Finn. They'd fetch a pretty penny, a pretty penny, I tell ye. I'd hae a go at grabbing 'em from that auld bawd's throat if I were nae a'feared her henchmen would nab me. They set up an awful squawk, they do, some of these auld bawds. They ainna near as helpless as they look.' So, ye see, that's how I knowed aboot 'em being purple and all—amethysts, I mean—and why this wench's eyes put me in mind of 'em. Och, she were a bonnie lass, she were. I ought to go back. I should hae asked her to come lie wie me. I took her hand, but she snatched it away. Ne'ertheless, I ought to hae asked her. She might hae agreed. Ye ne'er know."

"Well, what are ye waiting for—hic—Fitch? Go on, ask her."

"Finn, nae Fitch. Och, like as nae she's forgotten all aboot me. Still I ought to go back."

"Well, come on, Filmer. What are we waiting for? Let's go—hic—get her! Come on, Fiske, what do ye say? Where is this gel of yours?"

"Finn. Finn. Och, mon, she's nae in Inverness. She's miles—miles from here."

"Well, we got all night, ainna we, Filbert? What do ye—hic—say? We'll show her who'd too good for ye, and it willna be her, will it, Firmin?"

"Finn, mon! My name's Finn! *FINN!*"

"Well, ye needna get testy aboot it, Fimm. Fimm? That's an odd name. I was only trying to help ye."

"'Tis no use. She's too far away. Way to the north of

Scotland she is, in an auld, crumbling down fortress perched upon a cliff like an eagle. Got some auld laird to look after her, too. Nay, 'tis no use, I tell ye. 'Tis just no use."

"Och, cheer up, Fielding. We'll find us another wench—hic—just as good."

"I told ye my name was Finn! FINN!" The peddler suddenly became quite enraged. "And you're probably trying to steal my gel, too!"

"Nay, I wouldna do that, Fyfe."

At this the tinker jumped up and punched the other man in the nose, then passed out on the floor himself, unaware that a third man, who'd overheard the entire conversation, had slipped furtively out the back door of the tavern into the night.

Hugh Carmichael smiled evilly, and the man kneeling before him quaked with fear.

"Stop that quivering, mon!" the Earl of Dùndereen snapped impatiently. "Ye put me in mind of my foster brother Ian when he canna get a drink! There's no need for ye to be afraid anyway. Ye hae done well, verra well, indeed. In fact, I'm going to reward ye for your trouble. Twenty-five thousand marks I offered, and 25,000 marks ye will be paid. Here, take this note to Master Keane, who handles my accounts. Leslie will show ye the way and fix ye up wie a hot meal, a warm bed, and a wench, too."

"Och, thank ye, my lord. Thank ye, my lord." The man from the Inverness tavern bowed repeatedly, not believing his good fortune.

Hugh continued to grin until the door had closed, then his dark visage blackened angrily.

"Twenty-five thousand marks, indeed, to the likes of that scum. Connall, ye know what to do. 'Tis a worthless auld sot he is and nae like to be missed. Get rid of him, then report back here."

"Aye, my lord." Connall nodded, his hands already tightening with anticipation at slitting the poor informant's gullet.

"Ye are sure ye dinna want to go a'Maying, Mary?" Joanna raised one eyebrow inquisitively. "The bairns will be disappointed, and 'twould do ye good to get oot of the keep. No one will know us in Wick; there'll be so many strangers abroad."

"Nay, Joanna." Mary shook her head. "I promised Lord Duncan I would help him inventory some things this morning. He has some fine treasures, and I dinna believe he has any idea of their true worth. Some of them are quite valuable, although he persists in thinking the only priceless items 'hae come all the way from France,'" she laughed. "'Tis no doubt why his puir serving wenches were fooled so badly by the tinker. Besides, once the children get into Wick to see the festivities they willna miss me. Here." She pressed some coins into the maid's hand. "Hae a good time, and buy them all something frivolous for me."

Joanna smiled. "All right, if you're certain ye willna change your mind. Dinna look for us till late then. The bairns mean to visit e'ery carnival attraction in Wick, even though I hae attempted to dissuade them!"

Finally Joanna, the children, and Lord Duncan's men-at-arms departed for town, all laughing and shouting loudly as they went. Mary smiled as she waved good-bye to them from a window of the keep, thinking Joanna was going to have a great deal of difficulty restraining five unruly babes from going into the carnival booths to view God only knew what kind of monstrosities. Mary shivered slightly, recalling that day at the Inverness fair so long ago, then shook off the sudden morbid feeling of doom that crept over her at the thought as she joined the Baron. Now what had made her think of Hugh?

"Ye certainly hae some fine treasures, my lord," she said nearly an hour later as she catalogued another piece, a priceless Arabian scimitar with a gold, jewel-encrusted hilt.

"I got that when I fought against the Turks, damned infidels! All o'er the place," Lord Duncan growled. "'Twasna a true Crusade, of course, for they ended in 1369, but I was wie Varna in 1444 when we battled the Ottoman Empire. Aye, I was in my prime in those days, lassie, nae the decrepit auld war horse I am now.'' The laird's rheumy eyes glistened with excitement as he remembered the past.

"Willna ye tell me all aboot it, Lord Duncan?'' Mary prompted kindly, not mentioning her own adventure with the Turks; she wanted the Baron to think he was relating a special experience, for she knew it delighted him to relive his many past campaigns.

"Well, 'twas like this—'' he began, but was rudely interrupted by the whining Humphrey.

"My lord! My lord!''

"Well, what is it, Humphrey?'' Lord Duncan glared angrily at the openmouthed retainer.

Humphrey swallowed hard. "My lord, ye willna believe this—''

"Well, certainly I shall hae no chance to determine that if ye dinna tell me what 'tis ye are blathering aboot, mon! Oot wie it now! Dinna stand there gaping like the idiot ye are!''

"My—my lord. A large force is massing for an attack just ootside the castle walls.''

"Attack?'' The Baron was genuinely surprised. "What of the village, mon?''

"Apparently it holds no interest for the marauders, for they hae ignored it completely. 'Tis the fortress itself they mean to seize.''

"By God! I'll fix the bloody bastards! Take my keep will they? By God! I'll soon cut them down''—Lord Duncan brandished the scimitar violently—''whoe'er they are!''

"My lord, 'tis—'tis the Carmichaels,'' Humphrey managed to get out quaveringly.

"The Carmichaels!'' one hand went to Mary's throat.

The old laird gave her a sharp, piercing glance, then his face softened. "Dinna fash yourself, lassie.'' His gruff voice was kind. "I hae sworn to Hunter to protect ye, and so I shall. Dinna fear I shall turn ye o'er to them, for 'tis for ye they come, is it nae?''

"Ye—ye know?'' Mary gasped.

"Aye, I hae always known ye were a Carmichael wench, lass. 'Twas your eyes, of course, that gae ye away. Those damned accursed violet eyes. Ye couldna be aught else, for had ye been a MacBeth I should hae known of it."

"Then, why—why—"

"Later, lass. Right now I must see to my castle. By God! —I'm nae too auld for one last skirmish!"

Mary's heart pounded with fright as the elderly man left the room. The Carmichaels! The Carmichaels were attacking Torra nam Sian! Fear clutched her in its fist. Shock washed over her, stark and cruel. She could hear the terrified chatter of the women of the household as they scurried to the storeroom beneath the keep to barricade themselves within. Mary knew she should join them, but was drawn to watch the battle as she had always done at Bailekair, instead. She turned, gathering up the long folds of her *arascaid* as she hurried to ascend the stairs to the upper chambers. She ran along the corridor, flung open the door to her room, then slammed it shut, shooting the bolt home with a bang and fingers that trembled. She leaned against the locked barrier, shaking for a moment, then moved toward the balcony, shading her eyes against the glare of the sun as she stepped outside. Mary gasped again. Oh, thank God, Joanna had taken the children into Wick this morning. At least they would be safe! For Mary did not delude herself into thinking the aged Baron and his few men-at-arms, numbering no more than fifty at the most, could succeed in defending the crumbling walls of the old castle against the force of attackers she saw massing like ants far below. There must have been twenty-five score or more of them, all armored for battle.

They had come well-prepared for the assault, as though they'd had several weeks to plan the siege, for this was no idle raid. There were three great catapults and wagons of heavy stones with which to load the horrible machines; numerous long ladders with which to scale the fortress walls; several thick, solid battering-rams and a large hide-covered shield thirty feet in length and fifteen feet in width beneath which those who wielded the stout, hammering logs would hover for protection from the hot black pitch and arrows that would pour upon them from the ramparts of the keep. In addition, there were several smaller leather-bound screens behind which the archers upon the ground would stand with their deadly crossbows to pick off like flies the men who would defend the machicolated battlements of Torra nam Sian.

The battle would be long and bloody, lasting mayhap a fortnight if those inside the castle walls were lucky, a few days at most if they were not. And then—and then— Mary could not finish the thought. When would it begin? Tomorrow? The next day? The attackers would surely level the grounds first. They would not be able to roll the siege contraptions up to the bases of the walls otherwise. Oh, pray Joanna would come, see what was happening, and ride for help before the terrible assault started, before death crept up with its silencing hand to smother the screams of the men-at-arms forever!

Nay! This wasn't occurring! This wasn't real! This wasn't how it had been at Belgrade! But this was Scotland, and for some strange reason the purple-and-blue *breaçans* of the Carmichaels had moved forward to begin the attack! 'Twas too soon! They could not possibly be prepared yet! Mary felt that morbid tingle of foreboding chase down her spine once more. Something was wrong. Oh, God, what was it? If only she could find out what was wrong, Lord Duncan's men could arm themselves against it. If only she could make out the faces of the Carmichaels below, she might gain some idea as to what treachery was being planned. Were they Hugh's men? Ian's? Lord Gilchrist's? The manner of the battle would be determined by the laird who led them. Gilchrist would fight fairly, but Hugh or Ian—

The walls of the fortress shook as the first of the heavy stones fired from the catapults began to hammer against them, rolling this way and that, bouncing haphazardly over whatever lay in their mindless paths before they lumbered to a shuddering stop and were still. Shouts arose. Confusion reigned. Apparently the Carmichaels decided this ploy would not work, for the catapults were slowly repositioned, the focus of their targets changed. Again and again as the day wore on the vast, cumbersome machines were moved until at last the boulders began to strike with accuracy against the iron portcullis and the solid wooden doors of the keep itself. But the great iron bars of the gate held, although they were beaten almost flat from the continuous barrage of rocks.

Meanwhile the archers set up their screens a short distance behind the catapults, loosing hordes of long arrows from their crossbows toward the Baron's men positioned on the ramparts. Mary could thank God the Carmichaels had not yet been able to get close enough to set their shafts afire before releasing them. Still, like mindless beasts the attackers inched ever nearer as the hours passed, and the girl knew it was only a matter of time before flaming arrows would start to come over the walls to burn that which lay within, creating chaos and havoc among the inhabitants of Torra nam Sian as they left their posts to put out the blazes.

Even now some of the more hotheaded of the Carmichaels were running forward with the ladders with which they hoped to scale the outer defense, standing the long, runged poles up against the walls, climbing upon them like monkeys as they dodged and twisted to avoid being knocked from their perches.

Already the dead lay heavily where they had fallen. The MacBeths hung like broken puppets over the ramparts of the outer wall, arrows shot from the deadly crossbows protruding from their bodies. The Carmichaels sprawled upon the ground, many burned beyond all recognition from the pots of hot black pitch that had been poured upon them from the machicolated battlements. The blood ran red, its pungent odor mingling with the even more sickening smell of charred flesh. Mary fought back the vomit that rose quickly from her stomach at the nauseating aroma. Screams pierced the air, horrible cries of agony and low, keening moans of anguish. Smoke filled the azure sky that was slowly turning to a deepening orange as the sun sank lower and lower on the western horizon. The vapors stung the lass's eyes as they swept the horrible *mêlée*. Her eyes watered as the prickling acridity of the fumes rose from the blazing tar buckets. She blinked. Her eyes blurred, cleared, then misted once more. She rubbed them fiercely.

The Carmichaels were close enough now that she could see their battle-hungry faces. Oh, God! It was Hugh! Hugh, who led the marauding men. Even the black billowing furls could not disguise his powerful figure, dark and evil, astride his bold ebony destrier in the distance. His white teeth gleamed as he suddenly spied Mary's cringing figure upon the balcony. He threw back his head and laughed, then shouted. *"Buaidh no Bàs! Buaidh no Bàs!"* The Carmichael war cry rang out over the field.

His battle-ax flashed, silver and shining, beneath the warm spring setting sun. He was directing several men, some of whom bore a stout battering-ram. The others carried the blanketlike length of tanned leather hide to use as a roof to protect themselves from the burning pitch. It was a haphazard device, normally saved for late in the battle, when the walls were not so well-defended. Och, why wasn't Hugh waiting for the time when the siege contraptions, that could house as many as a hundred men in relative safety, could be rolled up to the castle walls? Again Mary was struck by the chilling thought that something was wrong, but what? She was not a soldier. She could not guess. All she had seen looked perfectly normal to her untrained eyes based on the past battles she had watched. But most of those had been mere raids. Only Belgrade had been different. Oh, God, beloved, where are ye? Ye would know what is wrong. Help me! Help me! But Hunter was far away and unaware of her plight.

The men inched forward beneath the shields of skins. The tar poured down, splattering off the cover. Great splotches of the molten liquid ran down the sides of the hide onto the hands and arms of the men who carried it. Those ravaged by its searing flame dropped their portions of the blanket, writhing in pain upon the ground where they'd fallen. The others came on, paying no attention to their fellow men-at-arms. The leather had been treated with something, Mary realized, for

478

although it smoked and stank, it did not burn. The iron portcullis and heavy wooden doors of Torra nam Sian shuddered as the battering-ram struck once and then again and again before Hugh's men were forced to retreat, looking like a huge porcupine beneath the arrows sticking up from the skin roof.

Hugh's men regrouped, readying themselves for another assault upon the keep's defenses. Once more the portcullis and doors, already severely weakened by the catapults, groaned under the strain of the battering ram beating against them. Mary could not see it, but a large, gaping hole had been gouged into the wood of one of the doors that had finally splintered and broken under the stress of the pounding. Hugh smiled at the sight, motioning toward another force of men nearby. Those with the battering-ram withdrew. The others crept forth, dragging two massive barrels of hot tar with them. Beneath the protective cover of the hide blanket they managed to pour some of the black oil into the hole and down the front of the door. They set the buckets, still half-full, beneath this, then one man with a smaller casket stepped forward.

Something snapped in Mary's brain as she saw the tiny tun. Suddenly she knew what was wrong, what had nagged at her all day in the back of her mind. The storeroom. The odd storeroom at Dùndereen, built off into the ground away from the main keep and all the other edifices, with only the very top feet of the structure protruding above the earth. The storeroom into which no torch, nor even a candle could be carried. The storeroom for which Hugh had flogged a man nearly to death for entering with a lighted pipe.

"Do ye want to blow us all to smithereens?" the Earl had cried with fear and anger and flayed the poor man unmercifully.

Black powder! It must be! Mary had heard tales of such, but had never seen the like. 'Twas said it was employed by those in league with the devil and came from a land far to the east filled with people whose eyes slanted like cats' orbs. God only knew how Hugh had obtained it! Black powder! Oh, God, no wonder Hugh did not care, had not waited for the siege machines to be rolled up to the walls. He had no need of them. If the stories Mary had heard were true, the outer defense would be blown to bits in seconds! The battle would be over before the sun finished setting in the red glowing sky! Oh, God!

The man with the casket began to sprinkle the stuff around the pool of pitch that dripped upon the earth from the hole in the door. He encompassed the two barrels half-filled with tar, then scattered the remainder of the tun along the ground. It curled like a dark snake in a trail of dull crystals to where Hugh stood. Mary's husband took a torch from one of his men and lit the coiled stuff. It flamed up like some magic fire of Angelica Fleming's, eating its way rapidly along itself, hissing and shooting sparks as it disappeared, scorching a long dark mark upon the earth.

"Oh, God, no!" Mary breathed and yelled a frantic warning, but it was too late.

The blazing length had reached the hot tar at last.

None was prepared for what happened then. The whole world exploded, sending scraps of metal, shards of wood, and gushing fountains of pitch spewing in every direction. One portion of the castle wall crumbled, stones flying and bouncing this way and that. The Carmichaels streamed through the opening that had been blasted into being, clamoring over the dead bodies and debris, swords mowing down the remaining MacBeths, who stood awed, stunned, and afraid.

Lord Duncan shouted orders frantically, getting as many of his men as possible behind the inner wall before closing up its gatehouse, knowing it was but a futile gesture of defense to gain time, for the battle had already been lost. Hugh's men picked up their battering ram to repeat the process with which they'd gained entry into the outer bailey to force their way into the inner ward. Mary heard the clatter of boots as they pelted up the stairway to the upper chambers of the keep. Moments later there was an urgent pounding upon her door.

"Mary, lass, 'tis Lord Duncan; open up!"

She ran hurriedly to draw the lock and fling open the door.

"Oh, my lord, what are we to do?"

He slammed the barrier shut, bolting it once more, his face

blackened with soot and grime, his *breacan* smeared with blood and dirt, his jaw set in a hard grim line.

"Dinna fash yourself, lass, for I'll defend ye till my last breath." His eyes were defeated but determined.

"Nay! Oh, Lord Duncan, nay! 'Tis me Hugh wants! Let me go to him, put an end to this destruction!"

"Nay, lass, I canna let ye sacrifice yourself for me and all for naught besides, for ye know they willna take us alive. I must try to save ye at least."

"But why? Why? We're all doomed! 'Tis useless and senseless, my lord, to try and continue. Get oot! Get oot, my lord, while ye may still escape!"

"Nay, I canna."

"But—but why?"

"If only so I may die wie peace of mind, lass. Ye see, Mary, years ago when Hunter's mother ran off from the castle, Ranald wanted to search for her. He knew she was ill and feared for her well-being, even if she managed to reach her own people, which we surmised was her intent. I was a hard mon, and I refused to permit him to follow her. I had always been against the match from the beginning. I locked Ranald in the keep's dungeon. I dinna realize how much he truly loved Laureen. Well, the gypsy ne'er returned. After several weeks I released Ranald. He immediately went to look for his bride, but—but she was dead, or at least he said she was when he came back to Torra nam Sian. After several months of brokenhearted grief Ranald went up to the northern tower and hanged himself. My conscience has troubled me o'er it e'er since. I felt responsible, ye see, for my kinsman's death and for depriving Hunter of both his parents.

"Then ye came, ye, wie your accursed violet Carmichael eyes, and Hunter loved ye, loved ye beyond all reason. I knew he must to hae risked death for ye, for that is what ye would hae brought him had our clan discovered it. But I was glad he'd found ye, Mary, even if ye were an enemy, for ye loved him as deeply as he did ye. I could see it on your face when ye looked at him. I dinna wish to make another mistake I would regret for the rest of what little life I had left to me.

Ye needed help, and so I gae it to ye, putting aside the feud that has raged between our two clans for nearly a hundred years. I'm nae sorry I did, lass, for ye and the others ye brought wie ye hae brightened my dreary days these past few months. I—I hae come to care for ye, lass, even if ye did let me win at chess!''

Mary stared at the old laird. He had known about her all along, and he had not betrayed her. Tears sprang to her eyes and trickled down her cheeks.

''Forgie me. Forgie me. I'm sorry, my lord, so verra sorry I hae repaid your kindness wie—wie—''

''Ye couldna hae foreseen this, lass, so I've naught for which to forgie ye. Come, Mary. Chin up now. 'Tis me who should apologize for nae taking better care of ye. Hunter will hae my head on a platter for this.'' He attempted to smile, but they both knew it was the end for the grey-haired Baron. He would never see Hunter again. ''This mon—this Hugh—will he slay ye, lass?''

''Nay, my lord. He's—he's my husband,'' Mary whispered bitterly and related the story of her past. ''So, ye see, Lord Duncan, ye needna fear for me. Hugh will but seek to punish me in some manner.''

''Och, Mary, Hunter will come for ye; I know it,'' the elderly man said when she'd finished speaking. ''A love such as that between him and ye canna be denied. Aye, between ye both ye will put an end to this feuding and the curse that has lain wie its dark sorrow upon us all. I'm only sorry I shallna live to see it.''

''Oh, my lord!''

''Dinna fret yourself, Mary. I'm an auld mon, lass. I hae lived a full life and hae few regrets.'' The shouts and sharp ring of spurs upon the stone floor of the main hall warned them the keep itself had been invaded. Boots strode, rough and discordant, up the stairs. Someone beat upon the door, began to throw his weight against it determinedly, shoulder making a dull thud upon the wood. ''Come, lassie,'' Lord Duncan smiled. ''Gie an auld mon a kiss to take into battle and remember ye by.''

Sobbing, Mary flung her arms about him and kissed him tenderly. "Good-bye, my lord. God be wie ye," she choked out as the chamber door at last snapped from its hinges and fell upon the floor to admit the bold black viciously smirking figure of her husband.

With the great, bellowing war cry of the MacBeths the old laird drew his sword and charged toward his enemy. The fight was swift and fatal, its outcome never in doubt. Moments later the Baron of Torra nam Sian lay dead among the ruins of his might fortress. Mary knelt, weeping, over his brave, lifeless body. She raised her blurred violet eyes to where Hugh hovered over her, wickedly leering at her as he wiped the blood from his blade and sheathed it.

"Dinna tell me that auld bastard had ye, too, whore," he sneered in greeting.

"Nay, he—he was but kind to me," she said before her dark cousin yanked her to her feet and dragged her screaming from the room.

"Well, madam." Hugh shook Mary roughly in the main hall after his search of the castle had ended and his men slaughtered the rest of the MacBeths, who'd refused to surrender, knowing death was preferable to being taken alive by their enemies. "Where is the whoreson Romany? Where is your lover, bitch?"

"He wasna my lover!" Mary lied. "Why dinna ye tell me he lived? Ye knew it! Nay, dinna seek to deny it, my lord, for the Romany told me of Euphemia MacBeth's and Ian's treachery. Ian would hae informed ye the MacBeth still lived, lived to take his revenge against us. Ye knew it! And yet ye said naught of it to me. 'Twas his kinsman who took Joanna and the bairns. I—I saw it in a dream, and I rode to Glenkirk to offer myself in their place, to save *your* child, Hugh!" Mary prayed he would believe her. "But I was too late. The Romany lived, and ye hadna warned me of it. He—he slew my bairns—"

"Nay!" Hugh's voice sounded strangled.

"Aye, they're dead! Dead! And the Romany—the Romany—"

She broke off as though unable to continue, not daring to look at Hugh's dark, angry visage.

"Kept ye alive to whore for him," he finished. "I ask ye again, bitch, where is he?"

"He—he tired of me and—and gae me to Lord Duncan—Oh, God, ye whoreson murderer! Ye killed my brother, dear Gordie, ye and Ian! And now *ye* hae slain an auld mon who was naught but more kind to me than you'll e'er know and ne'er even touched me." She buried her face in her hands, crying piteously.

"Lower your voice, bitch!" Hugh hissed, glancing around quickly to be sure none had heard Mary's accusation. He saw with relief his men were too busy raping the maids they'd discovered in the storeroom and consuming the ale and wine that had been found in the larder to pay any attention to their lord and his cowering lady. "Ye would believe the lies of a whoreson MacBeth aboot me and your brother?"

Mary made no reply, recognizing her life hung in the balance. Hugh would no doubt slay her where she stood if she persisted in her assertion, for he would have to shut her up, just as he had done Gordon. She trembled.

"I dinna know what to believe, my lord," she answered at last.

"Of course nae," he jeered. "Ye are quite mad. Mad, I know." His black eyes were hard as they raked her. "And none shall listen to ye if ye repeat your tale, I promise ye. I'll hae to lock ye away when we get home, else ye do some harm to yourself or another," he threatened silkily. "You're dangerous, quite dangerous indeed, methinks. No doubt ye murdered your own babes. Aye, you're crazy. 'Tis what a crazy woman would hae done. Aye, I remember when I was but a bairn at Dùndereen an auld bawd in our village went mad and killed her own children, all five of them. She chopped them up wie a butchering knife and buried them on a small plot of land behind her thatched hut. Aye, you're quite mad, Mary. I will, indeed, hae to put ye away. I hae missed ye, bitch. Did ye know that? I hae missed our nights together and the perversions wie which I pleasured myself upon your body. I hae found some new ones, Mary. Aye, I shall lock ye up when we get back to Dùndereen and show them to ye. None shall mind your screams—and I promise ye will scream, whore. But then a madwoman always does. . . ."

Mary cringed away from him in horror as his voice trailed off, evil in its insinuation, as he reached for her, his hands cupping her breasts with wicked promise as he bent to grind his mouth down hard upon her own, shutting off her breath, nearly choking her to death as his fingers moved up to tighten around her throat. She struggled desperately against him, hating him as he pinioned her wrists behind her back, then slapped her across the face brutally, swearing a muttered oath. His eyes bored down into hers as though he would have liked to kill her. He caught her golden hair roughly, twisting her head up to meet his jeering lips once more, tearing at her *arascaid* with his free hand, exposing her ripe, heaving mounds.

"Be still, bitch!" he snarled when she resisted, trying to yank away from him and pull the edges of her bodice together. "Be still, or I'll strip ye naked and gie ye to my men for sport!"

Mary ceased her futile attempts to escape him, trembling with rage and fear at her helplessness. He pushed her back upon a long hunting table at one end of the room. Dear God, he was going to rape her in the presence of all his men, some of whom were rutting away between the thighs of the captured serving maids, uncaring that the other men were lined up behind them awaiting their turns, wine and ale trickling from their lustful mouths as they watched the savage couplings, laughing as the women screamed and screamed at the indignities perpetrated upon their bodies. Mary moaned as Hugh lowered his mouth to one of her breasts, sucking at the nipple cruelly, biting her sharply with his teeth. She closed her eyes, feeling herself sinking into the horror of before. Her hands flailed about her wildly, weakly as she felt his bulging manhood pressed up against the softness of her thighs, felt his hands and knees begin to haul her *arascaid* up, pry her flanks apart. Her fingers curled into little claws. The knuckles of one hand hit some solid, metal object hurtfully. Her eyes flew open. It was a candle sconce of heavy gold. Her fingers stretched out desperately, closed around the ornate pedestal that rose up from the base of the thing in gentle, graceful curves. She half-raised herself against Hugh. He glanced up, wrathful and surprised at this new resistance. Mary smashed him in the face with the candelabra. He fell backward, his hands jammed upon his countenance to stop the flow of blood that spurted from his broken nose. He gave a cry of outrage, howling with ire as Mary rolled from the table and began to run.

She had freed Desmond from the debris of the ruined stables and mounted him before Hugh's men caught her, pulling her from the horse's back.

"Nay, dinna touch the bitch!" Hugh spat as he walked toward her slowly, menacingly, a cold damp rag pressed to his dark angry visage. "I'll punish her for the deed myself when we get home. Mount up! We'll start back for Dùndereen tonight. 'Tis a five-day ride from here, madam. Ye hae that long to wait—that long for your fear of me to grow like a snake crushing your heart wie'in your breast—that long to dwell upon the unpleasant things that I intend to do to ye when we arrive. Tonight was but a taste of what I hae in mind for ye, whore! God's wounds, but ye will pay for daring this," he said, indicating his broken, bleeding nose. "I'll hurt ye in ways ye ne'er dreamed possible, and when I'm through, I'll take ye abroad, to Spain, and sell ye to the first Moorish whorehouse dealer I find!"

Oh, God, please let this be a nightmare! Mary prayed feverishly. Please let me wake up and find myself safe in Hunter's arms! But she knew her husband's threats were only too real and that he would indeed carry them out without another thought. She trembled violently as she rode out through the sorrowful, ravaged walls of Torra nam Sian, Hugh Carmichael keeping pace ominously at her side.

*. . . for destruction will travel in her wake, and it must be borne.*

486

Joanna stared at the cataclysmic ruins of the fortress, a deep foreboding welling up inside her breast. She shook as she stepped down from Lord Duncan's carriage and made her way through the debris piled high at the place where the doors to the mighty castle had once stood.

"Mary?" Her voice echoed strangely in the night, quivering slightly. "Mary?"

"She's nae here." One of Lord Duncan's men came to inform the girl after the Baron's men-at-arms who had accompanied her that morning had searched the fortress thoroughly and reported the keep empty of all save dead bodies, one of which had been their lord, but none of which had belonged to the Lady Mary. "She may still be alive, my lady. Dinna despair. We'll find her."

Joanna's eyes were blinded by tears, and the children, upon gaining some small inkling of what had happened, set up a wail as well. The maid stumbled over a corpse in the half-light of the torches as she tried to return to the coach to comfort the bairns. The body rolled over, glaring up at her evilly. 'Twas Connall, Hugh Carmichael's master-at-arms.

"Oh, my God," the lass moaned in horror. "Hugh has her."

"Hugh?" Lord Duncan's man-at-arms questioned.

"'Tis too long a story to explain right now." Joanna attempted to regain control of herself, thinking rapidly, anxiously. She laid her hand on the man's arm. "Dickon, Sir Hunter's—wife is in grave danger. Ye and those few men who are left must escort myself and the children to—" To where? "To Lord Bothwell's castle in the Border Lands." The girl remembered Hunter's words to Mary about seeking Jane Gordon Hepburn's protection. "Your laird is dead. Ye are no longer bound to him. Aye, ye must take us to Bothwell, and pray the Hepburn will aid my lady!"

# Thirty-three

The long corridor danced with dark flickering shadows as Hugh made his way down the torch-lined hall of Dùndereen to the tower where he had thrown Mary upon their arrival at the keep and locked her in. Rudely he dismissed the guard at the door, then took the ring with its single key from a peg upon the wall.

Mary looked up with fear as he entered the room, for she had been anxiously awaiting his coming ever since dusk had settled upon the land and the moon had begun to creep upon silver feet through the one narrow window the circular chamber contained. For five days they had ridden across the Highlands before reaching Dùndereen, and not once had Hugh attempted to touch her. So tonight Mary had known he would come. Come to beat and abuse and rape her. She had shuddered at the prospect, quivered, and wept until she'd choked on her tears and rage at her helplessness. She could not bear it—not again. He had spoiled and sullied her once, broken her spirit, invaded her body, tortured her mind. He had reduced her to filth, and only Hunter's deep love and sensitivity had made her clean. She did not mean to suffer humiliation and degradation at Hugh's hands again—ever. But as his prisoner Mary had seen no way out for herself, no way—except one. She had agonized over her decision for hours as the time had passed and the twilight fallen and finally, with calm serenity, had reached the only conclusion acceptable to her tormented soul. She had decided to kill herself. It was a mortal sin, she knew, but she'd determined she'd rather be damned eternally than submit to Hugh Carmichael once more. Only the painful thought of leaving Hunter and her bairns forever had swayed her resolve, but then Mary had realized she could never face them again if she had to do it bruised and battered and stinking of Hugh's seed.

Only the horror of thinking she might not have the courage to carry out the fatal deed caused her violet eyes to leap with fright now as she gazed at her husband.

His feet were wide apart as he watched her. One hand rested on his swaggered hips; the other stroked his clan-belt lightly in anticipation, as though he were already savoring, in his brain, the things he intended to do to her. Not even the hunted, trapped look in Mary's eyes disturbed him. Indeed he took pleasure in seeing how she cowered before him across the room. His own black shards narrowed. He smirked as he saw her hand slide to her gold mesh girdle, her fingers wrap compulsively about her many-gemmed dirk. She pulled it from her belt, holding it warily. She was going to fight, by God. She was going to fight!

A surge of desire raced through Hugh's loins at the realization. How he wanted her. He was obsessed with her. For over three years, nearly four, he had lived without her and had not been able to banish the longing for her body that had engulfed his being each time he'd thought of her and determined to get her back. He'd relived their days and nights together over and over again in his mind, recalling how she'd writhed upon the floor as he'd beaten her, slashing her golden flesh with his leather clan-belt, punishing her for daring to think him tainted with his mother's madness. How he'd jammed his mouth down on hers until her lips had swollen from his harsh kisses. How he'd bruised her ripe breasts with his cruel, vicious hands. How he'd spread her pale flanks and hammered deep between them as she'd cried out, begging him for mercy. How he'd laughed and cut off her screams with his hard maleness before flipping her over to take her in a third, even more sordid manner. His manhood bulged against his codpiece as he remembered. Mary shivered at the sight.

Oh, God, gie me strength, and forgie my weakness, she prayed desperately, but 'tis too much to ask of me. I canna—willna!—bear it again!

"So, my wee half-wit, we are alone at last," Hugh said, his voice thick and hushed with lust. "I dreamed of ye these many nights past, and your verra nearness during our travels honed my desire to a feverish pitch. I would hae taken ye upon the road, but, of course, we couldna then hae enjoyed our little preliminaries."

"Dinna ye mean ye couldna hae enjoyed them, Hugh? After all, even the most brutal of your men would hae shuddered to see a lady of gentle birth so ill-treated and used."

"Lady?" he sniggered. "I thought we both understood ye are naught save a whore, Mary. A crazy whore who slew her own children and became so foully deranged even the Romany MacBeth could no longer stomach her."

"I dinna kill my bairns." Mary's words came through clenched teeth, for it was all she could do not to fling the fact that the children still lived in his smirking visage. "I told ye—"

"Do ye think I care what ye said? It suits my purposes to hae my men believe ye destroyed my babe and Edward's, whether ye did or nae. They're still dead either way, and I—I am wie'oot an heir, madam. 'Tis time, aye, I think 'tis time to get another one on ye." He began to remove his clothes slowly, his black raking eyes never leaving her frightened countenance.

"Nay, Hugh, you'll nae hae me again, not now or e'er," Mary said softly.

He laughed. The sound rang oddly, hollowly, evilly in the chamber. "Do ye really think ye can slay me wie that?" He indicated the dagger she wielded purposefully. "You'll be lucky to even wound me, bitch, and I shall delight in using it on ye once I hae wrested it from your grasp. Aye, we've nae played that sport, hae we, Mary? I'm good wie a dirk, verra good. I can cut ye up in all manners of ways. Oh, you'll survive of course, but I doubt you'll want to look in a mirror afterward—''

"I dinna intend the knife for ye, my lord," Mary responded with a strange coolness, feeling vaguely detached from the entire drama now that her mind was made up. Soon, soon she would be free—free forever from Hugh's cruel bondage and sadistic games. Her soul would be unchained to fly unfettered from all earthly trials. Her father, Edward, and her brother, dear Gordon, would be waiting for her. Aye, even now she could see them standing in the shadows just beyond, where they danced sadly upon the dark, grey green waves of the Loch Ness to the sorrowful music of the monster's woeful keening. " 'Tis for me. I would rather die than hae ye touch me again!" She raised the dagger, turning it inward so the blade pointed at herself, sharp and deadly as she lowered it until its finely honed tip pressed against the center of her chest between the soft golden mounds that rose and fell rapidly there.

Hugh hissed, a sudden swift intake of breath as he stared at her, mesmerized by her actions. "I canna believe ye will really do it." He was startled by the thought, for he did not want her to die. Nay, he wanted her to live and suffer!

"I will, I promise ye that. I will!"

He stiffened with anger, recognizing at last she spoke the truth. "There is no need to commit a mortal sin, whore. Ye hae saved yourself from my beastly attentions—for tonight at least! Aye, I shall leave ye here alone to dwell upon your perfidy. Ye would live the life of a nun? Well, then, madam, ye will! May your prayers provide ye sustenance, for I shallna—that is, until ye change your mind, bitch. And ye will. Ye will grow cold and hungry. 'Twillna be pleasant, slowly starving to death. Aye, ye will change your mind, and welcome my embrace before I'm through wie ye!"

"I shall use this dirk afore then, my lord, make no mistake aboot that!"

"Will ye? Well, we shall see, whore. Death is so—final,

Mary. Think aboot that. Ye willna be so bonnie once the worms hae finished wie ye!''

Then he turned on his heel and left her alone in the darkness of the tower. She waited and waited, but he did not come back, nor did Hugh send any supper to her. How long? How long, Mary thought desperately, can I hold oot against him before I am forced to plunge this dagger into my breast? Oh, beloved, where are ye? Where are ye? But there was no answer. Outside, upon the Highland moors, the heather was almost in full blossom, and still Hunter did not come.

The ship tossed and pitched upon the high seas, caught in the rough swell of a violent May storm. The rain battered the sails and deck, beating an ominous tattoo of spurts and splashes against the cloth that ripped and flapped in the high wind and the wood of the timbers that groaned and creaked as the vessel strained to stay afloat. The shouts of the sailors were lost over the roar of the gale and the thunder that crashed among the massing dark clouds. Lightning cracked, sending sparks of St. Elmo's green fire dancing along the lengths of rope that were lashed to the masts to hold the sails fast. At the ship's wheel the captain tried furiously to maintain his present heading, but 'twas useless. The vessel could not respond in the face of the relentless weather and was blown some distance off course again, nearing the shores of France rather than those of England, which had been the ship's final destination. Of her twin sister there was no sign. Had the other vessel been lost as well?

Hunter MacBeth lay on his back in his bunk, staring up at the low ceiling.

"She's veered off course again. The captain canna hold her," he remarked unnecessarily, for he knew Cadman too realized the ship had changed direction.

"He'll steer her around soon enough," the younger MacBeth offered for the sake of conversation.

"Nae in this storm."

Silence fell once more in the black gloom of the cabin. Though not by profession sailors, both the MacBeths had had enough sense not to attempt lighting a candle while the vessel was heaving upon the waves. The tallow would only have bounced about the room, possibly starting a fire on board.

"Damn Jamie," Hunter swore softly.

"Aye, this whole mission has been little more than a jest," Cadman agreed. "I've no stomach for it now. I do but long for my lassie and bairns."

"Aye." Hunter nodded.

Indeed the entire scheme had gone awry from its beginning. It had taken weeks to get the two ships provisioned and the entourage for the invasion into England assembled. The force itself had been small in numbers, for Jamie had not wished for open war with his enemy to the south, only to worry King Henry VII like a dog a bone. Undermanned, the group had at last set out, recognizing that if they were apprehended, the King of Scotland, quite possibly, intended to disavow any knowledge of the plan, thereby leaving them to England's mercy. Needless to say, morale had not been high at the onset and had only gotten discouragingly worse as the weeks had passed. Not only was Perkin Warbeck an impostor (which all knew, despite his protests to the contrary), but he was a damned poor sailor, besides. The Pretender had been sick for most of the voyage, puking up whatever food he'd managed to get down and making an absolute nuisance of himself as well. He'd insisted on being addressed as "Your Grace, King Richard III of England," even though 'twas the title the dead Prince's uncle had stolen and that, even less rightfully, belonged to the young impostor. Hunter had not understood how Kate Gordon had been able to stand the self-pitying wretch and liar; but somehow she had, for she'd remained constantly at her husband's side, cleaning up his vomit and soothing his whining complaints with tender words.

In March the first of the early spring rains had begun with their torrential high winds that set the waves to rolling wildly and tore at the sails of the vessels unmercifully, sending the ships way off course, blowing them almost to Cleves. They had started south once more, only to have one of the ships veer off the projected path of travel through the mistaken calculations of a drunken navigator, who was bent on directing the ship to Braganza. Then the Pretender had insisted they visit his "aunt" in Burgundy and would have sent the captains sailing up the Seine to accomplish this had not Hunter firmly countermanded the order. Lord, what a mess!

Hunter tapped his fingers impatiently along the side of his bunk. They would have to turn back. The wind was against them, had been against them from the beginning. James ought to have foreseen this, consulted his naval advisors before sending the vessels out. Aye, they would have to turn back to Scotland. To Scotland—and Mary.

Where was she now, his brave, bonnie lassie? Had Lord Duncan kept her safe as promised? Oh, how Hunter wished now he'd gone ahead and asked the Hepburn to take Mary and the others in, even though he'd known Lord Bothwell would have been forced to refuse the request. Oh, Mary! Mary! Even her name tormented Hunter. Day and night she had haunted him on this miserable voyage, filling up his senses with memories of her gilded being. Mary standing barefoot in the heather on the Highland moors, gold and purple like herself and just as sweetly fragrant as she turned and smiled at him before running to the shelter of his strong arms where he waited, cast in shadows, in the doorway of the kirk. Mary galloping toward him over the frozen, snow-covered ground, cloaked in frost and shrouded in mist as grey as the clouds that darkened his horizon each time she rode away. Mary, tall and proud in the box at the King's summer tourney, her long spun-gold tresses billowing about her lithe figure like a lover's caress in the wind, wrapping about his throat, lying dear and shorn in a jeweled casket at the Sultan's feet. Mary whirling challengingly, her violet eyes shooting sparks of desire as she danced at their gypsy wedding flirting with the black snaking whip he coiled about her expertly to draw her close. Mary laughing as he teased that soft place upon her shoulder, sobbing his name as he drove between her thighs, bringing her to glorious heights of rapture and surrender. Mary, flushed and trimphant as she handed him Magnus, their son.

My love! Ye are so real I can almost taste your scarlet mouth, feel the silky strands of your cascading mass of hair, touch your pale satin flesh. Oh, beloved!

Hunter jumped up from his bunk, determination setting his jaw in a hard line as he sought out the captain of the vessel, the wind nearly knocking him to his knees as he made his way above deck to the helm where the captain was struggling with the wheel. The rain pelted them both savagely.

"Turn this ship around, mon! Take her back to Scotland!" Hunter yelled above the raging torrent of the storm. "We canna land, and we're off course again. That young fool will see us in Burgundy or dead ere we reach our destination. Turn around, I say!"

"But—but, sir, King Richard—"

"King Richard be damned! 'Tis King Jamie's mon ye are. Do as I tell ye, or I'll hae your head on a platter, I promise ye. I am in charge of this mission. His Grace entrusted me wie the Pretender's safety. We canna land. We hae tried twice and failed. The winds are against us. The mission to England must be aborted until a future date. Now turn this ship around, and head for home!"

"Aye, sir. As ye wish, sir." The captain swallowed hard, wishing fervently he'd never undertaken this thankless task.

Hunter fought his way to the rail, his eyes raking the shifting, grey green waters of the brutally swirling sea far and beyond through the rain and mist. Beloved, I am coming home to ye. I am coming home!

In late June they landed at Berwick on the River Tweed, in spite of Perkin Warbeck's protests, complaints, and threats to report Hunter and Cadman both to the King for their "unspeakable conduct." The MacBeths did not care. They wanted only to get off the misfortunate vessel and away from the doomed impostor as quickly as possible. Berwick was not far from Patrick Hepburn's holding, Bothwell, and 'twas for this Hunter and Cadman rode after the others had set them and their destriers ashore, the young pretender insisting the rest continue on to Leith and from there to Edinburgh to present his case against the MacBeths to Jamie.

"That fool lad will wind up in the Tower," Cadman muttered as they spurred their steeds from the city limits.

"Methinks ye speak verily, brother," Hunter replied with a tight smile that did not quite reach the corners of his glittering eyes.

"James may truly be angry, Hunter. 'Twas a wee bit high-handed we both were wie that young mon and the captain, too. Lord! What a sorry tangle! I wish I'd kept my mouth shut, instead of adding my voice of discontent to your own."

"I dinna care. I hae a yearning for my lady and babes, and no mon will gainsay me."

"Aye, let us ride, sir, for my interests are the same as your own."

Dawn broke over the horizon as they picked their way through the Cheviot Hills that separated Scotland from England and made a jagged silhouette against the sweep of the sky, pale pink touched with fiery orange and just the barest hint of blue at the moment. To the south, just beyond the vast panorama of the hilly terrain, lay Northumberland, land of the mighty English Percys. To the west were the strongholds of the Hepburns and the Homes, the Scottish Border lords who each singly could rally four thousand men successfully to the King's cause or against him, as they had proven in the last rebellion.

The two men spoke little during the ride, each dwelling on his own thoughts in silence. There was no need to voice their fears aloud, for Hunter and Cadman had grown even more close as the years had passed and were more often than not in harmony with one another. They stopped twice, once along the roadside to eat the meal of hard bread, cheese, and dried meat they carried in their leather pouches from the ship, washing it down with cool water from a stream, and once at an inn in a small village to pass the night. There a couple of barmaids winked at them fetchingly, obviously more than willing to share the warmth of their beds that evening. Both men refused the invitation, but Hunter, recalling how years ago just such a woman had delayed him on his way to Stirling and how because of her he'd been caught in the summer storm and met Mary in the poor thatched hovel, gave each of the wenches a sovereign, watching with amusement as the maids bit into the coins wonderingly, not quite believing they were real.

"Why'd ye do that?" Cadman glanced at his kinsman questioningly.

Hunter smiled. "Because I once lied to ye, brother."

Cadman was puzzled. "Ye did? When?"

"When I told ye years ago Craigor could outrun the wind."

Understanding dawned. Cadman grinned.

"Just think, brother, if you'd nae had an ache in your loins for that bit of tavern fluff, you'd hae ne'er gotten drenched and found Mary."

"Aye, strange, isna it, the way little twists of fate change the courses of our lives, our destinies?"

"Aye," Cadman answered softly, thinking of how his lust for revenge had led him to Joanna.

Their mood pensive, the two men finished their ale in silence, then retired for the evening. They were up and moving again early the next morning, and by late afternoon could see Bothwell Castle looming ahead in the distance. The sight spurred them on.

"I'll warrant Patrick will be surprised to see us." Cadman's merry blue eyes twinkled at Hunter.

Hunter found for once he could not smile back at his engaging foster brother.

"I doubt the Hepburn's even in residence," he said grimly. "'Tis Jane I wish to see. Mayhap she can soothe Lord Bothwell's anger when he discovers we hae abandoned the mission and jumped ship, and he in turn will keep Jamie's wrath from descending upon us both just long enough for me to make certain Mary will be safe fore'er from Hugh Carmichael."

"Hunter, I beg of ye, dinna do aught rash in this matter. 'Tisna like ye to be so hotheaded."

"Ye wed a Carmichael woman, Cadman, and ye are under her spell as surely as I hae fallen under Mary's. Can ye nae understand the way I feel? Och, brother, what is it aboot them? I swear I love my lassie beyond all reason."

"Aye, I know what ye mean, and I hae oft asked myself that same question, but hae found no answer to it, unless 'tis that they are true and steadfast in their love, wild and passionate in their desire. Aye, they are fit mates for a mon, our Carmichael women."

"Methinks ye speak verily, sir," Hunter stated as they reached the outer gatehouse of Bothwell.

The two men were known to be particular friends of the Hepburn and were admitted without difficulty or question, then passed through to the inner bailey, where a couple of men-at-arms were explaining the rudiments of swordplay to a group of young lads, who were listening intently, eyes glowing with excitement as they attempted to mimic the older men's movements with their own small weapons. Even Hunter smiled at the sight, thinking how often Geoffrey and Ranald had gathered round him just so to learn what he might safely teach them about the basics of handling a sword or dirk. Two of the boys even reminded him of his sons. He neared the small circle from which shouts and laughter arose. Indeed it—it *was* Geoffrey and Ranald! Hunter's heart leapt to his throat, an icy chill of fey foreboding running up his spine as his oldest lad suddenly saw him and broke away from the others with a sobbing, heart-wrenching cry.

"Father! Oh, father! I knew ye would come! I knew it! Oh, father, Uncle Hugh killed Lord Duncan and took mama away from Torra nam Sian!"

Hunter's whole world shook and dropped out from beneath him as his belly began to churn sickeningly, and his hands tightened on his destrier's reins at the boy's words. Nay! Nay! 'Twasna true! 'Twasna true! He slid from the saddle to grasp the child to his pounding chest.

"Are—are ye sure, son?" He still dared to hope the lad was mistaken, though he knew in his heart Geoffrey spoke the truth.

"Aye, father. Oh, father, 'tis all my fault! Cousin Jo took us into Wick to go a'Maying, and I—I wasna there to protect mama as ye charged me to do! Uncle Hugh came while we were gone and blew up the fortress wie something. Dickon, one of Lord Duncan's men, called it 'black powder.' 'Twas— 'twas a terrible sight, father, the castle. There was blood and—and burned bodies e'erywhere. We looked and looked, but we couldna find mama. Cousin Jo recognized some of the dead men who—who were nae too—too—"

"I understand, son." Hunter realized the little boy was about to be sick at the memory. "Go on, Geoffrey."

"Och, father, they were Uncle Hugh's men. That's how we knew he'd taken mama away. I'm sorry, father. I wasna there—"

"Ye are nae to blame, son. There was naught ye could hae done." Hunter's dark visage was grim with fear as Joanna ran toward them from the keep.

"Jo!" Cadman caught her in his arms, nearly breaking her bones as he crushed her to him. "Thank God, ye are safe!"

Hunter stared at them and for one horrible moment wished it had been Joanna the Earl of Dùndereen had taken captive. He hated himself for the thought as soon as it occurred to him and repented his selfishness. Joanna guessed what he must be feeling and stepped forward hesitantly after gently disengaging herself from her husband's tight grasp. She laid her hand upon Hunter's arm.

"I'm sorry, Hunter," she spoke quietly, her honeyed eyes wide and frightened and filled with pity for him. "Geoffrey shouldna hae broken the news to ye so heedlessly. Och, if only she'd come a'Maying wie us— If only we'd known—I brought the bairns here. Lord Duncan's men escorted us. I dinna know what else to do—"

"Ye did all ye knew, Joanna." Hunter's face softened. "Dinna blame yourself." He was momentarily kind, for he realized the maid loved Mary, too, and beneath her solemn demeanor was desperately distraught with frantic worry and the fact that she had been helpless to do more. "God's blood! Two months! Nearly two months she has been in that whoreson's clutches! Has he harmed her? Is she still alive? Och, Joanna, do ye know aught of my lady?''

"She is alive, Hunter, but verra ill. Jane sent word to Patrick at Holyrood Palace when we arrived here. He rode to Dùndereen as soon as he was able. I believe he was sore grieved for ye both and his part in your separation. He found Mary near starved and—and—Och, Hunter, he says she is—is oot of her mind wie—wie madness!''

"Nay!"

"Aye, 'tis the God's truth, I swear it! Hugh—Hugh— Och, Hunter, ye dinna know what the Carmichael—what he—''

"Aye, Joanna, I *do* know— Oh, God, I'll kill him! If 'tis the last thing I ere do, I'll kill him!''

# Thirty-four

Time crawled by for Mary. Hugh kept her a prisoner in the castle keep, locked up in the tower both day and night, continuing his charade with the servants of her "madness," so that all were afraid to attend her or even to speak to her, thereby effectively cutting off any chance she might have gained for aid or escape. Alone, shut off from the rest of the world, devoid of news, even some small message or word that might have given her hope, she was slowly but surely dying. The hunger pains were not so bad—not now—not after more than a fortnight of fasting; but the thirst, dear God, the incredible thirst! Her tongue was so dry and swollen she could not speak; her lips too had swelled and cracked. Daily she grew weaker and weaker, not knowing how much longer she could hold out against her husband, who came each evening to gloat over her, taunt her, try to bully or wheedle her into changing her mind, depending upon his mood. But Mary only huddled in one corner with the knife pressed up against her breast, her violet eyes haunted and slowly losing all sense of reality. Only the fading memory of a tall dark man who had loved her once and been kind kept her alive.

She was exhausted from the strain of the constant vigil she maintained, resting only in snatches, fearing Hugh would come in while she slept, wrest the dagger from her grasp, and rape her. She did not close her eyes easily, and even when she was overcome by sheer fatigue, her wary dozing was troubled by a foreboding dream that came to her again and again during that time she spent in the tower a captive.

The dream was like her nightmare of that Lammas Eve so many years past, but different from it as well. Like the other it was dark in this dream, and the grey mist swirled about her so thickly she could scarcely see. But there the resemblance ended, for in this dream she was standing on the edge of the cliff overlooking the stormy, grey green waters of Loch Ness. From their murky whirling depths the black monster glided silently upward like a giant snake arising from the whitecapped waves. It crooned that same sad lament she had heard once before, weeping mournfully in the night. Ghosts danced about it on the lake. She recognized with a shock her father, Edward, and Gordon among them as they had looked in death, bloodied, with pain etched deeply into their faces. She called to them, but they could not hear her, perhaps could not even see her as she tried frantically to reach them only to find them always just beyond her grasp.

Only the girl, Anne MacBeth, came close, floating over the waters to run sorrowfully upon the golden sands of the beach, eyes upturned toward the cliff where Mary stood, a solitary shadow against the silver of the full moon. By the gleaming light Mary could see the crystal tears frozen on the MacBeth lass's cheeks. The maid's arms were uplifted, as though she were trying to tell Mary something, but could not speak. She seemed to be pointing toward the kirk—the kirk where Hunter and Mary had lain and loved.

Mary turned and walked toward the beckoning church, half-expecting, half-hoping to see Hunter there in its doorway waiting for her, but there was no sign of him, nor of his pale white destrier in the shadows. She walked on, and her heart leapt and sank in her breast, thudding hard and slowly with mounting terror. A strange empty ache filled her senses and made her sick at the pit of her belly. For there, in the small fenced yard behind the kirk where she had seldom been, lay a single grave.

Ominously it lured her, enticed her closer with its horrifying grip, so strong she could not escape it. On and on it pulled her toward itself until she stood upon its very mound, staring down at the grey granite marker at its fore. Her heart pounded violently in her breast, for the most macabre image was still to come.

She gazed at the stone and saw it was smooth, blank, unchiseled. There were no words upon the tomb to tell her to whom it belonged. Was it hers? Hunter's? Oh, God, who lay within that dark hole in the ground? She did not know. Mary only knew it waited for her and her alone. Then suddenly, as she watched it, the earth broke apart, and one bony hand reached forth from the grave, its index finger pointing toward the kirk eerily.

It was here Mary always awakened from the clutches of her nightmare in a cold sweat, heart beating as though it were going to burst within her breast, the screams tearing soundlessly from her throat.

What did it mean? God's wounds, what did it mean? Was she going to die? Or was it Hunter who already lay dead somewhere far beyond her reach? Was that what the terrifying dream was trying to tell her? Oh, God, no! No! she prayed fervently each time she awoke from its dreaded clutches. He's alive! He's alive! He will come for me; I know he will! She told herself over and over, tried to keep his dark handsome image from slipping from her mind.

But the heather bloomed purple on the Highland moors, and still Hunter did not come.

Mary grew gaunt and listless, a pale wraith of herself, a ravaged ghost of her former elusive, savage beauty. Dark rings formed beneath her violet eyes to match the haunting color of their irises. She felt trapped in the tower, doomed. She began to fear for her very sanity, to believe she truly was going crazy; and the thought compounded her horror. It was such a fine line, a slender threat that separated reality from the edge of madness. Hugh had driven her over its border once before, tormented her into that pit of blackness from which she'd thought there was to be no escape for her. Had he managed it again? Oh, dear Virgin Mary! Were her nightmares but dreams, or were they hallucinations?

One day she opened her mouth and found she could not speak, could force no sound from her lips, not even a silent scream. She froze at the realization, panicked before she remembered she'd had naught to drink for over a fortnight, had seen no one to talk to, not even a servant. Only Hugh came to the miserable chamber to stare at her and mock her, taunting them both with his evil suggestions, each knowing he feared now to carry them out—now that Mary's dirk lay between them. How cruelly he treated her, sometimes eating his evening meal a few feet from where she shivered against one wall, starving, dying of thirst, while he spilt his wine upon the floor carelessly, laughing as it ran red upon the stones like blood.

Mary never gave him the satisfaction of a reply, of seeing her waver from her purpose, only gazed at him steadily until he left her alone once more, whereupon she collapsed upon the floor and felt the black angel of Death hovering over her in the distance. How long could it continue? How long before Hugh's tales of her insanity were no longer lies, but truth? She tried to sing, to start her voice working again, but her vocal chords refused to respond. Nevertheless she kept hearing a strange mournful melody over and over again in her mind, as though someone were humming in her ear. It was some time before she realized the odd little song was the funeral dirge of the Loch Ness monster's weeping lament, and she wept, too, bittersweet tears of fright at the knowledge.

It was thus Patrick Hepburn found her when, after receiving his wife's urgent message and spending several days wrestling with his conscience, he finally rode to Dùndereen and demanded Hugh admit him to the tower wherein Mary was lodged at once, waving aside the Earl's protestations with an impatient motion of his hand.

"Dinna seek to bully me or play me for a fool, my lord," Lord Bothwell stated grimly, his eyes hard and cold as they raked the arrogant Carmichael. "For I amna an addle-wit, nor does your black visage make me quake in my boots, mon. Take me to the Lady Mary at once, or 'twillna go well for ye, I promise ye! Dinna forget I stand close to the King, my Lord Hugh, verra close indeed!"

Patrick stared at the pale, shadowed ghost of Mary Carmichael, and his heart ached for her. Hunter MacBeth had not lied about the laird of Dùndereen. The Hepburn wanted to slay the Earl himself as he bent to lift the man's wife to her feet. She doesna even know me, he thought. She isna even conscious. Her eyes flickered open briefly, and she made a weak, futile attempt to struggle against him, arms flailing about wildy as she searched for the dagger that had fallen from her desperate grasp.

"Lady Mary? Lady Mary. 'Tis I, Patrick Hepburn. Can ye hear me? Ye hae naught to fear from me, lass."

She was still once more, and he feared she had fainted again, then realized it was but taking time for her purple orbs to adjust to the light of the torches and grew even more angry upon recognizing she'd been kept in perpetual darkness, with only the narrow slit of her one window to brighten her dreary days. He shook her gently.

"Lady Mary. How long since ye hae eaten or drunk, lass? Can ye answer me?"

She gazed at him, wide-eyed, with amethyst jewels he could have jealously coveted, violet pools he could have gladly drowned in, and he understood then why Hunter MacBeth loved her so. It was those eyes. They were haunting, savage, beautiful, those accursed Carmichael eyes. They could drive a man out of his mind with wanting her.

She tried to speak; her voice croaked, rasped, made a small, pitiful sound.

"Water!" Lord Bothwell cried. "Water!"

He held the chalice to Mary's lips and raised her head so that she might drink, for she was too weak and exhausted by her ordeal to even manage that unaided.

"Slowly, lass, slowly, or you'll be sick," the Hepburn said gently.

"Patrick?" she managed at last, suddenly seeming to recognize him. "Oh, Patrick! Where is he? Why hasna he come?" she sobbed and flung her arms about Lord Bothwell's neck.

His own limbs tightened around her protectively as he crushed her to his chest and attempted to stifle her whispered outburst, her choking gasps. He stroked her hair lightly.

"Hush, lass, hush. Ye hae been ill. Ye must get well now. I am here to see ye do."

Somehow she understood him and the warning he sought to give her. She tried to pull herself together.

"Aye. I hae been ill." She shrank against him, suddenly observing Hugh standing in the doorway.

Patrick noted the frightened, flinching movement, turned wrathfully toward the Earl. "Is this how ye hae tended your 'sick' wife, mon? Locking her up in a dark room? Starving her to death? Refusing to quench her thirst? By God, I ought to flay ye alive for this! Get oot! Get oot of my sight at once! I am taking the Lady Mary downstairs. Hae another chamber prepared for her immediately. Christ's son! James will learn of this, my lord, I promise ye! I warn ye, ye had best treat your lady wie the kindness she warrants in the future, or ye will be the one who is 'ill,' my lord, I swear it! Sweet *Jesù!* Even a lowly animal deserved better than this!"

A room below on the second floor of the keep next to Lord Bothwell's was made ready, for Hugh was truly afraid of the second most powerful man in all Scotland. God only knew what the Hepburn intended to do to him, and Patrick *did* have the King's ear. Goddamn Mary! The bitch! The whore! Hugh ought to have killed her at Torra nam Sian! Now she was likely to escape his clutches again, the slut!

Patrick carried Mary downstairs and laid her tenderly upon the bed.. "Rest, my lady," he told her quietly. "Rest, and get well." Her closed eyes flew open in fear. She grabbed at him, frightened. "Nay, I'll nae leave ye. I gie ye my word, lass," he reassured her firmly.

Safe at last she slept and did not awaken again for many days. Delirious, she cried out often in her sleep, still terrified by her grueling ordeal. The Hepburn watched her ceaselessly, sadly, sending word to his anxious wife that Mary Carmichael was out of her mind, that her husband had tortured her beyond what she could endure; and Lord Bothwell did not know if she would live. Jane and Joanna read the solemn words contained in the scroll the messenger delivered and wept for their friend.

When Mary finally aroused herself once more, Patrick was still at her bedside. She managed a tremulous, timid smile.

"I hae been a sore trial to ye, my lord, I fear."

"Nay, Mary." He was kind and relieved to see some semblance of sanity in her violet eyes. "I ought to hae come sooner, for I am partially to blame for sending your knight from your side. 'Tis Jane ye hae to thank for my presence here, for 'twas she who wrote to me of your plight."

"She was e'er a good friend to me, my lord." Mary was quiet for a moment. Then she asked, "Joanna and the bairns—they are well?"

"Aye, Mary, and safe at Bothwell. I hae nae gi'en away your lie to Hugh aboot the babes."

"Thank ye, my lord."

She grew stronger as the days passed and was able to take some nourishment, first in the form of broths, then heavier meals later on as she regained her strength. Patrick remained with her constantly and had one of his men serve as their food-taster, for Lord Bothwell did not put it past the Earl of Dùndereen to poison both his wife and Jamie's man. When she was well enough, the Hepburn began to take Mary out for exercise upon the walkways of the battlements where she scanned the horizon anxiously for some sign of Hunter; but there was none.

"He will come, Mary." Patrick was certain of this, but the girl was not so sure anymore.

I shallna doubt him, she told herself over and over again. I doubted him once, and it nearly destroyed us both. I shallna doubt him again. He will come. He promised me he would. *When the heather blooms purple on the Highland moors,* he said. But she gazed out over the heaths, gold and violet in the full bloom of summer, and though her hope remained constant, her heart was heavy in her breast.

The Hepburn sent another message to his wife, informing her of Mary's progress; but Hugh, fearing Lord Bothwell wrote the King about the Earl's treatment of his Countess, dispatched his man, Leslie, after the page, whose final destination ended in a forest ditch rather than the Border Land castle toward which the young boy had ridden.

One day Mary coaxed Patrick into taking her riding. They cantered out over the wild sweep of terrain that rippled gently in the wind, clean and fresh with its sweet fragrance. They did not go far, for Mary was not fully recovered and tired easily, but she thought of the kirk in the distance and was reluctant to turn back, for she was certain 'twas there she would discover the answer to the riddle of her nightmare. Thereafter she plagued the Hepburn relentlessly until at last he consented one afternoon to ride with her to Mheadhoin, although he was uneasy about the prospect.

Mary's face was flushed, as though she had a fever, and her eyes were too bright as they galloped toward the ruins of the blackened village in the distance. Briefly Lord Bothwell recalled the stories of the plague that had claimed the town, the Black Death, and pondered momentarily if Mary had somehow contracted the disease, for she had told him she'd been there often in the past. He glanced at her and saw she was trembling, but then realized with relief she was but fatigued and overly excited, not ill at all. He wondered what lay at the abandoned sight to cause her fervor, but did not press her. Patrick Hepburn was naturally reticent himself and seldom pried into another's affairs without a specific purpose that more often than not concerned Scotland's politics. Mary, he felt certain, was not involved in any intrigue other than the strange legend she had related to him one evening.

They reached the cliff after a few hours of easy travel and halted, looking out over Loch Ness, which shone clear and blue in the dappled sunlight, not at all the menacing lake it was sometimes wont to be.

Lord Bothwell smiled. " 'Tisna as awesome as I feared from the tales I hae heard sung aboot it in the Border Lands. Is it true a wee beastie lives far beneath the waves?''

Mary's face was solemn when she replied, and Patrick realized the mighty Loch Ness was no laughing matter to the Highlanders. He sobered respectfully.

''Aye, there is a monster that lurks wie'in its depths,'' Mary spoke, ''but 'tis no 'wee beastie,' my lord, for I hae seen it. Once, many years ago, a great storm blew up as I was leaving Mheadhoin, and I saw it rise from the swirling whitecapped waters of the loch, nae still and blue as they are today, but angry massing torrents of fury, grey green in their tempestuous temper. 'Twas a giant thing—the monster—black as a world wie'oot a sun. Its head and neck resembled a great snake slithering upward from its coil, long and slender. But its body was huge, a hulking mass, rounded like a hump along its back. It cried oot; a strange weeping lament it sang, which carried eerily o'er the raging wind, sad and mournful. 'Tis said as long as there is death in the Highlands the monster will live on to chant its funeral dirge for those who hae died violently among us. Mayhap 'twill ne'er sleep.''

Mary shivered. Despite the bright afternoon, the Hepburn found himself shuddering also.

" 'Tis only a tale, lass,'' he said, trying to rid himself of the odd feeling that had settled upon him at her words.

"Aye, but I hae seen it,'' Mary insisted. "And there has been more than one puir Highlander cast into the loch's watery grave.'' She turned toward the kirk, her heart fluttering rapidly. "Wait here for me, Patrick. I want to go up alone.''

He nodded, glancing discreetly once more toward Loch Ness as she touched her whip lightly to Desmond's sides. Lord Bothwell wished a dark cloud had not suddenly chosen that moment to pass across the face of the sun.

Mary's horse picked its way gingerly up the small hill to

the cross-topped spire just upon the crest. The kirk, unlike the loch, did not look idyllic today, but was somehow ominous and forbidding from its perch upon the knoll. The edifice was not large, but had been built of the same grey granite as Bailekair and managed to appear just as imposing against the azure sky. The golden rays of the sun caught the panes of stained glass that still survived, glinting through the colors to cast rainbows of flashing brilliance. Like jeweled fingers, they grasped Mary. The effect was strangely cold, haughty, and regal, not gay and welcoming as it had been when Hunter had awaited her within the shadowed doorway. Mary quivered involuntarily. She reined Desmond up and dismounted slowly. Was it really here she had lain and loved with her Romany knight? Oh, Hunter, where are ye now, beloved? Why hae ye nae come to me as promised? Is this how ye felt so many long years past when ye waited for me, and I dinna come? Desperate? Hurting inside? Yearning for my nearness even as I ache for yours today?

The girl did not, at first, seek the inside of the kirk. Could her heart bear the pain she knew would engulf her very being when she entered the chapel to find it empty, bereft of Hunter's presence? Instead she walked softly around the church to the small yard at its back, pushed open the wrought-iron gate, and froze.

For the grave was there, just as she had seen it in her dream.

She wondered why she had never noticed it before, but then the mound was overgrown with ragged weeds and wild flowers that wafted gently in the breeze, and the tombstone had been weathered by time and the elements, leaving little more than a jagged rock thrusting upward from the earth at the head of the burial sight. She moved toward the thing, mesmerized, drawn by the grey granite stone at its fore. Just as in her dream the marker was blank or appeared so at first glance. But the closer Mary got the more plainly she was able to make out some faint etchings on the rock all the same. They were not deeply cut, as though whoever had put them there had been very old or weak. They apparently had been scratched on in fact with the edge of a dirk and not a proper chiseling tool at all.

Mary knelt upon the grave, trying to read the dim lines, but they did not form words at all. They seemed to be some kind of arrow. An arrow; that was all. An arrow pointing to the kirk just as the bony hand in Mary's dream had done. Whatever she was meant to find then lay not here, but in the church itself. Mary arose, brushing the dirt from her hands and knees, relieved the burial sight was not her own, nor Hunter's. That much at least she knew, for the grave was not recent; the weathered stone told her that.

She turned toward the chapel.

*Believe, and you will not fail. Believe, and you will not fail.*

She took a deep breath, braced herself to enter the kirk.

The church was more ravaged than ever, as though what little hope it had retained for its existence had disappeared with the lovers who'd come no more to its solitary haven. Birds nested in the high wooden rafters. Here and there spiders wove their webs in intricate designs, beautiful but deadly traps for whatever foolish insects might venture into the silken strands. Several more of the windowpanes had broken, leaving dark gaping holes amid the sunlit reds and greens and blues and purples of the glass that still remained. A few more of the pews had fallen prey to wood-rot. Grubs and ants worked busily to finish the decay. A small pile of scattered ashes from one of the fires Hunter had built to warm himself and Mary still charred the dais of the altar. The lass's heart turned over at the sight.

Having no idea for what she searched, Mary bent down to the floor and began to crawl along it, pulling at the oaken boards. Some were warped and came away easily in her hands; others were rotten and splintered when she grabbed them, leaving little prickly bits of stickers in her hands; still other panels were missing entirely.

For over an hour Mary searched, growing dirtier and more frustrated by the minute, while Patrick Hepburn waited outside upon the cliff. But he was a patient man. The intrigues of his life had taught him that and kept him in power when the overbold and those in too much of a hurry had fallen by the wayside. His only concern was that Mary would tire herself and have a relapse; so although he did not push her to leave, he did occasionally call out to be certain she was all right. Now and then his eyes would glint with amusement toward Hugh's men, who also waited some distance away and acted as guards and spies to be sure Lord Bothwell was not planning to spirit the Countess of Dùndereen away.

Mary discovered nothing beneath the floorboards except earth and the stone foundation of the building. Weary, disheartened, and thinking maybe she really *was* crazy, she left the kirk, warned by the lengthening shadows inside that dusk was almost upon the land. Tears stung her eyes at her failure; the Hepburn did not miss the bright, crystal droplets that splashed upon her cheeks.

"Whate'er 'tis, lass, you'll find it. We'll come back tomorrow."

The next day Mary arrived a little earlier and began to test the walls, knocking upon each grey stone rock by rock, listening intently, carefully for any hollow ring that would tell her one small boulder was but a façade; but this too proved fruitless.

They returned to Dùndereen that evening to find a Royal messenger awaiting Lord Bothwell. Patrick read the scroll silently, folded it up, and bade the page seek supper below in the main hall with his men.

"Mind ye dinna eat wie the laird's men, lad, but mine. They will look oot for ye." He gave the boy a sovereign.

"Thank ye, my lord." The page bowed politely.

"Is it—is it bad news, Patrick?" Mary questioned when the messenger had departed.

The Hepburn sighed. "I imagine that depends upon how ye look at it, Mary." His face was serious. "Hunter and Cadman hae abandoned the mission to England and jumped ship at Berwick. I am to return to Court at once."

Mary's heart leapt with sudden hope and then fear. One hand went to her throat. "Then—then Hunter may even now be on his way here!"

"That would be my guess, lass," Patrick replied. "Och, Mary, I hope he doesna do anything rash or foolish. He is much in love wie ye and has risked the King's wrath by his actions."

"Oh, Patrick, dinna leave me just yet. Canna ye see—'tis even more imperative I find the answer to the legend now! Please, take me back to the kirk just one more time before ye go. 'Twill be bad enough for me once ye hae gone, for I shall be alone again and at Hugh's mercy!"

"Hae no fear aboot that, Mary. I believe I hae sufficiently impressed upon the Earl that his well-being is directly dependent upon your own. I'm sorry, lass, but I canna take ye. I must obey Jamie's order."

"Oh, Patrick, please. One day might cool the King's anger against my beloved Romany knight; gie Hunter one more day to reach me—"

"And when he does, Mary—what of that? He canna hope to free ye, one mon alone against five hundred."

"That is why I *must* find the key to the puzzle of the curse, Patrick! It may be the answer, mine and Hunter's, to our future. Oh, please, Patrick!"

He considered this momentarily, then smiled slowly. "All right, lass. I ne'er could resist the pleading of a bonnie wench. But only one day, mind, and then I must go."

The following day Mary moved to the altar area she had previously avoided because it had been the love nest she'd shared with Hunter; its memories were still too vibrant, too alive to be easily forgotten, to be brought forth and relived with joy untinged by sadness.

Here the paneled walls had once been covered with beautiful, colorful pictures, intricately drawn and worked, depicting scenes from the life of Christ. Most of the paint had dulled with time, cracked and peeled; but what traces that still survived, despite the assaults of time, were lovely. Mary stood back, studying the artwork, wondering for a moment who had spent the many hours it must have taken to fill the large panels with the dramatic past of the kirk's savior. Then she began to tap each section much as she had done the stones.

Disheartened after several hours, she was just about to give up when she heard a dull thud that sounded different from the echo made by the rest of the panels. This scene was of Christ's birth, she noted absently, then her attention was caught by the tiny chest lying at the feet of one of the wise men who knelt before the King. There, cleverly interwoven into the painting of the jeweled casket, was an actual keyhole.

*Believe, and you will not fail.*

Trembling with excitement, Mary pulled the heavy gold chain Ashiyah had given her from around her neck, fumbling with the links impatiently when they became entangled with the locket with which Hunter had gifted her one Christmas here in the kirk so long ago. How ironic, almost fated it seemed now. She inserted the larger of the keys upon the necklace into the lock in the wall. It fit perfectly. Mary turned the key; a tiny door swung open from the wall. Inside was a small cupboard, she saw, that had originally been used to store the hosts for Mass. A small jeweled chest, similar to the one in the painting, now sat within.

The girl lifted it out carefully and placed it upon the altar, biting her lip with anticipation, her heart pounding. She then took the tinier of the two gold keys, put it in the lock of the casket, and turned. The crypt opened. Three scrolls of ancient, crumbling parchment lay within. Scarcely daring now to breathe, she picked the pages up gingerly, afraid they would disintegrate before her very eyes, unrolled them, read them. Tears of joy and sorrow streamed down her cheeks.

Minutes later Mary knew to whom the grave outside belonged and knew, too, the answer to the puzzle of the legend's curse.

Far and away a mountain lion screamed in the Highland hills.

# *Thirty-five*

Mary rewrapped the scrolls carefully, placed them back inside the chest, then closed the lid and locked it. Shaking, she took the casket from the kirk, knowing there were those in the Highlands who would slay her for its contents. Whom could she trust with the knowledge she carried in her hands? Patrick Hepburn? Lord Bothwell was the King's man and would have no hesitation in breaking open the crypt if he thought the peace in Scotland were at stake; and if he read the parchment pages inside, he would tell Jamie what they said. And the time was not yet ripe. . . . But there was no one else. She could not risk having the chest fall into Hugh Carmichael's hands. She shuddered just thinking of the repercussions were her husband to obtain the casket.

Mary mounted Desmond and rode slowly to where the Hepburn awaited. She would have to trust him.

"My lord," she said softly, "ye hae been verra kind to me these past few weeks. I've no doubt but what ye saved my sanity and life as well. I owe ye much, I know, but still I must ask one more favour of ye."

"Ye hae found that for which ye searched." It was a statement. "Then my day hasna been wasted, and the King's ire will be more easily borne. Name your boon, my lady." Lord Bothwell eyed the chest in her hands curiously, wondering what it contained.

The girl did not miss his inquisitive glance. "Patrick, I gie ye my word what lies herein has naught to do wie Scotland's welfare and must hae yours that ye willna seek to attain that which is wie'in. Will ye gie it, my lord?"

He gazed at her coolly for a moment, his eyes seeming to pierce her very soul as he pondered whether or not he could believe her. Mary trembled slightly, understanding why he had become so powerful. She felt he stripped her secrets from the innermost recesses of her mind. No wonder no prisoner could hold out for long against giving the Hepburn whatever information he desired. Finally Patrick nodded.

"All right, Mary, I gie ye my word. Now, what is it ye wish me to do wie the crypt then?"

"I want ye to take it wie ye when ye go. Keep it safe for me, my lord. Guard it wie your life, for its contents are precious to me and mine. I shall send to ye when the time is ripe for its opening and reveal what lies wie'in."

"I hope I may be there when that happens, Mary." He raised one eyebow questioningly.

"Patrick, if ye do this for me, I promise ye that."

"Verra well, then. Ye hae my word I will keep your secret safe till then."

Nevertheless, that evening as she watched him ride away from one of the squat towers of Dùndereen, Mary felt more helpless and desolate than she ever had in her life, and she hoped she had not made a mistake in letting him go.

Hunter MacBeth stared at the pale white castle in the distance, which sat like a hen upon a nest in the midst of the purple heather that swept across the Highland moors as far as the eye could see.

Ah, beloved, I hae nae failed ye—nae yet. I hae come while the heather—the sweet fragrance of ye—still blooms. I hae kept my vow.

Cadman's face, by his side, was grim. "Hunter, ye are mad, I tell ye! I beg of ye nae to do this." The younger man pleaded as he had for a fortnight, but knew his words were spoken in vain. Hunter's mind was made up, and Cadman recalled again the chilling oath that had led his kinsman to the wild, fatal scheme he had planned.

*If 'tis the last thing I e'er do, I'll kill him!*

"I hae no other choice." The Romany knight's dark visage was forbidding. "I am a broken clansman wie'oot an army to call up for my vengeance. I hae sworn to slay Hugh Carmichael and set Mary free fore'er. 'Twas a sacred oath I promised my beloved. I *must* see it through to the end, no matter the consequence to myself. And I must do it alone, brother."

"They will kill ye, Hunter! Ye canna hope to get oot alive!"

"I know, but I shall see Mary safe at least, someway, somehow. I shall hae that much. 'Tis enough. Tell her—" His voice tightened suddenly, but he mastered it once more. "Tell her I loved her, loved her more than my life—"

He did not finish, but set his gilded spurs to Craigor's sides, galloping over the gold-and-violet heath toward the woman who had branded his carnal mouth for her own and claimed his passionate heart for all time. *Oh, God, gie me strength,* he prayed, *make my sword-arm strong, stronger than Hugh Carmichael's. I ask nae for myself, Lord, but for Mary. Mary! Ah, Mary!* She was one in a million, his brave, bonnie lassie! His, and his alone, till death did them part! And death would be his that day, he knew. Straight toward the iron portcullis of Dùndereen he rode, with the knowledge lying heavily upon his heart and soul that he would not leave its walls alive. *'Tis for Mary I die. Mary, who is worth a thousand lives if I but had them to gie! Oh, beloved, forgie me, for ye must go on wie'oot me. I must set ye free to survive, to watch o'er our bairns and raise them to monhood, to teach them those things I hae treasured in my life—I love ye. I love ye! There will ne'er be aught for me save thee!*

She saw him coming. From the machicolated ramparts of the fortress she saw him coming, and her heart leapt with a joy she had never thought possible, then sank like a stone in her breast as she realized he was alone and understood his intent. Patrick Hepburn had read Hunter MacBeth a'right.

"Oh, God, no! No!" she cried aloud, running to the tower,

falling down the steep, winding steps in her haste to reach him, to somehow prevent him from his folly. They'll kill him! Oh, God, they'll kill him, and 'twill all be for naught, for I canna live wie'oot him! Oh, beloved, why hast thou done this mad thing?

But Mary was too late. Hunter had already demanded and received entrance to the castle, for Hugh's men had been so astonished and awed by the MacBeth's foolhardy arrogance that they had let him in. Hunter urged Craigor through the inner gatehouse and dismounted, his jaw set in a hard, determined line as he entered the keep itself, and the Carmichaels closed in warily around him. Her heart in her throat, Mary pushed and shoved her way through the crowd of men, cursing and slapping them when they would have restrained her. Wildly, wantonly she fought to gain her lover's side, uncaring that she would condemn herself to his fate by her actions.

"Go back!" Hunter warned hoarsely, more frightened than he had ever been in his life. "Go back!" But she paid him no heed.

"Hunter! Hunter!" She flung herself into his arms, weeping, sobbing, begging him to leave her, to try to escape while there was still time.

He held her close, crushing her to him fervently, catching great bunches of her golden hair in his hands as he stroked her, crooned softly in her ear, turned her face up to his to brush the crystal tears from her wide violet eyes, kiss tenderly the scarlet lips that trembled with love and fear for him.

"Ye are all right?"

"Aye. Patrick came, and I was spared."

"Oh, Mary, my tigress, my brave, bonnie lassie. I wasna worth your life! There was no need for ye to sacrifice yourself for me! Why did ye nae wait for me to free ye? Why did ye come down to me? Oh, God, beloved! They will slay us both now! Ye know that! Oh, my love, my maiden gold, my precious, foolish darling! Why? Why? I would ne'er hae asked this of ye!"

"Hush! Hush!" She smiled up at him tremulously, caressing

his face with her quivering, loving fingers, as though they had been alone in the main hall. "Didst truly believe I would let ye die alone? Oh, my life, I too love beyond all reason. I amna afraid." She squared her small shoulders proudly, and quoted, " 'Whither thou goest, I will go.' "

"Well, well. How verra touching. How verra touching, indeed." The Earl of Dùndereen swaggered slowly down the steps from the upstairs chambers. "I would ask to what do I owe this unexpected—pleasure, but I see there is no need. So, now I understand your great passion for the whore. Ye hae been lovers all along!" Hugh's dark visage was a tight, distorted mask of rage.

God's teeth! The man was either crazy or an utter fool to have come here alone! The Carmichael advanced toward the MacBeth stealthily, as a caged animal padding silently to crouch and spring upon its keeper. The two men stared at each other measuringly.

"Aye, 'tis me she loves," Hunter said softly. " 'Tis me she has always loved. Did ye really think I would let her go?"

"Love!" Hugh sneered scornfully. "Love is but a fool's notion, as I warned Mary once long ago. And ye, sir, are a verra great fool indeed. Well, whoreson, I hope she was better in your bed than she was in mine for ye to hae risked your neck for her." He grinned mockingly, wickedly. "Whate'er did ye hope to gain by coming here?"

Hunter smiled just as jeeringly in return. "My beloved's freedom from a swine who abused her in the foulest possible way. Ye are lower than a beast, Hugh Carmichael, and dinna deserve to be called a mon. I shall take the greatest pleasure in butchering ye like the pig ye are. Aye, let us begin, bastard, for the verra stench of ye sickens me!"

Hugh's face flushed with ire at the insulting words. "Are ye so eager to die then, whoreson?" he growled. "And ye, Mary, ye deceitful, lying bitch! Are ye so anxious to see your lover slain? I will kill him verra slowly, I promise ye, so ye may watch him suffer and know ye are helpless to prevent it. And perhaps while he's lying there, wie his life's blood draining from him, I'll pump another brat into your belly!"

Mary did not flinch from his evil leer, for Hunter had given her courage again. "Ye get a child on me, Hugh?" she spoke coldly. "Ha! I dinna know ye were capable of such. Ranald isna *your* son!"

It took a moment for the full import of her words to sink in, then suddenly Hugh understood. " 'Twas *his* bastard, and the bairn lives!" he breathed.

He went crazy, howled like a madman as he struck her down, a vicious blow across her face that sent her reeling dizzily to the floor. Hunter's temper snapped at that, and his anger knew no bounds. Berserk with wrath, he lunged forward, grabbing Hugh brutally about the throat, trying to choke the other man. The Carmichael men-at-arms closed in to restrain him, their blades held in readiness.

"Stand back!" Hunter hissed as he shoved Hugh against one wall roughly, fingers tightening cruelly into the Earl's flesh. "This is between me and your laird, unless, of course, he is too much of a coward to fight me!"

Hugh's black shards narrowed dangerously. One hand flew to the hilt of his sword. The tension in the hall was so thick it could have been cut with a knife. Mary shivered. Oh, God, dinna let them duel, she prayed feverishly, for the longer they taunt one another, the longer my beloved and I shall live; and we hae so much to live for, Lord. Oh, why? Why has Hunter done this mad thing? We shall ne'er leave here alive—

Hunter stayed the Carmichael's movement with a quick, savage twist of the Earl's wrist. The Romany knight stepped away, helping the trembling Mary to stand, before drawing the single steel mesh gauntlet from his hand. His violet eyes glittering with deadly intent, Hunter hit Hugh Carmichael across his dark smirking visage, splitting open the laird's lip.

"That was for Mary," the MacBeth snarled, then flung the glove upon the floor. "Pick it up," he ordered softly. "Pick it up! Or are ye so lacking in honor ye canna?"

Hugh swooped up the glove, tossing it back to the Romany knight sharply, striking Hunter in the chest.

"Your challenge is accepted, bastard! But 'tis a whore ye

die for, ye son of a bitch! Remember that when I send ye to your grave. A whore I—''

Hunter struck him again to silence him, then loosed his sword from its scabbard, saluting briefly. ''On guard!'' the MacBeth spat. ''I hae waited a long time for this and hae much for which to repay ye!''

The two men engaged arms, blades slashing furiously at one another, the clash of the shining metal ringing to the rafters of the hall as they battled. The duel was deadly, for neither man was armored. Hunter had known Hugh would not be dressed in a full coat of mail in his own fortress and so had foregone his own, honorable as always, wearing only the traditional gauntlet with which to challenge his opponent. The swords scraped against one another, parrying, thrusting as the foes danced lightly, warily upon booted feet, muscles straining in their forearms from the force required to wield the heavy weapons. Several times one or the other surged forward only to meet with a wall or floor where his enemy had once stood. When this happened, sparks flew up from the gleaming silver steel as it scratched along the surfaces of the stones like flint.

Hugh sidestepped a wicked onslaught neatly, and Hunter's blade sliced a torch from its sconce with a hiss. The tallow bounced against one wall, then tumbled down to roll and skip across the floor, sending waves of flame in this direction and that. Several of the onlooking men-at-arms scrambled hastily to extinguish the blaze, but the combatants paid no attention, each grimly intent on slaying the other.

Hunter pressed his attack, driving the Earl up the staircase that wound its way up one side of the hall. For one precarious moment the two men dueled dangerously close to the edge of the steps where, lacking any balustrade, one or the other might have fallen some distance to the floor below, possibly to his death. The swords flew, cutting slithering swathes and arcs in the air, came together, disengaged, then clattered into a brief union at the hilts as each man tried to gain enough leverage to push the other over the side of the staircase. Hugh hovered too close for comfort for one fleeting second before he shifted his weight, regaining his balance as the two enemies reversed positions. Hunter laughed mockingly, wiping the sweat from his eyes during the small respite.

"'Tisna quite the same this time, is it, bastard?" he jeered at the panting Earl. "Ye hae nae the advantage of haeing run me to the ground like a dog. How does it feel, whoreson, to fight a real mon?"

Hugh did not answer. He was too busy trying to ward off another devilish assault, for, indeed, the two men were evenly matched; and the Carmichael who had begun the battle so confidently had now actually started to wonder whether or not his life was, in fact, in peril. He felt himself slammed against the wall as the MacBeth's sword seared his shoulder, then withdrew. The Earl jumped back to avoid another hit, lost his footing, and toppled down the steps.

"Bind it!" Hunter commanded curtly as he reached the bottom of the stairs, towering like a demon over his wounded opponent. The Romany knight smiled, a hard, tight, hateful grin, but his amethyst eyes glittered darkly, murderously, as he recalled the words with which the Carmichael had taunted him that day outside of Stirling. "I'm of no mind to slip on your blood," Hunter purred silkily, insolently.

With a deft movement Hugh ripped a shred of cloth from his *breacan* and tied off the deep, jagged cut to stanch the flow of blood.

"Ye hae a remarkable memory for a fool," he gasped raggedly.

"Aye," Hunter rejoined. "One that hasna forgotten your cowardice that day, nor the scar I wear across my belly because of it!"

The weapons began to sing their death song once again. Mary trembled convulsively as the slight breeze they stirred whispered through her mass of golden hair, teasing her cruelly with its mournful dirge. Dear God! It sounded like the strange weeping lament of the Loch Ness monster, but for whom did the funeral bell toll? Sweet *Jesù!* Nae for Hunter! Pray, God, nae Hunter! Her breath caught in her throat as she watched him beat off a merciless attack, saw the powerful muscles ripple in his back, remembered how many times she had lain beneath him and felt the taut cords flutter just so under the gentle caress of her hands before her fingers had tightened into his flesh, nails clawing little furrows in the bronze of him as she'd urged him on.

Hugh was tiring; she could tell. He was not used to battling a left-handed foe and had begun to breathe heavily as he maneuvered his weighty blade.

Kill him! Kill him, Hunter! Mary's mind screamed, but she did not shout the words aloud, for fear of distracting her beloved's attention, thereby costing him his life.

The Earl had started to swing his broadsword wildly now, like a battle-ax which was his favorite weapon and with which he was more proficient. It veered toward Hunter's neck. The MacBeth ducked quickly, rolling to one side. The blade hit the side of the staircase with a mighty whack, shattering from the force of the blow. Hugh flung away the useless sword and drew his dirk as the Romany knight bounded hastily to his feet in one graceful leap. Hunter smiled cruelly, and Mary shuddered at seeing the savage beast inside him unleashed in full force as he closed in for the kill, tossing away his blade and yanking his own dagger from its sheath.

Oh, God, Mary moaned and bit her lip, for a fight with dirks in close quarters was the deadliest duel of all.

The two men circled warily, then moved in, nearing each other murderously, for the daggers were short and had to be used quickly and skillfully at close range. Hunter's blade shot out; Hugh jumped back. The MacBeth threw his body at the Carmichael's before the Earl had time to recover. The two enemies fell to the floor, grappling as they rolled over and over, each trying to force his dirk up between the flesh pressed on flesh. One of the daggers emerged from the tumbling *mêlée* and skidded across the floor. Mary gave a small, involuntary cry, for she could not tell to which man it had belonged.

Then suddenly Hunter was on top of Hugh, driving his blade home into the Earl's naked throat. Blood spurted and then gushed like water from a fountain from the mortal blow, splattering the Romany knight's *breacan* and hands as they pulled the dirk free. Hugh made an odd, strangled, gurgling sound, shuddered, and lay still. The MacBeth disentangled himself from the Carmichael's corpse, then rose unsteadily to his feet.

Mary stared at the black evil figure of Hugh Carmichael upon the floor, thought of all the pain and heartache he had caused her. Was he really dead? She had to be certain—Why, she never knew, but she went crazy then. With a sob of outrage she drew her dagger, running forward to kneel over his fallen body, stabbing him again and again in the chest, the belly; weeping, moaning, screaming hysterically, shaking with fear and fury. She stabbed him for Magnus, for Edward, for Gordon, for Hunter, and for herself, over and over, unaware of the massive amount of blood that poured forth in a torrent, splashing upon her hair, her face, her fingers as they wielded the dirk, seeping down from Hugh's corpse in little rivulets, darkening the hard rock floor of the main hall of Dùndereen with stains that would never be washed clean.

"Oh, beloved." Hunter's purple eyes were filled with pity as he watched her, for he had seen this type of thing happen many times before on the battlefield. He bent to pull her away amid the horrified gazes of the Carmichael men-at-arms. "He's dead, beloved," he said gently. "He'll ne'er hurt ye again."

Tenderly Hunter wrapped his arms about Mary's trembling form, held her close, and kissed her lovingly before Hugh's men surrounded them and closed in to cut the lovers down.

# Thirty-six

Ian Carmichael staggered drunkenly through the wine cellar of Bailekair. Goddamn it! Where in the hell were the serving wenches when ye needed one? Christ! He needed a drink. Badly. Had needed one ever since he'd come upon Euphemia MacBeth's battered, broken body upon the shores of Loch Ness at the bottom of the cliff. What had happened to bring her to such an end he had never discovered. He'd only known she was dead. Dead! His greedy little Effie would come to him no more. He'd left her there. He'd had to. What other choice had there been for him? He could not bury her at Bailekair nor even explain how he'd come to know her. He'd ridden toward home, choking, feeling as though his lungs were going to burst within his chest any minute. He hadn't been able to breathe, so terrible had the shock of Euphemia's death and loss been to him, so horrible had the indignity of having to leave her there unshriven affected him. He was nothing without her. Nothing! His mother's pawn. His mother, who bullied him, taunted him, made him feel like a fool! It had been Effie who'd made him strong, made him feel like a man. Oh, God, Effie! Effie!

"Effie?" Ian raised his eyes to a shadow in one corner of the dark cellar. He lifted his candle higher. "Effie, is that ye? Oh, Effie!" he stumbled toward her.

She was gone. She had disappeared. Ian began to panic.

He just *had* to find her! She was the only woman who aroused him fully, encouraged him to stand up to his domineering mother. Suddenly he smiled, shaking his head gently.

"Dinna tease me, Effie," he crooned, realizing her game at last, for she had always been a saucy minx, secreting herself away for him to find her, then giggling and clapping her hands with delight when he pulled her from her hiding place. "I'm going to get ye, lass. 'Tisna nice to tease me when ye know I hunger for ye so. Come oot! Come oot where'er ye are!"

But only silence greeted his demand. Ian tiptoed through the cellar, slowly peeking around a timbered pole in hopes of catching her in the middle of changing her position, which she often did, even though he protested 'twas cheating. He heard a slight pattering upon the floor, a light skittering across the stones. Effie! She was so thin. Why, she weighed scarcely a mite! Aye, there she was. She'd hidden in that barrel over there. Ian was sure of it.

"Ahaha!" With a shout of glee he pried open the lid, stared down at the sparkling, crystal ale that lay within, as clear as a shaded mountain pool.

Aye, she was there all right! Swimming fine and naked, enticing him in with one beckoning hand, luring him to join her, running her tongue sensuously over her smiling lips.

"Effie!" He plunged into the glistening diamond liquid and, in his drunken stupor, drowned.

"Cadman." Joanna stared sorrowfully at Hunter MacBeth's diminishing figure. "We canna let him do this. He'll be slain—I know he will!—and Mary will ne'er forgie us for nae preventing him from doing this mad thing. She wouldna want him to sacrifice himself for her. Her life wouldna be worth living wie'oot him. He's her world, Cadman. E'erything she's e'er been, she's been for him. E'erything she's e'er done, e'erything she's e'er suffered, e'erything she's e'er gi'en up has been for him. Ride after him quickly! Dinna let him do this crazy thing!"

"I canna, Jo. I would I could, but I canna. Hunter is a

mon, lass, more of a mon than most; and a mon must do what he thinks is right.''

"But he's her whole world, Cadman! She willna go on wie'oot him!"

"Jo, I fear neither one of them will get oot of Dùndereen alive."

"Dear God!'' the maid gasped, her honeyed eyes wide with terror. "Oh, Cadman, my husband, we must do *something!* I—I feel so helpless. Oh, sweet *Jesù!* I canna imagine them dead. Oh, the puir bairns. What will I say to them? Cadman, please, think of something we can do to help Hunter and Mary. I'll ne'er forgie myself otherwise—'' Her voice broke as to his dismay she began to weep uncontrollably.

"Nor will I. Be quiet, Jo! Crying willna help, and your sobs may draw attention to ourselves. I love them both as dearly as ye.'' His face was somber. "Shush now, and let me think.''

Half-choking, Joanna finally managed to stifle the wrenching, muffled sounds arising from her throat.

"They do hae one chance, Jo,'' Cadman spoke slowly, "but 'tis a small one, so I dinna wish for ye to set your hopes too high.''

"Tell me! Tell me anyway! Oh, anything, no matter how slender, just to hae a chance at saving them!"

"Well, if the Earl is honest, and there is a fair duel between him and Hunter, and if my foster brother manages to slay Hugh Carmichael, then there will be no one in power at Dùndereen, for we must assume the Earl's men dinna and willna obey Mary, especially under the circumstances. Now your lady isna a mere woman to be slain wie'oot another thought. She is the daughter of an Earl and the Countess of Dùndereen, besides. She must be brought up before some sort of clan council for her crimes, no matter how hastily assembled. Since if Hugh Carmichael is killed by my kinsman, there will be no one in authority at the keep to preside o'er such a council, we may presume Mary and probably Hunter, since they will want to torture him verra slowly before he dies, will be transferred to another fortress wie a high-ranking laird.''

''Ian! Ian at Bailekair!'' Joanna's face began to light up. ''He's closest to Dùndereen.''

''Aye, that would be my guess also, lass. Mayhap, if all goes right, somewhere between the two places we can at least get some word to Hunter and Mary, let them know we stand ready to aid them, so they dinna gie up hope.''

''Aye, but how?''

''Jo, is there anyone hereaboots whom ye trust absolutely, who would be willing to do anything for Mary, regardless of the situation, and keep silent aboot it, besides?''

''Mistress Flora! Mistress Flora and her husband, Alan. She's Mary's auld nanna, and both she and Alan loved and reared Mary since my lady was but a bairn.''

''Good. Let us ride to her cottage then. We'll need some other clothes. Peasant dress so we may mingle wie the crofters who work the land at Dùndereen. If we keep quiet and stay low, I doubt we'll be noticed that way.''

The villagers of Dùndereen ceased working in the fields as the small cavalcade passed them by in grim silence. The Carmichael men stern and forbidding. The Earl of Dùndereen's dead body hanging over his big black destrier. The Romany MacBeth and his lover, the betrayer Mary Carmichael, riding, side-by-side, to Bailekair where their punishment would be meted out, for a laird was needed to sit in judgment over one of such rank as Mary. But all knew what the outcome would be. Burning at the stake for the witch, Mary Carmichael; and hanging for the interloper, Sir Hunter MacBeth, with disembowelment while he still lived, dangling at the end of a rope.

Some of the peasants pelted the two with rocks, tomatoes, and other assorted odds and ends, for though they'd had no love for the Earl, the crofters hated the MacBeths with an even greater passion. Some ran forward to spit upon the lovers and curse them evilly. Mary tried unsuccessfully to ward off one woman, kicking out at the screeching virago

527

with a booted foot, but the maid was persistent, yelling at her vilely, screaming ugly words of hate and venom as she clawed at Mary's bloodstained *arascaid* and yanked at her leather-shod feet. Mary glanced down at the serf coldly and gasped aloud as her violet eyes met Joanna's doe brown ones.

*Joanna!* Mary mouthed the name silently, but smothered the word as soon as it formed on her lips at the girl's warning shake of her head.

"Wicked tart! Cheap hussy!" Joanna cat-called loudly as she ripped off a piece of Mary's dress. "Shameless wanton! Evil slut!" Then swiftly under her breath as she snatched the shawl from Mary's shoulders, she whispered, "We shall do what we can to help ye. Dinna lose faith!"

Imperceptibly Mary nodded, giving the lass a grateful look, trying to smile bravely, but there were tears in her amethyst jewels all the same. To keep up the charade Mary twisted her bound hands from the pommel of her saddle, as though she were attempting to grab back her *tonnag*. With a start she saw the emerald ring upon her fourth finger.

*If e'er ye hae need of me, send it. I vow I will come wie the King's army if necessary.*

Alinor! Dear Alinor!

"Joanna, the ring," Mary breathed softly. "The ring! Alinor! Take it to Alinor!"

For one horrible eternity Joanna did not understand, then at last she caught the drift of Mary's quiet outburst.

"Betrayer of our clan! Repent! Repent now before ye die!" Joanna shouted with a hiss as she tore the ring from Mary's hand and concealed it beneath the folds of her shawl before any others could see.

Mary heaved a sigh of relief and kicked out gently at the girl. Joanna fell to the ground.

"May ye burn at the stake for your sins, lowly whore!" The maid shook one fist threateningly at Mary and continued to mumble horrible curses after the passing party.

Joanna clutched the ring to her bosom, scurrying with an exaggerated humped back and limp beneath her tattered *tonnag* across the road to where another stooped peasant awaited. Unnoticed by the other crofters, the two disappeared into the trees at the edge of the field, where their horses were tethered. There Joanna held up the ring for her husband's inspection.

"Mary wants me to take this to Alinor, Cadman. Charlie's wife must know or hae something my lady believes will help them. Oh, God, they're going to die! We've got to help them somehow, or they're going to die! And Eadar Da Voe is so far away!"

"As is Edinburgh," Cadman observed with a sinking heart. "I know Jamie owes Hunter, but the King will ne'er come in time and mayna come at all if he is still angry wie us o'er the mission to England. I canna even be certain His Grace is at Holyrood Palace. 'Tis summer, and Jamie loves to hunt—"

"Oh, Cadman, ride quickly. Ride to Glenkirk, for I canna; they would slay me on sight. 'Tis closer. Lady Sophia loved ye and Hunter of auld. She may send aid, even if 'twill only delay the end for them a little. We need time! I shall go to Eadar Da Voe—"

"Och, Jo, ye canna possibly hope to get there alone, and the MacBeths may kill me the moment I am wie'in their walls!"

"Ne'ertheless we must try! They'll die otherwise. Och, Cadman, we love them both too much nae to try!"

"Aye, but, oh, God, I love ye, too, Jo!"

"Cadman, we shallna be able to live wie ourselves if we dinna make some attempt to save Hunter and Mary. What will there be for us then—wie their deaths on our consciences for the rest of our lives? I canna bear it, I tell ye!"

"Nor can I. Oh, God, take care, my sweet. Kiss me quickly for luck, then be off wie ye."

Joanna raised herself on tiptoe to place her lips tenderly, feverishly against her husband's own. "I love ye, Cadman. I hae come to love ye more than life itself. Remember that if—if I dinna—dinna see ye again. Oh, Godspeed, my heart! Fare thee well."

Chaos reigned at Bailekair. Ian had been found dead, drowned in a tun of ale; and now the men-at-arms of Dùndereen had arrived, bringing their laird's dead body and Mary and her lover with them. And through it all Lady Margaret stood like a queen, the sole victor, triumphant in her glory, in this her finest hour. 'Twas hers! Bailekair was hers at last! No matter that Andrew, the elder twin by thirty minutes, would inherit the title. He would not take it, for Harold would not be able to stand it, and the twins never did anything that might cause trouble between them. They were too close. Aye, Margaret ruled supreme at the massive fortress she had coveted, lied for, betrayed for, and would have killed for if necessary.

"Lay my son and nephew oot in the main hall," she directed, "and throw those two in the castle dungeon." She gave Mary a smug, scathing glance. "We want them to die slowly, verra slowly indeed; but first our kinsmen must hae proper burials. There must be no honor shirked for my son and nephew. That bitch and her whoreson lover willna rot—nae for a while yet anyway."

Mary shuddered as the men who had once called her their lady grabbed her roughly, fondling her crudely as they passed her from man to man amidst the shouts and jeers of the onlookers, while Hunter strained furiously against the relentless grasp of those who held him tightly. He feared he would see his beloved raped by them all before his very eyes and be powerless to prevent it. Indeed that might have been Mary's fate had not Alan suddenly appeared and intervened.

"For shame!" the dead Lion of Bailekair's old master-at-arms cried as he entered the hall. "Hae ye no sense of decency or honor among ye that ye make sport of the auld laird's only daughter, whate'er her crime? Hae ye no respect for Magnus's love for his bonnie lassie that ye would rape her in his own castle? For shame, I say! Leave the wench be, and return to your duties else the auld Earl rise up from his grave to haunt ye for holding his glorious memory so cheap!"

Here and there the men began to lower their heads shamefacedly, shuffle their feet sheepishly, for indeed there was not a one among them who had not loved and respected the Lion of Bailekair. Some of them recalled dandling his only daughter upon their knee during her childhood and were sickened by the thought of what they'd almost done, would have done had not Alan protested. One by one they turned away.

"Dinna let this auld fool sway ye if ye want the whore." Lady Margaret ran after them, sorry they were not to humiliate and degrade her daughter after all, for the Countess of Bailekair had actually been licking her lips as she'd contemplated the prospect, savored Mary's horror in her mind.. "She's naught but a whore," Lady Margaret cried beseechingly, but she was not able to stop the men-at-arms from returning to their duties. "Take her away!" She glared evilly at Mary when the hall was nearly empty. "I canna abide the sight of the slut!"

But as the men who remained led Mary and Hunter away the Countess shivered, for the MacBeth's accursed eyes had had murder in them when he'd looked at her, raking her body insolently and finding it wanting before he'd thrown back his head and laughed scornfully. He'll pay for that insult! Margaret vowed, the vulgar whoreson! Still, she suddenly felt hot and flushed, and her heart beat strangely in her breast. God's blood, but Mary's lover had been attractive!

The dungeons were dark and damp. The heavy wooden doors leading to the slimy staircase below squeaked and moaned on the iron hinges that had grown rusty from lack of use, for few were taken prisoner in the Highlands, where the wild, savage clansmen preferred to make the solving of their quarrels permanent. The rats squealed wrathfully at the intrusion of the small group into their nesting place and pattered away hurriedly from the bright flame of the torches, tails slithering with a shuddering hiss across the moist stone floor. Mary clung closely to Hunter's side as they descended the steep dank steps, trying not to slip and fall, for if the drop did not kill them, the sharp jagged rocks below would not doubt cripple them for life.

Nae that it matters, Mary thought wryly, for we are to die

anyway, and better the end be merciful. She trembled, remembering her mother's hate-filled face, and knew death at the Countess's hands would be very slow and excruciatingly painful.

The men-at-arms opened one of the cell doors, shoved Mary and Hunter inside, then slammed the barrier shut, not even leaving them a single torch with which to see by.

"Tigress?" Hunter called softly in the darkness.

"I am here, beloved."

Following the sound of her voice he managed to reach her side. "Are ye all right, Mary?"

"Aye, except that I canna feel my hands."

" 'Tis the ropes. They are bound too tightly and hae cut off your circulation. Here, let me see if I can get them undone, and then ye can free me."

In silence he worked patiently at the knots he could not see, twisting them this way and that until finally they loosened, and the coarse hemp fell from Mary's hands. She rubbed her chafed wrists vigorously until the blood began to flow normally once more, then moved to free Hunter in the same fashion. Afterward they stumbled around in the darkness, investigating the cell inch by inch. As far as they could determine there was no way out for them. The floor and all four walls were solid rock; the barred door was of heavy oak, thick and impenetrable. Mary felt her heart sink once more as they sat down upon the hard, wide board that hung from massive, iron chains from one wall and served as a bed. Hunter's strong sword-arm closed around her slightly shaking figure tightly, drawing her near; she took comfort in his presence.

"How—how long do ye think we hae?" she asked, her voice small and tremulous in the blackness, even though she knew the answer to her question as well as he.

"Three, maybe four days at the most. Oh, God, beloved! I ne'er meant for this to happen."

"I amna afraid. We shalna be parted, my love, nae even in death."

Dusk closed over the Highlands, enveloping the vast, sweeping moors and rugged, purple mountains in an eerie shroud of grey that gleamed an odd fiery silver in the light of the twilight moon shot through with the flaming orange of the sun that still lingered briefly on the western horizon. The effect was almost unnerving as Cadman stared up at the forbidding spires of Glenkirk Castle looming ominously just ahead in the distance, always so welcoming in the past and now a stranger to the young MacBeth who had once called it home. He wondered if he would leave the fortress of his youth and manhood alive, ever see his gentle, fawnlike Joanna again. Well, there was no help for it. A man must do what he must do, and Cadman knew his wife was right. He could not live with the thought that he had not tried to aid his foster brother (who had saved his life more than once in many a battle) on his conscience. He took a deep breath, set his gilded spurs to Logie's sides, and shouted his name out loudly to the sentries.

Far and away Joanna, for the first time in her life, laid her whip cruelly about her mount's sides. The pretty, fine-boned brown mare, Maeve, which Cadman had given her, lengthened its stride as it galloped recklessly over the Highland moors in the ghostly twilight, traveling ever southward to Eadar Da Voe.

"Hurry! Hurry! Hurry!" the maid chanted grimly under her breath as she pressed the palfrey on, keeping a sharp watch for wandering marauders in all directions, brigands who would set upon her, rape and slay her without another thought.

Och, had she taken leave of her senses? She could not possibly hope to reach the Murray stronghold set upon the eastern shores of Scotland alone, a solitary woman, fair game for any lone, desperate cutthroat or drunken men-at-arms looking for a chance bit of sport. She yanked the horse up abruptly, intending to go back to her husband, to tell Cadman 'twas futile, the plan they had made, as mad as Hunter's own crazy scheme that had gotten them all into this sad tangle.

Then Joanna thought of Mary's frightened, tearstained face and knew she must continue. She raised her whip determinedly once more.

The guards at the gatehouse of Glenkirk were surprised and confused to observe Cadman MacBeth below, alone, upon his great chestnut destrier with its wild mane and flowing tail of ebony, waiting expectantly before the heavy, wooden doors of the castle. Some thought him a loyal clansman still and were for opening the portcullis at once. Others suspected him of being a broken man and were also for admitting him, but only to bring him to trial before a clan council and see him hanged for his perfidy. Still others had believed him dead these many years past and claimed he was a ghost come to haunt them who could simply pass right through the gatehouse if he so desired.

Finally one man smarter than the rest pointed out that Cadman had always been a favorite of the Lady Sophia and that broken man, ghost, or no, he ought to be taken straight away to the Countess of Glenkirk, who would hear his story and decide what should be done. The others hastily agreed to this idea, for though Lord Angus's son, Stephen, was their true laird, they all knew who really reigned at Glenkirk, and she would have their heads on a platter if they displeased her.

They cranked up the iron portcullis and opened the doors to the fortress, then surrounded Cadman warily as he slowly cantered in, dismounted, and asked for the Lady Sophia. They escorted him to the Countess's presence, breathing a sigh of relief when, after gazing at him for some minutes, stunned, their lady flung herself into Cadman's arms, kissed him with a mother's own love and began to weep softly on his shoulder.

"Oh, Cadman! Is it really ye?" Sophia gasped, wiping at her tear-filled eyes. "I canna believe it after all these years. Let me look at ye, son. Oh, Cadman!"

"My lady. My lady. 'Tis good to see ye," he said, his own voice choked with emotion as he gently disengaged himself from her embrace to kneel at her feet and do her homage.

"Och, get up, my foster son, rise! I wouldna hae ye bow so low before me."

"I owe ye that, my lady, and more for ye know what I am and what I hae done," he spoke softly.

"I only know ye had your reasons for it and wouldna hae betrayed our clan, nor brought shame upon us. Rise up, Cadman, and tell me why ye hae come."

"Send for Stephen, my lady, for this concerns him also."

Cadman waited until the Countess's eldest son had come to the main hall before he poured himself a chalice of wine and began to relate his tale.

Joanna managed to get as far as some miles outside of Glasgow before the terrible thing she had feared all along became a reality. There were seven of them, and they spied her with delight, spurring their steeds after her furiously galloping figure in hot pursuit as they gave chase, rowdily shouting and laughing, made brash and insensitive by the liquor they'd consumed in a nearby tavern, thinking only of easing their lust. She was grateful they were men-at-arms and not bandits, for they would not be as likely to kill her after using her if they caught up with her. She glanced back anxiously over one shoulder, saw them drawing closer, heard them howling with glee. She whipped Maeve brutally, fearing all the while she would ride the gentle mare to death if they kept up this grueling pace, but it was no use anyway. The small palfrey was no match for the thundering destriers, and soon Joanna was surrounded by the wine-stupored men. They grabbed at the horse's bridle, slowing the steed to a halt, then reached for the girl, who lashed out at them bravely with her riding crop as they hooted and cat-called lewd jests at her distress. They yanked the quirt easily from her trembling hands, then pulled her from the mare's back, tearing at her garments as they passed her from man to man, arguing over who was to be first with her.

Dimly through her fright Joanna recognized the *breacan* of the MacDonalds and realized they must be the Earl of Wynd Cheathaich's men, for David MacDonald's keep lay not far from Glasgow.

"Stop it! Stop it!" she cried, hanging on to the slender thread of hope her knowledge of their laird had given her and wishing fervently she might be able to reason with the drunken men. "Wouldst rape your own kin?"

"Kin, lads! Do ye hear that? The lass claims she is kin to us!" one man shouted, laughing as though this were a great joke.

"I *am!*" Joanna insisted. "Are ye nae the Earl of Wynd Cheathaich's men-at-arms?" she asked desperately.

"Why, our fame has preceded us, lads!" another man yelled, the headiness of the liquor making him dizzy with foolishness.

"Och, ye are! Ye are!" Joanna tried helplessly to make them listen, her heart growing cold at the thought of her fate if she failed.

"And what if we are?"

"Hear me, and dinna do this thing, for I promise ye will rue it. I am wife to Sir Cadman MacBeth, brother of Grace MacBeth MacDonald, your laird's lady."

"Och, the wench lies!" one man more lustful than the others spat. "Let's get on wie it. My codpiece is nigh to bursting at the seams!"

"And what if she isna?" another more sober countered cautiously. "Lord David would take it verra ill, indeed, if the gel speaks the truth and we harm her."

The other men began to mutter among themselves; obviously the thought of their Earl's rage were they to rape his kinswoman was enough to cool their ardor considerably.

"Och, the laird isna likely to learn of it. Besides, the wench lies, I'm telling ye!"

"Well, there is one way to find oot," another declared. "We shall take her to the laird. If she isna who she claims to be, the Earl willna mind if we hae our way wie her afterward. Better safe than sorry, eh, lads?"

"Aye!" The others took up the cry.

With a slightly more gentle and respectful manner they threw Joanna upon her mare's back and led her toward Wynd Cheathaich.

At Glenkirk Lady Sophia paled visibly as Cadman finished his story. The one hand the Countess held to her slender throat trembled. She muffled a small moan as it escaped her lips, but she did not weep as her son feared she might; for he too had been moved by the heart-wrenching tale his kinsman had related.

"Ye hae done wrong, Cadman, both ye and Hunter," Stephen said slowly, "yet, still, 'tis hard for me to fault ye. We MacBeths are a passionate lot, more oft ruled by our hearts than our heads, methinks. Och, mother." He turned to the Countess. "What is to be done? If there were no bairns from these alliances, I could see my way clear as to my actions in the matter, but both Hunter's and Cadman's blood has mingled wie the Carmichael lasses' own. Their babes are our kinsmen, regardless of the circumstances." *Her blood will be your blood. . . .* "I canna, in good conscience, allow their parents to be slain, mother, whate'er they hae done."

"Nor can I," the saintly Lady Sophia with a backbone of steel replied. "Call up your men-at-arms, my son. We must attack Bailekair at dawn!"

At Wynd Cheathaich Joanna knelt before David MacDonald to tell her story and beg his assistance in escorting her safely to Eadar Da Voe. He pondered her tale thoughtfully, for he had reason to believe her, knowing of Hunter MacBeth's love for the Lady Mary; but he had never seen Joanna and wished to assure himself 'twasna just a ruse on the maid's part to spare himself the unwelcome attentions of his men, so he hesitated in his answer. Grace MacBeth MacDonald gazed quietly at the young lass who claimed to be her brother's wife, saw Cadman's ring upon the girl's hand, and stated firmly,

"I believe her, David." Grace rose from her chair, walked slowly to where Joanna knelt upon the floor, her head bowed low, and raised the maid to her feet, looking steadily into the lass's doe brown eyes before she kissed Joanna quickly on both cheeks and said, "Welcome to our home, dear sister. Rest assured my husband will gie ye the aid for which ye ask."

And the Earl of Wynd Cheathaich, who held sway ove
kings, but could deny his fragile, dovelike wife nothing
shouted, "Sir Kevin! Sir Giles! Sir Chauncey! Make ready t
escort the Dame Joanna to Eadar Da Voe on the morrow, an
assemble the remainder of my men for a detachment to b
dispatched to Bailekair immediately." He turned to Joanna
"I myself shall lead my troops to lay siege to your lady'
castle. I hae no hopes of winning the battle, but I may buy y
and Hunter and Mary some time."

"I shall ride with my brother's wife to Eadar Da Voe."
Grace spoke in a tone that David realized would brook n
argument.

"See ye take care, my lady."

At dawn that following morning the MacBeths began thei
assault upon Bailekair's defenses; David MacDonald and hi
men set out for the fortress deep in the Highlands; and Joanna
and Grace, accompanied by no less than fifty outriders
galloped furiously toward Eadar Da Voe.

In the dungeons of the castle of her birth Mary and Hunte
clung to one another tightly and waited, preparing themselve
for death.


# Thirty-seven


"Do ye remember the first time I saw ye, lass, that day o
the summer storm so many years past?" Hunter asked quietly
in the darkness.

"Aye." Mary tried to smile, but he could not see her. How
like him to attempt to ease her pain and fear by recalling
happy memories. "Nine years ago it has been—so much
time, beloved, and yet so verra little."

"Methinks we hae had more in those nine years than mos

538

people do in a lifetime, Mary. Ye were so verra bonnie, that day; ye took my breath away. How I wanted ye.''

"And ye so dark and handsome, so verra proud and arrogant, my love. I might hae killed ye. Och, how I shudder to think of it, to realize the love and passion I might ne'er hae known then.''

"Nine years, and I do but hunger more for ye, beloved. Each day, each hour, each minute that has passed in our lives my love for ye has grown stronger, deeper. Och, ye are a witch, Mary Carmichael, the wisest of enchantresses; for ye hae chained my heart fore'er wie the binding spell of your love. Aye, ye hae been a fit mate for me, my dearest maiden gold, worth all I hae had to gie and more.''

"And ye hae been my life, Hunter MacBeth, for I would only hae existed wie'oot ye by my side. Do ye remember—do ye remember once I asked ye to love me as though it were to be the last time?''

"Aye.''

"I want ye to do that now. I want ye to love me for the last time, for all time as I love ye, my life.''

"Then come unto my arms, tigress; but nae for the last time. Nay, we shall pretend 'tis just the beginning for us, nae the end; and I will love ye as a young mon does in the first blush of his youth, when love is precious and sweet and wie'oot pain. Aye, that is how I will love ye, Mary, for no mon holds his love more dear than I.''

He laid her down upon the hard, board bed of their tiny cell, his movements slow and sweet and tender, as though he were, indeed, a young man discovering her womanhood for the first time, as though they had all the time in the world.

He touched her softly in the blackness, tracing every curve of her beautiful face with wonder, as though he had been blind and she fresh and new to him and he seeing her with his hands for the first time, exploring every aspect of her silken skin: her temples, her eyelids, her nose, her cheeks, her mouth. Oh, most especially her mouth, those sweet, tender, trembling lips that parted gently for his own as he bent his head and kissed her, tasting of her lightly, then drinking

539

deeper and deeper until he felt as though he were drowning as the roar of passion closed over him like an engulfing tide. He kissed her throat, her ears, burying his dark visage in the mass of her cascading golden hair, breathing in the scent of her perfume sharply, sadly, for the heather fragrance reminded him of the purple Highland moors they would not see again.

Slowly he removed her clothes, as though she had been a queen and he her slave preparing her for a ritual bath, kissing every line of her lithe figure as he revealed it, picturing it in his mind without a single flaw, for he could not see her in the darkness, but it did not matter. His memory was faultless; he knew and loved her so well, had spent so many hours, days, years knowing her and loving her in the most intimate fashion.

His hands swept to her breasts, fondling them caressingly, stroking the rosy nipples that sprang to life at his touch, covering them gently with his mouth, lips sucking as Mary moaned softly with pleasure, feeling little tingles of fire race through her blood. His mouth moved lower. His tongue teased the small indentation in her belly, trailed down along her thighs, then crept its way back up to venture over the swelling mound between her flanks, seek the warm, moist hollow that lay within. He felt that soft place quiver beneath his lips in the blackness as one hand slid down to ease the ache for him he knew had started there. He raised his head as Mary's fingers wrapped themselves in his rich mahogany hair to draw him close.

Languidly she began to peel off his garments as he had done hers, seeing him too in her mind, strong, dark, and virile; his flesh marked with the white battle scars that proclaimed him as a warrior. He would have covered her body with his own when she had finished, but she pushed at his chest gently until he lay beside her, feeling her begin to explore him as he had done her, the wetness of her thighs pressed against his own as she kissed him, caressing his face with her hands, tracing the carnal outline of his mouth with her fingers and then her tongue before she sought the inside of his lips like a curious young maiden.

Her mouth fluttered downward over his bronzed breast, and he shuddered slightly with anticipation as he realized where it traveled, gasping as her lips closed over his swollen manhood. Her tongue swirled about him in delicious ravishment until he caught her to him, pulling her up, rolling her over so that she was spread beneath him, breathless, as she awaited his clean swift penetration.

He plunged into the warm, inviting pool of her, diving ever downward to the very core of her being, drowning in her, feeling the surging waves of her close over him, sucking him down into the whirling depths of her innermost self as she rushed up to meet him as a thundering surf crashing upon a beach again and again.

How they reveled in each other! Reached the glorious heights of ecstasy they had always known together before floating back down to reality, back to the dark dank cell that held them prisoner. Hunter kissed the bittersweet tears from Mary's cheeks, but they did not speak. They had no need of words. They had never had need of them. They lay together quietly in the silence, their hearts pounding slower and slower, each knowing their love had cost them their lives and not caring, for whatever the price, it had been worth it for them both.

They hae come, Mary thought dully as she stirred in Hunter's arms. They hae come to torture and slay us. This is the end. But the heavy wooden door did not open; only the small, iron grill halfway up its length was shoved aside with a grinding rasp.

"My lady! My lady! Can ye hear me?"

Mary jumped up, puzzled, and ran quickly toward the sound of the young voice, fumbling to pull on her *arascaid* to hide her nakedness.

"Aye."

" 'Tis I, Collie. I hae brought ye something to eat and drink and a candle, my lady, so ye mayna hae to remain in darkness." The boy handed the steaming plates, cool mugs, and the tallow as well as a flint through the narrow slit, his own torch providing a small amount of light for Mary to see by and take the provisions he offered.

"Collie, what are ye doing here?"

"I tagged along when the Earl's men brought ye to Bailekair. They dinna take any notice of me in the confusion. Ye were kind to me, my lady, smashing my head wie that vase afore ye escaped that time long past. The Earl would hae had me flogged to death were it nae for that," he explained as Mary almost smiled. Only a servant would have thought a cracked skull a generosity under the circumstances. "I had a monstrous bump on my brow, my lady, so the laird knew I'd been taken unawares. He demoted me to pot boy for two months afterward, but at least I wasna flayed alive. He was cruel wie his whip when he was angry, he was; and I thank ye for sparing me that. Anyway, I couldna rest easy last night, nae knowing your fate down here, my lady. I heard in the kitchen that auld bawd—begging your pardon, my lady—the Countess said ye were nae to be brought food nor drink, in order to wear down your resistance to the torture she has planned for ye. So first chance I got, I smuggled this stuff oot, told them 'twas for some men-at-arms. I'm sorry I dinna hae the key to this door, or I'd let ye oot, besides. In all the confusion I doubt anyone would even notice, and ye could escape."

"Confusion? What confusion? Collie, what is happening up there?"

"Lord, my lady. The MacBeths hae attacked the fortress, and they do say the Earl of Wynd Cheathaich, the MacDonald, has joined the assault. E'eryone is in a terrible uproar o'er it, for the castle hasna been besieged in years."

Mary heard a sharp intake of breath behind her and realized Hunter had awakened and caught the boy's words. The Romany knight moved on cat's feet toward the grate.

"Lad, are ye certain 'tis the keep itself and nae the village that is under assault?"

"Aye, sir, verra sure. They canna even hold the Earls' funerals for all the ruckus. Her ladyship is in a horrible rage, I tell ye."

"I can imagine," Mary spoke dryly, but hope soared in her breast all the same. "Did they say what they intended to do with Sir Hunter and myself, Collie?"

"Nay, my lady. The Countess was all for killing ye right away, but Sir Alan told her that ye would keep and that they dinna hae time to carry oot a burning and a hanging under the circumstances, much less spare the men her ladyship wanted to come down and torture ye for awhile."

Oh, thank God for Alan, Mary thought. If I live through this, someway, somehow, I'll see he and Mistress Flora ne'er want for aught again!

"I must go now, my lady, in case someone comes to check on ye, though I think it unlikely. I'll try to bring ye food and drink when I can and candles too. I'm sorry there's just the one, but 'twas all I dared snatch from a sconce."

"That's all right, Collie. Ye hae done more than enough for us. Thank ye. Thank ye, lad. God bless ye," Mary said fervently, but the boy was already gone. She turned to Hunter. "What do ye make of it, beloved?"

"I dinna know, except that somehow, someway Cadman and Joanna hae performed a miracle!"

The battle between the Carmichaels, MacBeths, and MacDonalds raged furiously. For nearly a fortnight it raged, but at its end Bailekair still stood strong, its walls unravaged, and the dead of the three clans lay heavily upon the bloodied ground. But there was no victory for either side, for Alinor came, true to her word, with not only her father's men, but the King and the Hepburn as well. Both of them had gone to Eadar Da Voe to discuss the failure of the mission to England with the powerful Earl Murray and had still been at the keep when Joanna and Grace had arrived, begging aid.

Jamie put a halt to the fighting at once and bade Bailekair throw open its gates. Then for the first time in nearly a hundred years outside of Court the Carmichaels and MacBeths were assembled together under one roof, wary, hostile, but even more afraid of the King's obvious wrath as he stared at them from the head of the main hall after restoring order to the fortress and commanding them inside the castle to hear his words of displeasure. He spoke very quietly, but his voice shook with anger, and none present was deceived by his outwardly calm demeanor.

"Look ye at the scourge of death and destruction your feud and hatred hae wrought, the blood that has run red upon the ground, the sorrow ye hae reaped from the bitter harvest ye hae sown. I am ashamed—ashamed! do ye ken?—to call ye my people! If we canna hae peace among our own, but discord in its stead, how can we hope to stand strong and united against those of other nations who would oppose us, would burn our homes, rape our women, slay our men, and wrest our beloved Scotland from our verra grasp? I would lead ye to victory, and ye would drag me down to defeat wie your petty quarrel! Ye disgust and enrage me wie your feud, make me ill unto death wie your hatred! And ye would destroy the love two among ye hae found wie one another, a love so great I vow someday a bard will write of it so that all may learn of the hope eternal that sprang from the seeds of your bitter animosity. What hae ye done wie them? Where are Sir Hunter MacBeth and Lady Mary Carmichael?"

Immediately a babble of accusations, explanations, and outrage arose, ringing the very rafters of the hall with its outcry.

"Silence!" James thundered. "I'll nae listen to your entreaties, for ye will but seek to lay the blame upon each other. Nor shall I stand by and hear ye malign those two who hae dared to defy ye wie their love for one another; for your tongues will bear naught save vicious malice, vile and vulgar, for that which ye canna understand." He turned to Lord Bothwell grimly. "See they are found at once—if they're still alive, if these fools hae nae slain them." He glared at those in the great chamber. "And bring them here, so these—petty cowards," he sneered the words disdainfully, "may recognize true heart and courage hereafter."

Then he sat down to wait, and none dared break the stillness that enveloped the main hall again.

Mary and Hunter entered the room slowly, scarcely daring to believe they were free, were not to die after all, that the King himself had come to their defense. Hand-in-hand they walked toward their ruler proudly, heads held high, Mary clutching tightly the chest Patrick Hepburn had returned to her safekeeping. Halfway down the vast chamber there came a small commotion at the doors of the castle. All eyes turned toward the sound as Jane Hepburn burst through the barriers grandly. Her husband had hastily scrawled a message before leaving Eadar Da Voe, telling her to journey to Bailekair posthaste, bringing the MacBeth children with her.

"Mama! Father!" The lovers' bairns ran to their parents to be swooped up joyfully into welcoming arms, crushed to breasts that breathed raggedly with overwhelming emotion. Mary and Hunter buried their faces in their babes' soft, downy hair to hide the feeling that welled up inside them, while Cadman and Joanna hugged their own twins close at one end of the hall.

Then gently Mary and Hunter set their children down and moved to kneel before the King, whose own eyes were suspiciously moist.

"Look ye upon these two," Jamie commanded as he gazed at the bowed heads before him, "and heed well the lesson of the love they hae shared between them, even in the face of death, for they alone are your salvation. Rise up, Sir Hunter MacBeth and Lady Mary Carmichael, for your love is the single burning flame of hope amidst this tragic and sorry feud, a hope the auld witch gae ye all when she laid her curse upon ye if only ye hadna been too blind to see it. Aye, there *is* an answer to the puzzle of the curse, and the Hepburn tells me Mary holds its key. So I ask ye, my lady, to unlock the riddle of the maze that has tangled up your lives."

And so in the silence that followed Jamie's startling pronouncement, with Hunter at her side and her bairns at her feet, Mary Carmichael told the story of the legend up to her finding of the casket she held now in her hands.

"This small chest"—she displayed the box aloft for all to see—"contains the answer to the puzzle of the legend. But before I open it to reveal that which lies wie'in I want to tell ye this: Grizel dinna curse us. We cursed ourselves with our bitter feud and hatred and destroyed all that was precious between two people who loved as passionately as Hunter MacBeth and I love each other. Now I shall finish the story of the legend, for its curse has lain too long upon us.

"James Carmichael dinna kidnap Anne MacBeth as we all hae thought these many years past, for they were lovers, even as Hunter and I." *As 'twas in the beginning, so will it be again.* "But a feud lay between the two clans, and they could see no way for their love to succeed in the face of its enmity. They were desperate wie longing for one another and vowed to defy their clans, once more even as Hunter and I. They wed in secret, and Anne went wie James willingly that night he rode up to the walls of Glenkirk to claim her as his bride and bring her home to Bailekair.

"But his brother, Robert of Dùndereen, accompanied him on the raid; and when Robert learned of the marriage, the two men quarreled. They dueled upon the ramparts of Bailekair because James refused to ransom Anne back to her kinsmen, who had laid siege to the castle. 'Twas Robert who was slain and whose body was flung o'er the high battlements of the fortress to the corpse-laden ground where the dead of the Carmichaels and MacBeths sprawled, pitiful and ugly.

"The gentle Anne could not bear the suffering and mortal fate she and James had brought to so many wie their great love for one another, so she left him, intending to enter a nunnery to repent her sin." . . . *accursed amongst thy people for another's sin, the same of which will be his own in the end.* "But she was heavy wie child and couldna travel far, so she rode to the kirk at Mheadhoin where she and James had lain and loved in secret; and there she died. She died, but the child of their brief, passionate union lived—lived and survived.

"Anne's faithful nanna, the gypsy Grizel, was in attendance at the babe's birth. She took the child to Torra nam Sian, far to the north of Scotland where none was likely to guess its true origins and slay it. She persuaded a young MacBeth kinswoman, whose own bairn had died, to take the babe in and raise it as her own. Then Grizel returned to Mheadhoin, where she laid her curse upon us all.

"The name of the child born to James Carmichael and Anne MacBeth was George, he who first bore the accursed violet eyes and was Hunter's grandfather. I tell ye all, the blood of the Carmichaels flows in the veins of Hunter MacBeth as surely as does the blood of the MacBeths. His great-grandfather was my own. By that blood, lineage, and heritage, Sir Hunter MacBeth is the true Earl of Bailekair!"

*And all that he gains will be his from the beginning.*

What should he have felt? Shock, surprise, disbelief? Oddly enough Hunter felt none of those things. It was as though he had always guessed, had always known somehow, someway, because he was so much a part of Mary and she of him. An earl! He was an earl, but he did not care. He had never despised, nor despaired of his low rank like Cadman. Only an immense joy that Mary would never have to leave Bailekair again filled Hunter's heart to overflowing. He clasped her hand tightly in understanding as she continued, her voice throbbing with love and passion for him and her proud castle.

"Open the casket. The certificates of marriage, birth, and Grizel's letter are all wie'in. All I say is truth. The blood of the Carmichaels and MacBeths has mingled for all time. What say ye? Will ye slay Hunter and our sons? Will ye slay the children of Cadman MacBeth and Joanna Carmichael, his wife? If ye kill us all, ye canna undo what has been done, what love alone has wrought, for love is the answer to the puzzle of the curse of the legend. Ye must forget your feud, bury your hate, and forgie one another." *Forgie. Forgie that a weary, troubled soul may rest in peace and walk no more amongst ye.* "If ye dinna, I warn ye even as Grizel did, ye will destroy us all! I ask again, what say ye?"

A strange, uneasy silence held the crowd gathered in the vast hall as though the shadow of the old gypsy herself had enshrouded them. Then one man braver than the rest stepped forward, and Mary had never loved her brother more than in that moment when Charlie Carmichael held out his hand to her beloved Romany knight and said,

"I am proud to call ye brother, my Lord Hunter MacBeth, Earl of Bailekair."

"Nay! Nay!" Lady Margaret saw her whole empire crumbling at her feet. "Ye hae ruined e'erything, ye bitch! Ye hae destroyed all I hae e'er worked for!"

She ran toward Mary furiously, demented in her rage, her dagger upraised in one hand that curled like a claw around the hilt of the blade. Hunter moved to halt the Countess's violent onslaught, but not quickly enough to spare his beloved. The dirk plunged with searing agony into Mary's breast. The last thing she remembered was her dear Romany knight—nay, her *lord*, she corrected herself hazily—bending over her, saying over and over again,

"Oh, tigress, ye canna die now after all we hae lived through together!"

# Thirty-eight

Mary Carmichael did not die, and she never knew afterward which of the two necklaces she wore always beneath the bodice of her *arascaid* had been the one that had saved her life: the keys that had unlocked the puzzle of the legend or the locket Hunter had given her one Christmas so many years past. She liked to think the links of both had intertwined to spare her, for Lady Margaret's dagger had glanced off the gold metal to slide downward, cutting a light, jagged wound just beneath Mary's breastbone. It was strange that when it healed, it resembled the scar Hunter bore upon his own belly.

The evil Countess herself was dead. When she learned Mary lived, she drank a chalice of hemlock, fatally poisoning herself after confessing it had been she who'd drugged

Magnus's wine that evening so long ago. Mary guessed her mother's end was fitting after all.

Peace lay over the Highlands now. The Carmichaels and MacBeths had sworn to forever end the feud between them, vowing their oaths before the King himself; and Jamie was content as his eyes fell upon the bowed heads of Hunter and Mary kneeling before him, the last two to pledge their fealty and peace.

*Yet as sorrow lingers, so joy will come, but only when ye hae turned full circle. When the stormy seas hae brought him who left ye home again once more, two will kneel before their sovereign lord, who will lay his hands upon them and bless them for all time, as two were once blessed by another.*

Aye, the joy Grizel had promised had come at last.

"Rise, Lord Hunter MacBeth, Earl of Bailekair, and Lady Mary Carmichael," the King toned most royally, then sighed with playful ruefulness and said, "Hunter, I am in your debt, and I mislike it more than I can say. It has troubled my conscience sorely, I tell ye, this debt of mine."

"How so, Your Grace?" The newly confirmed Earl of Bailekair was puzzled. "If a debt has been owed me, ye hae more than repaid it."

"Nay, Hunter. 'Tis the boon of which I speak. The boon I once offered ye and that ye refused. I still owe ye that and would set matters a'right, so my favor is once more yours for the asking."

"Sire, I am flattered, but truly there is naught I would hae. If 'twould please, Your Grace, howe'er"—he had not missed Jamie's darkening frown—"I would gie my boon to Mary as a wedding present, for though I hae nae yet asked her, I hope she is soon to become my bride."

"Ye hae nae yet asked her!" the King burst out sputtering with mock rage. "Well, for God's sake, mon! What are ye waiting for? The bonniest lass in all Scotland, and ye hae nae yet asked for her hand! Ye'd best hurry up wie it then, my lord, or I swear I'll hae her myself, for she has oft tempted me in the past, I promise ye. Kneel down, my lord, now, and speak what I know is in your heart."

549

Solemnly Hunter went down in courtly fashion upon one knee before Mary and took her hand. "Lady Mary Kathryn Carmichael, I love ye. I love ye more than my life. Will ye do me the honor of becoming my wife?"

"Aye, my lord, I will."

A great cheer rang out from the Carmichaels and MacBeths gathered in the great hall of Bailekair at this, and 'twas all Jamie could do to restore order.

"Well, lass." He turned to Mary kindly when all were quiet once more. "What will ye hae?"

"I hae so much now, Sire," the girl murmured, gazing at her family and friends. Hunter and their children, Geoffrey, Ranald, and Magnus. Patrick and Jane Hepburn. David and Grace MacDonald. Charlie and Alinor Carmichael. Cadman and Joanna MacBeth. Cadman and Joanna, the two who had loved Hunter and Mary so dearly, stood by them unfailingly through it all, and asked naught in return for their unwavering devotion. Cadman and Joanna, two unwanted bastards who had loved and lost so cruelly and found one another to love again. "Aye, aye, Your Grace, I *do* hae a boon to request!" Mary's face suddenly lit up with excitement.

"Name it, and 'tis yours then." The King's eyes twinkled merrily with happiness and curiosity. "But if 'tis Fleming's estates, ye canna hae those, for I hae pardoned his lordship—again!"

"Nay, Sire. 'Tis Dùndereen I would hae."

"Dùndereen, Mary?"

"Och, nay for myself, Your Grace," she reassured him hastily lest he think her a greedy subject. "Nay, I ask that the titles of Earl and Countess of Dùndereen and all their holdings be bestowed upon Cadman and Joanna MacBeth!"

"Oh, nay, Mary! 'Tis Geoffrey's inheritance!" Joanna cried out, thunderstruck.

"Edward ne'er wanted it and wouldna hae wanted it for his son," Mary replied calmly, her mind made up. "If ye and Cadman and Hunter are willing, I would see Edward's bairn troth-plighted to your Janet, and we shall build them a keep where our lands join."

A muscle in Cadman's jaw worked queerly. Tears stung his dark blue eyes as he knelt at Mary's feet and placed his lips against her hands. "Mary. Mary. I—I—"

"Rise, my Lord Cadman MacBeth, Earl of Dùndereen," James managed to get out softly, his voice choked with emotion, overwhelmed by his subjects. He rubbed his own eyes and cleared his throat. "Earls ye and Hunter may be, but there is still the matter of Perkin Warbeck to discuss!"

"Oh, Sire." The two men groaned as the King pretended to scowl at them both ominously.

But Jamie could not keep up the charade for long. He laughed uproariously at the sight of the shamefaced countenances of his Earls, then snapped impudently, "I wish ye had thrown that young mon o'erboard, for he has tried my patience sorely!"

Hunter MacBeth and Mary Carmichael were wed Lammas Day, August 1, 1495, in the kirk at Mheadhoin. It seemed fitting somehow that the legend that had begun there end there too.

The Highland moors of Scotland were gold and purple in their beauty as the two lovers rode sedately up the hill to its crest where the cross-topped spire of the chapel stood tall and proud against the sweep of the breathtaking azure sky filled with puffy wisps of white clouds. The still Loch Ness far below shown clear and blue beneath the dappled sunlight, and only once during the ceremony that bound her forever to Hunter did Mary believe she heard in the distance a strange triumphant cry of glory that could only have come from the monster of the lake.

After the solemn but joyous ritual had ended the newly wed couple walked hand-in-hand to stand before the solitary grave in the fenced yard behind the kirk, place bunches of sweet flowers upon the single mound, and pay their quiet respects to the brave, bonnie lassie who lay untroubled now within for all eternity.

The newlyweds had had chiseled upon the granite that very day as their gift to the past:

ANNE LEAH MACBETH CARMICHAEL

Countess of Bailekair

Beloved wife of James George Carmichael
Earl of Bailekair

1382–1397

R.I.P.

" 'Tis o'er. The legend has ended," Mary whispered softly as she gazed at the stone. "Nay, beloved," Hunter smiled down at her, his glittering violet eyes darkening in a way that made her heart begin to pound slowly. "The legend is just beginning."

# *Author's Note*

All persons in this book are fictitious with the exception of such historical figures mentioned as the Kings and Queens of various countries, the Earls of Angus, Huntly, and Bothwell, and the Ladies Gordon, etc. Any instances in which their lives intermingle with those of the characters are pure invention, although the Battle of Sauchieburn (Scotland), the events leading up to it, and its final outcome at Beaton's Mill are fact. The murderer of King James III of Scotland, however, was never in truth discovered. There were several skirmishes between the Hungarians and the Turks over the city of Belgrade during the years covered herein, but the one the author has described is fictional. Perkin Warbeck, a pretender to the crown of England, made two aborted attempts to invade that country, the first in 1493, the second in 1495, before he finally succeeded in 1497. He was aided at various times in his plot by King James IV of Scotland, and the author could not resist incorporating one of these attempts into her tale, although she has altered the true facts to suit her story.

In reality, during the fifteenth century, the members of the Carmichael family were septs of the Clans MacDougall and Stewart. The members of the MacBeth family were septs of the Clans MacBain, MacDonald, and MacLean. Neither family was a separate clan unto itself. For purposes of this novel, however, the author has chosen to portray them as such, and no resemblance, intended or otherwise, to the real families of Carmichael and MacBeth of the fifteenth century should be looked for by the reader. The Clans Murray and MacDonald did exist, but the persons portrayed herein as belonging to them did not.

The author has, in addition, taken the liberty of providing both major clans with mottos, war cries, shields, plant-badges, and *breacan* colors, choosing those she found most pleasing. They are not meant to be authentic, as both families of today now have their own tartans, etc. The author has used the terms "shield" and "coat of arms" interchangeably, because during this time period the shield was the coat of arms. Occasionally, though this was relatively rare at this point in history, the shield was topped by a helmet with mantling. The full armorial bearings or achievement (consisting of the shield, helmet, mantling, crown or coronet, crest, supporters, compartment, motto, and sometimes knightly order) with which we are familiar today came in to being at a much later date and for this reason is not employed herein.

It should also be stated the use of family surnames was not prevalent at this time, and the author has employed them merely to prevent the reader from becoming confused. And although Gaelic was the language spoken in the Scottish Highlands during the fifteenth century, the author has used the English versions of given names, feeling they would be more familiar to the reader. Almost all of them, however, may be translated into the Gaelic tongue.

The castles of Bailekair, Dùndereen, Glenkirk, and any others stated as being part of the Carmichael or MacBeth holdings, the castles of the Clans Murray and MacDonald, the town of Mheadhoin, and the kirk exist only in the author's imagination.

Rebecca Brandewyne

# Regarding the Clans

### THE CLAN CARMICHAEL

| | |
|---|---|
| Motto: | *Nunquam obliviscar* (I will never forget) |
| War cry: | *Buaidh no Bàs* (Victory or Death) |

Shield:    *Or a cross purpure* surmounted of a winged *or* unicorn\* *rampant argent, armed* and *crined or*, issuing from a cloud *azure*, the *dexter* foreleg bearing a broadsword *argent* and *or*

(A field of gold subdivided by a purple cross which center bears a rearing silver or white unicorn\* having gold wings, horn, hooves, mane, and tail, standing atop a blue cloud, its right foreleg holding a silver-bladed sword with a gold hilt)

\*On the Chief of the clan's shield *only* the unicorn wears a gold coronet

Plant-badge:    Purple Heather

Clan Colors:    Purple and Blue

# THE CLAN MacBETH

| | |
|---|---|
| Motto: | Touch not the *catt bot* a *targe* (Touch not the cat without a shield) |
| War cry: | *A* MacBeth! *A* MacBeth! (To MacBeth! or To me!) |
| Shield: | *Per pale gyronny or* and *sable*, and *or;* the *sinister* surmounted of a mountain-cat* *salient sable*, *inflamed proper*, the *sinister* foreleg bearing a Highland *targe*, the *dexter vert*, the *sinister gules*, *bordure sable* |
| | (A field halved, the right side consisting of four triangles alternating of gold and black to form two squares or quarters, the left side solid of gold which center bears a leaping black mountain cat* depicted as in flames represented in their natural colouring, its left foreleg holding a small, round Highland shield with right side of green, left side of red, and bordered all around of black) |
| | *On the Chief of the clan's shield *only* the mountain cat wears a red coronet |
| Plant-badge: | Scots Pine |
| Clan Colors: | Red and Green |

# THE BEST OF BESTSELLERS
# FROM WARNER BOOKS

### A STRANGER IN THE MIRROR
*by Sidney Sheldon*                     *(A36-492, $3.95)*

Toby Temple—super star and super bastard, adored by his vast TV and movie public yet isolated from real, human contact by his own suspicion and distrust. Jill Castle—she came to Hollywood to be a star and discovered she had to buy her way with her body. In a world of predators, they are bound to each other by a love so ruthless and strong, that is more than human—and less.

### BLOODLINE
*by Sidney Sheldon*                     *(A36-491, $3.95)*

When the daughter of one of the world's richest men inherits his multi-billion-dollar business, she inherits his position at the top of the company and at the top of the victim's list of his murderer! "An intriguing and entertaining tale."

—*Publishers Weekly*

### RAGE OF ANGELS
*by Sidney Sheldon*                     *(A36-214, $3.95)*

A breath-taking novel that takes you behind the doors of the law and inside the heart and mind of Jennifer Parker. She rises from the ashes of her own courtroom disaster to become one of America's most brilliant attorneys. Her story is interwoven with that of two very different men of enormous power. As Jennifer inspires both men to passion, each is determined to destroy the other—and Jennifer, caught in the crossfire, becomes the ultimate victim.

# BEST OF BESTSELLERS
# FROM WARNER BOOKS

### THE FAN
*by Bob Randall*                    (95-887, $2.75)

The Fan: warm and admiring, then arrogantly suggestive; then obscene, and finally, menacing. Plunging a dawdy Broadway actress into a shocking nightmare. "A real nail-biter...works to perfection as it builds to a surprising climax...the tension is killing."                    —*Saturday Review*

### FORT APACHE, THE BRONX
*by Heywood Gould*                    (95-618, $2.75)

They were only rookies...two green cops blown away on the killer walkways of the Bronx. Now the Force is on the prowl under a tough new captain who is determined to shape up his last command for losers where life is mean, death is often murder, and the law of the jungle is the only law.

### SEE THE KID RUN
*by Bob Ottum*                    (95-123, $2.75)

A chilling race through the dark side of New York with a kid you'll never forget! Wanted: Elvis Presley Reynolds, aged 14½, who dreams of Mark Cross, Brooks Brothers and the Plaza—where one day soon he'll pass as "Somebody." He's an urban urchin with bottomless eyes and an incredible ambition to escape to the good life while there's still time.

### THE TUESDAY BLADE
*By Bob Ottum*                    (95-643, $2.75)

"We're looking for one guy carrying seven razors or seven guys carrying one razor each." That's how a cop summed up the case. But the killer they were tracking was just one girl—big, beautiful and armed with THE TUESDAY BLADE. "My current reading favorite...makes 'Death Wish' look like a kindergarten exercise."
                    —Liz Smith, *New York News*